SHIRLEY & JAMILA

save their summer

by Gillian Goerz

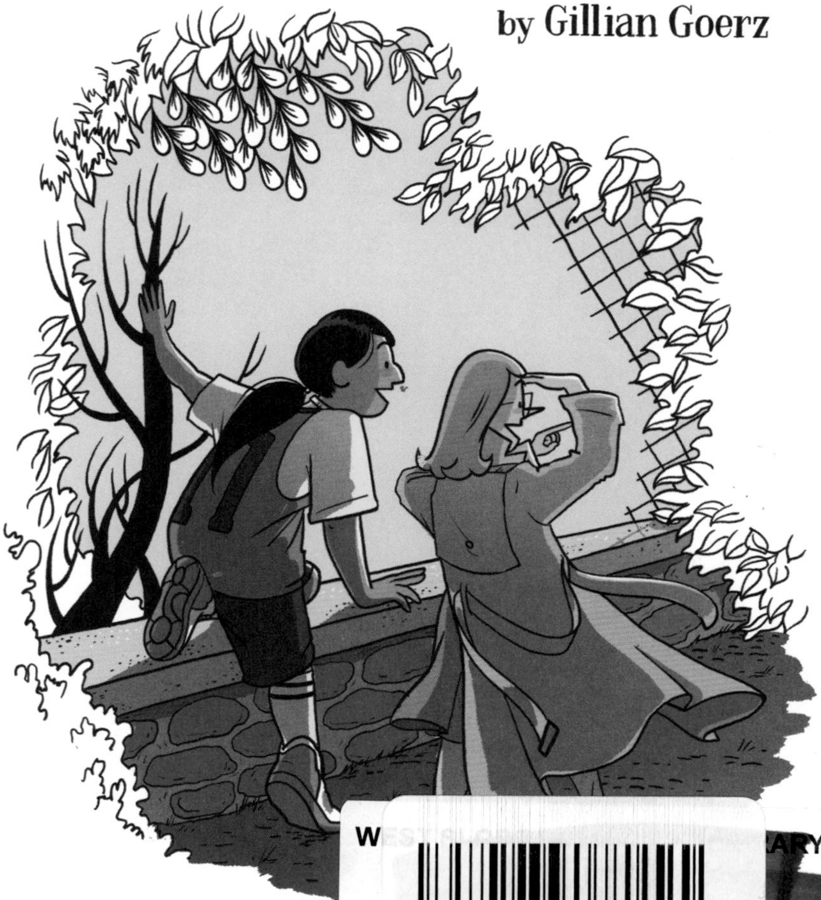

Dial Books

TO THE FRIENDSHIPS THAT CHANGED
ME FOR THE BETTER
—G.G.

Dial Books for Young Readers
An imprint of Penguin Random House LLC, New York

Visit us online at penguinrandomhouse.com

Library of Congress Cataloging-in-Publication Data is available.

Hardcover ISBN 9780525552857

5 7 9 10 8 6 4

Paperback ISBN 9780525552864

4th Printing
GFV
Manufactured in Italy

Design by Jennifer Kelly and Gillian Goerz
Text set in GG Sans with permission of the author

Produced with the support of the City of Toronto through the
Toronto Arts Council and the Ontario Arts Council

TORONTO
ARTS
COUNCIL

FUNDED BY
THE CITY OF
TORONTO

ONTARIO ARTS COUNCIL
CONSEIL DES ARTS DE L'ONTARIO
an Ontario government agency
un organisme du gouvernement de l'Ontario

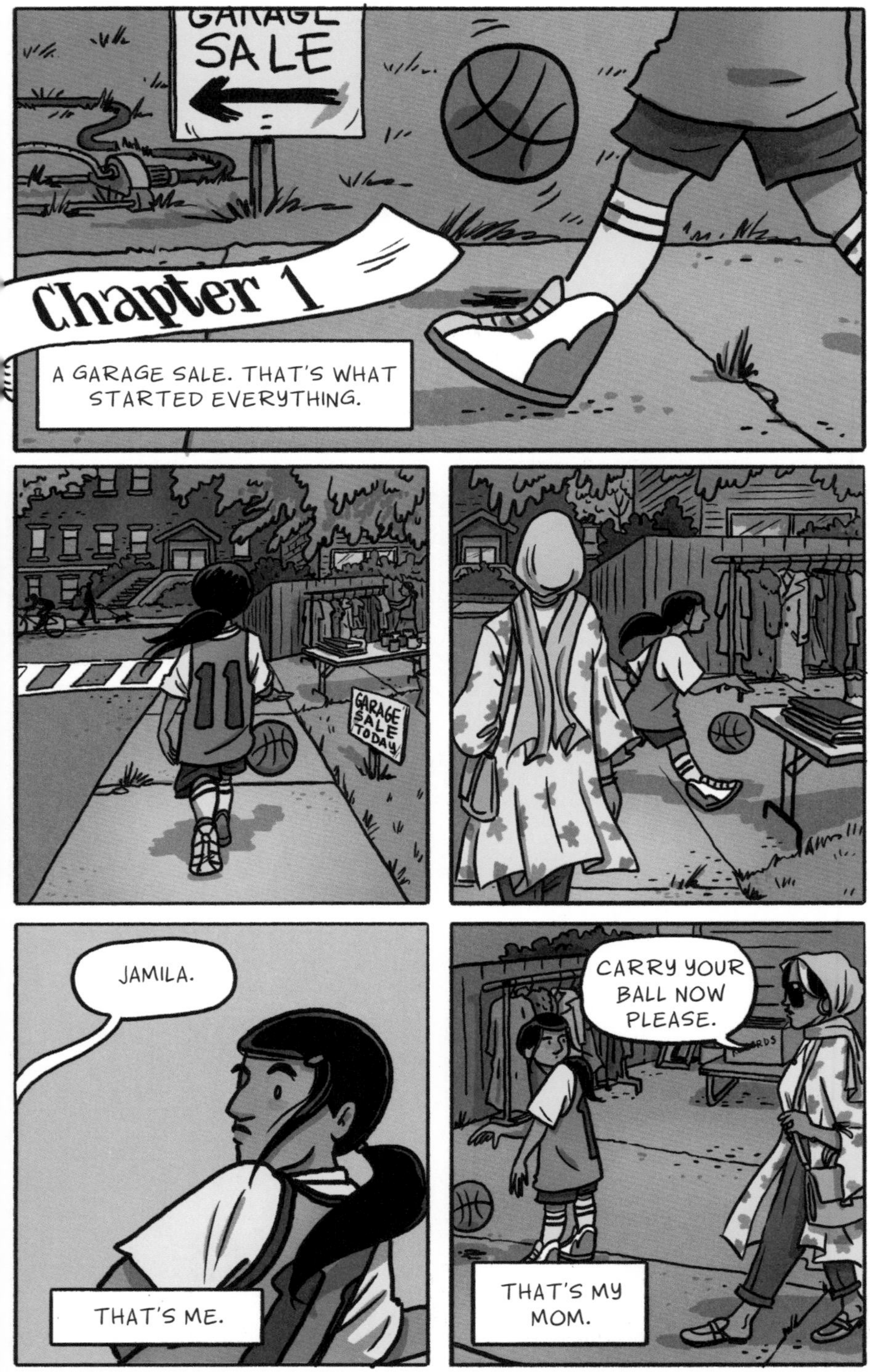
GARAGE SALE
Chapter 1
A GARAGE SALE. THAT'S WHAT STARTED EVERYTHING.
GARAGE SALE TODAY
JAMILA.
THAT'S ME.
CARRY YOUR BALL NOW PLEASE.
THAT'S MY MOM.

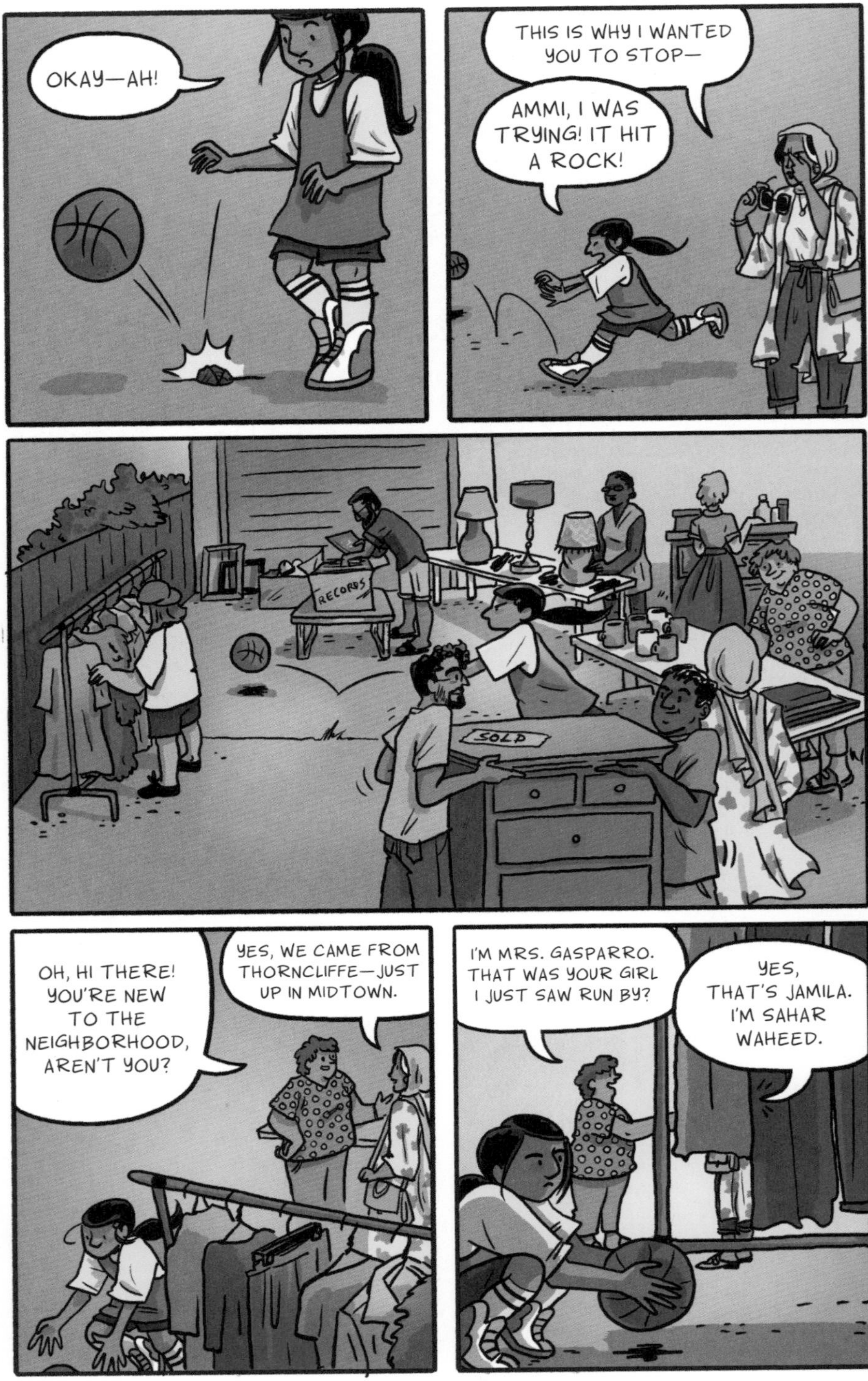
OKAY—AH!
THIS IS WHY I WANTED YOU TO STOP—
AMMI, I WAS TRYING! IT HIT A ROCK!
RECORDS
SOLD
OH, HI THERE! YOU'RE NEW TO THE NEIGHBORHOOD, AREN'T YOU?
YES, WE CAME FROM THORNCLIFFE—JUST UP IN MIDTOWN.
I'M MRS. GASPARRO. THAT WAS YOUR GIRL I JUST SAW RUN BY?
YES, THAT'S JAMILA. I'M SAHAR WAHEED.

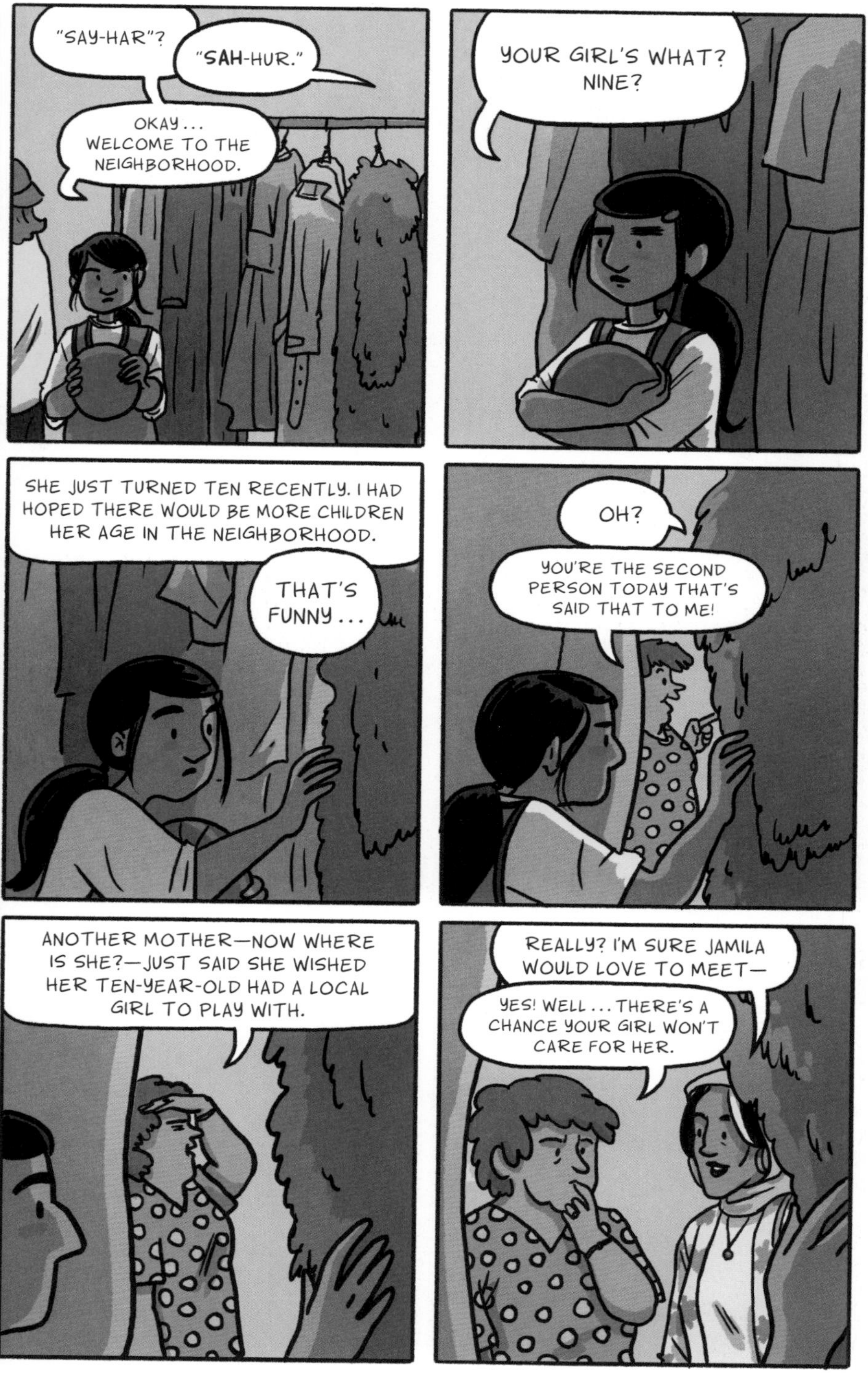
"SAY-HAR"?
"SAH-HUR."
OKAY... WELCOME TO THE NEIGHBORHOOD.
YOUR GIRL'S WHAT? NINE?
SHE JUST TURNED TEN RECENTLY. I HAD HOPED THERE WOULD BE MORE CHILDREN HER AGE IN THE NEIGHBORHOOD.
THAT'S FUNNY...
OH?
YOU'RE THE SECOND PERSON TODAY THAT'S SAID THAT TO ME!
ANOTHER MOTHER—NOW WHERE IS SHE?—JUST SAID SHE WISHED HER TEN-YEAR-OLD HAD A LOCAL GIRL TO PLAY WITH.
REALLY? I'M SURE JAMILA WOULD LOVE TO MEET—
YES! WELL... THERE'S A CHANCE YOUR GIRL WON'T CARE FOR HER.

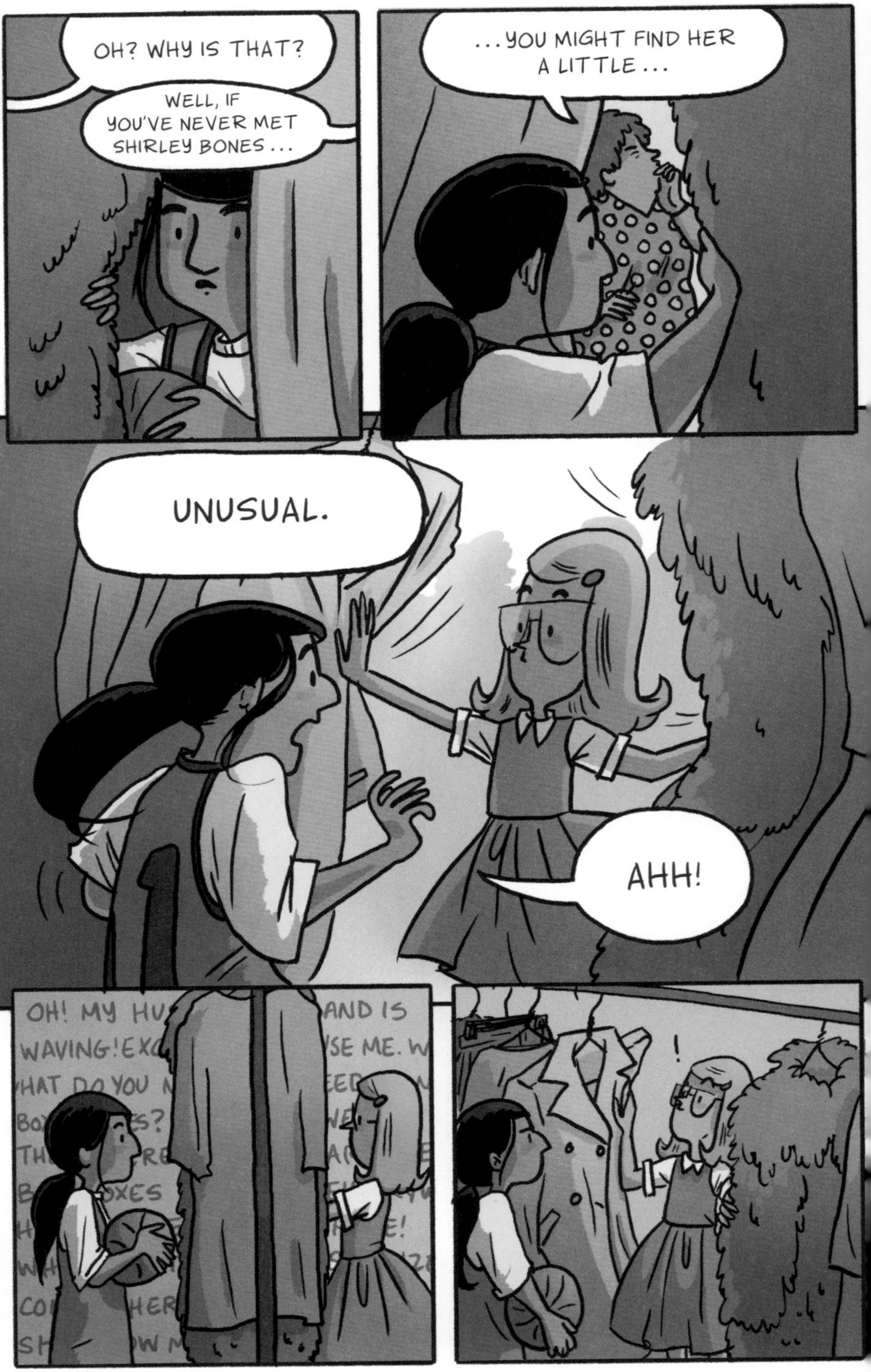
OH? WHY IS THAT?
WELL, IF YOU'VE NEVER MET SHIRLEY BONES . . .
. . . YOU MIGHT FIND HER A LITTLE . . .
UNUSUAL.
AHH!
!

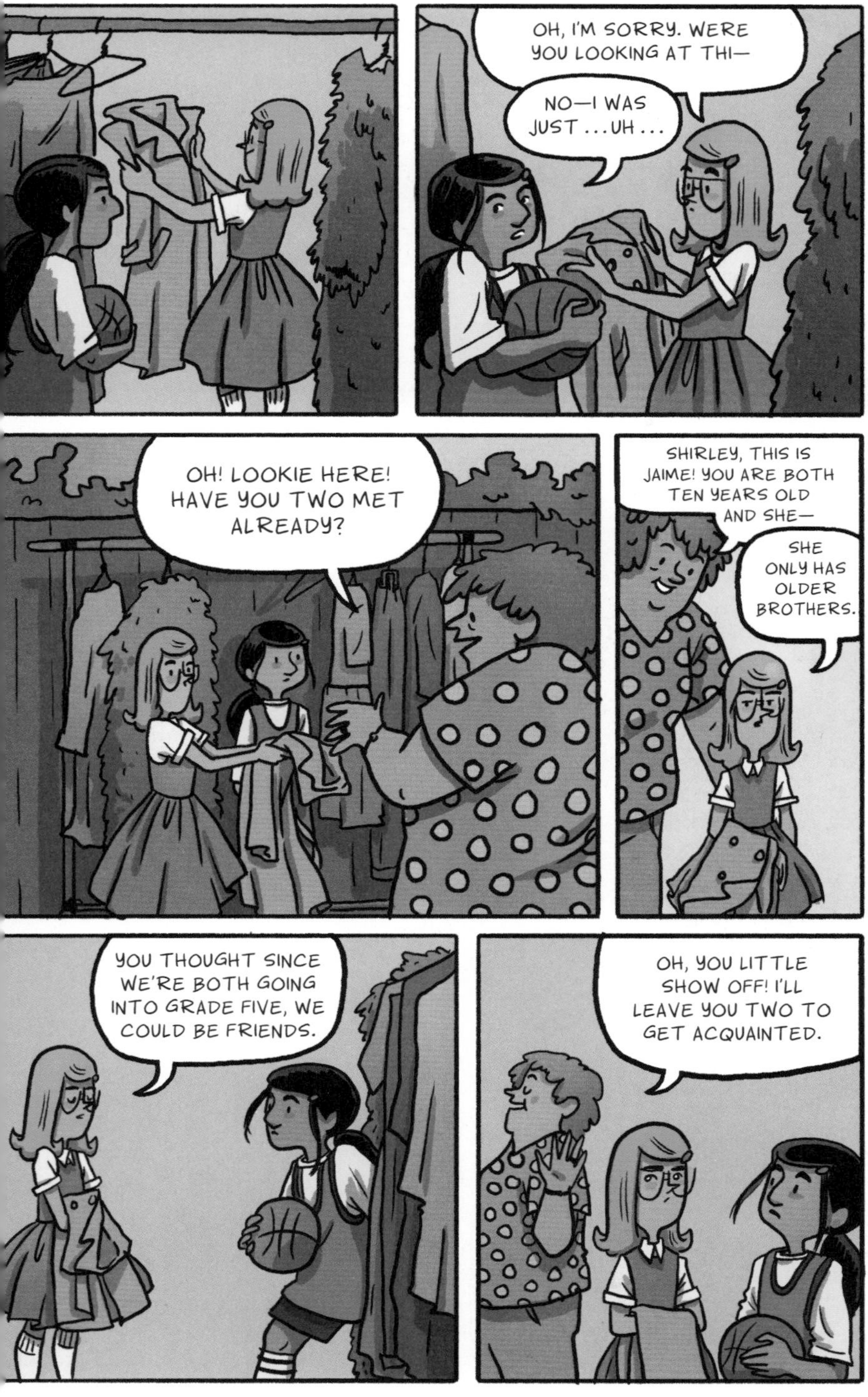
OH, I'M SORRY. WERE YOU LOOKING AT THI—
NO—I WAS JUST . . . UH . . .
OH! LOOKIE HERE! HAVE YOU TWO MET ALREADY?
SHIRLEY, THIS IS JAIME! YOU ARE BOTH TEN YEARS OLD AND SHE—
SHE ONLY HAS OLDER BROTHERS.
YOU THOUGHT SINCE WE'RE BOTH GOING INTO GRADE FIVE, WE COULD BE FRIENDS.
OH, YOU LITTLE SHOW OFF! I'LL LEAVE YOU TWO TO GET ACQUAINTED.

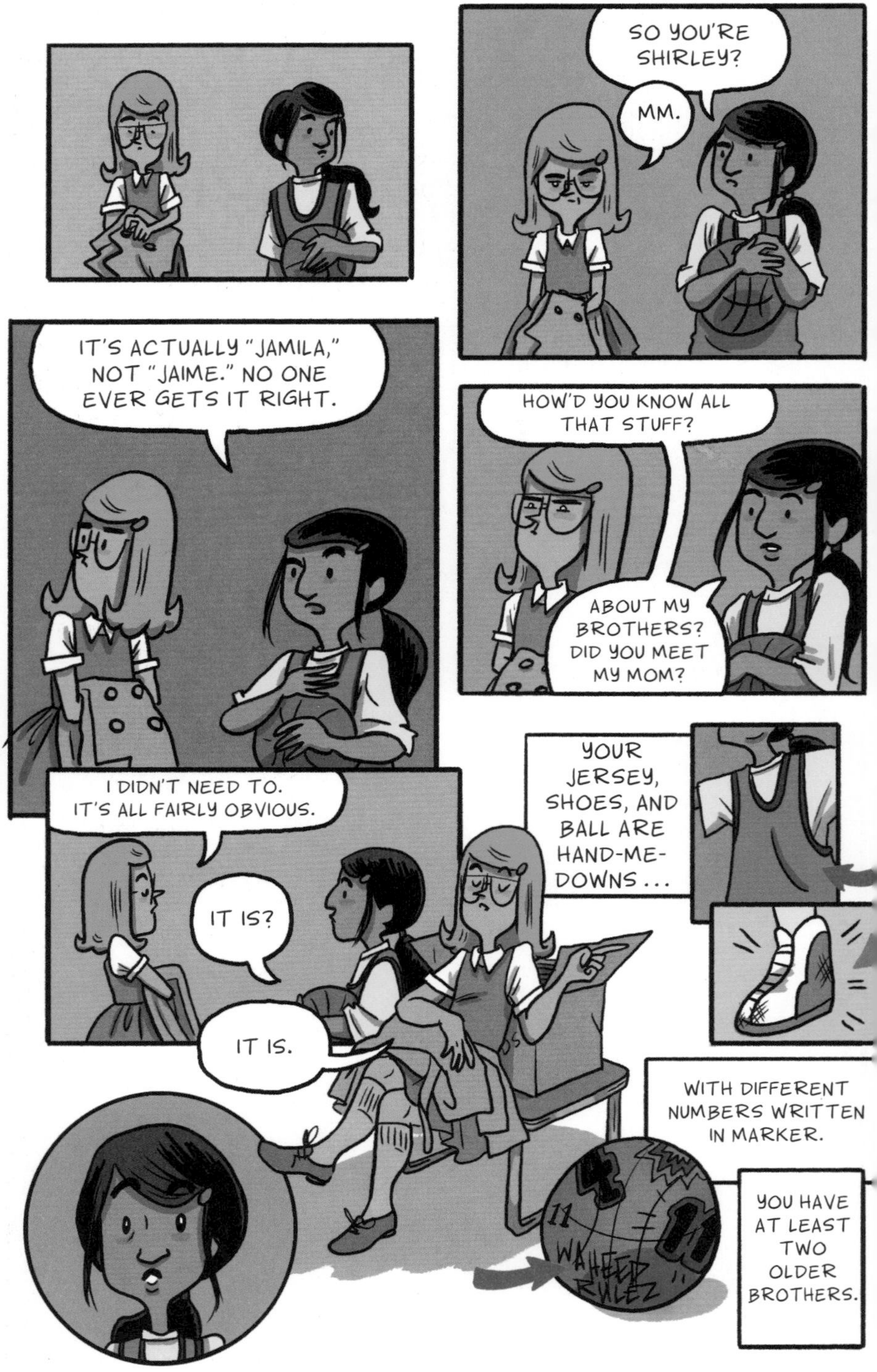
SO YOU'RE SHIRLEY?
MM.
IT'S ACTUALLY "JAMILA," NOT "JAIME." NO ONE EVER GETS IT RIGHT.
HOW'D YOU KNOW ALL THAT STUFF?
ABOUT MY BROTHERS? DID YOU MEET MY MOM?
I DIDN'T NEED TO. IT'S ALL FAIRLY OBVIOUS.
IT IS?
IT IS.
YOUR JERSEY, SHOES, AND BALL ARE HAND-ME-DOWNS . . .
WITH DIFFERENT NUMBERS WRITTEN IN MARKER.
11
WAHEED RULEZ
YOU HAVE AT LEAST TWO OLDER BROTHERS.

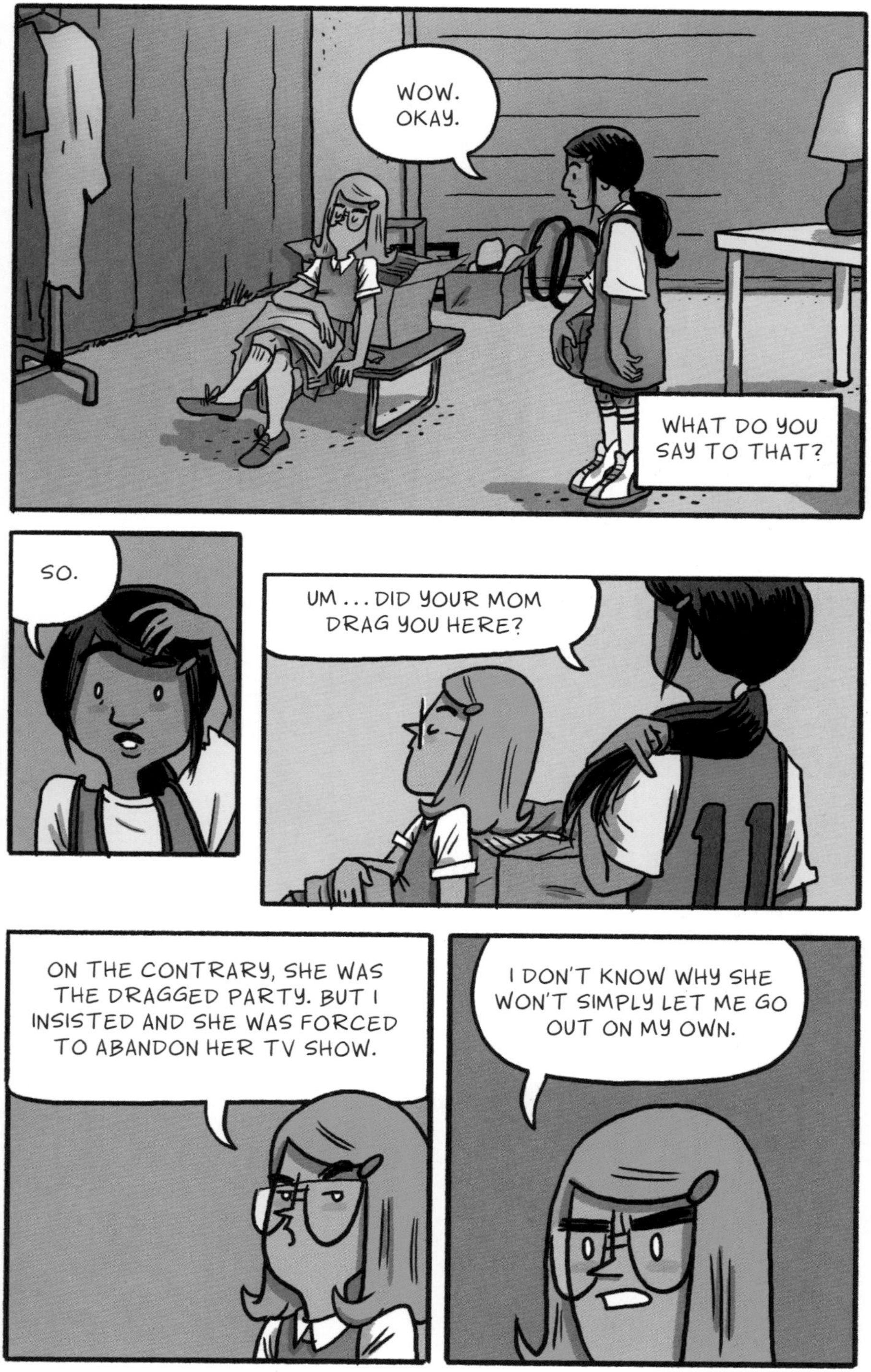
WOW. OKAY.
WHAT DO YOU SAY TO THAT?
SO.
UM . . . DID YOUR MOM DRAG YOU HERE?
ON THE CONTRARY, SHE WAS THE DRAGGED PARTY. BUT I INSISTED AND SHE WAS FORCED TO ABANDON HER TV SHOW.
I DON'T KNOW WHY SHE WON'T SIMPLY LET ME GO OUT ON MY OWN.

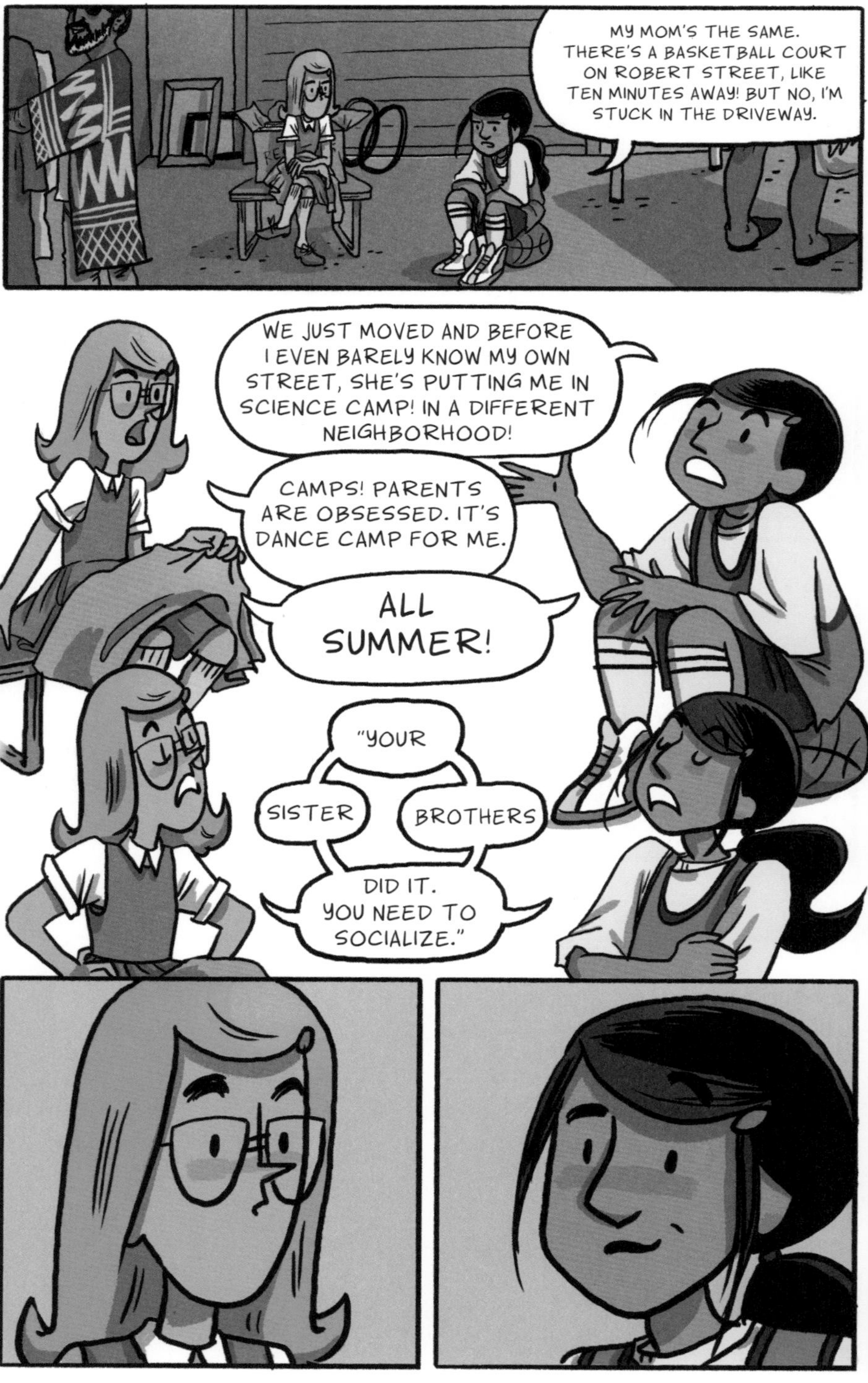

MY MOM'S THE SAME. THERE'S A BASKETBALL COURT ON ROBERT STREET, LIKE TEN MINUTES AWAY! BUT NO, I'M STUCK IN THE DRIVEWAY.
WE JUST MOVED AND BEFORE I EVEN BARELY KNOW MY OWN STREET, SHE'S PUTTING ME IN SCIENCE CAMP! IN A DIFFERENT NEIGHBORHOOD!
CAMPS! PARENTS ARE OBSESSED. IT'S DANCE CAMP FOR ME.
ALL SUMMER!
"YOUR
SISTER
BROTHERS
DID IT. YOU NEED TO SOCIALIZE."

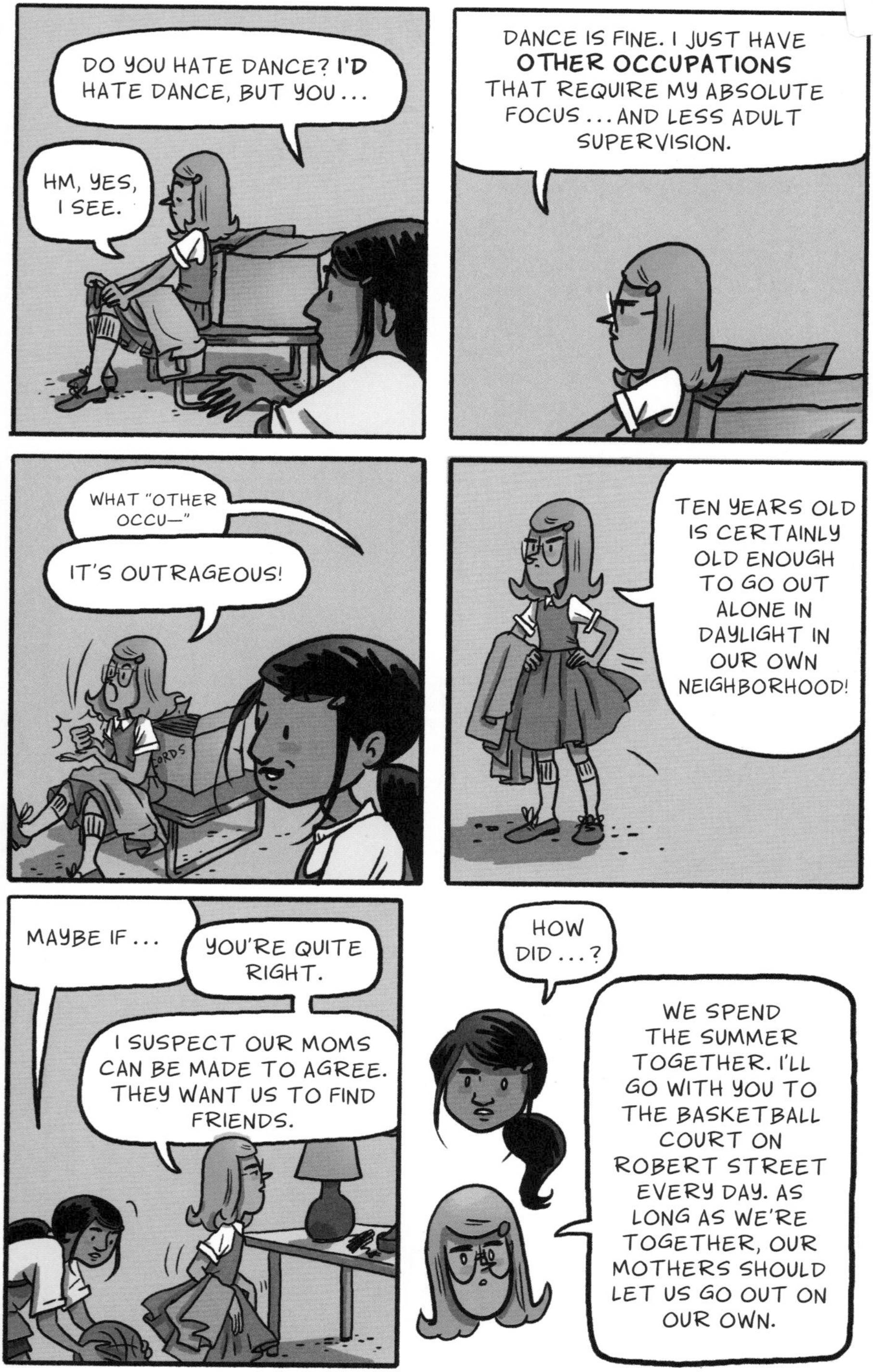
DO YOU HATE DANCE? **I'D** HATE DANCE, BUT YOU . . .
HM, YES, I SEE.
DANCE IS FINE. I JUST HAVE **OTHER OCCUPATIONS** THAT REQUIRE MY ABSOLUTE FOCUS . . . AND LESS ADULT SUPERVISION.
WHAT "OTHER OCCU—"
IT'S OUTRAGEOUS!
TEN YEARS OLD IS CERTAINLY OLD ENOUGH TO GO OUT ALONE IN DAYLIGHT IN OUR OWN NEIGHBORHOOD!
MAYBE IF . . .
YOU'RE QUITE RIGHT.
I SUSPECT OUR MOMS CAN BE MADE TO AGREE. THEY WANT US TO FIND FRIENDS.
HOW DID . . . ?
WE SPEND THE SUMMER TOGETHER. I'LL GO WITH YOU TO THE BASKETBALL COURT ON ROBERT STREET EVERY DAY. AS LONG AS WE'RE TOGETHER, OUR MOTHERS SHOULD LET US GO OUT ON OUR OWN.

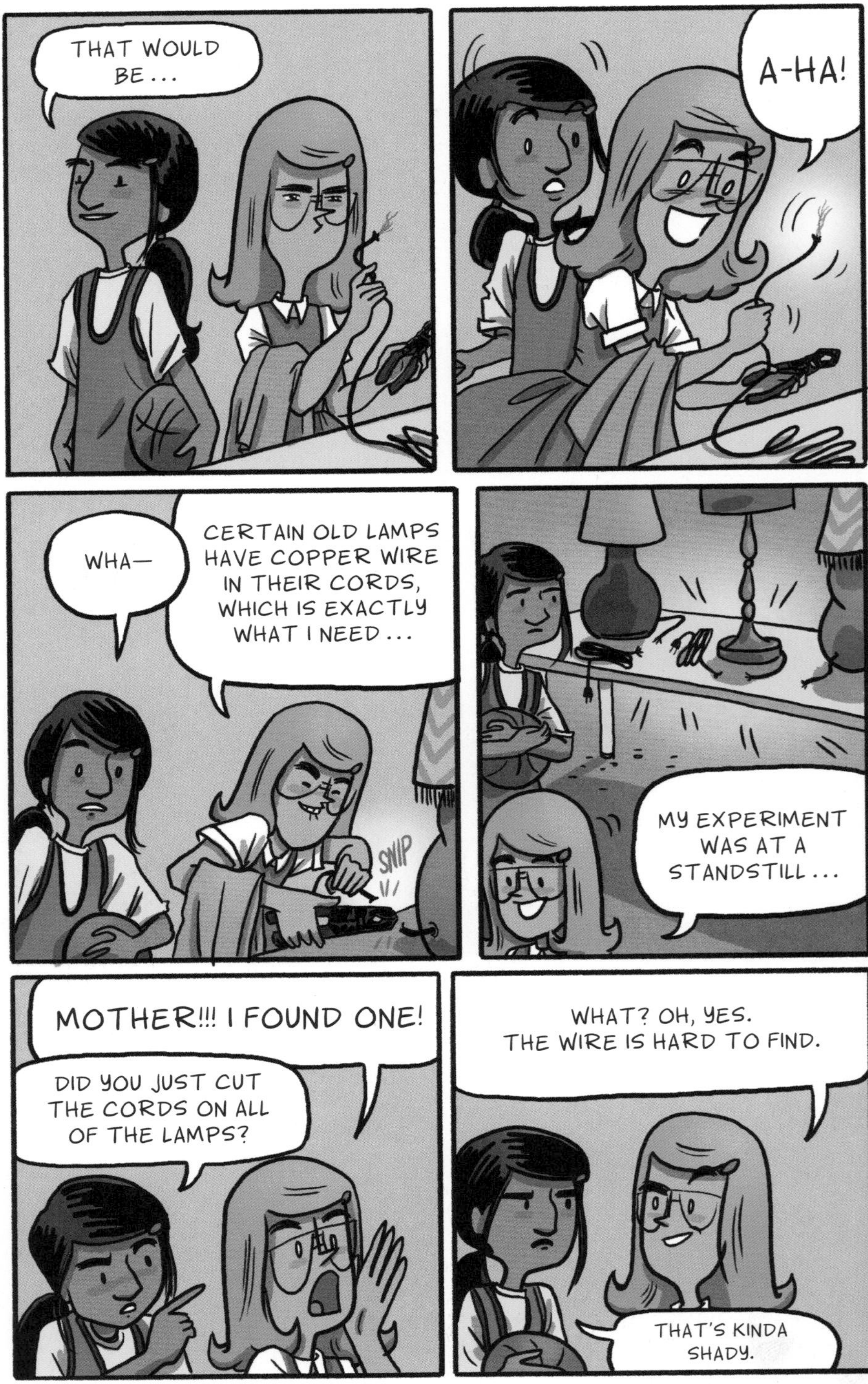
THAT WOULD BE...
A-HA!
WHA—
CERTAIN OLD LAMPS HAVE COPPER WIRE IN THEIR CORDS, WHICH IS EXACTLY WHAT I NEED...
SNIP
MY EXPERIMENT WAS AT A STANDSTILL...
MOTHER!!! I FOUND ONE!
DID YOU JUST CUT THE CORDS ON ALL OF THE LAMPS?
WHAT? OH, YES. THE WIRE IS HARD TO FIND.
THAT'S KINDA SHADY.

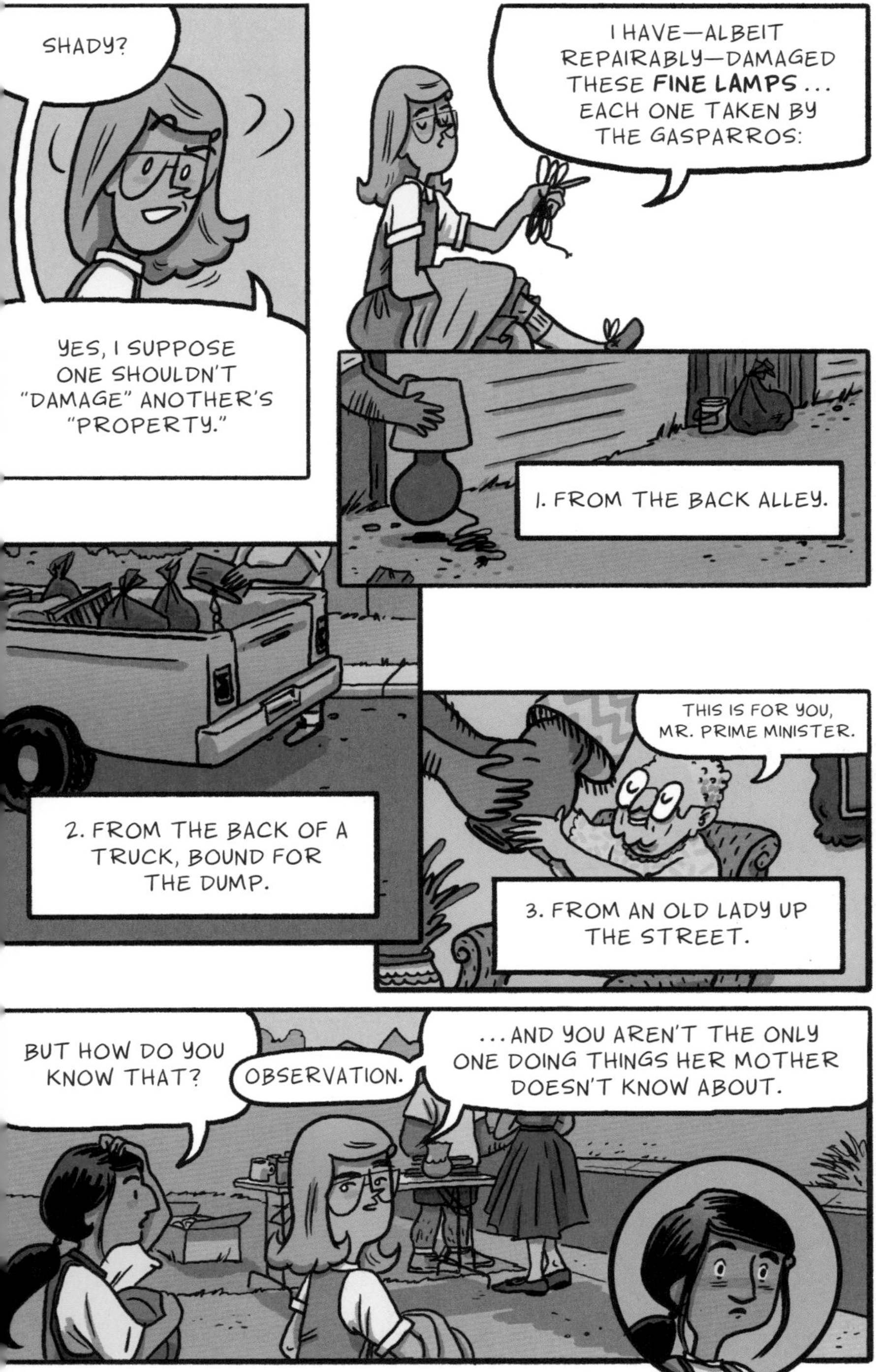
SHADY?
YES, I SUPPOSE ONE SHOULDN'T "DAMAGE" ANOTHER'S "PROPERTY."
I HAVE—ALBEIT REPAIRABLY—DAMAGED THESE **FINE LAMPS** . . . EACH ONE TAKEN BY THE GASPARROS:
1. FROM THE BACK ALLEY.
2. FROM THE BACK OF A TRUCK, BOUND FOR THE DUMP.
THIS IS FOR YOU, MR. PRIME MINISTER.
3. FROM AN OLD LADY UP THE STREET.
BUT HOW DO YOU KNOW THAT?
OBSERVATION.
. . . AND YOU AREN'T THE ONLY ONE DOING THINGS HER MOTHER DOESN'T KNOW ABOUT.

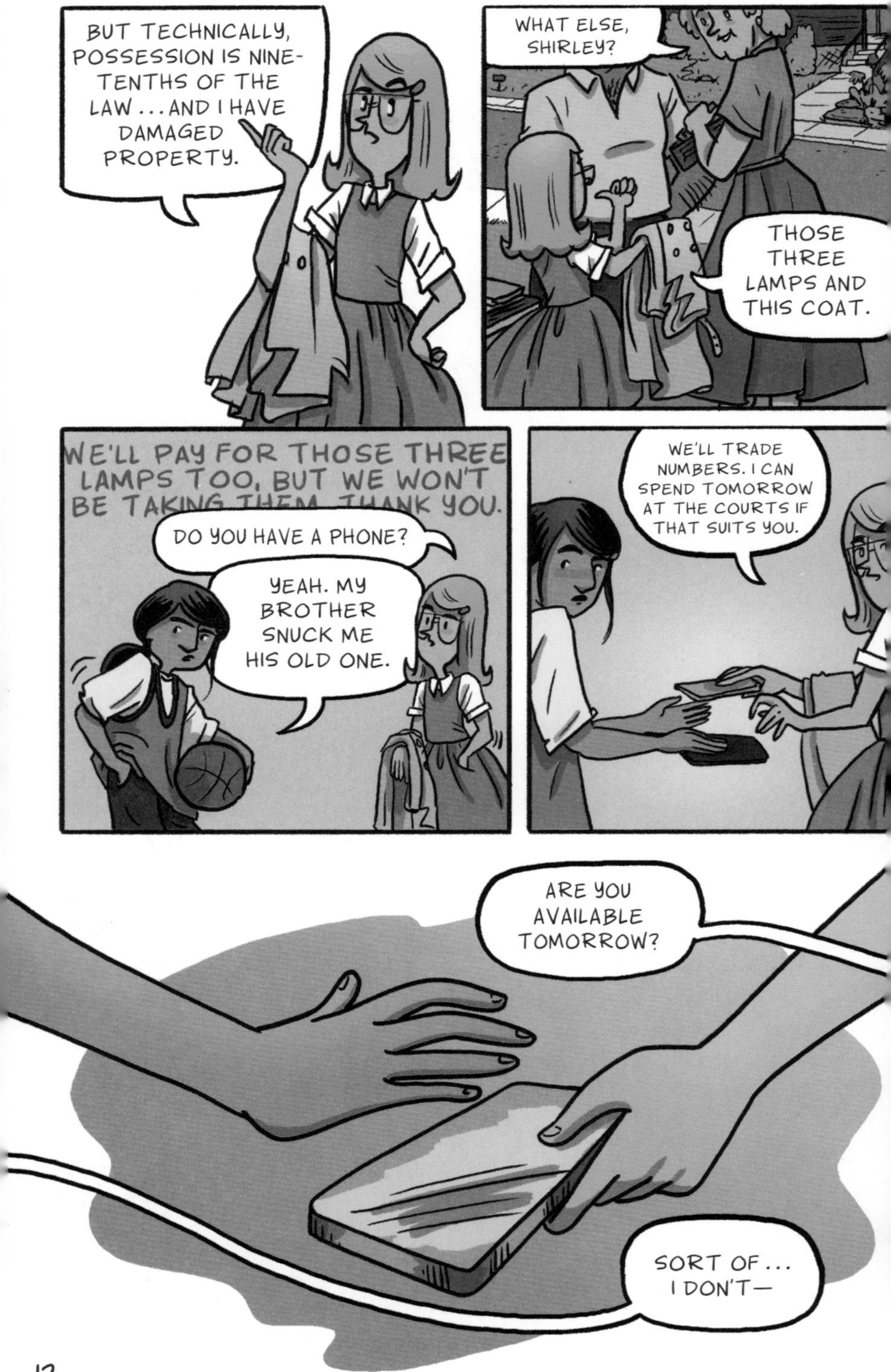
BUT TECHNICALLY, POSSESSION IS NINE-TENTHS OF THE LAW . . . AND I HAVE DAMAGED PROPERTY.
WHAT ELSE, SHIRLEY?
THOSE THREE LAMPS AND THIS COAT.
WE'LL PAY FOR THOSE THREE LAMPS TOO, BUT WE WON'T BE TAKING THEM, THANK YOU.
DO YOU HAVE A PHONE?
YEAH. MY BROTHER SNUCK ME HIS OLD ONE.
WE'LL TRADE NUMBERS. I CAN SPEND TOMORROW AT THE COURTS IF THAT SUITS YOU.
ARE YOU AVAILABLE TOMORROW?
SORT OF . . . I DON'T—

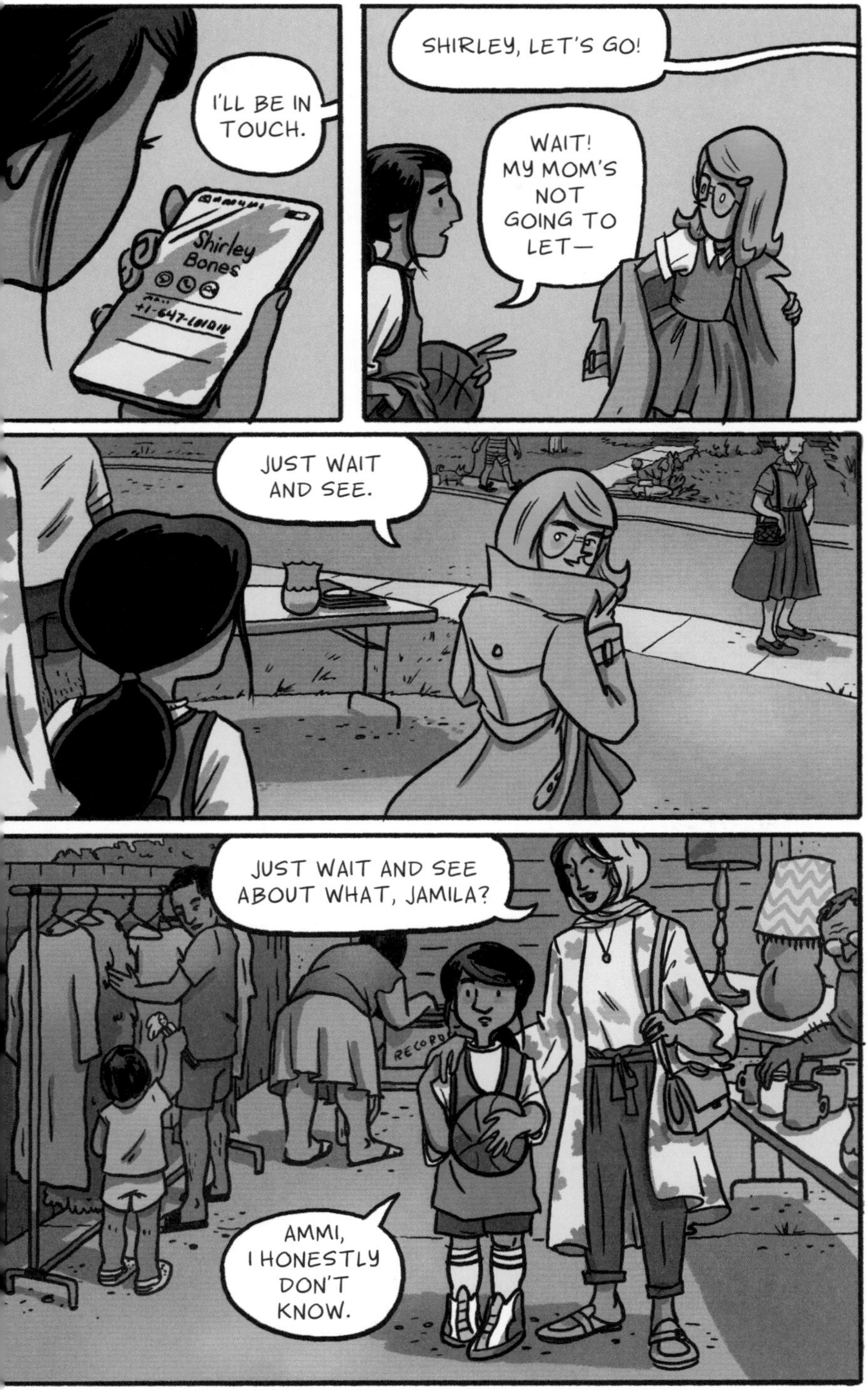
I'LL BE IN TOUCH.
Shirley Bones
SHIRLEY, LET'S GO!
WAIT! MY MOM'S NOT GOING TO LET—
JUST WAIT AND SEE.
JUST WAIT AND SEE ABOUT WHAT, JAMILA?
AMMI, I HONESTLY DON'T KNOW.

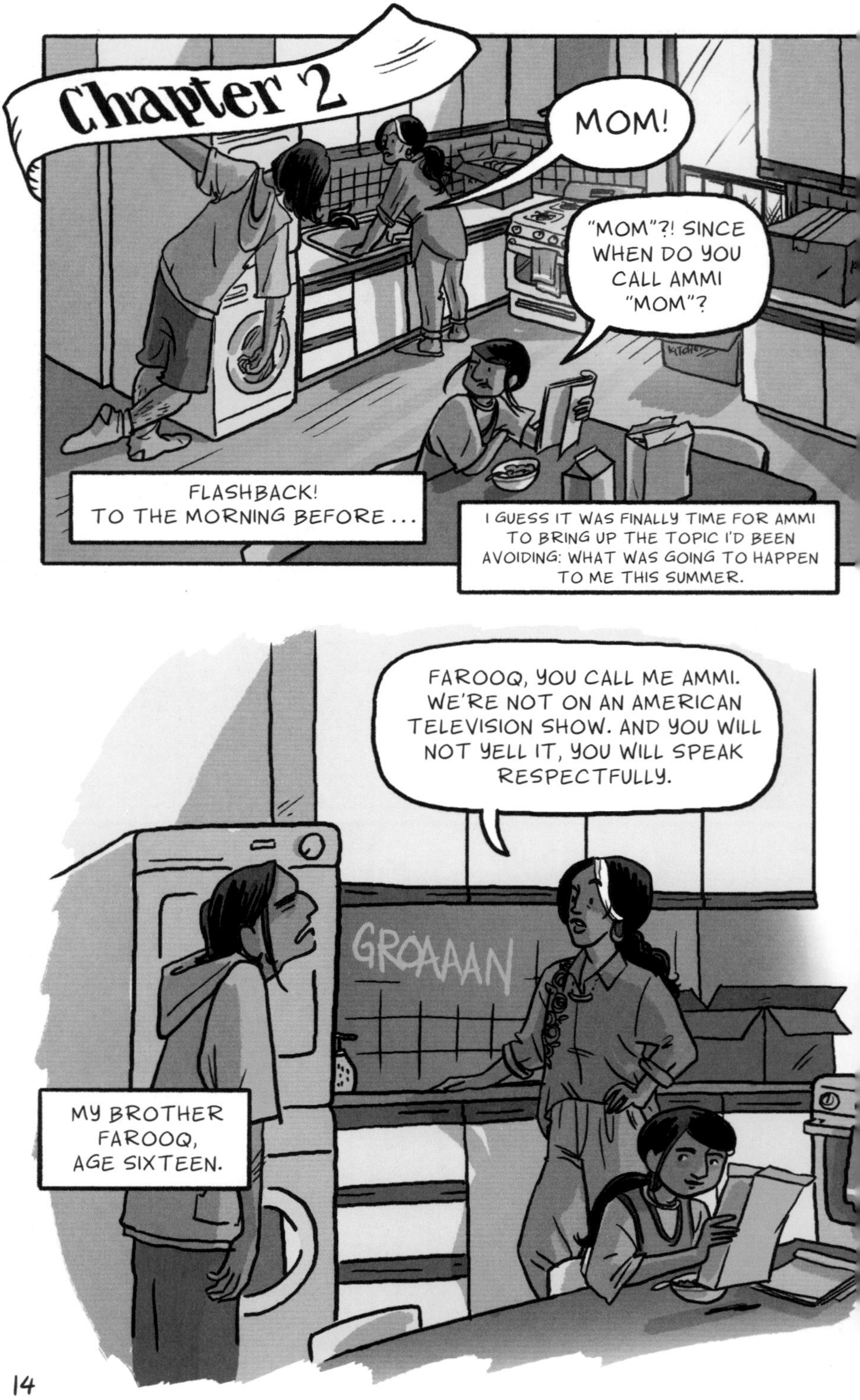
Chapter 2
MOM!
"MOM"?! SINCE WHEN DO YOU CALL AMMI "MOM"?
FLASHBACK! TO THE MORNING BEFORE . . .
I GUESS IT WAS FINALLY TIME FOR AMMI TO BRING UP THE TOPIC I'D BEEN AVOIDING: WHAT WAS GOING TO HAPPEN TO ME THIS SUMMER.
FAROOQ, YOU CALL ME AMMI. WE'RE NOT ON AN AMERICAN TELEVISION SHOW. AND YOU WILL NOT YELL IT, YOU WILL SPEAK RESPECTFULLY.
GROAAAN
MY BROTHER FAROOQ, AGE SIXTEEN.

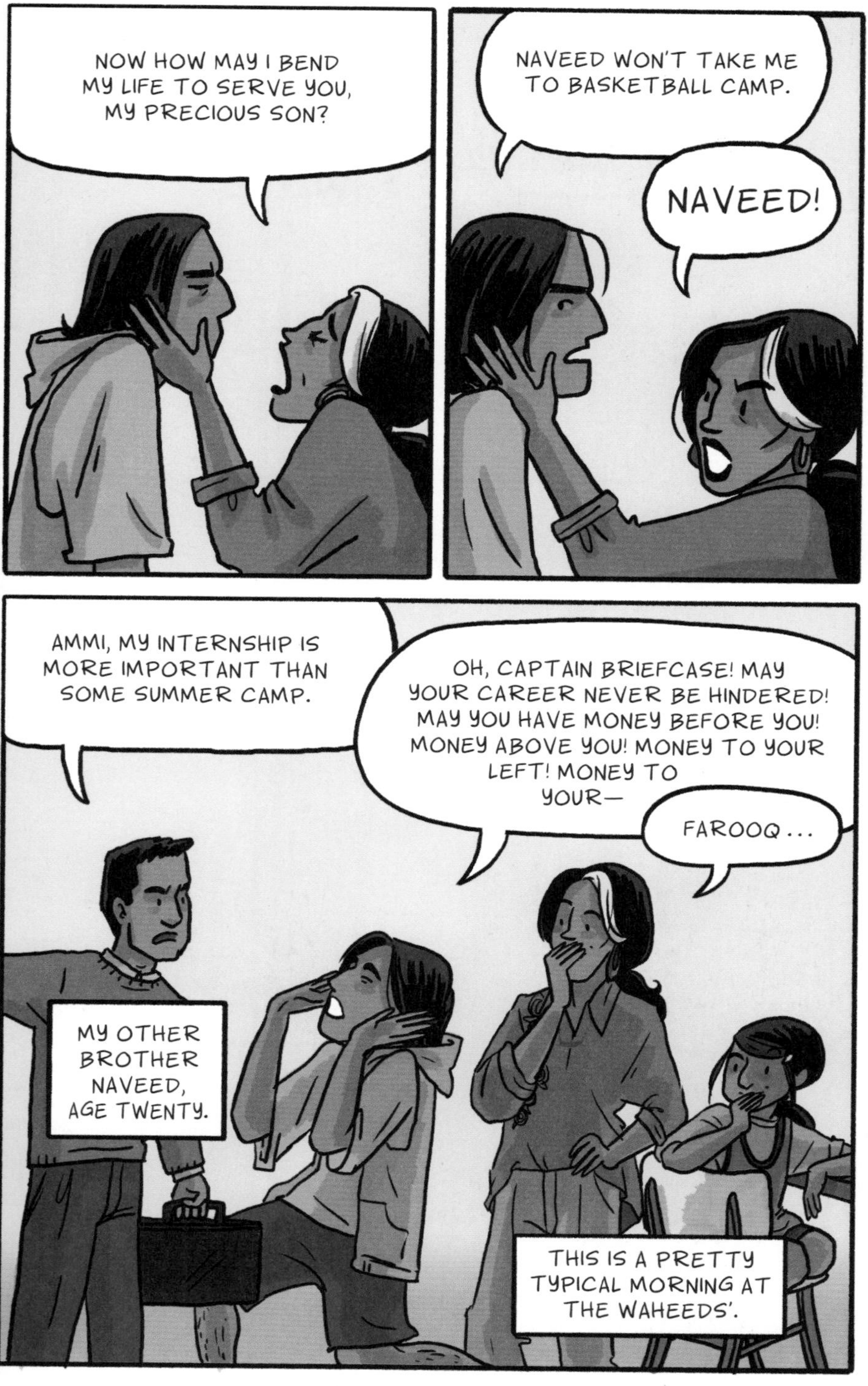
NOW HOW MAY I BEND MY LIFE TO SERVE YOU, MY PRECIOUS SON?
NAVEED WON'T TAKE ME TO BASKETBALL CAMP.
NAVEED!
AMMI, MY INTERNSHIP IS MORE IMPORTANT THAN SOME SUMMER CAMP.
OH, CAPTAIN BRIEFCASE! MAY YOUR CAREER NEVER BE HINDERED! MAY YOU HAVE MONEY BEFORE YOU! MONEY ABOVE YOU! MONEY TO YOUR LEFT! MONEY TO YOUR—
FAROOQ . . .
MY OTHER BROTHER NAVEED, AGE TWENTY.
THIS IS A PRETTY TYPICAL MORNING AT THE WAHEEDS'.

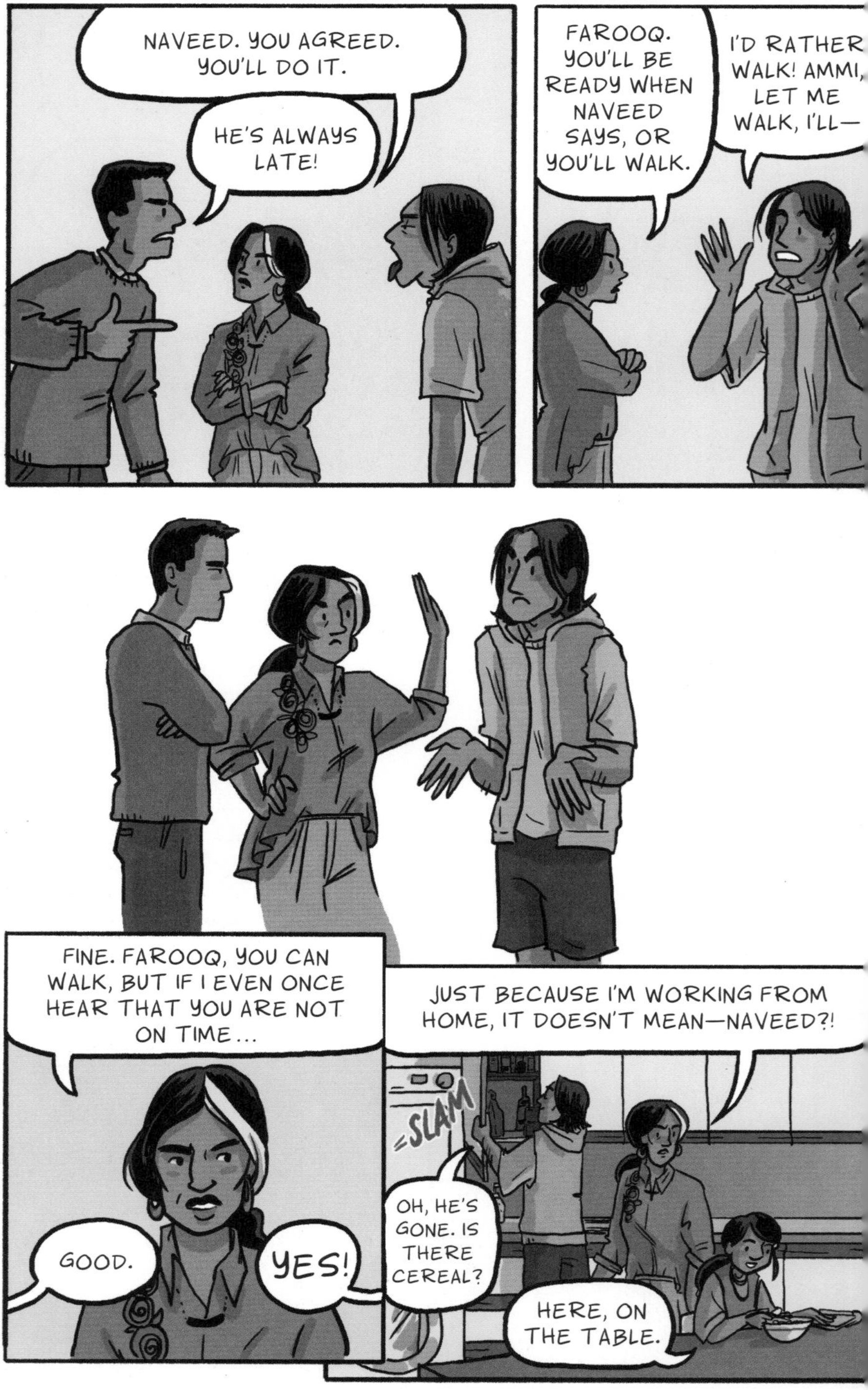
NAVEED. YOU AGREED. YOU'LL DO IT.
HE'S ALWAYS LATE!
FAROOQ. YOU'LL BE READY WHEN NAVEED SAYS, OR YOU'LL WALK.
I'D RATHER WALK! AMMI, LET ME WALK, I'LL—
FINE. FAROOQ, YOU CAN WALK, BUT IF I EVEN ONCE HEAR THAT YOU ARE NOT ON TIME...
GOOD.
YES!
JUST BECAUSE I'M WORKING FROM HOME, IT DOESN'T MEAN—NAVEED?!
SLAM
OH, HE'S GONE. IS THERE CEREAL?
HERE, ON THE TABLE.

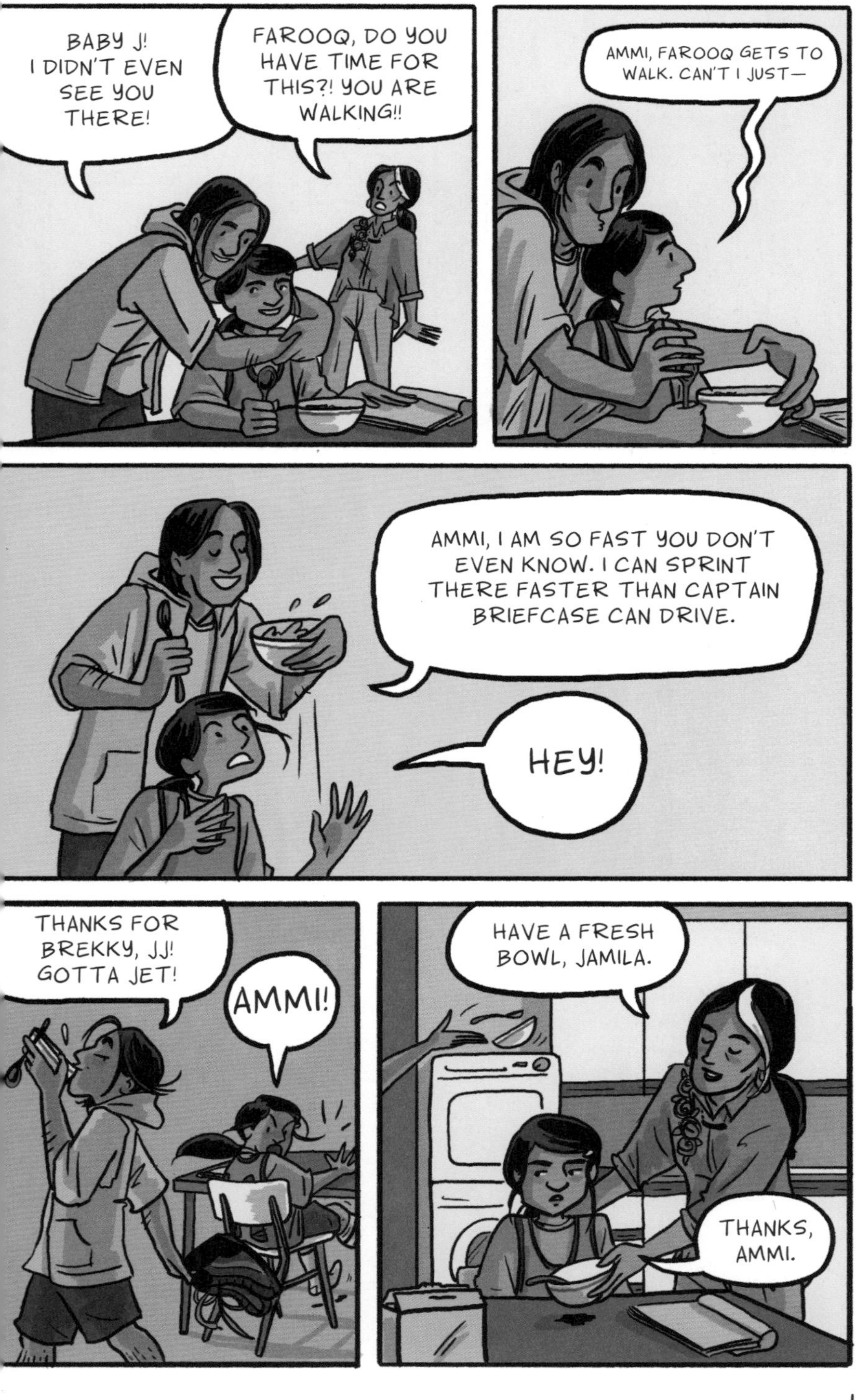
BABY J! I DIDN'T EVEN SEE YOU THERE!
FAROOQ, DO YOU HAVE TIME FOR THIS?! YOU ARE WALKING!!
AMMI, FAROOQ GETS TO WALK. CAN'T I JUST—
AMMI, I AM SO FAST YOU DON'T EVEN KNOW. I CAN SPRINT THERE FASTER THAN CAPTAIN BRIEFCASE CAN DRIVE.
HEY!
THANKS FOR BREKKY, JJ! GOTTA JET!
AMMI!
HAVE A FRESH BOWL, JAMILA.
THANKS, AMMI.

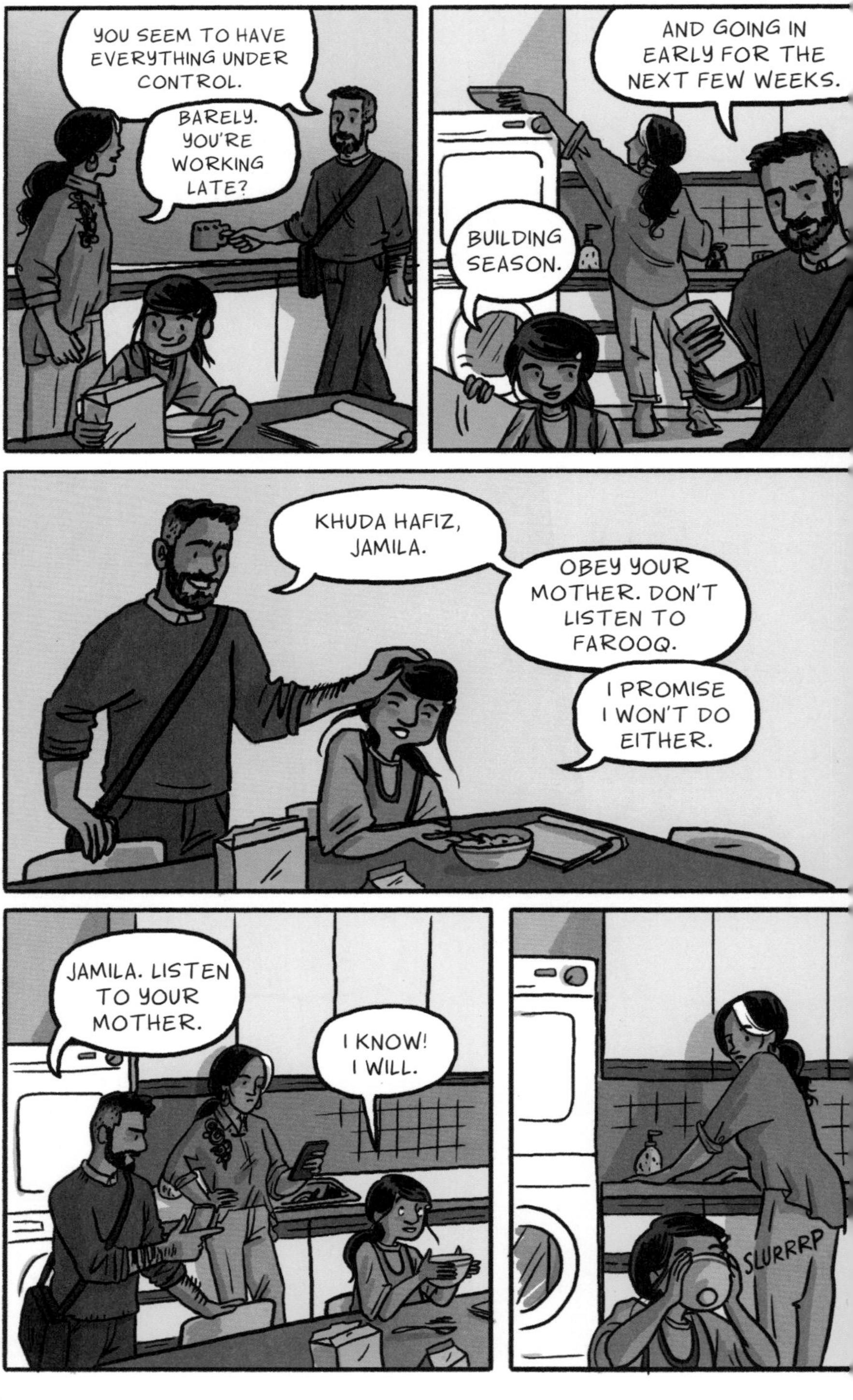
YOU SEEM TO HAVE EVERYTHING UNDER CONTROL.
BARELY. YOU'RE WORKING LATE?
AND GOING IN EARLY FOR THE NEXT FEW WEEKS.
BUILDING SEASON.
KHUDA HAFIZ, JAMILA.
OBEY YOUR MOTHER. DON'T LISTEN TO FAROOQ.
I PROMISE I WON'T DO EITHER.
JAMILA. LISTEN TO YOUR MOTHER.
I KNOW! I WILL.
SLURRRP

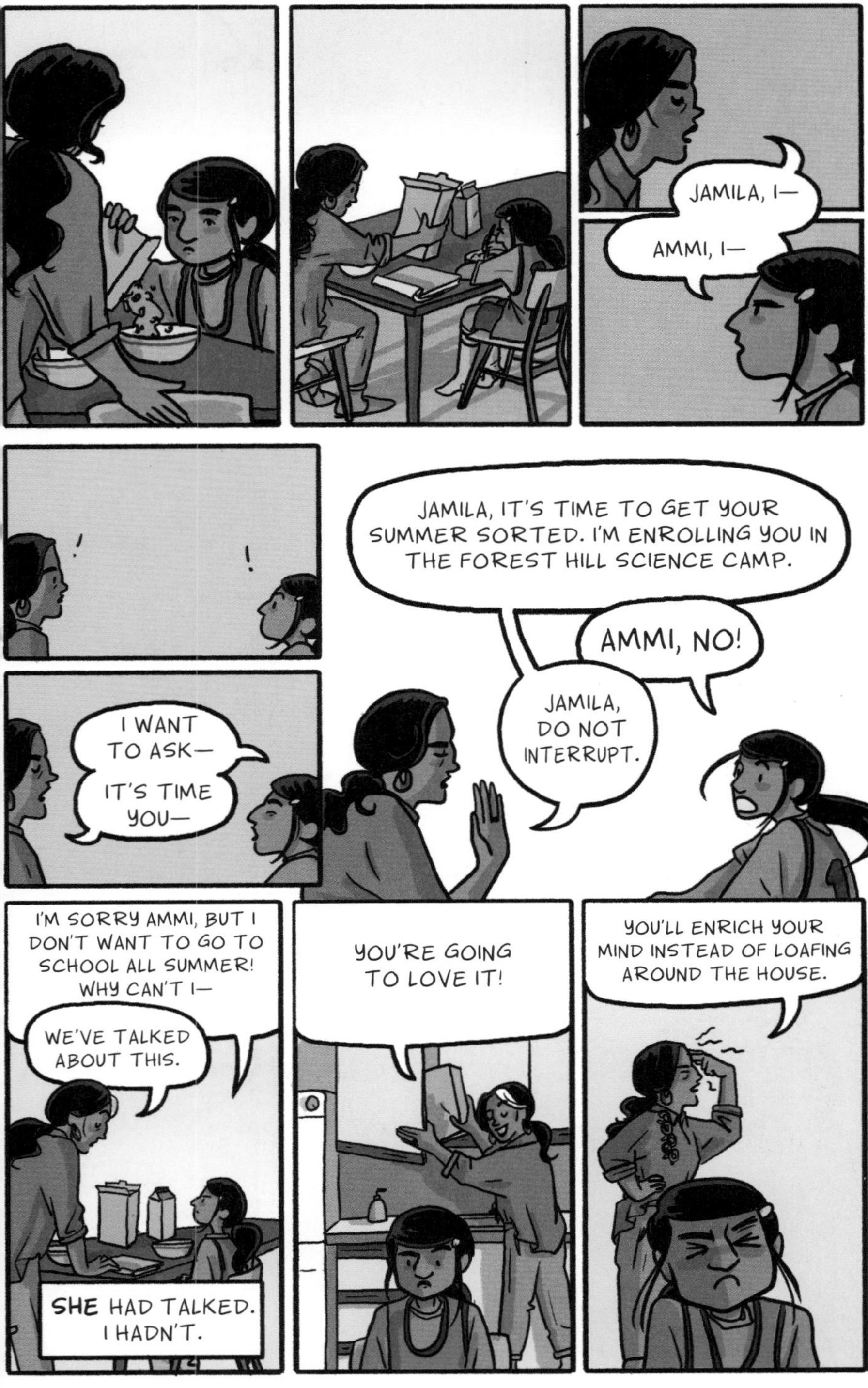
JAMILA, I—
AMMI, I—
!
!
JAMILA, IT'S TIME TO GET YOUR SUMMER SORTED. I'M ENROLLING YOU IN THE FOREST HILL SCIENCE CAMP.
I WANT TO ASK—
IT'S TIME YOU—
AMMI, NO!
JAMILA, DO NOT INTERRUPT.
I'M SORRY AMMI, BUT I DON'T WANT TO GO TO SCHOOL ALL SUMMER! WHY CAN'T I—
WE'VE TALKED ABOUT THIS.
SHE HAD TALKED. I HADN'T.
YOU'RE GOING TO LOVE IT!
YOU'LL ENRICH YOUR MIND INSTEAD OF LOAFING AROUND THE HOUSE.

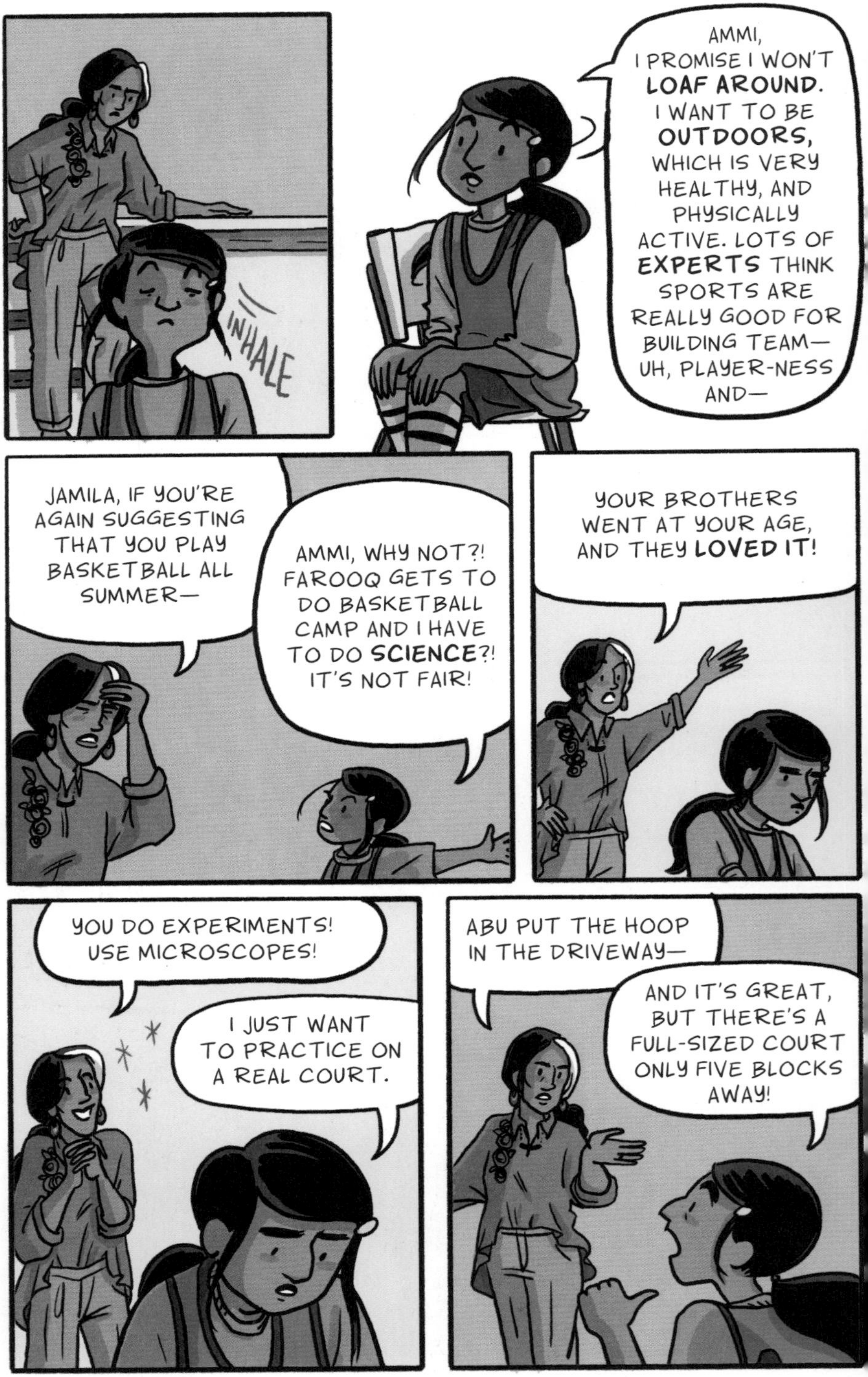
INHALE
AMMI, I PROMISE I WON'T LOAF AROUND. I WANT TO BE OUTDOORS, WHICH IS VERY HEALTHY, AND PHYSICALLY ACTIVE. LOTS OF EXPERTS THINK SPORTS ARE REALLY GOOD FOR BUILDING TEAM— UH, PLAYER-NESS AND—
JAMILA, IF YOU'RE AGAIN SUGGESTING THAT YOU PLAY BASKETBALL ALL SUMMER—
AMMI, WHY NOT?! FAROOQ GETS TO DO BASKETBALL CAMP AND I HAVE TO DO SCIENCE?! IT'S NOT FAIR!
YOUR BROTHERS WENT AT YOUR AGE, AND THEY LOVED IT!
YOU DO EXPERIMENTS! USE MICROSCOPES!
I JUST WANT TO PRACTICE ON A REAL COURT.
ABU PUT THE HOOP IN THE DRIVEWAY—
AND IT'S GREAT, BUT THERE'S A FULL-SIZED COURT ONLY FIVE BLOCKS AWAY!

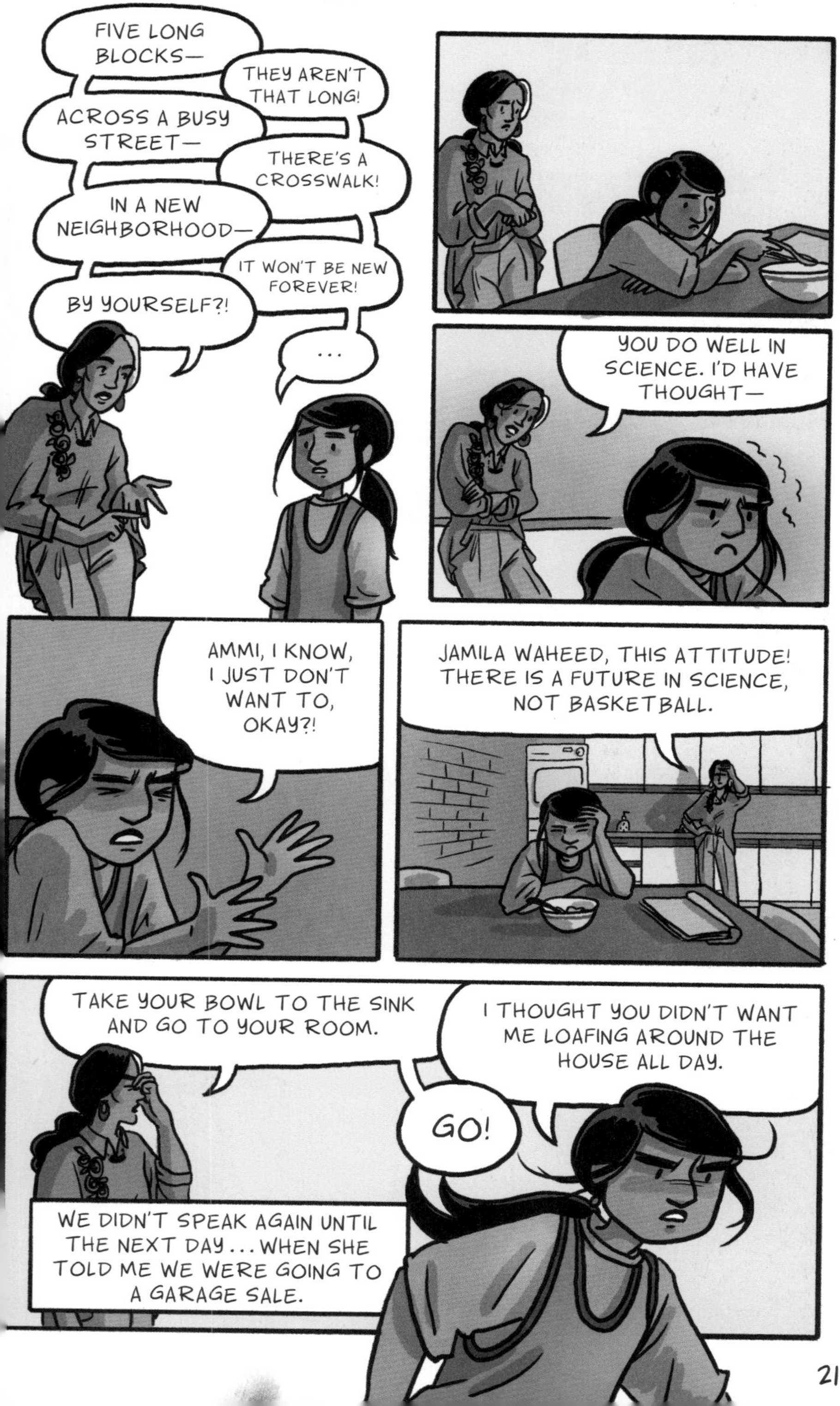
FIVE LONG BLOCKS—
THEY AREN'T THAT LONG!
ACROSS A BUSY STREET—
THERE'S A CROSSWALK!
IN A NEW NEIGHBORHOOD—
IT WON'T BE NEW FOREVER!
BY YOURSELF?!
...
YOU DO WELL IN SCIENCE. I'D HAVE THOUGHT—
AMMI, I KNOW, I JUST DON'T WANT TO, OKAY?!
JAMILA WAHEED, THIS ATTITUDE! THERE IS A FUTURE IN SCIENCE, NOT BASKETBALL.
TAKE YOUR BOWL TO THE SINK AND GO TO YOUR ROOM.
I THOUGHT YOU DIDN'T WANT ME LOAFING AROUND THE HOUSE ALL DAY.
GO!
WE DIDN'T SPEAK AGAIN UNTIL THE NEXT DAY . . . WHEN SHE TOLD ME WE WERE GOING TO A GARAGE SALE.

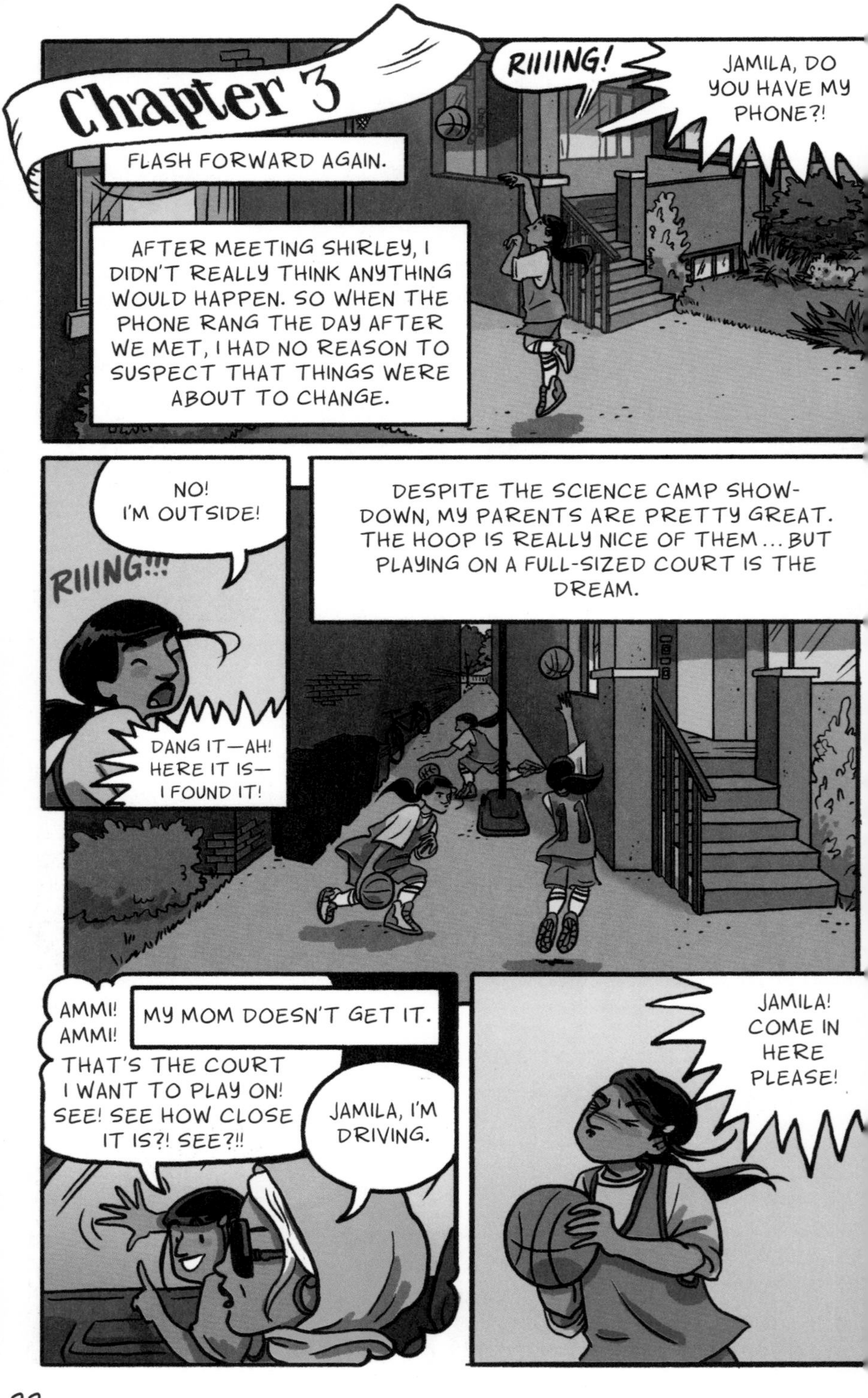
Chapter 3
FLASH FORWARD AGAIN.
AFTER MEETING SHIRLEY, I DIDN'T REALLY THINK ANYTHING WOULD HAPPEN. SO WHEN THE PHONE RANG THE DAY AFTER WE MET, I HAD NO REASON TO SUSPECT THAT THINGS WERE ABOUT TO CHANGE.
RIIING!
JAMILA, DO YOU HAVE MY PHONE?!
NO! I'M OUTSIDE!
RIIING!!!
DANG IT—AH! HERE IT IS— I FOUND IT!
DESPITE THE SCIENCE CAMP SHOW-DOWN, MY PARENTS ARE PRETTY GREAT. THE HOOP IS REALLY NICE OF THEM... BUT PLAYING ON A FULL-SIZED COURT IS THE DREAM.
MY MOM DOESN'T GET IT.
AMMI! AMMI!
THAT'S THE COURT I WANT TO PLAY ON! SEE! SEE HOW CLOSE IT IS?! SEE?!!
JAMILA, I'M DRIVING.
JAMILA! COME IN HERE PLEASE!

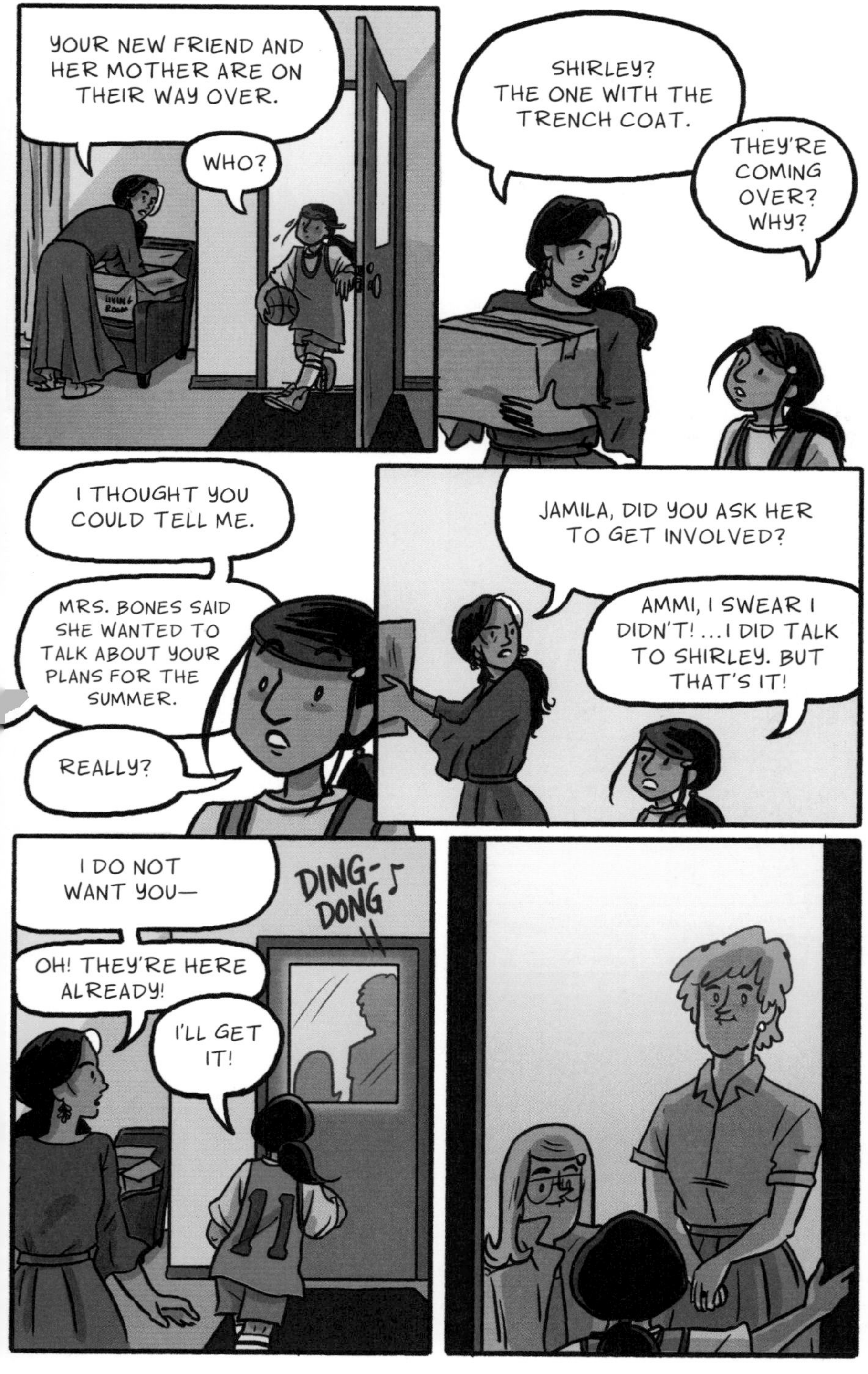
YOUR NEW FRIEND AND HER MOTHER ARE ON THEIR WAY OVER.
WHO?
SHIRLEY? THE ONE WITH THE TRENCH COAT.
THEY'RE COMING OVER? WHY?
I THOUGHT YOU COULD TELL ME.
MRS. BONES SAID SHE WANTED TO TALK ABOUT YOUR PLANS FOR THE SUMMER.
REALLY?
JAMILA, DID YOU ASK HER TO GET INVOLVED?
AMMI, I SWEAR I DIDN'T! ...I DID TALK TO SHIRLEY. BUT THAT'S IT!
I DO NOT WANT YOU—
DING-DONG
OH! THEY'RE HERE ALREADY!
I'LL GET IT!

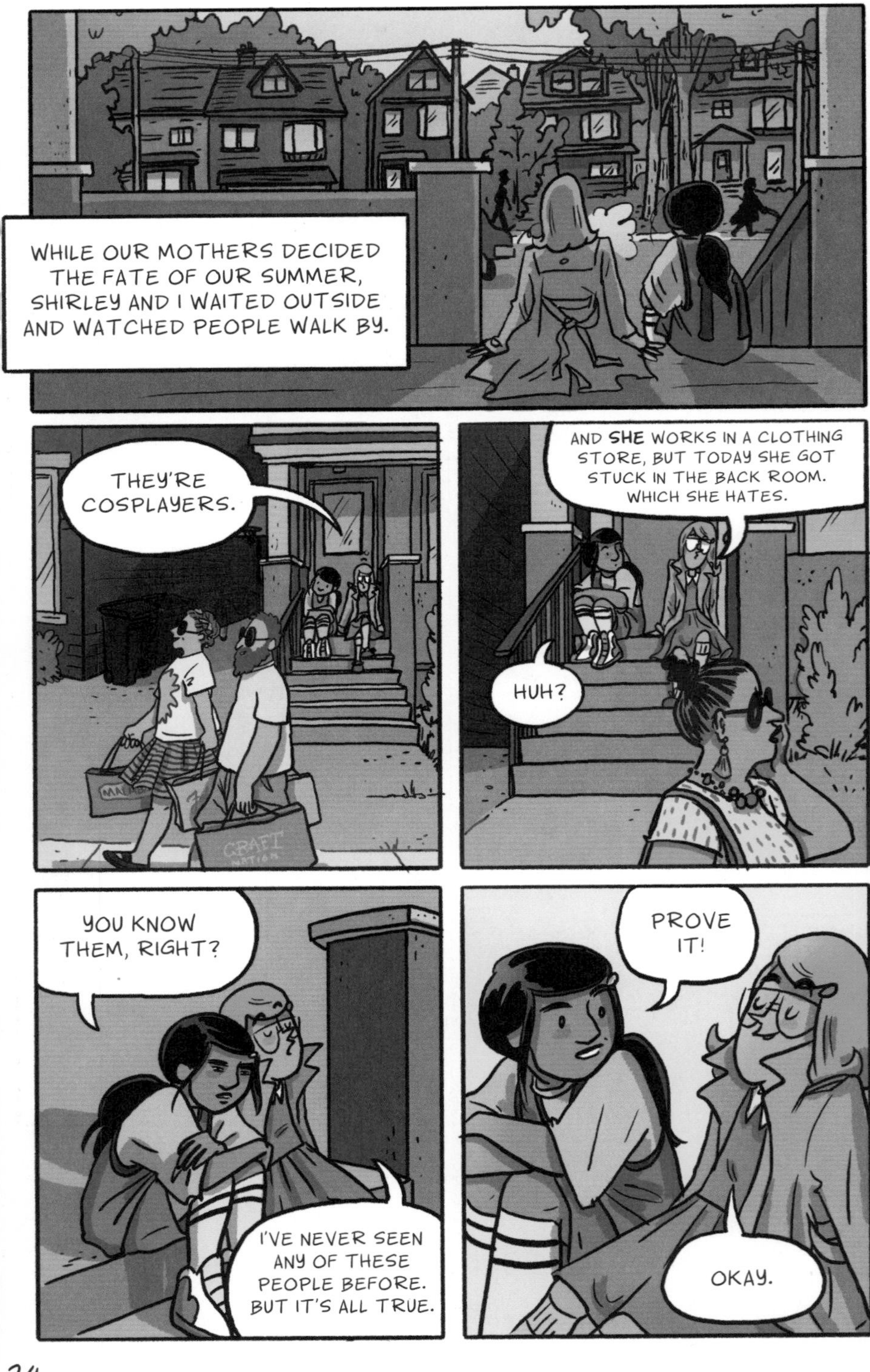

WHILE OUR MOTHERS DECIDED THE FATE OF OUR SUMMER, SHIRLEY AND I WAITED OUTSIDE AND WATCHED PEOPLE WALK BY.
THEY'RE COSPLAYERS.
AND **SHE** WORKS IN A CLOTHING STORE, BUT TODAY SHE GOT STUCK IN THE BACK ROOM. WHICH SHE HATES.
HUH?
YOU KNOW THEM, RIGHT?
I'VE NEVER SEEN ANY OF THESE PEOPLE BEFORE. BUT IT'S ALL TRUE.
PROVE IT!
OKAY.

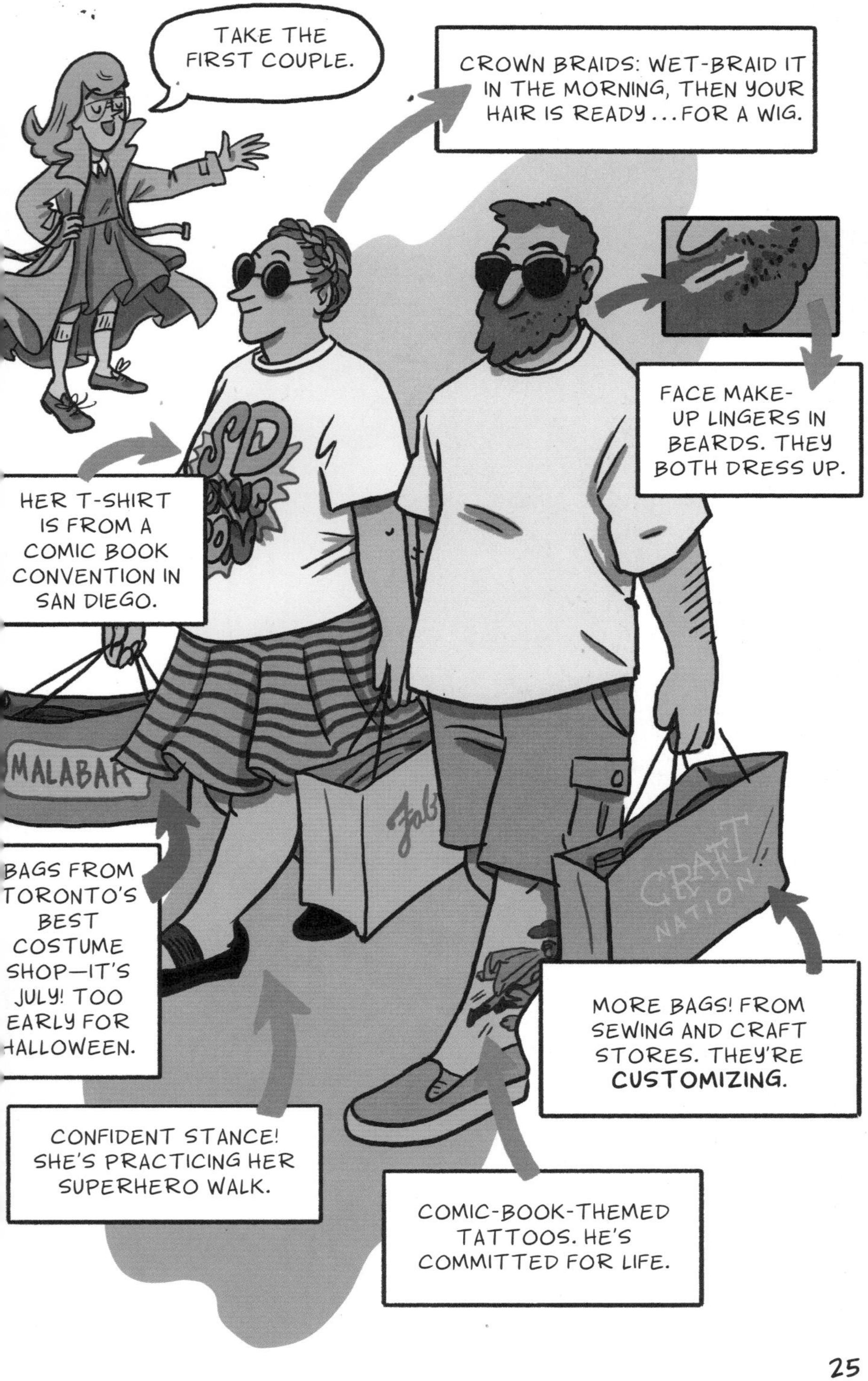
TAKE THE FIRST COUPLE.
CROWN BRAIDS: WET-BRAID IT IN THE MORNING, THEN YOUR HAIR IS READY . . . FOR A WIG.
FACE MAKE-UP LINGERS IN BEARDS. THEY BOTH DRESS UP.
HER T-SHIRT IS FROM A COMIC BOOK CONVENTION IN SAN DIEGO.
MALABAR
BAGS FROM TORONTO'S BEST COSTUME SHOP—IT'S JULY! TOO EARLY FOR HALLOWEEN.
CRAFT NATION
MORE BAGS! FROM SEWING AND CRAFT STORES. THEY'RE **CUSTOMIZING**.
CONFIDENT STANCE! SHE'S PRACTICING HER SUPERHERO WALK.
COMIC-BOOK-THEMED TATTOOS. HE'S COMMITTED FOR LIFE.

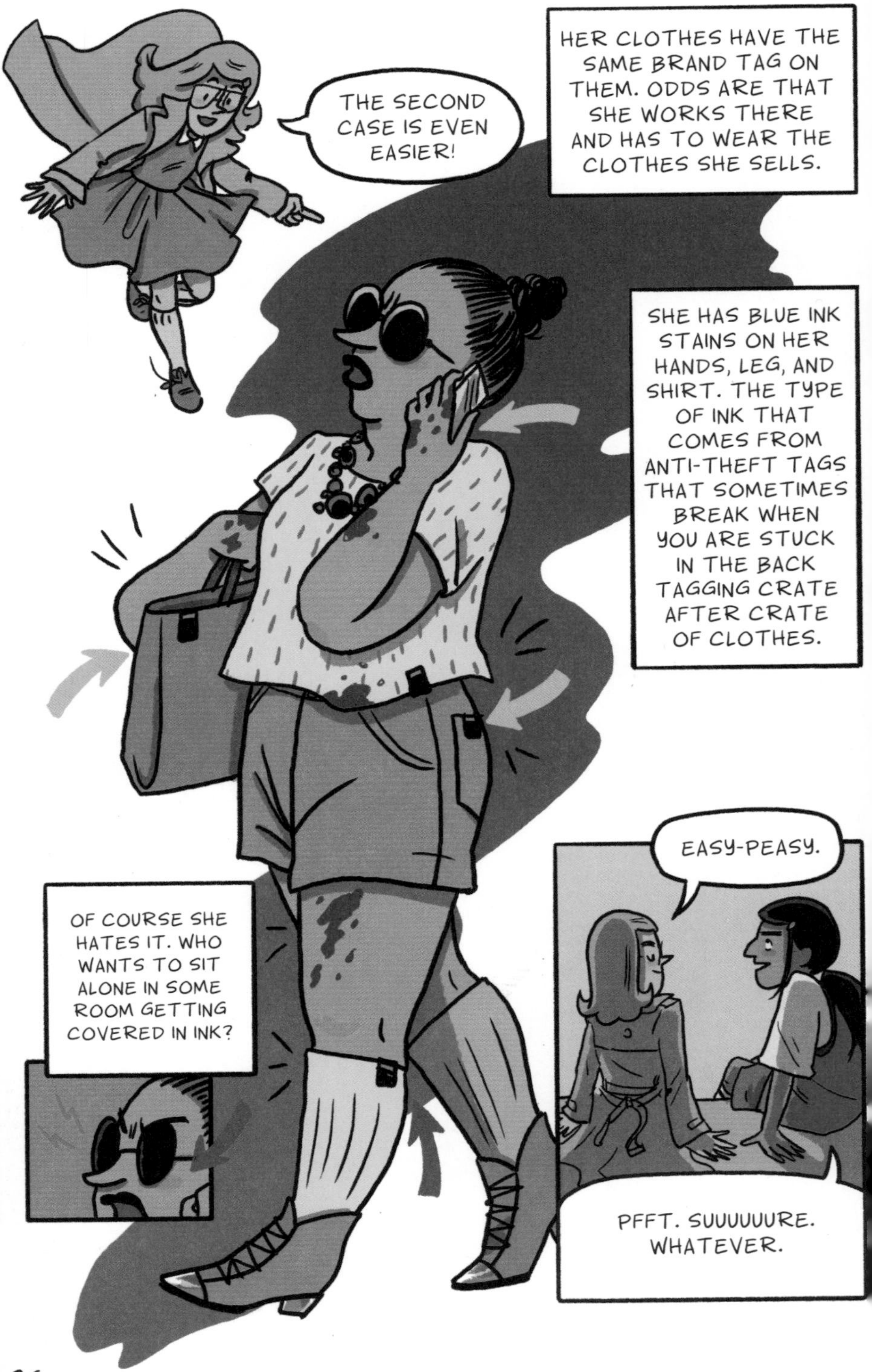
THE SECOND CASE IS EVEN EASIER!
HER CLOTHES HAVE THE SAME BRAND TAG ON THEM. ODDS ARE THAT SHE WORKS THERE AND HAS TO WEAR THE CLOTHES SHE SELLS.
SHE HAS BLUE INK STAINS ON HER HANDS, LEG, AND SHIRT. THE TYPE OF INK THAT COMES FROM ANTI-THEFT TAGS THAT SOMETIMES BREAK WHEN YOU ARE STUCK IN THE BACK TAGGING CRATE AFTER CRATE OF CLOTHES.
OF COURSE SHE HATES IT. WHO WANTS TO SIT ALONE IN SOME ROOM GETTING COVERED IN INK?
EASY-PEASY.
PFFT. SUUUUUURE. WHATEVER.

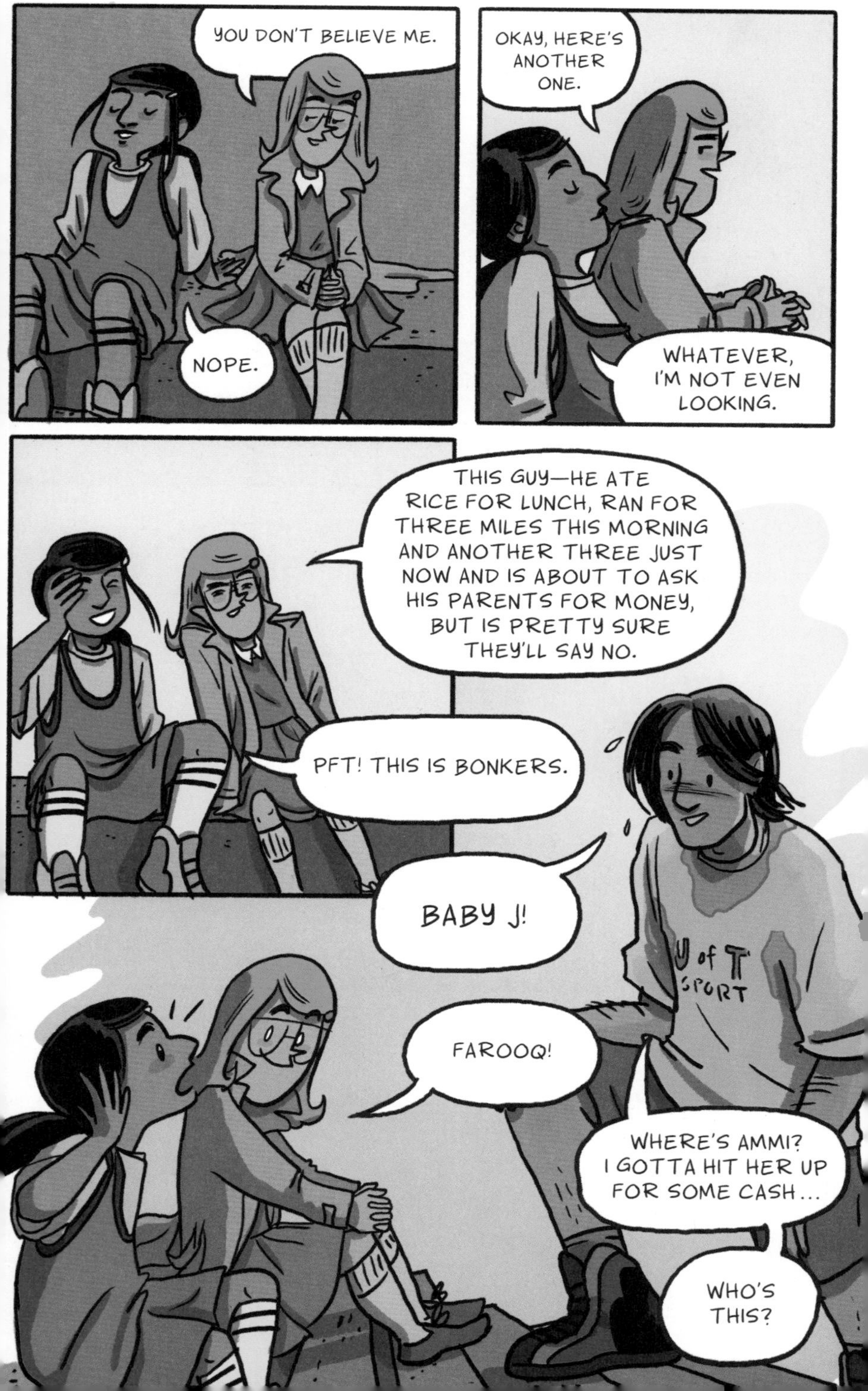
YOU DON'T BELIEVE ME.
NOPE.
OKAY, HERE'S ANOTHER ONE.
WHATEVER, I'M NOT EVEN LOOKING.
THIS GUY—HE ATE RICE FOR LUNCH, RAN FOR THREE MILES THIS MORNING AND ANOTHER THREE JUST NOW AND IS ABOUT TO ASK HIS PARENTS FOR MONEY, BUT IS PRETTY SURE THEY'LL SAY NO.
PFT! THIS IS BONKERS.
BABY J!
U of T SPORT
FAROOQ!
WHERE'S AMMI? I GOTTA HIT HER UP FOR SOME CASH...
WHO'S THIS?

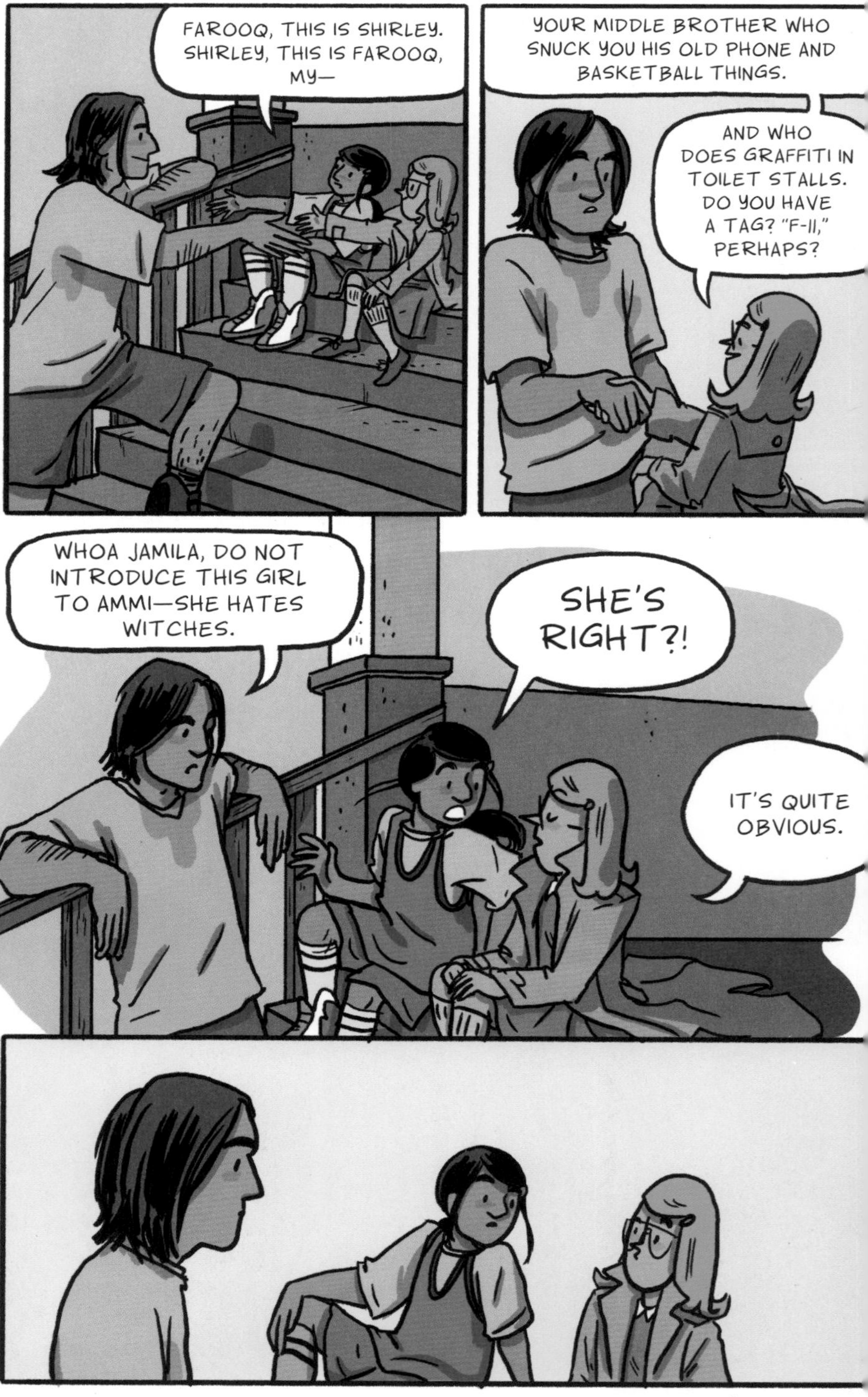
FAROOQ, THIS IS SHIRLEY. SHIRLEY, THIS IS FAROOQ, MY—
YOUR MIDDLE BROTHER WHO SNUCK YOU HIS OLD PHONE AND BASKETBALL THINGS.
AND WHO DOES GRAFFITI IN TOILET STALLS. DO YOU HAVE A TAG? "F-11," PERHAPS?
WHOA JAMILA, DO NOT INTRODUCE THIS GIRL TO AMMI—SHE HATES WITCHES.
SHE'S RIGHT?!
IT'S QUITE OBVIOUS.

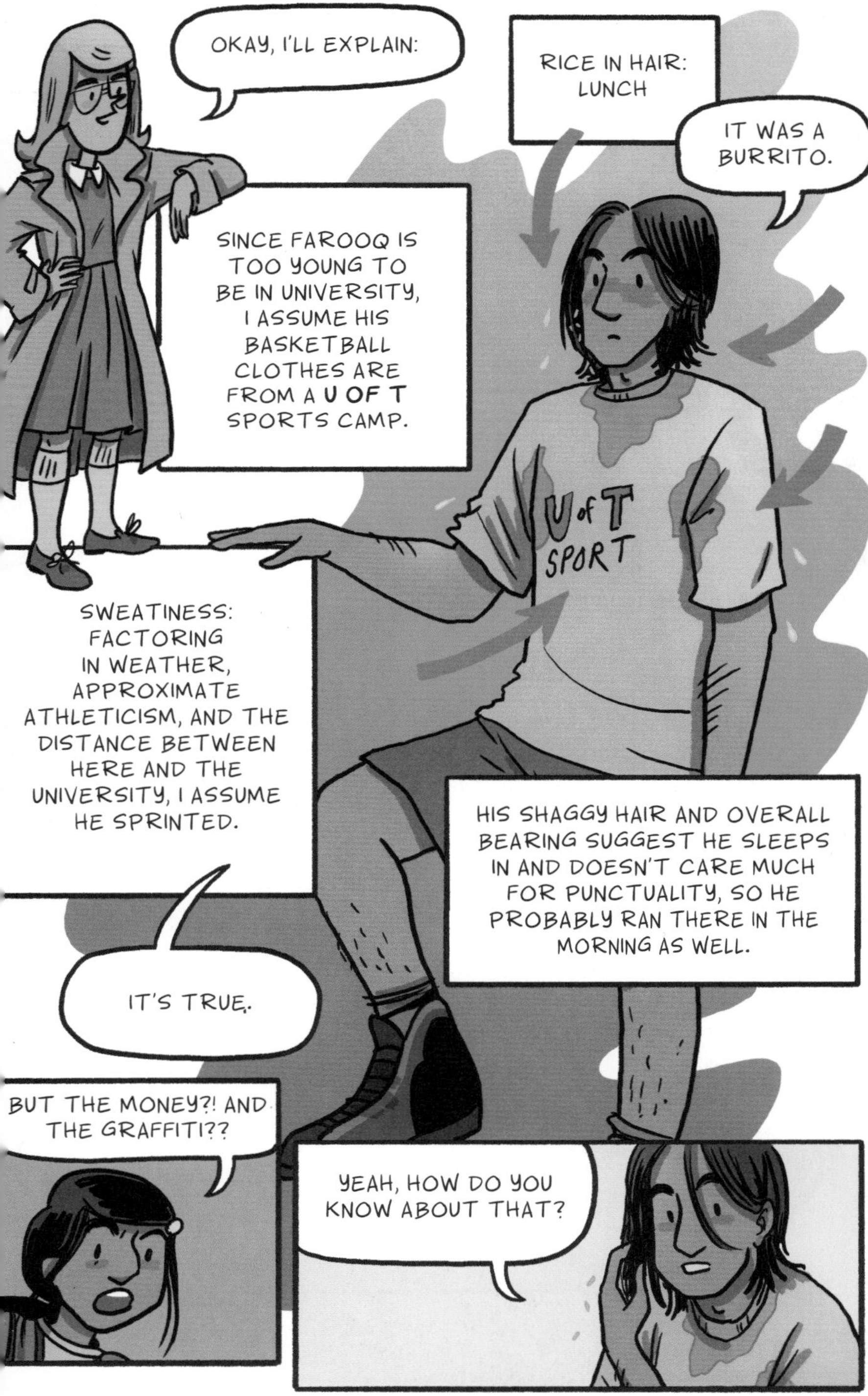
OKAY, I'LL EXPLAIN:
RICE IN HAIR: LUNCH
IT WAS A BURRITO.
SINCE FAROOQ IS TOO YOUNG TO BE IN UNIVERSITY, I ASSUME HIS BASKETBALL CLOTHES ARE FROM A **U OF T** SPORTS CAMP.
U of T SPORT
SWEATINESS: FACTORING IN WEATHER, APPROXIMATE ATHLETICISM, AND THE DISTANCE BETWEEN HERE AND THE UNIVERSITY, I ASSUME HE SPRINTED.
HIS SHAGGY HAIR AND OVERALL BEARING SUGGEST HE SLEEPS IN AND DOESN'T CARE MUCH FOR PUNCTUALITY, SO HE PROBABLY RAN THERE IN THE MORNING AS WELL.
IT'S TRUE.
BUT THE MONEY?! AND THE GRAFFITI??
YEAH, HOW DO YOU KNOW ABOUT THAT?

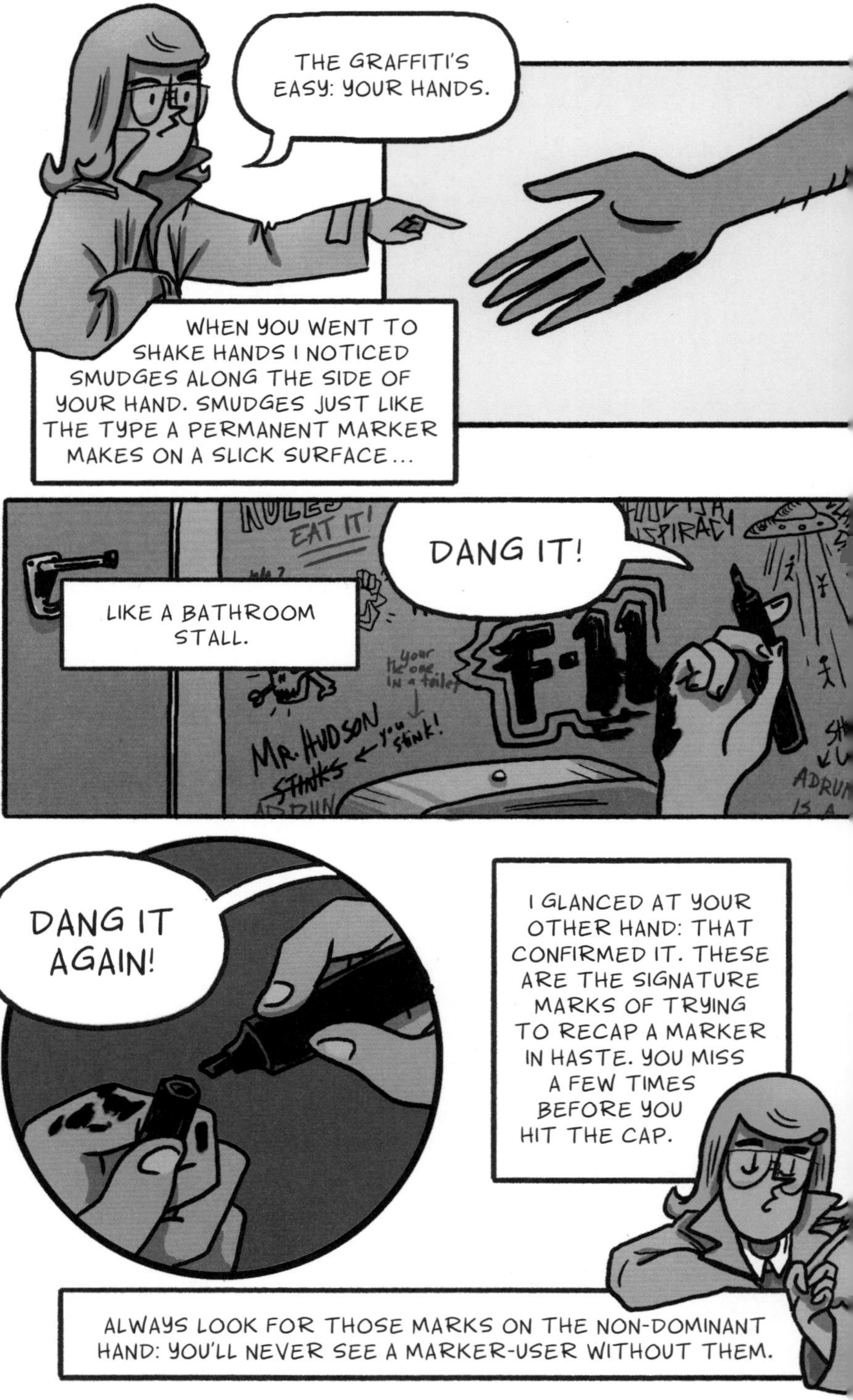
THE GRAFFITI'S EASY: YOUR HANDS.
WHEN YOU WENT TO SHAKE HANDS I NOTICED SMUDGES ALONG THE SIDE OF YOUR HAND. SMUDGES JUST LIKE THE TYPE A PERMANENT MARKER MAKES ON A SLICK SURFACE...
LIKE A BATHROOM STALL.
DANG IT!
EAT IT!
F-11
MR. HUDSON
STINKS
you stink!
DANG IT AGAIN!
I GLANCED AT YOUR OTHER HAND: THAT CONFIRMED IT. THESE ARE THE SIGNATURE MARKS OF TRYING TO RECAP A MARKER IN HASTE. YOU MISS A FEW TIMES BEFORE YOU HIT THE CAP.
ALWAYS LOOK FOR THOSE MARKS ON THE NON-DOMINANT HAND: YOU'LL NEVER SEE A MARKER-USER WITHOUT THEM.

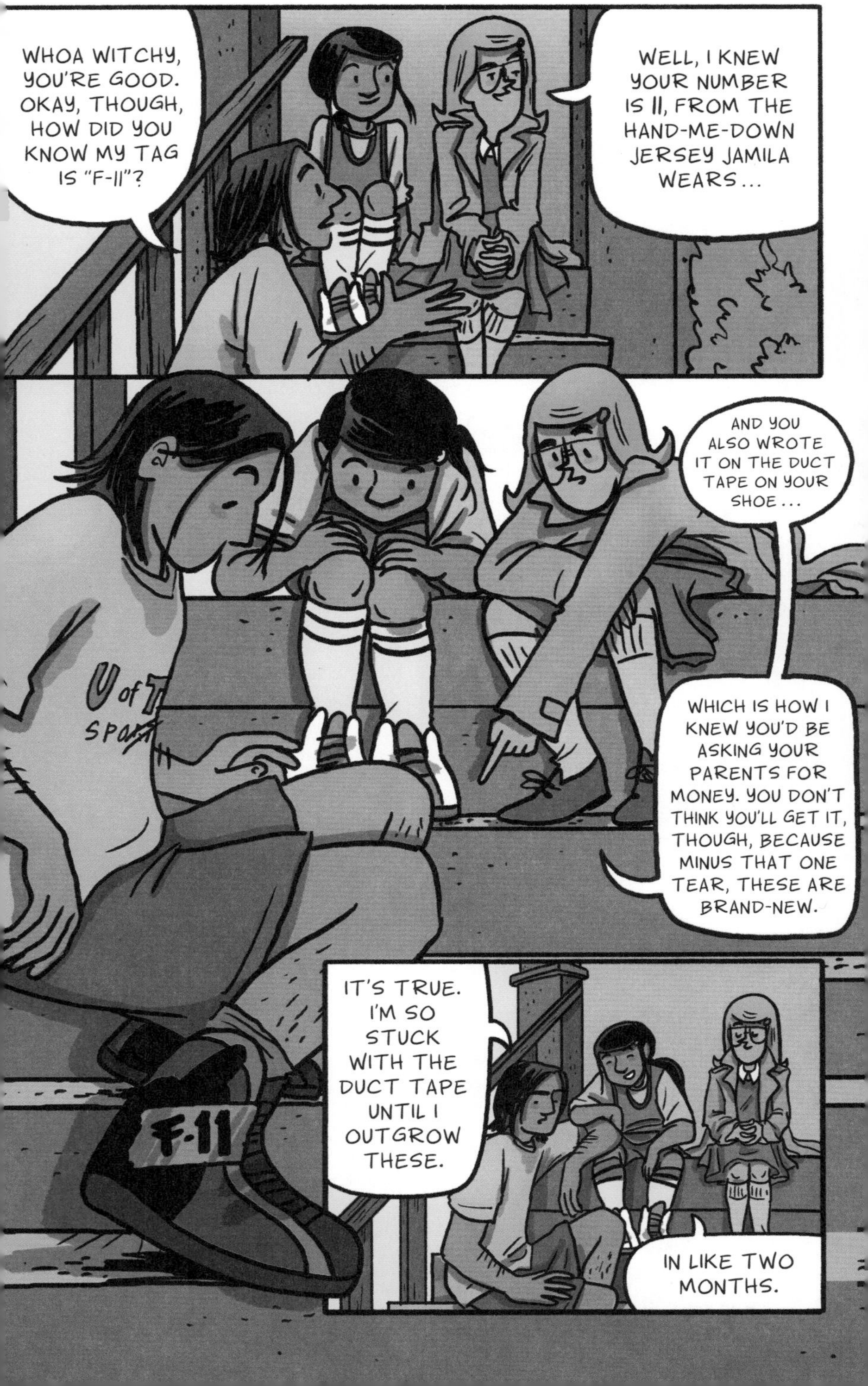
WHOA WITCHY, YOU'RE GOOD. OKAY, THOUGH, HOW DID YOU KNOW MY TAG IS "F-11"?
WELL, I KNEW YOUR NUMBER IS 11, FROM THE HAND-ME-DOWN JERSEY JAMILA WEARS...
AND YOU ALSO WROTE IT ON THE DUCT TAPE ON YOUR SHOE...
WHICH IS HOW I KNEW YOU'D BE ASKING YOUR PARENTS FOR MONEY. YOU DON'T THINK YOU'LL GET IT, THOUGH, BECAUSE MINUS THAT ONE TEAR, THESE ARE BRAND-NEW.
F-11
IT'S TRUE. I'M SO STUCK WITH THE DUCT TAPE UNTIL I OUTGROW THESE.
IN LIKE TWO MONTHS.

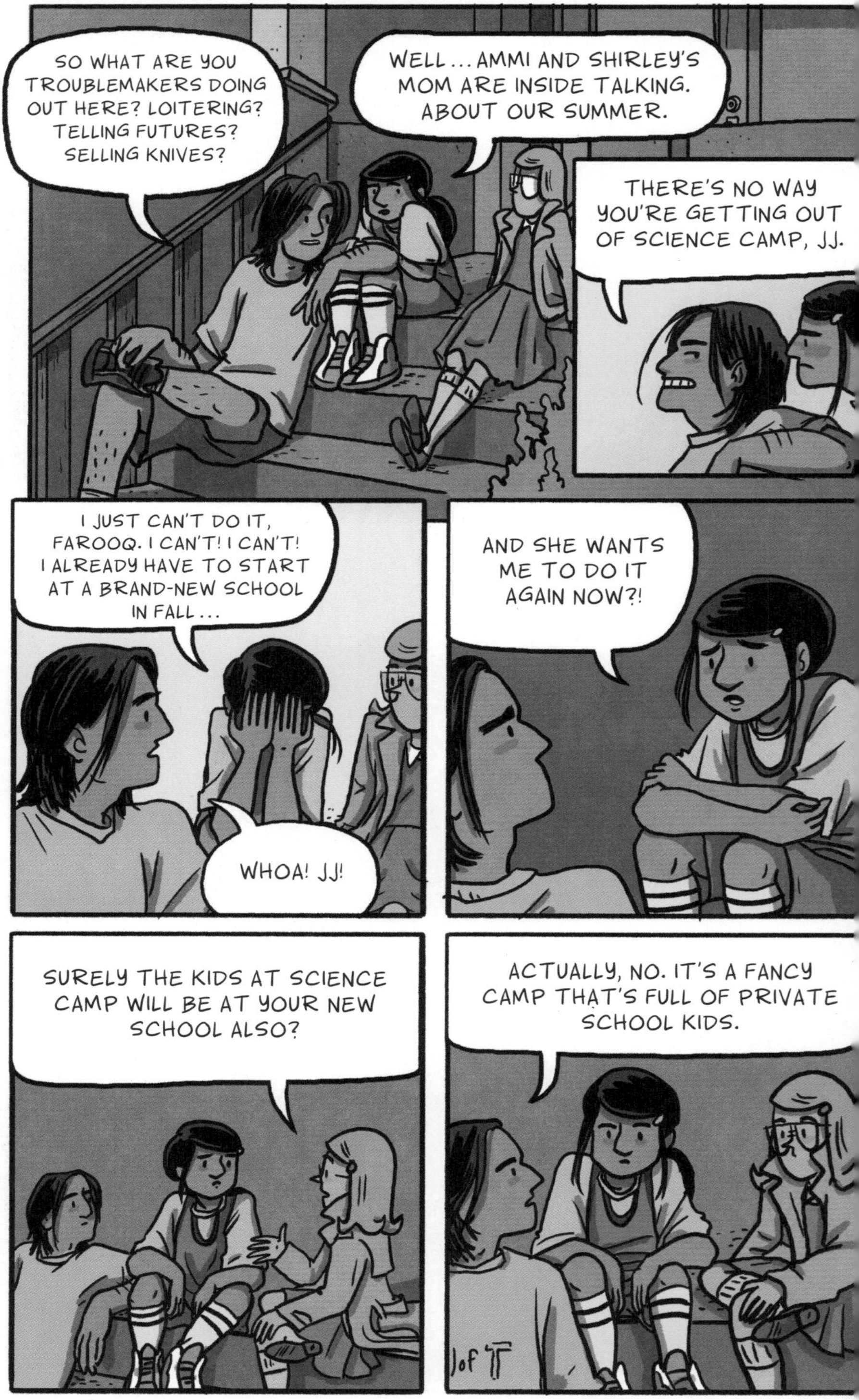
SO WHAT ARE YOU TROUBLEMAKERS DOING OUT HERE? LOITERING? TELLING FUTURES? SELLING KNIVES?
WELL ... AMMI AND SHIRLEY'S MOM ARE INSIDE TALKING. ABOUT OUR SUMMER.
THERE'S NO WAY YOU'RE GETTING OUT OF SCIENCE CAMP, JJ.
I JUST CAN'T DO IT, FAROOQ. I CAN'T! I CAN'T! I ALREADY HAVE TO START AT A BRAND-NEW SCHOOL IN FALL ...
WHOA! JJ!
AND SHE WANTS ME TO DO IT AGAIN NOW?!
SURELY THE KIDS AT SCIENCE CAMP WILL BE AT YOUR NEW SCHOOL ALSO?
ACTUALLY, NO. IT'S A FANCY CAMP THAT'S FULL OF PRIVATE SCHOOL KIDS.

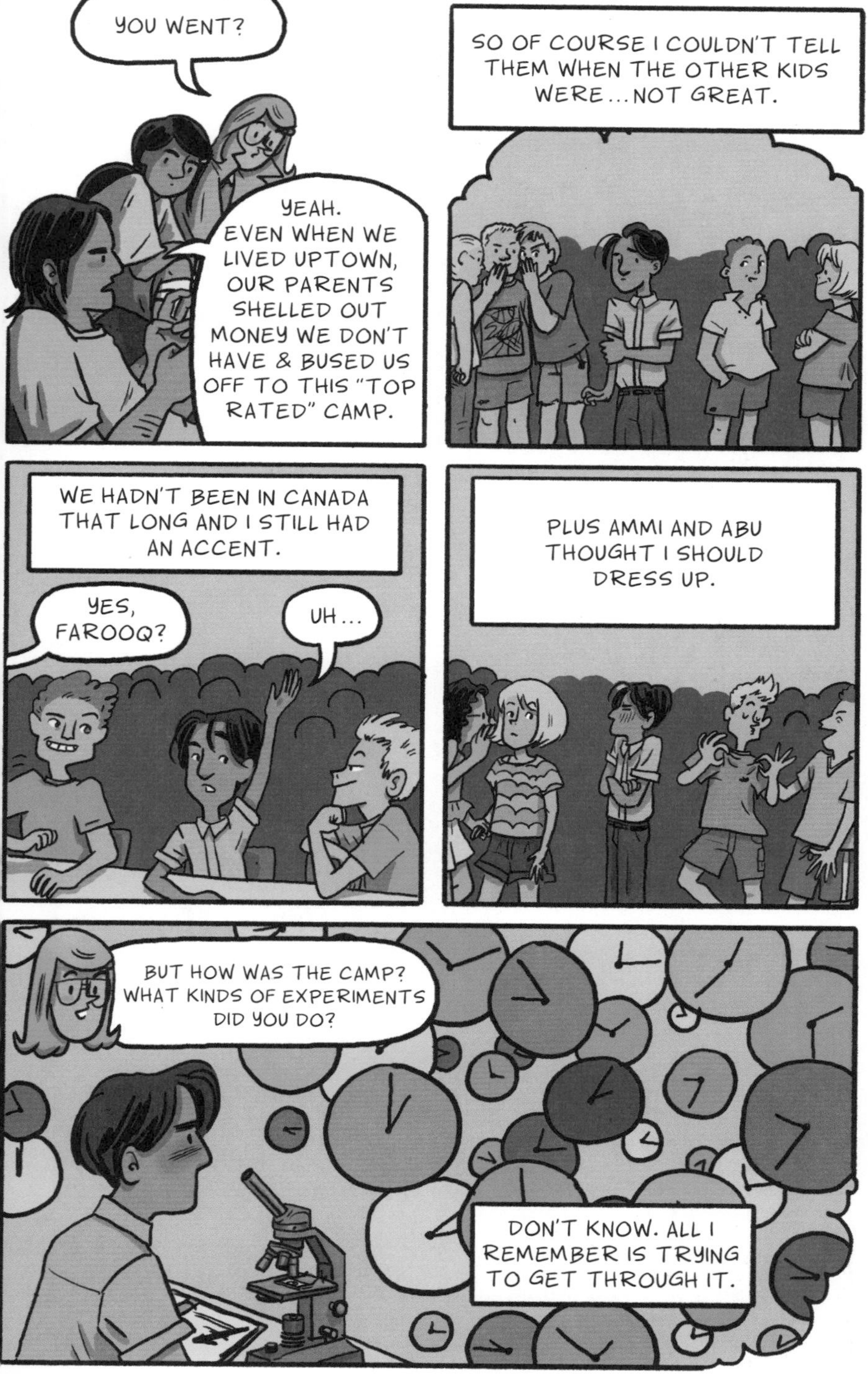

YOU WENT?
YEAH. EVEN WHEN WE LIVED UPTOWN, OUR PARENTS SHELLED OUT MONEY WE DON'T HAVE & BUSED US OFF TO THIS "TOP RATED" CAMP.
SO OF COURSE I COULDN'T TELL THEM WHEN THE OTHER KIDS WERE... NOT GREAT.
WE HADN'T BEEN IN CANADA THAT LONG AND I STILL HAD AN ACCENT.
YES, FAROOQ?
UH...
PLUS AMMI AND ABU THOUGHT I SHOULD DRESS UP.
BUT HOW WAS THE CAMP? WHAT KINDS OF EXPERIMENTS DID YOU DO?
DON'T KNOW. ALL I REMEMBER IS TRYING TO GET THROUGH IT.

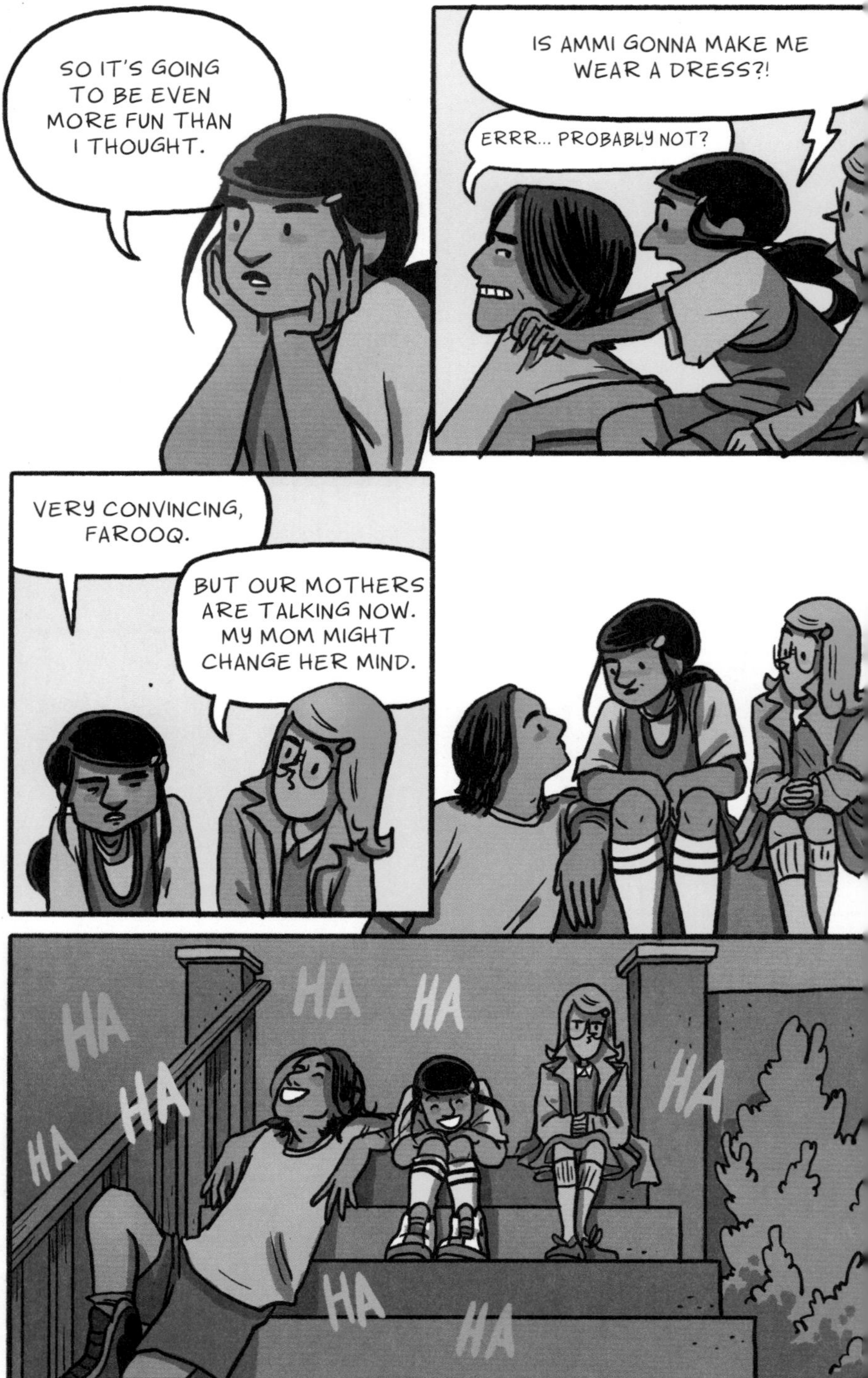
SO IT'S GOING TO BE EVEN MORE FUN THAN I THOUGHT.
IS AMMI GONNA MAKE ME WEAR A DRESS?!
ERRR... PROBABLY NOT?
VERY CONVINCING, FAROOQ.
BUT OUR MOTHERS ARE TALKING NOW. MY MOM MIGHT CHANGE HER MIND.
HA HA HA HA HA HA HA HA HA

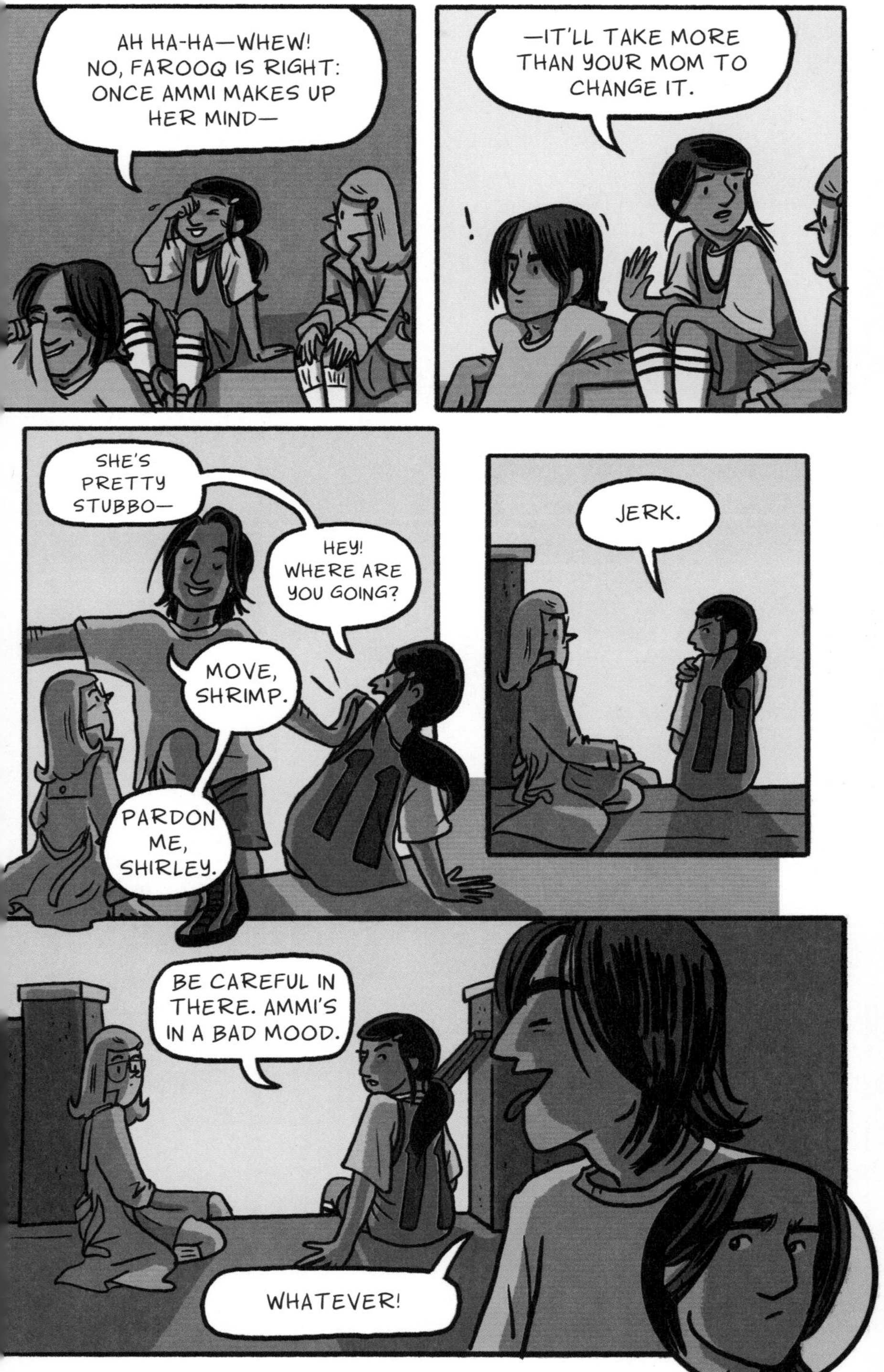
AH HA-HA—WHEW! NO, FAROOQ IS RIGHT: ONCE AMMI MAKES UP HER MIND—
—IT'LL TAKE MORE THAN YOUR MOM TO CHANGE IT.
!
SHE'S PRETTY STUBBO—
HEY! WHERE ARE YOU GOING?
MOVE, SHRIMP.
PARDON ME, SHIRLEY.
JERK.
BE CAREFUL IN THERE. AMMI'S IN A BAD MOOD.
WHATEVER!

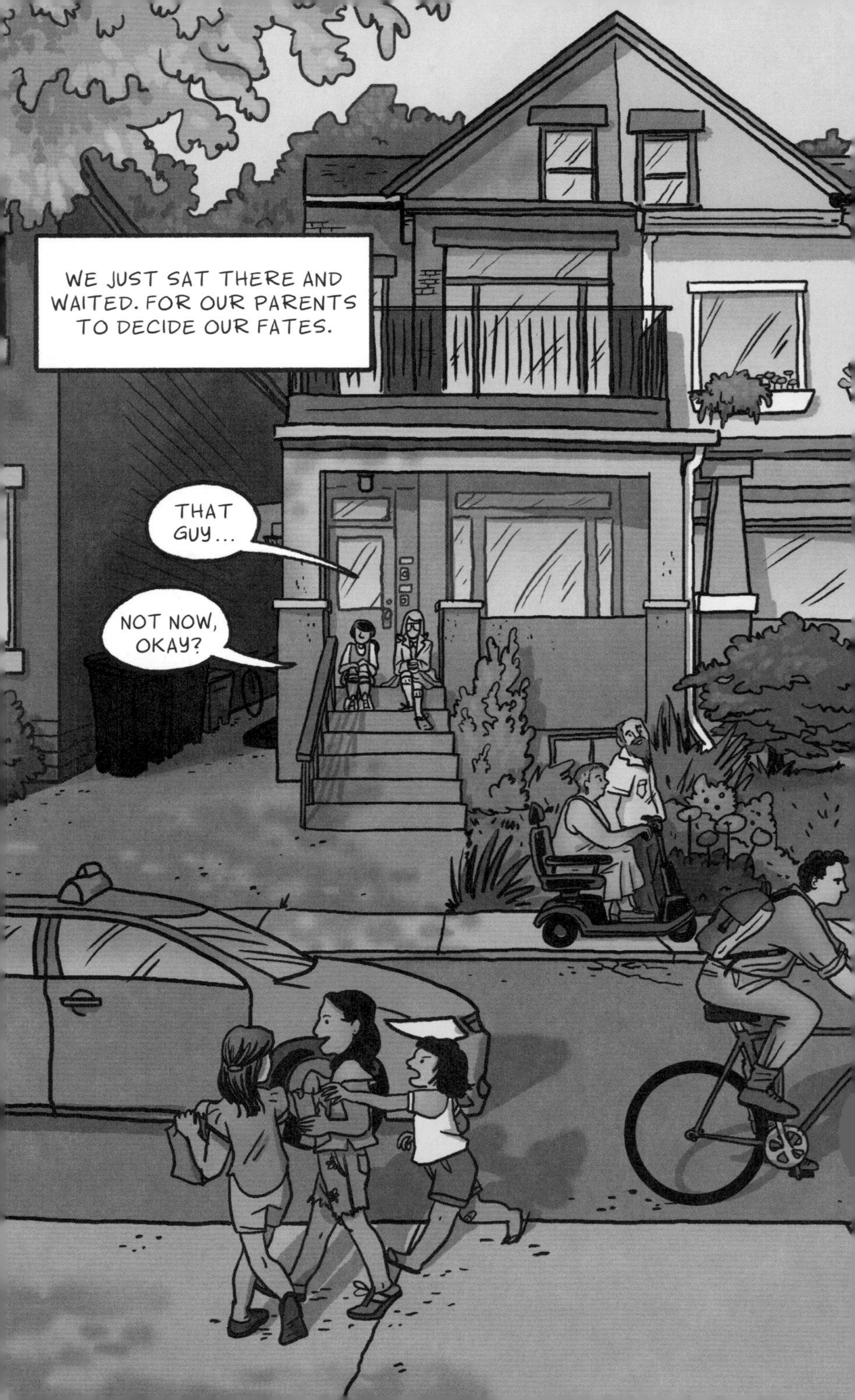
WE JUST SAT THERE AND WAITED. FOR OUR PARENTS TO DECIDE OUR FATES.
THAT GUY...
NOT NOW, OKAY?

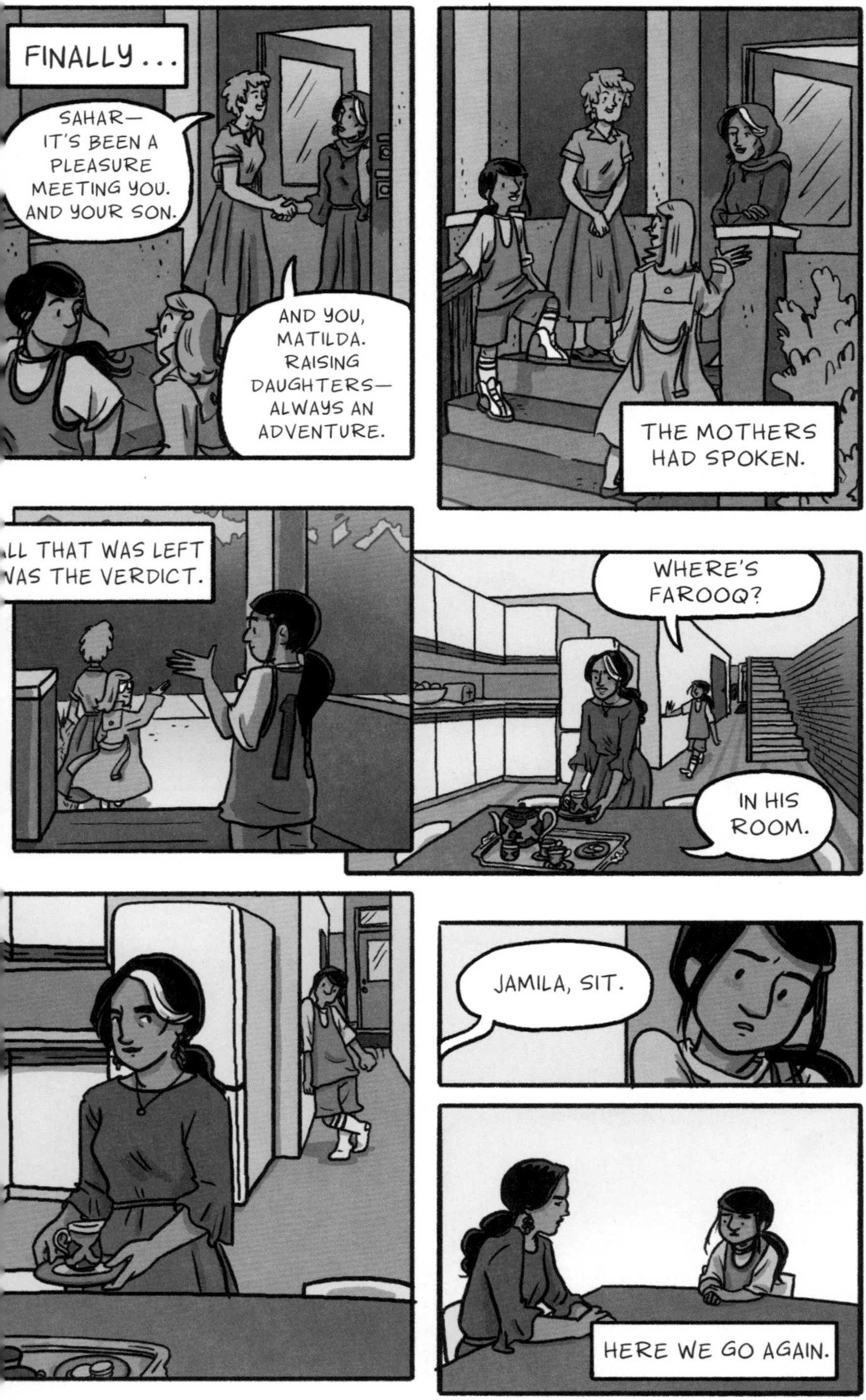
FINALLY . . .
SAHAR— IT'S BEEN A PLEASURE MEETING YOU. AND YOUR SON.
AND YOU, MATILDA. RAISING DAUGHTERS— ALWAYS AN ADVENTURE.
THE MOTHERS HAD SPOKEN.
LL THAT WAS LEFT VAS THE VERDICT.
WHERE'S FAROOQ?
IN HIS ROOM.
JAMILA, SIT.
HERE WE GO AGAIN.

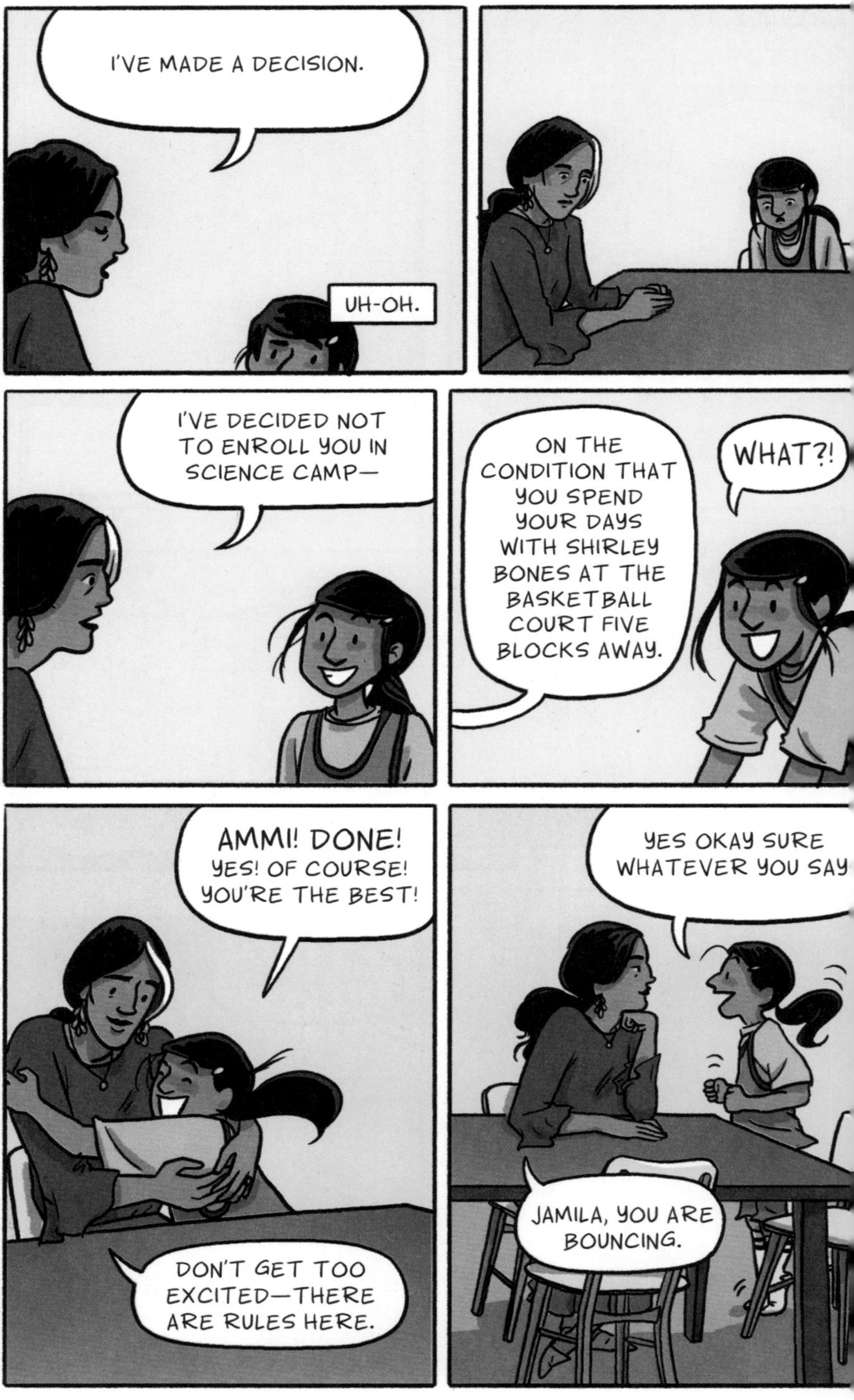
I'VE MADE A DECISION.
UH-OH.
I'VE DECIDED NOT TO ENROLL YOU IN SCIENCE CAMP—
ON THE CONDITION THAT YOU SPEND YOUR DAYS WITH SHIRLEY BONES AT THE BASKETBALL COURT FIVE BLOCKS AWAY.
WHAT?!
AMMI! DONE! YES! OF COURSE! YOU'RE THE BEST!
DON'T GET TOO EXCITED—THERE ARE RULES HERE.
YES OKAY SURE WHATEVER YOU SAY
JAMILA, YOU ARE BOUNCING.

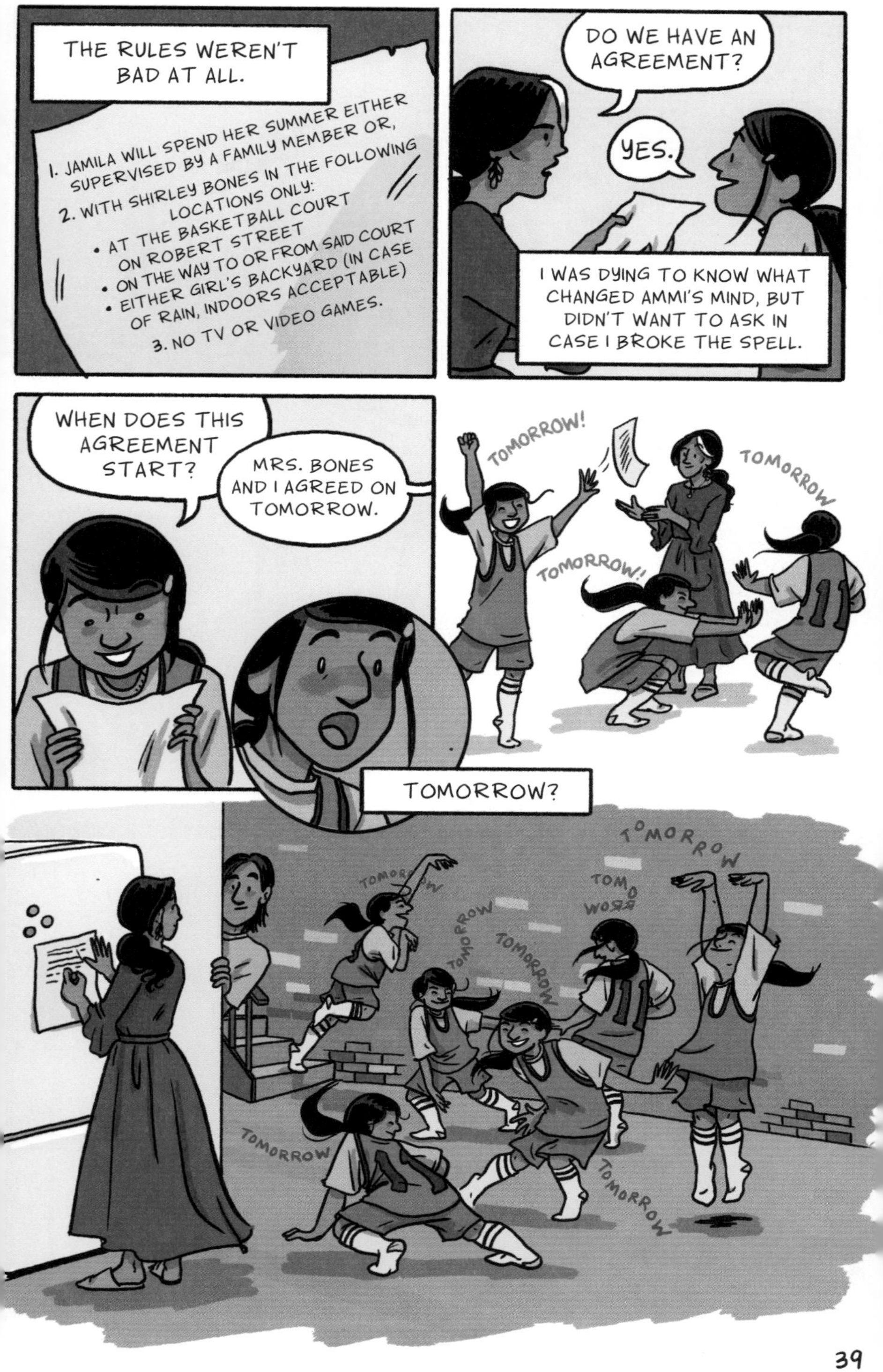
THE RULES WEREN'T BAD AT ALL.
1. JAMILA WILL SPEND HER SUMMER EITHER SUPERVISED BY A FAMILY MEMBER OR,
2. WITH SHIRLEY BONES IN THE FOLLOWING LOCATIONS ONLY:
• AT THE BASKETBALL COURT ON ROBERT STREET
• ON THE WAY TO OR FROM SAID COURT
• EITHER GIRL'S BACKYARD (IN CASE OF RAIN, INDOORS ACCEPTABLE)
3. NO TV OR VIDEO GAMES.
DO WE HAVE AN AGREEMENT?
YES.
I WAS DYING TO KNOW WHAT CHANGED AMMI'S MIND, BUT DIDN'T WANT TO ASK IN CASE I BROKE THE SPELL.
WHEN DOES THIS AGREEMENT START?
MRS. BONES AND I AGREED ON TOMORROW.
TOMORROW?
TOMORROW!
TOMORROW
TOMORROW!!
TOMORROW
TOMORROW
TOMORROW
TOMORROW
TOMORROW
TOMORROW
TOMORROW
TOMORROW

Chapter 4

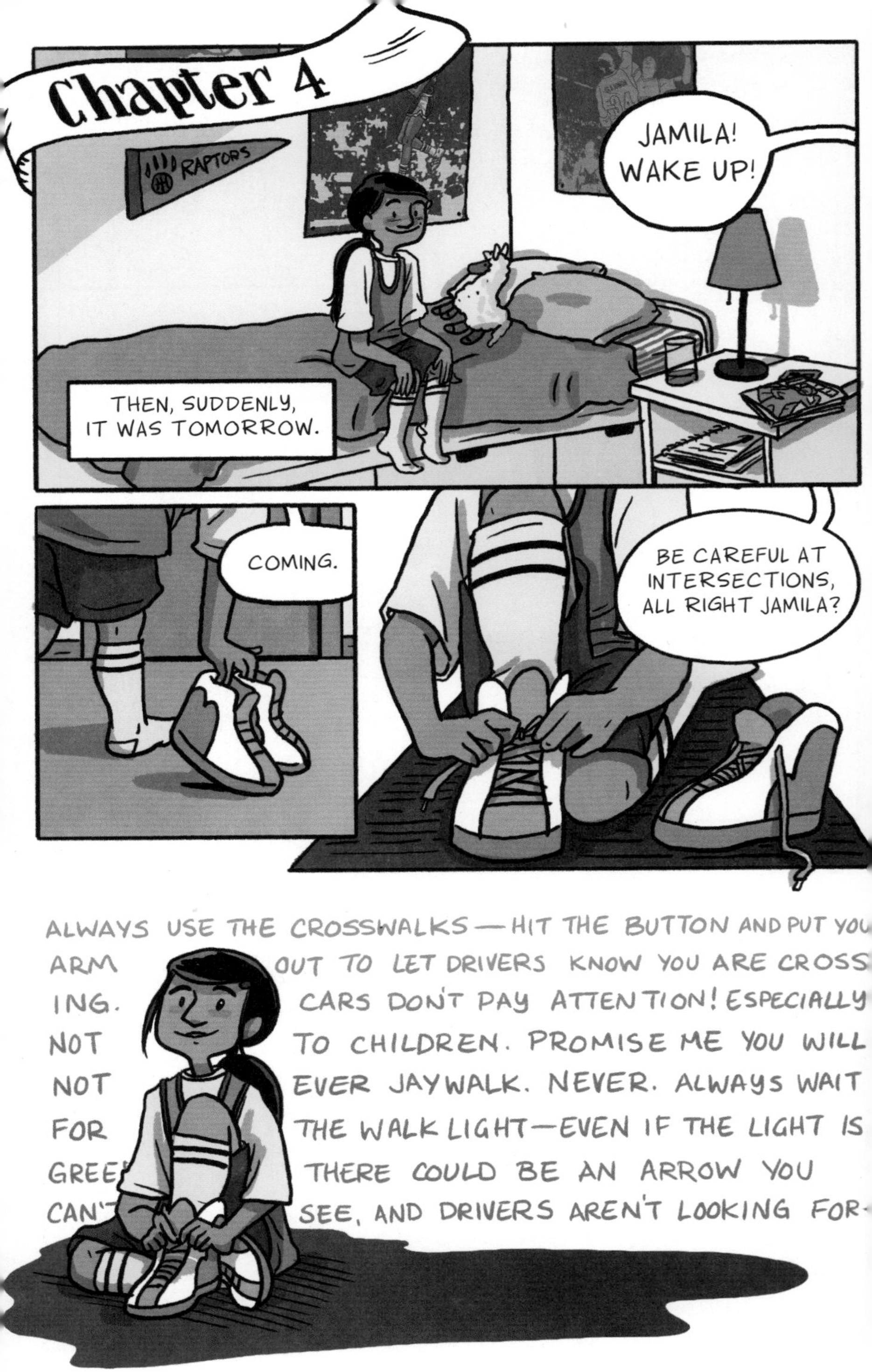
RAPTORS
THEN, SUDDENLY, IT WAS TOMORROW.
JAMILA! WAKE UP!
COMING.
BE CAREFUL AT INTERSECTIONS, ALL RIGHT JAMILA?
ALWAYS USE THE CROSSWALKS—HIT THE BUTTON AND PUT YOU
ARM OUT TO LET DRIVERS KNOW YOU ARE CROSS
ING. CARS DON'T PAY ATTENTION! ESPECIALLY
NOT TO CHILDREN. PROMISE ME YOU WILL
NOT EVER JAYWALK. NEVER. ALWAYS WAIT
FOR THE WALK LIGHT—EVEN IF THE LIGHT IS
GREE THERE COULD BE AN ARROW YOU
CAN' SEE, AND DRIVERS AREN'T LOOKING FOR-

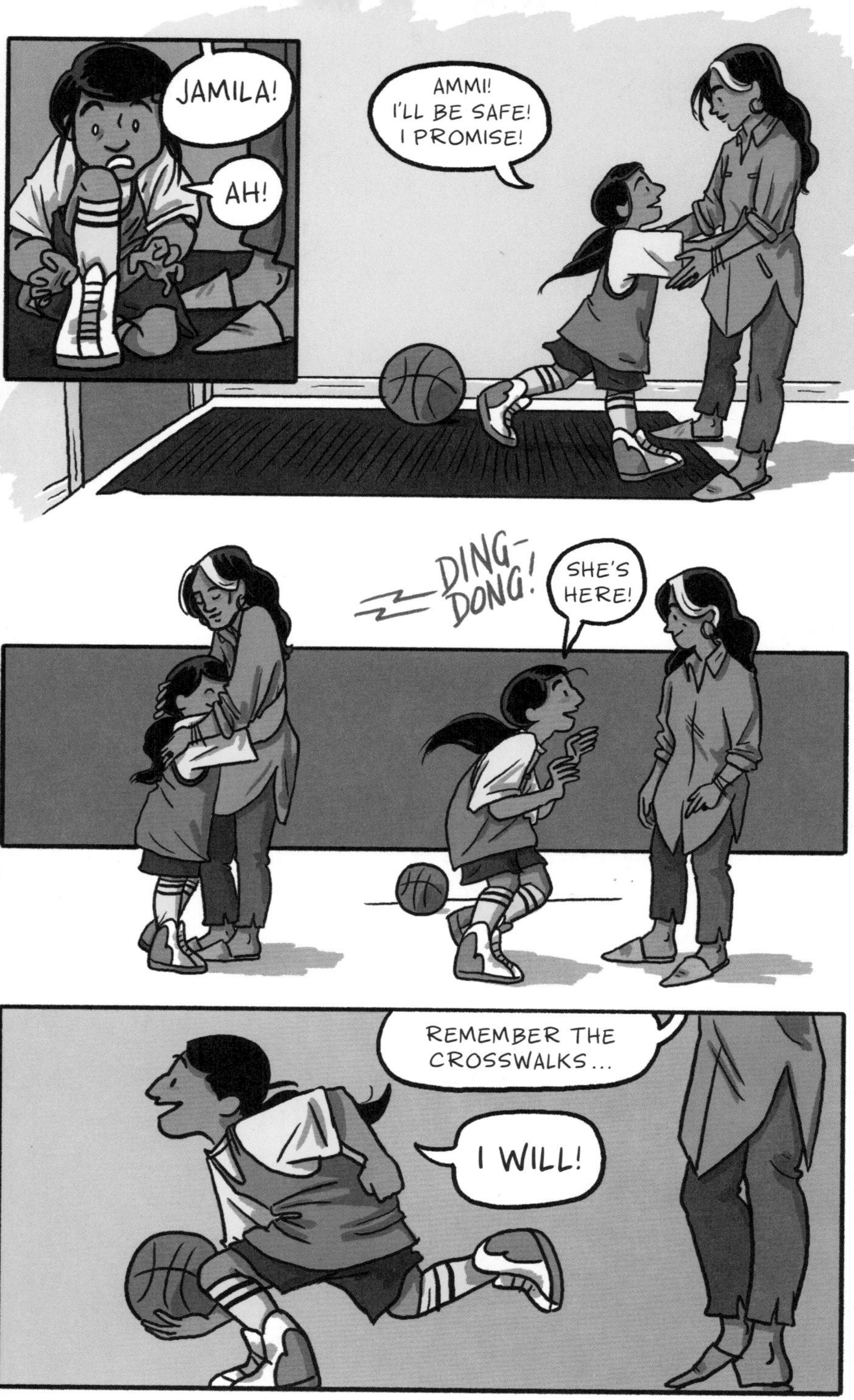
JAMILA!
AH!
AMMI! I'LL BE SAFE! I PROMISE!
DING-DONG!
SHE'S HERE!
REMEMBER THE CROSSWALKS...
I WILL!

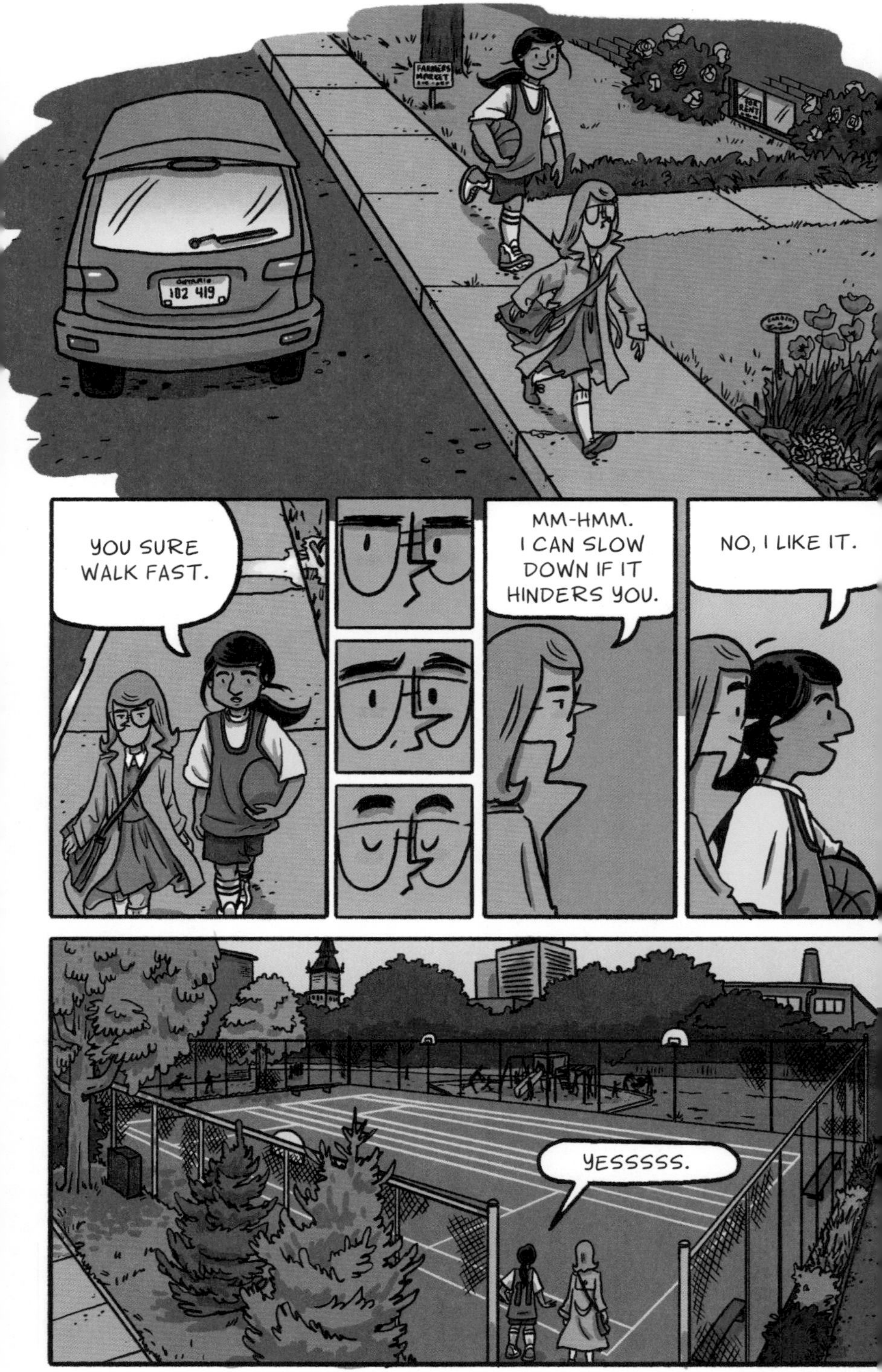
YOU SURE WALK FAST.
MM-HMM. I CAN SLOW DOWN IF IT HINDERS YOU.
NO, I LIKE IT.
YESSSSS.

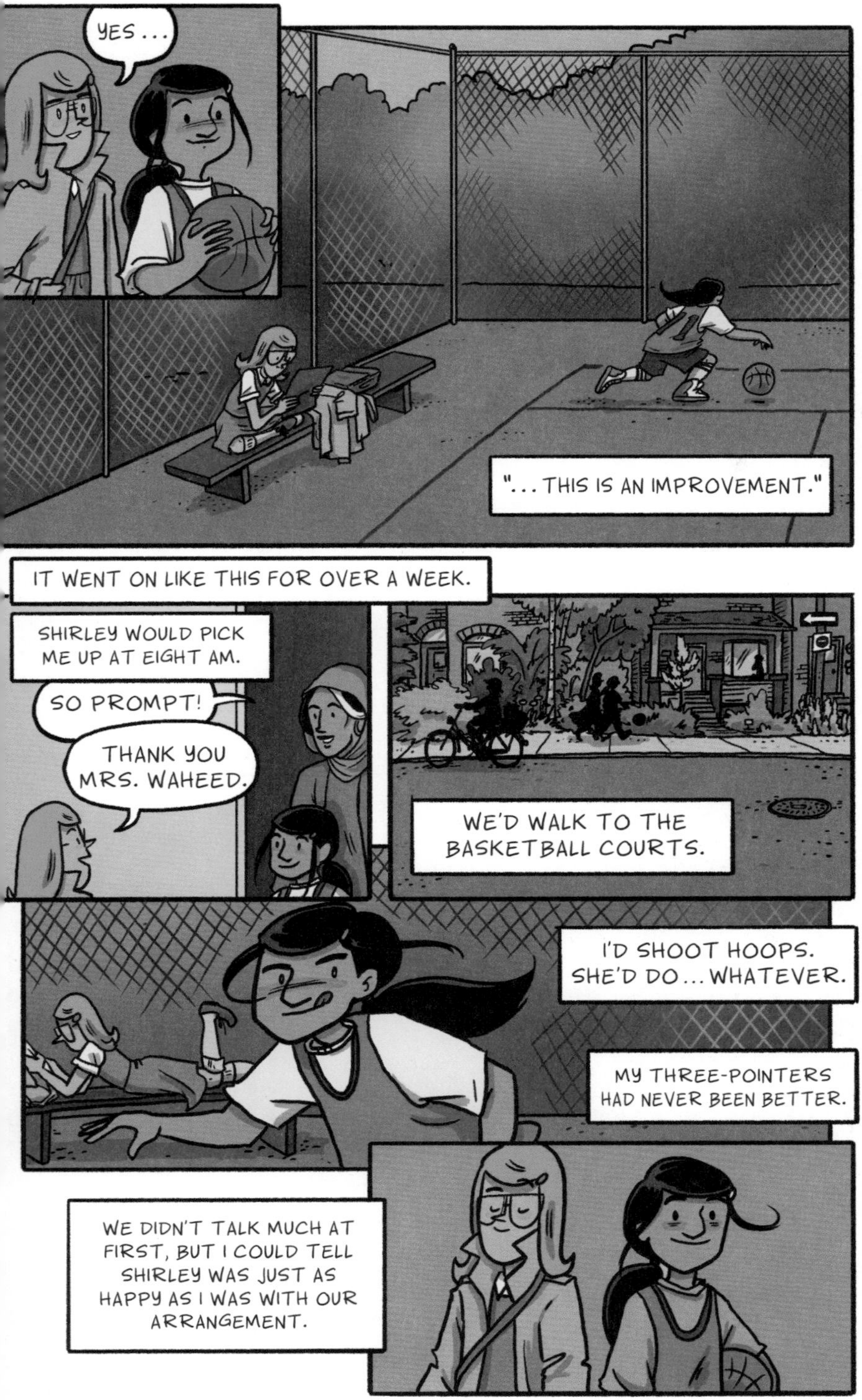
YES . . .
". . . THIS IS AN IMPROVEMENT."
IT WENT ON LIKE THIS FOR OVER A WEEK.
SHIRLEY WOULD PICK ME UP AT EIGHT AM.
SO PROMPT!
THANK YOU MRS. WAHEED.
WE'D WALK TO THE BASKETBALL COURTS.
I'D SHOOT HOOPS. SHE'D DO . . . WHATEVER.
MY THREE-POINTERS HAD NEVER BEEN BETTER.
WE DIDN'T TALK MUCH AT FIRST, BUT I COULD TELL SHIRLEY WAS JUST AS HAPPY AS I WAS WITH OUR ARRANGEMENT.

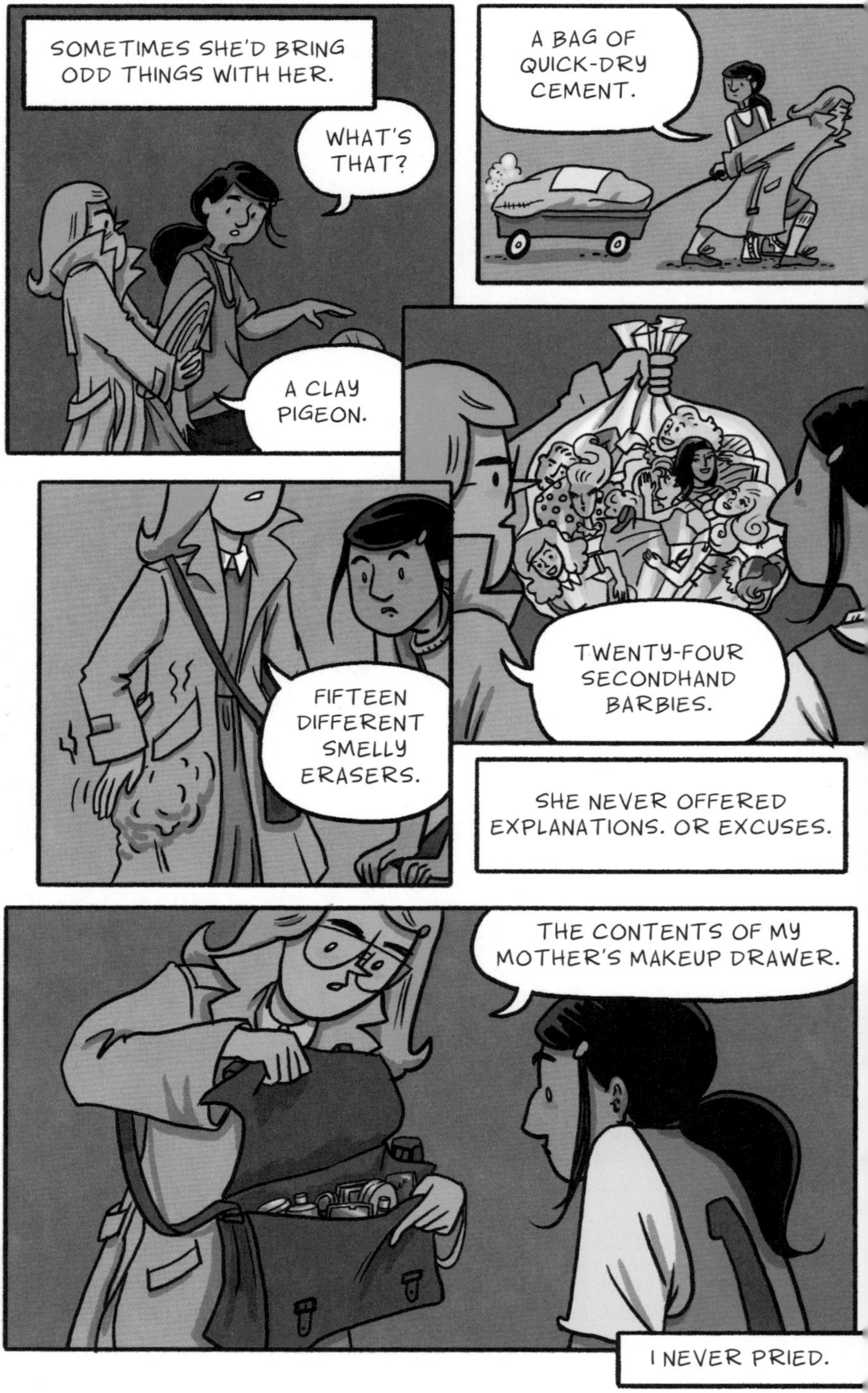
SOMETIMES SHE'D BRING ODD THINGS WITH HER.
WHAT'S THAT?
A CLAY PIGEON.
A BAG OF QUICK-DRY CEMENT.
TWENTY-FOUR SECONDHAND BARBIES.
FIFTEEN DIFFERENT SMELLY ERASERS.
SHE NEVER OFFERED EXPLANATIONS. OR EXCUSES.
THE CONTENTS OF MY MOTHER'S MAKEUP DRAWER.
I NEVER PRIED.

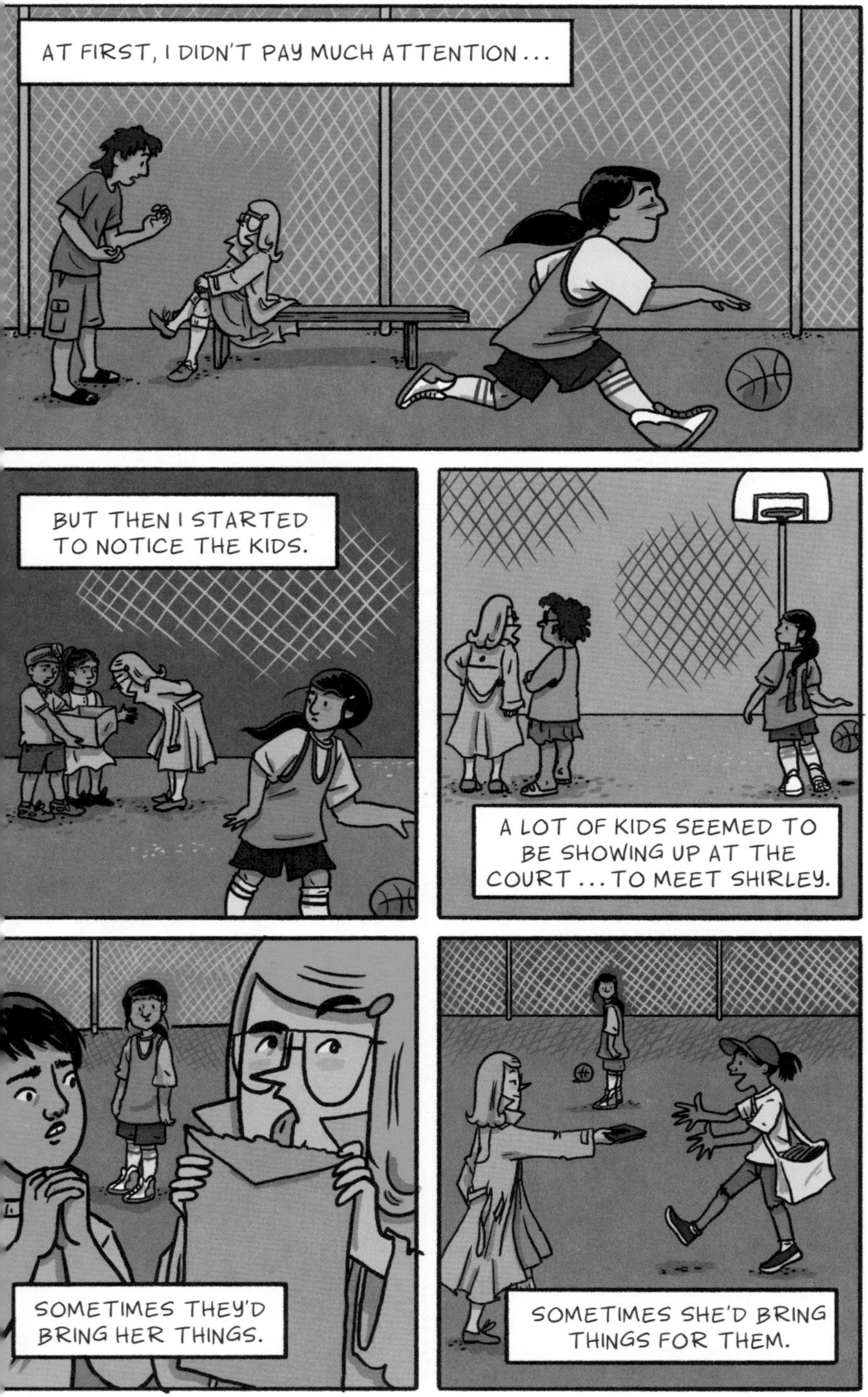
AT FIRST, I DIDN'T PAY MUCH ATTENTION . . .
BUT THEN I STARTED TO NOTICE THE KIDS.
A LOT OF KIDS SEEMED TO BE SHOWING UP AT THE COURT . . . TO MEET SHIRLEY.
SOMETIMES THEY'D BRING HER THINGS.
SOMETIMES SHE'D BRING THINGS FOR THEM.

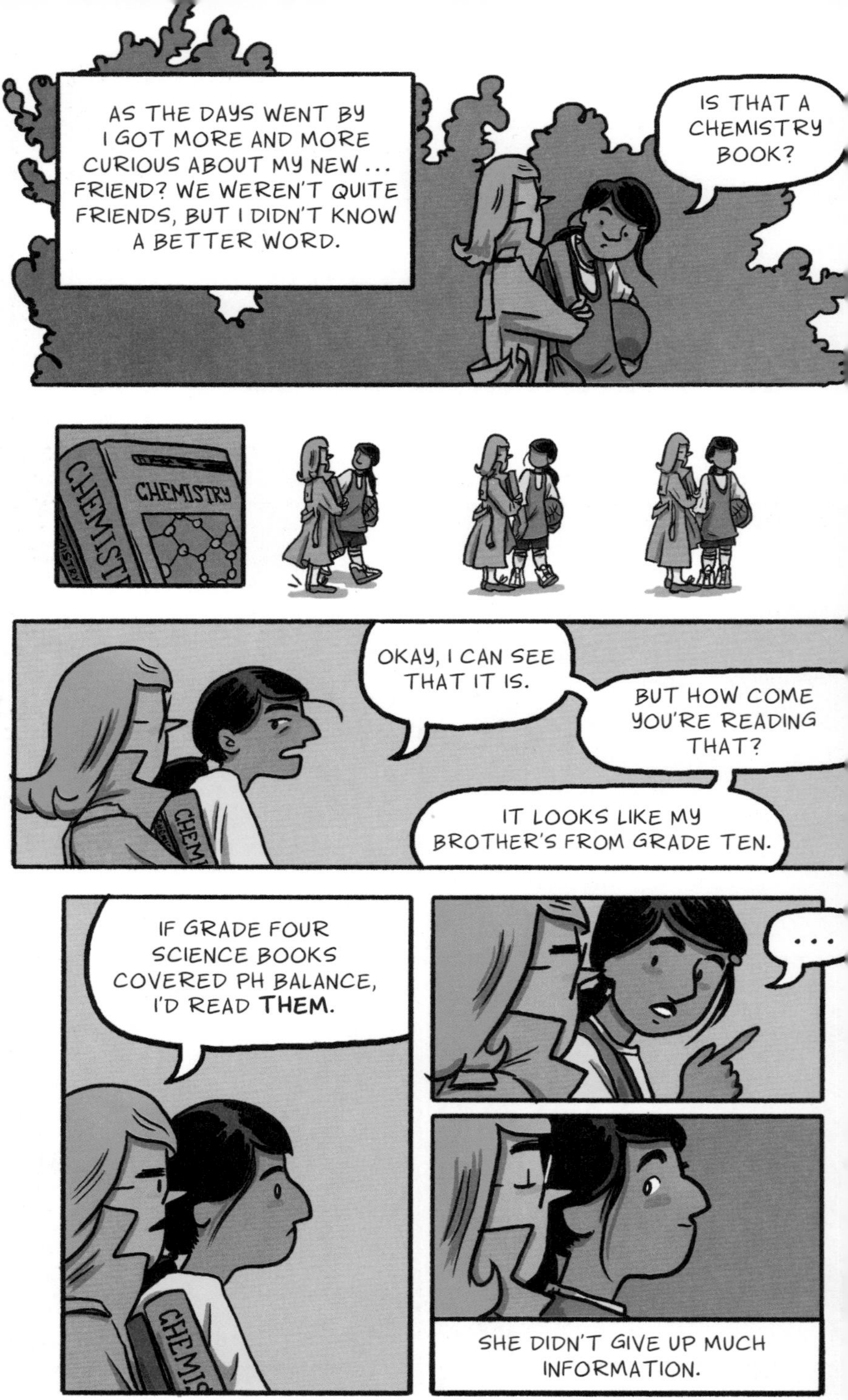
AS THE DAYS WENT BY I GOT MORE AND MORE CURIOUS ABOUT MY NEW ... FRIEND? WE WEREN'T QUITE FRIENDS, BUT I DIDN'T KNOW A BETTER WORD.
IS THAT A CHEMISTRY BOOK?
CHEMISTRY
CHEMISTRY
OKAY, I CAN SEE THAT IT IS.
BUT HOW COME YOU'RE READING THAT?
IT LOOKS LIKE MY BROTHER'S FROM GRADE TEN.
IF GRADE FOUR SCIENCE BOOKS COVERED PH BALANCE, I'D READ **THEM.**
...
SHE DIDN'T GIVE UP MUCH INFORMATION.

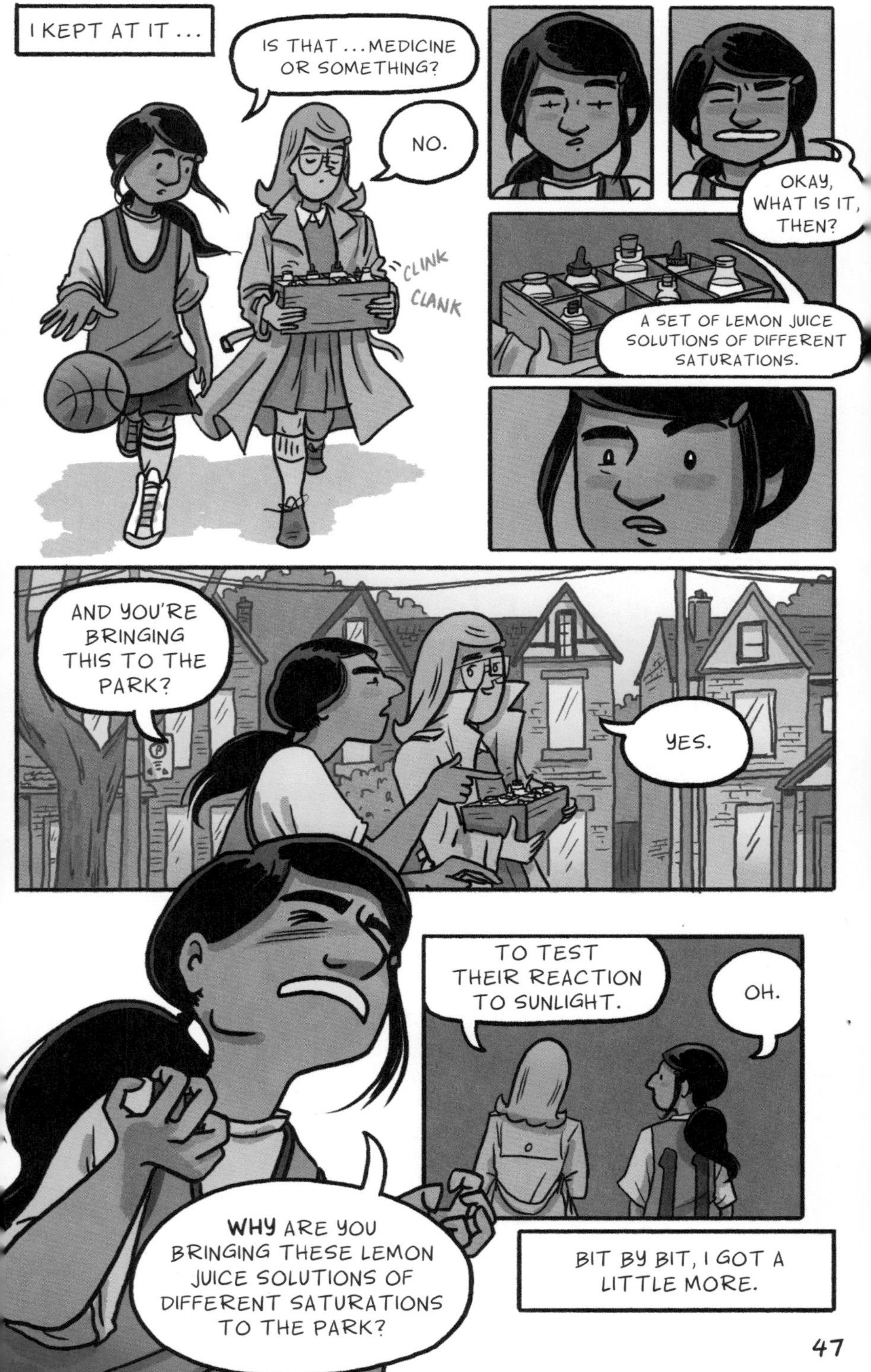

I KEPT AT IT . . .
IS THAT . . . MEDICINE OR SOMETHING?
NO.
CLINK
CLANK
OKAY, WHAT IS IT, THEN?
A SET OF LEMON JUICE SOLUTIONS OF DIFFERENT SATURATIONS.
AND YOU'RE BRINGING THIS TO THE PARK?
YES.
WHY ARE YOU BRINGING THESE LEMON JUICE SOLUTIONS OF DIFFERENT SATURATIONS TO THE PARK?
TO TEST THEIR REACTION TO SUNLIGHT.
OH.
BIT BY BIT, I GOT A LITTLE MORE.

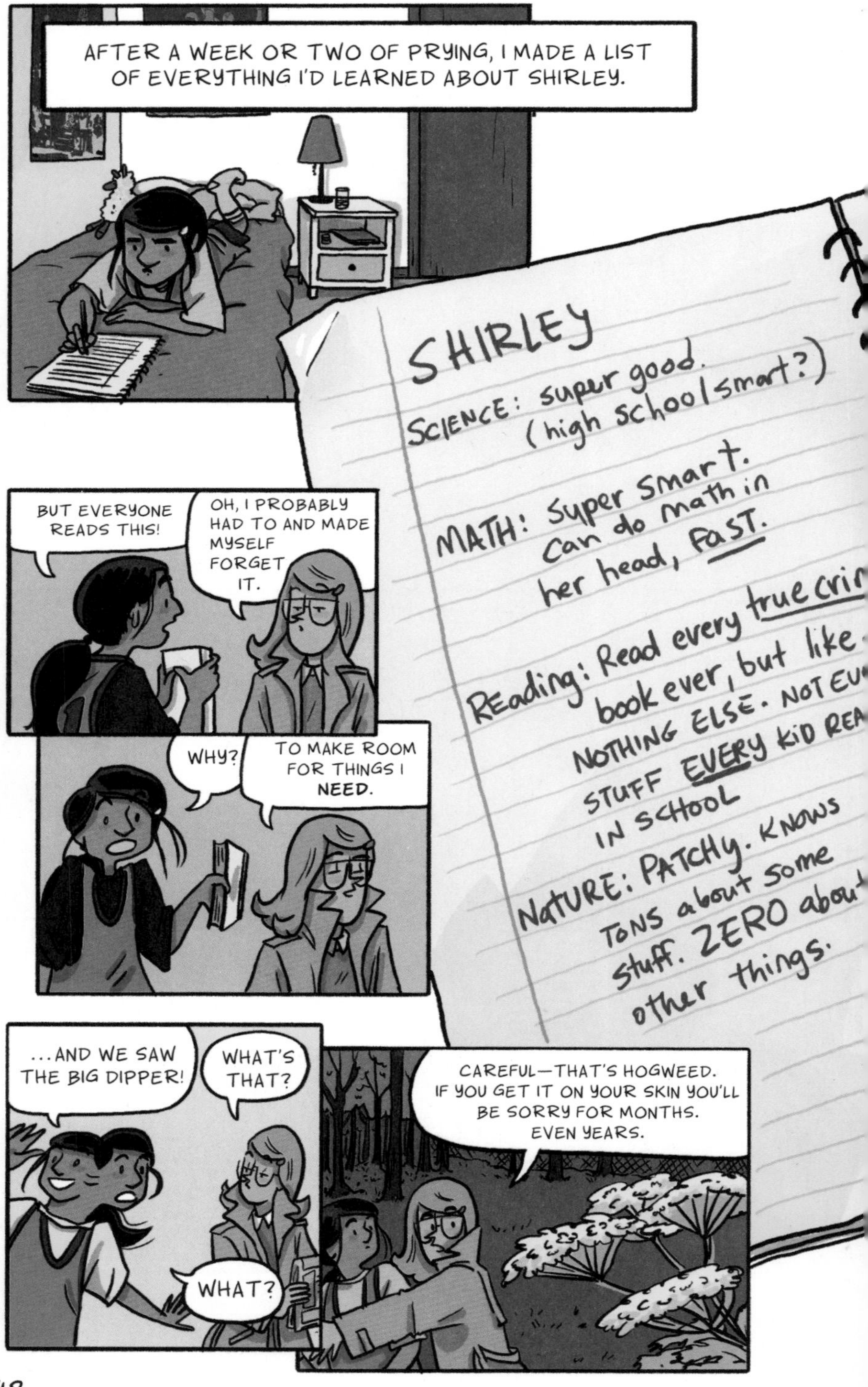
AFTER A WEEK OR TWO OF PRYING, I MADE A LIST OF EVERYTHING I'D LEARNED ABOUT SHIRLEY.
SHIRLEY
SCIENCE: super good. (high school smart?)
MATH: Super Smart. Can do math in her head, FAST.
Reading: Read every true crim
book ever, but like
NOTHING ELSE. NOT EV
STUFF EVERY KID REA
IN SCHOOL
NATURE: PATCHY. KNOWS TONS about some stuff. ZERO about other things.
BUT EVERYONE READS THIS!
OH, I PROBABLY HAD TO AND MADE MYSELF FORGET IT.
WHY?
TO MAKE ROOM FOR THINGS I NEED.
...AND WE SAW THE BIG DIPPER!
WHAT'S THAT?
WHAT?
CAREFUL—THAT'S HOGWEED. IF YOU GET IT ON YOUR SKIN YOU'LL BE SORRY FOR MONTHS. EVEN YEARS.

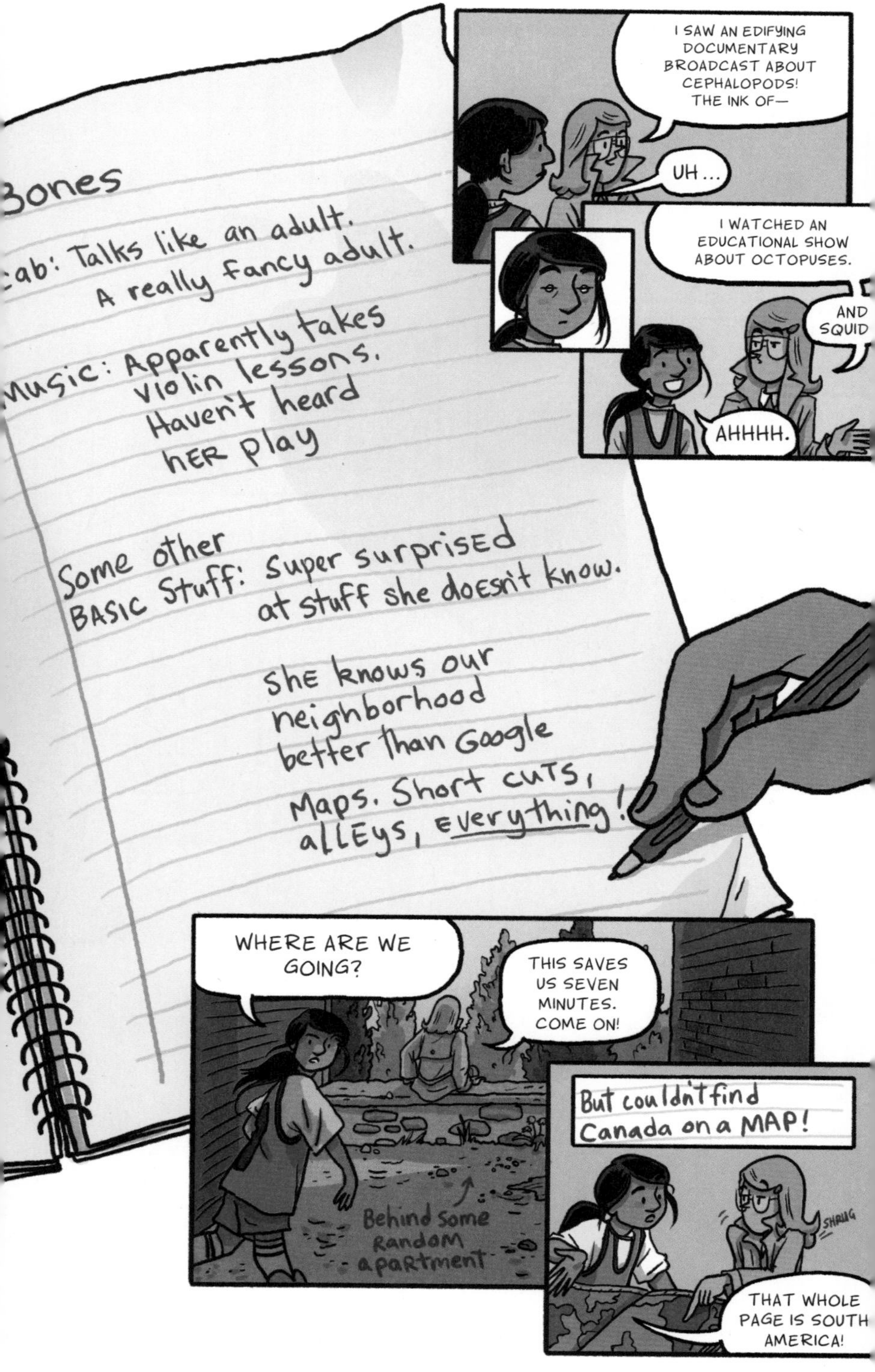
Bones
Cab: Talks like an adult. A really fancy adult.
I SAW AN EDIFYING DOCUMENTARY BROADCAST ABOUT CEPHALOPODS! THE INK OF—
UH...
I WATCHED AN EDUCATIONAL SHOW ABOUT OCTOPUSES.
AND SQUID
AHHHH.
Music: Apparently takes violin lessons. Haven't heard her play
Some other BASIC Stuff: Super surprised at stuff she doesn't know.
She knows our neighborhood better than Google Maps. Short cuts, alleys, everything!
WHERE ARE WE GOING?
THIS SAVES US SEVEN MINUTES. COME ON!
Behind some random apartment
But couldn't find Canada on a MAP!
SHRUG
THAT WHOLE PAGE IS SOUTH AMERICA!

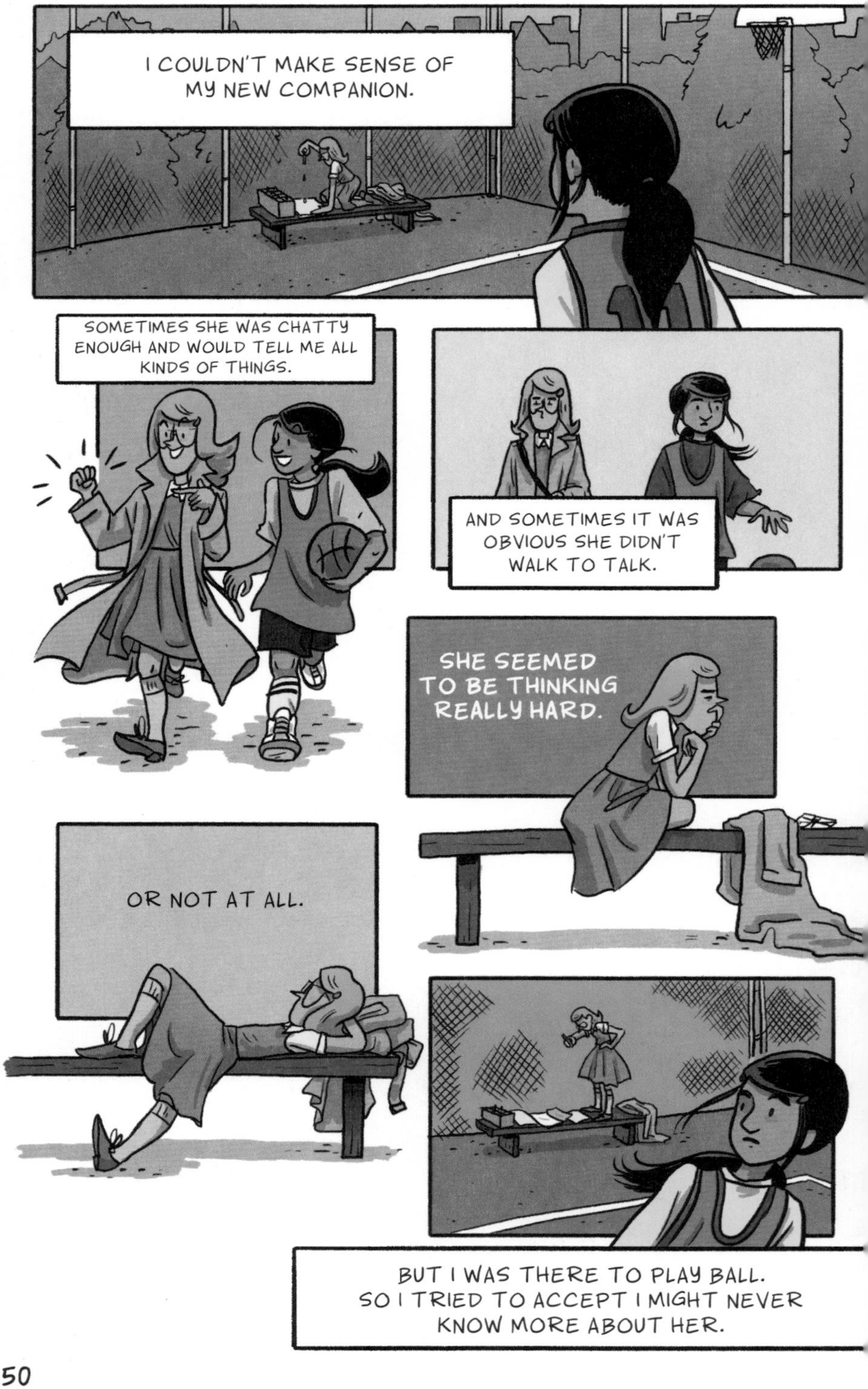
I COULDN'T MAKE SENSE OF MY NEW COMPANION.
SOMETIMES SHE WAS CHATTY ENOUGH AND WOULD TELL ME ALL KINDS OF THINGS.
AND SOMETIMES IT WAS OBVIOUS SHE DIDN'T WALK TO TALK.
SHE SEEMED TO BE THINKING REALLY HARD.
OR NOT AT ALL.
BUT I WAS THERE TO PLAY BALL. SO I TRIED TO ACCEPT I MIGHT NEVER KNOW MORE ABOUT HER.

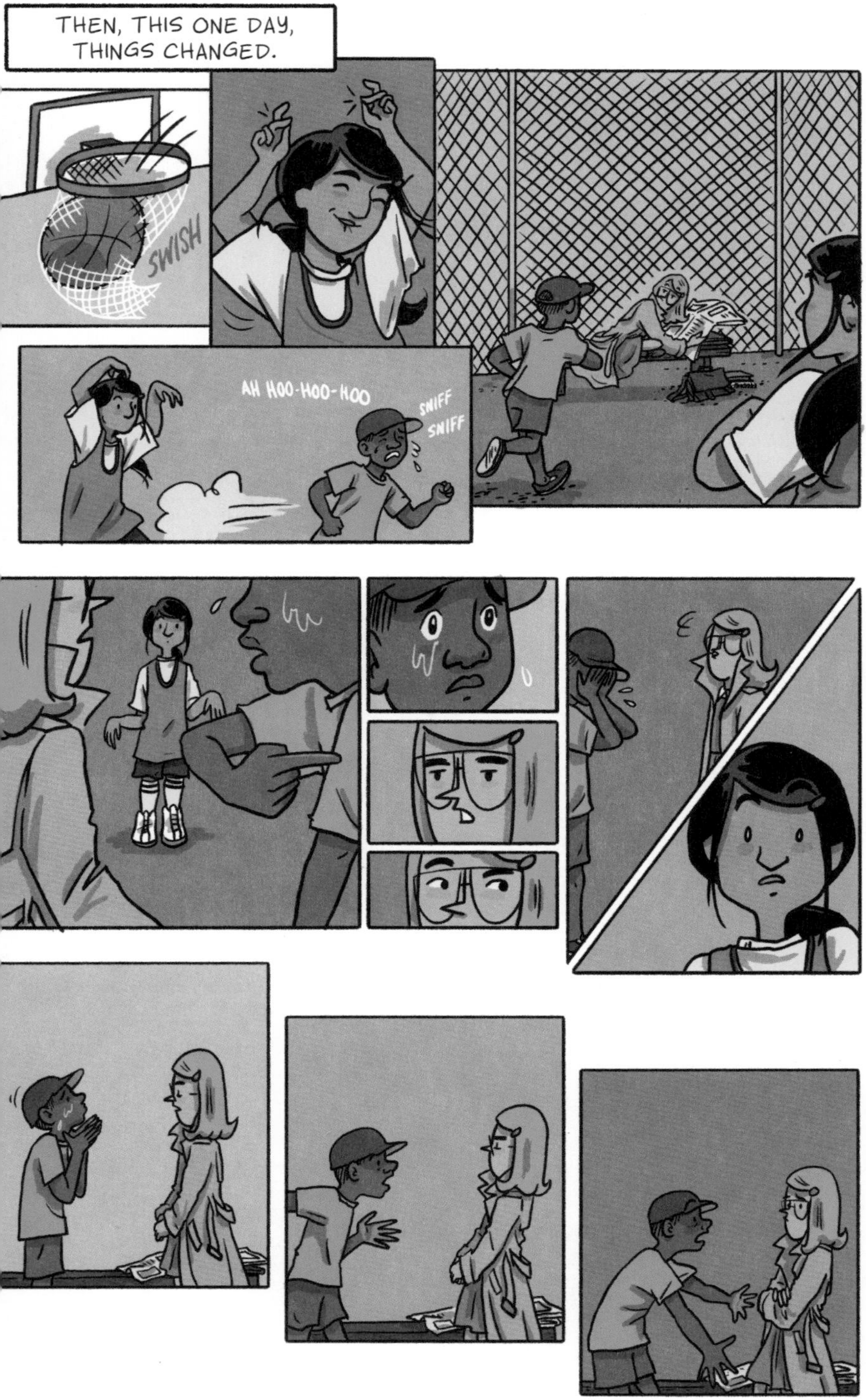
THEN, THIS ONE DAY,
THINGS CHANGED.
SWISH
AH HOO-HOO-HOO
SNIFF
SNIFF

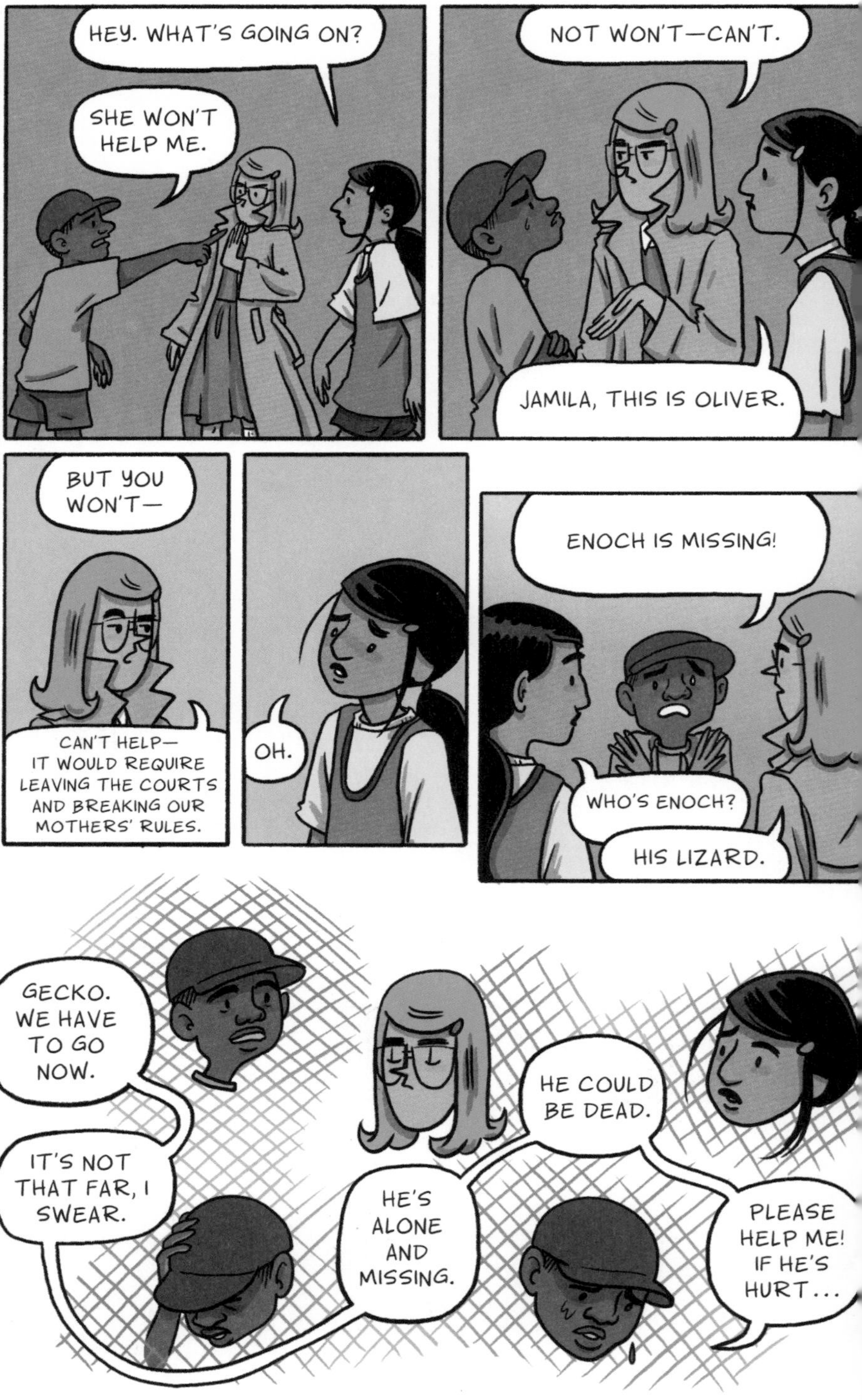
HEY. WHAT'S GOING ON?
SHE WON'T HELP ME.
NOT WON'T—CAN'T.
JAMILA, THIS IS OLIVER.
BUT YOU WON'T—
CAN'T HELP— IT WOULD REQUIRE LEAVING THE COURTS AND BREAKING OUR MOTHERS' RULES.
OH.
ENOCH IS MISSING!
WHO'S ENOCH?
HIS LIZARD.
GECKO. WE HAVE TO GO NOW.
IT'S NOT THAT FAR, I SWEAR.
HE'S ALONE AND MISSING.
HE COULD BE DEAD.
PLEASE HELP ME! IF HE'S HURT...

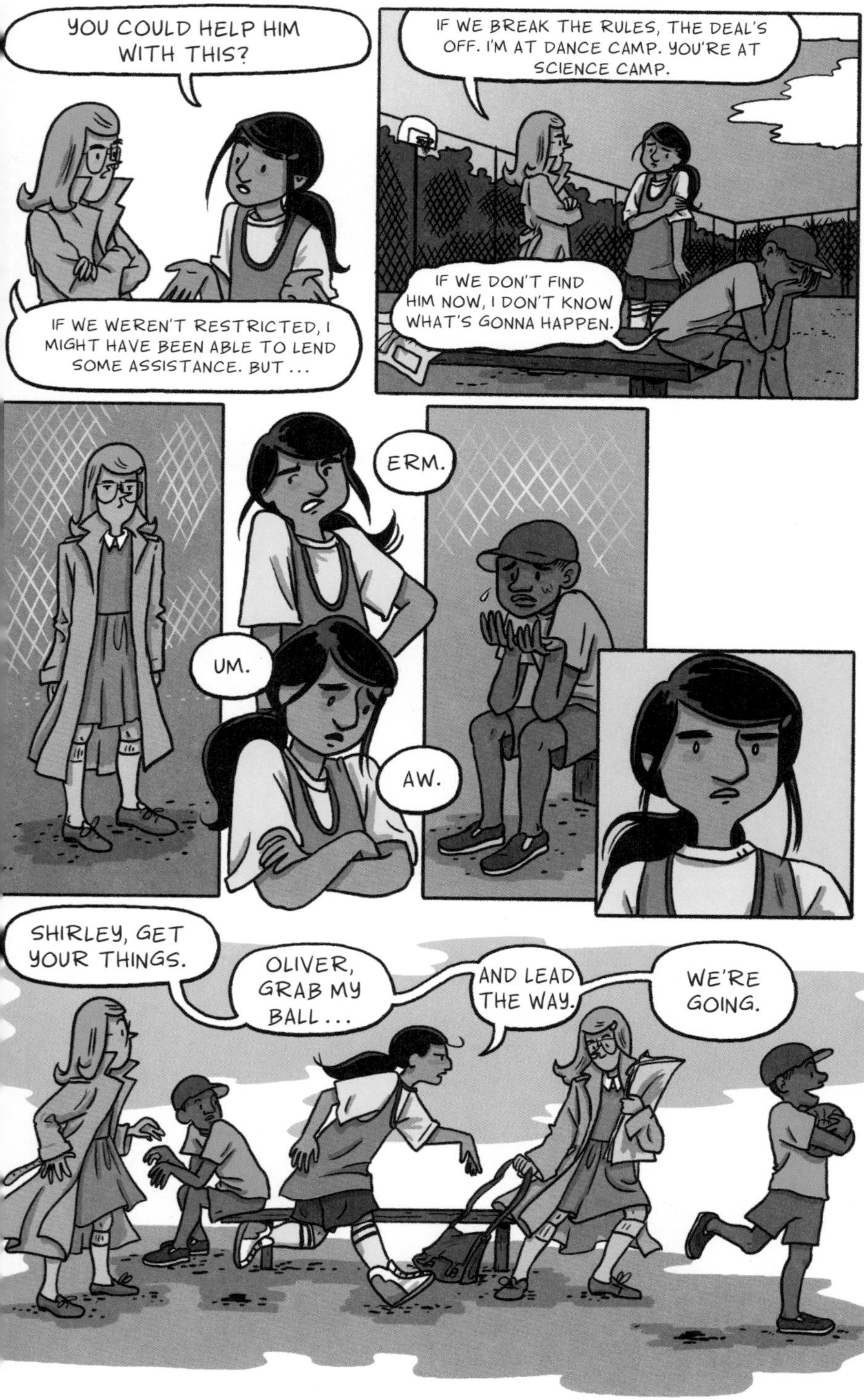
YOU COULD HELP HIM WITH THIS?
IF WE WEREN'T RESTRICTED, I MIGHT HAVE BEEN ABLE TO LEND SOME ASSISTANCE. BUT . . .
IF WE BREAK THE RULES, THE DEAL'S OFF. I'M AT DANCE CAMP. YOU'RE AT SCIENCE CAMP.
IF WE DON'T FIND HIM NOW, I DON'T KNOW WHAT'S GONNA HAPPEN.
ERM.
UM.
AW.
SHIRLEY, GET YOUR THINGS.
OLIVER, GRAB MY BALL . . .
AND LEAD THE WAY.
WE'RE GOING.

Chapter 5

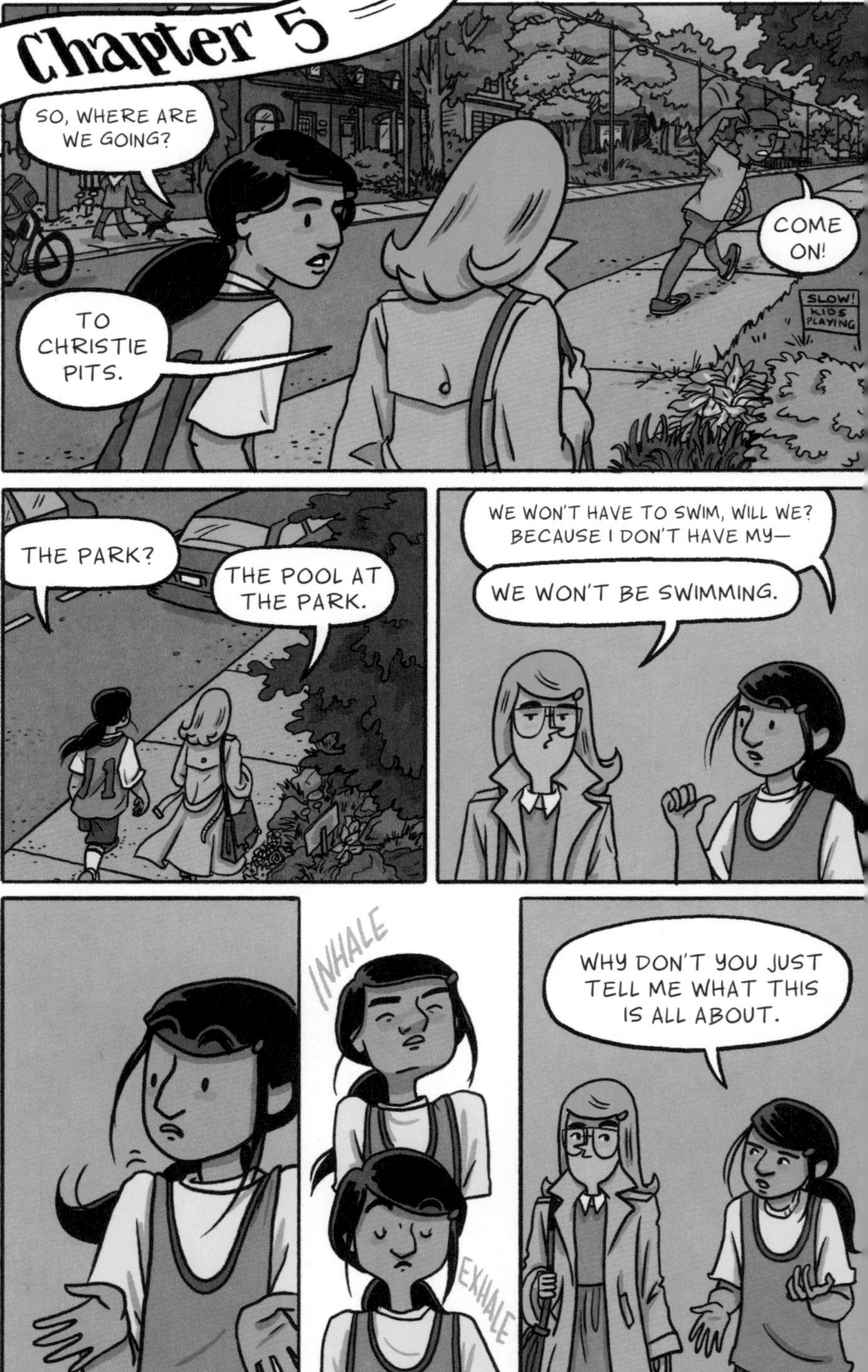
SO, WHERE ARE WE GOING?
COME ON!
SLOW! KIDS PLAYING
TO CHRISTIE PITS.
THE PARK?
THE POOL AT THE PARK.
WE WON'T HAVE TO SWIM, WILL WE? BECAUSE I DON'T HAVE MY—
WE WON'T BE SWIMMING.
INHALE
EXHALE
WHY DON'T YOU JUST TELL ME WHAT THIS IS ALL ABOUT.

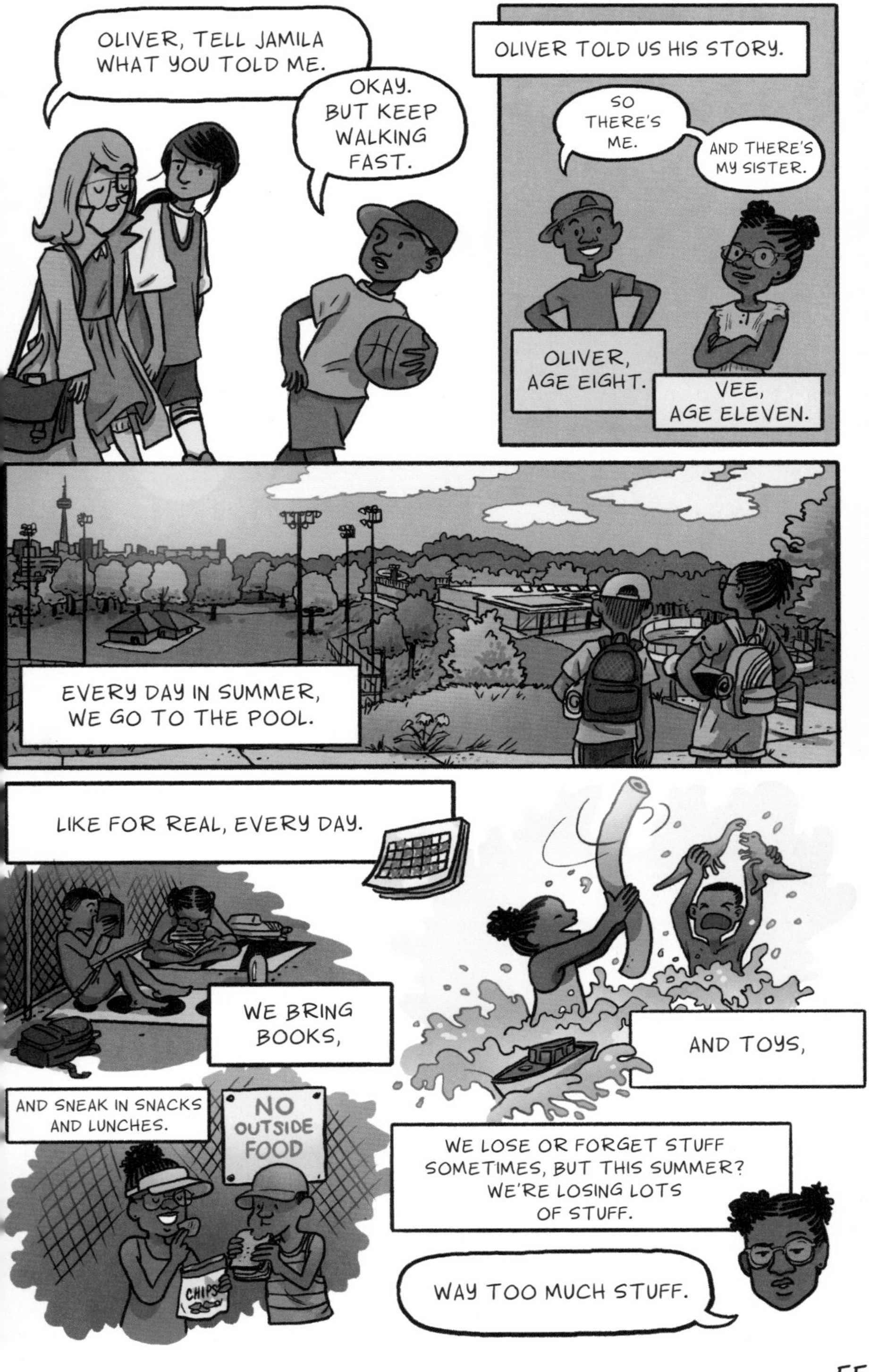
OLIVER, TELL JAMILA WHAT YOU TOLD ME.
OKAY. BUT KEEP WALKING FAST.
OLIVER TOLD US HIS STORY.
SO THERE'S ME.
AND THERE'S MY SISTER.
OLIVER, AGE EIGHT.
VEE, AGE ELEVEN.
EVERY DAY IN SUMMER, WE GO TO THE POOL.
LIKE FOR REAL, EVERY DAY.
WE BRING BOOKS,
AND TOYS,
AND SNEAK IN SNACKS AND LUNCHES.
NO OUTSIDE FOOD
CHIPS
WE LOSE OR FORGET STUFF SOMETIMES, BUT THIS SUMMER? WE'RE LOSING LOTS OF STUFF.
WAY TOO MUCH STUFF.

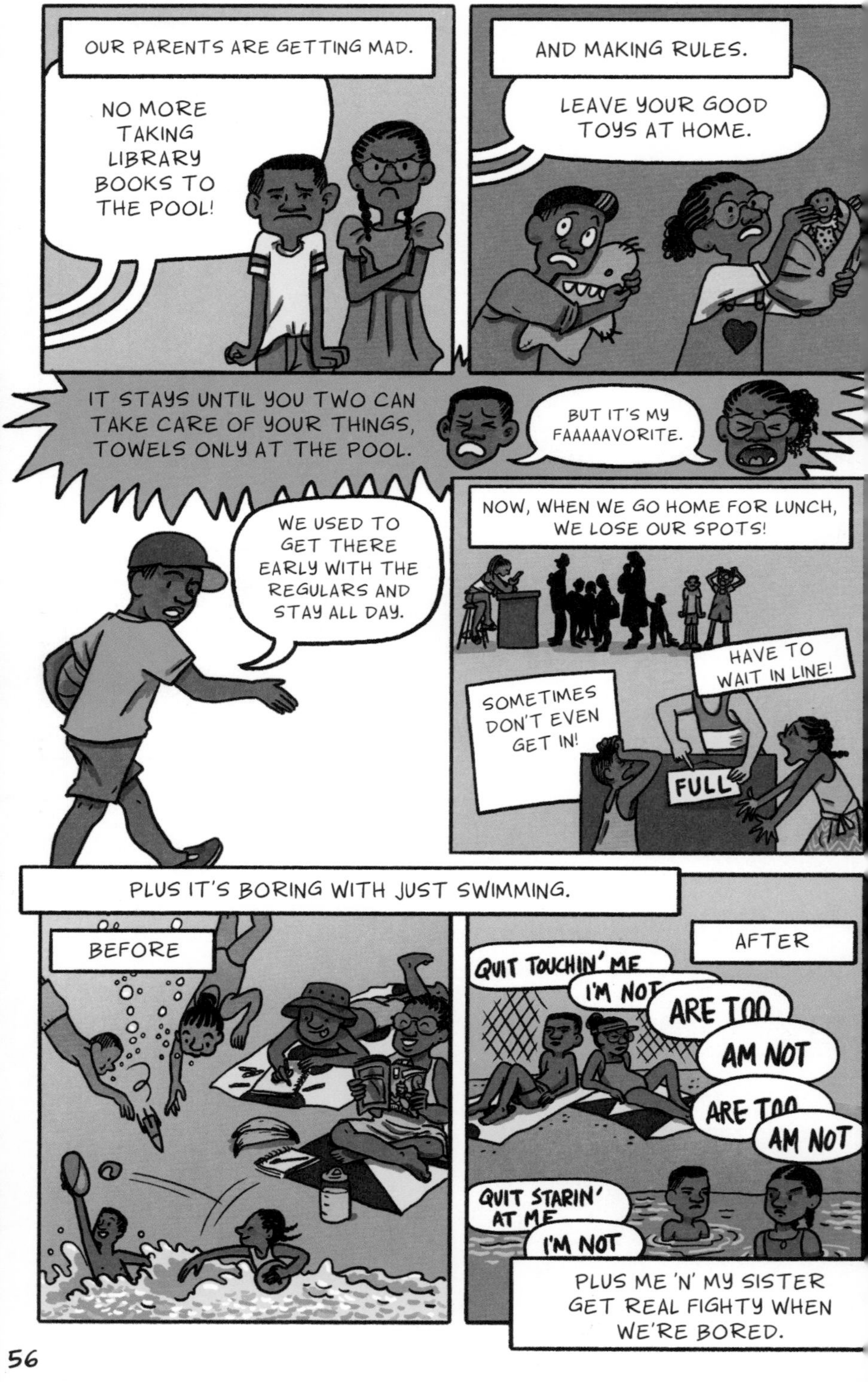
OUR PARENTS ARE GETTING MAD.
NO MORE TAKING LIBRARY BOOKS TO THE POOL!
AND MAKING RULES.
LEAVE YOUR GOOD TOYS AT HOME.
IT STAYS UNTIL YOU TWO CAN TAKE CARE OF YOUR THINGS, TOWELS ONLY AT THE POOL.
BUT IT'S MY FAAAAAVORITE.
WE USED TO GET THERE EARLY WITH THE REGULARS AND STAY ALL DAY.
NOW, WHEN WE GO HOME FOR LUNCH, WE LOSE OUR SPOTS!
HAVE TO WAIT IN LINE!
SOMETIMES DON'T EVEN GET IN!
FULL
PLUS IT'S BORING WITH JUST SWIMMING.
BEFORE
AFTER
QUIT TOUCHIN' ME
I'M NOT
ARE TOO
AM NOT
ARE TOO
AM NOT
QUIT STARIN' AT ME
I'M NOT
PLUS ME 'N' MY SISTER GET REAL FIGHTY WHEN WE'RE BORED.

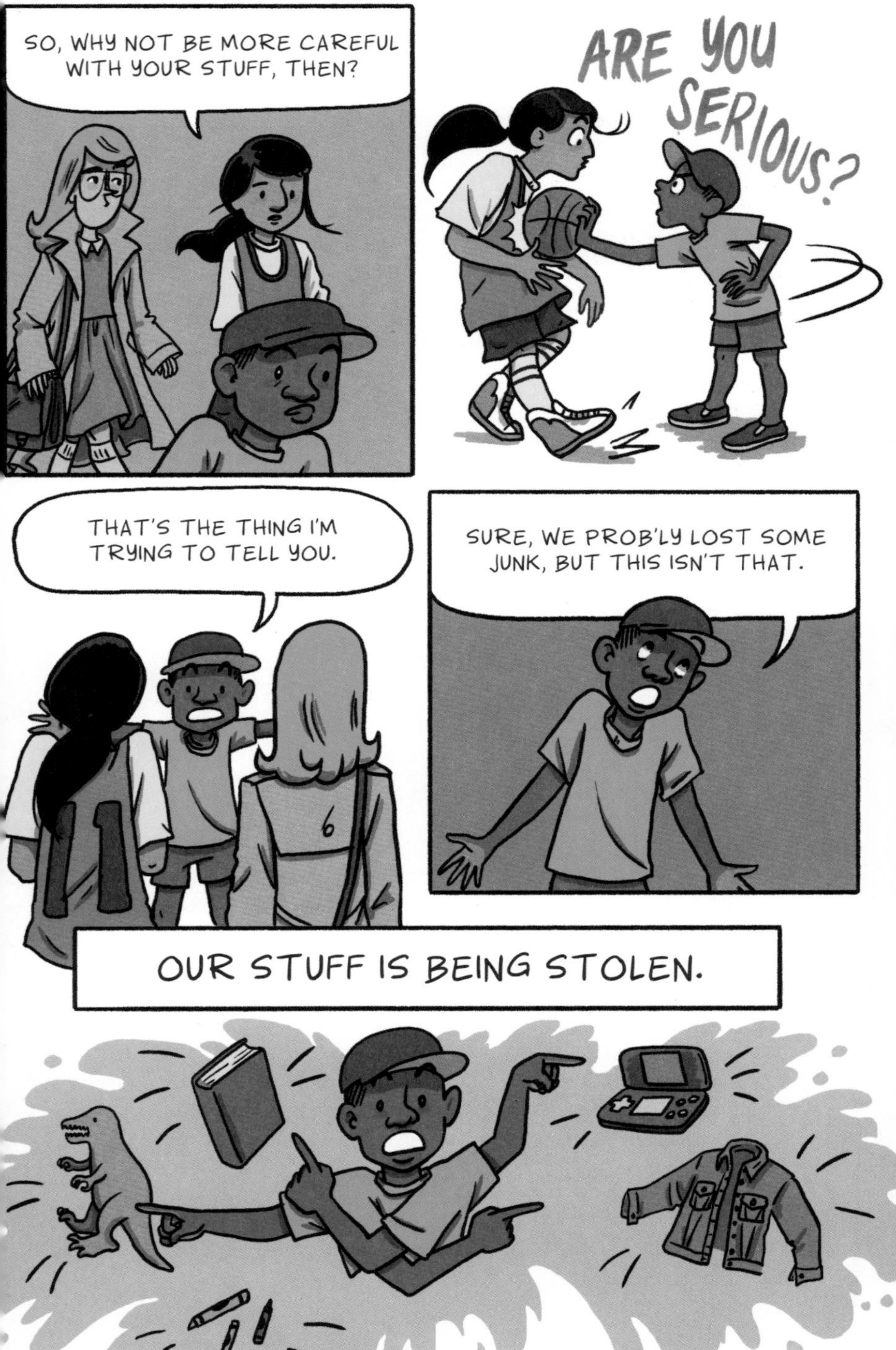
SO, WHY NOT BE MORE CAREFUL WITH YOUR STUFF, THEN?
ARE YOU SERIOUS?
THAT'S THE THING I'M TRYING TO TELL YOU.
SURE, WE PROB'LY LOST SOME JUNK, BUT THIS ISN'T THAT.
OUR STUFF IS BEING STOLEN.

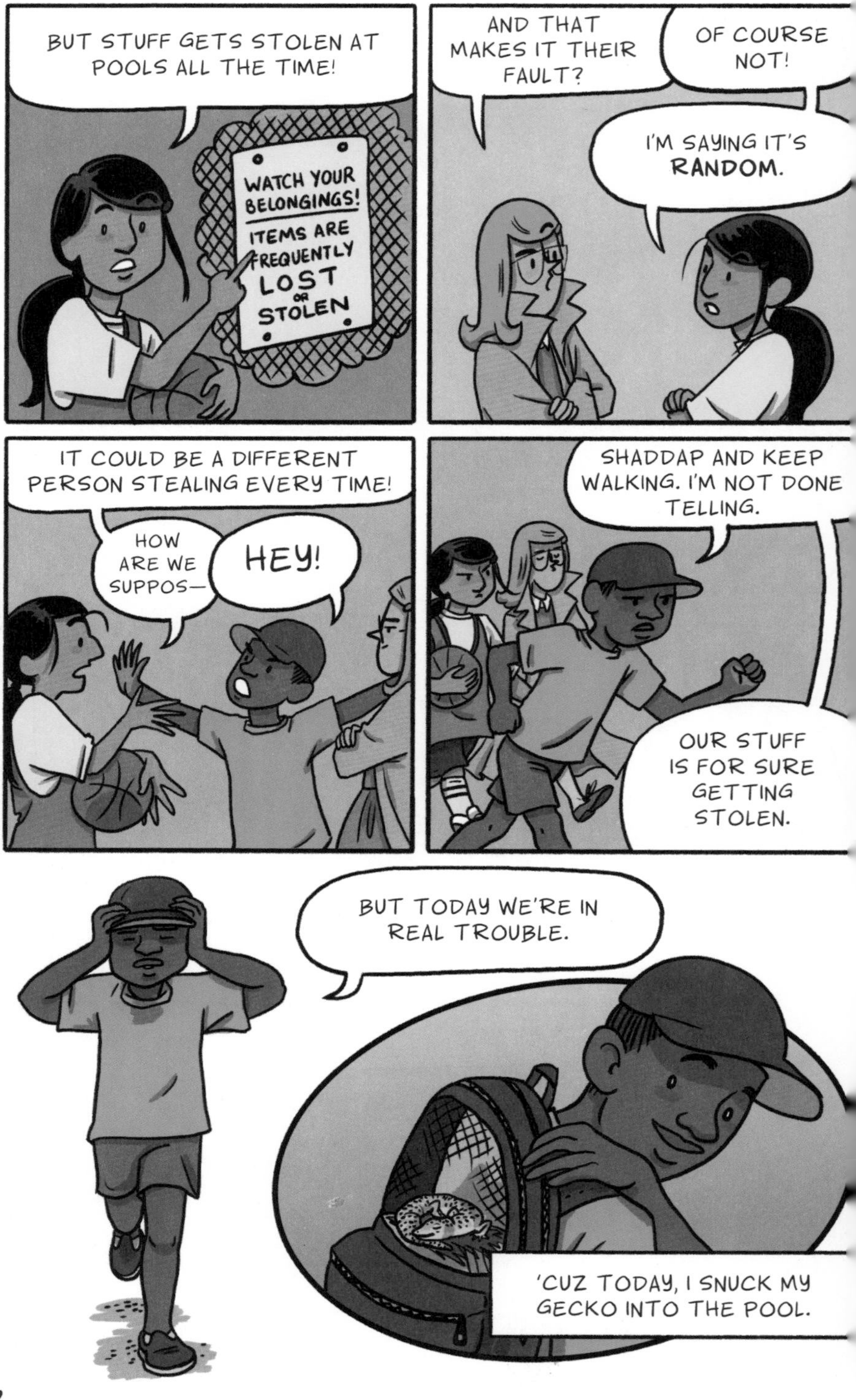
BUT STUFF GETS STOLEN AT POOLS ALL THE TIME!
WATCH YOUR BELONGINGS!
ITEMS ARE FREQUENTLY LOST OR STOLEN
AND THAT MAKES IT THEIR FAULT?
OF COURSE NOT!
I'M SAYING IT'S RANDOM.
IT COULD BE A DIFFERENT PERSON STEALING EVERY TIME!
HOW ARE WE SUPPOS—
HEY!
SHADDAP AND KEEP WALKING. I'M NOT DONE TELLING.
OUR STUFF IS FOR SURE GETTING STOLEN.
BUT TODAY WE'RE IN REAL TROUBLE.
'CUZ TODAY, I SNUCK MY GECKO INTO THE POOL.

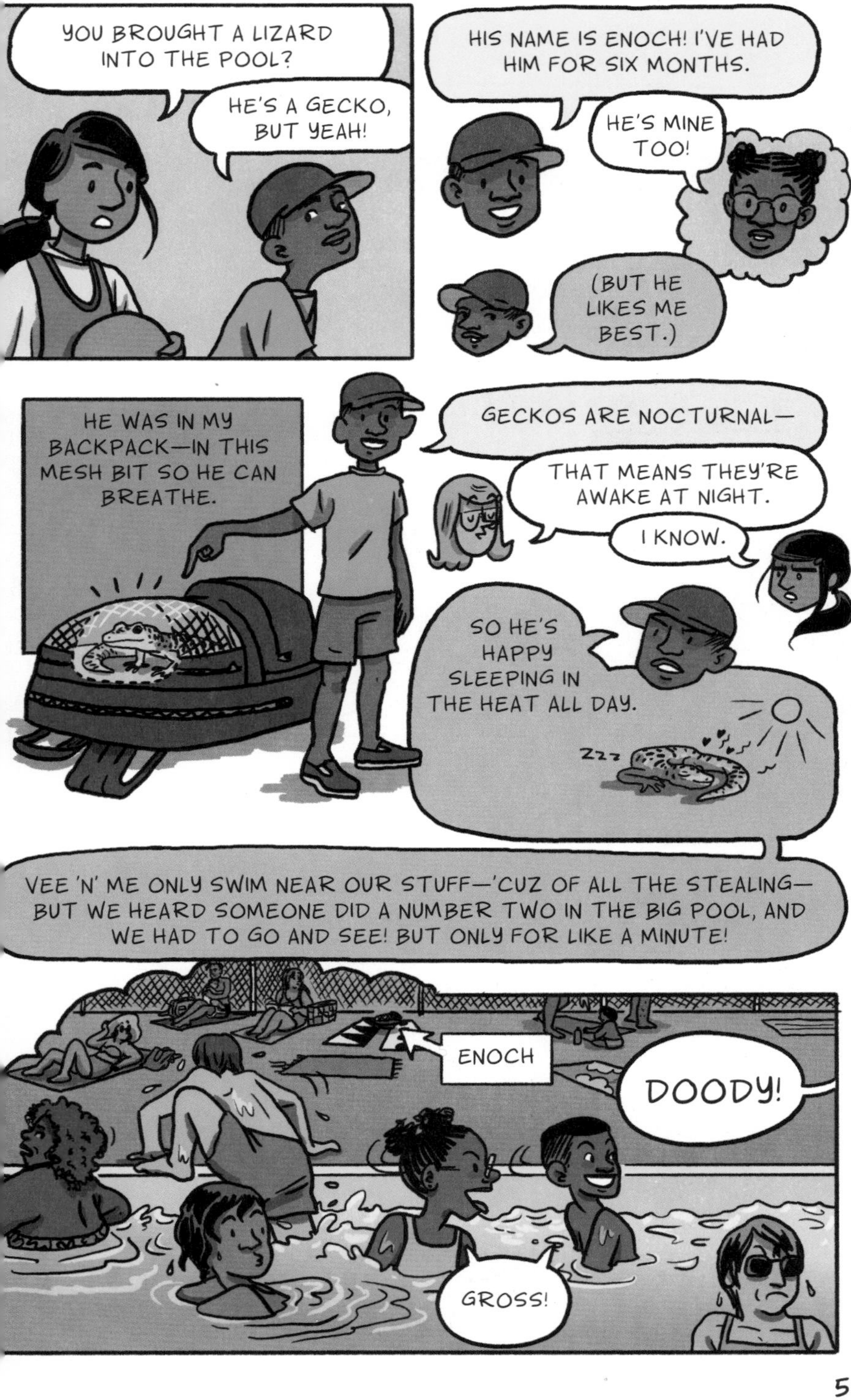
YOU BROUGHT A LIZARD INTO THE POOL?
HE'S A GECKO, BUT YEAH!
HIS NAME IS ENOCH! I'VE HAD HIM FOR SIX MONTHS.
HE'S MINE TOO!
(BUT HE LIKES ME BEST.)
HE WAS IN MY BACKPACK—IN THIS MESH BIT SO HE CAN BREATHE.
GECKOS ARE NOCTURNAL—
THAT MEANS THEY'RE AWAKE AT NIGHT.
I KNOW.
SO HE'S HAPPY SLEEPING IN THE HEAT ALL DAY.
ZZZ
VEE 'N' ME ONLY SWIM NEAR OUR STUFF—'CUZ OF ALL THE STEALING—BUT WE HEARD SOMEONE DID A NUMBER TWO IN THE BIG POOL, AND WE HAD TO GO AND SEE! BUT ONLY FOR LIKE A MINUTE!
ENOCH
DOODY!
GROSS!

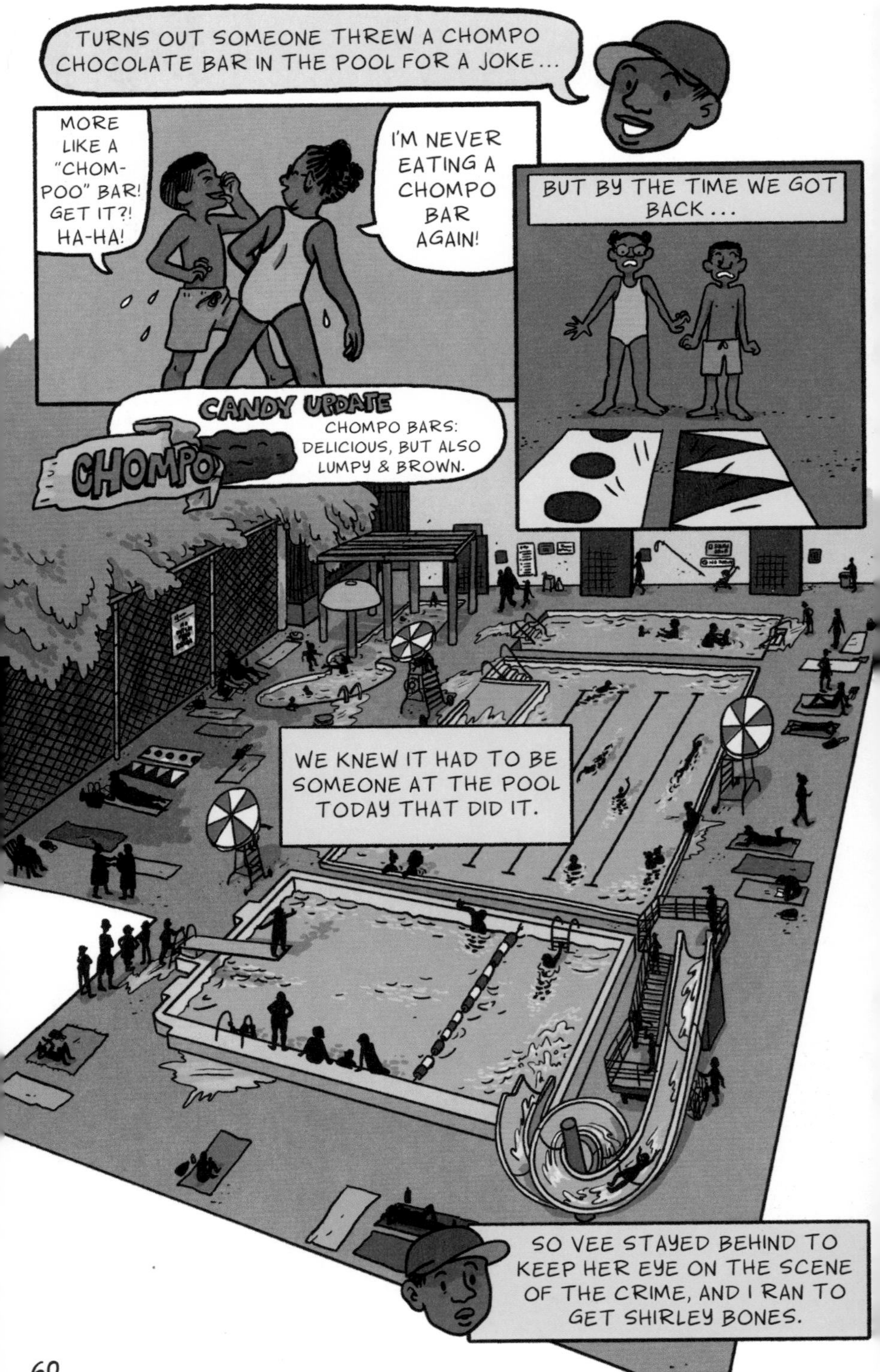
TURNS OUT SOMEONE THREW A CHOMPO CHOCOLATE BAR IN THE POOL FOR A JOKE...
MORE LIKE A "CHOM-POO" BAR! GET IT?! HA-HA!
I'M NEVER EATING A CHOMPO BAR AGAIN!
BUT BY THE TIME WE GOT BACK...
CANDY UPDATE
CHOMPO BARS: DELICIOUS, BUT ALSO LUMPY & BROWN.
CHOMPO
WE KNEW IT HAD TO BE SOMEONE AT THE POOL TODAY THAT DID IT.
SO VEE STAYED BEHIND TO KEEP HER EYE ON THE SCENE OF THE CRIME, AND I RAN TO GET SHIRLEY BONES.

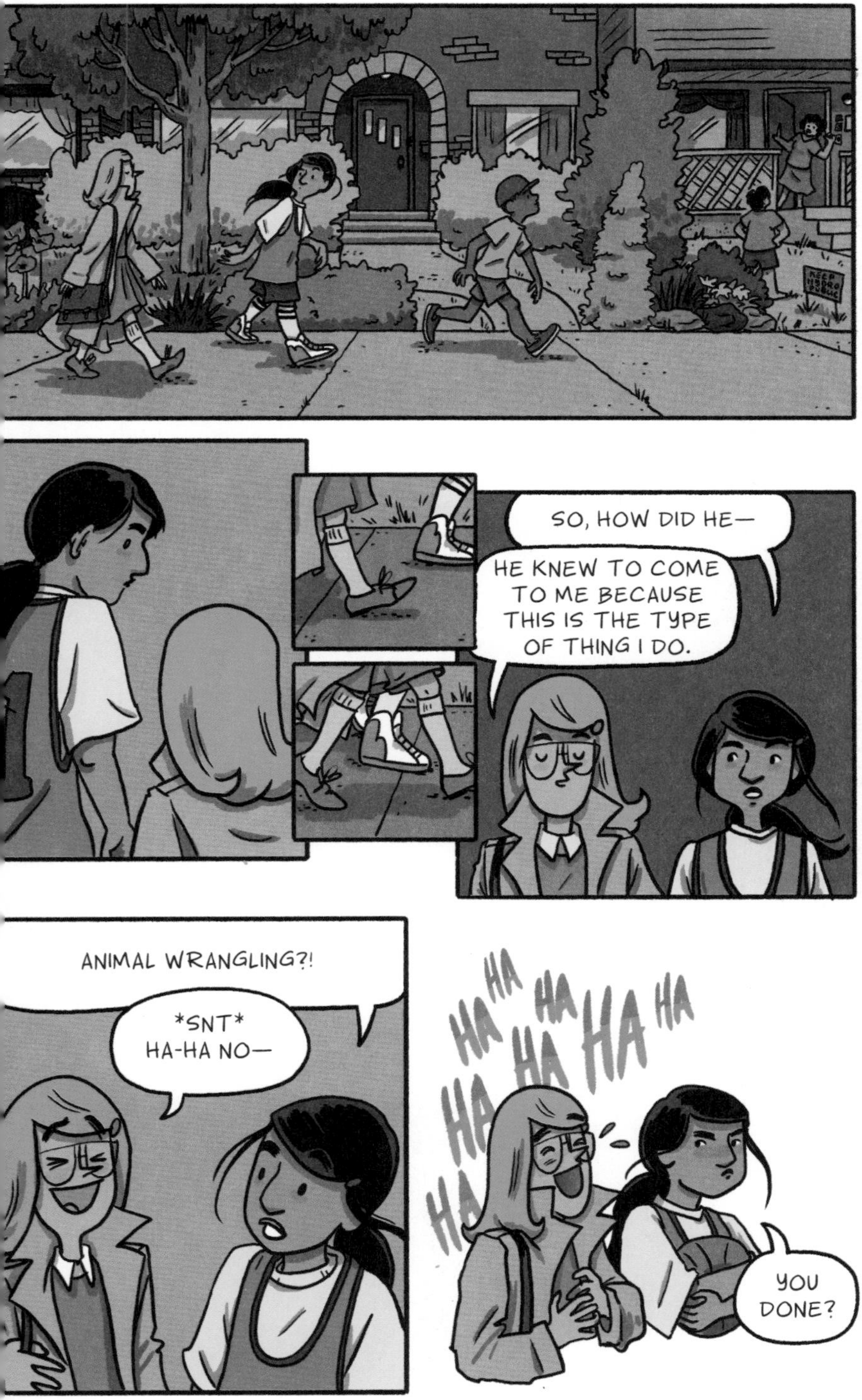
KEEP HYDRO PUBLIC
SO, HOW DID HE—
HE KNEW TO COME TO ME BECAUSE THIS IS THE TYPE OF THING I DO.
ANIMAL WRANGLING?!
SNT HA-HA NO—
HA HA HA HA HA HA HA HA HA HA
YOU DONE?

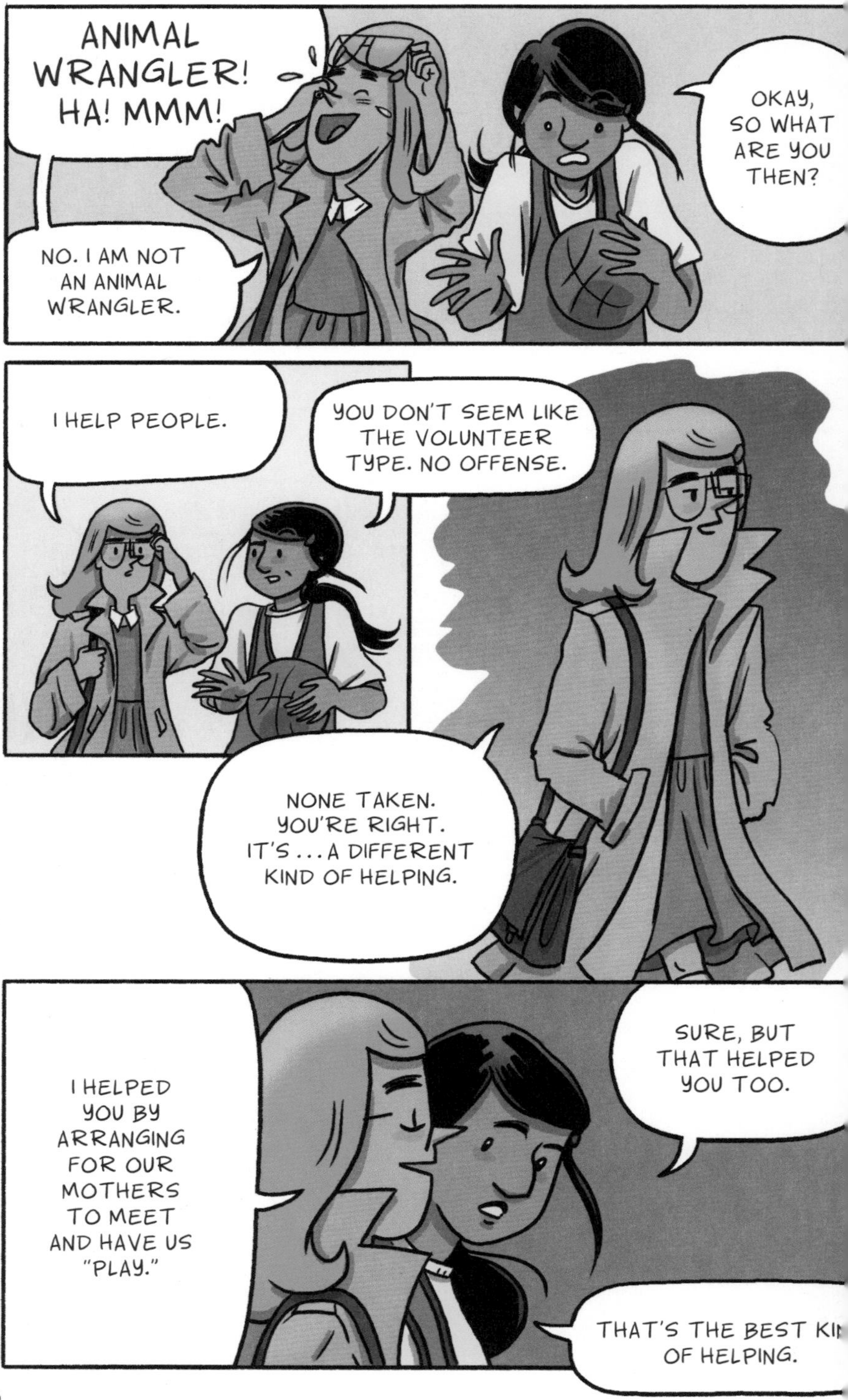

ANIMAL WRANGLER! HA! MMM!
NO. I AM NOT AN ANIMAL WRANGLER.
OKAY, SO WHAT ARE YOU THEN?
I HELP PEOPLE.
YOU DON'T SEEM LIKE THE VOLUNTEER TYPE. NO OFFENSE.
NONE TAKEN. YOU'RE RIGHT. IT'S . . . A DIFFERENT KIND OF HELPING.
I HELPED YOU BY ARRANGING FOR OUR MOTHERS TO MEET AND HAVE US "PLAY."
SURE, BUT THAT HELPED YOU TOO.
THAT'S THE BEST KI
OF HELPING.

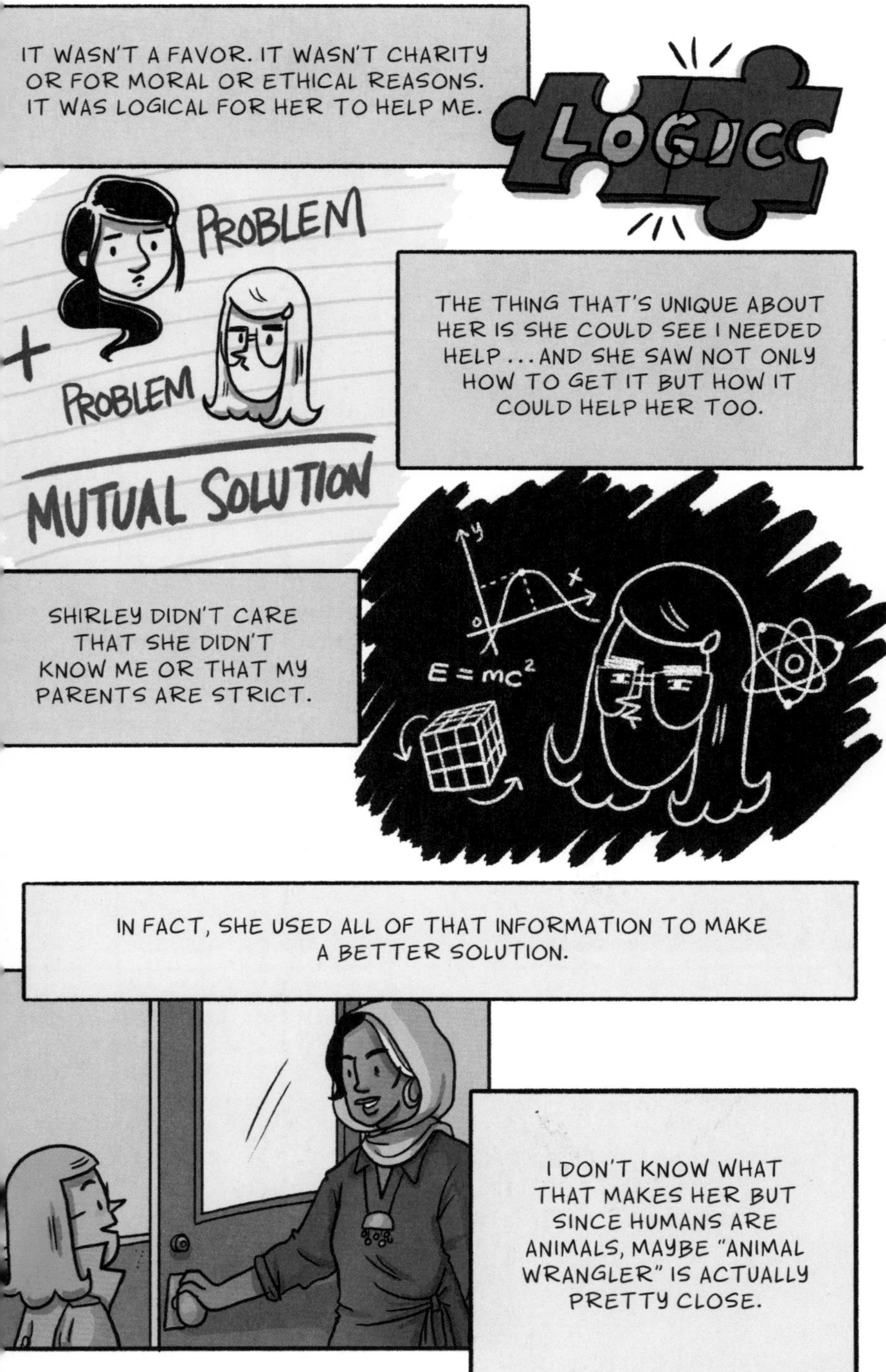
IT WASN'T A FAVOR. IT WASN'T CHARITY OR FOR MORAL OR ETHICAL REASONS. IT WAS LOGICAL FOR HER TO HELP ME.
LOGIC
PROBLEM
+
PROBLEM
MUTUAL SOLUTION
THE THING THAT'S UNIQUE ABOUT HER IS SHE COULD SEE I NEEDED HELP . . . AND SHE SAW NOT ONLY HOW TO GET IT BUT HOW IT COULD HELP HER TOO.
SHIRLEY DIDN'T CARE THAT SHE DIDN'T KNOW ME OR THAT MY PARENTS ARE STRICT.
y
x
0
E = mc²
IN FACT, SHE USED ALL OF THAT INFORMATION TO MAKE A BETTER SOLUTION.
I DON'T KNOW WHAT THAT MAKES HER BUT SINCE HUMANS ARE ANIMALS, MAYBE "ANIMAL WRANGLER" IS ACTUALLY PRETTY CLOSE.

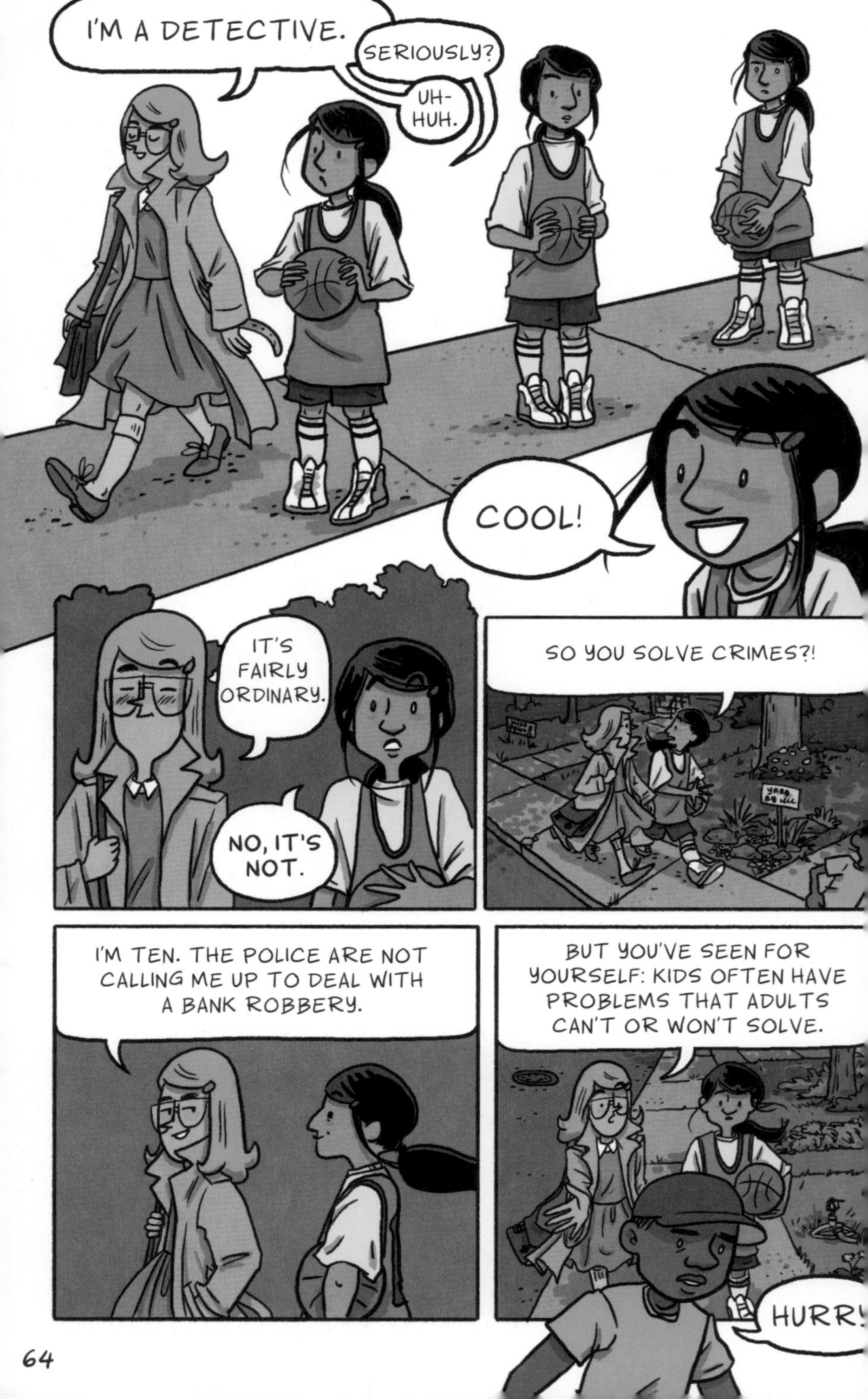
I'M A DETECTIVE.
SERIOUSLY?
UH-HUH.
COOL!
IT'S FAIRLY ORDINARY.
NO, IT'S NOT.
SO YOU SOLVE CRIMES?!
I'M TEN. THE POLICE ARE NOT CALLING ME UP TO DEAL WITH A BANK ROBBERY.
BUT YOU'VE SEEN FOR YOURSELF: KIDS OFTEN HAVE PROBLEMS THAT ADULTS CAN'T OR WON'T SOLVE.
HURR!

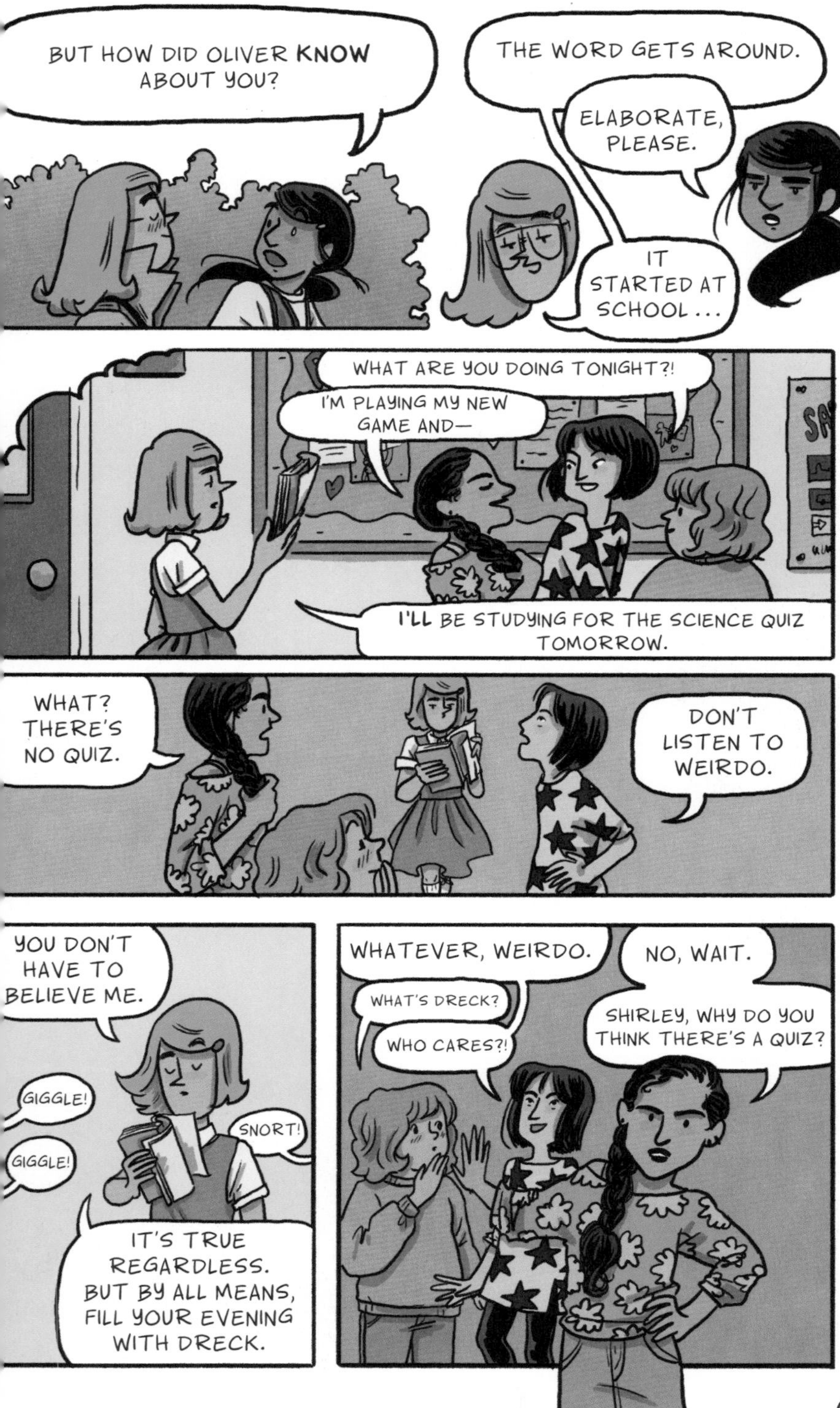
BUT HOW DID OLIVER **KNOW** ABOUT YOU?
THE WORD GETS AROUND.
ELABORATE, PLEASE.
IT STARTED AT SCHOOL . . .
WHAT ARE YOU DOING TONIGHT?!
I'M PLAYING MY NEW GAME AND—
I'LL BE STUDYING FOR THE SCIENCE QUIZ TOMORROW.
WHAT? THERE'S NO QUIZ.
DON'T LISTEN TO WEIRDO.
YOU DON'T HAVE TO BELIEVE ME.
GIGGLE!
SNORT!
GIGGLE!
IT'S TRUE REGARDLESS. BUT BY ALL MEANS, FILL YOUR EVENING WITH DRECK.
WHATEVER, WEIRDO.
NO, WAIT.
WHAT'S DRECK?
WHO CARES?!
SHIRLEY, WHY DO YOU THINK THERE'S A QUIZ?

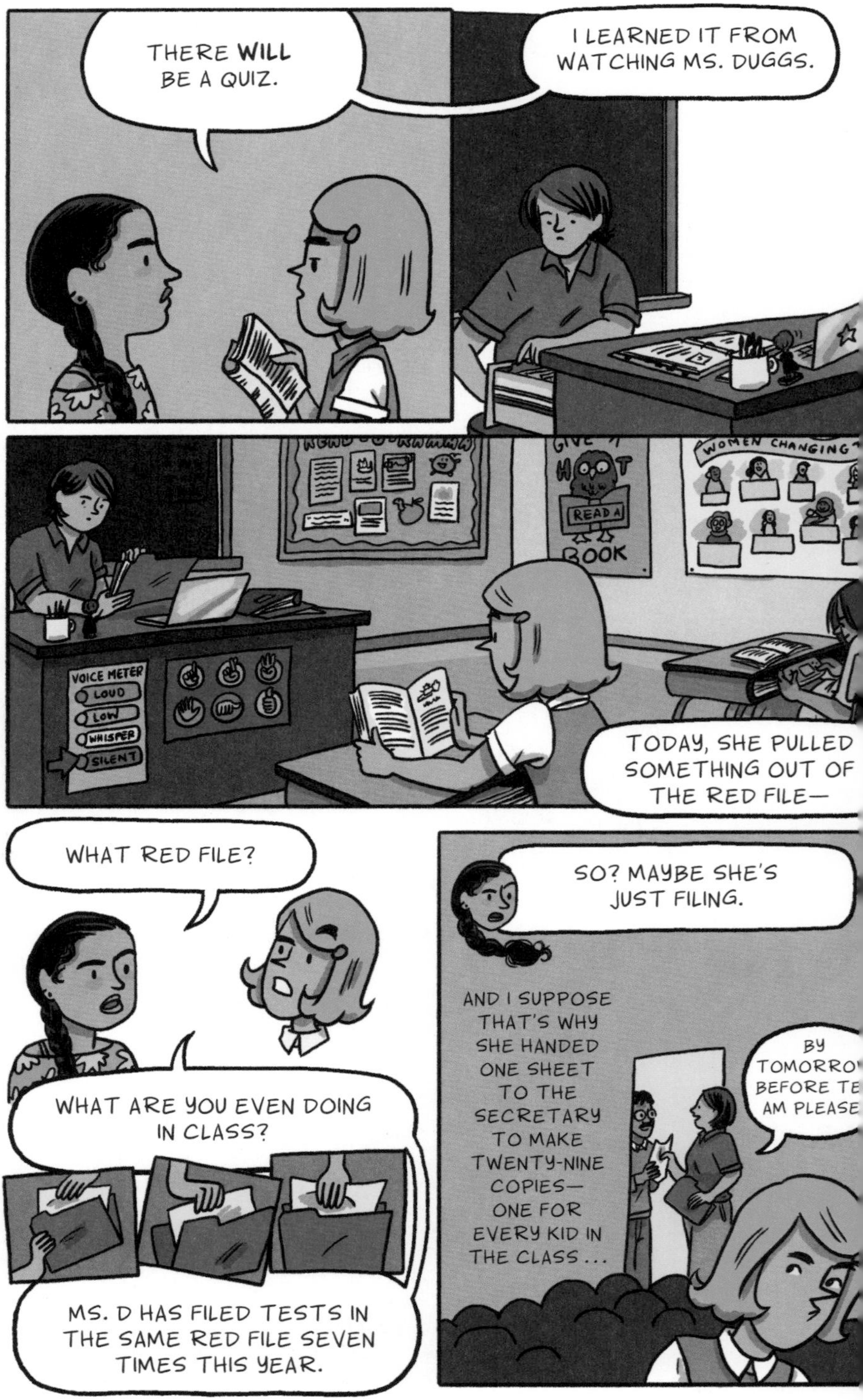

THERE **WILL** BE A QUIZ.
I LEARNED IT FROM WATCHING MS. DUGGS.
VOICE METER
LOUD
LOW
WHISPER
SILENT
READ A
BOOK
WOMEN CHANGING
TODAY, SHE PULLED SOMETHING OUT OF THE RED FILE—
WHAT RED FILE?
WHAT ARE YOU EVEN DOING IN CLASS?
MS. D HAS FILED TESTS IN THE SAME RED FILE SEVEN TIMES THIS YEAR.
SO? MAYBE SHE'S JUST FILING.
AND I SUPPOSE THAT'S WHY SHE HANDED ONE SHEET TO THE SECRETARY TO MAKE TWENTY-NINE COPIES— ONE FOR EVERY KID IN THE CLASS . . .
BY TOMORRO BEFORE TE AM PLEASE

MS. DUGGS NEEDS HER COPIES BY TEN AM.

BETWEEN TEN AND LUNCH WE HAVE TWO SUBJECTS:

SCIENCE AND LANGUAGE ARTS. WE JUST HAD A TEST IN LANGUAGE ARTS EIGHT DAYS AGO.

TOMORROW WE'RE HAVING A POP QUIZ. IN SCIENCE.

SINCE MICHAYLA WAS SICK FOR TWO DAYS...

AND GABRIELLA, YOU AND SHAY PASSED NOTES FOR THE LAST THREE SCIENCE LESSONS...

(AND YOU BOTH GET C'S IN SCIENCE)...

YOU MAY WANT TO STUDY.

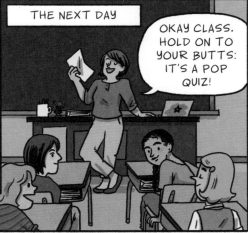

THE NEXT DAY

OKAY CLASS. HOLD ON TO YOUR BUTTS: IT'S A POP QUIZ!

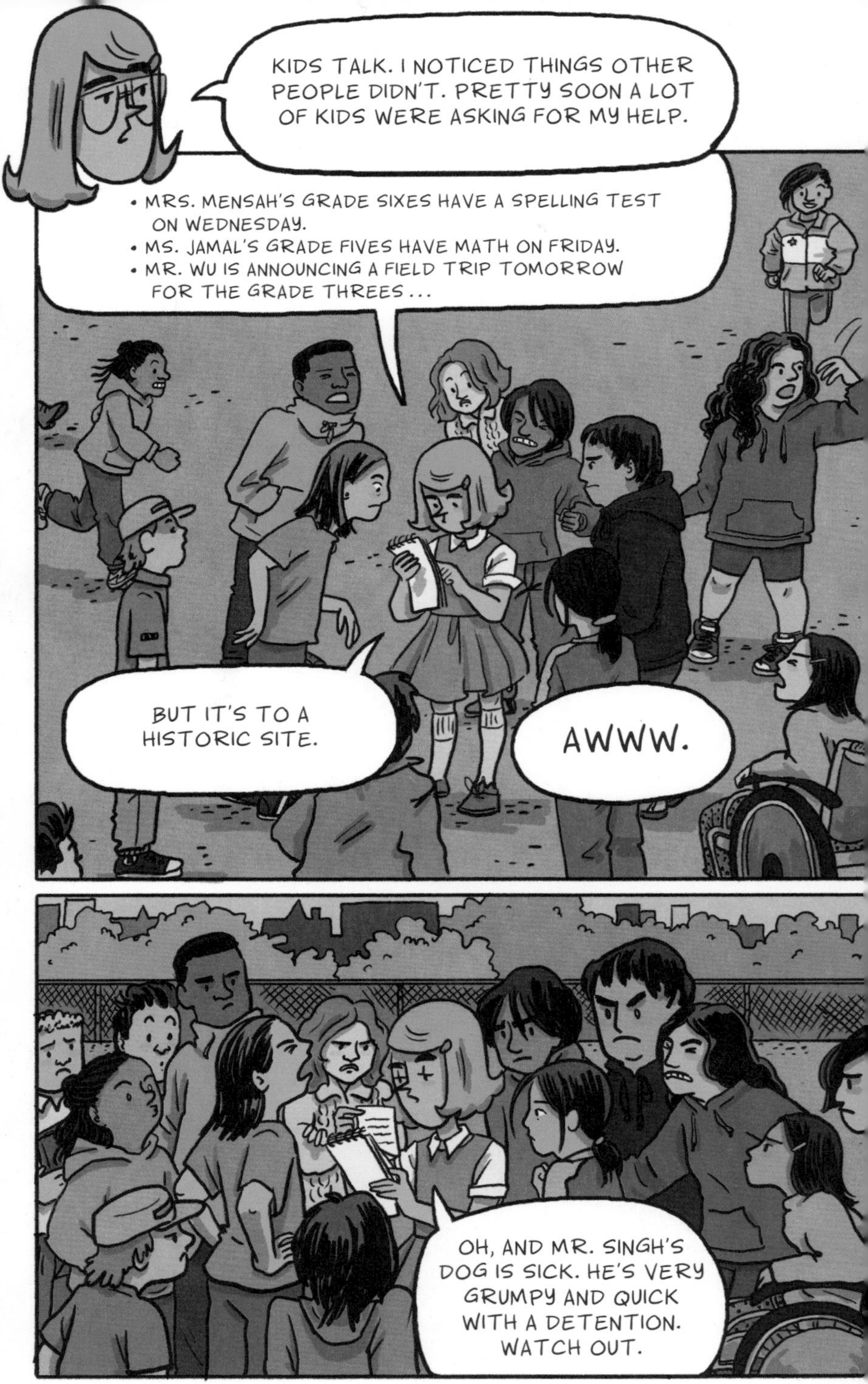
KIDS TALK. I NOTICED THINGS OTHER PEOPLE DIDN'T. PRETTY SOON A LOT OF KIDS WERE ASKING FOR MY HELP.
• MRS. MENSAH'S GRADE SIXES HAVE A SPELLING TEST ON WEDNESDAY.
• MS. JAMAL'S GRADE FIVES HAVE MATH ON FRIDAY.
• MR. WU IS ANNOUNCING A FIELD TRIP TOMORROW FOR THE GRADE THREES . . .
BUT IT'S TO A HISTORIC SITE.
AWWW.
OH, AND MR. SINGH'S DOG IS SICK. HE'S VERY GRUMPY AND QUICK WITH A DETENTION. WATCH OUT.

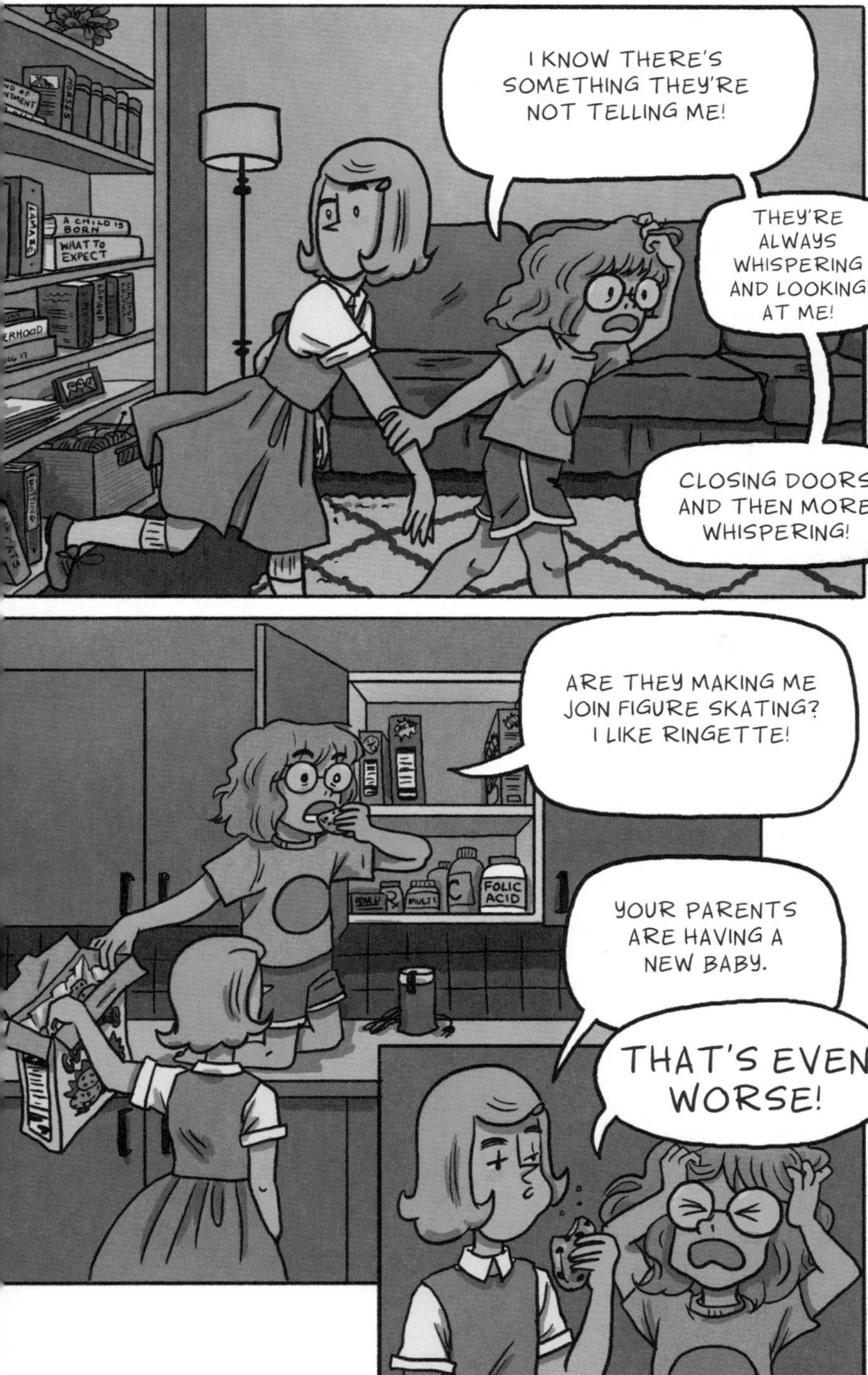
A CHILD IS BORN
WHAT TO EXPECT
I KNOW THERE'S SOMETHING THEY'RE NOT TELLING ME!
THEY'RE ALWAYS WHISPERING AND LOOKING AT ME!
CLOSING DOORS AND THEN MORE WHISPERING!
ARE THEY MAKING ME JOIN FIGURE SKATING? I LIKE RINGETTE!
FOLIC ACID
YOUR PARENTS ARE HAVING A NEW BABY.
THAT'S EVEN WORSE!

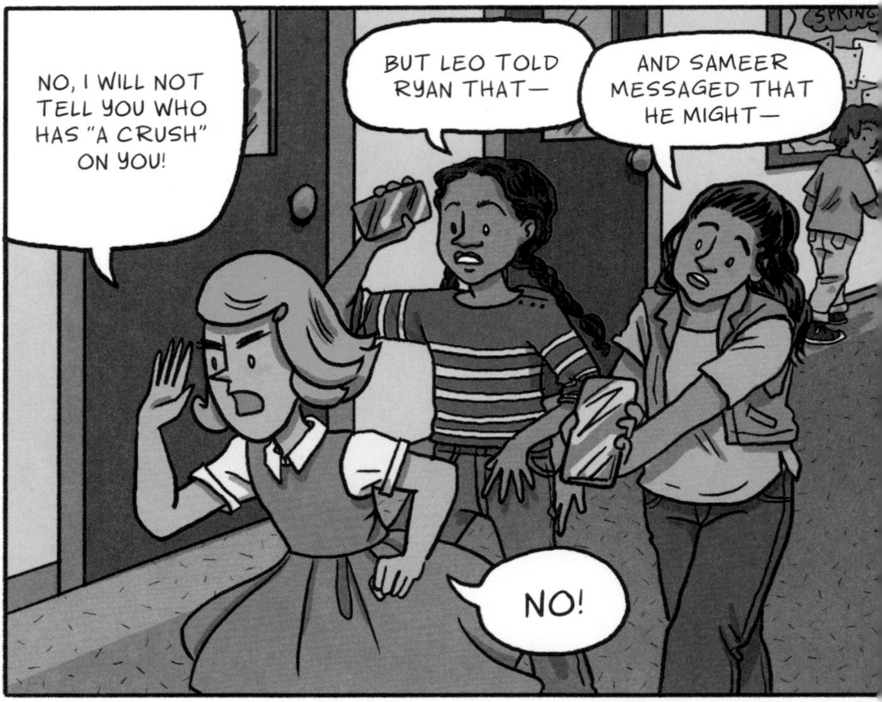
NO, I WILL NOT TELL YOU WHO HAS "A CRUSH" ON YOU!
BUT LEO TOLD RYAN THAT—
AND SAMEER MESSAGED THAT HE MIGHT—
NO!

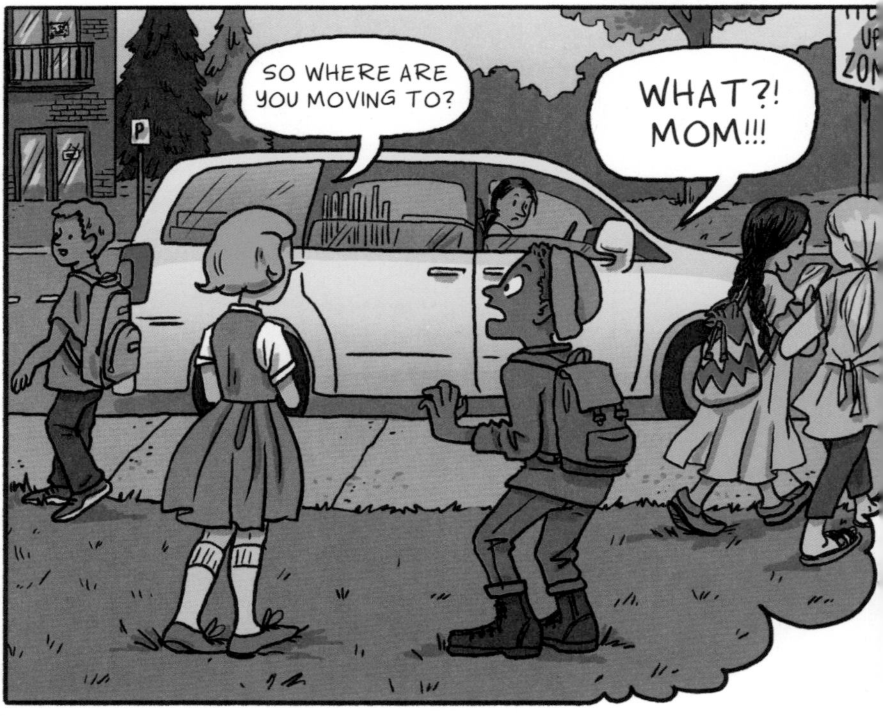
SO WHERE ARE YOU MOVING TO?
WHAT?! MOM!!!

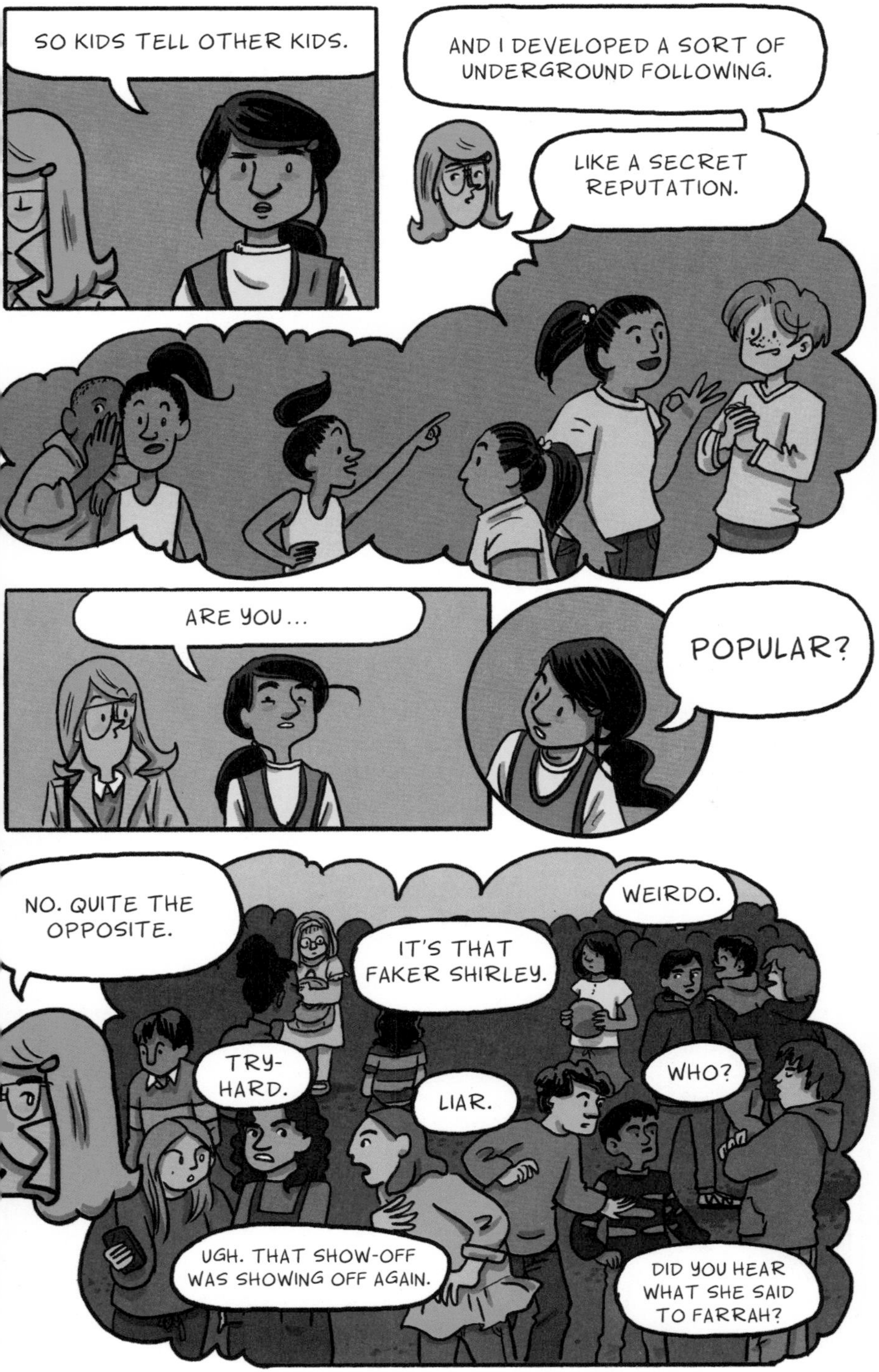
SO KIDS TELL OTHER KIDS.
AND I DEVELOPED A SORT OF UNDERGROUND FOLLOWING.
LIKE A SECRET REPUTATION.
ARE YOU...
POPULAR?
NO. QUITE THE OPPOSITE.
WEIRDO.
IT'S THAT FAKER SHIRLEY.
TRY-HARD.
WHO?
LIAR.
UGH. THAT SHOW-OFF WAS SHOWING OFF AGAIN.
DID YOU HEAR WHAT SHE SAID TO FARRAH?

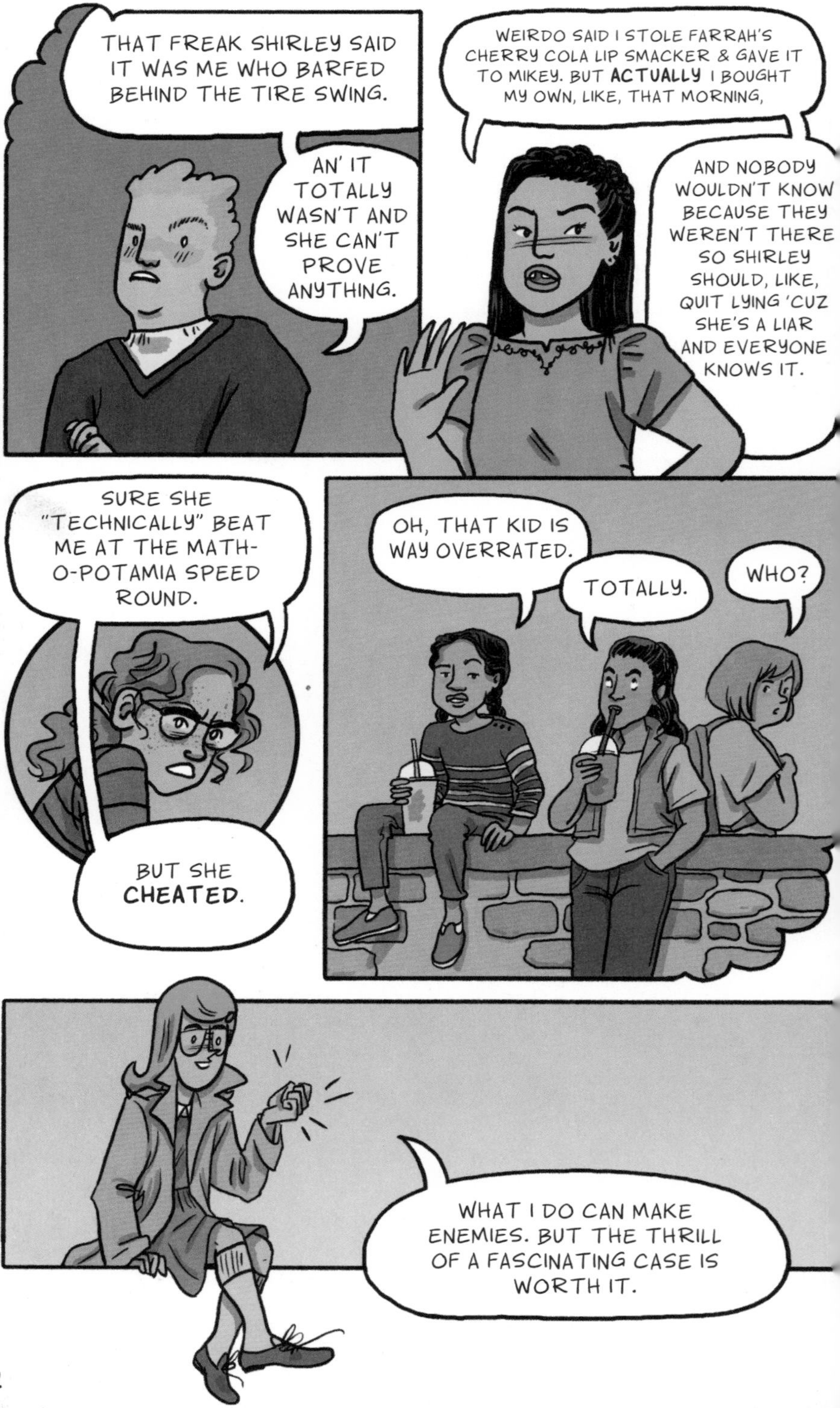
THAT FREAK SHIRLEY SAID IT WAS ME WHO BARFED BEHIND THE TIRE SWING.
AN' IT TOTALLY WASN'T AND SHE CAN'T PROVE ANYTHING.
WEIRDO SAID I STOLE FARRAH'S CHERRY COLA LIP SMACKER & GAVE IT TO MIKEY. BUT ACTUALLY I BOUGHT MY OWN, LIKE, THAT MORNING,
AND NOBODY WOULDN'T KNOW BECAUSE THEY WEREN'T THERE SO SHIRLEY SHOULD, LIKE, QUIT LYING 'CUZ SHE'S A LIAR AND EVERYONE KNOWS IT.
SURE SHE "TECHNICALLY" BEAT ME AT THE MATH-O-POTAMIA SPEED ROUND.
BUT SHE CHEATED.
OH, THAT KID IS WAY OVERRATED.
TOTALLY.
WHO?
WHAT I DO CAN MAKE ENEMIES. BUT THE THRILL OF A FASCINATING CASE IS WORTH IT.

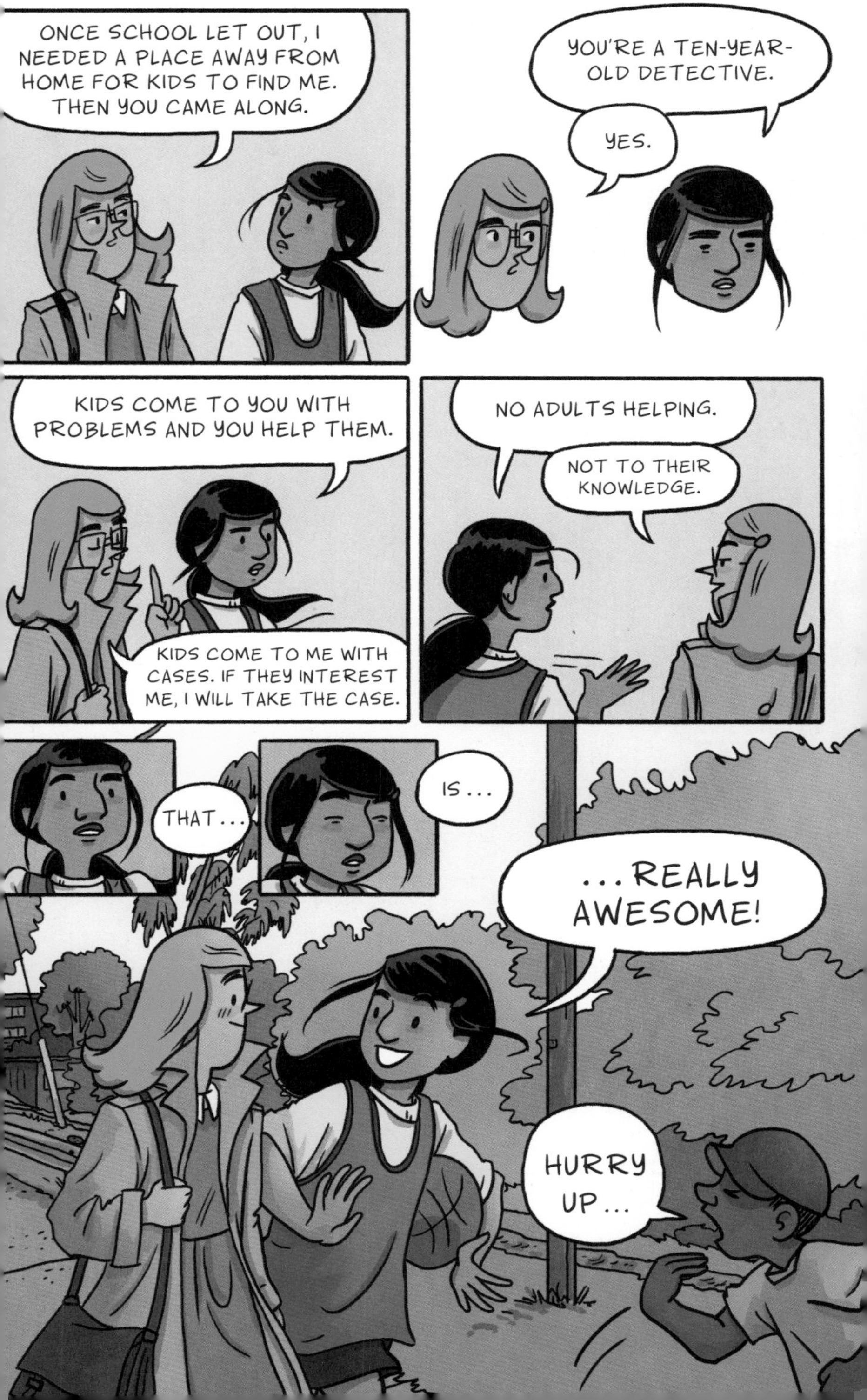
ONCE SCHOOL LET OUT, I NEEDED A PLACE AWAY FROM HOME FOR KIDS TO FIND ME. THEN YOU CAME ALONG.
YOU'RE A TEN-YEAR-OLD DETECTIVE.
YES.
KIDS COME TO YOU WITH PROBLEMS AND YOU HELP THEM.
KIDS COME TO ME WITH CASES. IF THEY INTEREST ME, I WILL TAKE THE CASE.
NO ADULTS HELPING.
NOT TO THEIR KNOWLEDGE.
THAT...
IS...
...REALLY AWESOME!
HURRY UP...

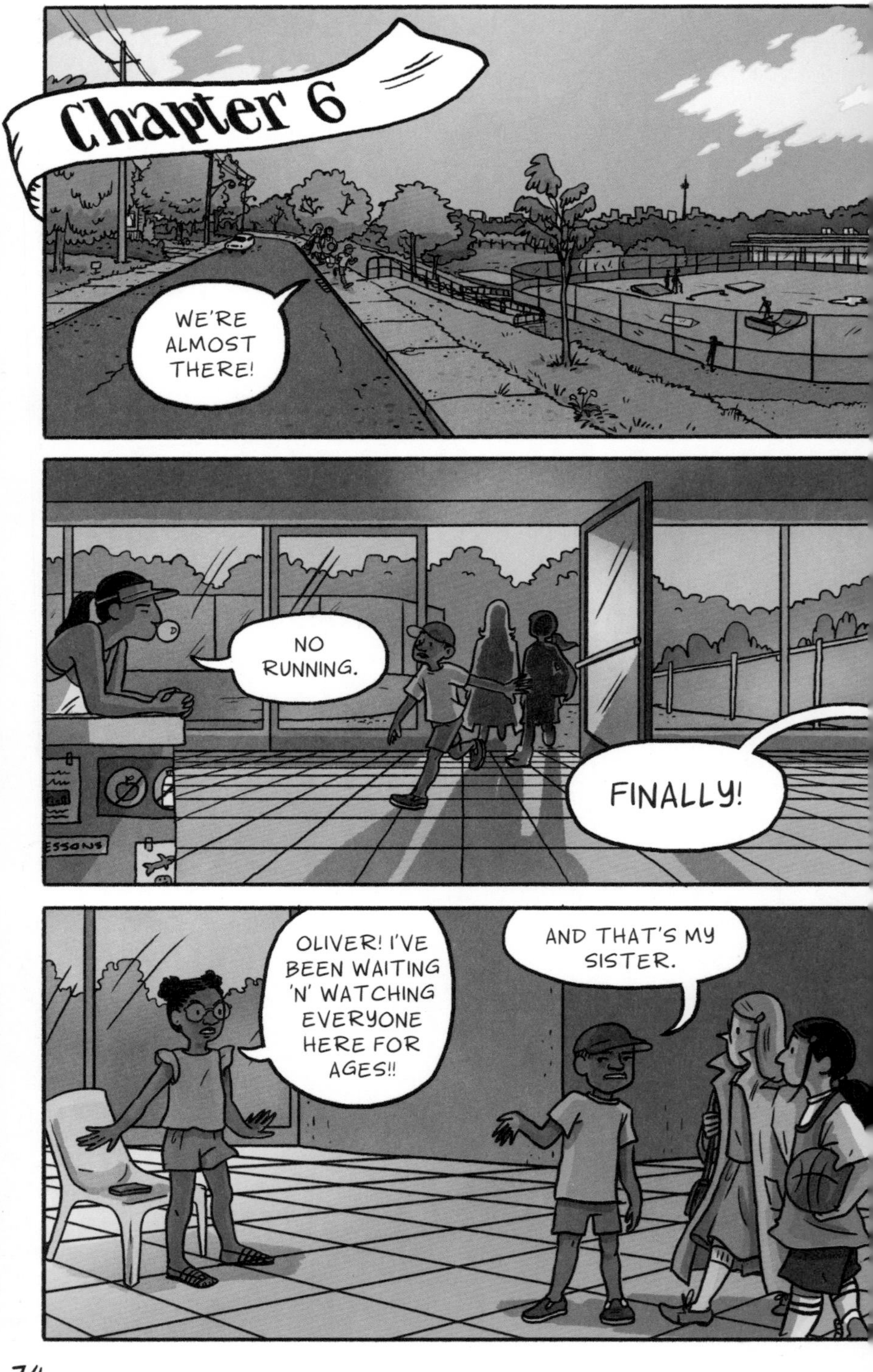
Chapter 6
WE'RE ALMOST THERE!
NO RUNNING.
FINALLY!
OLIVER! I'VE BEEN WAITING 'N' WATCHING EVERYONE HERE FOR AGES!!
AND THAT'S MY SISTER.

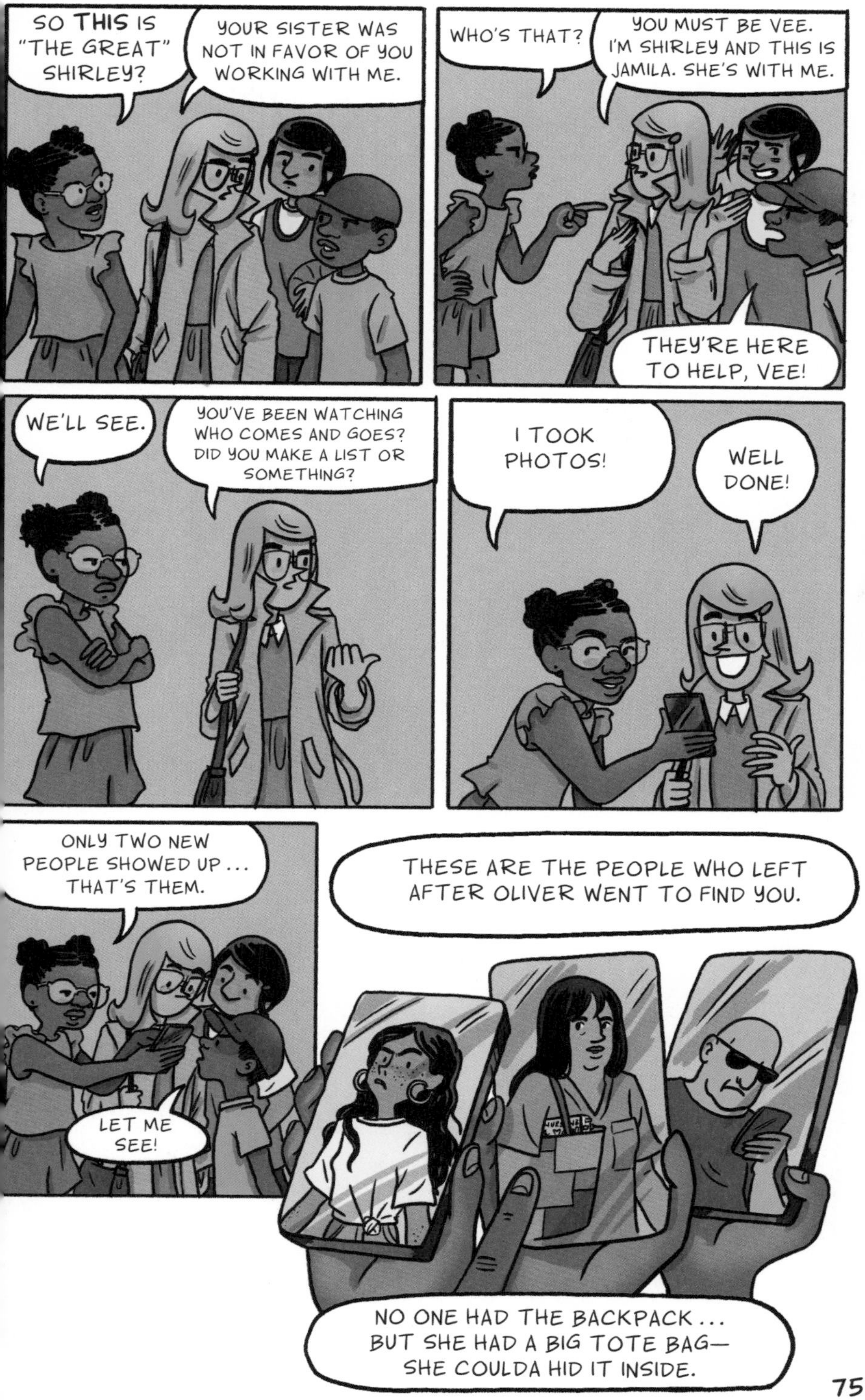
SO THIS IS "THE GREAT" SHIRLEY?
YOUR SISTER WAS NOT IN FAVOR OF YOU WORKING WITH ME.
WHO'S THAT?
YOU MUST BE VEE. I'M SHIRLEY AND THIS IS JAMILA. SHE'S WITH ME.
THEY'RE HERE TO HELP, VEE!
WE'LL SEE.
YOU'VE BEEN WATCHING WHO COMES AND GOES? DID YOU MAKE A LIST OR SOMETHING?
I TOOK PHOTOS!
WELL DONE!
ONLY TWO NEW PEOPLE SHOWED UP . . . THAT'S THEM.
LET ME SEE!
THESE ARE THE PEOPLE WHO LEFT AFTER OLIVER WENT TO FIND YOU.
NO ONE HAD THE BACKPACK . . . BUT SHE HAD A BIG TOTE BAG— SHE COULDA HID IT INSIDE.

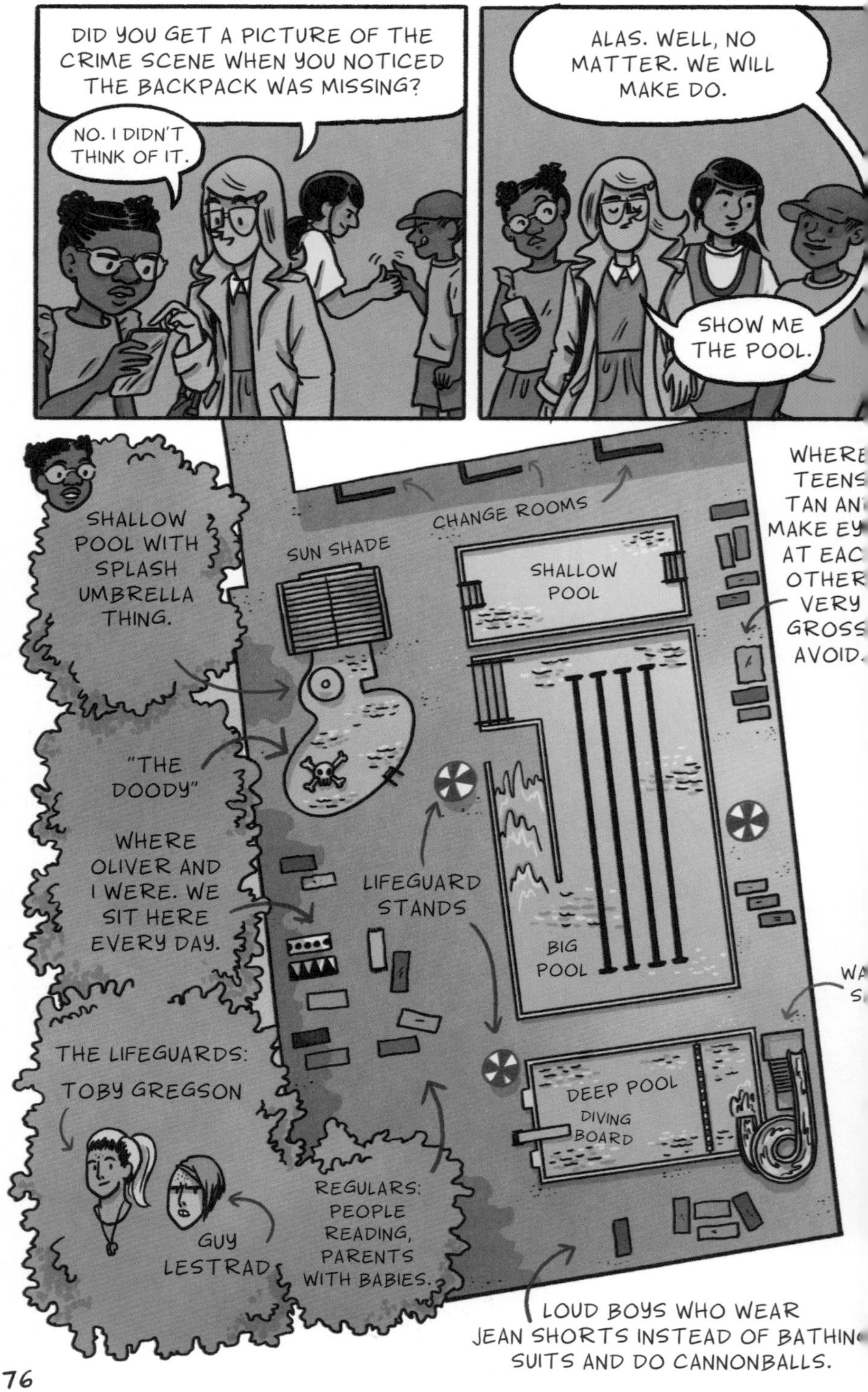

DID YOU GET A PICTURE OF THE CRIME SCENE WHEN YOU NOTICED THE BACKPACK WAS MISSING?
NO. I DIDN'T THINK OF IT.
ALAS. WELL, NO MATTER. WE WILL MAKE DO.
SHOW ME THE POOL.
CHANGE ROOMS
SUN SHADE
SHALLOW POOL WITH SPLASH UMBRELLA THING.
SHALLOW POOL
WHERE TEENS TAN AN MAKE EY AT EAC OTHER VERY GROSS AVOID.
"THE DOODY"
WHERE OLIVER AND I WERE. WE SIT HERE EVERY DAY.
LIFEGUARD STANDS
BIG POOL
THE LIFEGUARDS:
TOBY GREGSON
GUY LESTRAD
REGULARS: PEOPLE READING, PARENTS WITH BABIES.
DEEP POOL
DIVING BOARD
LOUD BOYS WHO WEAR JEAN SHORTS INSTEAD OF BATHIN SUITS AND DO CANNONBALLS.

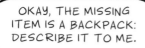OKAY, THE MISSING ITEM IS A BACKPACK: DESCRIBE IT TO ME.

IT'S NAVY BLUE,

WITH A MESH COMPARTMENT.

THOSE ARE OUR TOWELS.

WOULDN'T ENOCH GET SQUISHED IN THERE?

NO, IT'S FOAM THAT HOLDS ITS SHAPE. THE MESH PART IS LIKE A LITTLE GECKO APARTMENT!

SO, WHAT ARE YOU GOING TO **DO**?

FIRST, FIND OUT WHAT "THE PROFESSIONALS" KNOW.

TOBY'S OKAY, BUT LESTRAD'S A REAL JERK.

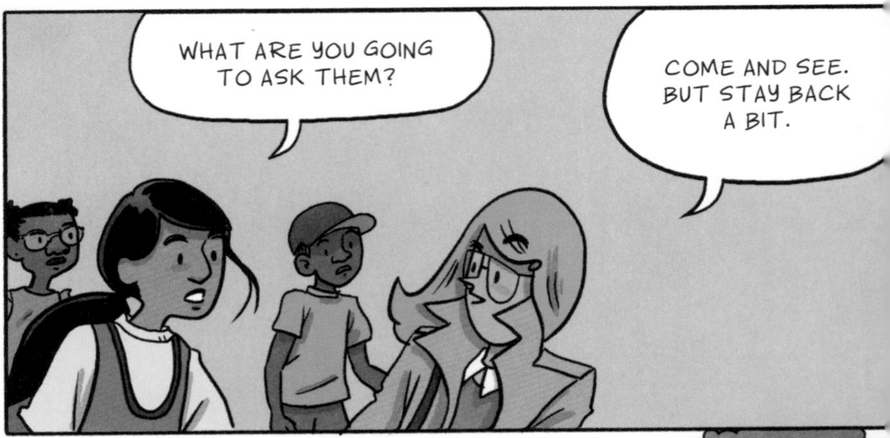
WHAT ARE YOU GOING TO ASK THEM?
COME AND SEE. BUT STAY BACK A BIT.

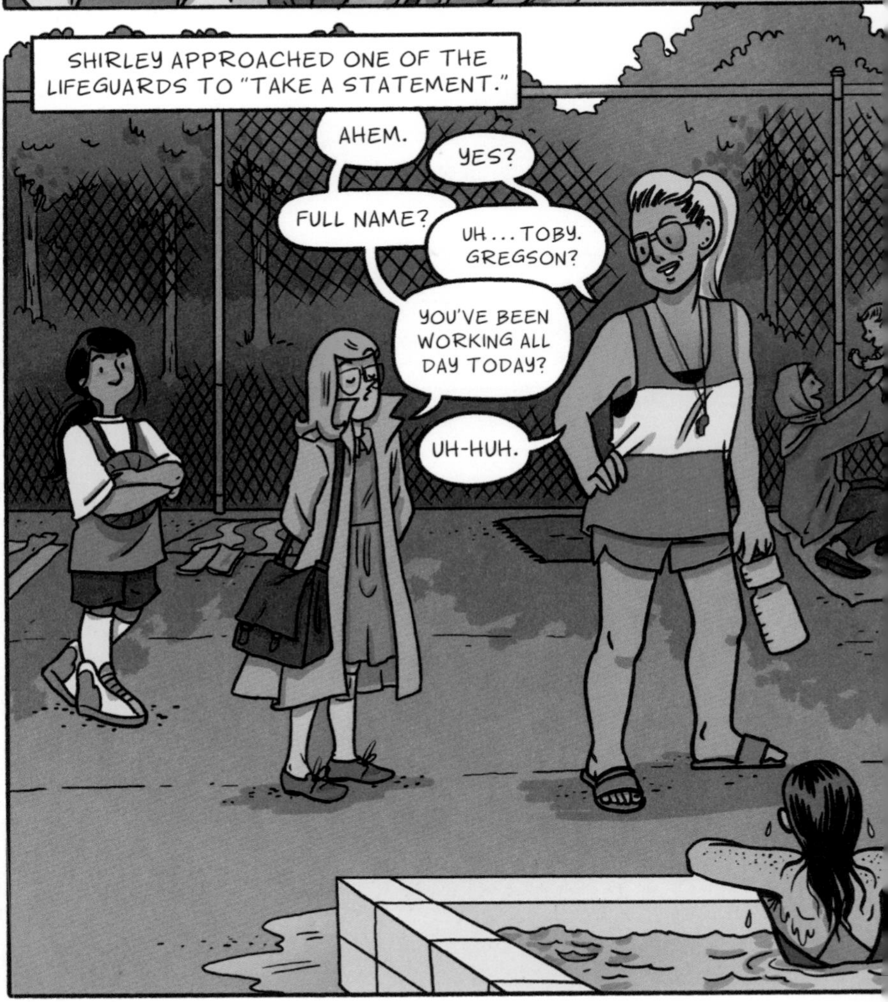
SHIRLEY APPROACHED ONE OF THE LIFEGUARDS TO "TAKE A STATEMENT."
AHEM.
YES?
FULL NAME?
UH... TOBY. GREGSON?
YOU'VE BEEN WORKING ALL DAY TODAY?
UH-HUH.

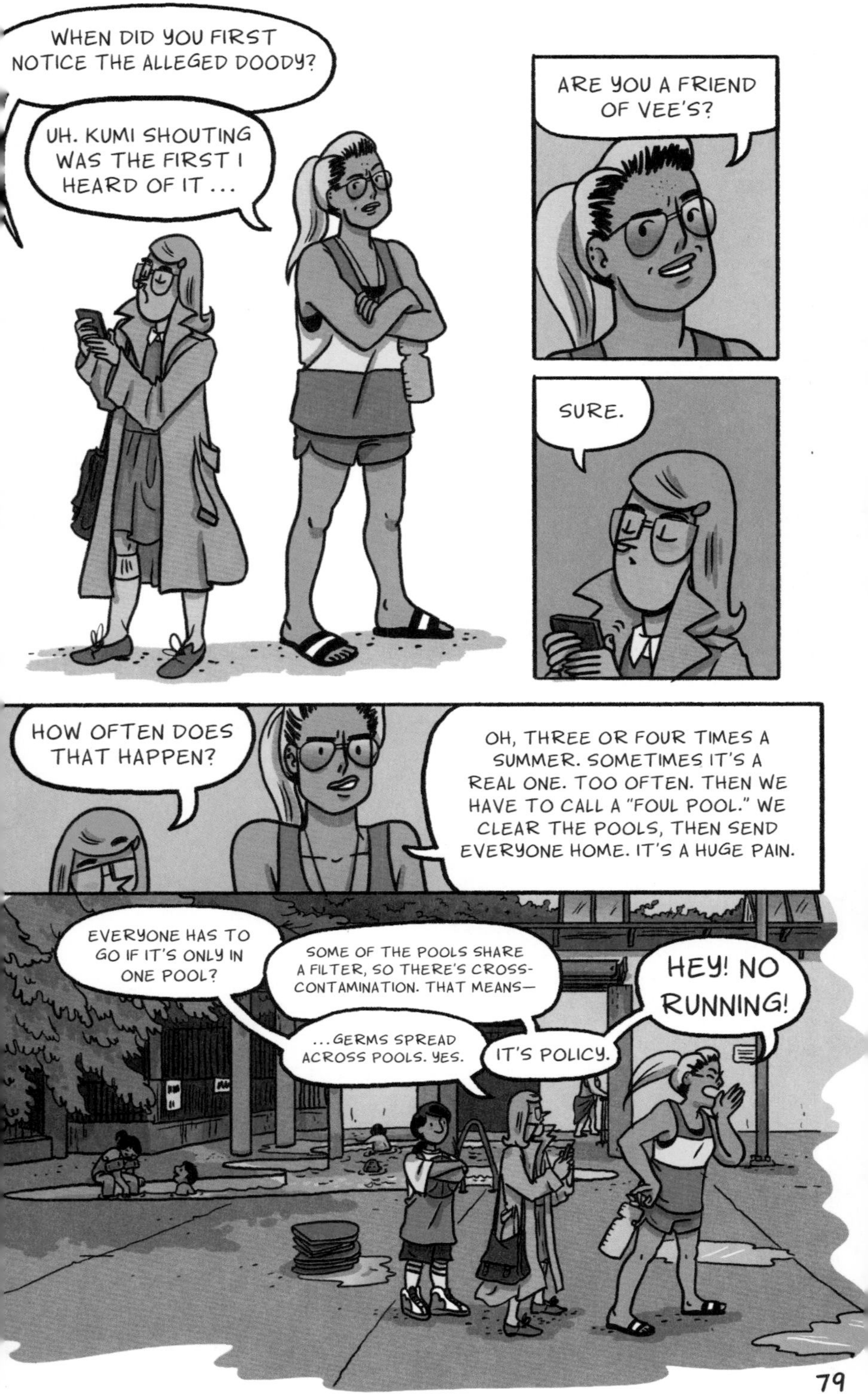
WHEN DID YOU FIRST NOTICE THE ALLEGED DOODY?
UH. KUMI SHOUTING WAS THE FIRST I HEARD OF IT . . .
ARE YOU A FRIEND OF VEE'S?
SURE.
HOW OFTEN DOES THAT HAPPEN?
OH, THREE OR FOUR TIMES A SUMMER. SOMETIMES IT'S A REAL ONE. TOO OFTEN. THEN WE HAVE TO CALL A "FOUL POOL." WE CLEAR THE POOLS, THEN SEND EVERYONE HOME. IT'S A HUGE PAIN.
EVERYONE HAS TO GO IF IT'S ONLY IN ONE POOL?
SOME OF THE POOLS SHARE A FILTER, SO THERE'S CROSS-CONTAMINATION. THAT MEANS—
. . . GERMS SPREAD ACROSS POOLS. YES.
IT'S POLICY.
HEY! NO RUNNING!

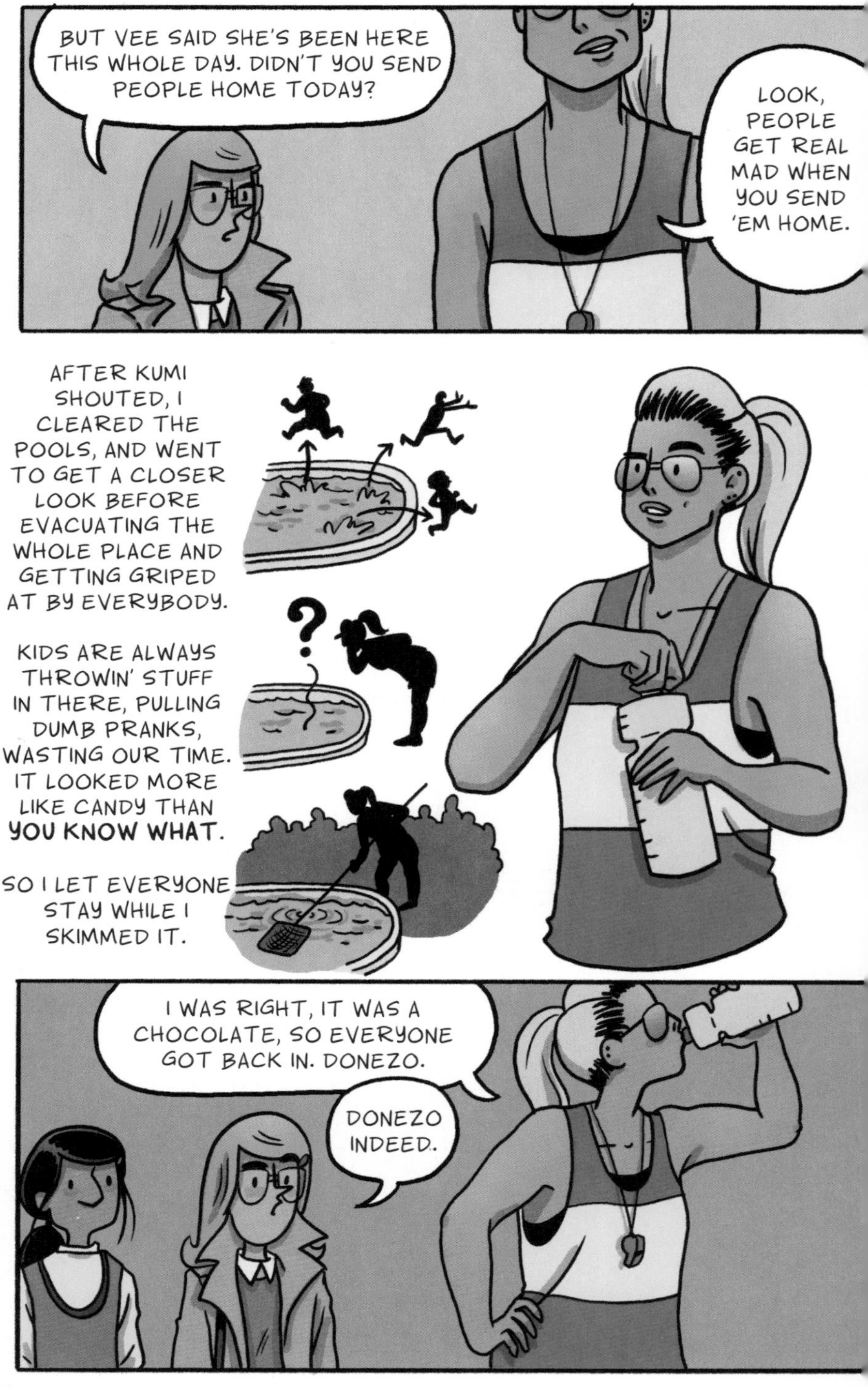
BUT VEE SAID SHE'S BEEN HERE THIS WHOLE DAY. DIDN'T YOU SEND PEOPLE HOME TODAY?
LOOK, PEOPLE GET REAL MAD WHEN YOU SEND 'EM HOME.
AFTER KUMI SHOUTED, I CLEARED THE POOLS, AND WENT TO GET A CLOSER LOOK BEFORE EVACUATING THE WHOLE PLACE AND GETTING GRIPED AT BY EVERYBODY.
KIDS ARE ALWAYS THROWIN' STUFF IN THERE, PULLING DUMB PRANKS, WASTING OUR TIME. IT LOOKED MORE LIKE CANDY THAN **YOU KNOW WHAT**.
SO I LET EVERYONE STAY WHILE I SKIMMED IT.
?
I WAS RIGHT, IT WAS A CHOCOLATE, SO EVERYONE GOT BACK IN. DONEZO.
DONEZO INDEED.

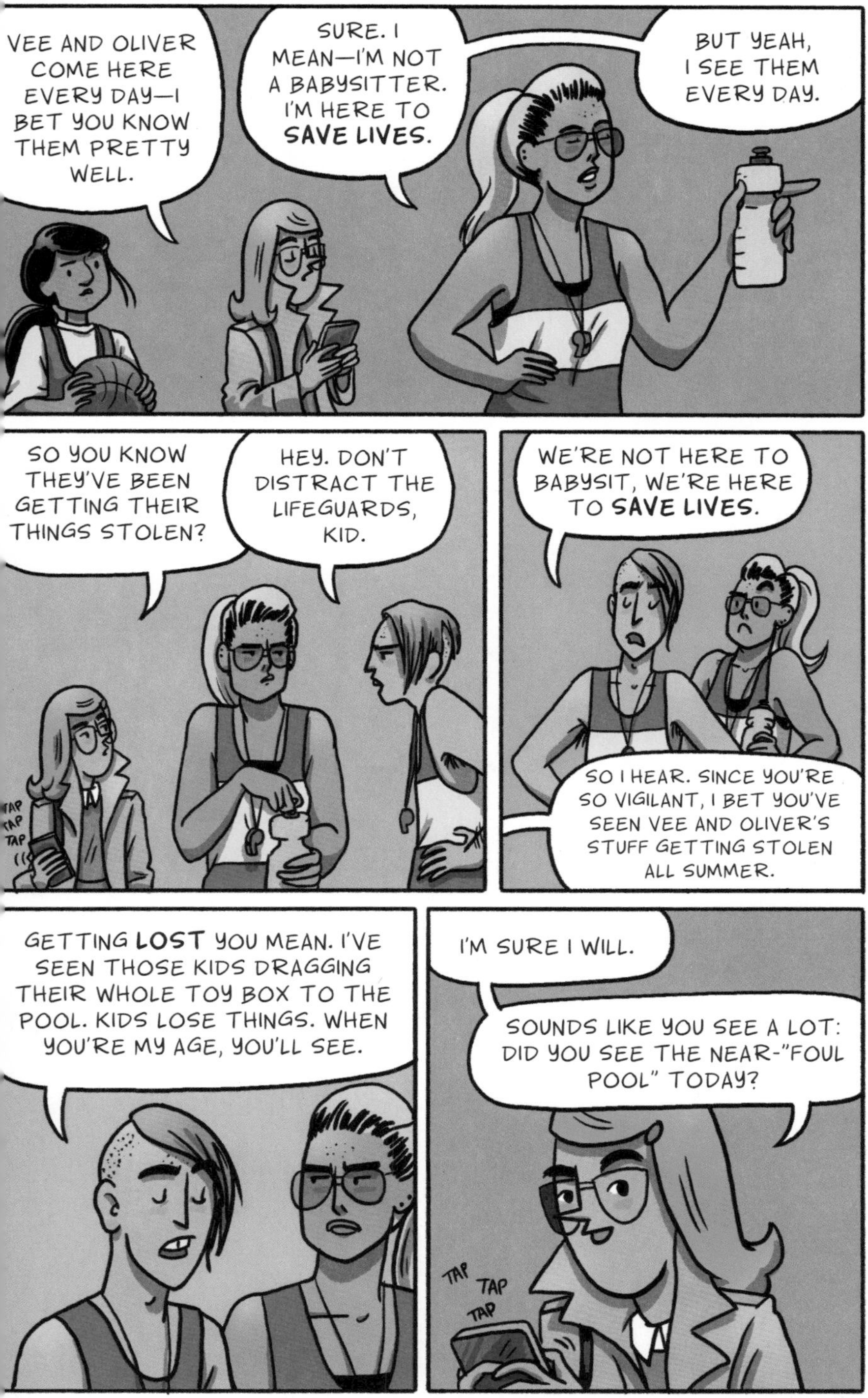
VEE AND OLIVER COME HERE EVERY DAY—I BET YOU KNOW THEM PRETTY WELL.
SURE. I MEAN—I'M NOT A BABYSITTER. I'M HERE TO **SAVE LIVES**.
BUT YEAH, I SEE THEM EVERY DAY.
SO YOU KNOW THEY'VE BEEN GETTING THEIR THINGS STOLEN?
HEY. DON'T DISTRACT THE LIFEGUARDS, KID.
TAP TAP TAP
WE'RE NOT HERE TO BABYSIT, WE'RE HERE TO **SAVE LIVES**.
SO I HEAR. SINCE YOU'RE SO VIGILANT, I BET YOU'VE SEEN VEE AND OLIVER'S STUFF GETTING STOLEN ALL SUMMER.
GETTING **LOST** YOU MEAN. I'VE SEEN THOSE KIDS DRAGGING THEIR WHOLE TOY BOX TO THE POOL. KIDS LOSE THINGS. WHEN YOU'RE MY AGE, YOU'LL SEE.
I'M SURE I WILL.
SOUNDS LIKE YOU SEE A LOT: DID YOU SEE THE NEAR-"FOUL POOL" TODAY?
TAP TAP TAP

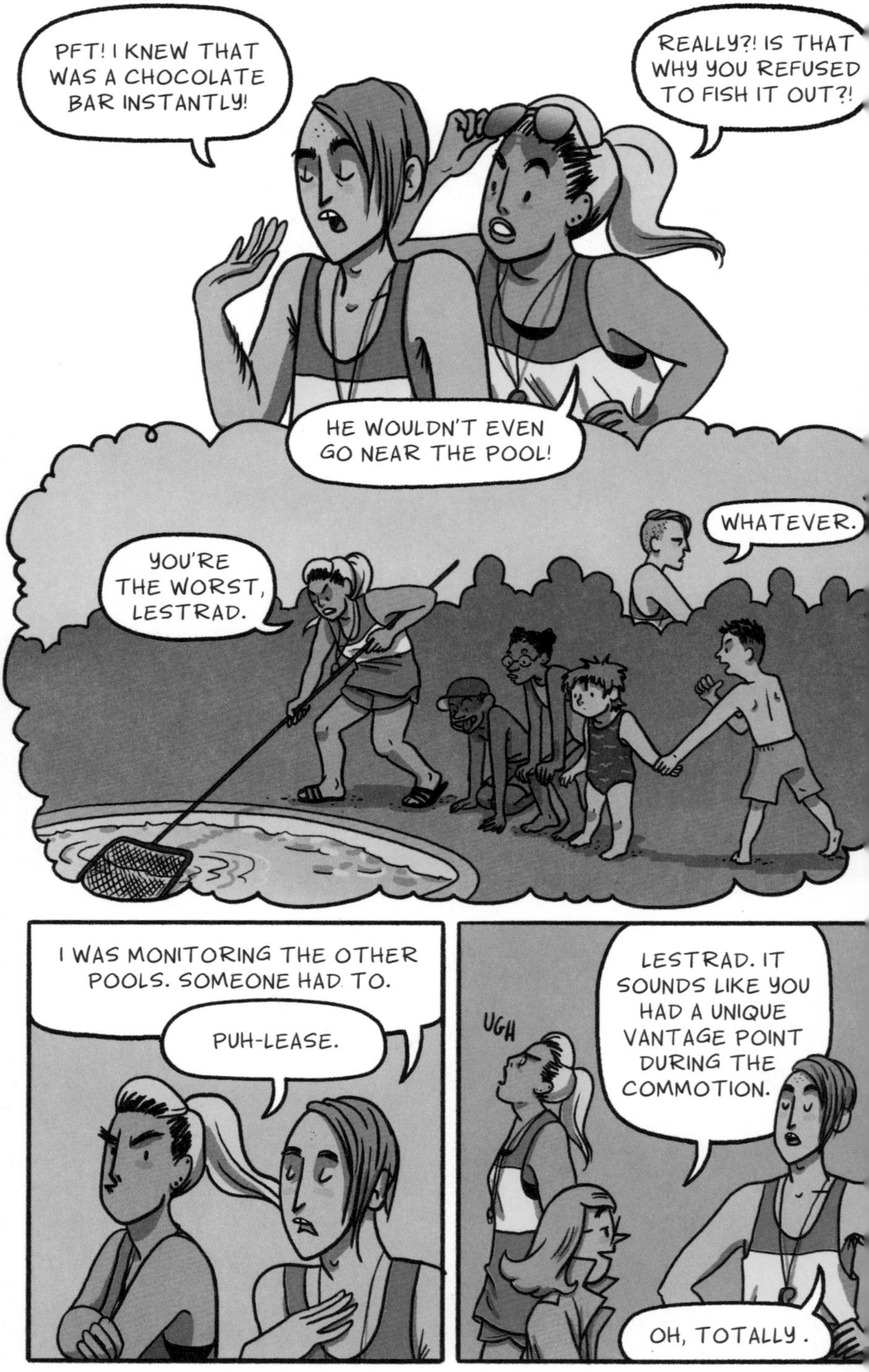
PFT! I KNEW THAT WAS A CHOCOLATE BAR INSTANTLY!
REALLY?! IS THAT WHY YOU REFUSED TO FISH IT OUT?!
HE WOULDN'T EVEN GO NEAR THE POOL!
YOU'RE THE WORST, LESTRAD.
WHATEVER.
I WAS MONITORING THE OTHER POOLS. SOMEONE HAD TO.
PUH-LEASE.
UGH
LESTRAD. IT SOUNDS LIKE YOU HAD A UNIQUE VANTAGE POINT DURING THE COMMOTION.
OH, TOTALLY.

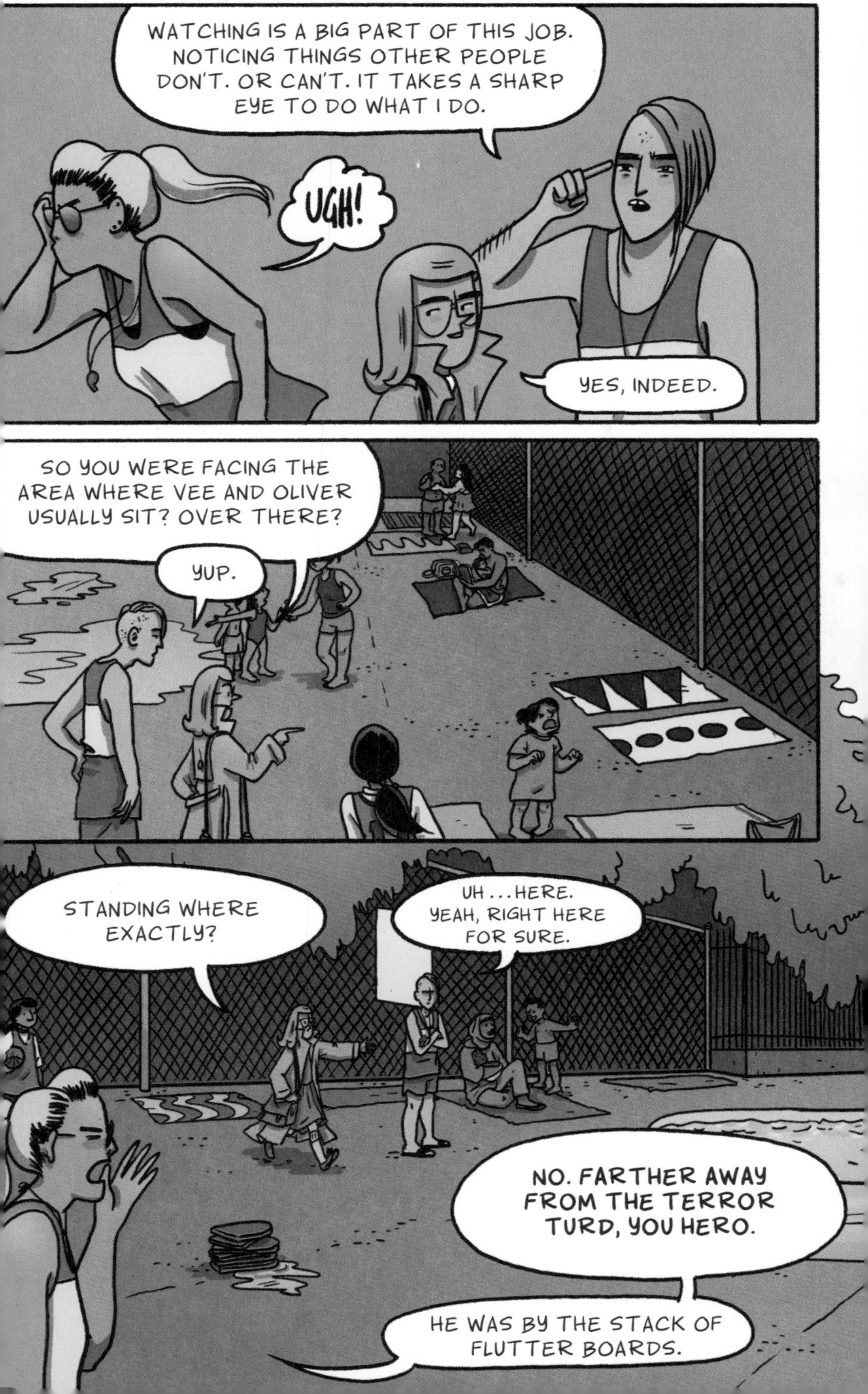
WATCHING IS A BIG PART OF THIS JOB. NOTICING THINGS OTHER PEOPLE DON'T. OR CAN'T. IT TAKES A SHARP EYE TO DO WHAT I DO.
UGH!
YES, INDEED.
SO YOU WERE FACING THE AREA WHERE VEE AND OLIVER USUALLY SIT? OVER THERE?
YUP.
STANDING WHERE EXACTLY?
UH . . . HERE. YEAH, RIGHT HERE FOR SURE.
NO. FARTHER AWAY FROM THE TERROR TURD, YOU HERO.
HE WAS BY THE STACK OF FLUTTER BOARDS.

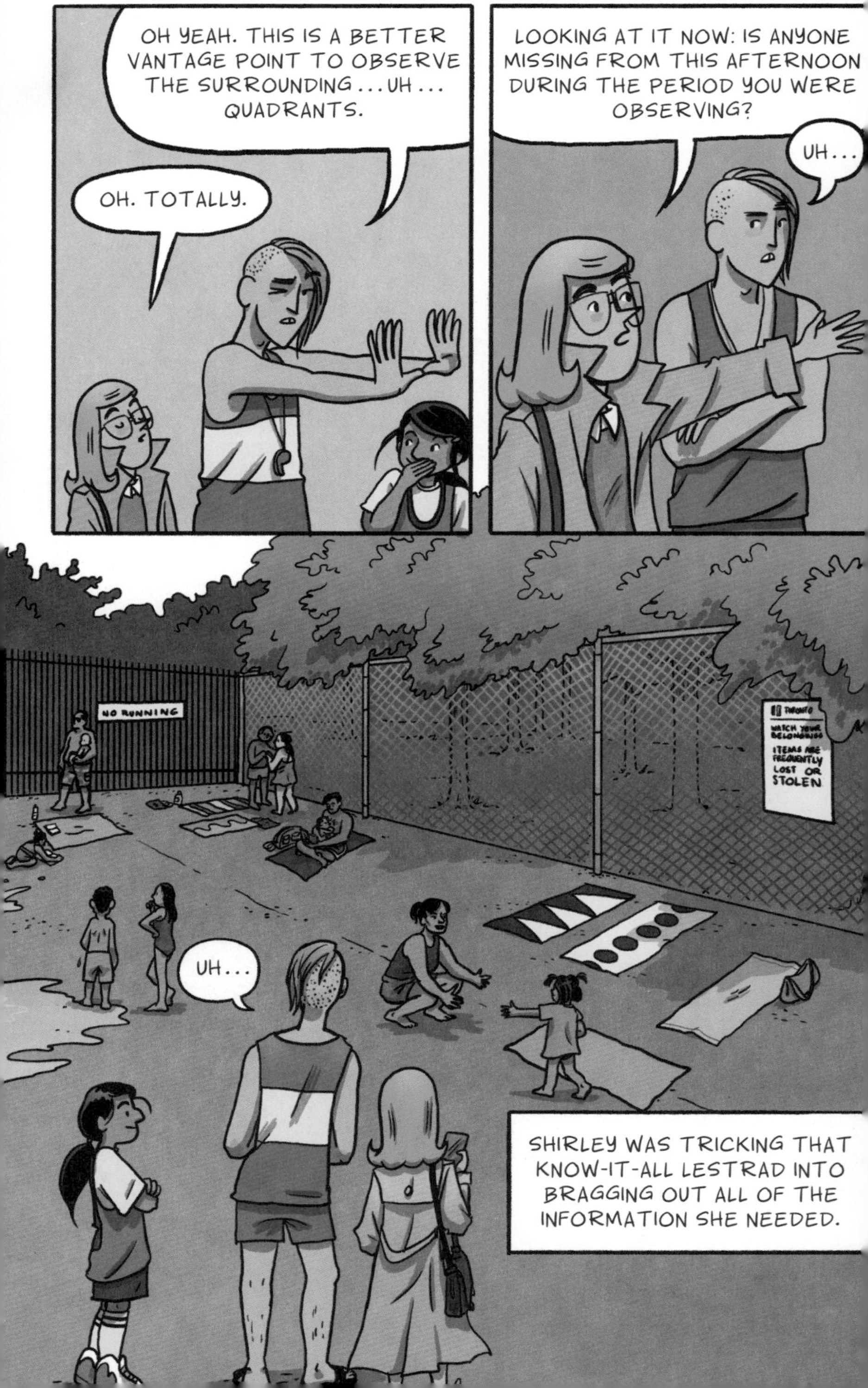
OH YEAH. THIS IS A BETTER VANTAGE POINT TO OBSERVE THE SURROUNDING . . . UH . . . QUADRANTS.
OH. TOTALLY.
LOOKING AT IT NOW: IS ANYONE MISSING FROM THIS AFTERNOON DURING THE PERIOD YOU WERE OBSERVING?
UH . . .
NO RUNNING
ITEMS ARE FREQUENTLY LOST OR STOLEN
UH . . .
SHIRLEY WAS TRICKING THAT KNOW-IT-ALL LESTRAD INTO BRAGGING OUT ALL OF THE INFORMATION SHE NEEDED.

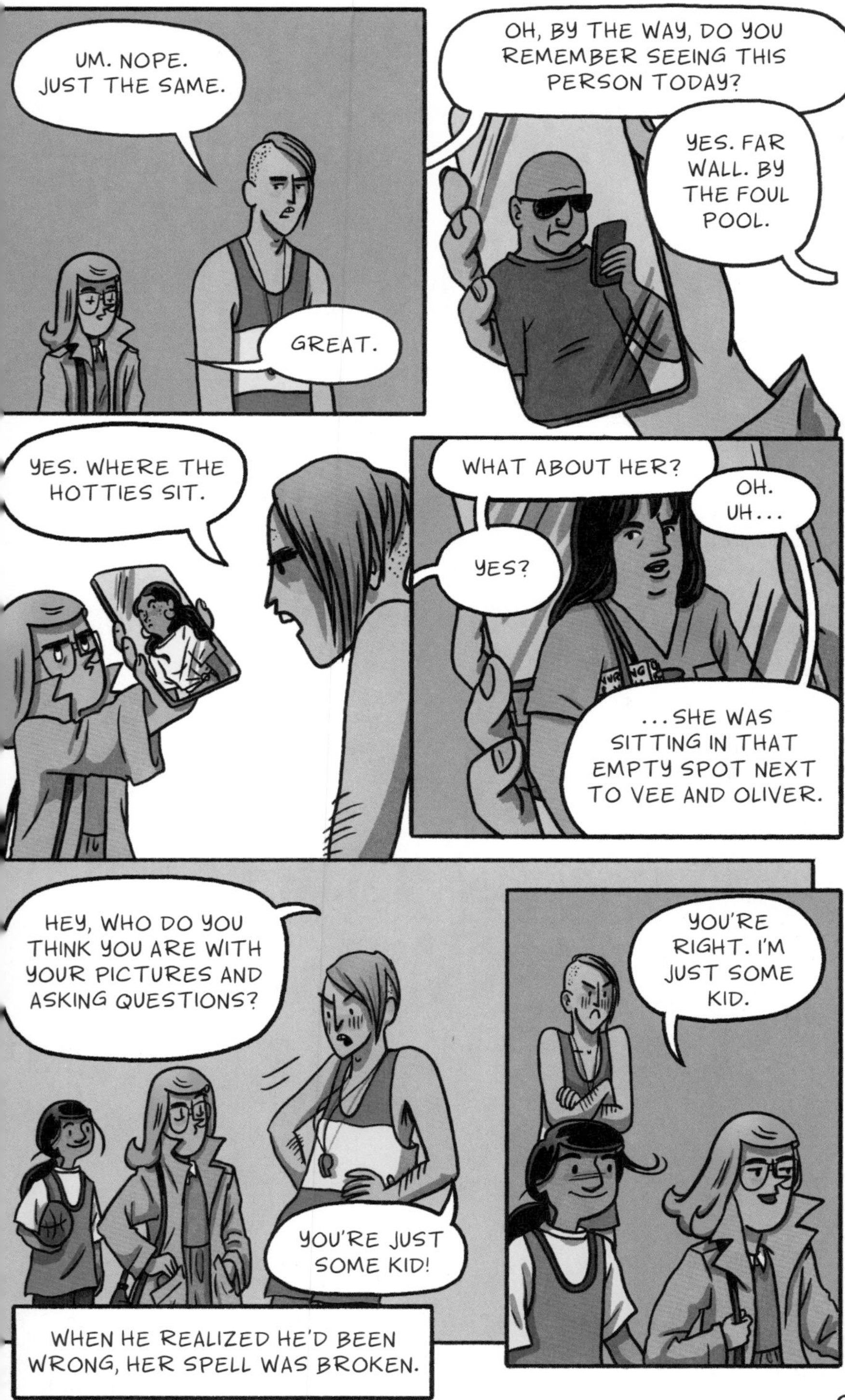
UM. NOPE. JUST THE SAME.
GREAT.
OH, BY THE WAY, DO YOU REMEMBER SEEING THIS PERSON TODAY?
YES. FAR WALL. BY THE FOUL POOL.
YES. WHERE THE HOTTIES SIT.
WHAT ABOUT HER?
YES?
OH. UH...
...SHE WAS SITTING IN THAT EMPTY SPOT NEXT TO VEE AND OLIVER.
HEY, WHO DO YOU THINK YOU ARE WITH YOUR PICTURES AND ASKING QUESTIONS?
YOU'RE JUST SOME KID!
WHEN HE REALIZED HE'D BEEN WRONG, HER SPELL WAS BROKEN.
YOU'RE RIGHT. I'M JUST SOME KID.

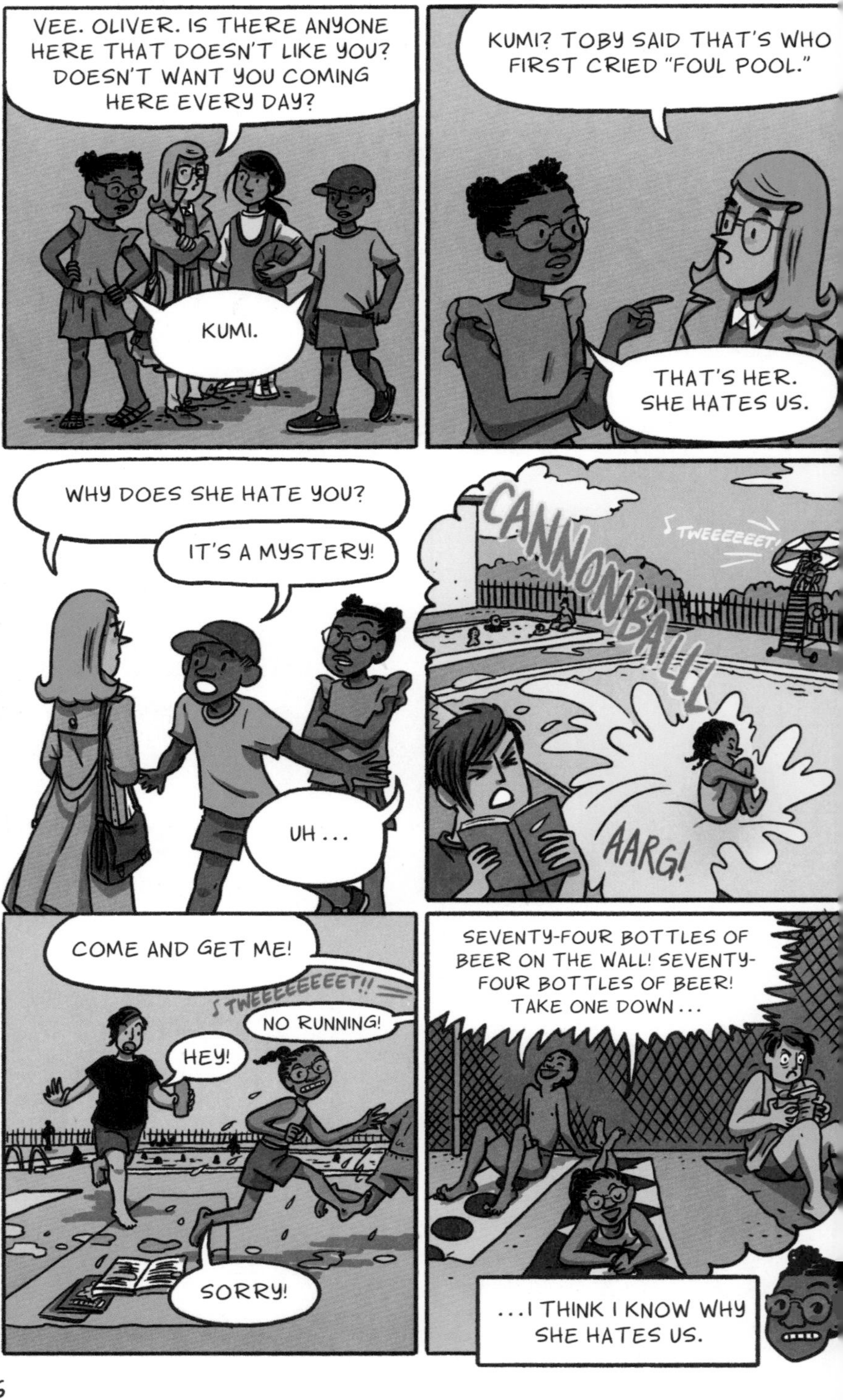
VEE. OLIVER. IS THERE ANYONE HERE THAT DOESN'T LIKE YOU? DOESN'T WANT YOU COMING HERE EVERY DAY?
KUMI.
KUMI? TOBY SAID THAT'S WHO FIRST CRIED "FOUL POOL."
THAT'S HER. SHE HATES US.
WHY DOES SHE HATE YOU?
IT'S A MYSTERY!
UH . . .
CANNONBALL!
TWEEEEEET!
AARG!
COME AND GET ME!
TWEEEEEEEET!!
NO RUNNING!
HEY!
SORRY!
SEVENTY-FOUR BOTTLES OF BEER ON THE WALL! SEVENTY-FOUR BOTTLES OF BEER! TAKE ONE DOWN . . .
. . . I THINK I KNOW WHY SHE HATES US.

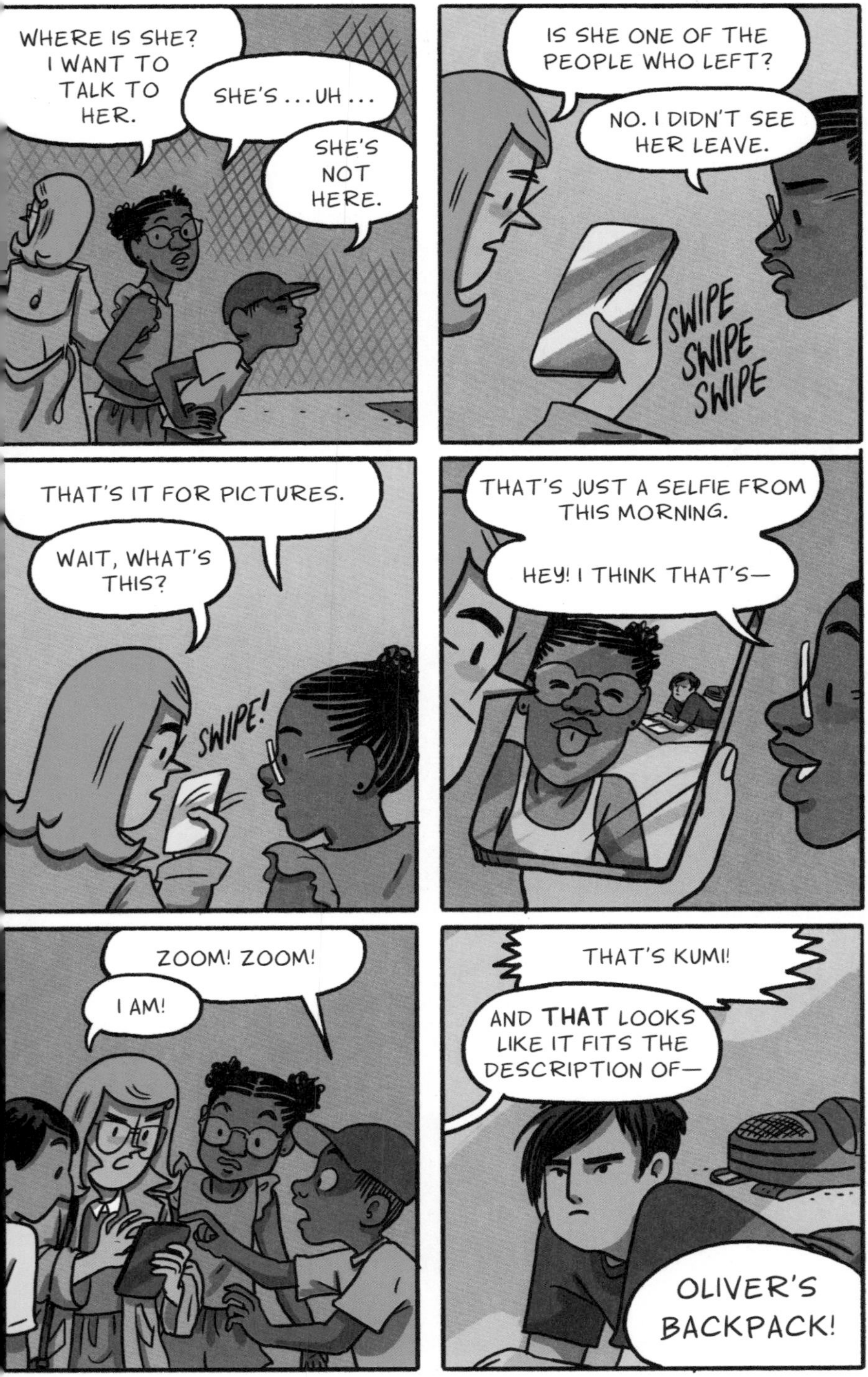
WHERE IS SHE? I WANT TO TALK TO HER.
SHE'S . . . UH . . .
SHE'S NOT HERE.
IS SHE ONE OF THE PEOPLE WHO LEFT?
NO. I DIDN'T SEE HER LEAVE.
SWIPE
SWIPE
SWIPE
THAT'S IT FOR PICTURES.
WAIT, WHAT'S THIS?
SWIPE!
THAT'S JUST A SELFIE FROM THIS MORNING.
HEY! I THINK THAT'S—
ZOOM! ZOOM!
I AM!
THAT'S KUMI!
AND **THAT** LOOKS LIKE IT FITS THE DESCRIPTION OF—
OLIVER'S BACKPACK!

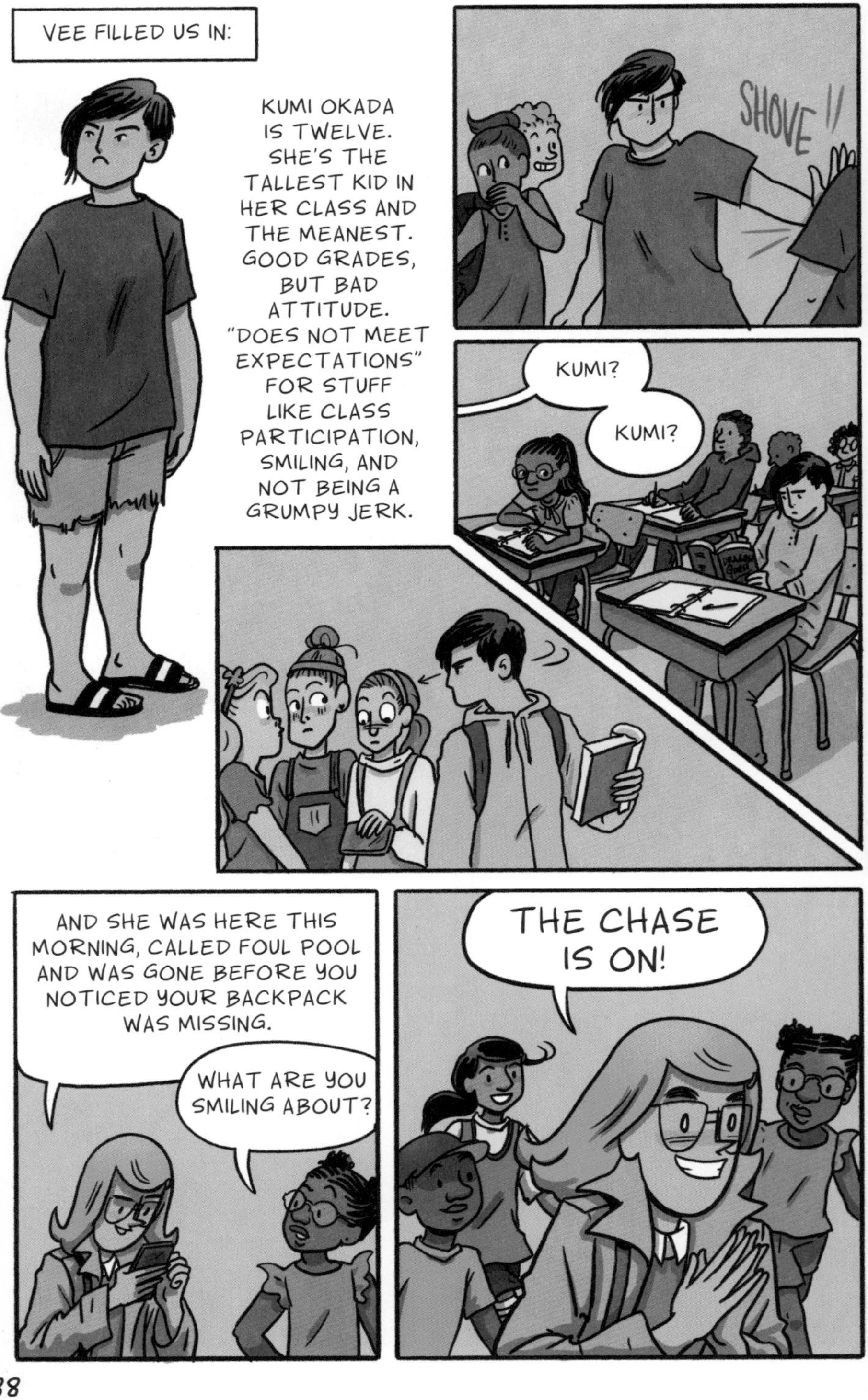
VEE FILLED US IN:
KUMI OKADA IS TWELVE. SHE'S THE TALLEST KID IN HER CLASS AND THE MEANEST. GOOD GRADES, BUT BAD ATTITUDE. "DOES NOT MEET EXPECTATIONS" FOR STUFF LIKE CLASS PARTICIPATION, SMILING, AND NOT BEING A GRUMPY JERK.
SHOVE!!
KUMI?
KUMI?
AND SHE WAS HERE THIS MORNING, CALLED FOUL POOL AND WAS GONE BEFORE YOU NOTICED YOUR BACKPACK WAS MISSING.
WHAT ARE YOU SMILING ABOUT?
THE CHASE IS ON!

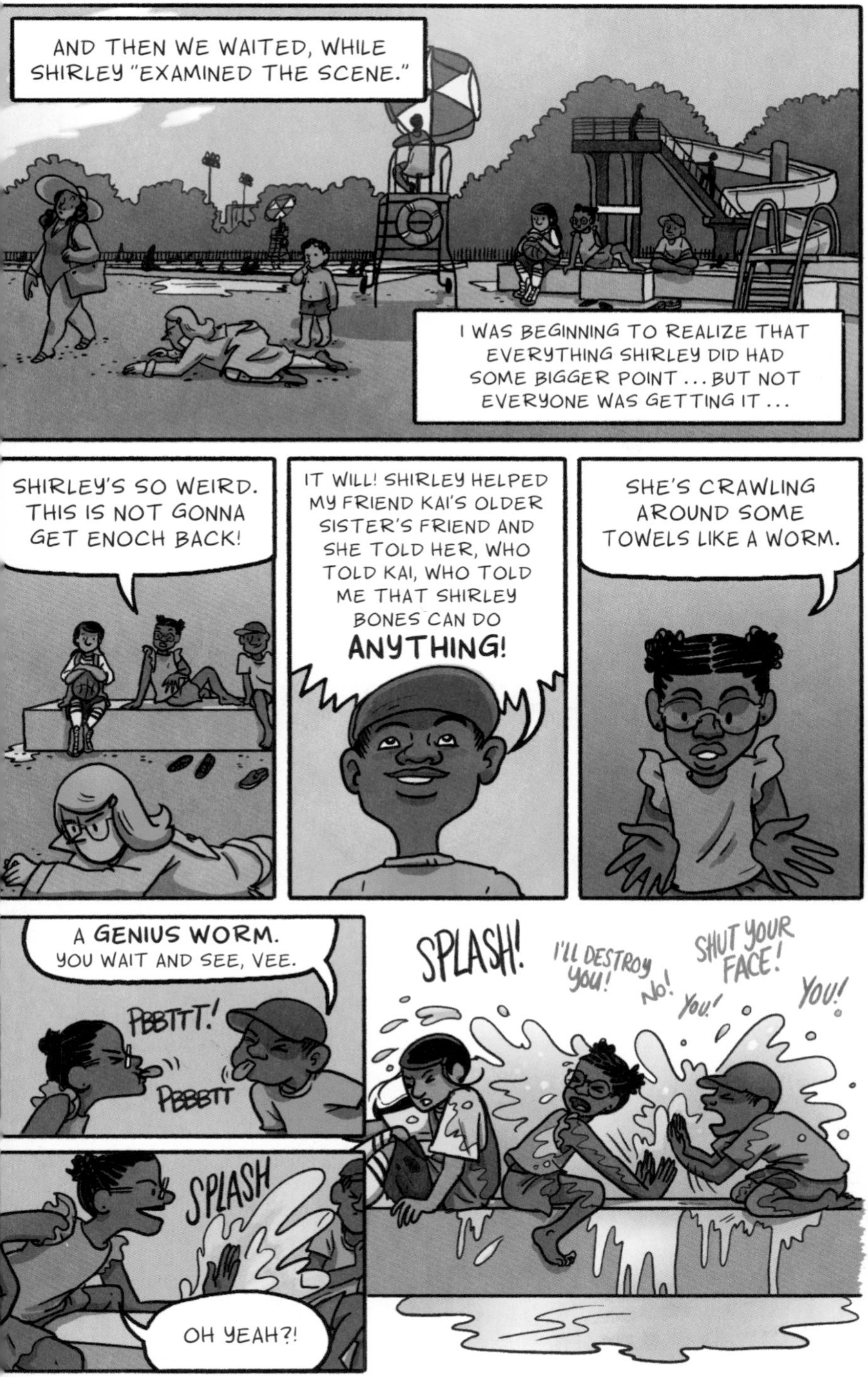
AND THEN WE WAITED, WHILE SHIRLEY "EXAMINED THE SCENE."
I WAS BEGINNING TO REALIZE THAT EVERYTHING SHIRLEY DID HAD SOME BIGGER POINT . . . BUT NOT EVERYONE WAS GETTING IT . . .
SHIRLEY'S SO WEIRD. THIS IS NOT GONNA GET ENOCH BACK!
IT WILL! SHIRLEY HELPED MY FRIEND KAI'S OLDER SISTER'S FRIEND AND SHE TOLD HER, WHO TOLD KAI, WHO TOLD ME THAT SHIRLEY BONES CAN DO ANYTHING!
SHE'S CRAWLING AROUND SOME TOWELS LIKE A WORM.
A GENIUS WORM. YOU WAIT AND SEE, VEE.
PBBTTT!
PBBBTT
SPLASH
OH YEAH?!
SPLASH!
I'LL DESTROY YOU!
NO!
SHUT YOUR FACE!
YOU!
YOU!

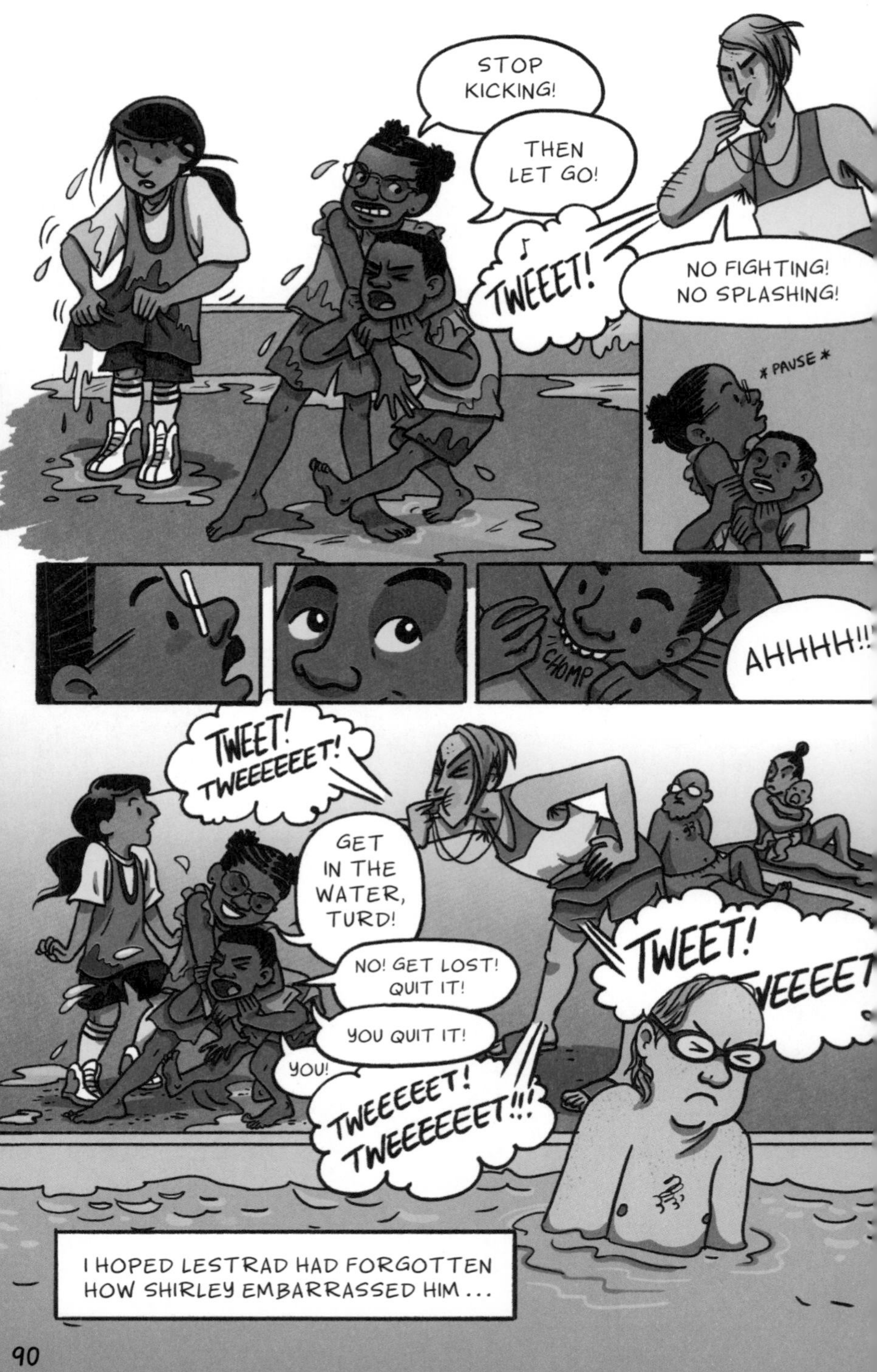
STOP KICKING!
THEN LET GO!
TWEEET!
NO FIGHTING! NO SPLASHING!
PAUSE
CHOMP
AHHHH!!
TWEET! TWEEEEEET!
GET IN THE WATER, TURD!
NO! GET LOST! QUIT IT!
YOU QUIT IT!
YOU!
TWEET!
TWEEEEET! TWEEEEEET!!!
I HOPED LESTRAD HAD FORGOTTEN HOW SHIRLEY EMBARRASSED HIM . . .

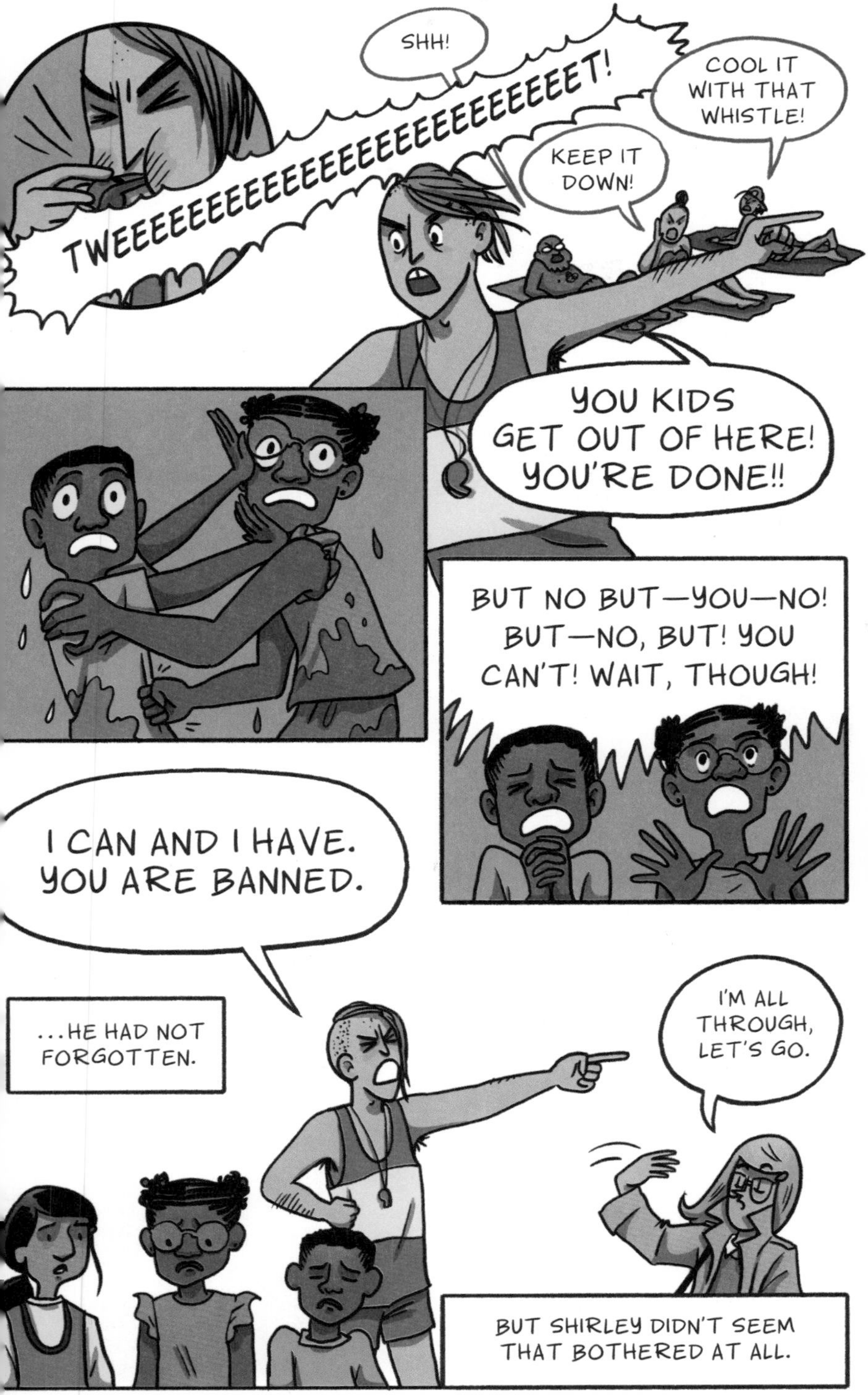
TWEEEEEEEEEEEEEEEEEEEEEEEEEEET!
SHH!
COOL IT WITH THAT WHISTLE!
KEEP IT DOWN!
YOU KIDS GET OUT OF HERE! YOU'RE DONE!!
BUT NO BUT—YOU—NO! BUT—NO, BUT! YOU CAN'T! WAIT, THOUGH!
I CAN AND I HAVE. YOU ARE BANNED.
...HE HAD NOT FORGOTTEN.
I'M ALL THROUGH, LET'S GO.
BUT SHIRLEY DIDN'T SEEM THAT BOTHERED AT ALL.

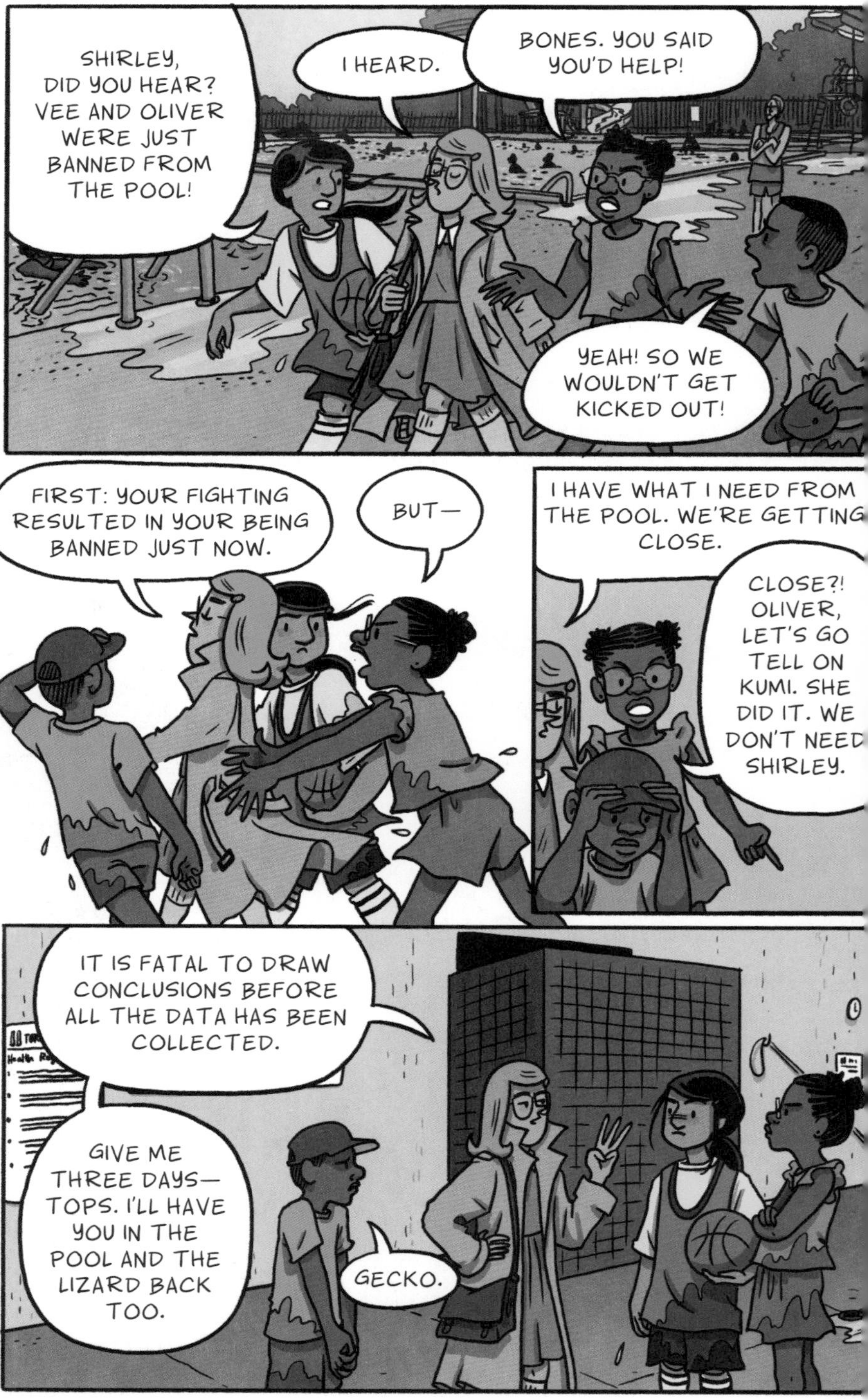
SHIRLEY, DID YOU HEAR? VEE AND OLIVER WERE JUST BANNED FROM THE POOL!
I HEARD.
BONES. YOU SAID YOU'D HELP!
YEAH! SO WE WOULDN'T GET KICKED OUT!
FIRST: YOUR FIGHTING RESULTED IN YOUR BEING BANNED JUST NOW.
BUT—
I HAVE WHAT I NEED FROM THE POOL. WE'RE GETTING CLOSE.
CLOSE?! OLIVER, LET'S GO TELL ON KUMI. SHE DID IT. WE DON'T NEED SHIRLEY.
IT IS FATAL TO DRAW CONCLUSIONS BEFORE ALL THE DATA HAS BEEN COLLECTED.
GIVE ME THREE DAYS— TOPS. I'LL HAVE YOU IN THE POOL AND THE LIZARD BACK TOO.
GECKO.

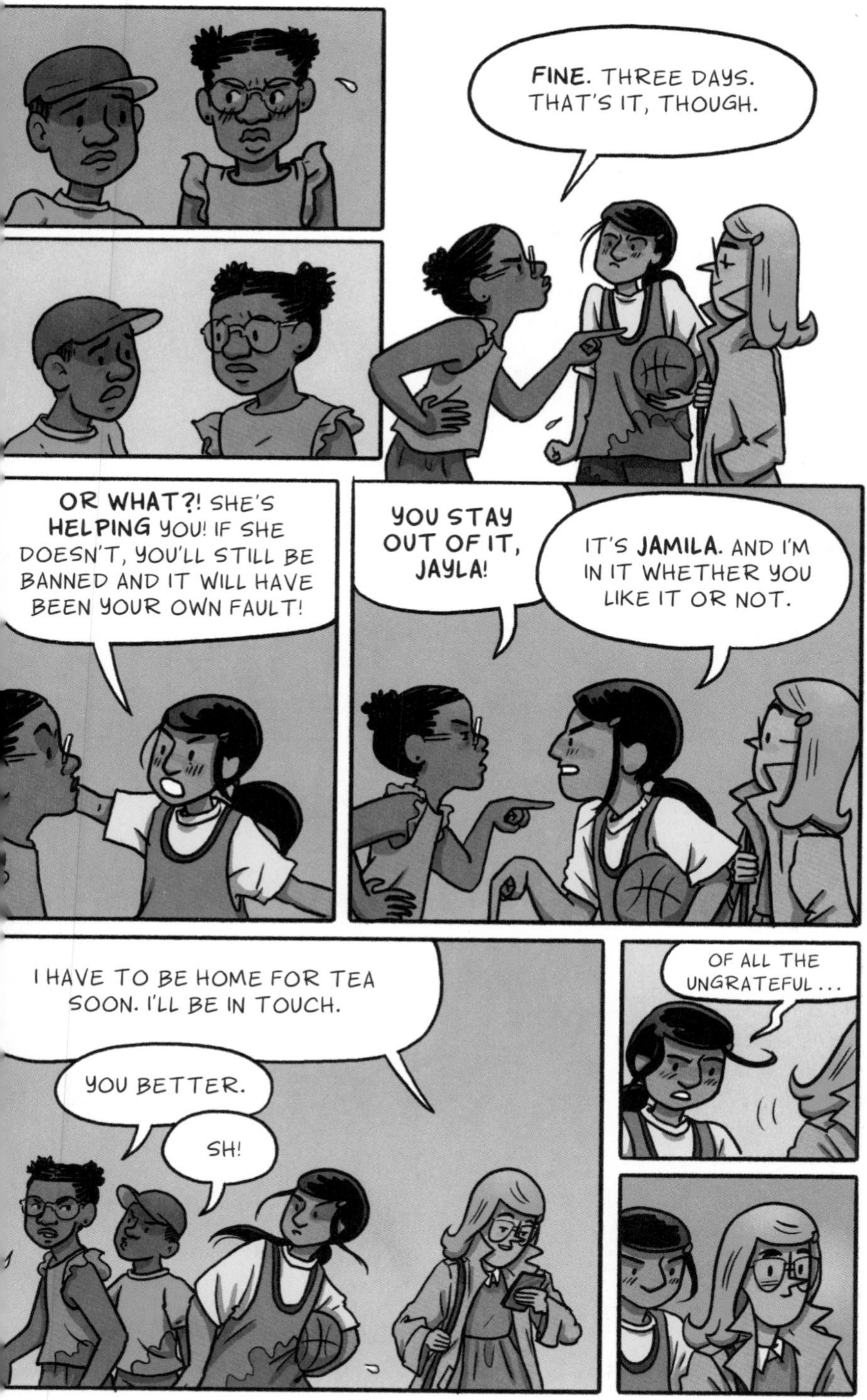
FINE. THREE DAYS. THAT'S IT, THOUGH.
OR WHAT?! SHE'S HELPING YOU! IF SHE DOESN'T, YOU'LL STILL BE BANNED AND IT WILL HAVE BEEN YOUR OWN FAULT!
YOU STAY OUT OF IT, JAYLA!
IT'S JAMILA. AND I'M IN IT WHETHER YOU LIKE IT OR NOT.
I HAVE TO BE HOME FOR TEA SOON. I'LL BE IN TOUCH.
YOU BETTER.
SH!
OF ALL THE UNGRATEFUL . . .

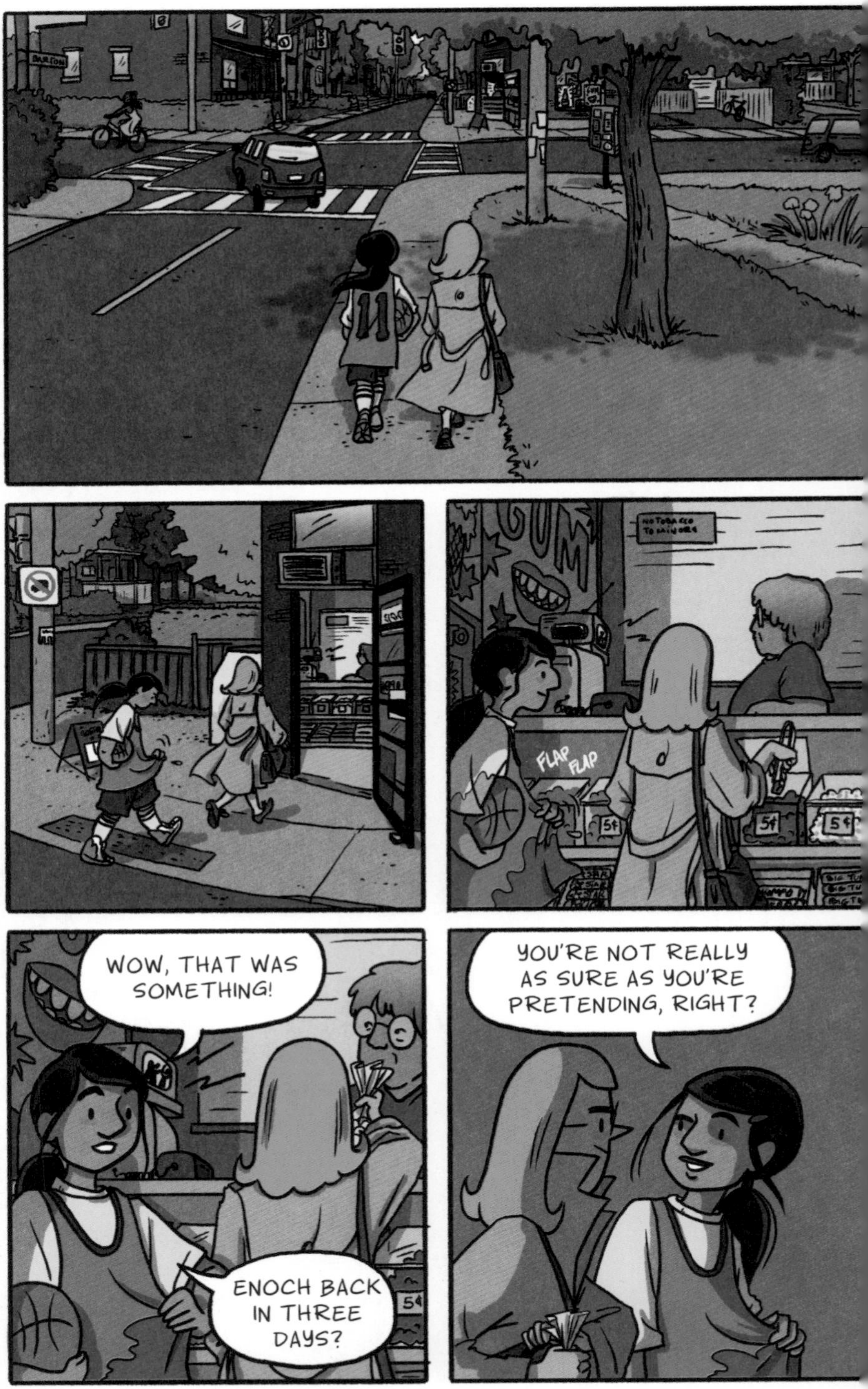
BURTON
NO TOBACCO TO MINORS
GUM
FLAP FLAP
5¢
5¢
5¢
WOW, THAT WAS SOMETHING!
ENOCH BACK IN THREE DAYS?
YOU'RE NOT REALLY AS SURE AS YOU'RE PRETENDING, RIGHT?

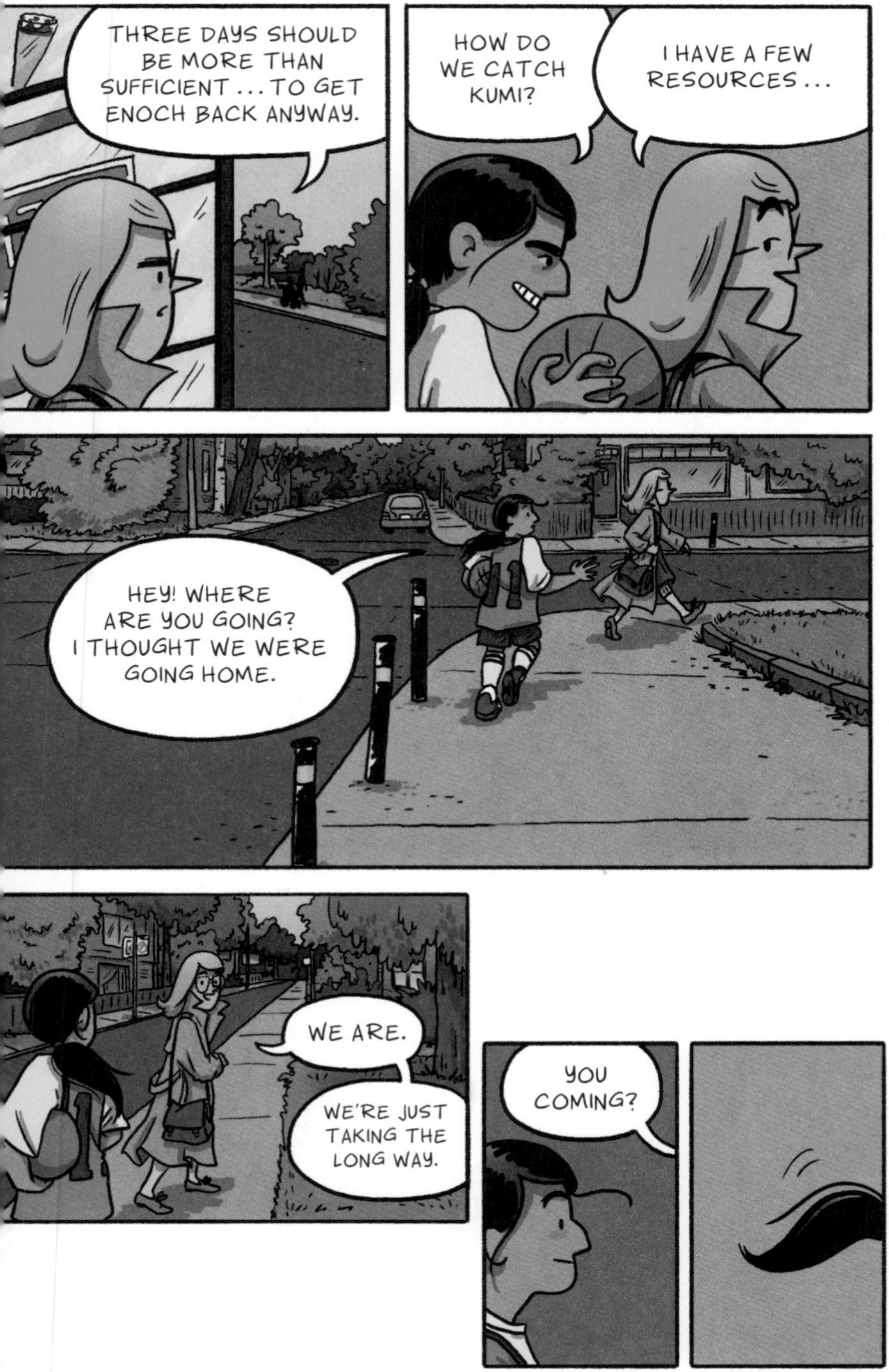
THREE DAYS SHOULD BE MORE THAN SUFFICIENT . . . TO GET ENOCH BACK ANYWAY.
HOW DO WE CATCH KUMI?
I HAVE A FEW RESOURCES . . .
HEY! WHERE ARE YOU GOING? I THOUGHT WE WERE GOING HOME.
WE ARE.
WE'RE JUST TAKING THE LONG WAY.
YOU COMING?

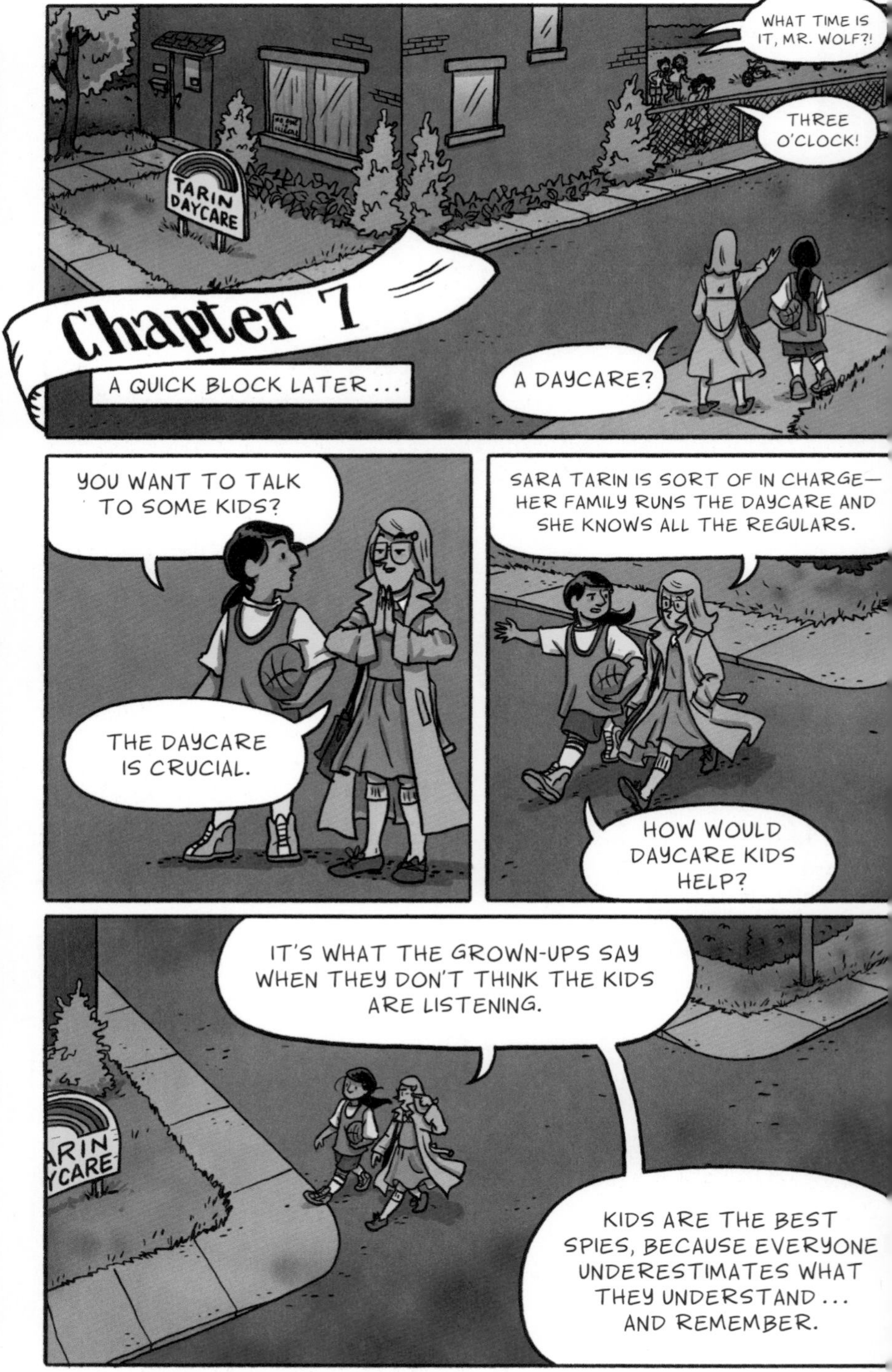
TARIN DAYCARE
WHAT TIME IS IT, MR. WOLF?!
THREE O'CLOCK!
Chapter 7
A QUICK BLOCK LATER . . .
A DAYCARE?
YOU WANT TO TALK TO SOME KIDS?
THE DAYCARE IS CRUCIAL.
SARA TARIN IS SORT OF IN CHARGE— HER FAMILY RUNS THE DAYCARE AND SHE KNOWS ALL THE REGULARS.
HOW WOULD DAYCARE KIDS HELP?
IT'S WHAT THE GROWN-UPS SAY WHEN THEY DON'T THINK THE KIDS ARE LISTENING.
KIDS ARE THE BEST SPIES, BECAUSE EVERYONE UNDERESTIMATES WHAT THEY UNDERSTAND . . . AND REMEMBER.

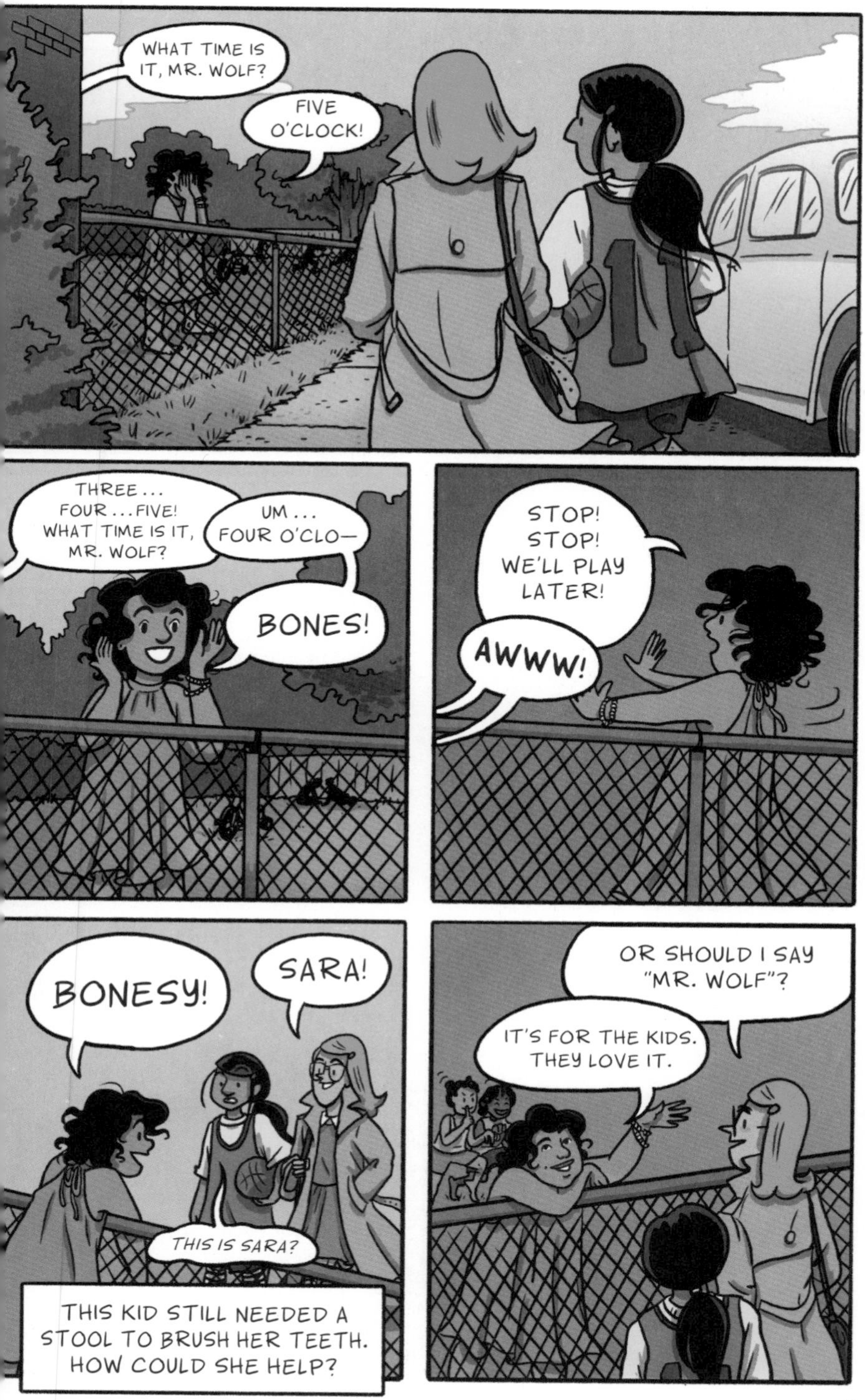
WHAT TIME IS IT, MR. WOLF?
FIVE O'CLOCK!
THREE... FOUR...FIVE! WHAT TIME IS IT, MR. WOLF?
UM... FOUR O'CLO—
BONES!
STOP! STOP! WE'LL PLAY LATER!
AWWW!
BONESY!
SARA!
THIS IS SARA?
THIS KID STILL NEEDED A STOOL TO BRUSH HER TEETH. HOW COULD SHE HELP?
OR SHOULD I SAY "MR. WOLF"?
IT'S FOR THE KIDS. THEY LOVE IT.

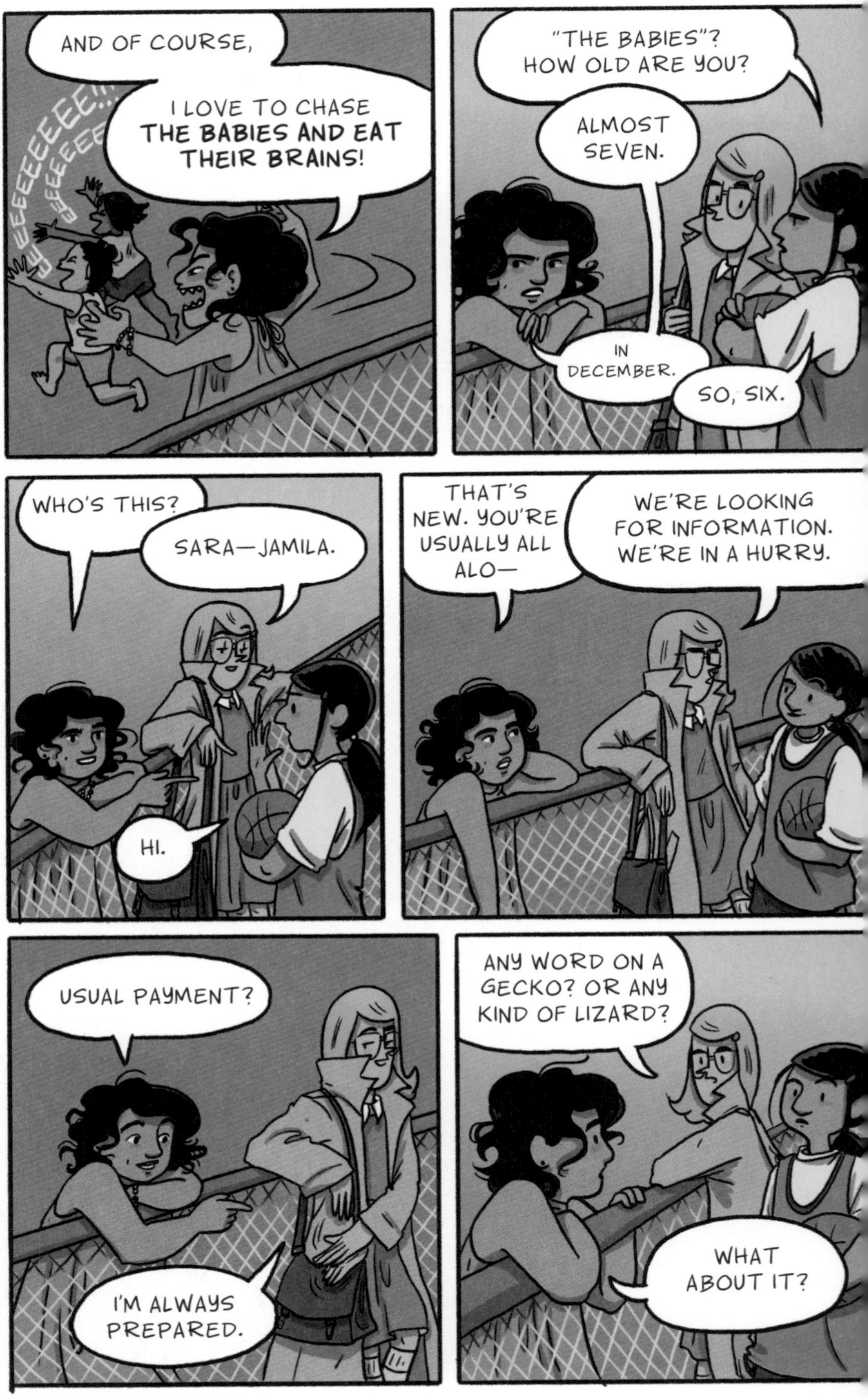
AND OF COURSE,
I LOVE TO CHASE THE BABIES AND EAT THEIR BRAINS!
"THE BABIES"? HOW OLD ARE YOU?
ALMOST SEVEN.
IN DECEMBER.
SO, SIX.
WHO'S THIS?
SARA—JAMILA.
HI.
THAT'S NEW. YOU'RE USUALLY ALL ALO—
WE'RE LOOKING FOR INFORMATION. WE'RE IN A HURRY.
USUAL PAYMENT?
I'M ALWAYS PREPARED.
ANY WORD ON A GECKO? OR ANY KIND OF LIZARD?
WHAT ABOUT IT?

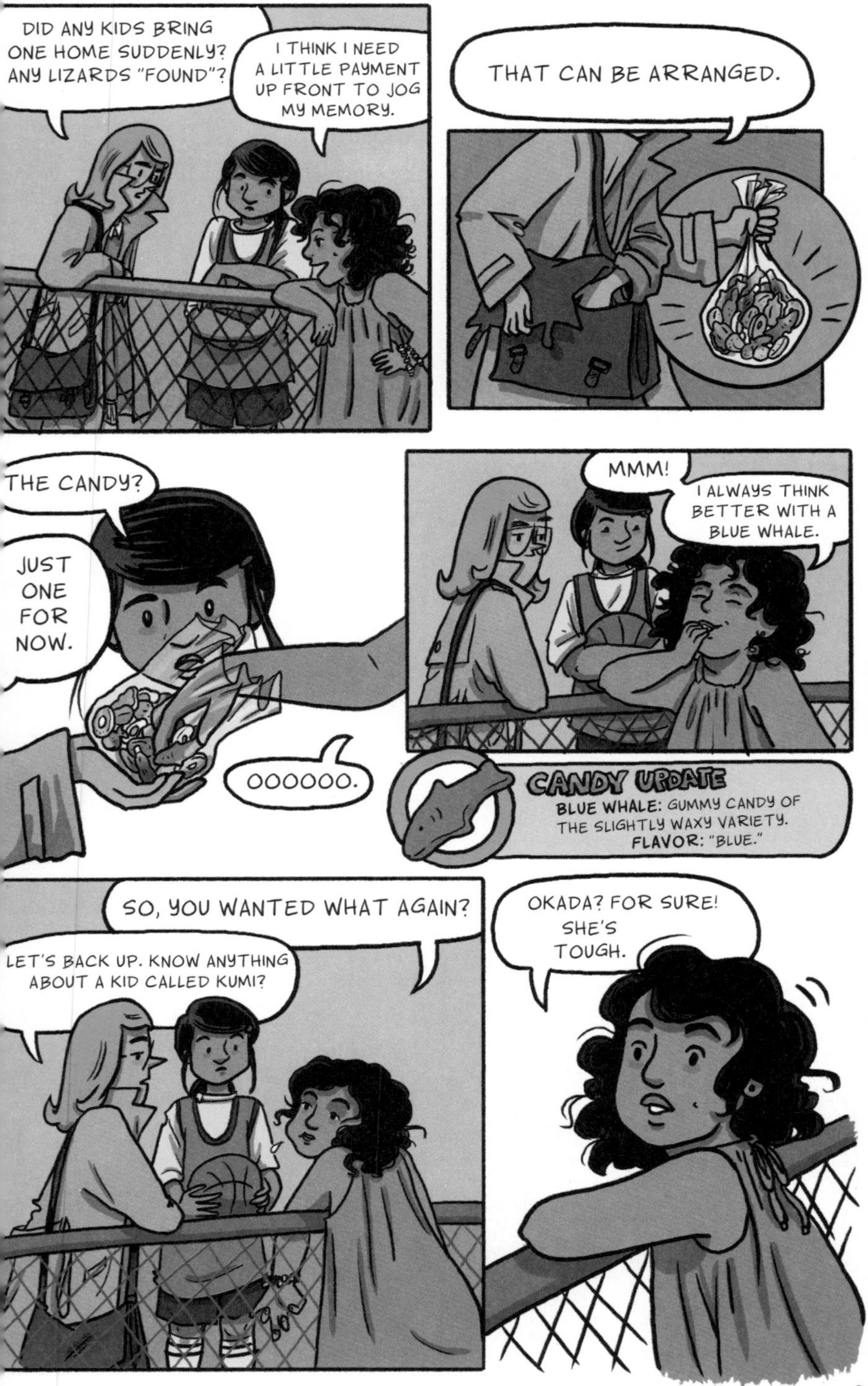
DID ANY KIDS BRING ONE HOME SUDDENLY? ANY LIZARDS "FOUND"?
I THINK I NEED A LITTLE PAYMENT UP FRONT TO JOG MY MEMORY.
THAT CAN BE ARRANGED.
THE CANDY?
JUST ONE FOR NOW.
OOOOOO.
MMM!
I ALWAYS THINK BETTER WITH A BLUE WHALE.
CANDY UPDATE
BLUE WHALE: GUMMY CANDY OF THE SLIGHTLY WAXY VARIETY.
FLAVOR: "BLUE."
SO, YOU WANTED WHAT AGAIN?
LET'S BACK UP. KNOW ANYTHING ABOUT A KID CALLED KUMI?
OKADA? FOR SURE! SHE'S TOUGH.

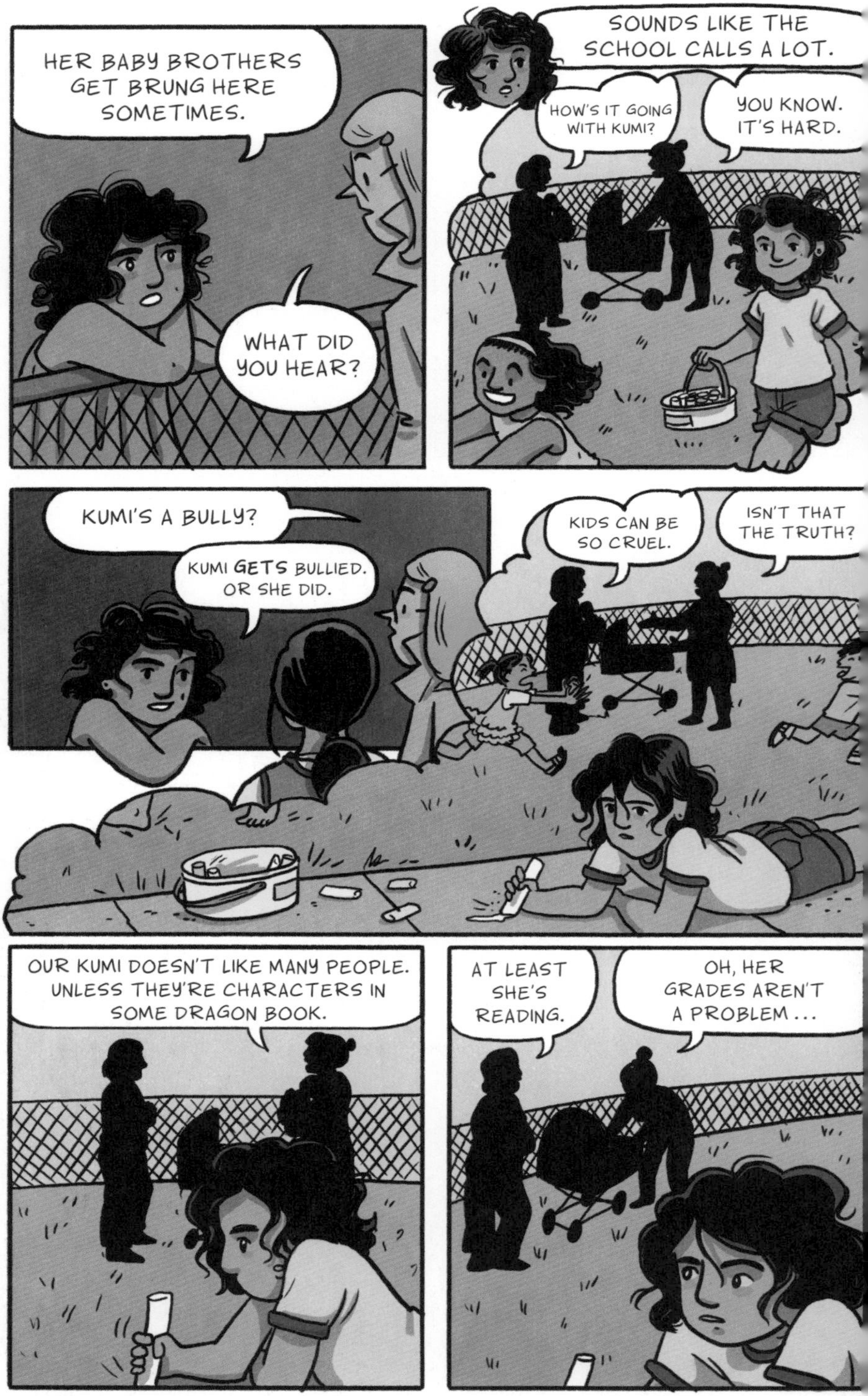
HER BABY BROTHERS GET BRUNG HERE SOMETIMES.
WHAT DID YOU HEAR?
SOUNDS LIKE THE SCHOOL CALLS A LOT.
HOW'S IT GOING WITH KUMI?
YOU KNOW. IT'S HARD.
KUMI'S A BULLY?
KUMI GETS BULLIED. OR SHE DID.
KIDS CAN BE SO CRUEL.
ISN'T THAT THE TRUTH?
OUR KUMI DOESN'T LIKE MANY PEOPLE. UNLESS THEY'RE CHARACTERS IN SOME DRAGON BOOK.
AT LEAST SHE'S READING.
OH, HER GRADES AREN'T A PROBLEM . . .

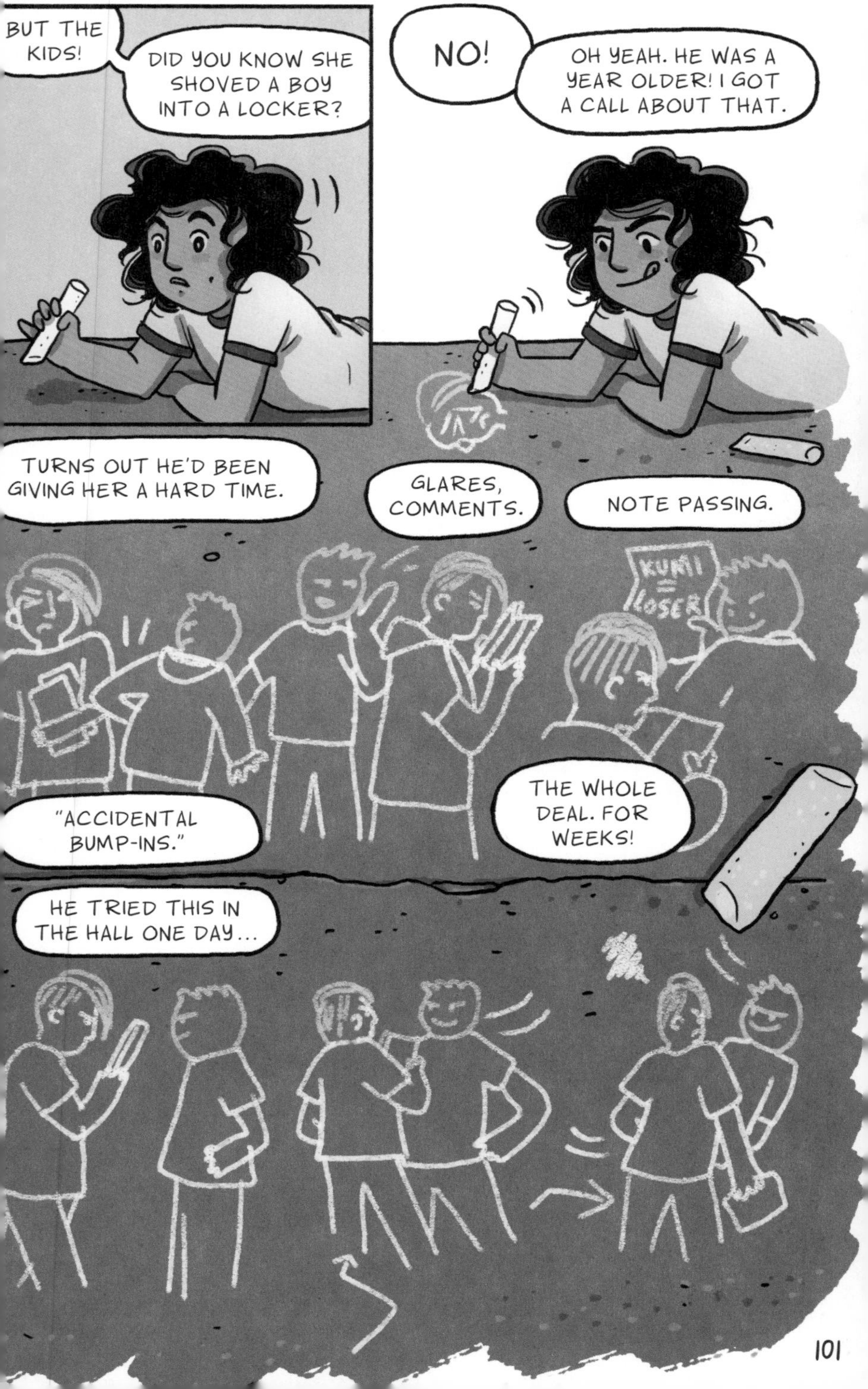

BUT THE KIDS!
DID YOU KNOW SHE SHOVED A BOY INTO A LOCKER?
NO!
OH YEAH. HE WAS A YEAR OLDER! I GOT A CALL ABOUT THAT.
TURNS OUT HE'D BEEN GIVING HER A HARD TIME.
GLARES, COMMENTS.
NOTE PASSING.
KUMI = LOSER
"ACCIDENTAL BUMP-INS."
THE WHOLE DEAL. FOR WEEKS!
HE TRIED THIS IN THE HALL ONE DAY...

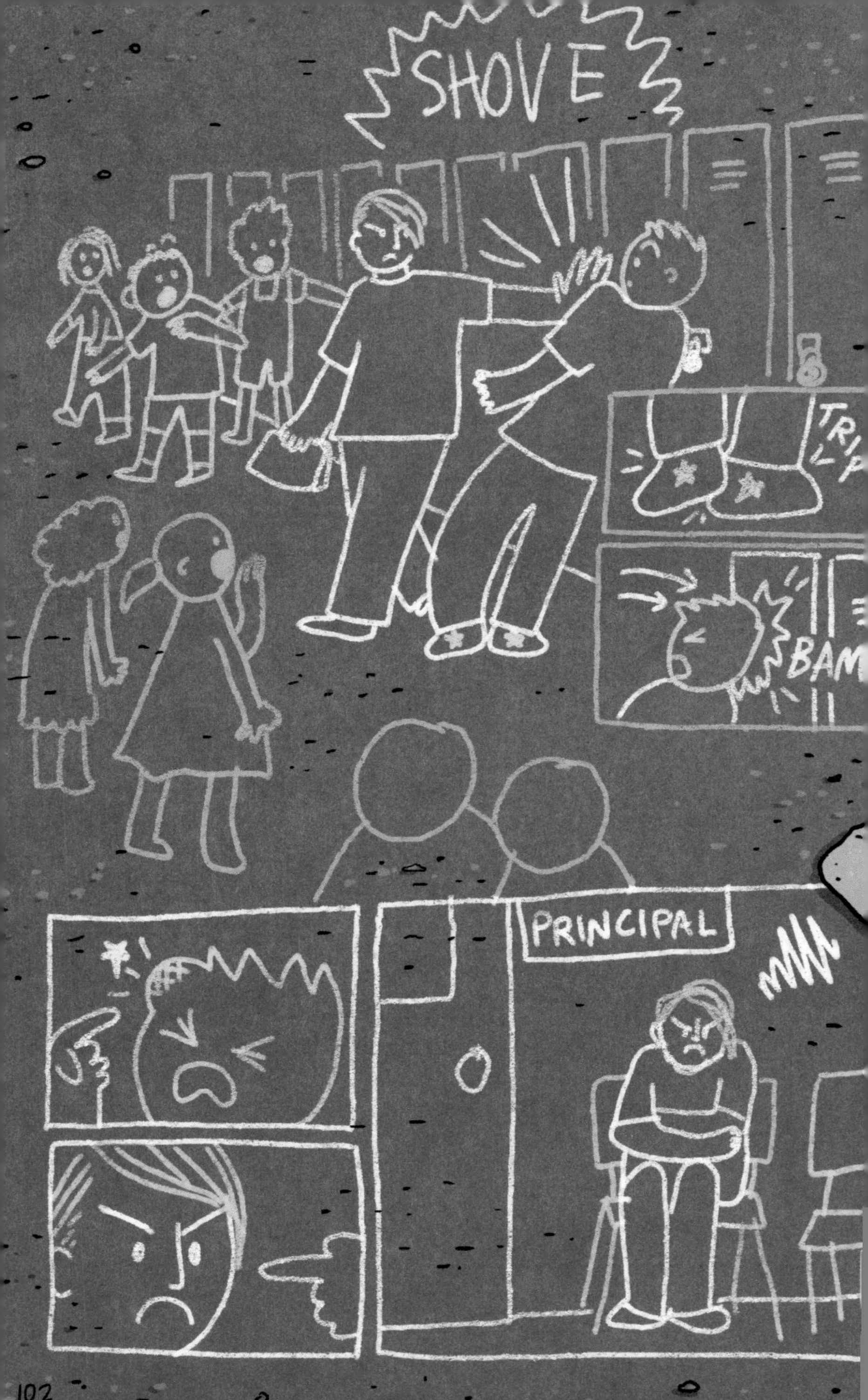
SHOVE
TRIP
BAM
PRINCIPAL

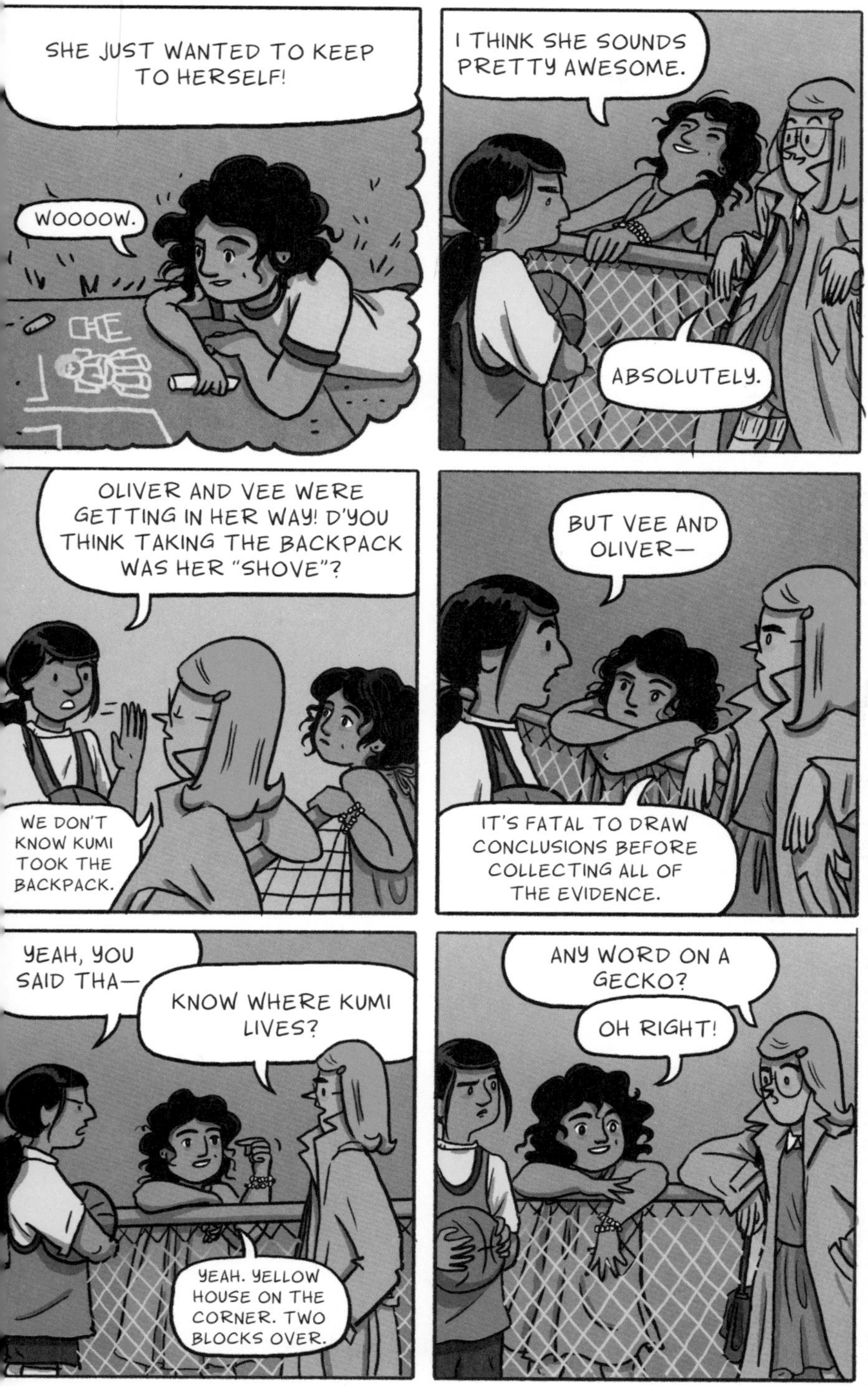
SHE JUST WANTED TO KEEP TO HERSELF!
WOOOOW.
I THINK SHE SOUNDS PRETTY AWESOME.
ABSOLUTELY.
OLIVER AND VEE WERE GETTING IN HER WAY! D'YOU THINK TAKING THE BACKPACK WAS HER "SHOVE"?
WE DON'T KNOW KUMI TOOK THE BACKPACK.
BUT VEE AND OLIVER—
IT'S FATAL TO DRAW CONCLUSIONS BEFORE COLLECTING ALL OF THE EVIDENCE.
YEAH, YOU SAID THA—
KNOW WHERE KUMI LIVES?
YEAH. YELLOW HOUSE ON THE CORNER. TWO BLOCKS OVER.
ANY WORD ON A GECKO?
OH RIGHT!

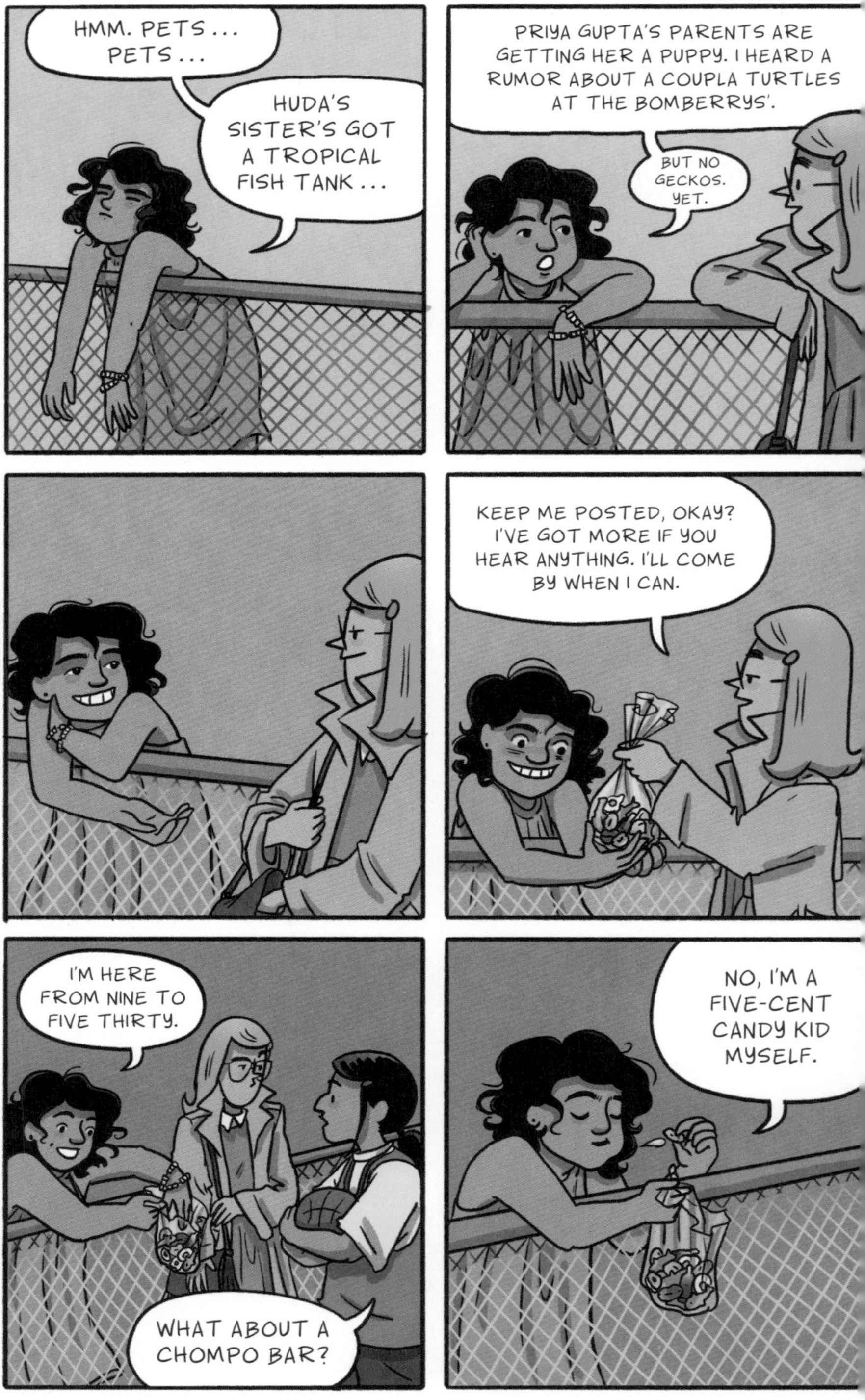
HMM. PETS...
PETS...
HUDA'S SISTER'S GOT A TROPICAL FISH TANK...
PRIYA GUPTA'S PARENTS ARE GETTING HER A PUPPY. I HEARD A RUMOR ABOUT A COUPLA TURTLES AT THE BOMBERRYS'.
BUT NO GECKOS. YET.
KEEP ME POSTED, OKAY? I'VE GOT MORE IF YOU HEAR ANYTHING. I'LL COME BY WHEN I CAN.
I'M HERE FROM NINE TO FIVE THIRTY.
WHAT ABOUT A CHOMPO BAR?
NO, I'M A FIVE-CENT CANDY KID MYSELF.

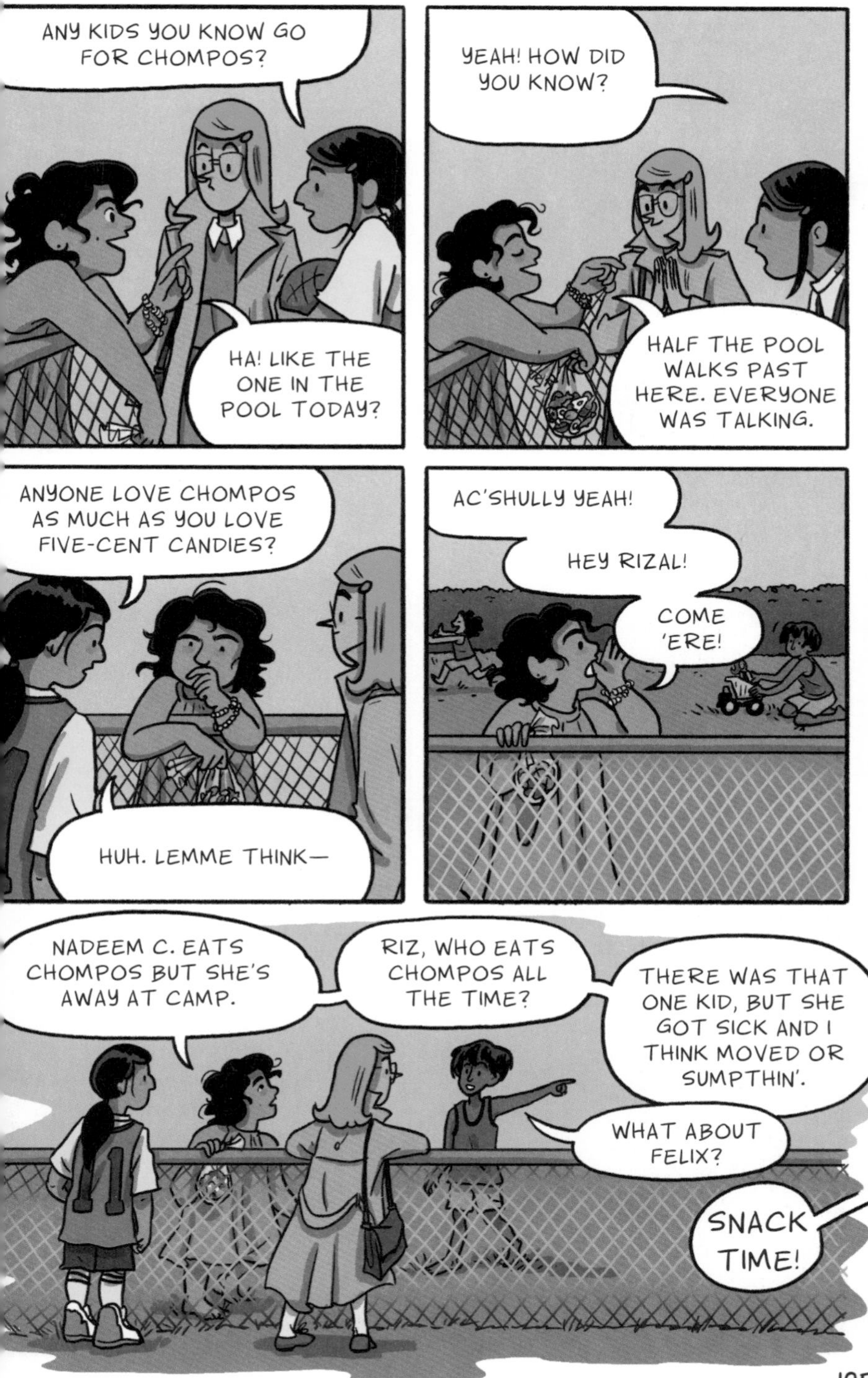
ANY KIDS YOU KNOW GO FOR CHOMPOS?
HA! LIKE THE ONE IN THE POOL TODAY?
YEAH! HOW DID YOU KNOW?
HALF THE POOL WALKS PAST HERE. EVERYONE WAS TALKING.
ANYONE LOVE CHOMPOS AS MUCH AS YOU LOVE FIVE-CENT CANDIES?
HUH. LEMME THINK—
AC'SHULLY YEAH!
HEY RIZAL!
COME 'ERE!
NADEEM C. EATS CHOMPOS BUT SHE'S AWAY AT CAMP.
RIZ, WHO EATS CHOMPOS ALL THE TIME?
THERE WAS THAT ONE KID, BUT SHE GOT SICK AND I THINK MOVED OR SUMPTHIN'.
WHAT ABOUT FELIX?
SNACK TIME!

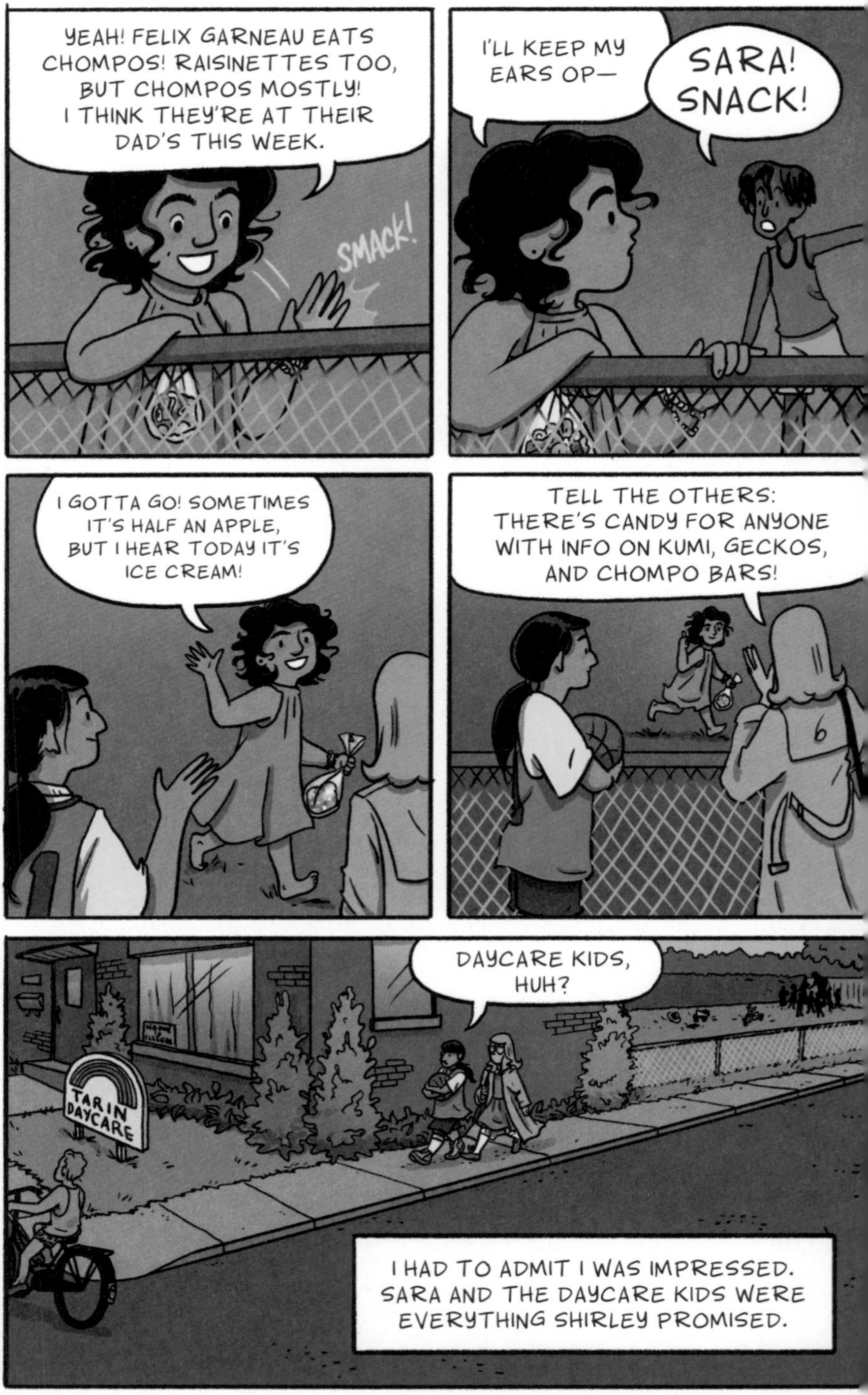

YEAH! FELIX GARNEAU EATS CHOMPOS! RAISINETTES TOO, BUT CHOMPOS MOSTLY! I THINK THEY'RE AT THEIR DAD'S THIS WEEK.
SMACK!
I'LL KEEP MY EARS OP—
SARA! SNACK!
I GOTTA GO! SOMETIMES IT'S HALF AN APPLE, BUT I HEAR TODAY IT'S ICE CREAM!
TELL THE OTHERS: THERE'S CANDY FOR ANYONE WITH INFO ON KUMI, GECKOS, AND CHOMPO BARS!
TARIN DAYCARE
DAYCARE KIDS, HUH?
I HAD TO ADMIT I WAS IMPRESSED. SARA AND THE DAYCARE KIDS WERE EVERYTHING SHIRLEY PROMISED.

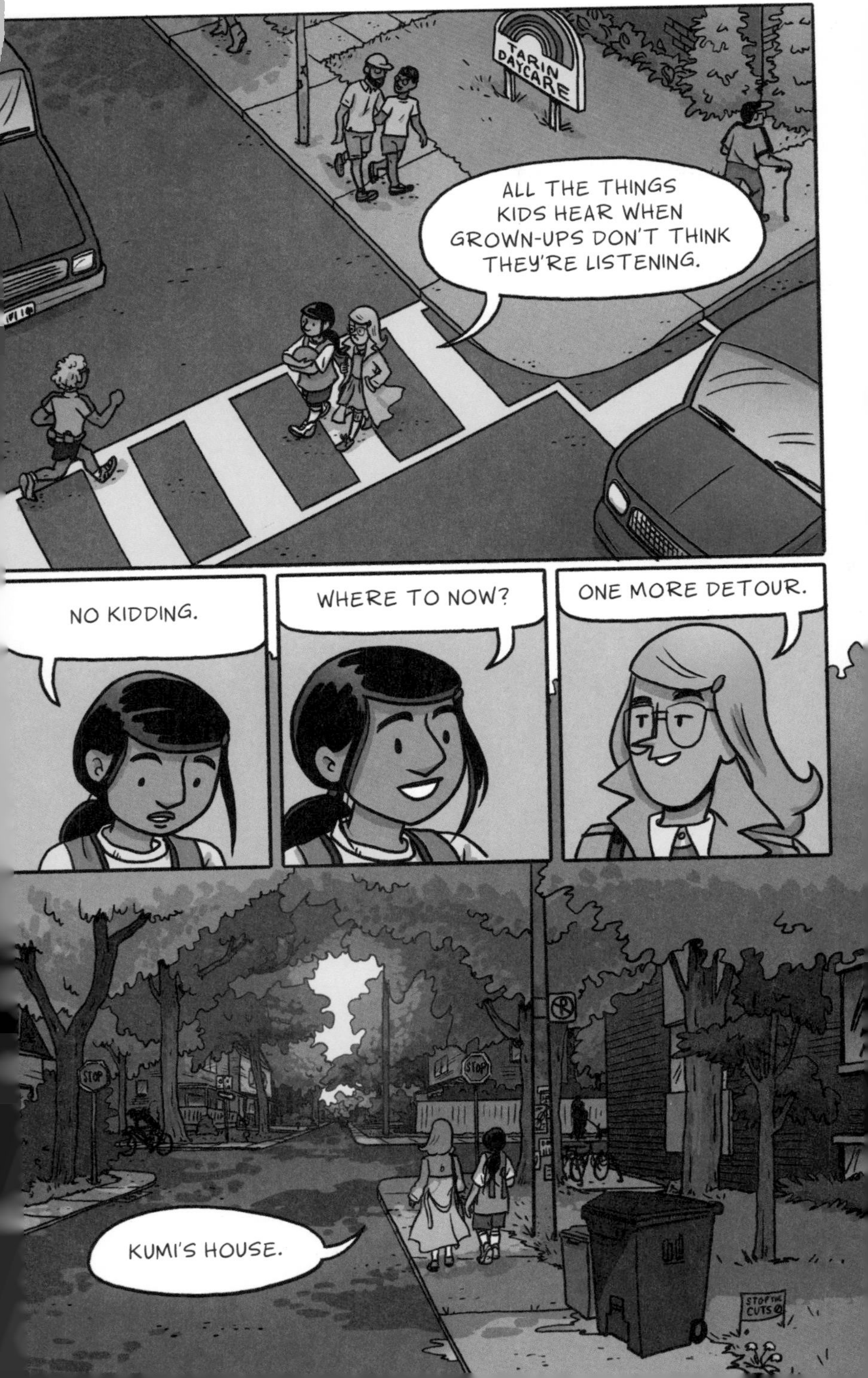
TARIN DAYCARE
ALL THE THINGS KIDS HEAR WHEN GROWN-UPS DON'T THINK THEY'RE LISTENING.
NO KIDDING.
WHERE TO NOW?
ONE MORE DETOUR.
KUMI'S HOUSE.

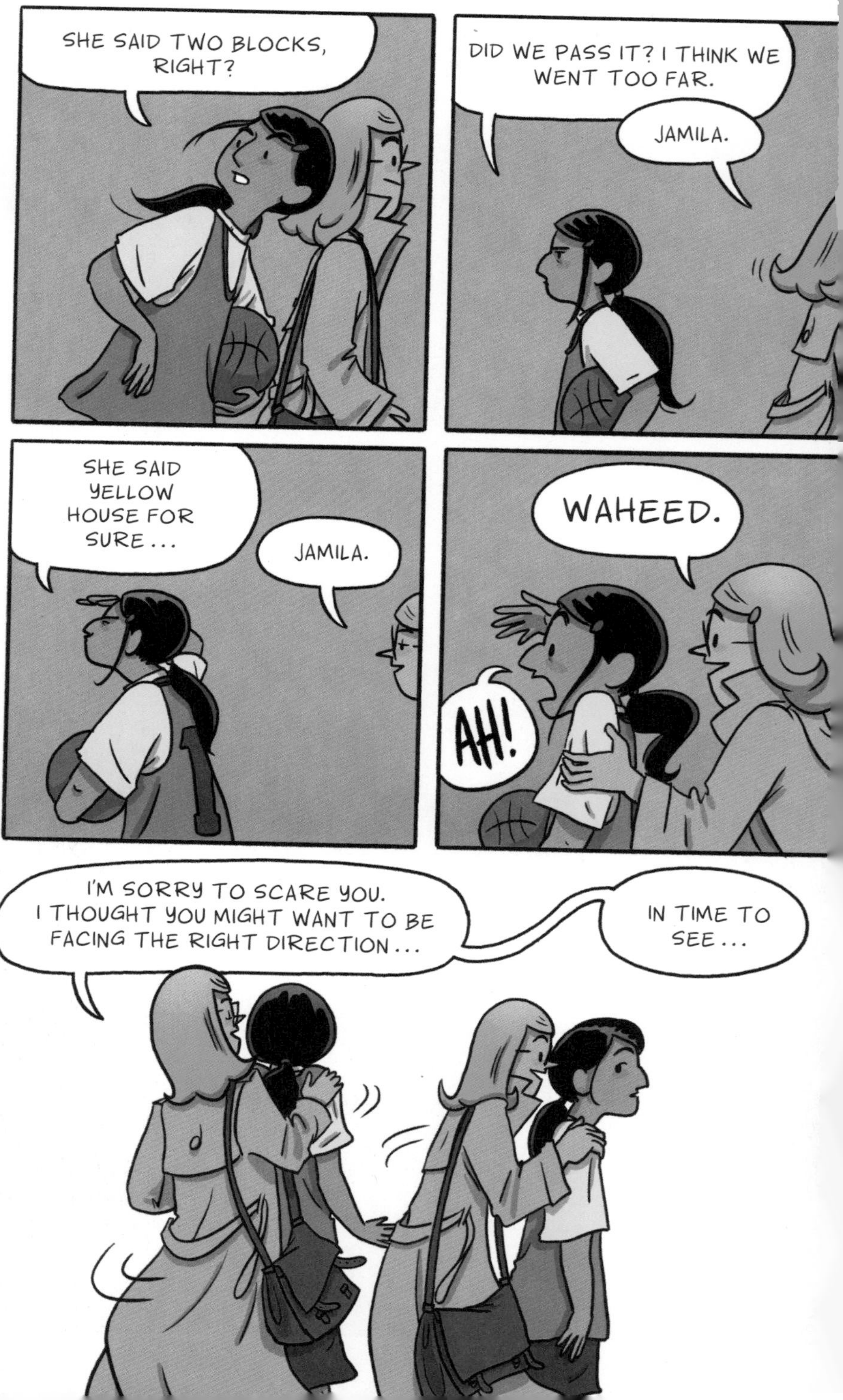
SHE SAID TWO BLOCKS, RIGHT?
DID WE PASS IT? I THINK WE WENT TOO FAR.
JAMILA.
SHE SAID YELLOW HOUSE FOR SURE...
JAMILA.
WAHEED.
AH!
I'M SORRY TO SCARE YOU. I THOUGHT YOU MIGHT WANT TO BE FACING THE RIGHT DIRECTION...
IN TIME TO SEE...

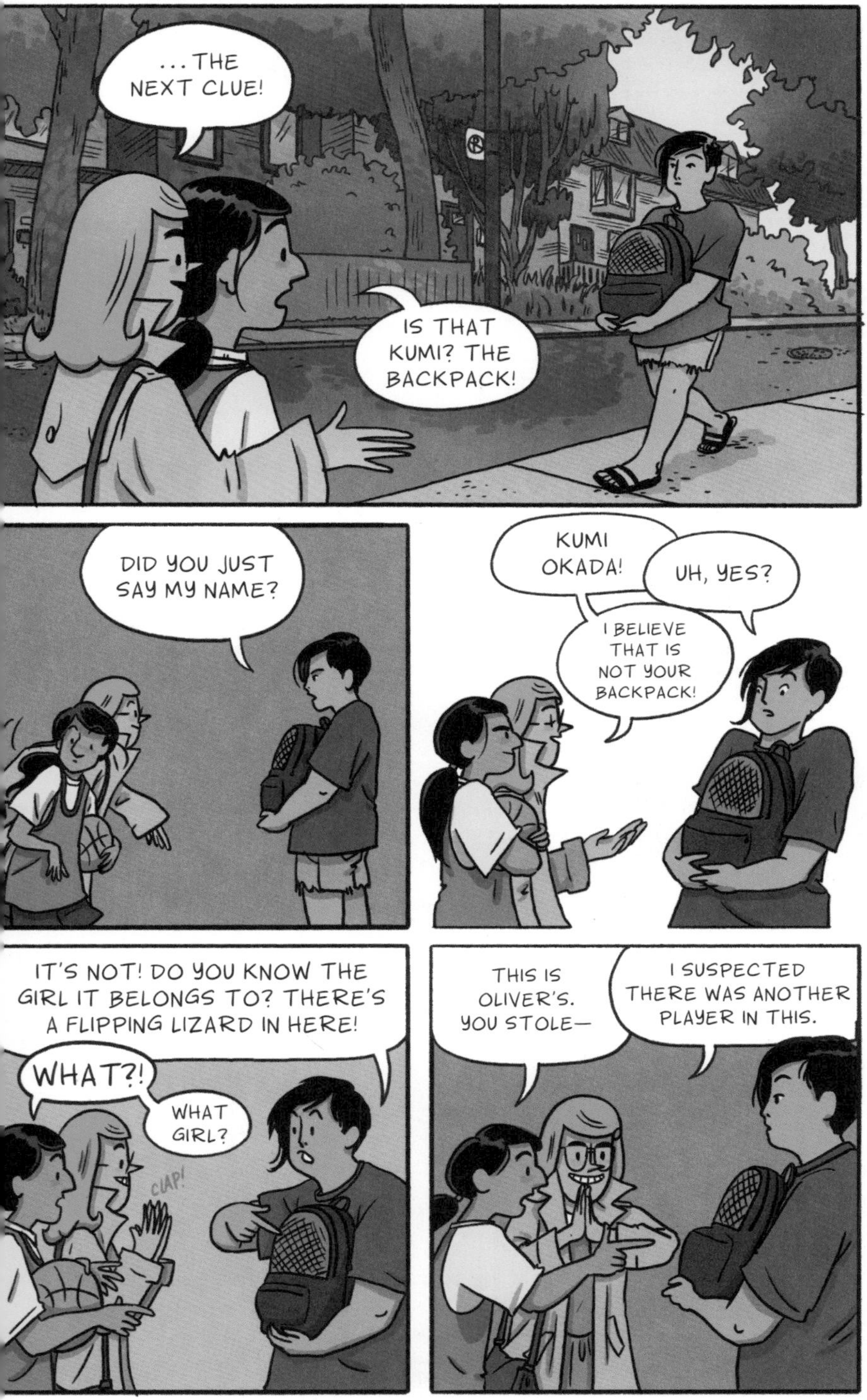
...THE
NEXT CLUE!
IS THAT
KUMI? THE
BACKPACK!
DID YOU JUST
SAY MY NAME?
KUMI
OKADA!
UH, YES?
I BELIEVE
THAT IS
NOT YOUR
BACKPACK!
IT'S NOT! DO YOU KNOW THE
GIRL IT BELONGS TO? THERE'S
A FLIPPING LIZARD IN HERE!
WHAT?!
WHAT
GIRL?
CLAP!
THIS IS
OLIVER'S.
YOU STOLE—
I SUSPECTED
THERE WAS ANOTHER
PLAYER IN THIS.

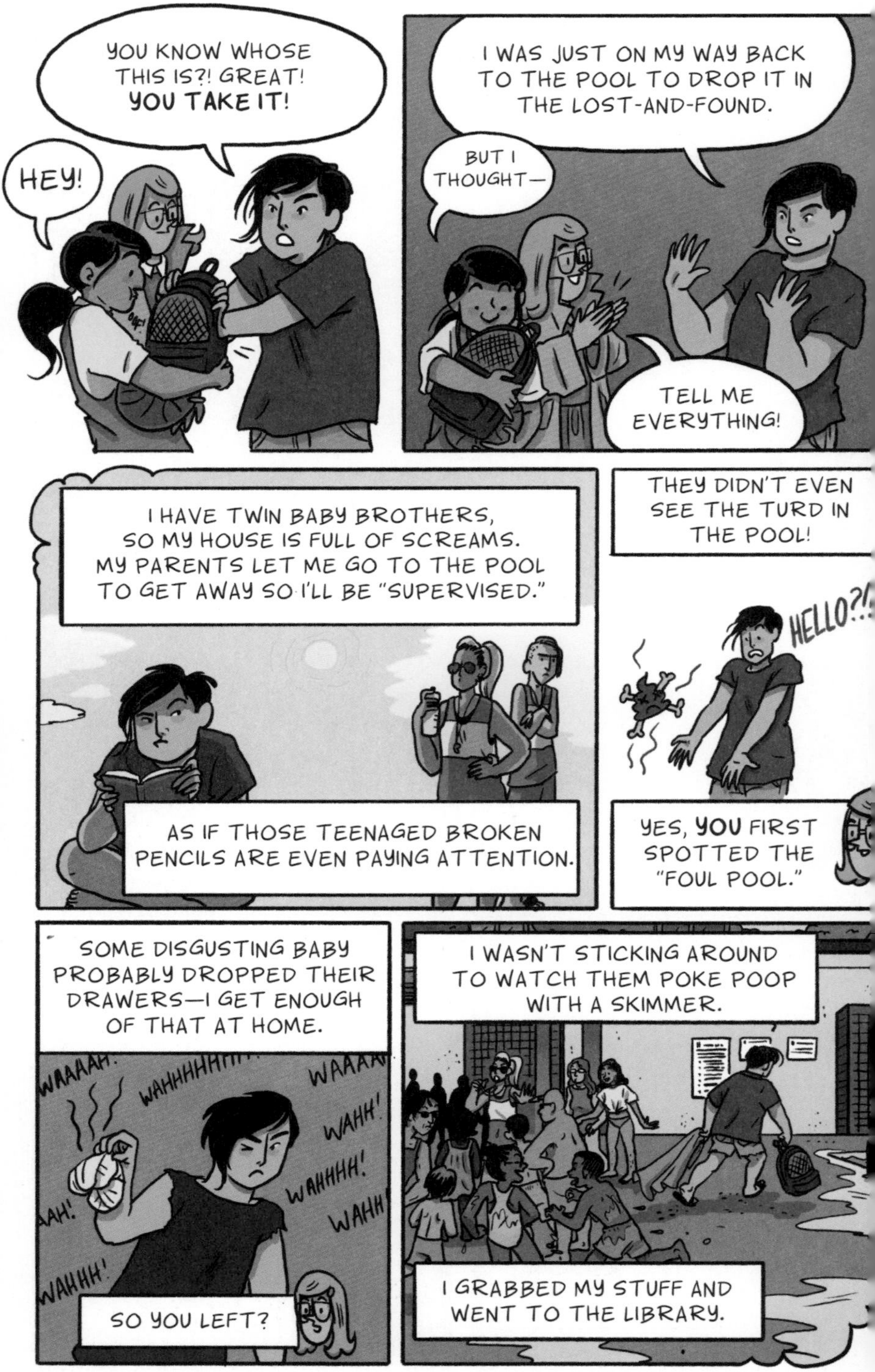
YOU KNOW WHOSE THIS IS?! GREAT! **YOU TAKE IT!**
HEY!
I WAS JUST ON MY WAY BACK TO THE POOL TO DROP IT IN THE LOST-AND-FOUND.
BUT I THOUGHT—
TELL ME EVERYTHING!
I HAVE TWIN BABY BROTHERS, SO MY HOUSE IS FULL OF SCREAMS. MY PARENTS LET ME GO TO THE POOL TO GET AWAY SO I'LL BE "SUPERVISED."
AS IF THOSE TEENAGED BROKEN PENCILS ARE EVEN PAYING ATTENTION.
THEY DIDN'T EVEN SEE THE TURD IN THE POOL!
HELLO?!
YES, **YOU** FIRST SPOTTED THE "FOUL POOL."
SOME DISGUSTING BABY PROBABLY DROPPED THEIR DRAWERS—I GET ENOUGH OF THAT AT HOME.
WAAAAH!
WAHHHHHH!
WAAAA!
WAHH!
WAHHHH!
AAH!
WAHH!
WAHHH!
SO YOU LEFT?
I WASN'T STICKING AROUND TO WATCH THEM POKE POOP WITH A SKIMMER.
I GRABBED MY STUFF AND WENT TO THE LIBRARY.

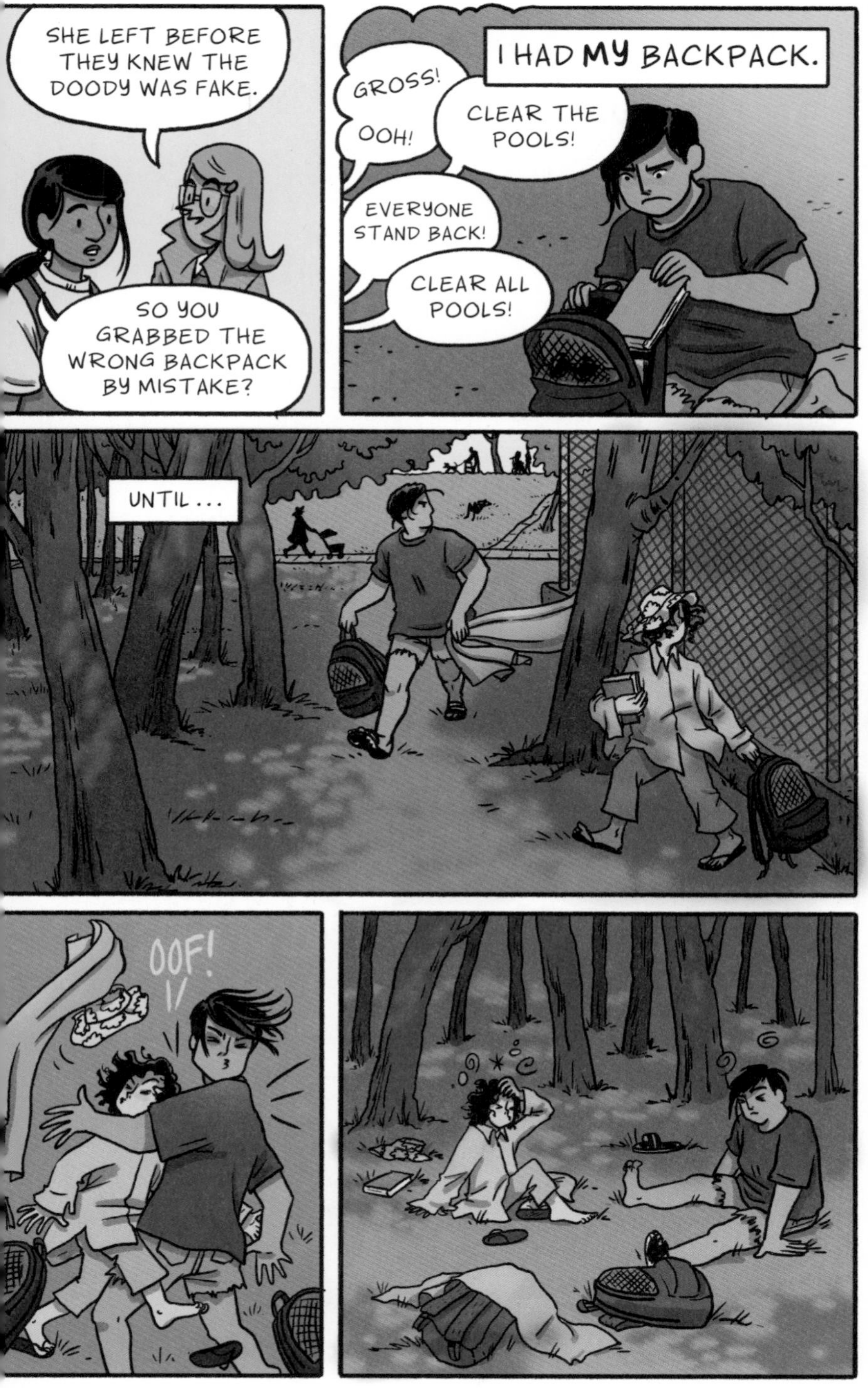
SHE LEFT BEFORE THEY KNEW THE DOODY WAS FAKE.
SO YOU GRABBED THE WRONG BACKPACK BY MISTAKE?
I HAD MY BACKPACK.
GROSS!
OOH!
CLEAR THE POOLS!
EVERYONE STAND BACK!
CLEAR ALL POOLS!
UNTIL . . .
OOF!

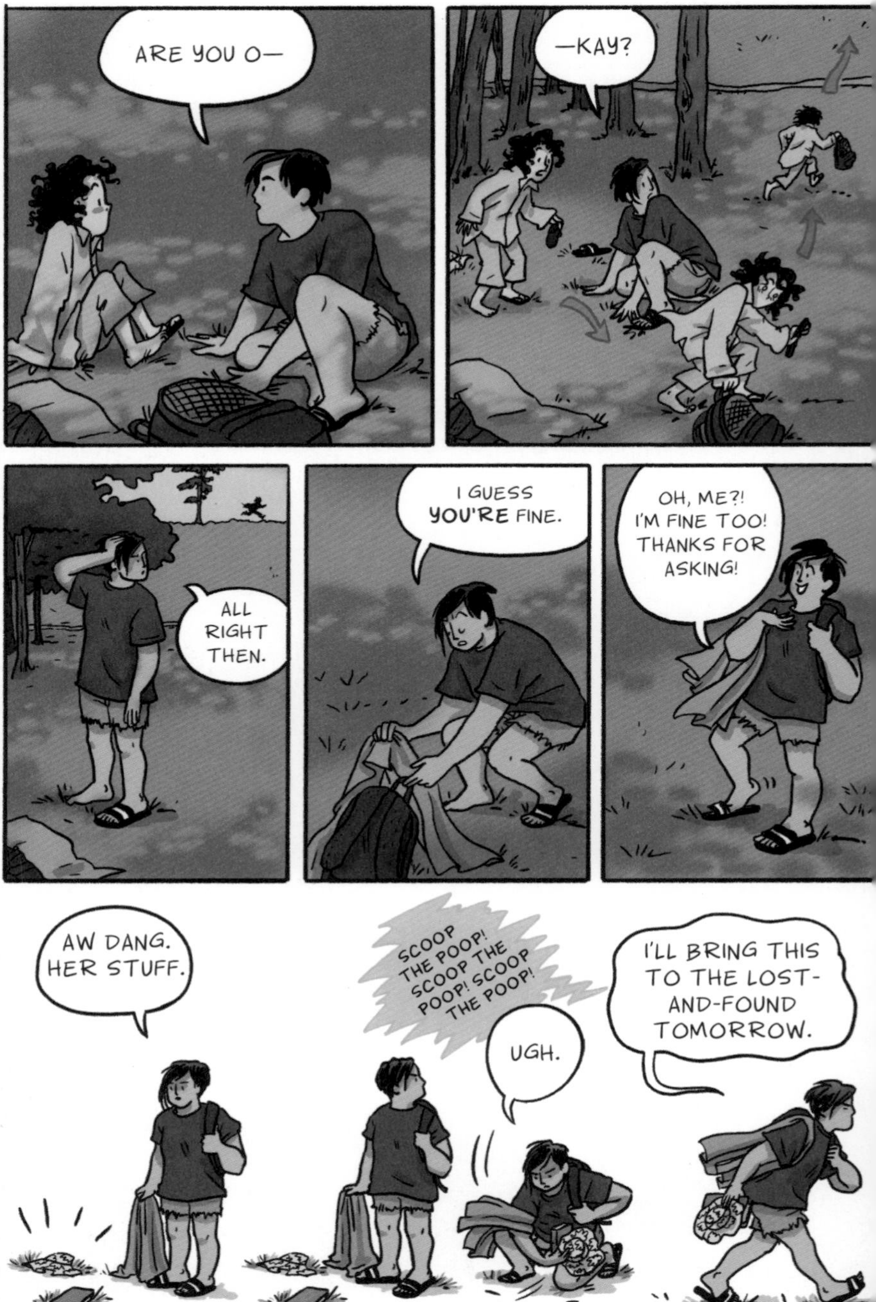
ARE YOU O—
—KAY?
ALL RIGHT THEN.
I GUESS YOU'RE FINE.
OH, ME?! I'M FINE TOO! THANKS FOR ASKING!
AW DANG. HER STUFF.
SCOOP THE POOP! SCOOP THE POOP! SCOOP THE POOP!
UGH.
I'LL BRING THIS TO THE LOST-AND-FOUND TOMORROW.

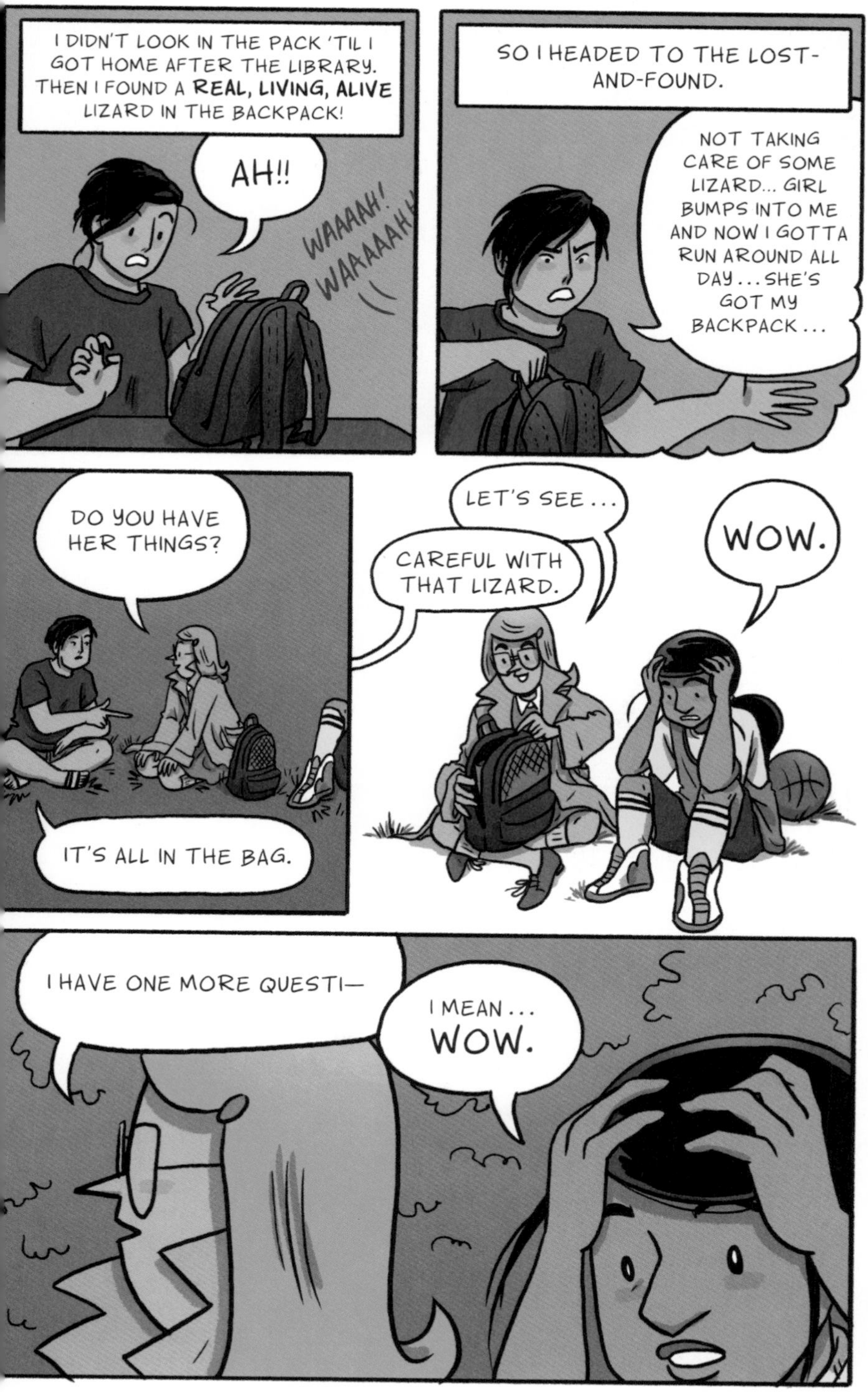
I DIDN'T LOOK IN THE PACK 'TIL I GOT HOME AFTER THE LIBRARY. THEN I FOUND A **REAL, LIVING, ALIVE** LIZARD IN THE BACKPACK!
AH!!
WAAAAH! WAAAAAH
SO I HEADED TO THE LOST-AND-FOUND.
NOT TAKING CARE OF SOME LIZARD... GIRL BUMPS INTO ME AND NOW I GOTTA RUN AROUND ALL DAY... SHE'S GOT MY BACKPACK...
DO YOU HAVE HER THINGS?
IT'S ALL IN THE BAG.
LET'S SEE...
CAREFUL WITH THAT LIZARD.
WOW.
I HAVE ONE MORE QUESTI—
I MEAN... WOW.

I HAD IT ALL WRONG.

WHAT? OH, YES. YOU DID.

SO, MY QUESTION:

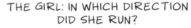
THE GIRL: IN WHICH DIRECTION DID SHE RUN?

ALONG BARTON STREET, TOWARD THE CONVENIENCE STORE.

EAST.

IT REALLY IS GETTING LATE—WE BOTH SHOULD GET HOME.

YOU'RE TAKING ENOCH?

YES. I'LL LET OLIVER AND VEE KNOW HE'S SAFE.

WHAT ABOUT MY BAG?

I DON' KNOW. Y

SHIRLEY GOT KUMI'S CONTACT INFORMATION AND WE HEADED HOME.

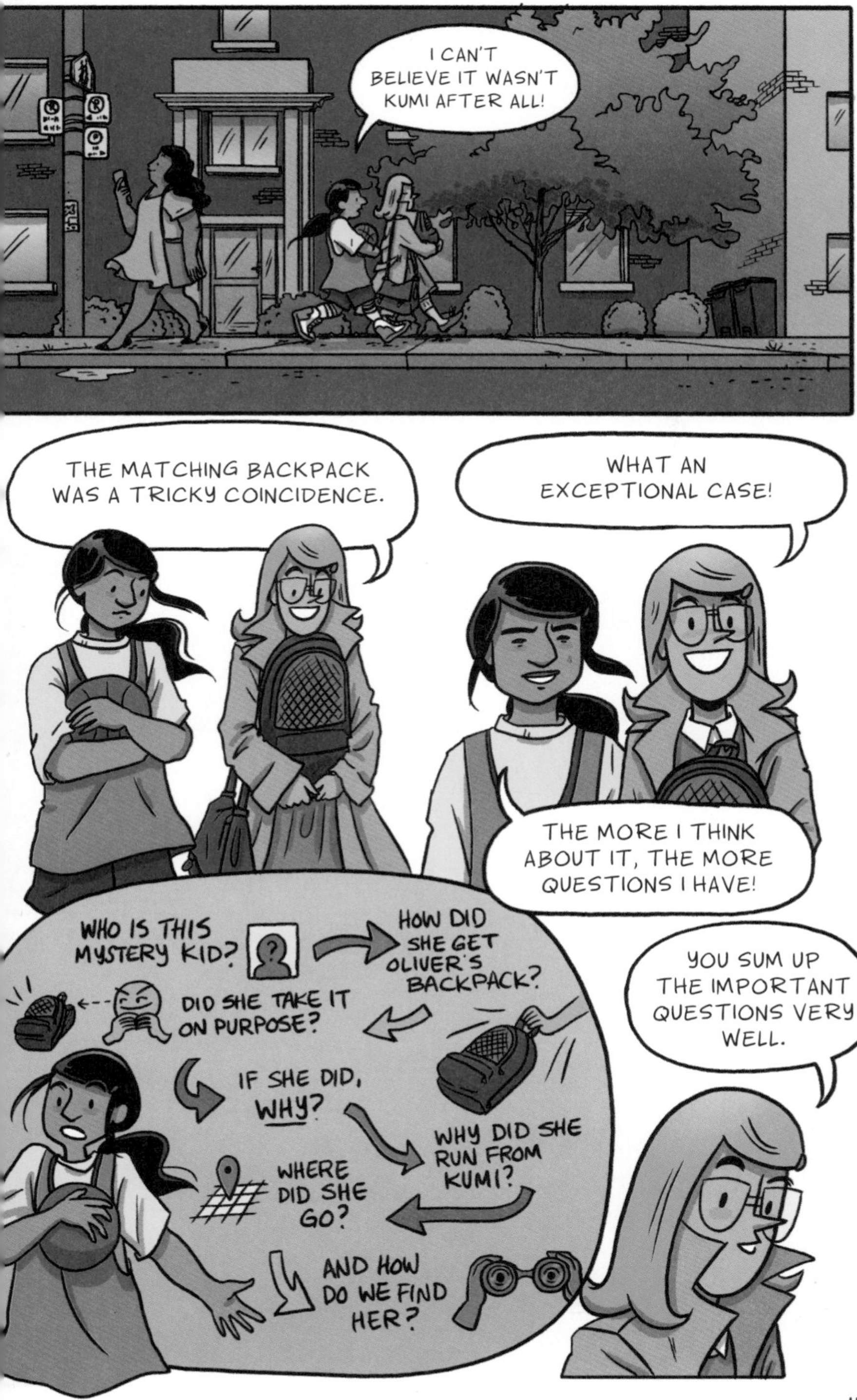
I CAN'T BELIEVE IT WASN'T KUMI AFTER ALL!
THE MATCHING BACKPACK WAS A TRICKY COINCIDENCE.
WHAT AN EXCEPTIONAL CASE!
THE MORE I THINK ABOUT IT, THE MORE QUESTIONS I HAVE!
WHO IS THIS MYSTERY KID?
HOW DID SHE GET OLIVER'S BACKPACK?
DID SHE TAKE IT ON PURPOSE?
IF SHE DID, WHY?
WHY DID SHE RUN FROM KUMI?
WHERE DID SHE GO?
AND HOW DO WE FIND HER?
YOU SUM UP THE IMPORTANT QUESTIONS VERY WELL.

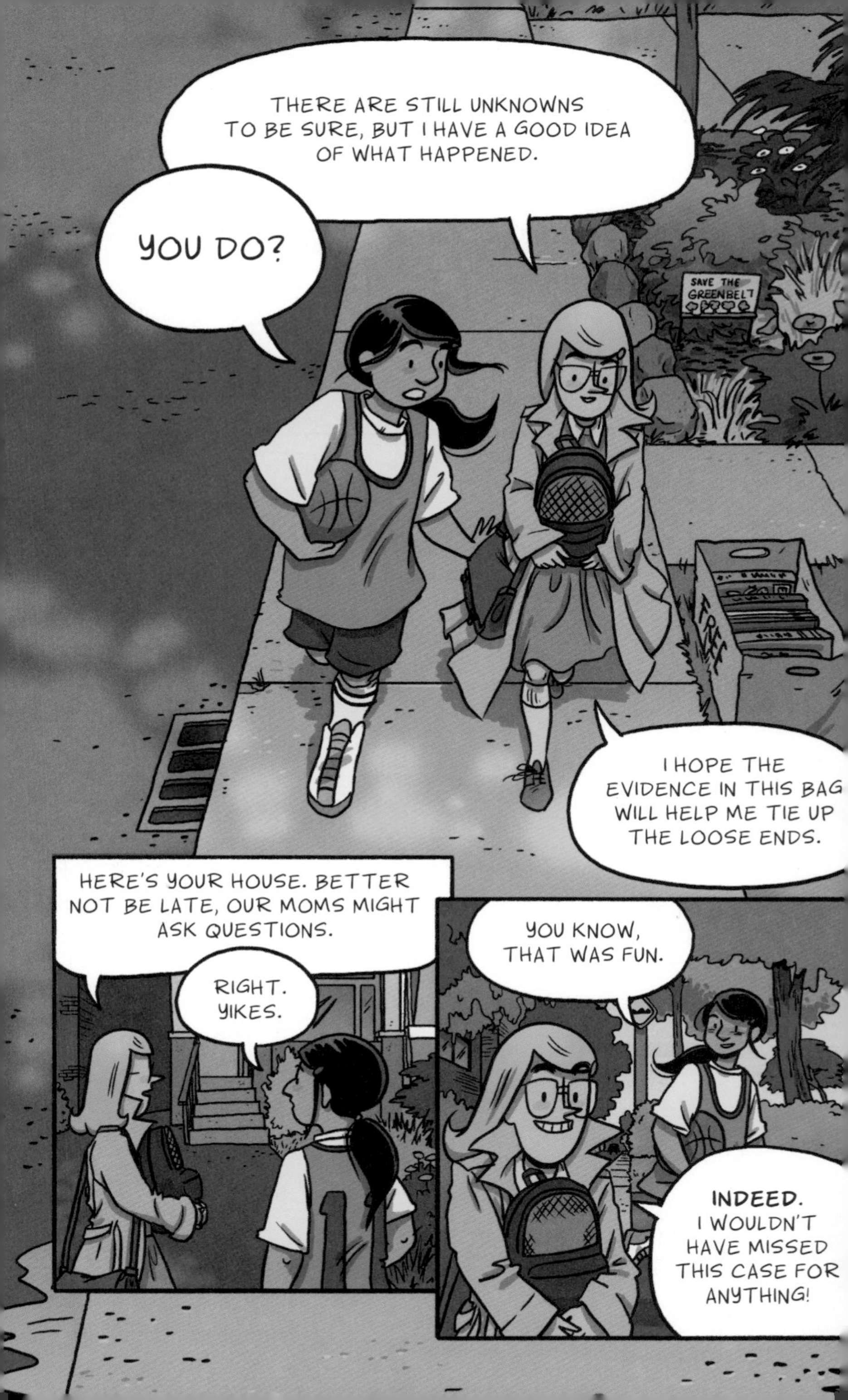
THERE ARE STILL UNKNOWNS TO BE SURE, BUT I HAVE A GOOD IDEA OF WHAT HAPPENED.
YOU DO?
SAVE THE GREENBELT
FREE
I HOPE THE EVIDENCE IN THIS BAG WILL HELP ME TIE UP THE LOOSE ENDS.
HERE'S YOUR HOUSE. BETTER NOT BE LATE, OUR MOMS MIGHT ASK QUESTIONS.
RIGHT. YIKES.
YOU KNOW, THAT WAS FUN.
INDEED. I WOULDN'T HAVE MISSED THIS CASE FOR ANYTHING!

Chapter 8

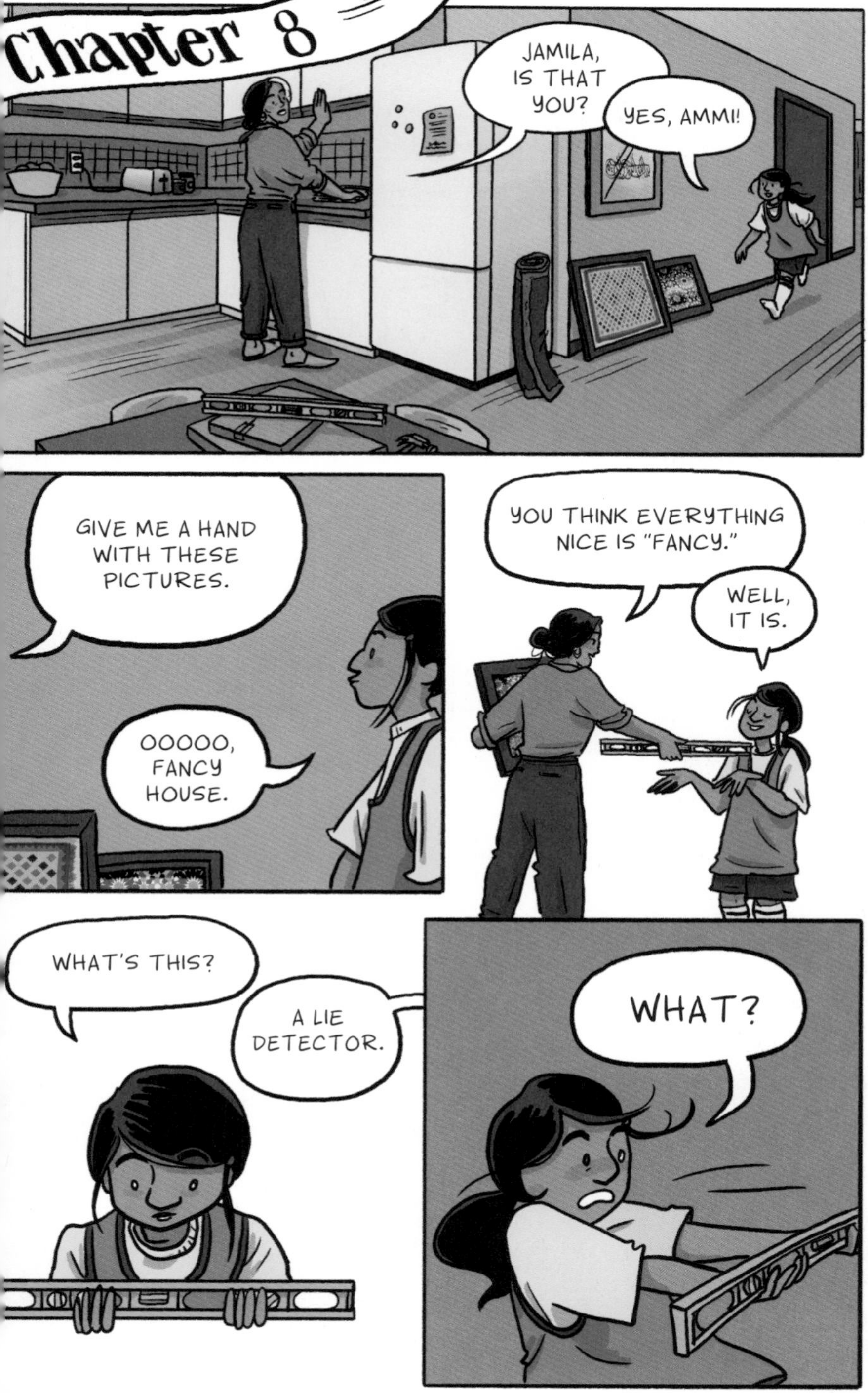

JAMILA, IS THAT YOU?
YES, AMMI!
GIVE ME A HAND WITH THESE PICTURES.
OOOOO, FANCY HOUSE.
YOU THINK EVERYTHING NICE IS "FANCY."
WELL, IT IS.
WHAT'S THIS?
A LIE DETECTOR.
WHAT?

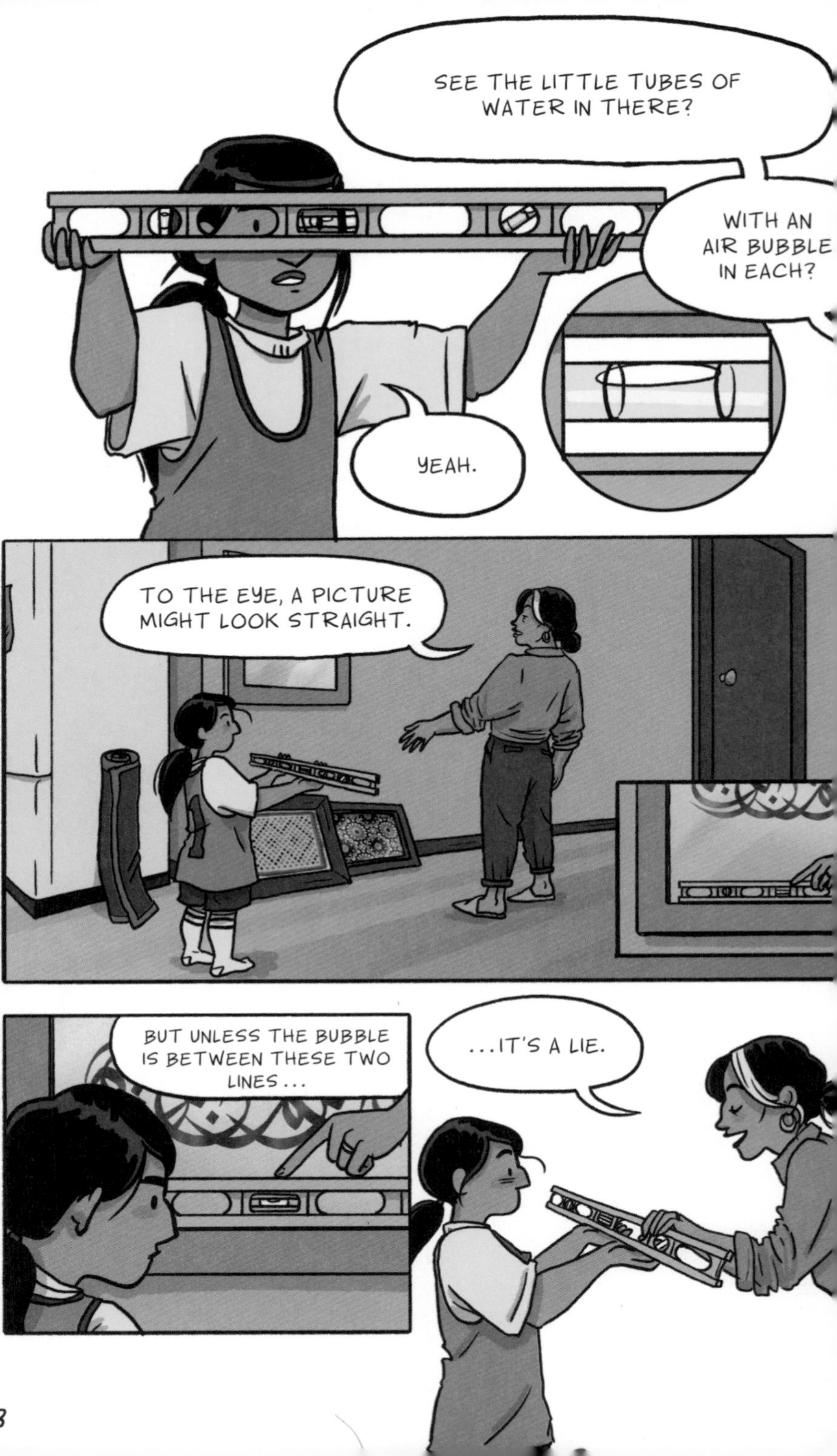
SEE THE LITTLE TUBES OF WATER IN THERE?
WITH AN AIR BUBBLE IN EACH?
YEAH.
TO THE EYE, A PICTURE MIGHT LOOK STRAIGHT.
BUT UNLESS THE BUBBLE IS BETWEEN THESE TWO LINES...
...IT'S A LIE.

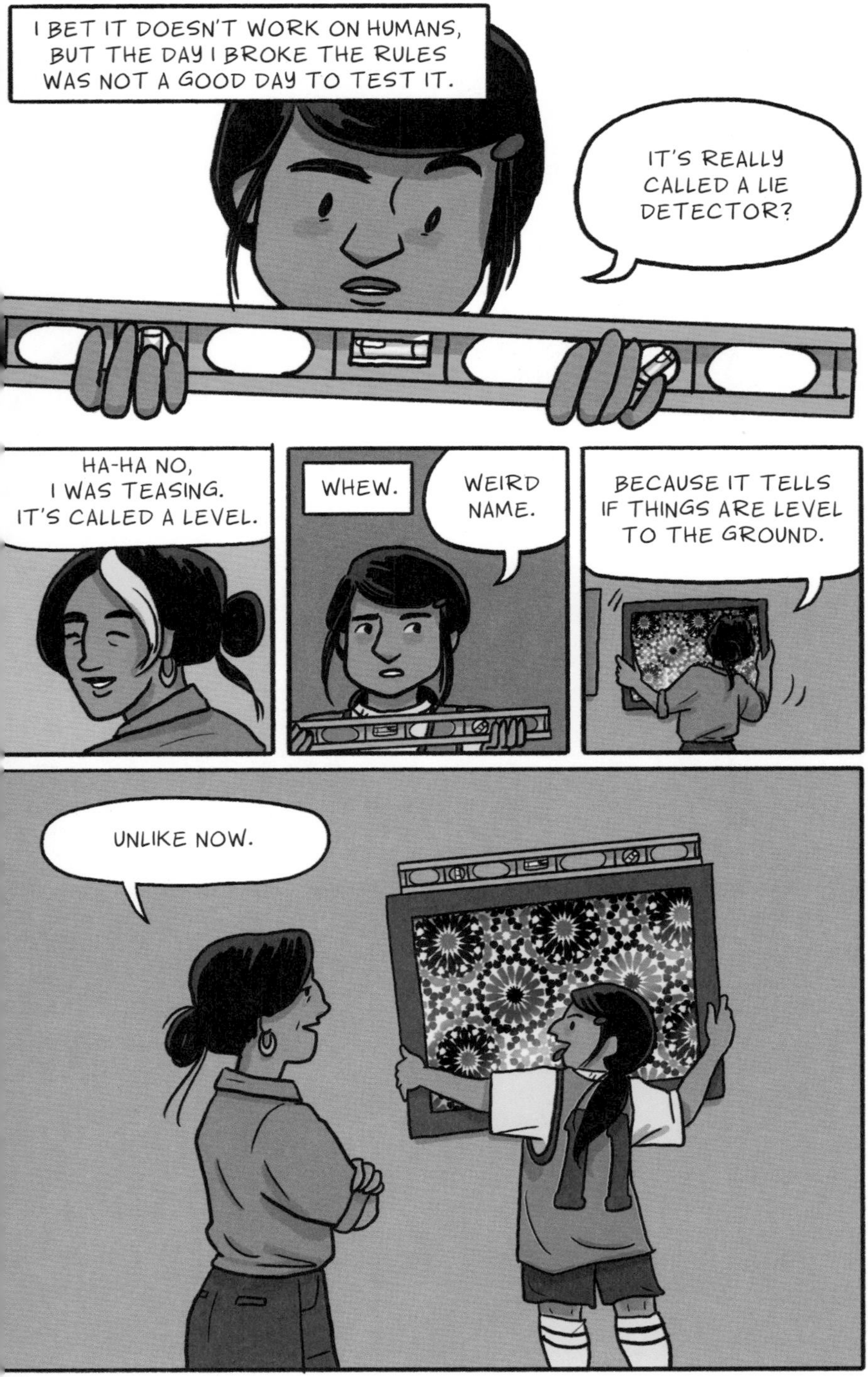
I BET IT DOESN'T WORK ON HUMANS, BUT THE DAY I BROKE THE RULES WAS NOT A GOOD DAY TO TEST IT.
IT'S REALLY CALLED A LIE DETECTOR?
HA-HA NO, I WAS TEASING. IT'S CALLED A LEVEL.
WHEW.
WEIRD NAME.
BECAUSE IT TELLS IF THINGS ARE LEVEL TO THE GROUND.
UNLIKE NOW.

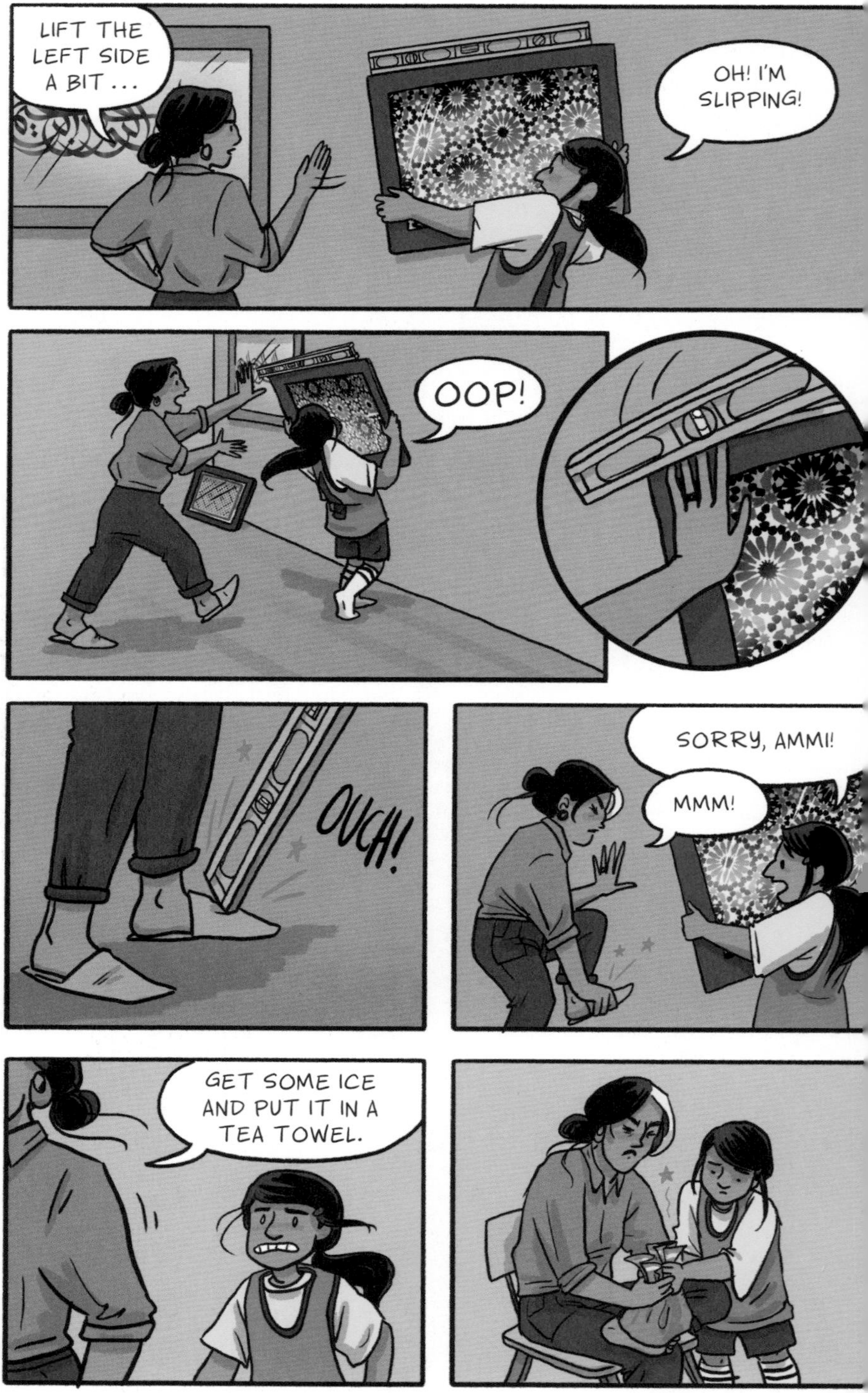
LIFT THE LEFT SIDE A BIT . . .
OH! I'M SLIPPING!
OOP!
OUCH!
SORRY, AMMI!
MMM!
GET SOME ICE AND PUT IT IN A TEA TOWEL.

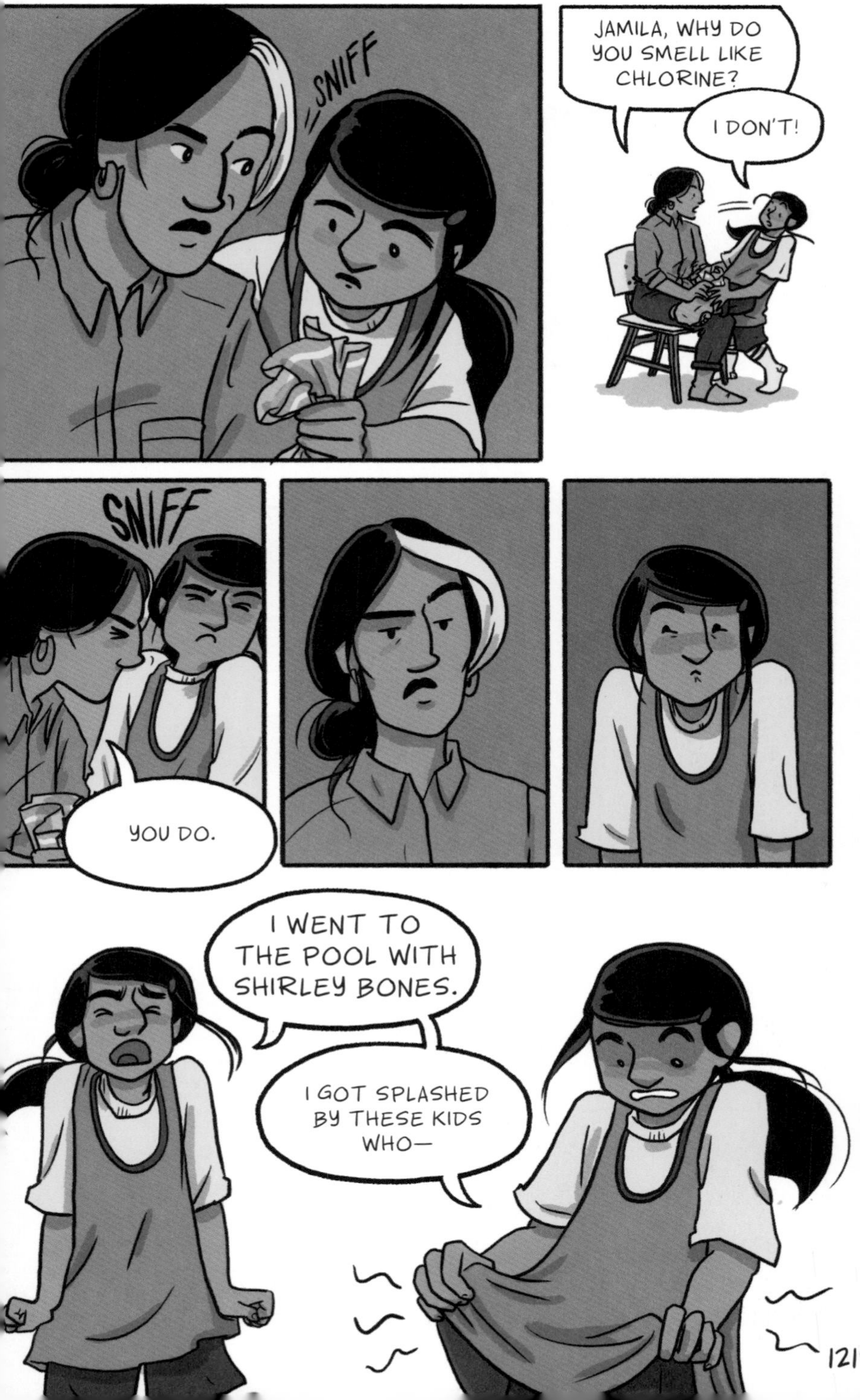
SNIFF
JAMILA, WHY DO YOU SMELL LIKE CHLORINE?
I DON'T!
SNIFF
YOU DO.
I WENT TO THE POOL WITH SHIRLEY BONES.
I GOT SPLASHED BY THESE KIDS WHO—

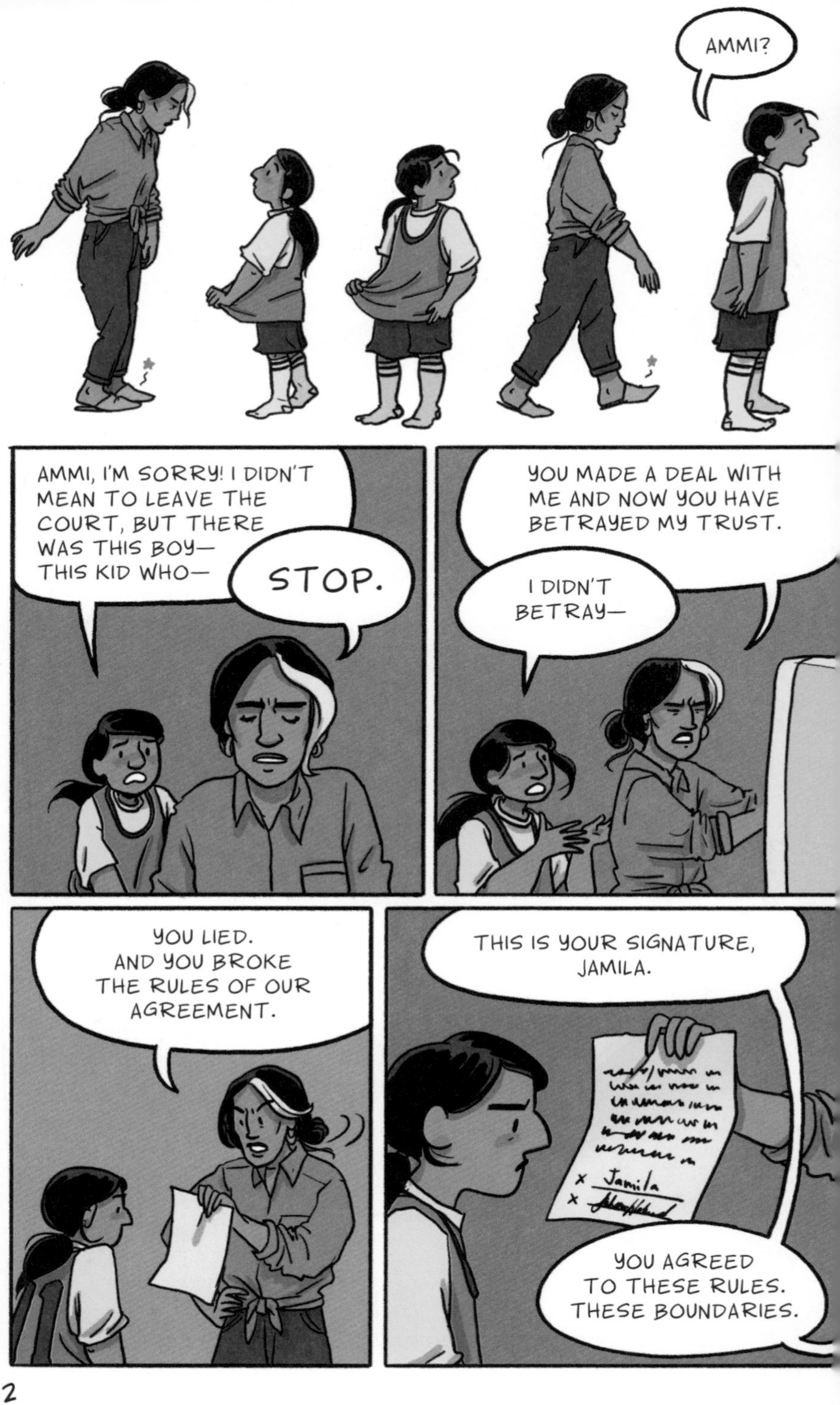
AMMI?
AMMI, I'M SORRY! I DIDN'T MEAN TO LEAVE THE COURT, BUT THERE WAS THIS BOY— THIS KID WHO—
STOP.
YOU MADE A DEAL WITH ME AND NOW YOU HAVE BETRAYED MY TRUST.
I DIDN'T BETRAY—
YOU LIED. AND YOU BROKE THE RULES OF OUR AGREEMENT.
THIS IS YOUR SIGNATURE, JAMILA.
Jamila
YOU AGREED TO THESE RULES. THESE BOUNDARIES.

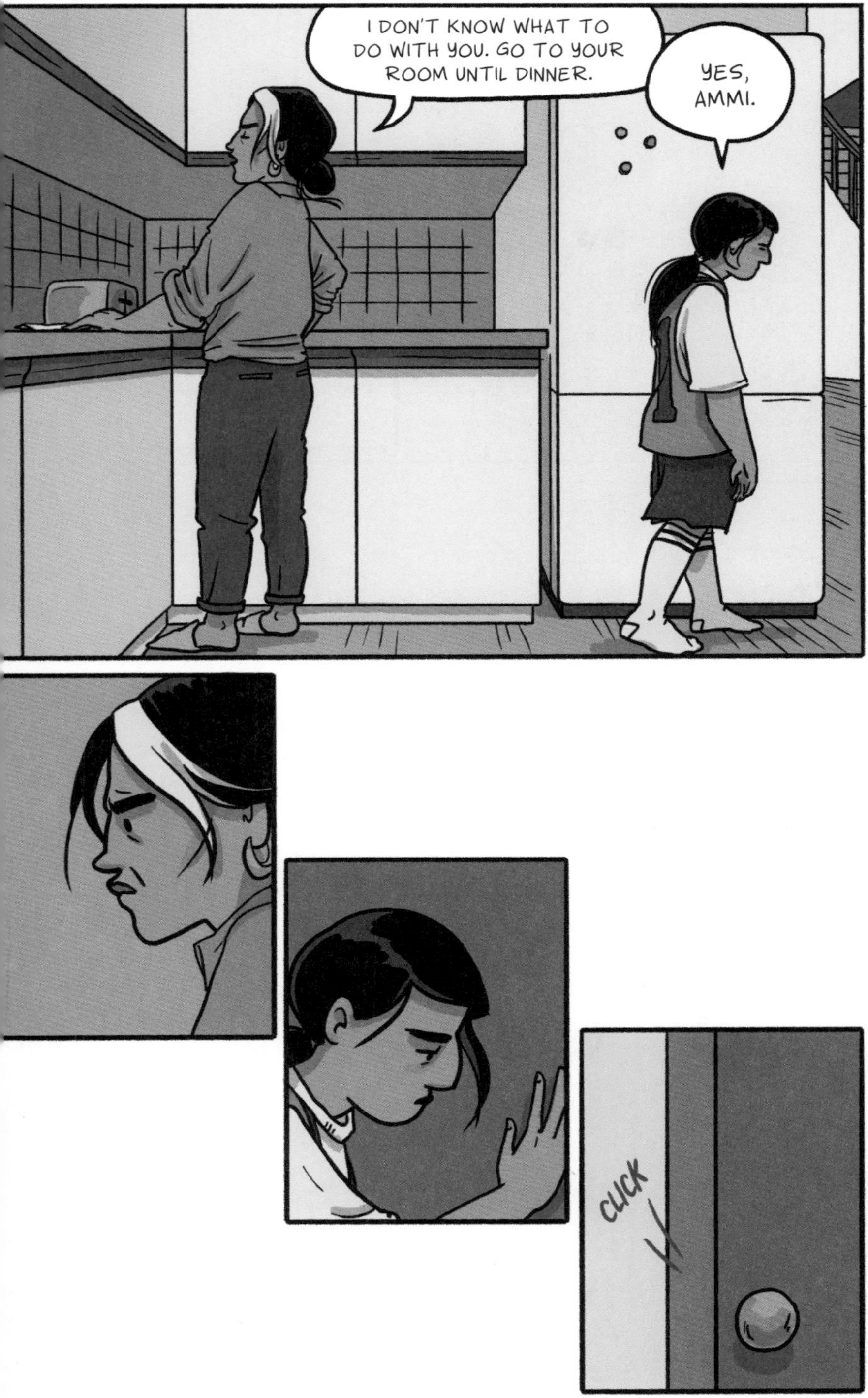
I DON'T KNOW WHAT TO DO WITH YOU. GO TO YOUR ROOM UNTIL DINNER.
YES, AMMI.
CLICK

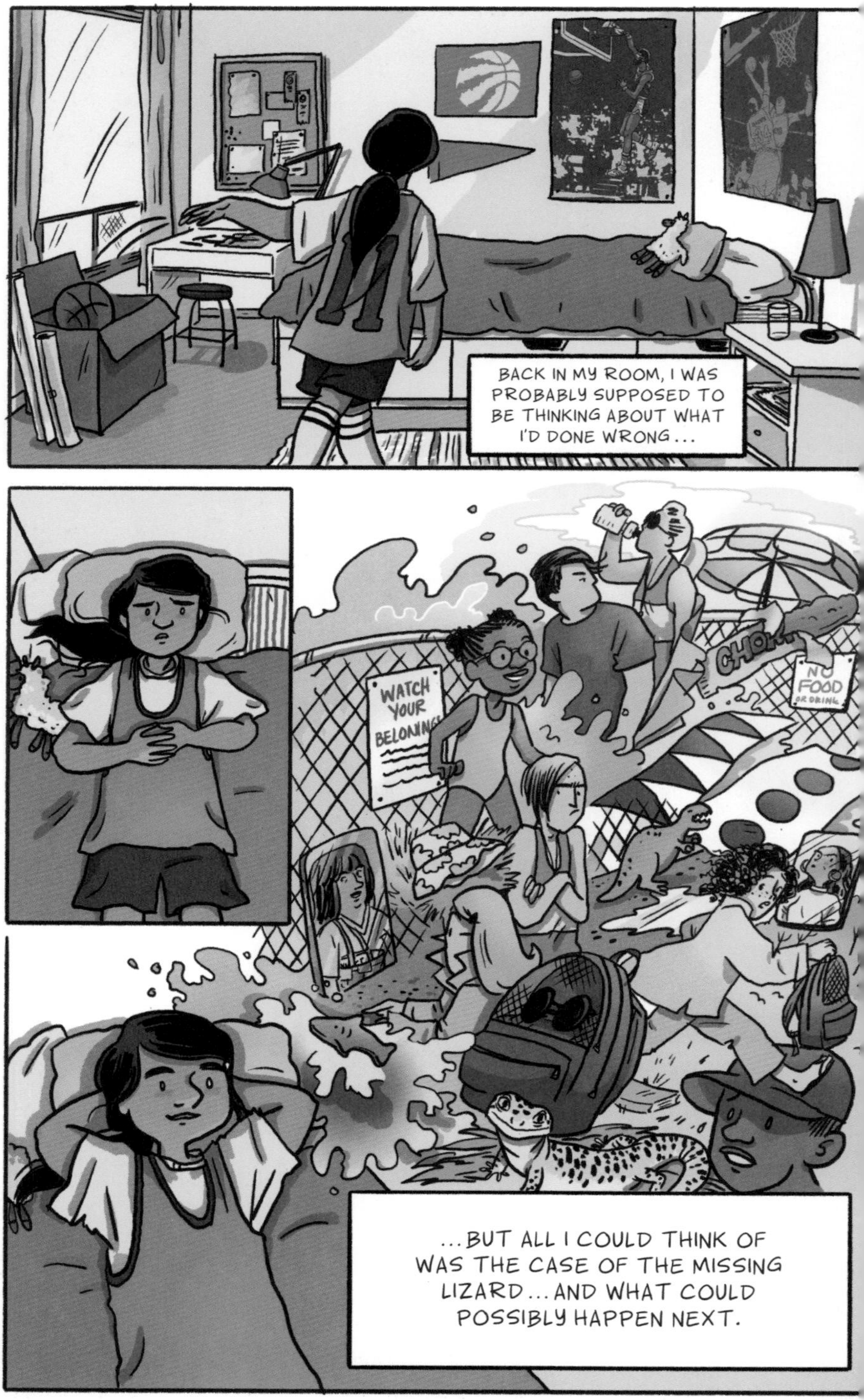
BACK IN MY ROOM, I WAS PROBABLY SUPPOSED TO BE THINKING ABOUT WHAT I'D DONE WRONG...
WATCH YOUR
NO FOOD
...BUT ALL I COULD THINK OF WAS THE CASE OF THE MISSING LIZARD... AND WHAT COULD POSSIBLY HAPPEN NEXT.

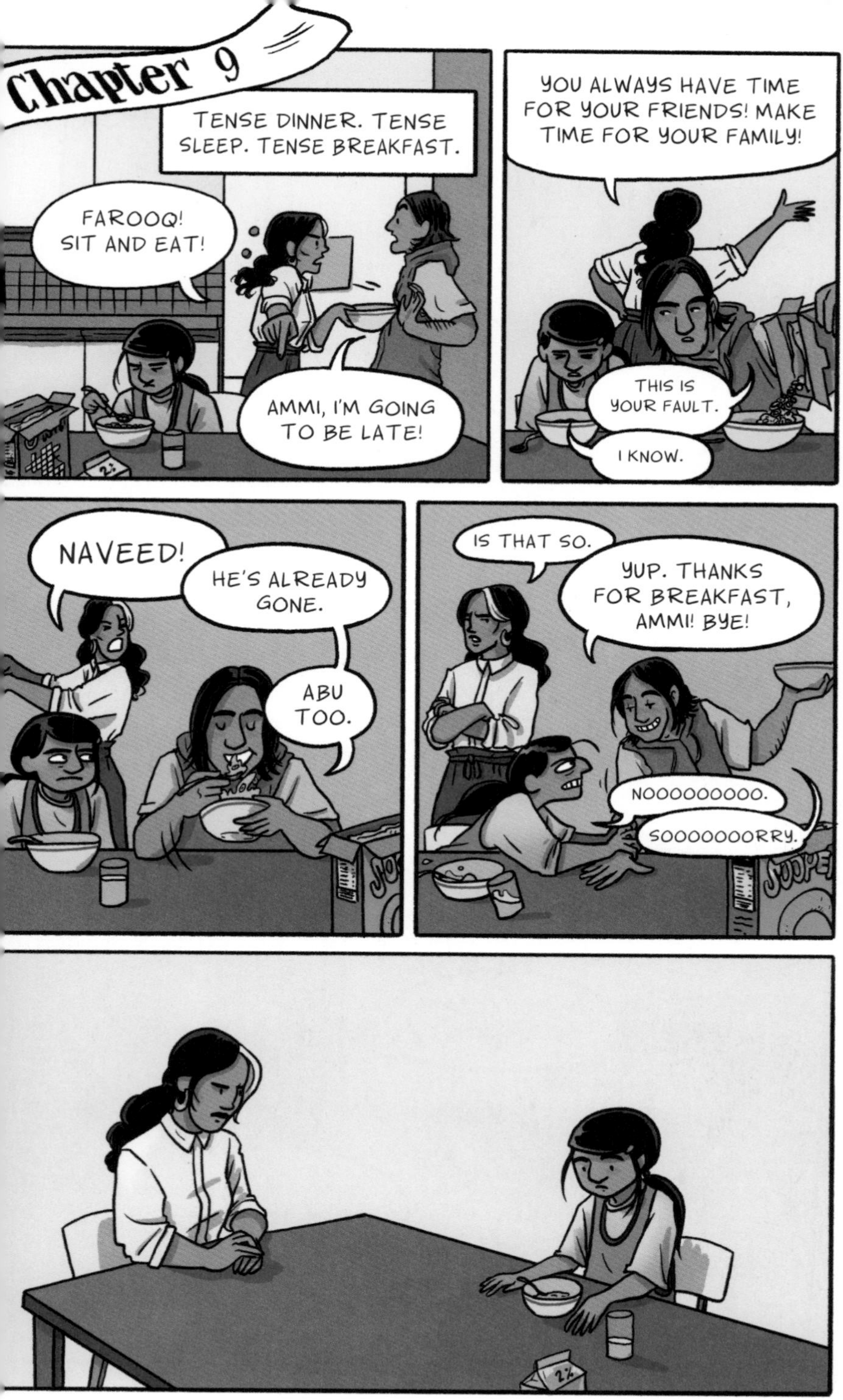
Chapter 9
TENSE DINNER. TENSE SLEEP. TENSE BREAKFAST.
FAROOQ! SIT AND EAT!
AMMI, I'M GOING TO BE LATE!
YOU ALWAYS HAVE TIME FOR YOUR FRIENDS! MAKE TIME FOR YOUR FAMILY!
THIS IS YOUR FAULT.
I KNOW.
NAVEED!
HE'S ALREADY GONE.
ABU TOO.
IS THAT SO.
YUP. THANKS FOR BREAKFAST, AMMI! BYE!
NOOOOOOOOO.
SOOOOOOORRY.

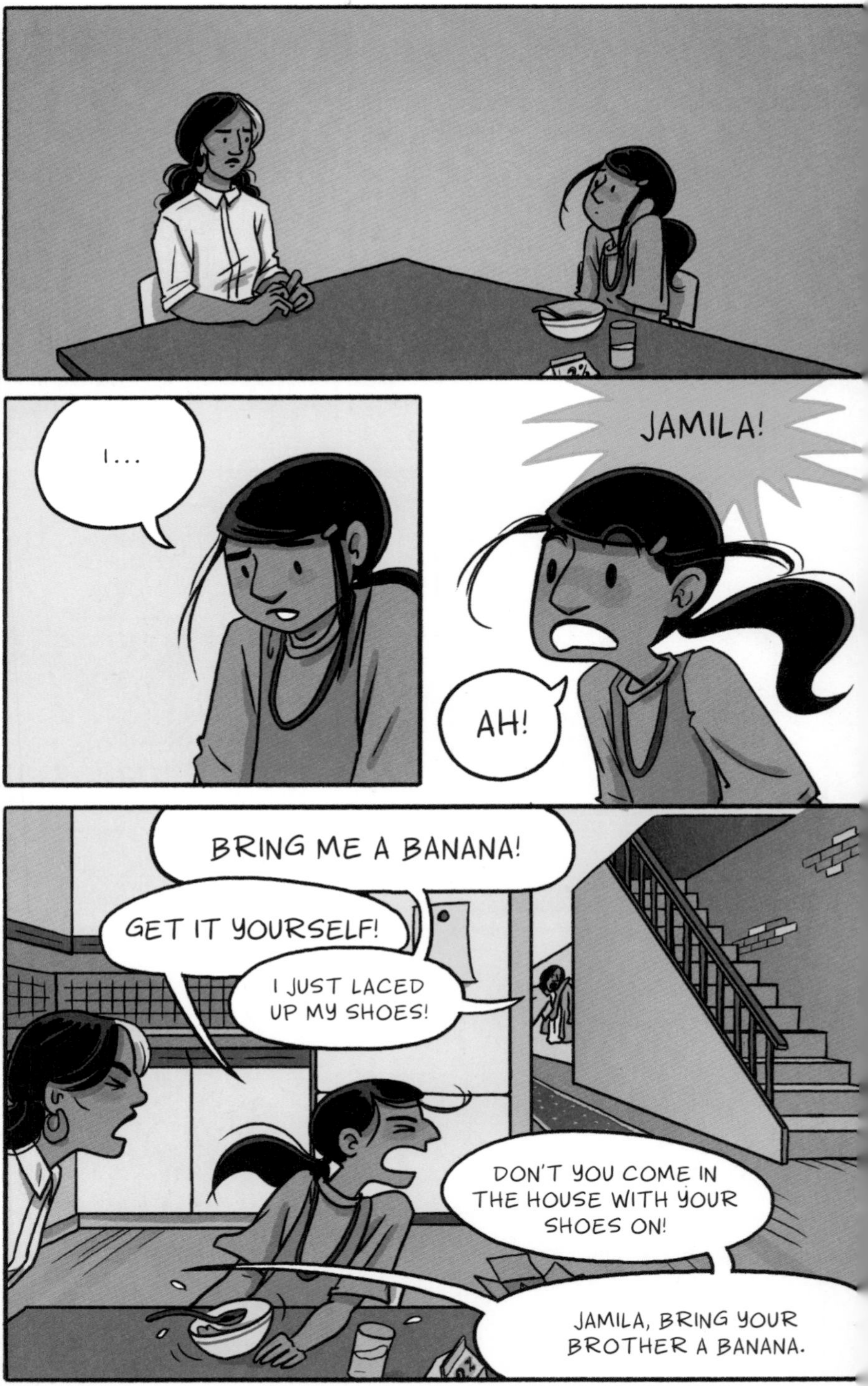
I...
JAMILA!
AH!
BRING ME A BANANA!
GET IT YOURSELF!
I JUST LACED UP MY SHOES!
DON'T YOU COME IN THE HOUSE WITH YOUR SHOES ON!
JAMILA, BRING YOUR BROTHER A BANANA.

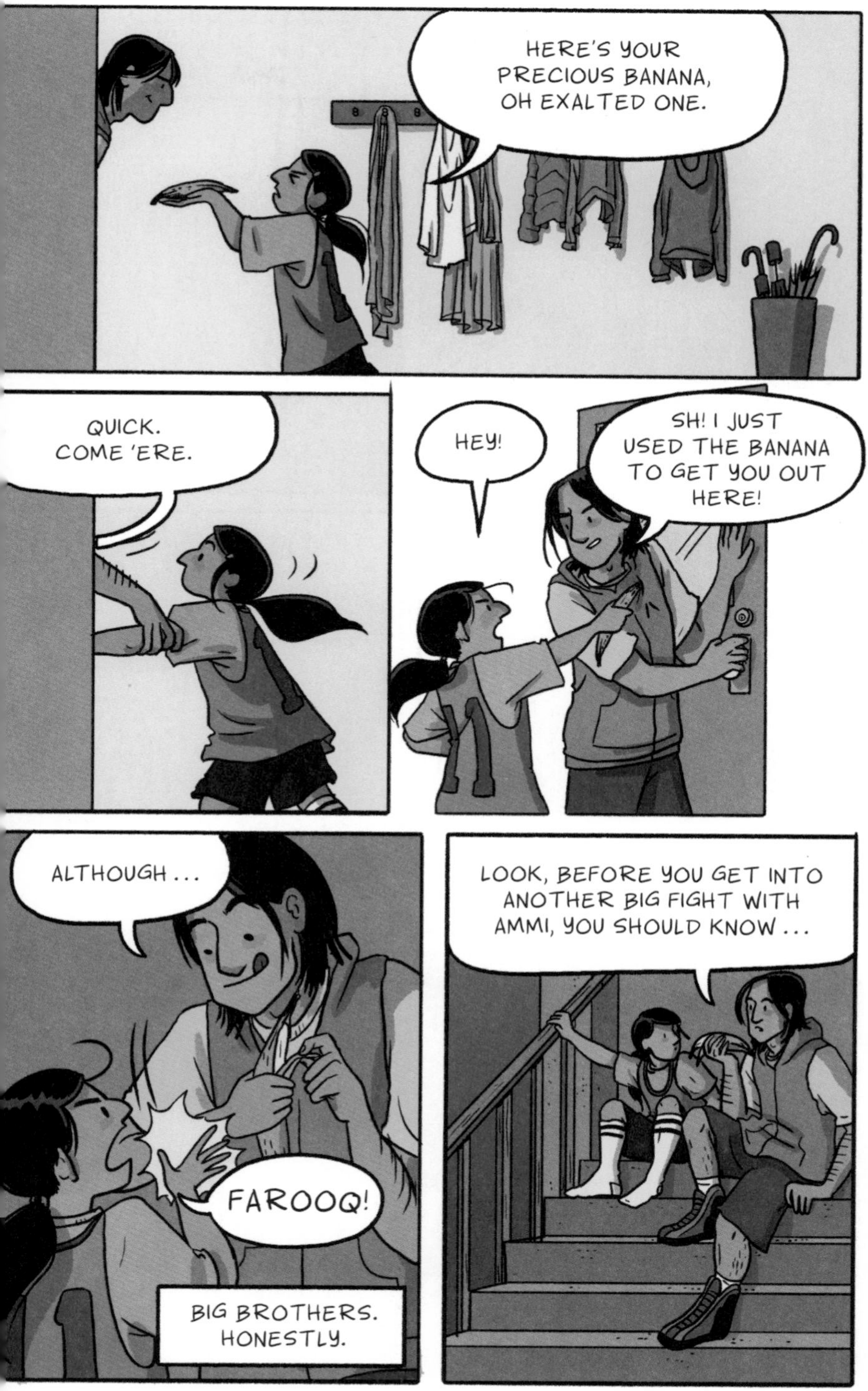
HERE'S YOUR PRECIOUS BANANA, OH EXALTED ONE.
QUICK. COME 'ERE.
HEY!
SH! I JUST USED THE BANANA TO GET YOU OUT HERE!
ALTHOUGH . . .
FAROOQ!
BIG BROTHERS. HONESTLY.
LOOK, BEFORE YOU GET INTO ANOTHER BIG FIGHT WITH AMMI, YOU SHOULD KNOW . . .

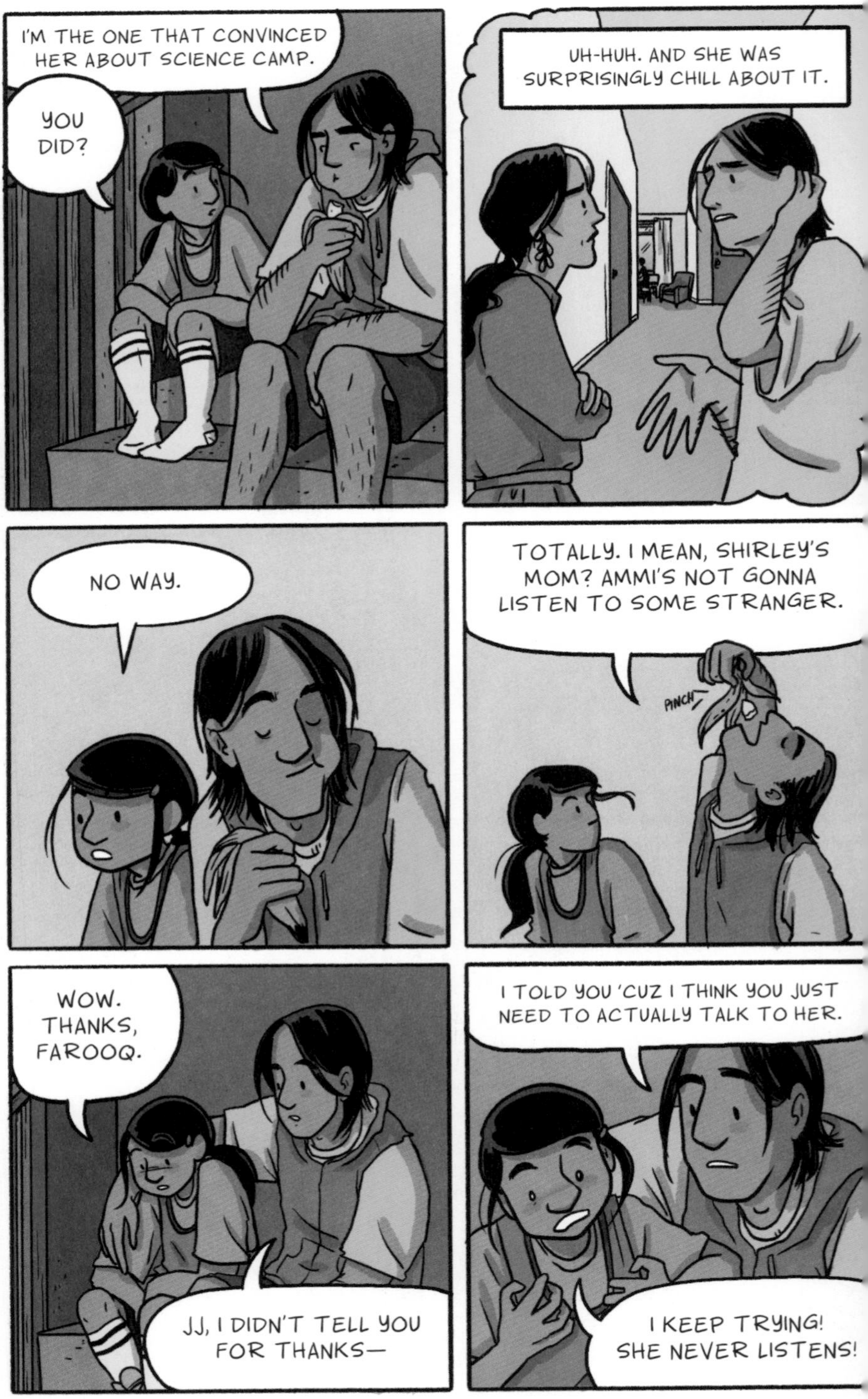
I'M THE ONE THAT CONVINCED HER ABOUT SCIENCE CAMP.
YOU DID?
UH-HUH. AND SHE WAS SURPRISINGLY CHILL ABOUT IT.
NO WAY.
TOTALLY. I MEAN, SHIRLEY'S MOM? AMMI'S NOT GONNA LISTEN TO SOME STRANGER.
PINCH
WOW. THANKS, FAROOQ.
JJ, I DIDN'T TELL YOU FOR THANKS—
I TOLD YOU 'CUZ I THINK YOU JUST NEED TO ACTUALLY TALK TO HER.
I KEEP TRYING! SHE NEVER LISTENS!

I KNOW, BUT SHE LISTENED THIS ONE TIME. SO MAYBE SHE WILL AGAIN...?

WHY'D YOU SNEAK OFF ANYWAY? YOU KNOW AMMI'S THE WORLD'S BEST DETECTIVE.

HA! NOT ANYMORE.

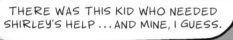

THERE WAS THIS KID WHO NEEDED SHIRLEY'S HELP...AND MINE, I GUESS.

SEE! IT'S NOT LIKE YOU TO SNEAK OFF FOR PRANKS

(LIKE I WOULD HAVE).

TELL HER THAT!

I TRIED YESTERDAY!

I KNOW, BUT SHE'S COOLED OFF BY NOW.

I GOTTA GO. I REALLY AM LATE.

SMACK

TRY HER AGAIN!

HEY!

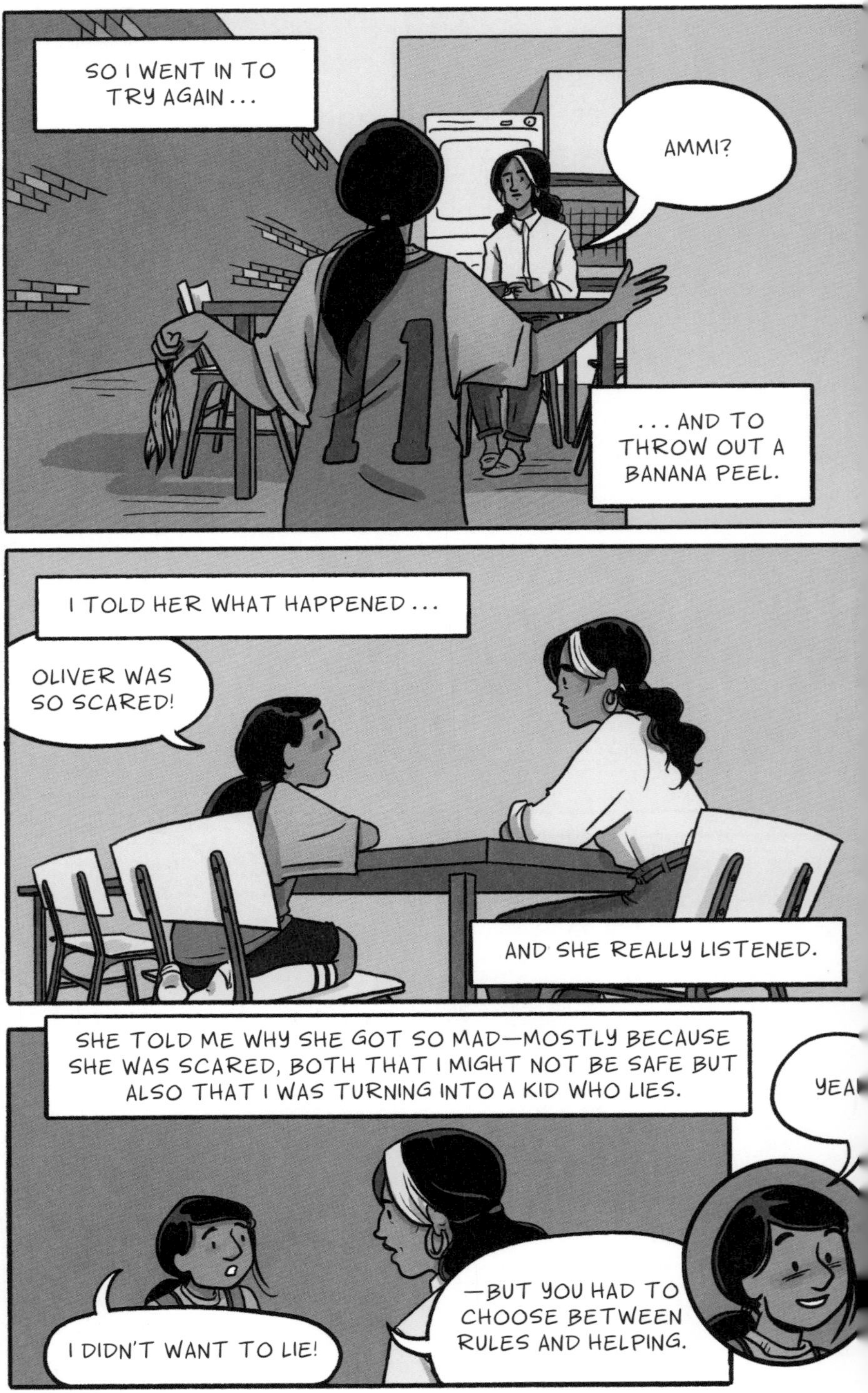
SO I WENT IN TO TRY AGAIN . . .
AMMI?
. . . AND TO THROW OUT A BANANA PEEL.
I TOLD HER WHAT HAPPENED . . .
OLIVER WAS SO SCARED!
AND SHE REALLY LISTENED.
SHE TOLD ME WHY SHE GOT SO MAD—MOSTLY BECAUSE SHE WAS SCARED, BOTH THAT I MIGHT NOT BE SAFE BUT ALSO THAT I WAS TURNING INTO A KID WHO LIES.
I DIDN'T WANT TO LIE!
—BUT YOU HAD TO CHOOSE BETWEEN RULES AND HELPING.

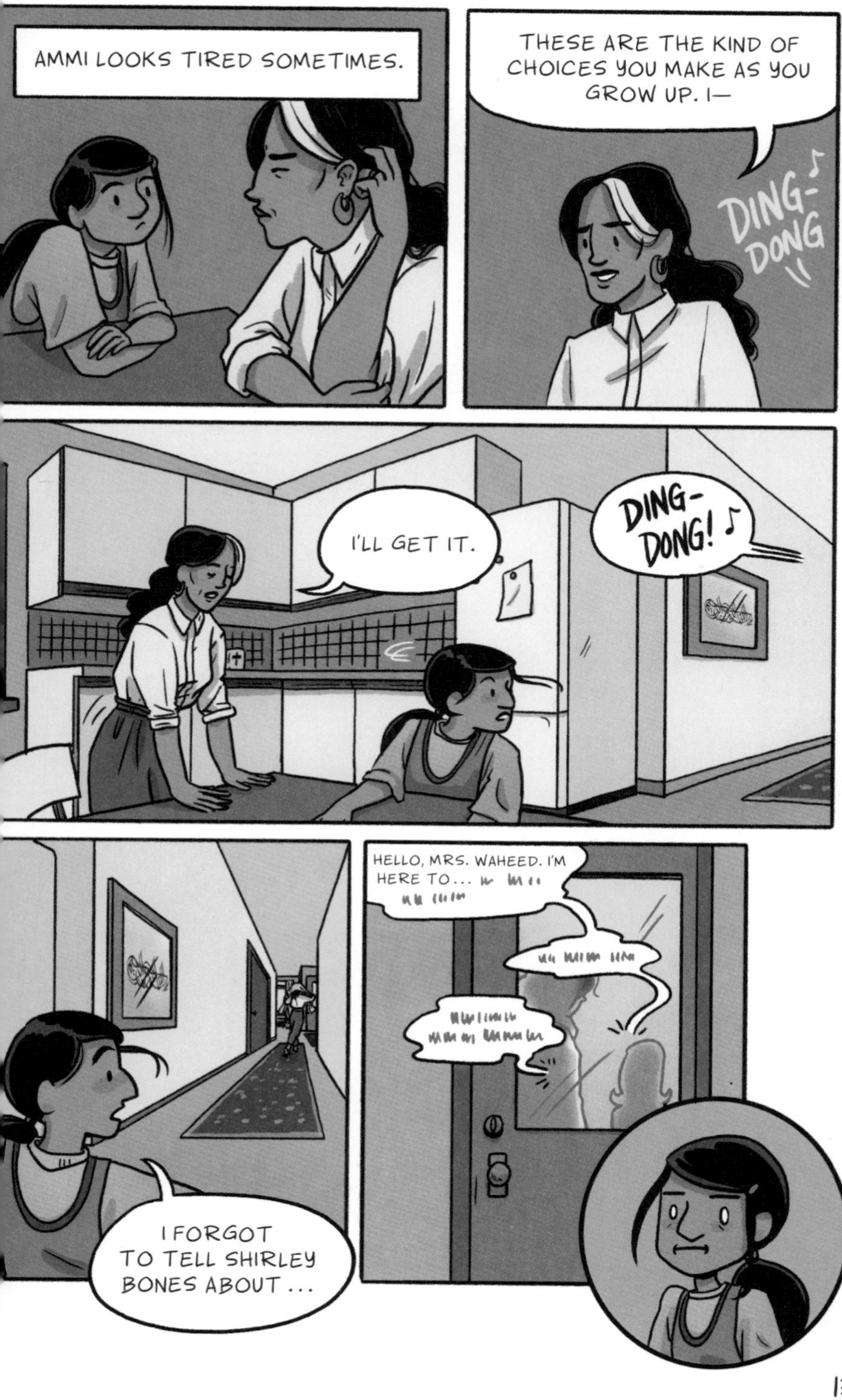
AMMI LOOKS TIRED SOMETIMES.
THESE ARE THE KIND OF CHOICES YOU MAKE AS YOU GROW UP. I—
DING-DONG
I'LL GET IT.
DING-DONG!
HELLO, MRS. WAHEED. I'M HERE TO...
I FORGOT TO TELL SHIRLEY BONES ABOUT...

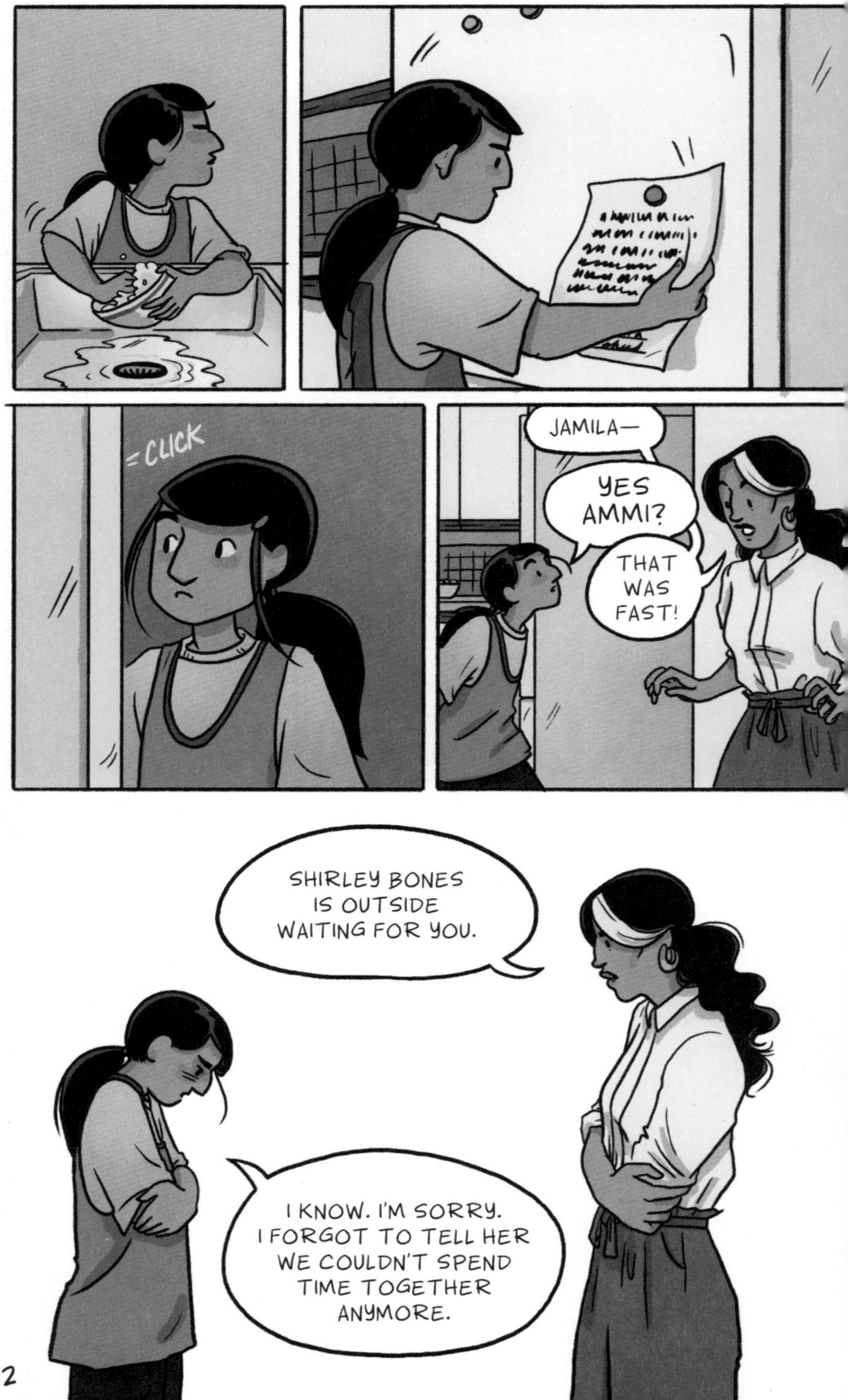
CLICK
JAMILA—
YES AMMI?
THAT WAS FAST!
SHIRLEY BONES IS OUTSIDE WAITING FOR YOU.
I KNOW. I'M SORRY. I FORGOT TO TELL HER WE COULDN'T SPEND TIME TOGETHER ANYMORE.

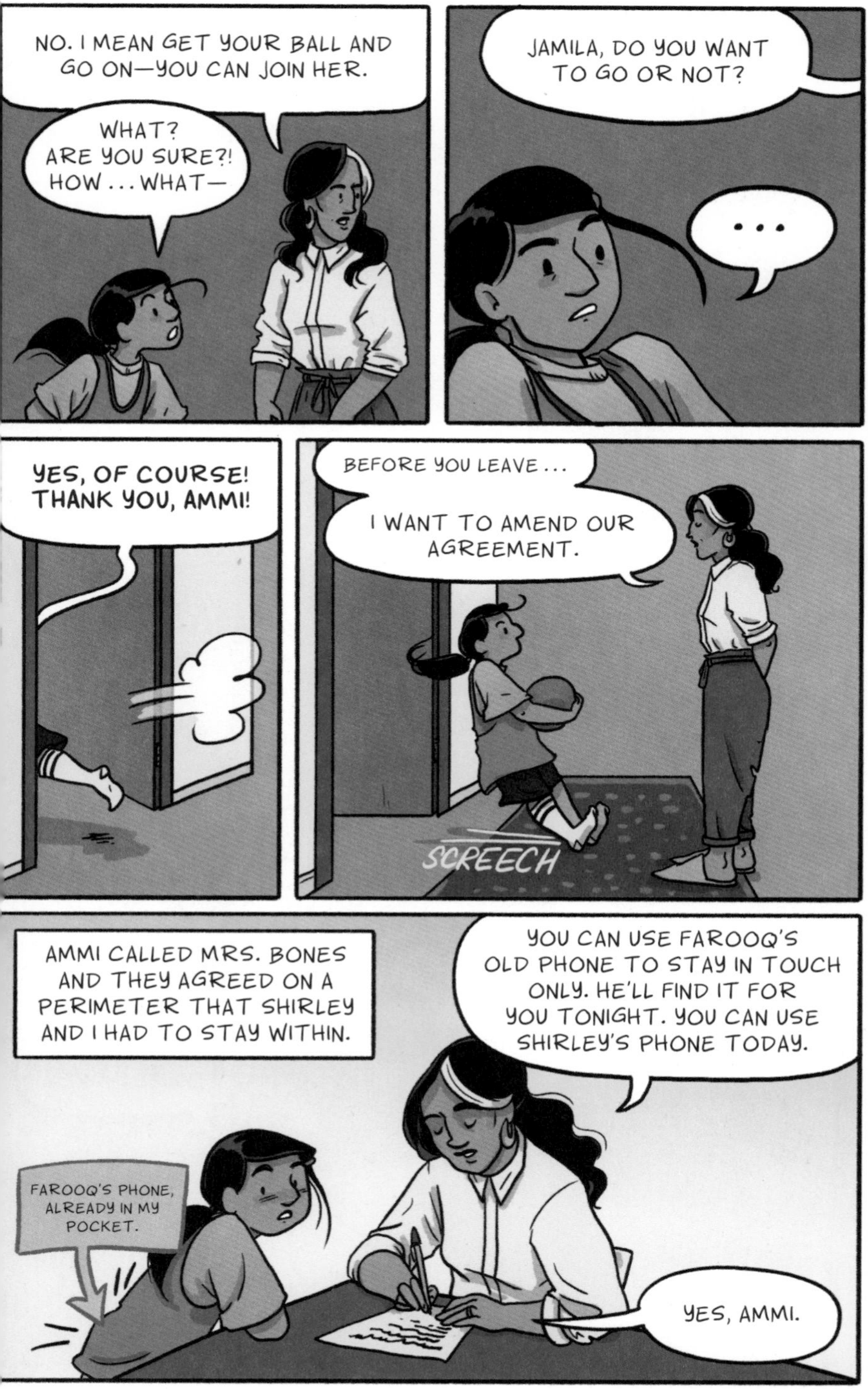
NO. I MEAN GET YOUR BALL AND GO ON—YOU CAN JOIN HER.
WHAT? ARE YOU SURE?! HOW . . . WHAT—
JAMILA, DO YOU WANT TO GO OR NOT?
. . .
YES, OF COURSE! THANK YOU, AMMI!
BEFORE YOU LEAVE . . .
I WANT TO AMEND OUR AGREEMENT.
SCREECH
AMMI CALLED MRS. BONES AND THEY AGREED ON A PERIMETER THAT SHIRLEY AND I HAD TO STAY WITHIN.
YOU CAN USE FAROOQ'S OLD PHONE TO STAY IN TOUCH ONLY. HE'LL FIND IT FOR YOU TONIGHT. YOU CAN USE SHIRLEY'S PHONE TODAY.
FAROOQ'S PHONE, ALREADY IN MY POCKET.
YES, AMMI.

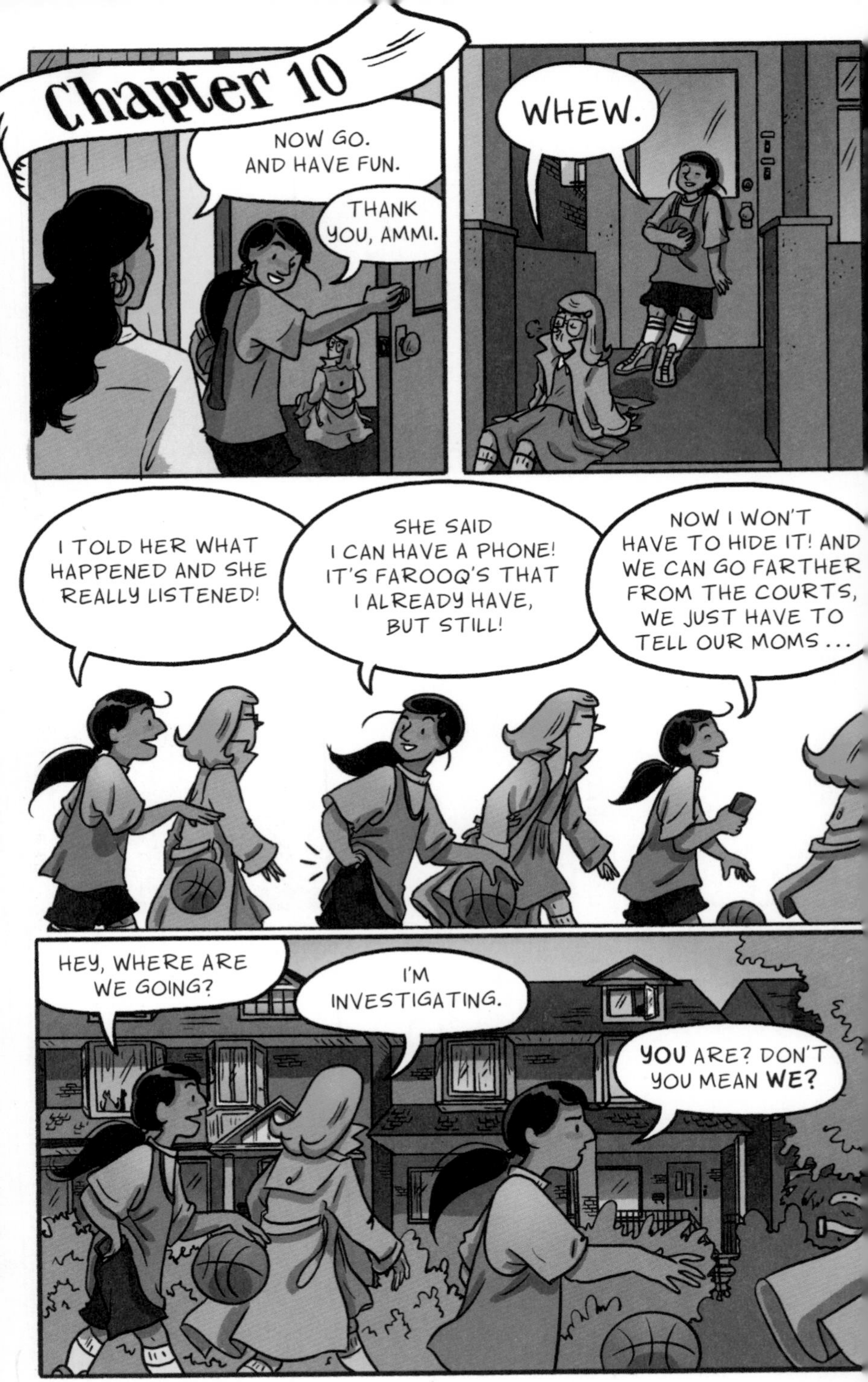
Chapter 10
NOW GO. AND HAVE FUN.
THANK YOU, AMMI.
WHEW.
I TOLD HER WHAT HAPPENED AND SHE REALLY LISTENED!
SHE SAID I CAN HAVE A PHONE! IT'S FAROOQ'S THAT I ALREADY HAVE, BUT STILL!
NOW I WON'T HAVE TO HIDE IT! AND WE CAN GO FARTHER FROM THE COURTS, WE JUST HAVE TO TELL OUR MOMS . . .
HEY, WHERE ARE WE GOING?
I'M INVESTIGATING.
YOU ARE? DON'T YOU MEAN **WE**?

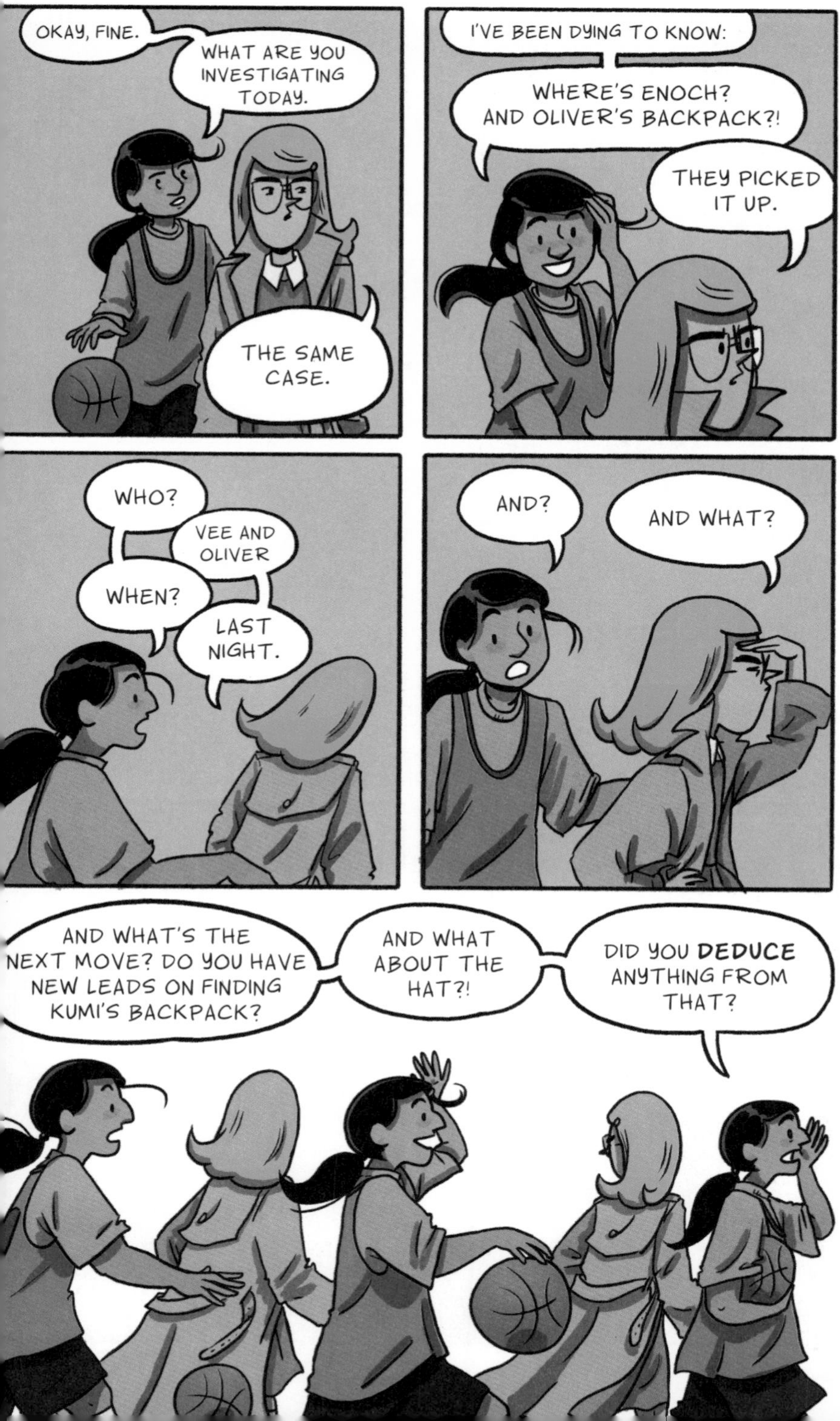
OKAY, FINE.
WHAT ARE YOU INVESTIGATING TODAY.
THE SAME CASE.
I'VE BEEN DYING TO KNOW:
WHERE'S ENOCH? AND OLIVER'S BACKPACK?!
THEY PICKED IT UP.
WHO?
VEE AND OLIVER
WHEN?
LAST NIGHT.
AND?
AND WHAT?
AND WHAT'S THE NEXT MOVE? DO YOU HAVE NEW LEADS ON FINDING KUMI'S BACKPACK?
AND WHAT ABOUT THE HAT?!
DID YOU **DEDUCE** ANYTHING FROM THAT?

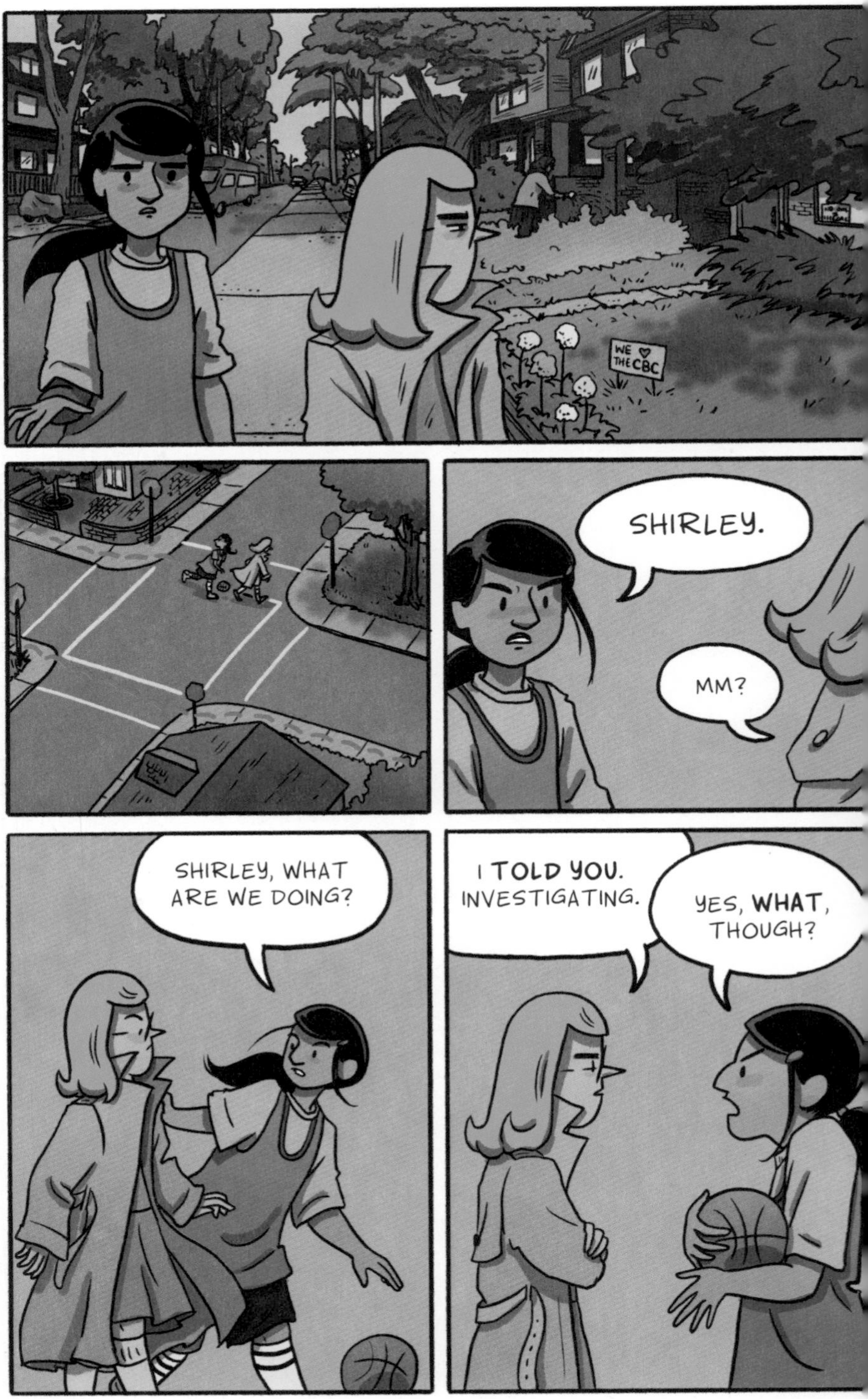
WE ♥ THE CBC
SHIRLEY.
MM?
SHIRLEY, WHAT ARE WE DOING?
I **TOLD YOU.** INVESTIGATING.
YES, **WHAT**, THOUGH?

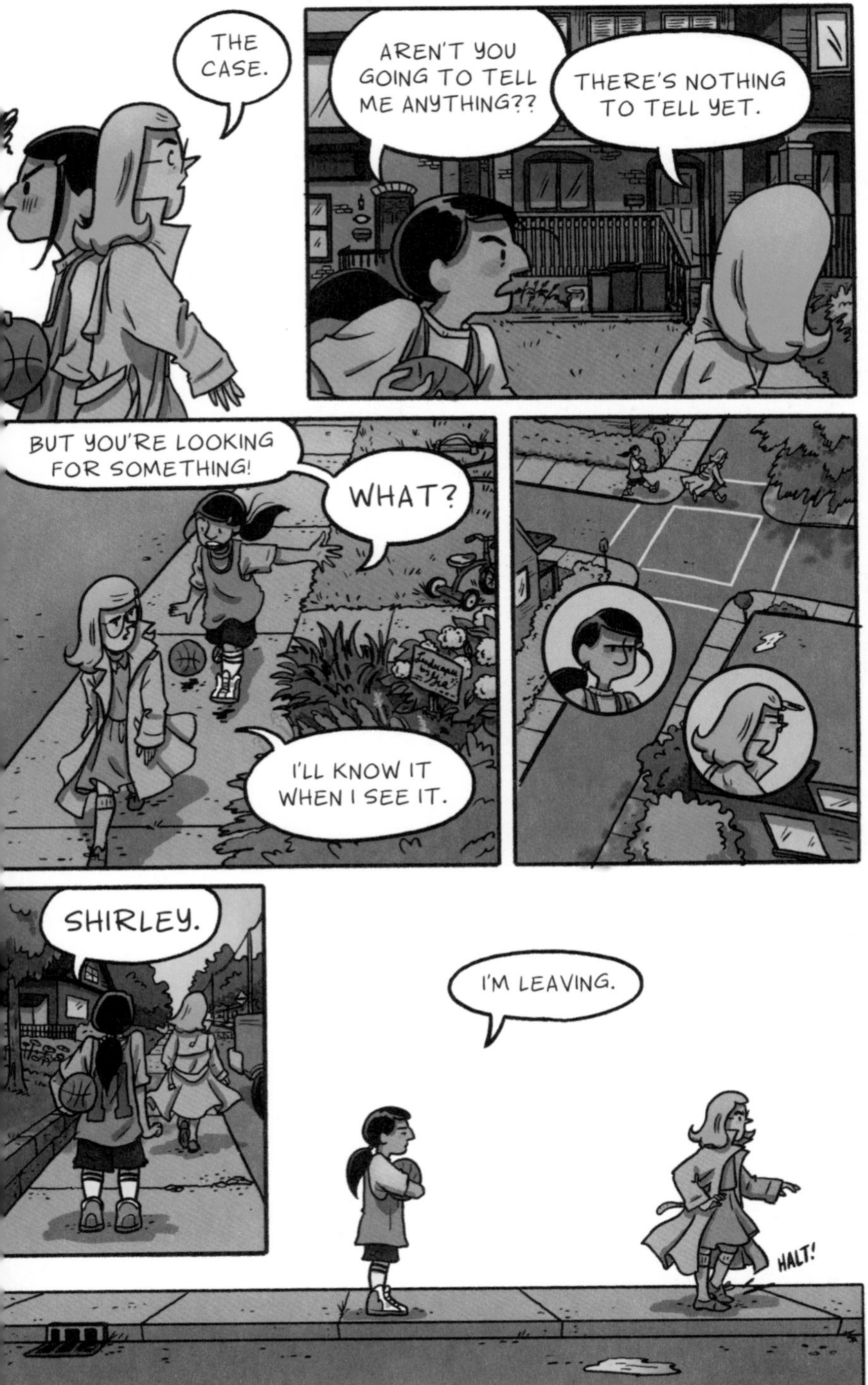
THE CASE.
AREN'T YOU GOING TO TELL ME ANYTHING??
THERE'S NOTHING TO TELL YET.
BUT YOU'RE LOOKING FOR SOMETHING!
WHAT?
I'LL KNOW IT WHEN I SEE IT.
SHIRLEY.
I'M LEAVING.
HALT!

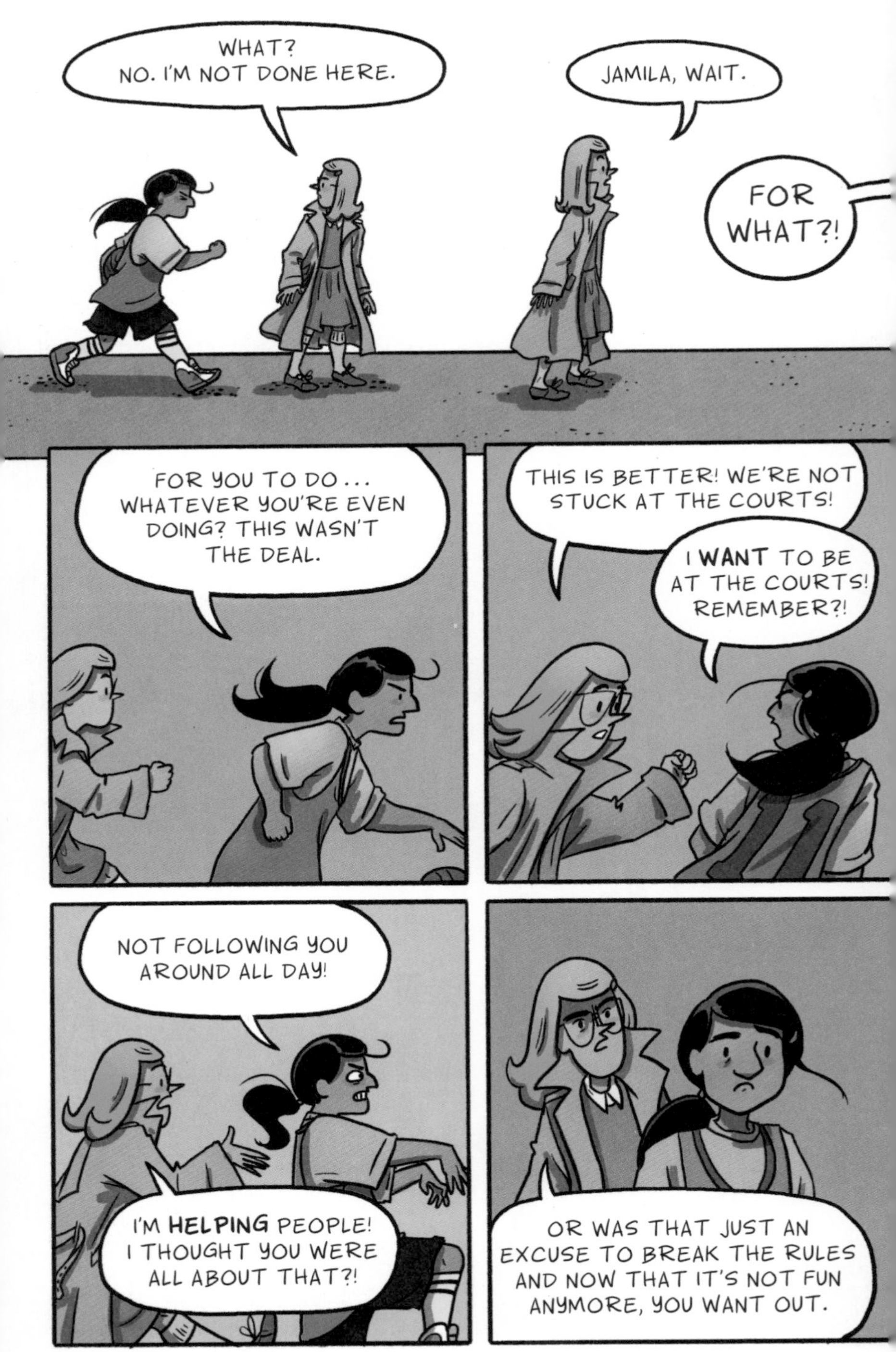
WHAT?
NO. I'M NOT DONE HERE.
JAMILA, WAIT.
FOR WHAT?!
FOR YOU TO DO... WHATEVER YOU'RE EVEN DOING? THIS WASN'T THE DEAL.
THIS IS BETTER! WE'RE NOT STUCK AT THE COURTS!
I **WANT** TO BE AT THE COURTS! REMEMBER?!
NOT FOLLOWING YOU AROUND ALL DAY!
I'M **HELPING** PEOPLE! I THOUGHT YOU WERE ALL ABOUT THAT?!
OR WAS THAT JUST AN EXCUSE TO BREAK THE RULES AND NOW THAT IT'S NOT FUN ANYMORE, YOU WANT OUT.

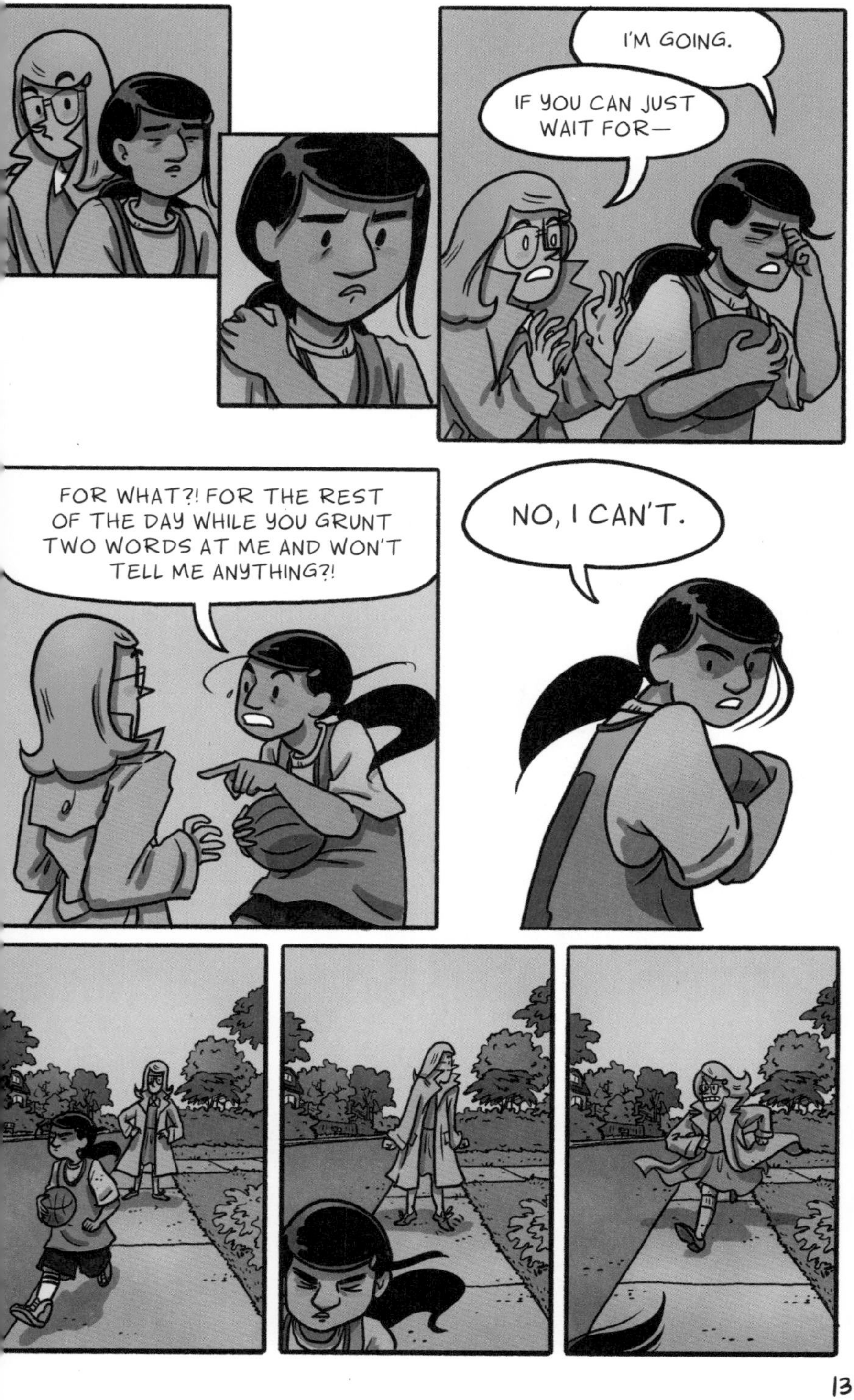
I'M GOING.
IF YOU CAN JUST WAIT FOR—
FOR WHAT?! FOR THE REST OF THE DAY WHILE YOU GRUNT TWO WORDS AT ME AND WON'T TELL ME ANYTHING?!
NO, I CAN'T.

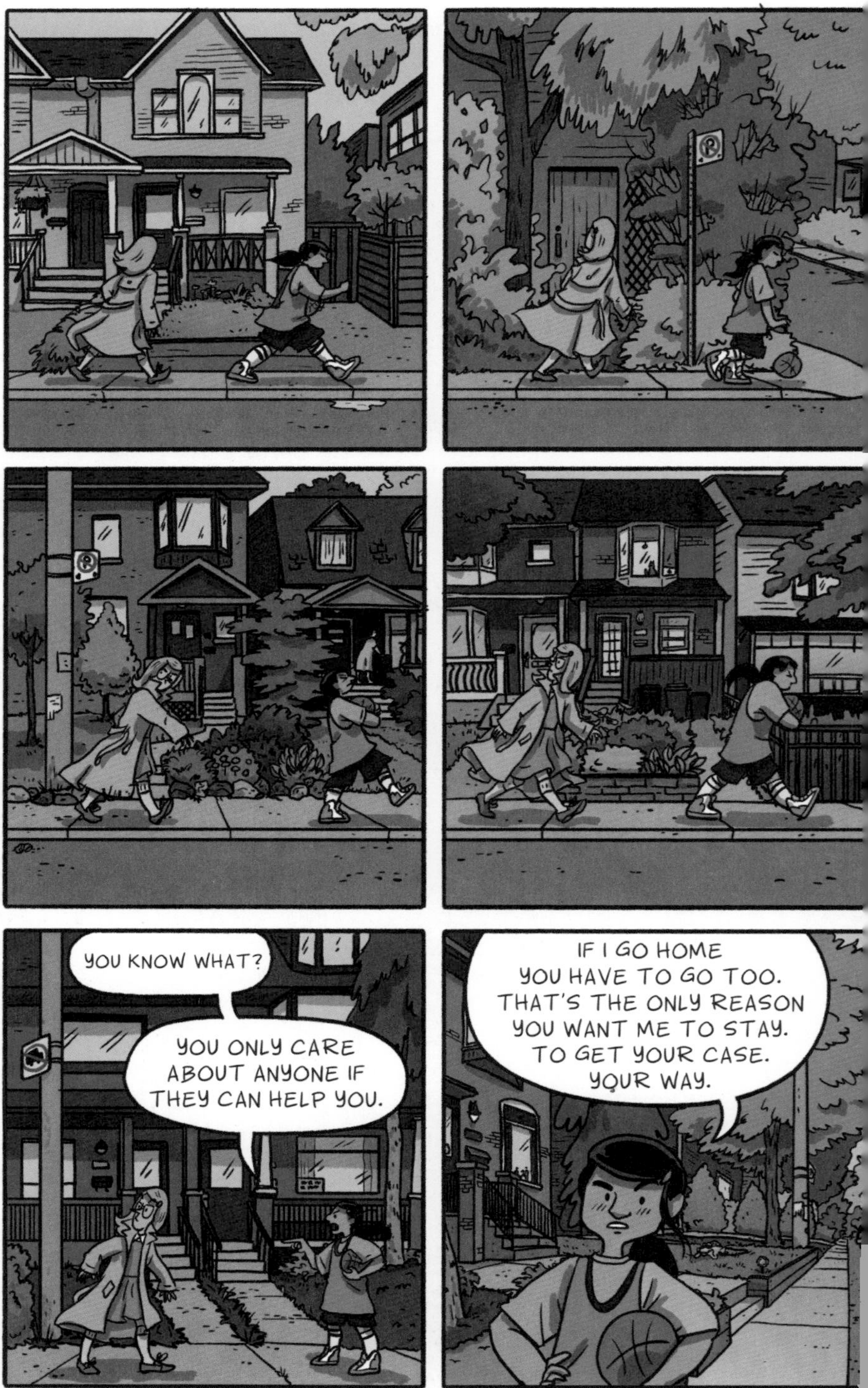
YOU KNOW WHAT?
YOU ONLY CARE ABOUT ANYONE IF THEY CAN HELP YOU.
IF I GO HOME YOU HAVE TO GO TOO. THAT'S THE ONLY REASON YOU WANT ME TO STAY. TO GET YOUR CASE. YOUR WAY.

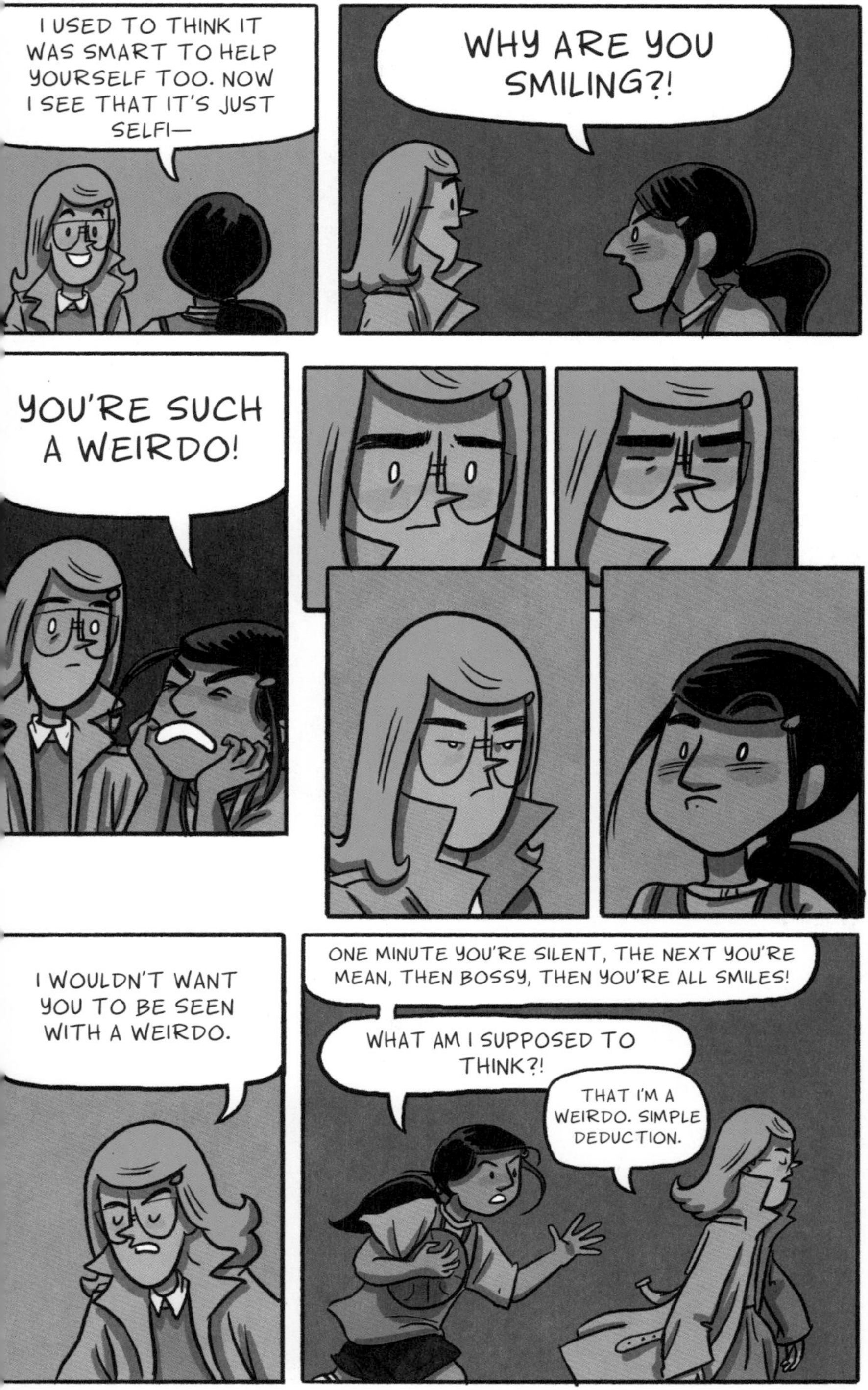
I USED TO THINK IT WAS SMART TO HELP YOURSELF TOO. NOW I SEE THAT IT'S JUST SELFI—
WHY ARE YOU SMILING?!
YOU'RE SUCH A WEIRDO!
I WOULDN'T WANT YOU TO BE SEEN WITH A WEIRDO.
ONE MINUTE YOU'RE SILENT, THE NEXT YOU'RE MEAN, THEN BOSSY, THEN YOU'RE ALL SMILES!
WHAT AM I SUPPOSED TO THINK?!
THAT I'M A WEIRDO. SIMPLE DEDUCTION.

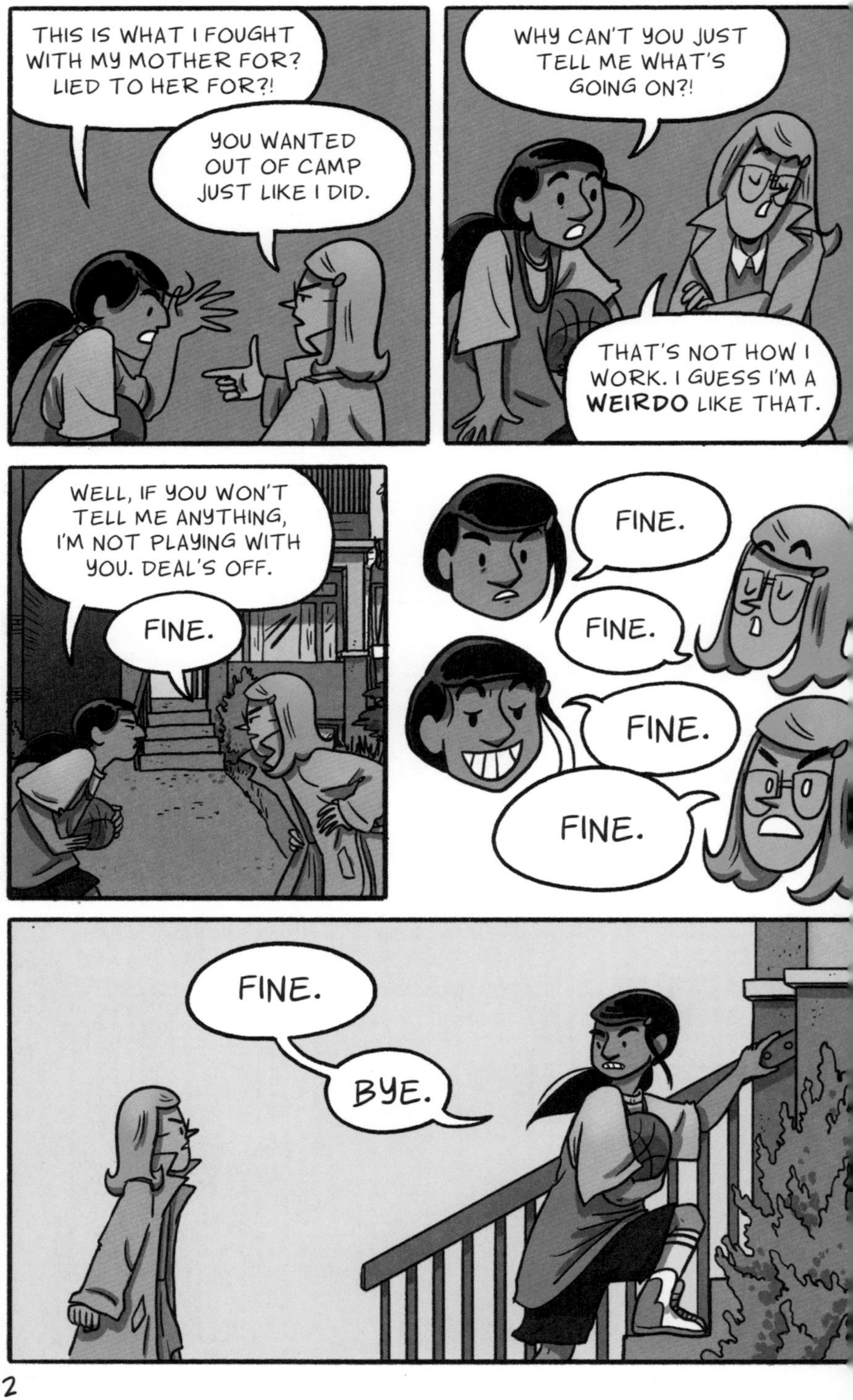
THIS IS WHAT I FOUGHT WITH MY MOTHER FOR? LIED TO HER FOR?!
YOU WANTED OUT OF CAMP JUST LIKE I DID.
WHY CAN'T YOU JUST TELL ME WHAT'S GOING ON?!
THAT'S NOT HOW I WORK. I GUESS I'M A **WEIRDO** LIKE THAT.
WELL, IF YOU WON'T TELL ME ANYTHING, I'M NOT PLAYING WITH YOU. DEAL'S OFF.
FINE.
FINE.
FINE.
FINE.
FINE.
FINE.
BYE.

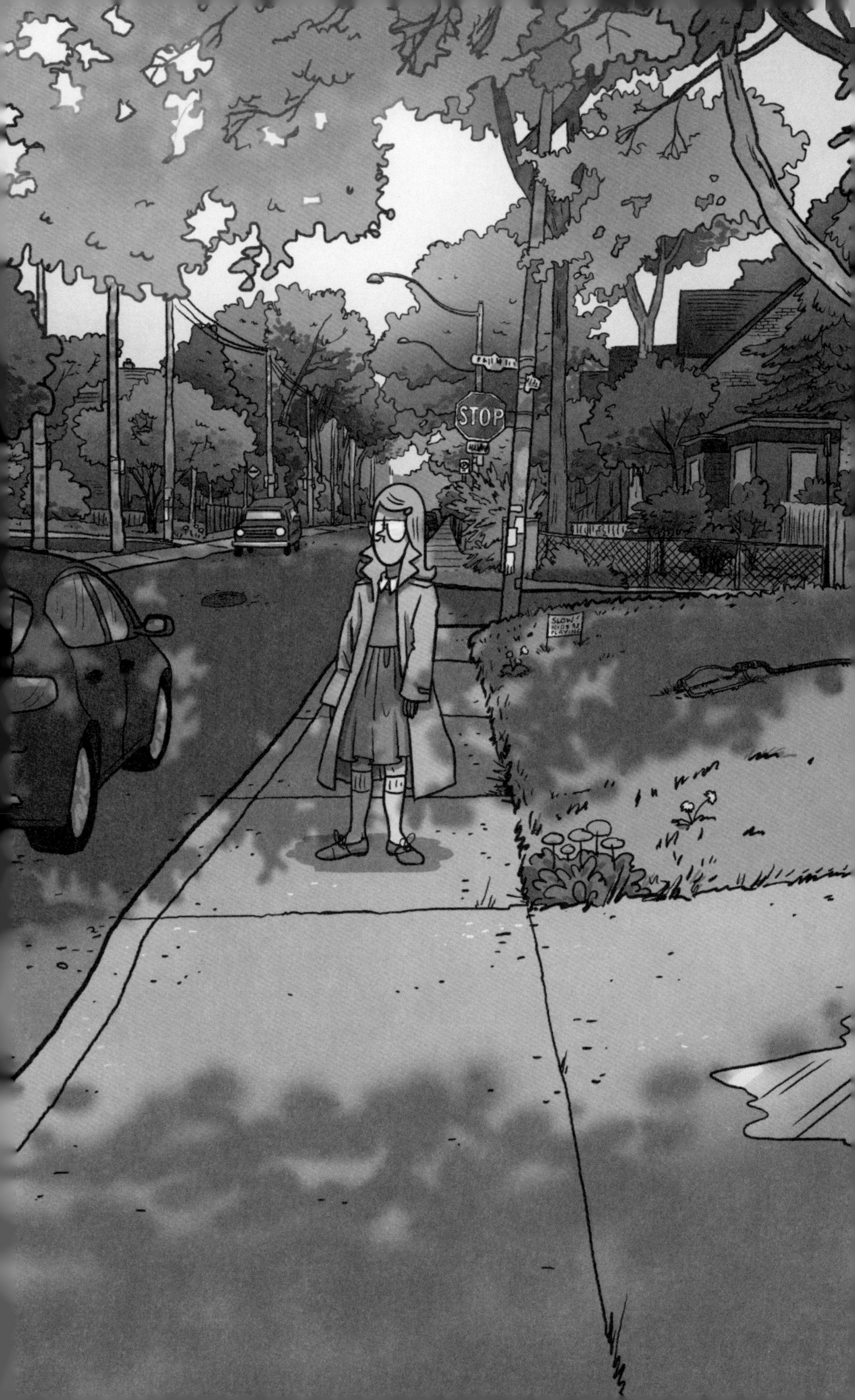
STOP
SLOW!

Chapter 11

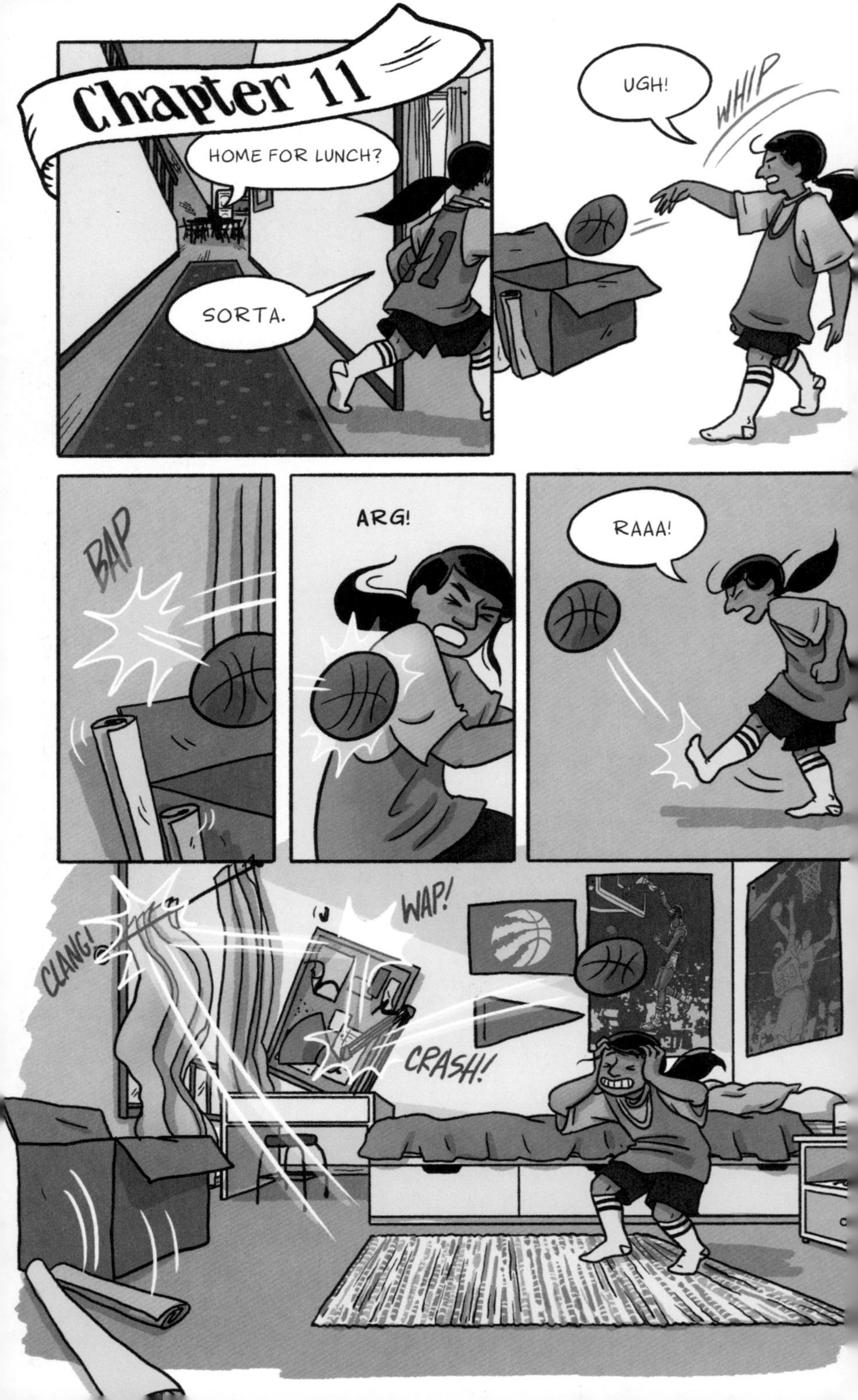
HOME FOR LUNCH?
SORTA.
UGH!
WHIP
BAP
ARG!
RAAA!
CLANG!
WAP!
CRASH!

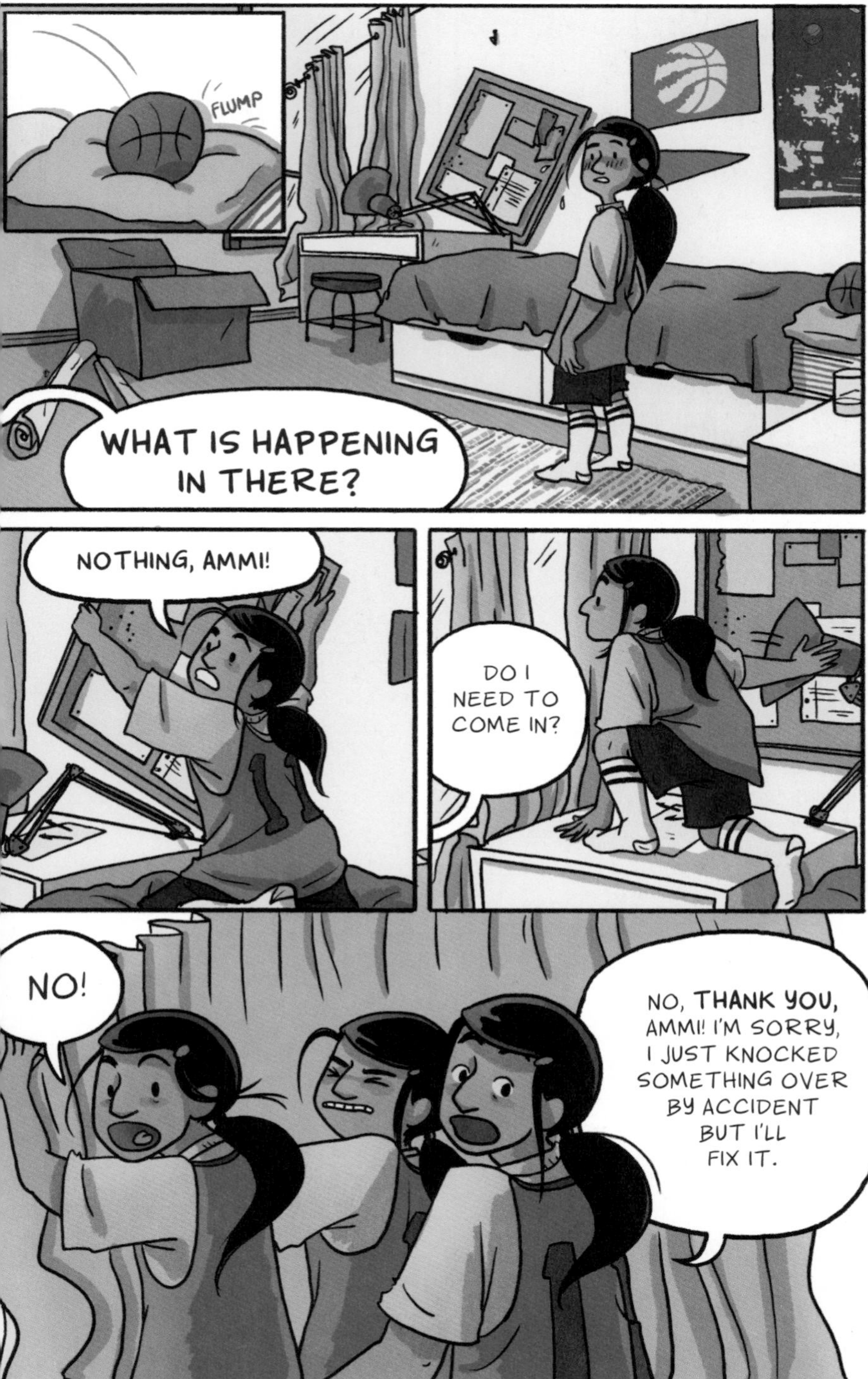
FLUMP
WHAT IS HAPPENING IN THERE?
NOTHING, AMMI!
DO I NEED TO COME IN?
NO!
NO, THANK YOU, AMMI! I'M SORRY, I JUST KNOCKED SOMETHING OVER BY ACCIDENT BUT I'LL FIX IT.

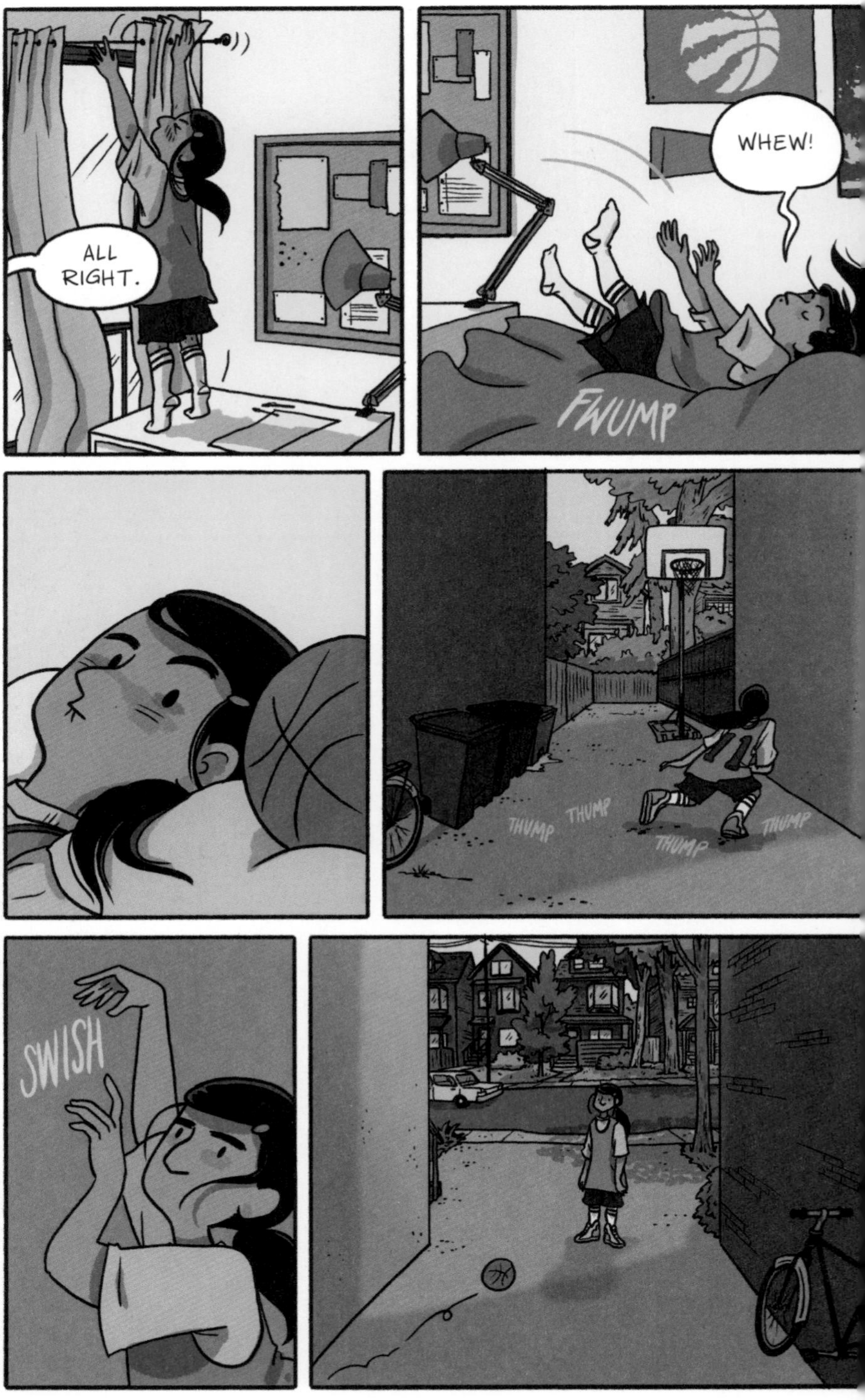
ALL RIGHT.
WHEW!
FWUMP
THUMP
THUMP
THUMP
THUMP
SWISH

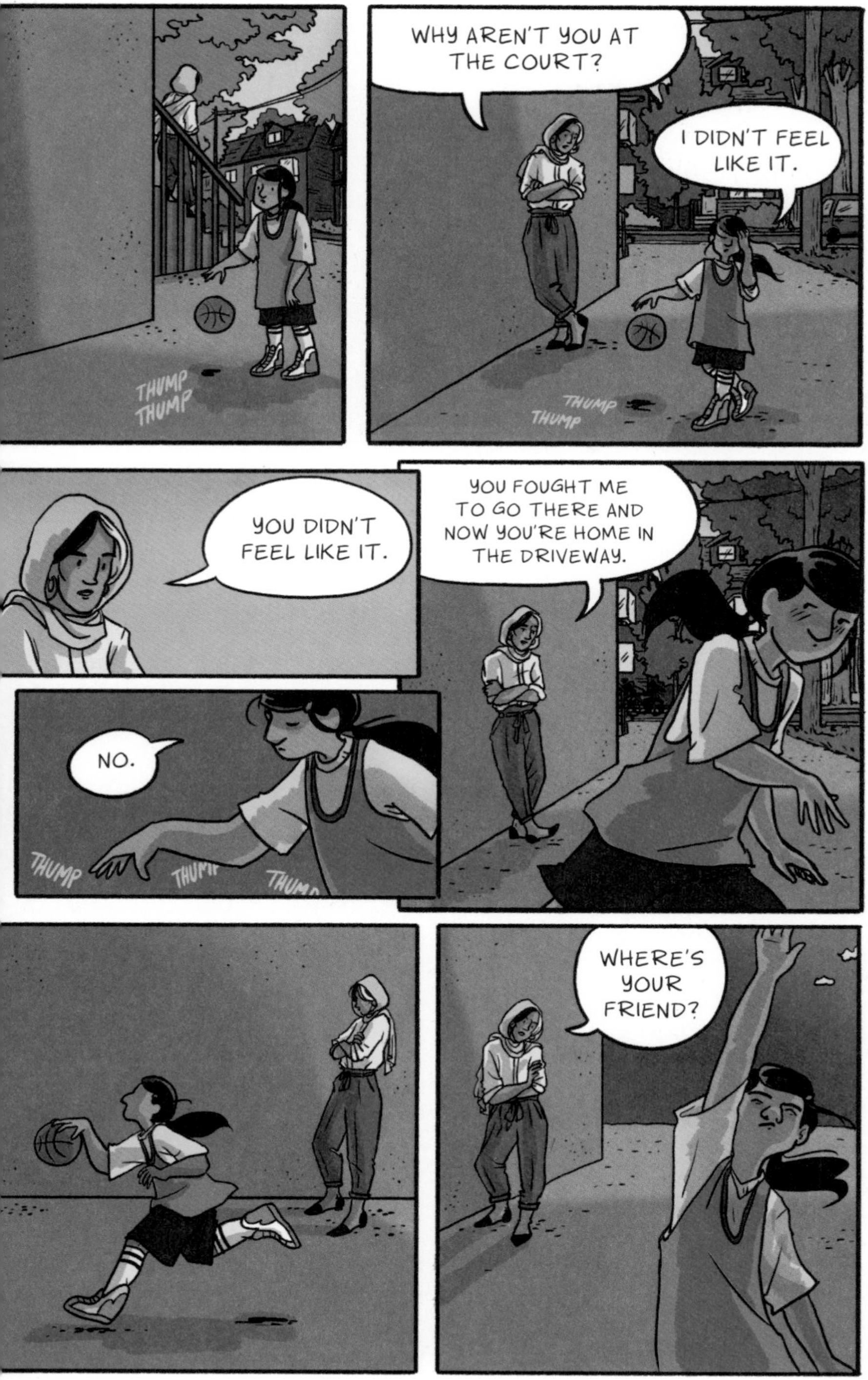
THUMP
THUMP
WHY AREN'T YOU AT THE COURT?
I DIDN'T FEEL LIKE IT.
THUMP
THUMP
YOU DIDN'T FEEL LIKE IT.
YOU FOUGHT ME TO GO THERE AND NOW YOU'RE HOME IN THE DRIVEWAY.
NO.
THUMP
WHERE'S YOUR FRIEND?

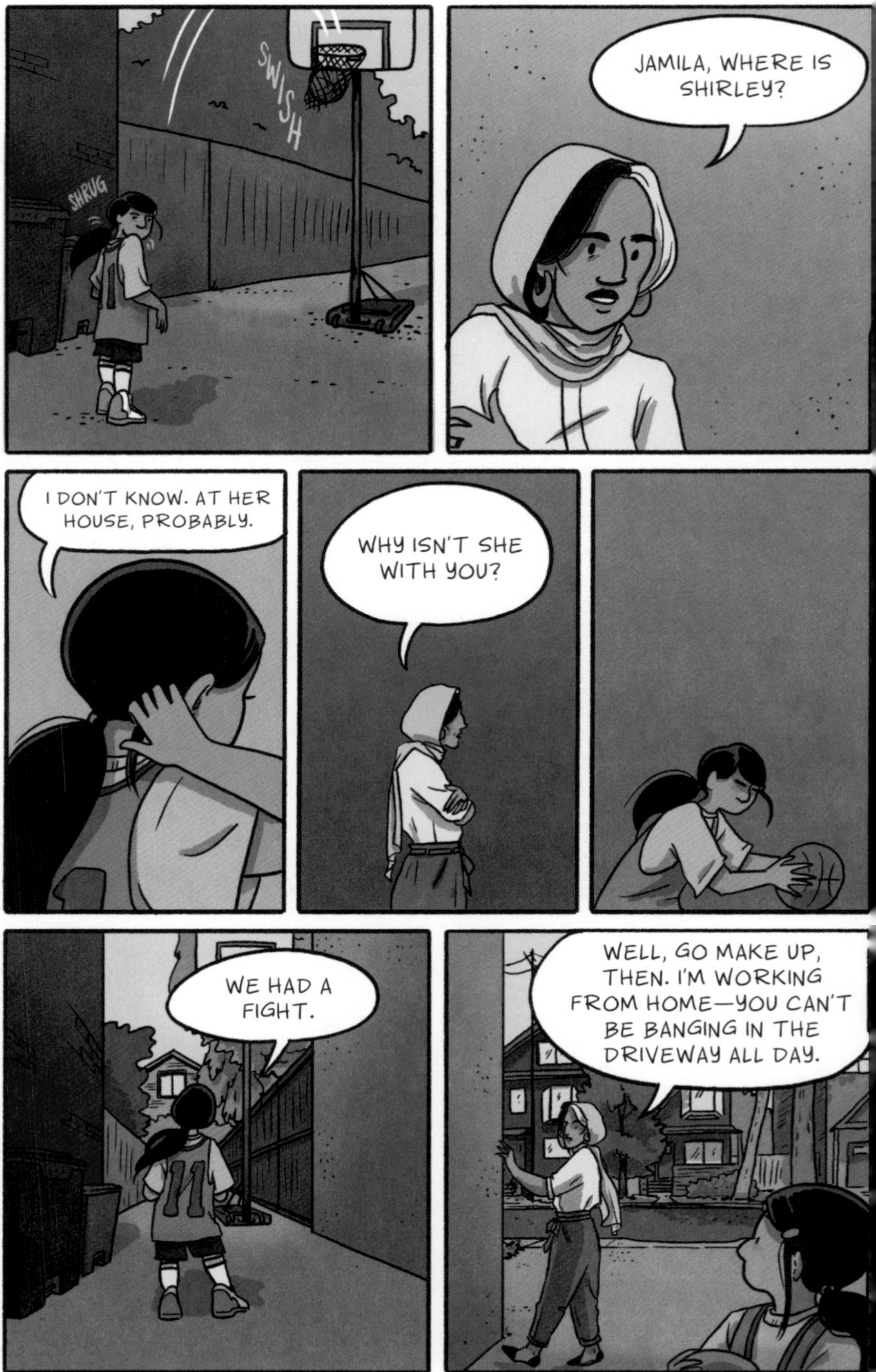
SWISH
SHRUG
JAMILA, WHERE IS SHIRLEY?
I DON'T KNOW. AT HER HOUSE, PROBABLY.
WHY ISN'T SHE WITH YOU?
WE HAD A FIGHT.
WELL, GO MAKE UP, THEN. I'M WORKING FROM HOME—YOU CAN'T BE BANGING IN THE DRIVEWAY ALL DAY.

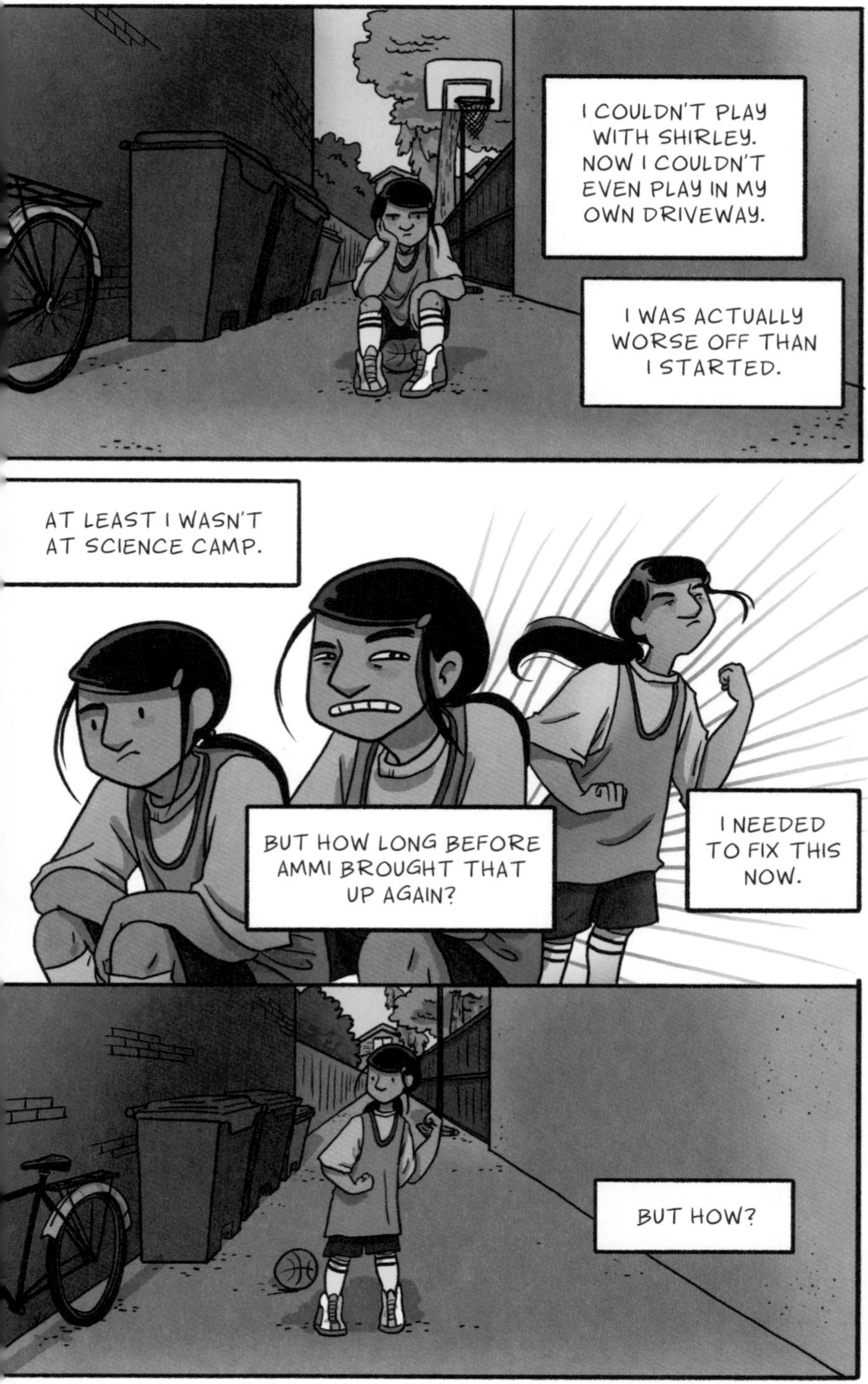
I COULDN'T PLAY WITH SHIRLEY. NOW I COULDN'T EVEN PLAY IN MY OWN DRIVEWAY.
I WAS ACTUALLY WORSE OFF THAN I STARTED.
AT LEAST I WASN'T AT SCIENCE CAMP.
BUT HOW LONG BEFORE AMMI BROUGHT THAT UP AGAIN?
I NEEDED TO FIX THIS NOW.
BUT HOW?

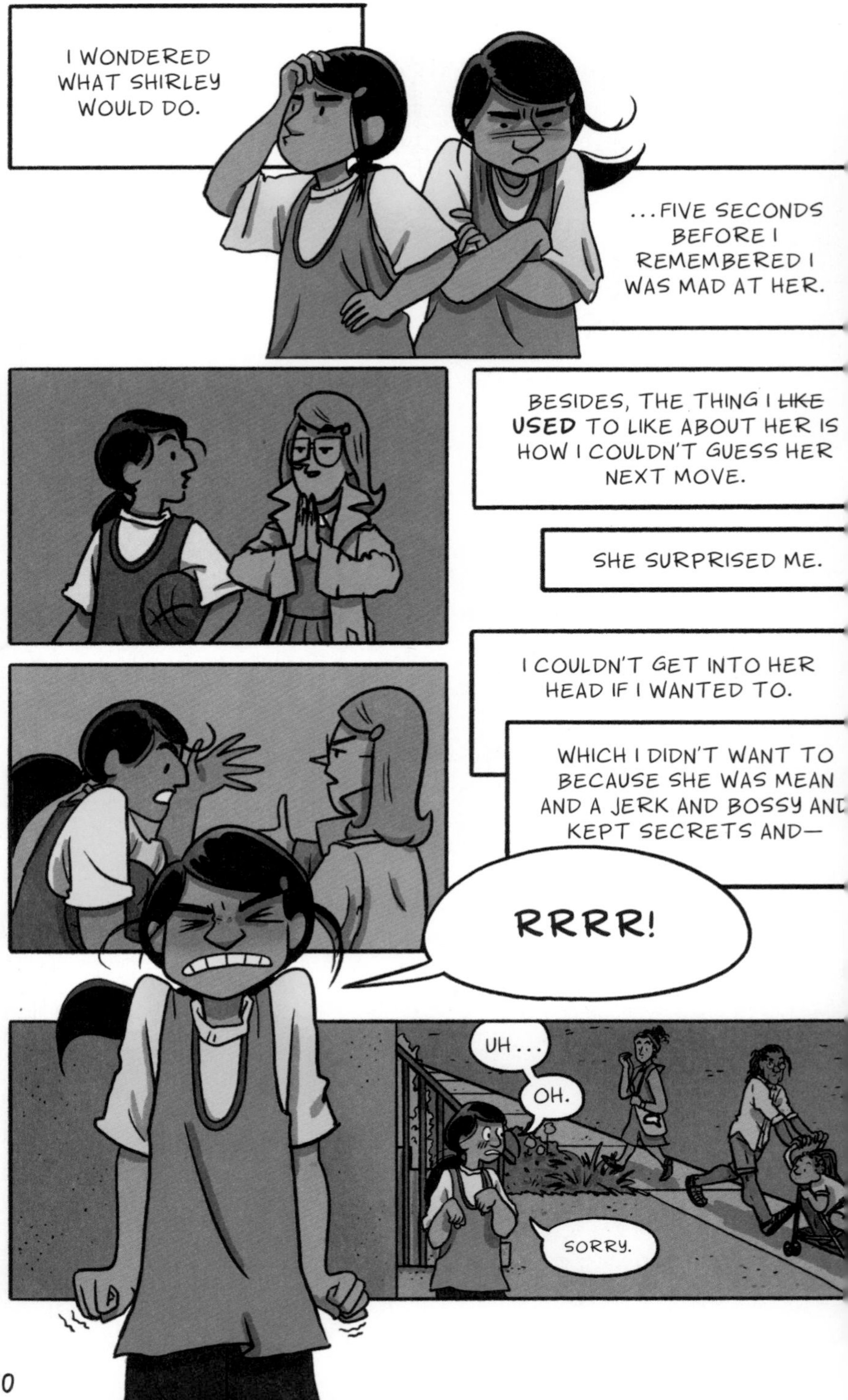
I WONDERED WHAT SHIRLEY WOULD DO.
...FIVE SECONDS BEFORE I REMEMBERED I WAS MAD AT HER.
BESIDES, THE THING I ~~LIKE~~ **USED** TO LIKE ABOUT HER IS HOW I COULDN'T GUESS HER NEXT MOVE.
SHE SURPRISED ME.
I COULDN'T GET INTO HER HEAD IF I WANTED TO.
WHICH I DIDN'T WANT TO BECAUSE SHE WAS MEAN AND A JERK AND BOSSY AND KEPT SECRETS AND—
RRRR!
UH...
OH.
SORRY.

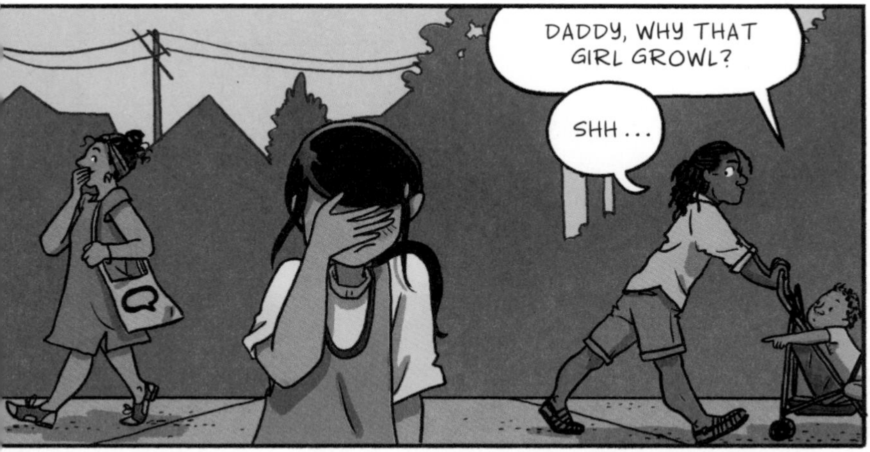
DADDY, WHY THAT GIRL GROWL?
SHH . . .

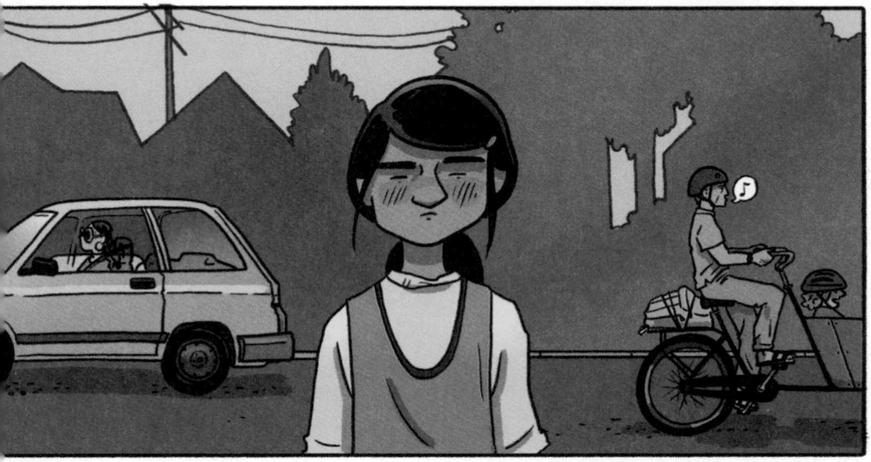

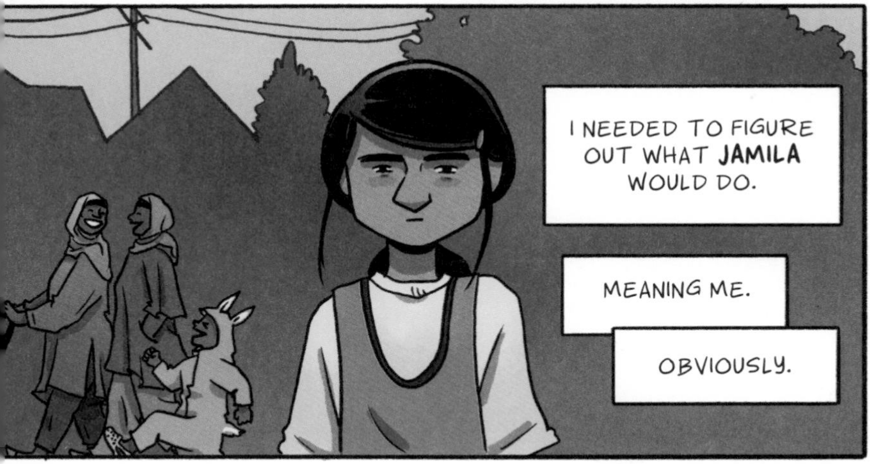
I NEEDED TO FIGURE OUT WHAT **JAMILA** WOULD DO.
MEANING ME.
OBVIOUSLY.

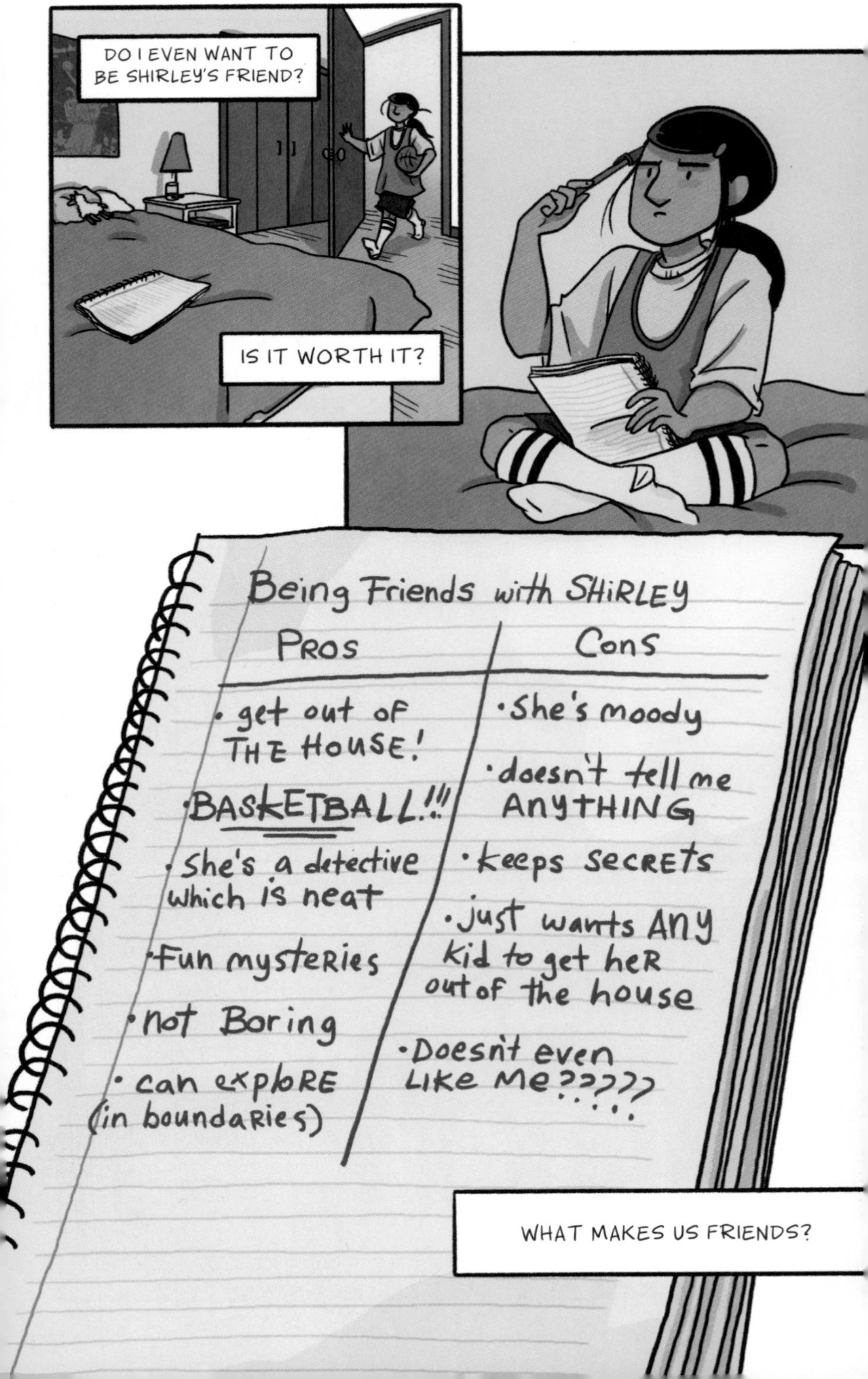
DO I EVEN WANT TO BE SHIRLEY'S FRIEND?
IS IT WORTH IT?
Being Friends with SHIRLEY
PROS
Cons
• get out of THE HOUSE!
• BASKETBALL!!!
• She's a detective which is neat
• Fun mysteries
• not Boring
• can explore (in boundaries)
• She's moody
• doesn't tell me ANYTHING
• keeps secrets
• just wants ANY kid to get her out of the house
• Doesn't even Like Me?????
WHAT MAKES US FRIENDS?

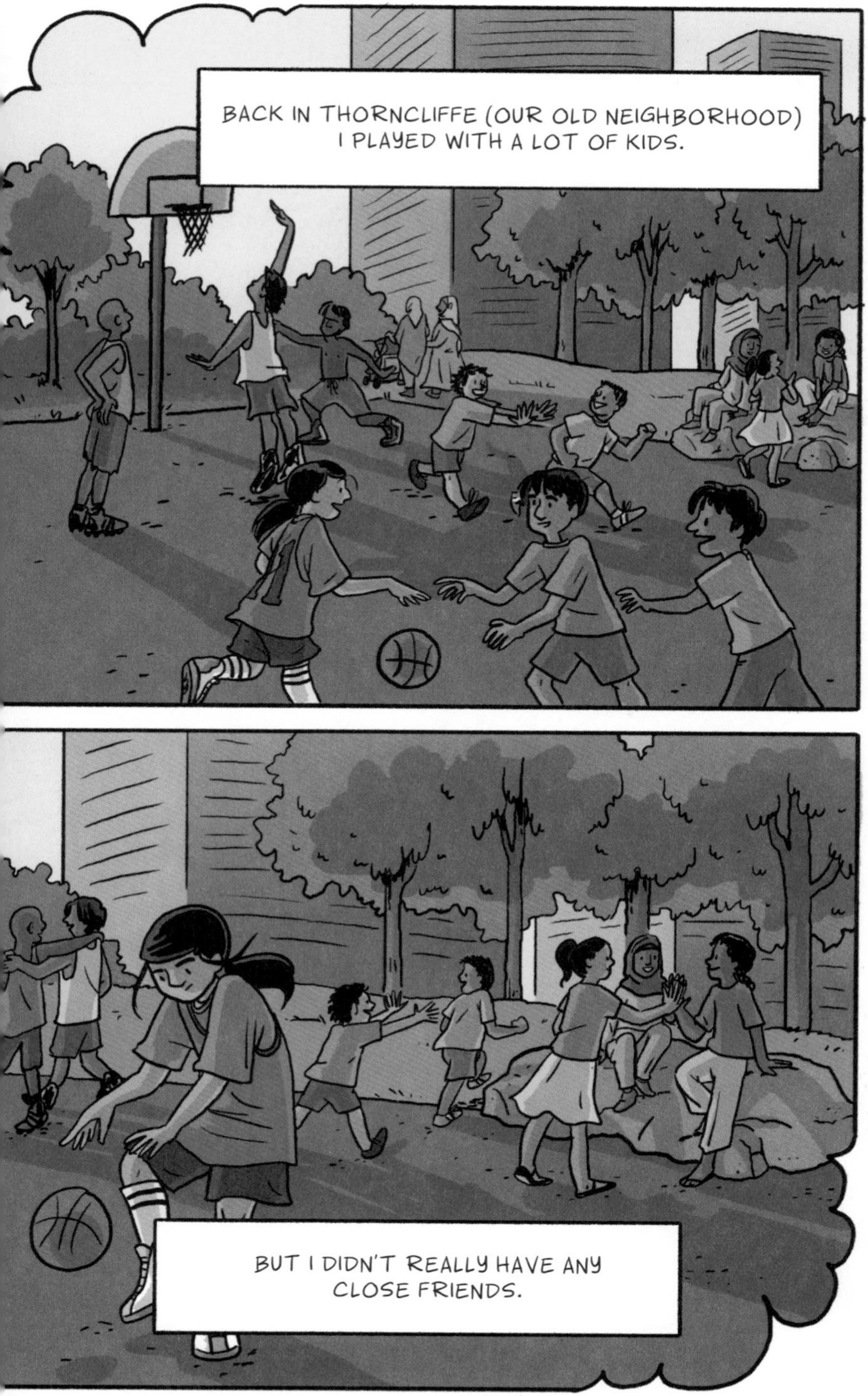
BACK IN THORNCLIFFE (OUR OLD NEIGHBORHOOD) I PLAYED WITH A LOT OF KIDS.
BUT I DIDN'T REALLY HAVE ANY CLOSE FRIENDS.

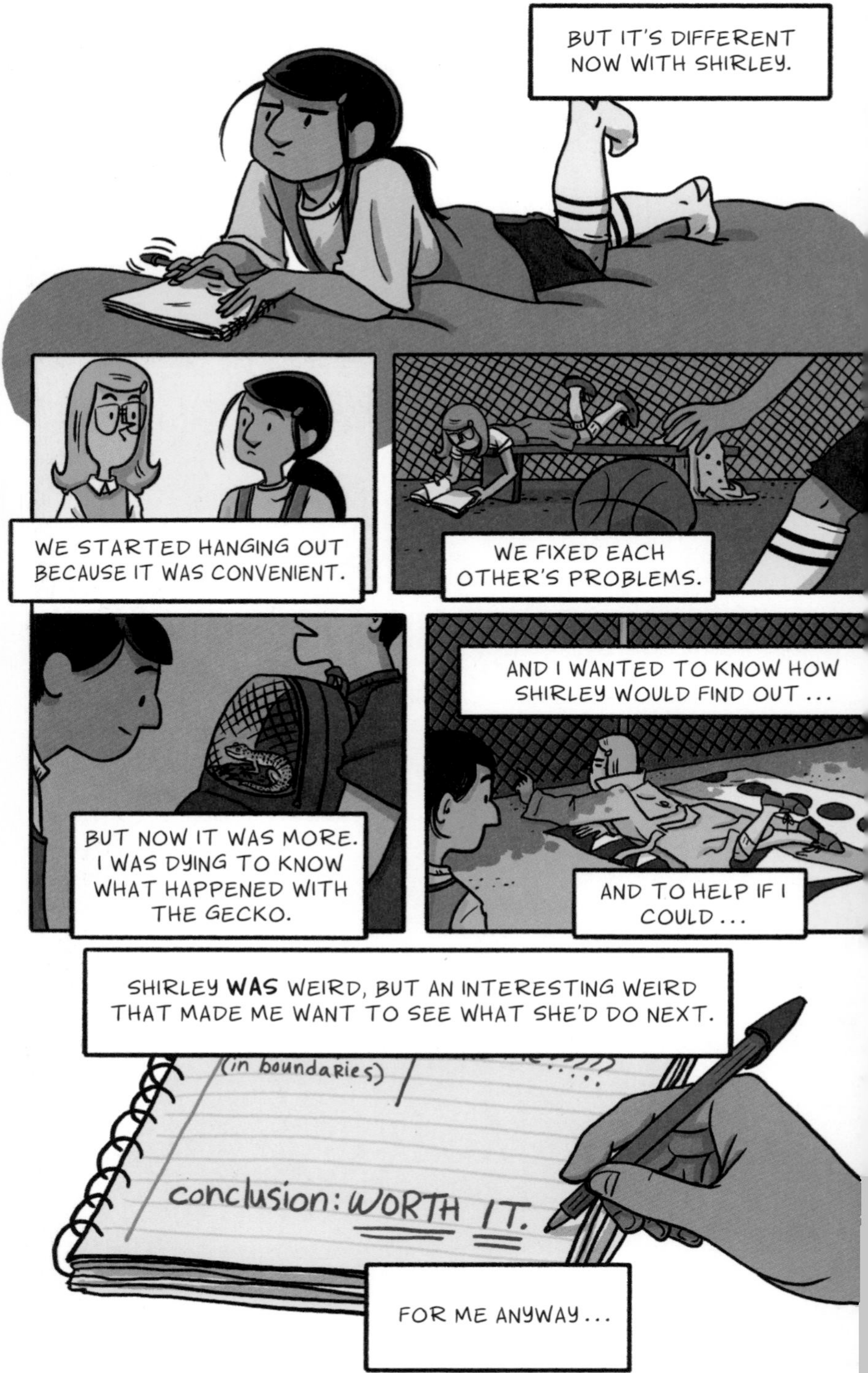
BUT IT'S DIFFERENT NOW WITH SHIRLEY.
WE STARTED HANGING OUT BECAUSE IT WAS CONVENIENT.
WE FIXED EACH OTHER'S PROBLEMS.
BUT NOW IT WAS MORE. I WAS DYING TO KNOW WHAT HAPPENED WITH THE GECKO.
AND I WANTED TO KNOW HOW SHIRLEY WOULD FIND OUT . . .
AND TO HELP IF I COULD . . .
SHIRLEY **WAS** WEIRD, BUT AN INTERESTING WEIRD THAT MADE ME WANT TO SEE WHAT SHE'D DO NEXT.
(in boundaries)
conclusion: WORTH IT.
FOR ME ANYWAY . . .

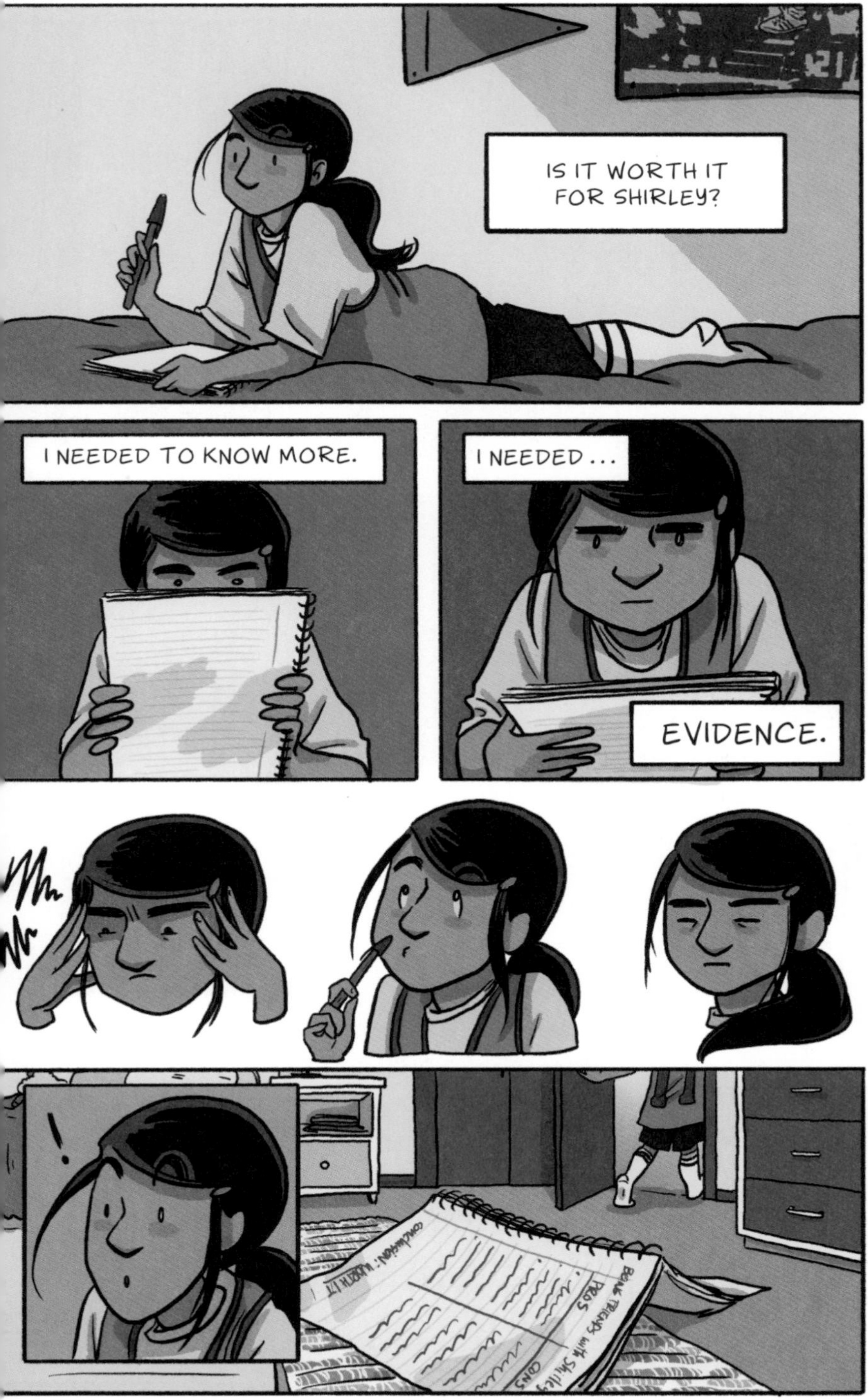
IS IT WORTH IT FOR SHIRLEY?
I NEEDED TO KNOW MORE.
I NEEDED . . .
EVIDENCE.
!
BEING FRIENDS with Shirley
PROS
CONS
conclusion: WORTH IT

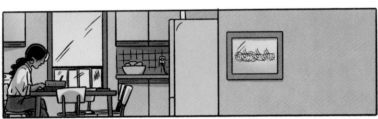

CAN I HELP YOU WITH SOMETHING, JAMILA?

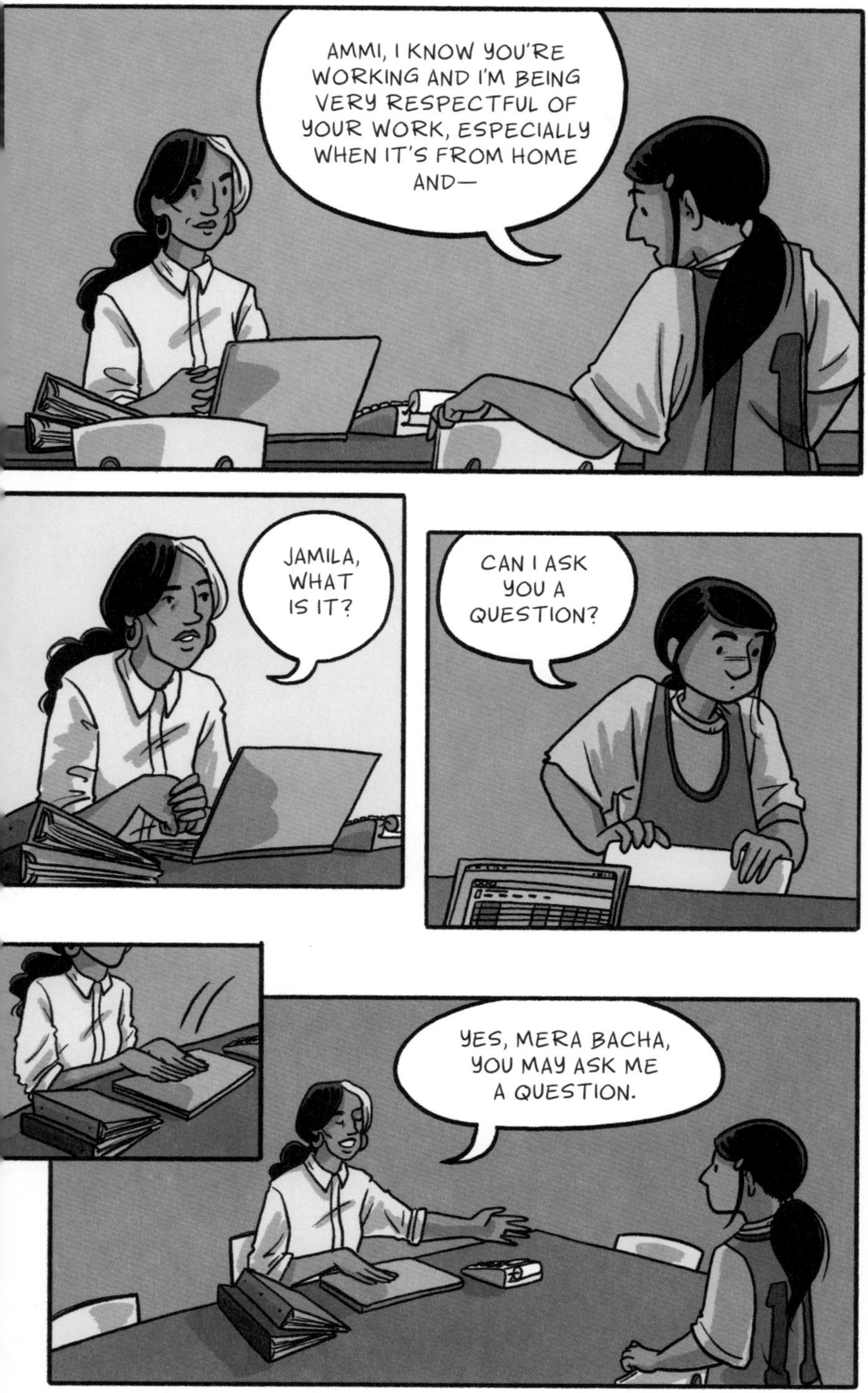
AMMI, I KNOW YOU'RE WORKING AND I'M BEING VERY RESPECTFUL OF YOUR WORK, ESPECIALLY WHEN IT'S FROM HOME AND—
JAMILA, WHAT IS IT?
CAN I ASK YOU A QUESTION?
YES, MERA BACHA, YOU MAY ASK ME A QUESTION.

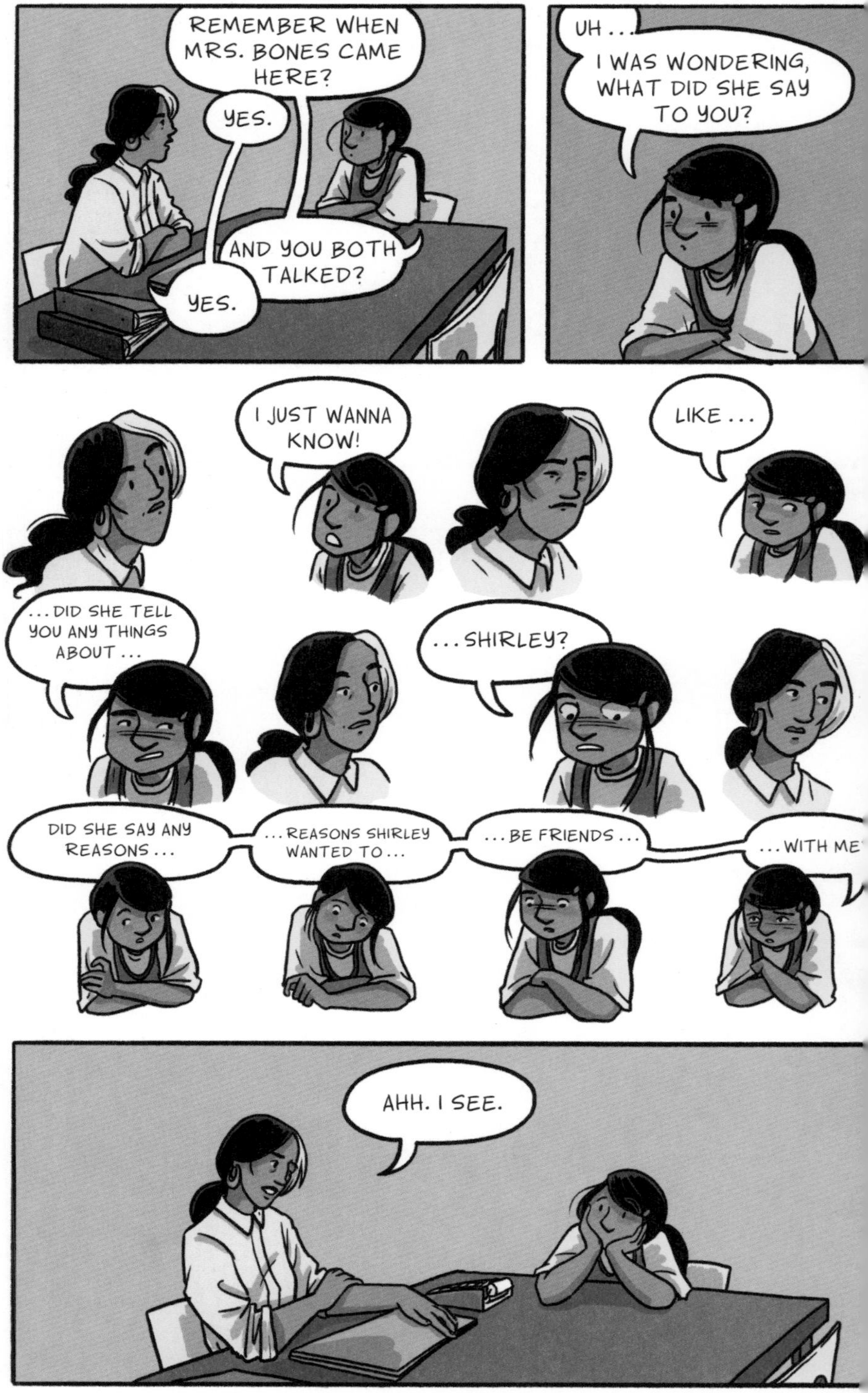
REMEMBER WHEN MRS. BONES CAME HERE?
YES.
AND YOU BOTH TALKED?
YES.
UH . . .
I WAS WONDERING, WHAT DID SHE SAY TO YOU?
I JUST WANNA KNOW!
LIKE . . .
. . . DID SHE TELL YOU ANY THINGS ABOUT . . .
. . . SHIRLEY?
DID SHE SAY ANY REASONS . . .
. . . REASONS SHIRLEY WANTED TO . . .
. . . BE FRIENDS . . .
. . . WITH ME
AHH. I SEE.

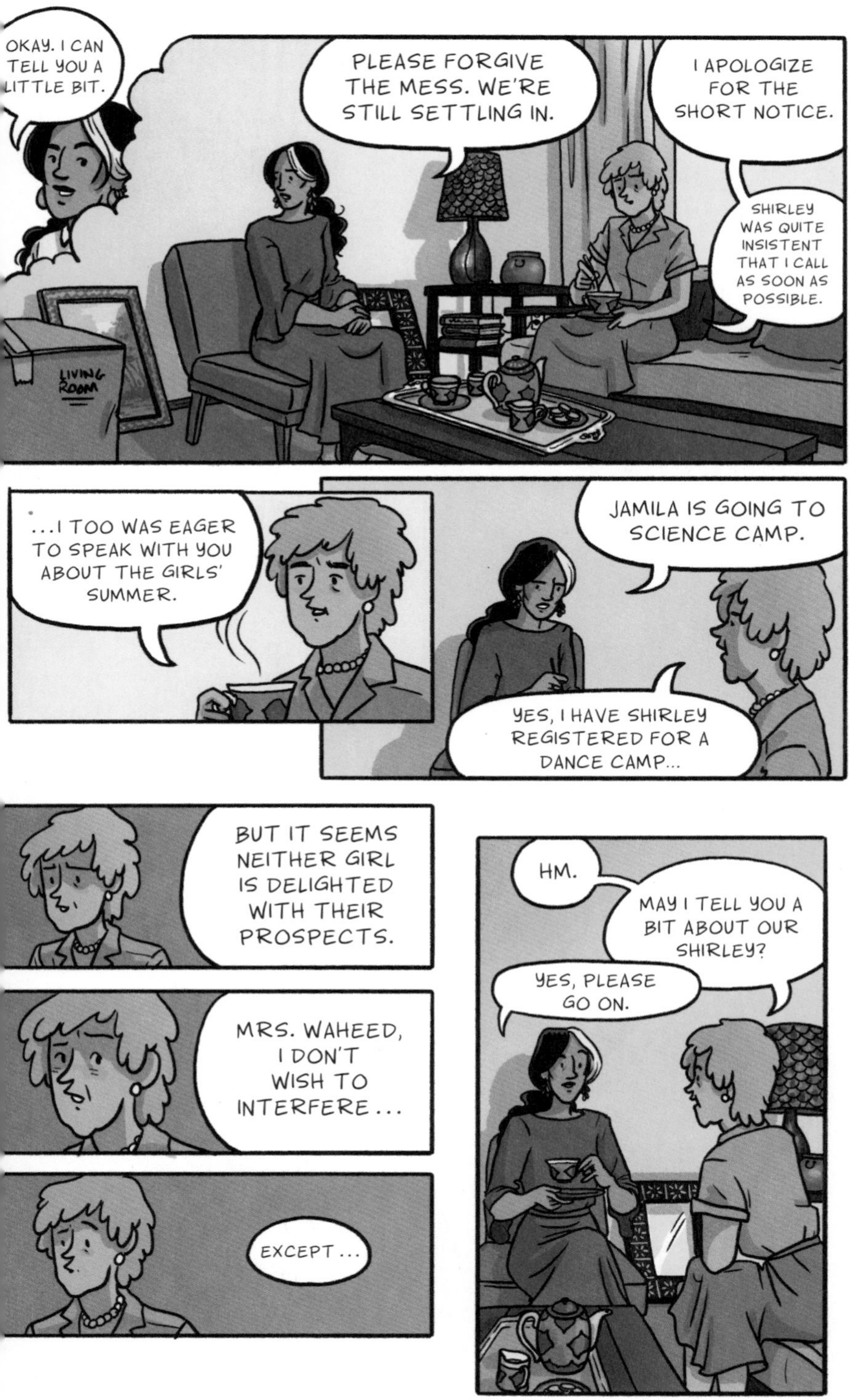
OKAY. I CAN TELL YOU A LITTLE BIT.
PLEASE FORGIVE THE MESS. WE'RE STILL SETTLING IN.
I APOLOGIZE FOR THE SHORT NOTICE.
SHIRLEY WAS QUITE INSISTENT THAT I CALL AS SOON AS POSSIBLE.
LIVING ROOM
...I TOO WAS EAGER TO SPEAK WITH YOU ABOUT THE GIRLS' SUMMER.
JAMILA IS GOING TO SCIENCE CAMP.
YES, I HAVE SHIRLEY REGISTERED FOR A DANCE CAMP...
BUT IT SEEMS NEITHER GIRL IS DELIGHTED WITH THEIR PROSPECTS.
MRS. WAHEED, I DON'T WISH TO INTERFERE...
EXCEPT...
HM.
MAY I TELL YOU A BIT ABOUT OUR SHIRLEY?
YES, PLEASE GO ON.

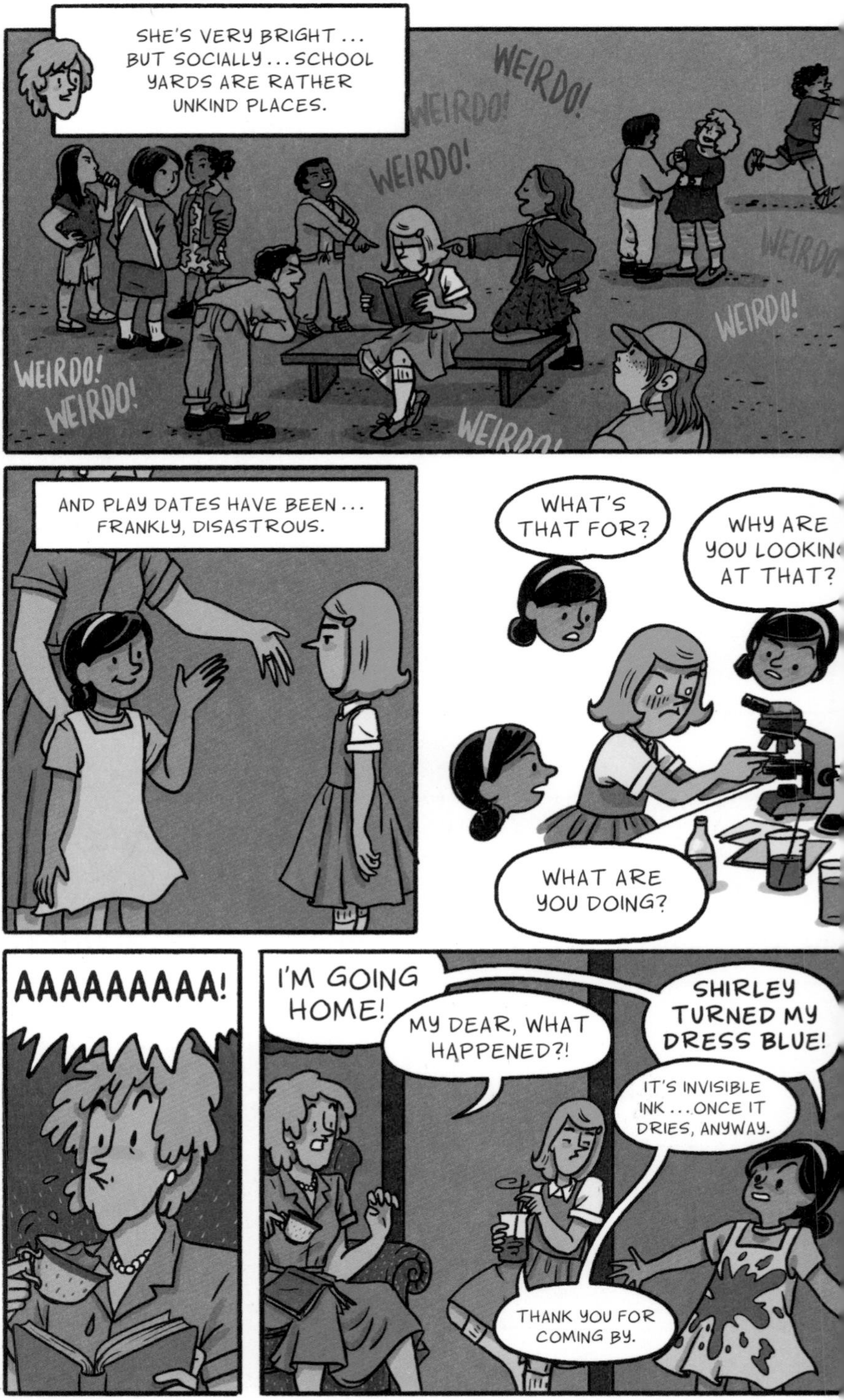
SHE'S VERY BRIGHT ... BUT SOCIALLY ... SCHOOL YARDS ARE RATHER UNKIND PLACES.
WEIRDO!
WEIRDO!
WEIRDO!
WEIRDO!
WEIRDO!
WEIRDO!
WEIRDO!
AND PLAY DATES HAVE BEEN ... FRANKLY, DISASTROUS.
WHAT'S THAT FOR?
WHY ARE YOU LOOKING AT THAT?
WHAT ARE YOU DOING?
AAAAAAAAA!
I'M GOING HOME!
MY DEAR, WHAT HAPPENED?!
SHIRLEY TURNED MY DRESS BLUE!
IT'S INVISIBLE INK ... ONCE IT DRIES, ANYWAY.
THANK YOU FOR COMING BY.

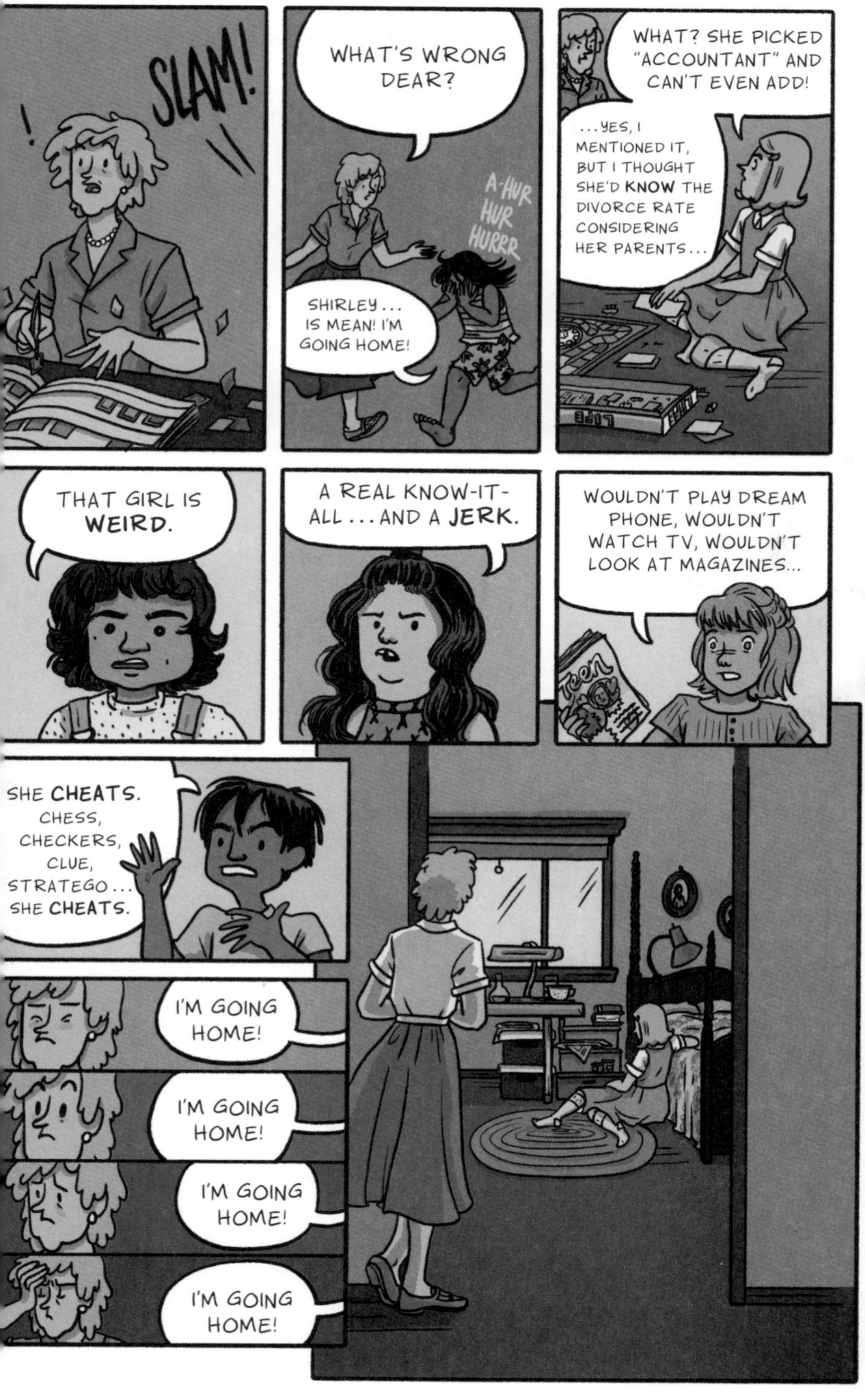
SLAM!
!
WHAT'S WRONG DEAR?
A-HUR HUR HURRR
SHIRLEY... IS MEAN! I'M GOING HOME!
WHAT? SHE PICKED "ACCOUNTANT" AND CAN'T EVEN ADD!
...YES, I MENTIONED IT, BUT I THOUGHT SHE'D KNOW THE DIVORCE RATE CONSIDERING HER PARENTS...
THAT GIRL IS WEIRD.
A REAL KNOW-IT-ALL... AND A JERK.
WOULDN'T PLAY DREAM PHONE, WOULDN'T WATCH TV, WOULDN'T LOOK AT MAGAZINES...
Teen
SHE CHEATS. CHESS, CHECKERS, CLUE, STRATEGO... SHE CHEATS.
I'M GOING HOME!
I'M GOING HOME!
I'M GOING HOME!
I'M GOING HOME!

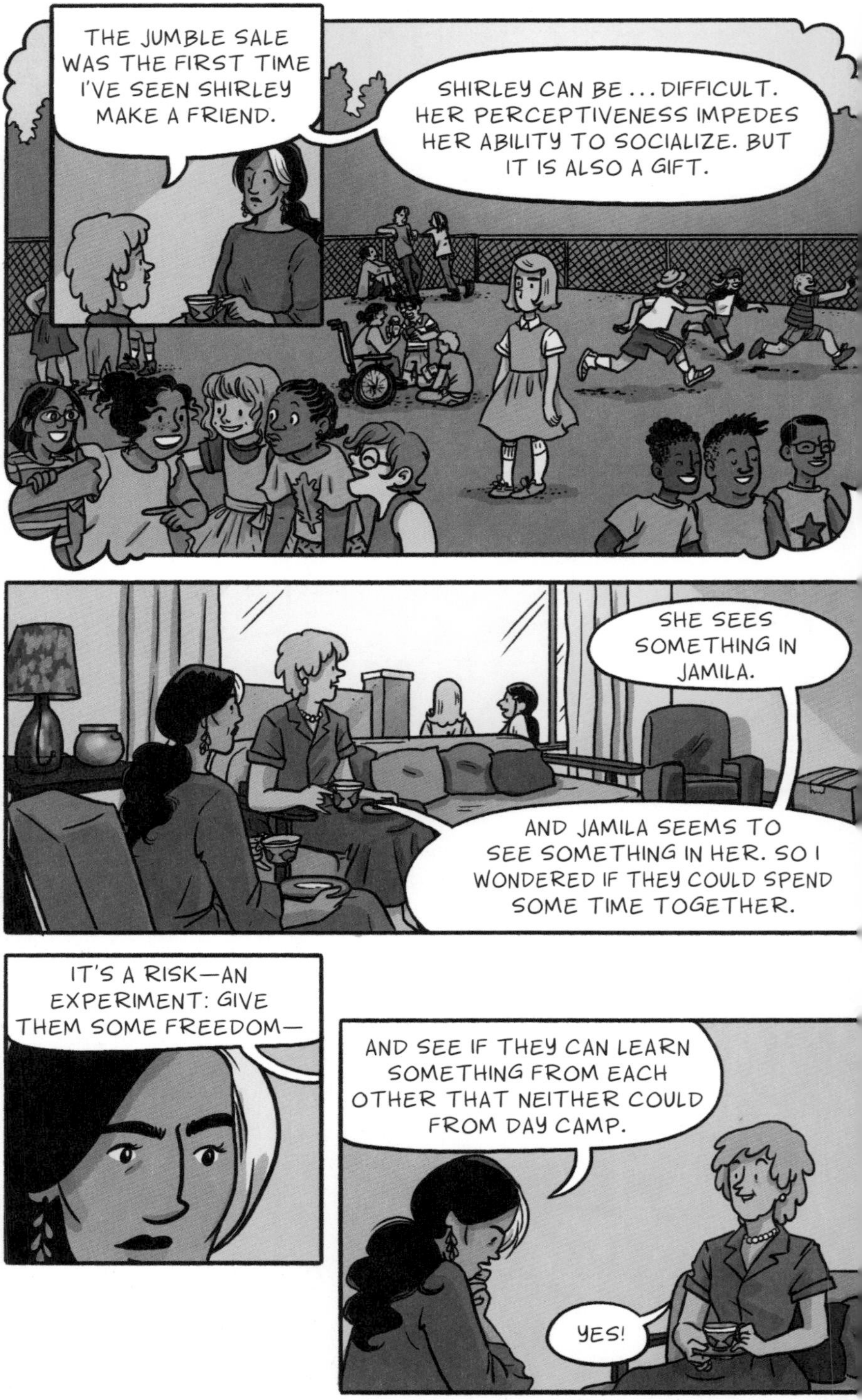
THE JUMBLE SALE WAS THE FIRST TIME I'VE SEEN SHIRLEY MAKE A FRIEND.
SHIRLEY CAN BE . . . DIFFICULT. HER PERCEPTIVENESS IMPEDES HER ABILITY TO SOCIALIZE. BUT IT IS ALSO A GIFT.
SHE SEES SOMETHING IN JAMILA.
AND JAMILA SEEMS TO SEE SOMETHING IN HER. SO I WONDERED IF THEY COULD SPEND SOME TIME TOGETHER.
IT'S A RISK—AN EXPERIMENT: GIVE THEM SOME FREEDOM—
AND SEE IF THEY CAN LEARN SOMETHING FROM EACH OTHER THAT NEITHER COULD FROM DAY CAMP.
YES!

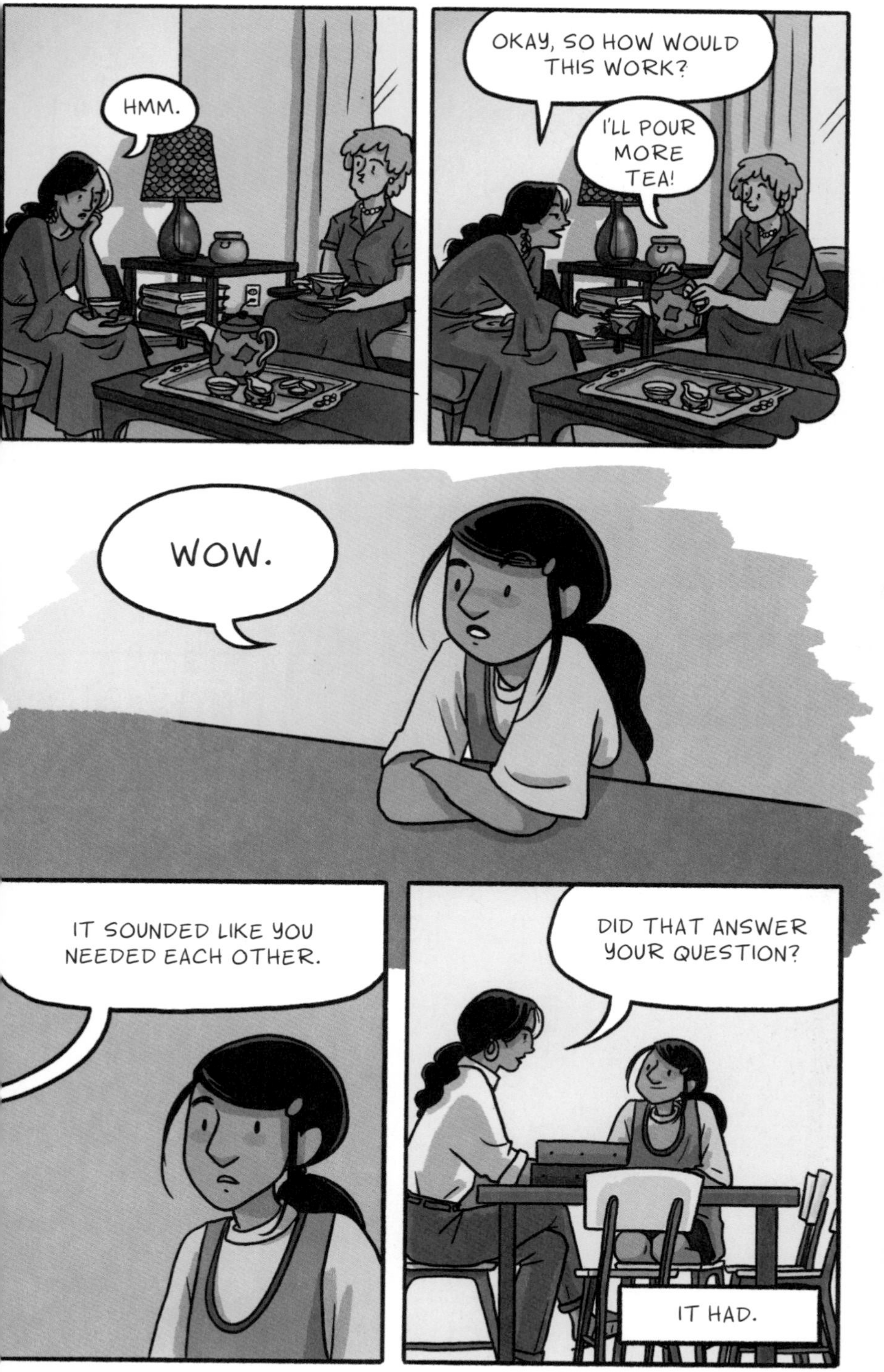
HMM.
OKAY, SO HOW WOULD THIS WORK?
I'LL POUR MORE TEA!
WOW.
IT SOUNDED LIKE YOU NEEDED EACH OTHER.
DID THAT ANSWER YOUR QUESTION?
IT HAD.

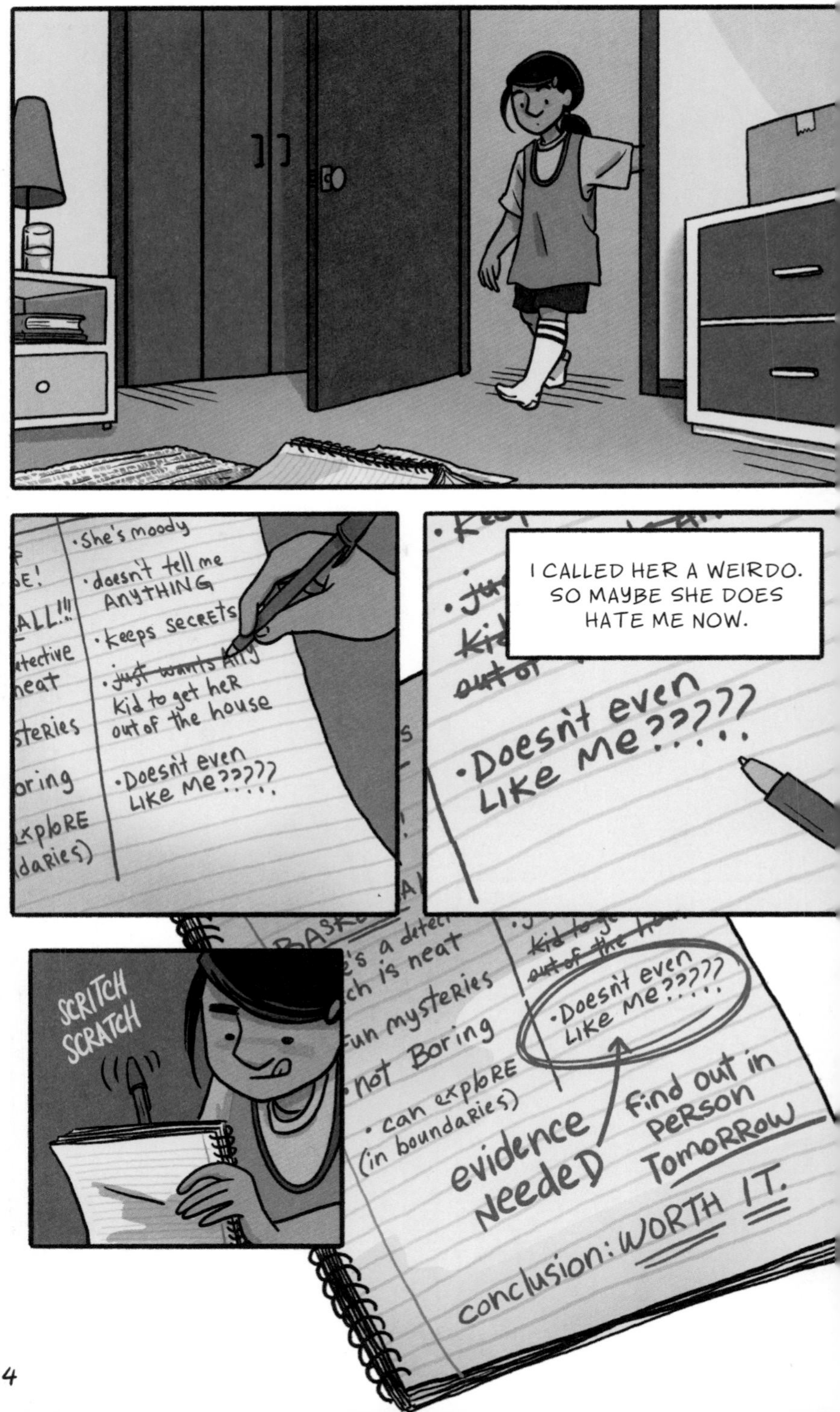
·She's moody
·doesn't tell me ANYTHING
·keeps secrets
·just wants Any kid to get her out of the house
·Doesn't even Like Me?????.....
I CALLED HER A WEIRDO. SO MAYBE SHE DOES HATE ME NOW.
·Doesn't even Like Me?????.....
SCRITCH SCRATCH
Fun mysteries
·not Boring
·can explore (in boundaries)
·Doesn't even Like Me?????.....
evidence needed
Find out in person tomorrow
conclusion: WORTH IT.

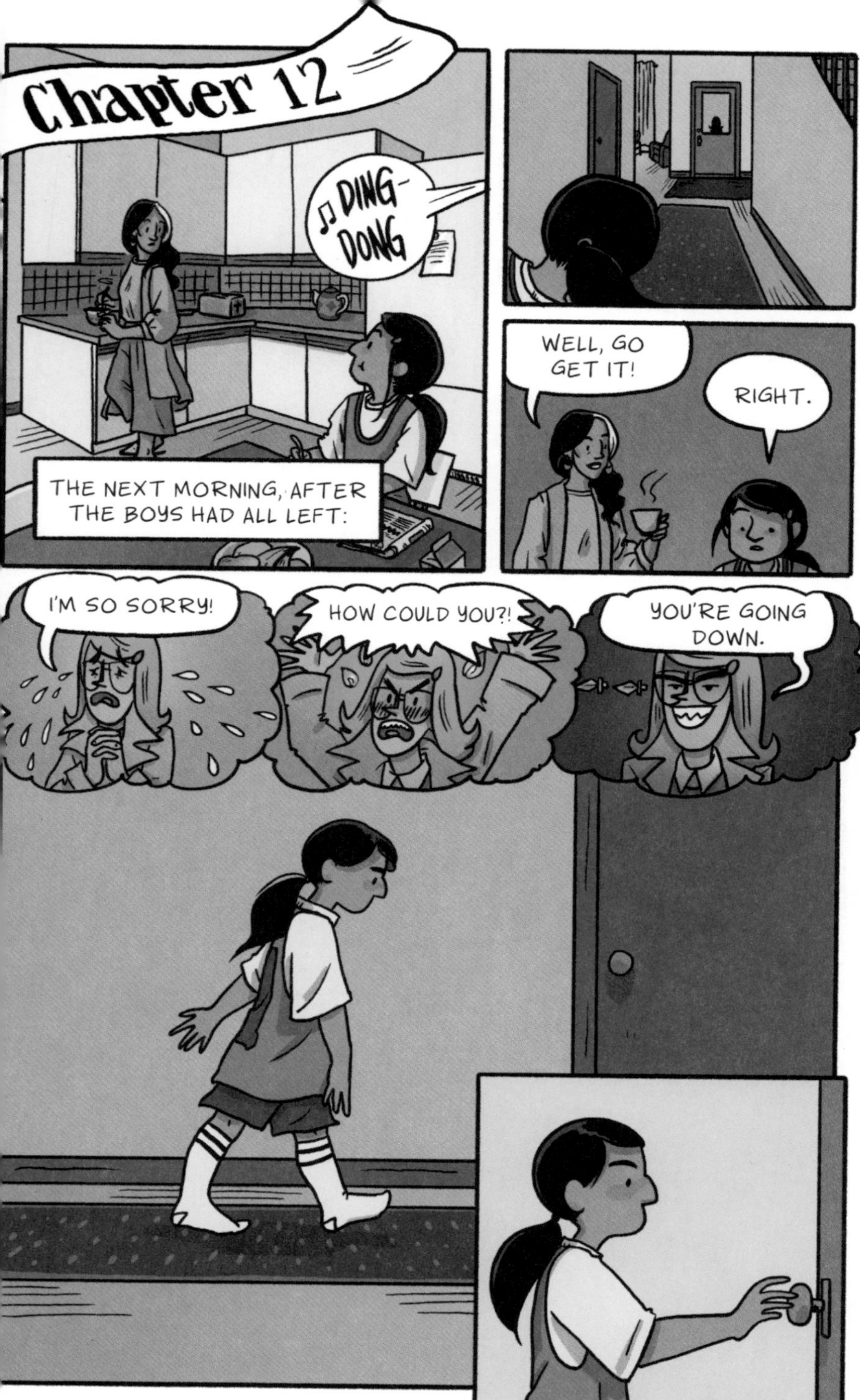
Chapter 12
♫ DING-DONG
THE NEXT MORNING, AFTER THE BOYS HAD ALL LEFT:
WELL, GO GET IT!
RIGHT.
I'M SO SORRY!
HOW COULD YOU?!
YOU'RE GOING DOWN.

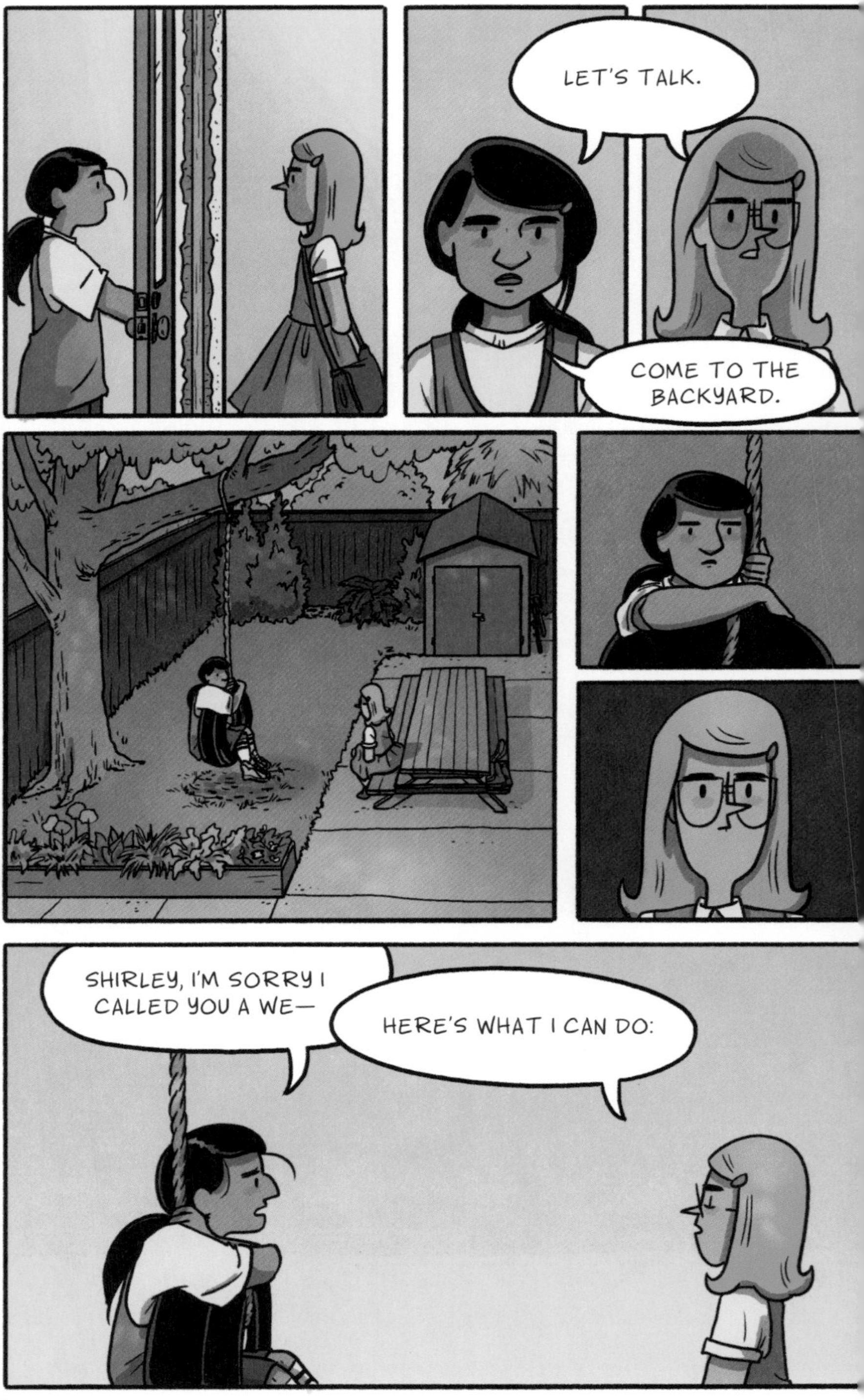
LET'S TALK.
COME TO THE BACKYARD.
SHIRLEY, I'M SORRY I CALLED YOU A WE—
HERE'S WHAT I CAN DO:

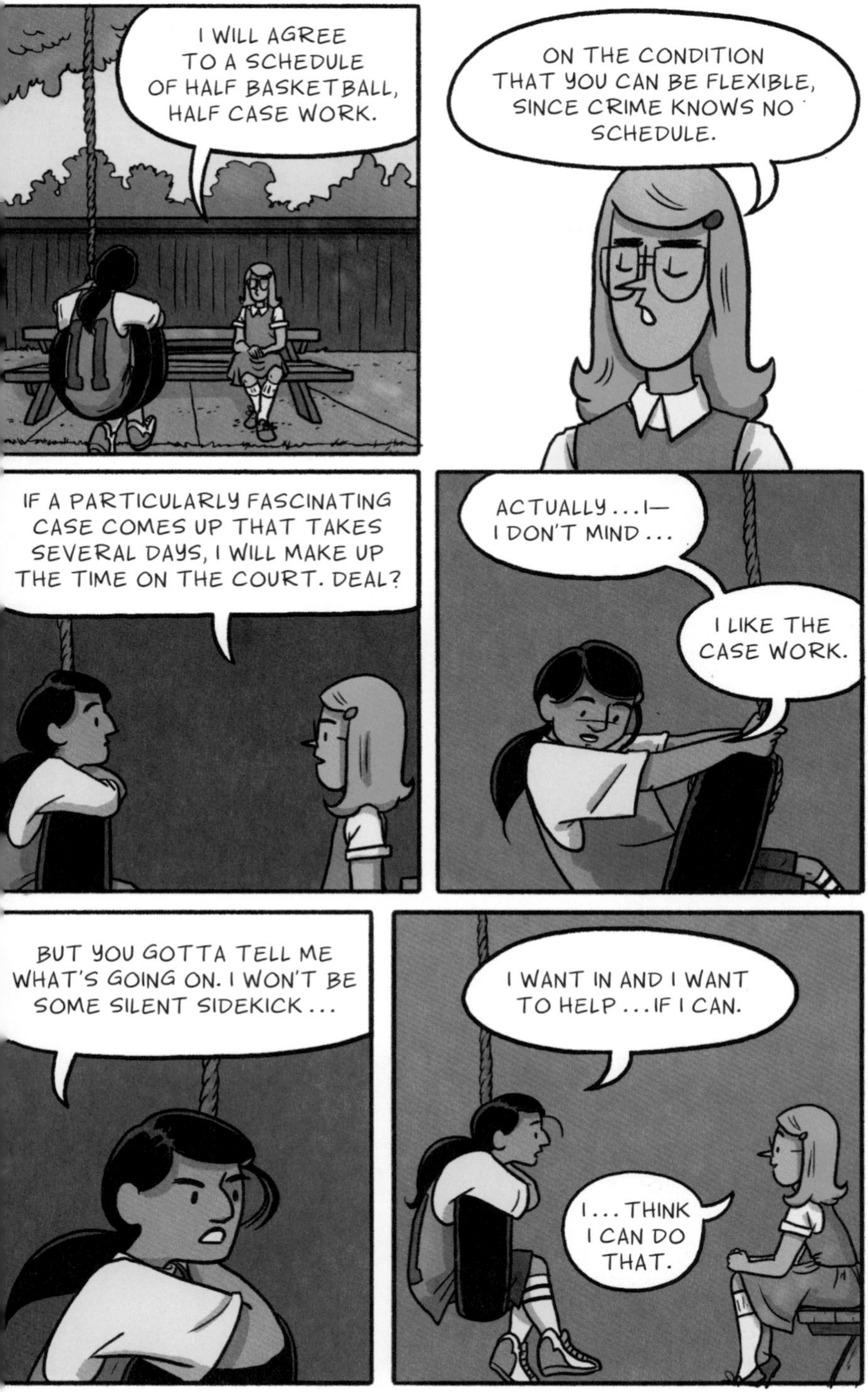
I WILL AGREE TO A SCHEDULE OF HALF BASKETBALL, HALF CASE WORK.
ON THE CONDITION THAT YOU CAN BE FLEXIBLE, SINCE CRIME KNOWS NO SCHEDULE.
IF A PARTICULARLY FASCINATING CASE COMES UP THAT TAKES SEVERAL DAYS, I WILL MAKE UP THE TIME ON THE COURT. DEAL?
ACTUALLY . . . I— I DON'T MIND . . .
I LIKE THE CASE WORK.
BUT YOU GOTTA TELL ME WHAT'S GOING ON. I WON'T BE SOME SILENT SIDEKICK . . .
I WANT IN AND I WANT TO HELP . . . IF I CAN.
I . . . THINK I CAN DO THAT.

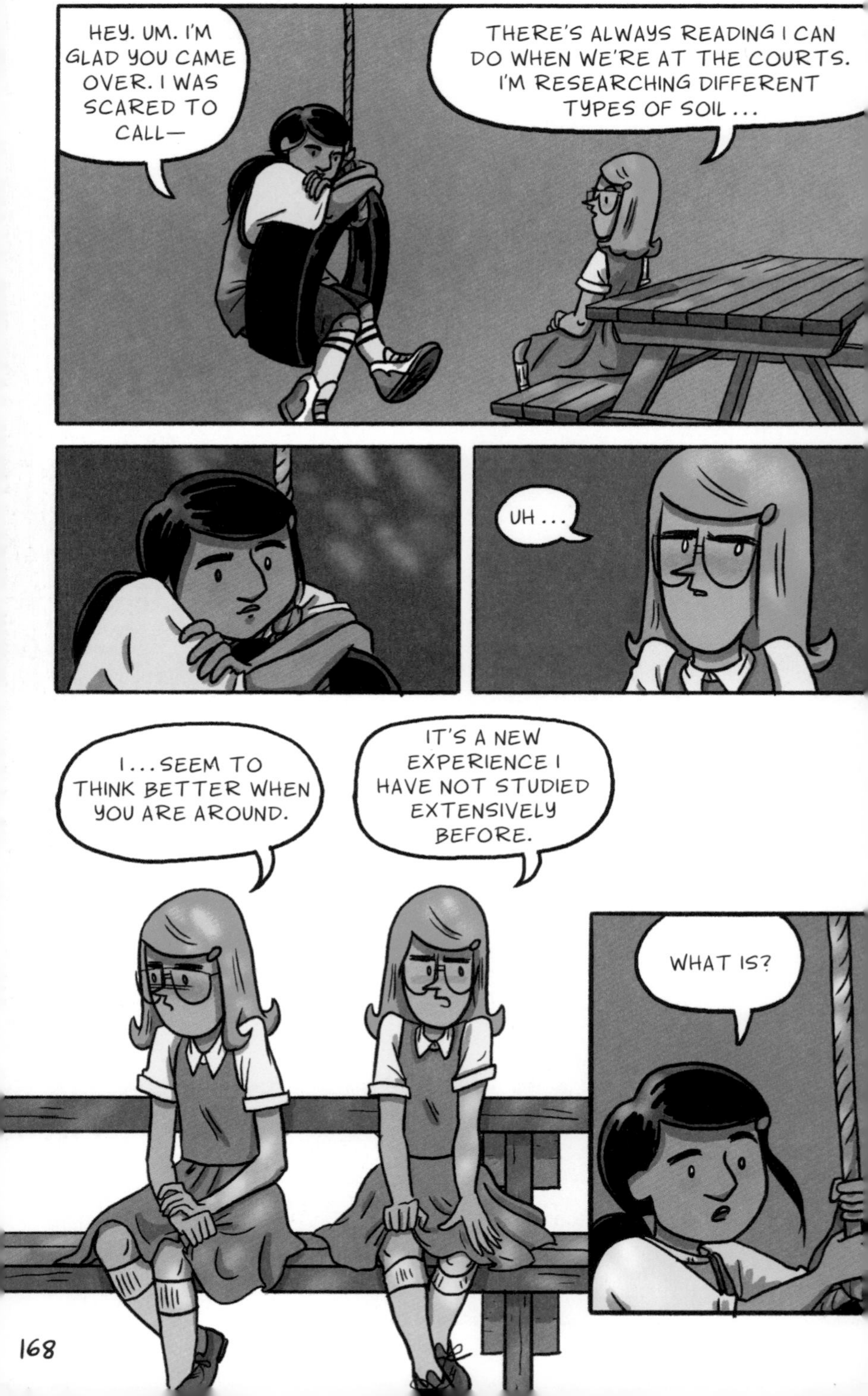
HEY. UM. I'M GLAD YOU CAME OVER. I WAS SCARED TO CALL—
THERE'S ALWAYS READING I CAN DO WHEN WE'RE AT THE COURTS. I'M RESEARCHING DIFFERENT TYPES OF SOIL . . .
UH . . .
I . . . SEEM TO THINK BETTER WHEN YOU ARE AROUND.
IT'S A NEW EXPERIENCE I HAVE NOT STUDIED EXTENSIVELY BEFORE.
WHAT IS?

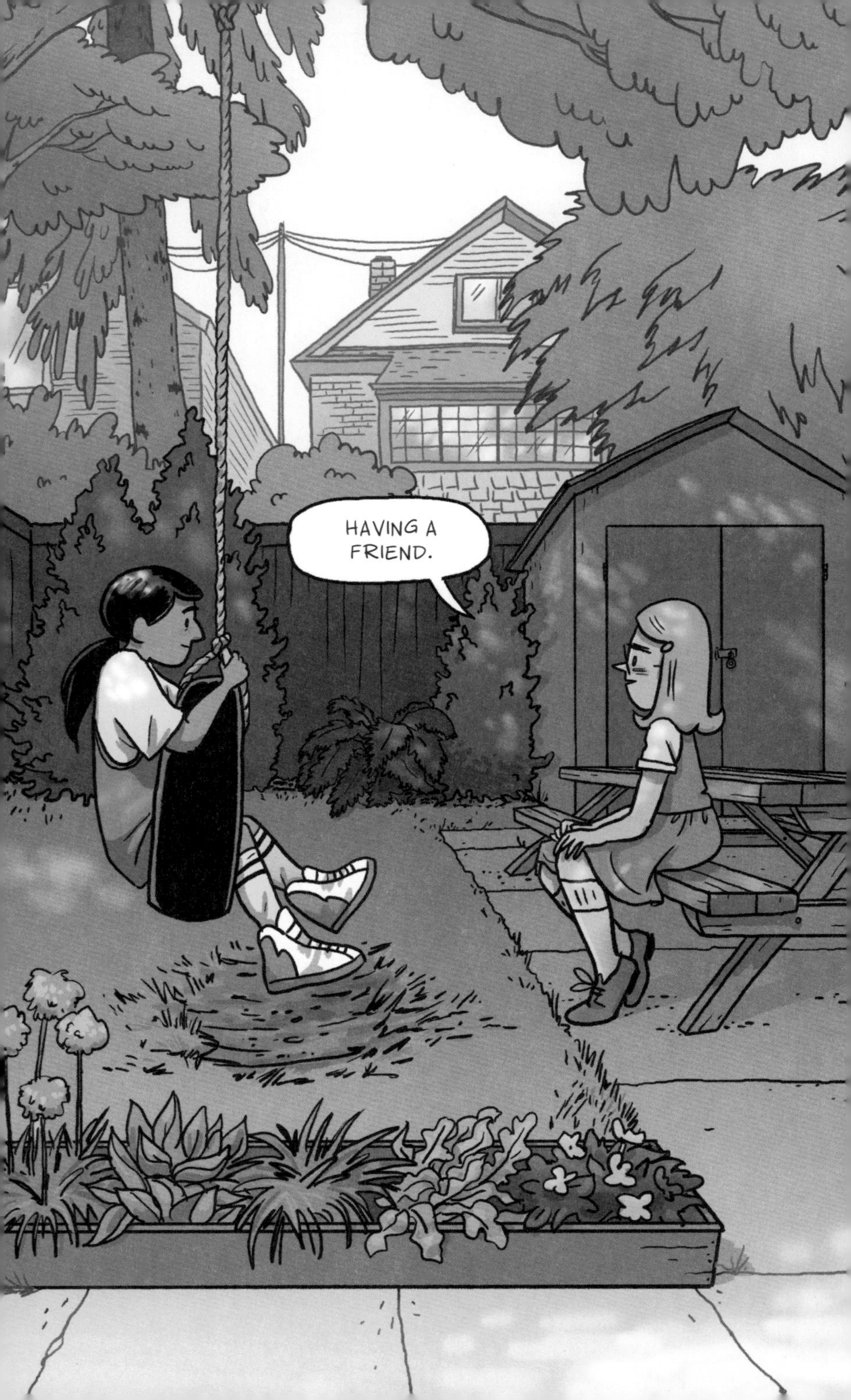
HAVING A FRIEND.

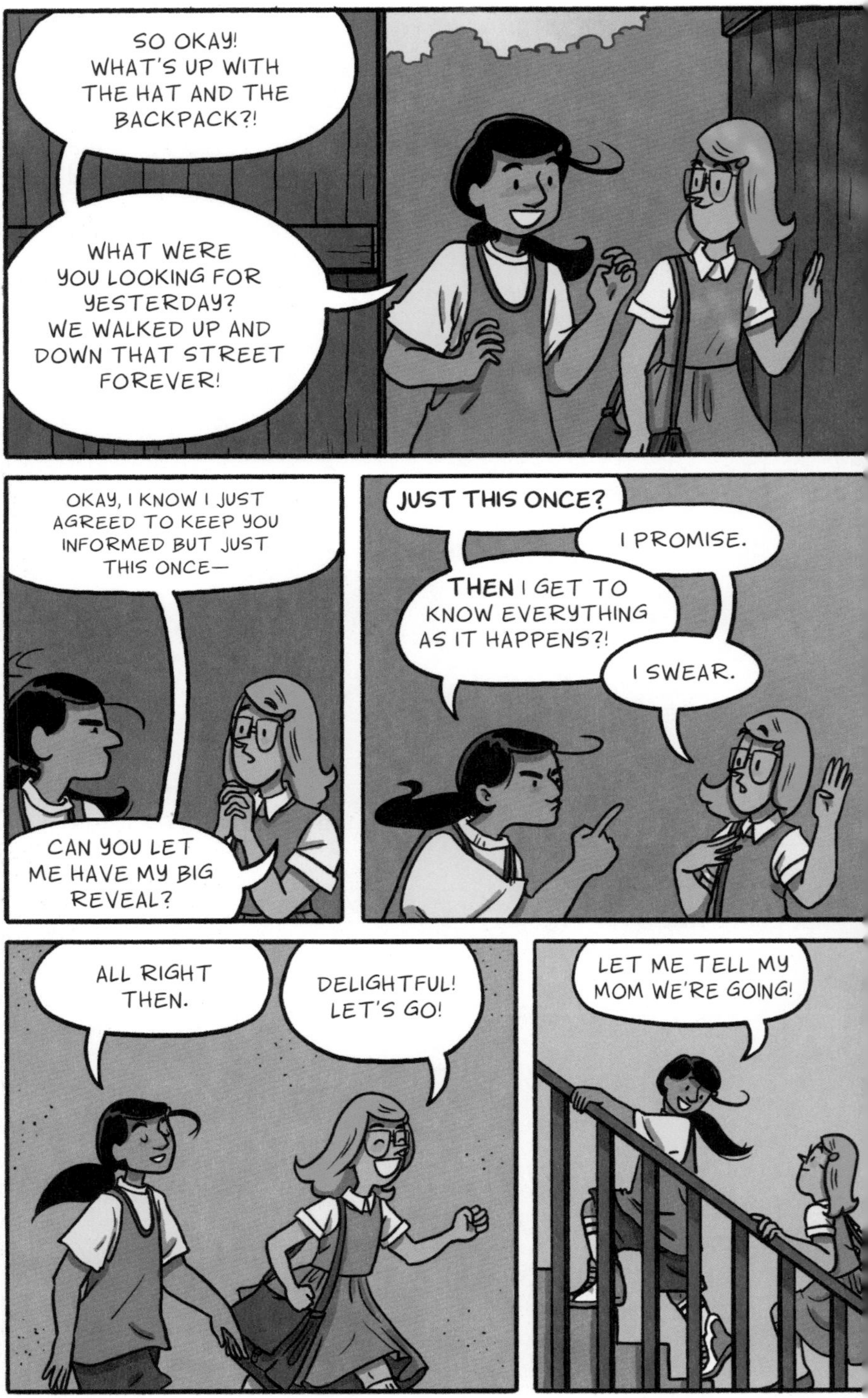
SO OKAY! WHAT'S UP WITH THE HAT AND THE BACKPACK?!
WHAT WERE YOU LOOKING FOR YESTERDAY? WE WALKED UP AND DOWN THAT STREET FOREVER!
OKAY, I KNOW I JUST AGREED TO KEEP YOU INFORMED BUT JUST THIS ONCE—
CAN YOU LET ME HAVE MY BIG REVEAL?
JUST THIS ONCE?
I PROMISE.
THEN I GET TO KNOW EVERYTHING AS IT HAPPENS?!
I SWEAR.
ALL RIGHT THEN.
DELIGHTFUL! LET'S GO!
LET ME TELL MY MOM WE'RE GOING!

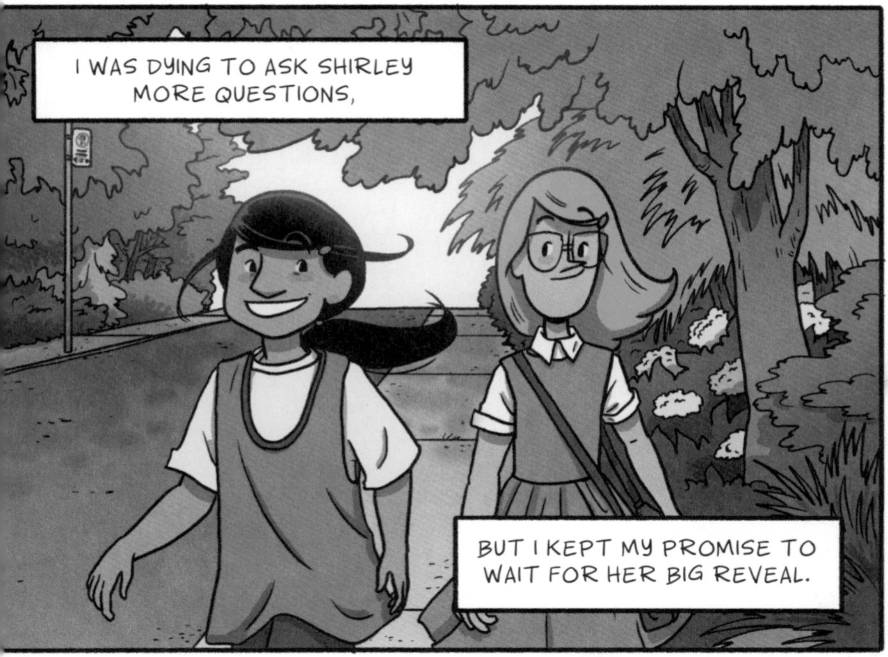
I WAS DYING TO ASK SHIRLEY MORE QUESTIONS,
BUT I KEPT MY PROMISE TO WAIT FOR HER BIG REVEAL.

Chapter 13

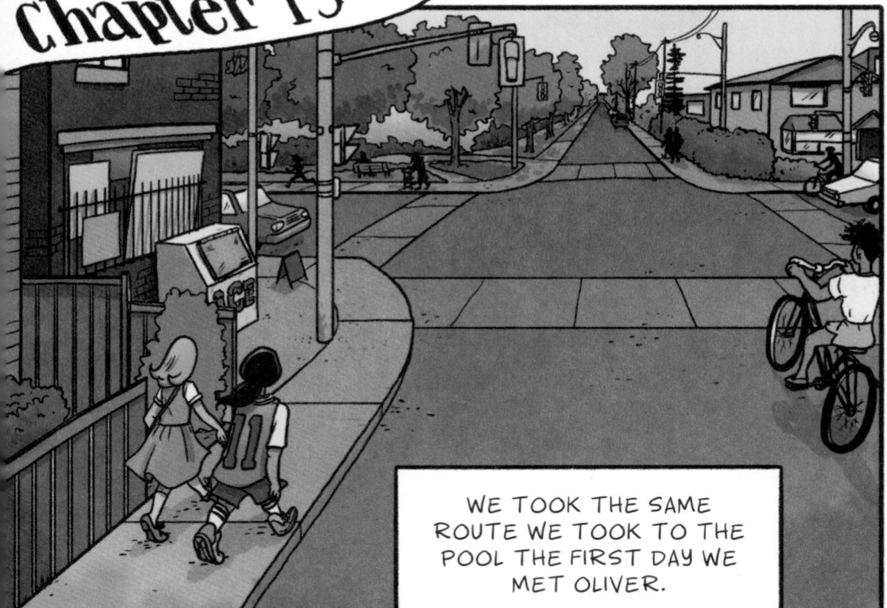
WE TOOK THE SAME ROUTE WE TOOK TO THE POOL THE FIRST DAY WE MET OLIVER.

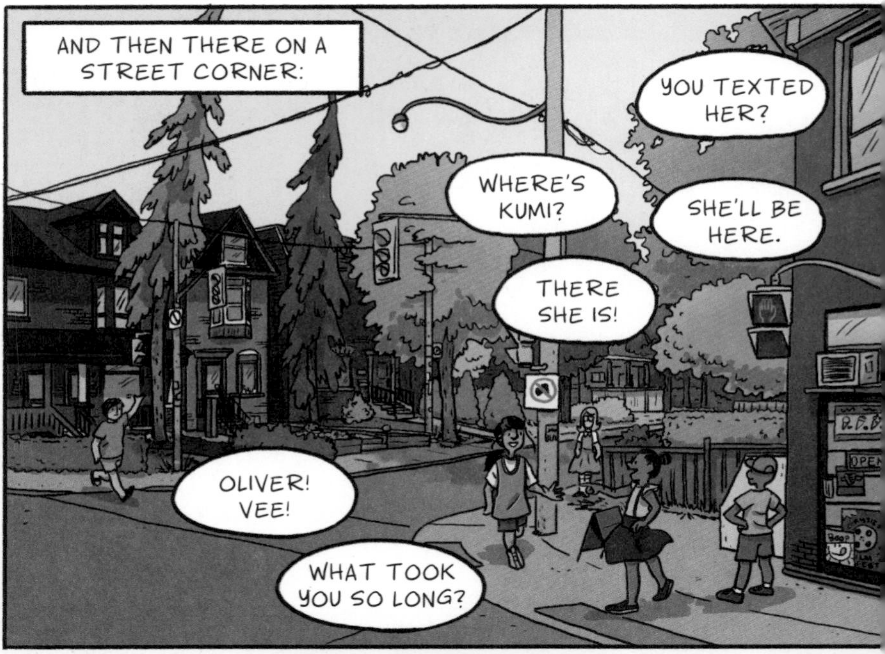
AND THEN THERE ON A STREET CORNER:
YOU TEXTED HER?
WHERE'S KUMI?
SHE'LL BE HERE.
THERE SHE IS!
OLIVER! VEE!
WHAT TOOK YOU SO LONG?

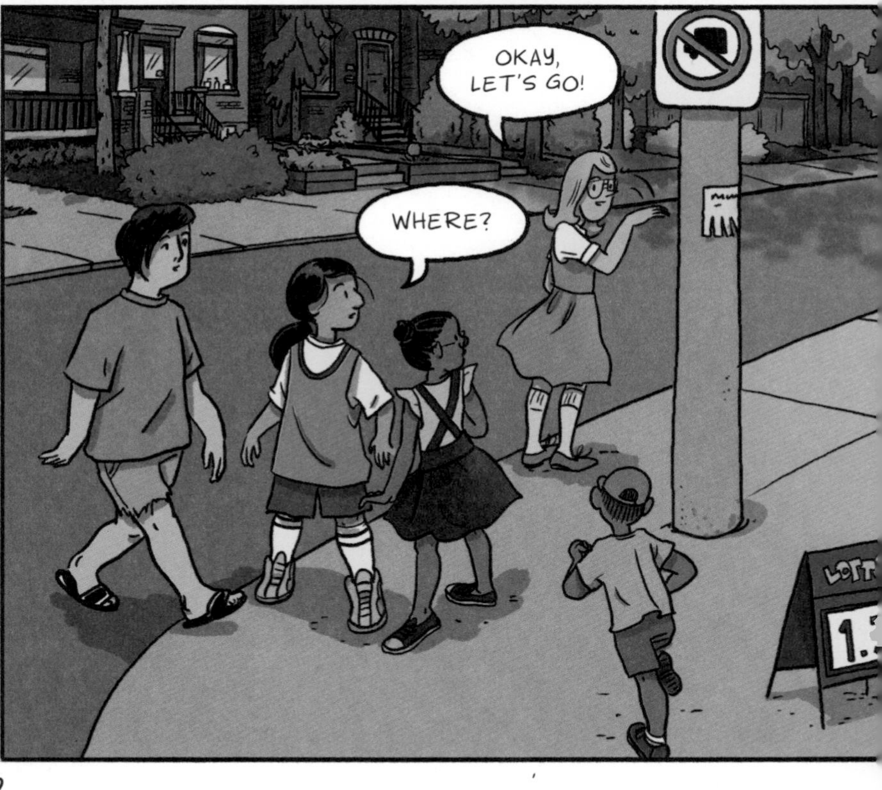
OKAY, LET'S GO!
WHERE?

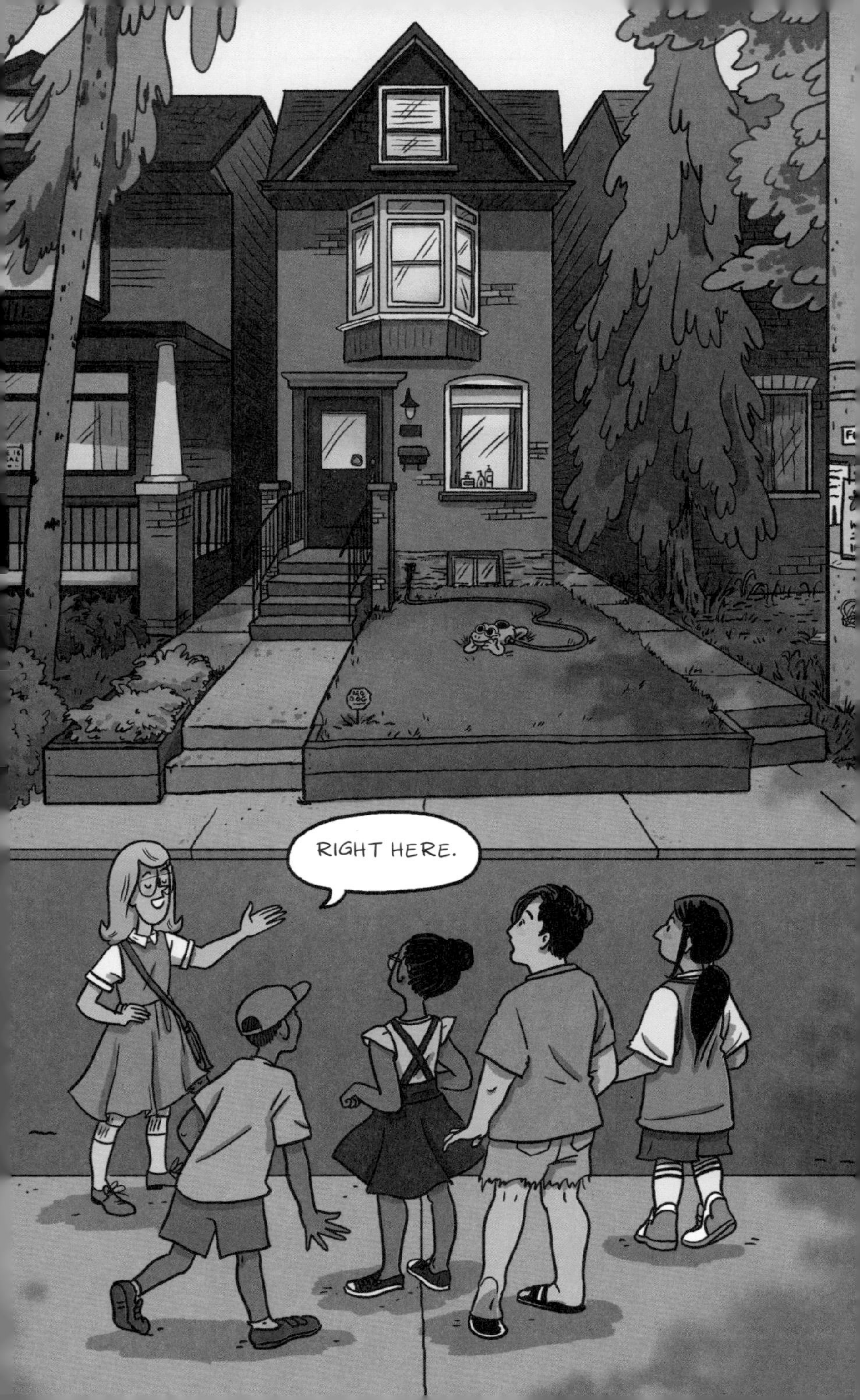
RIGHT HERE.

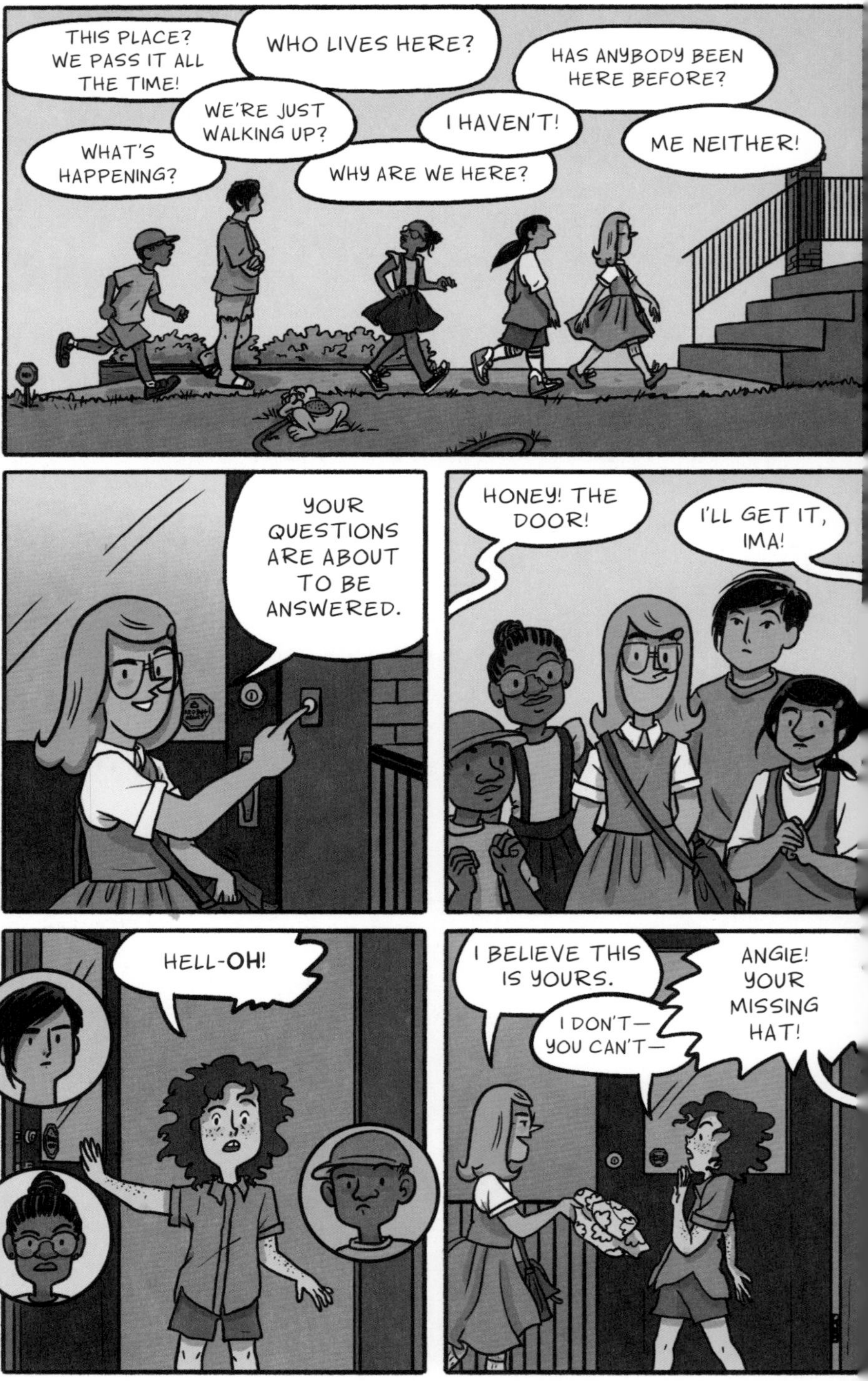
THIS PLACE? WE PASS IT ALL THE TIME!
WHO LIVES HERE?
HAS ANYBODY BEEN HERE BEFORE?
WE'RE JUST WALKING UP?
I HAVEN'T!
ME NEITHER!
WHAT'S HAPPENING?
WHY ARE WE HERE?
YOUR QUESTIONS ARE ABOUT TO BE ANSWERED.
HONEY! THE DOOR!
I'LL GET IT, IMA!
HELL-**OH**!
I BELIEVE THIS IS YOURS.
I DON'T— YOU CAN'T—
ANGIE! YOUR MISSING HAT!

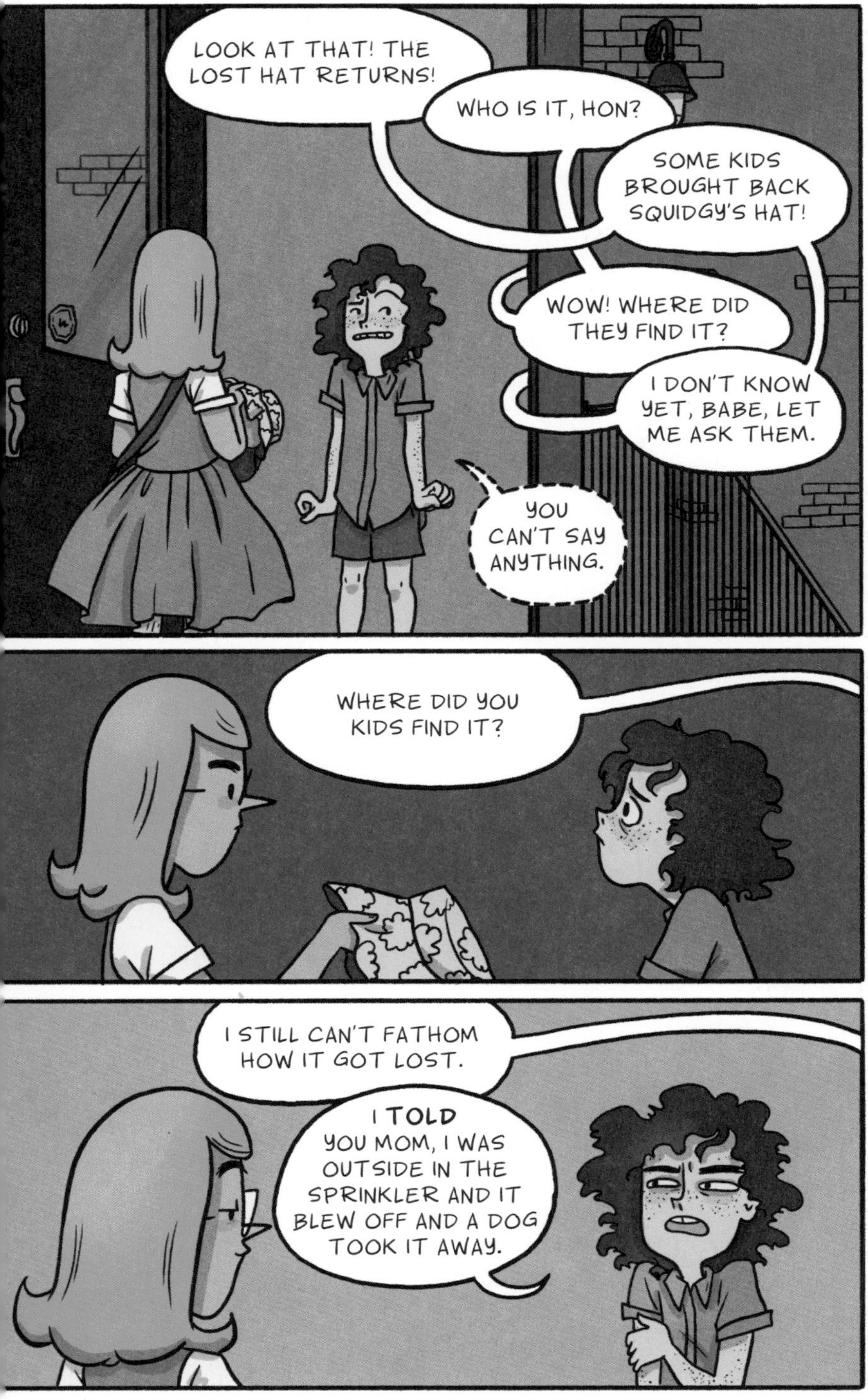
LOOK AT THAT! THE LOST HAT RETURNS!
WHO IS IT, HON?
SOME KIDS BROUGHT BACK SQUIDGY'S HAT!
WOW! WHERE DID THEY FIND IT?
I DON'T KNOW YET, BABE, LET ME ASK THEM.
YOU CAN'T SAY ANYTHING.
WHERE DID YOU KIDS FIND IT?
I STILL CAN'T FATHOM HOW IT GOT LOST.
I **TOLD** YOU MOM, I WAS OUTSIDE IN THE SPRINKLER AND IT BLEW OFF AND A DOG TOOK IT AWAY.

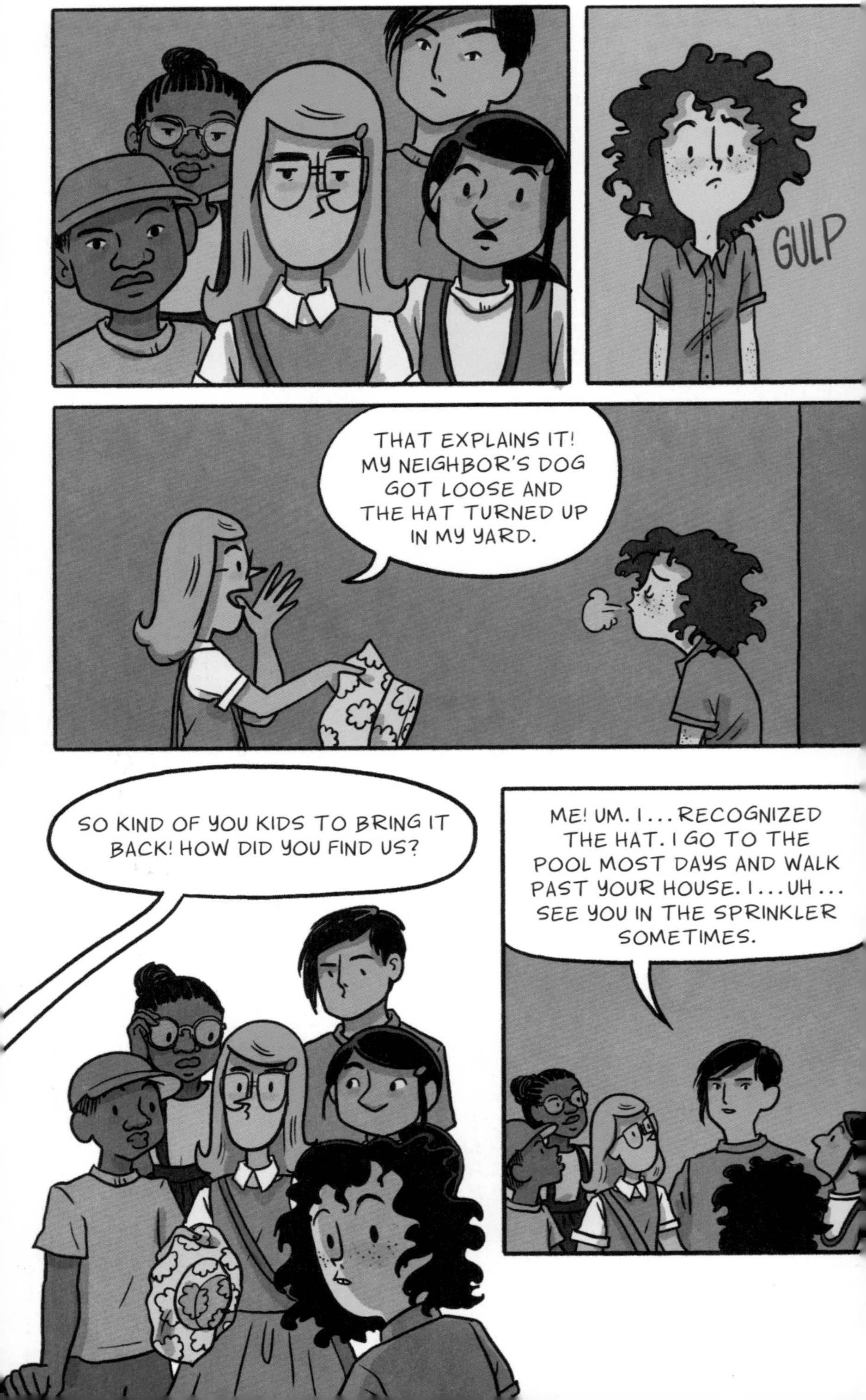
GULP
THAT EXPLAINS IT! MY NEIGHBOR'S DOG GOT LOOSE AND THE HAT TURNED UP IN MY YARD.
SO KIND OF YOU KIDS TO BRING IT BACK! HOW DID YOU FIND US?
ME! UM. I . . . RECOGNIZED THE HAT. I GO TO THE POOL MOST DAYS AND WALK PAST YOUR HOUSE. I . . . UH . . . SEE YOU IN THE SPRINKLER SOMETIMES.

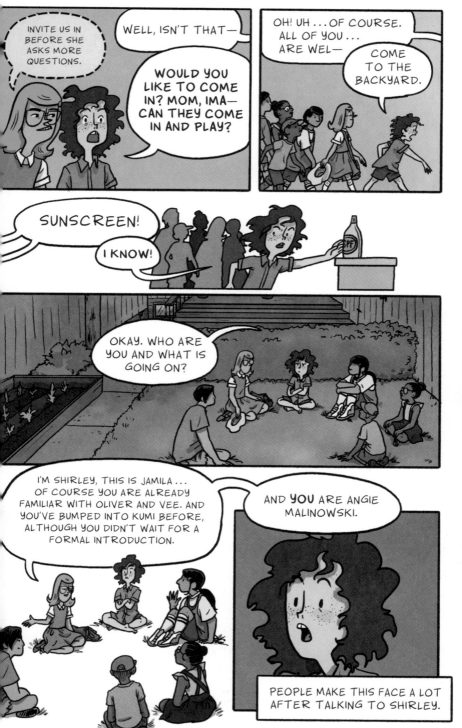

INVITE US IN BEFORE SHE ASKS MORE QUESTIONS.

WELL, ISN'T THAT—

WOULD YOU LIKE TO COME IN? MOM, IMA— CAN THEY COME IN AND PLAY?

OH! UH...OF COURSE. ALL OF YOU... ARE WEL—

COME TO THE BACKYARD.

SUNSCREEN!

I KNOW!

OKAY. WHO ARE YOU AND WHAT IS GOING ON?

I'M SHIRLEY, THIS IS JAMILA... OF COURSE YOU ARE ALREADY FAMILIAR WITH OLIVER AND VEE. AND YOU'VE BUMPED INTO KUMI BEFORE, ALTHOUGH YOU DIDN'T WAIT FOR A FORMAL INTRODUCTION.

AND **YOU** ARE ANGIE MALINOWSKI.

PEOPLE MAKE THIS FACE A LOT AFTER TALKING TO SHIRLEY.

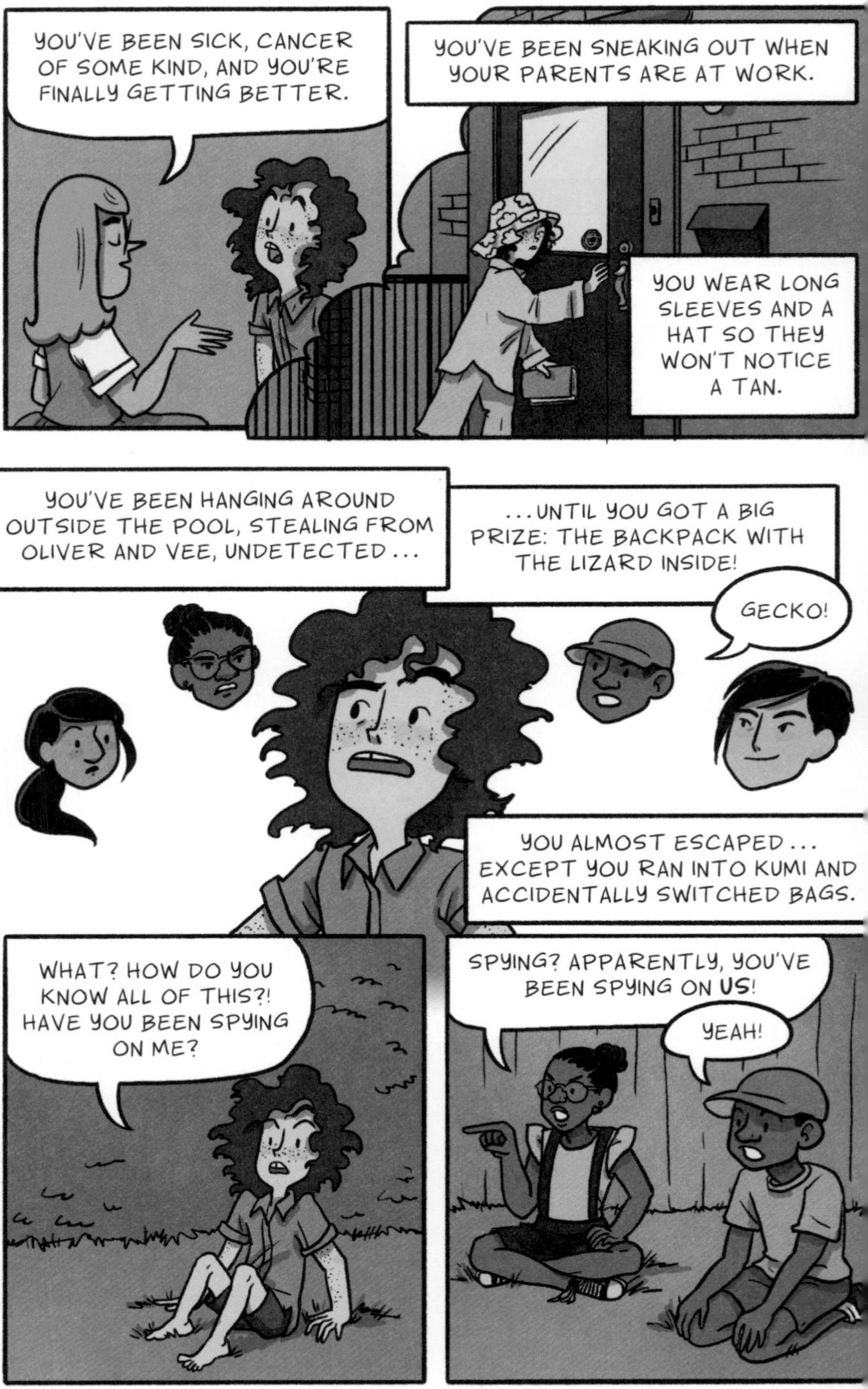
YOU'VE BEEN SICK, CANCER OF SOME KIND, AND YOU'RE FINALLY GETTING BETTER.
YOU'VE BEEN SNEAKING OUT WHEN YOUR PARENTS ARE AT WORK.
YOU WEAR LONG SLEEVES AND A HAT SO THEY WON'T NOTICE A TAN.
YOU'VE BEEN HANGING AROUND OUTSIDE THE POOL, STEALING FROM OLIVER AND VEE, UNDETECTED . . .
. . . UNTIL YOU GOT A BIG PRIZE: THE BACKPACK WITH THE LIZARD INSIDE!
GECKO!
YOU ALMOST ESCAPED . . . EXCEPT YOU RAN INTO KUMI AND ACCIDENTALLY SWITCHED BAGS.
WHAT? HOW DO YOU KNOW ALL OF THIS?! HAVE YOU BEEN SPYING ON ME?
SPYING? APPARENTLY, YOU'VE BEEN SPYING ON US!
YEAH!

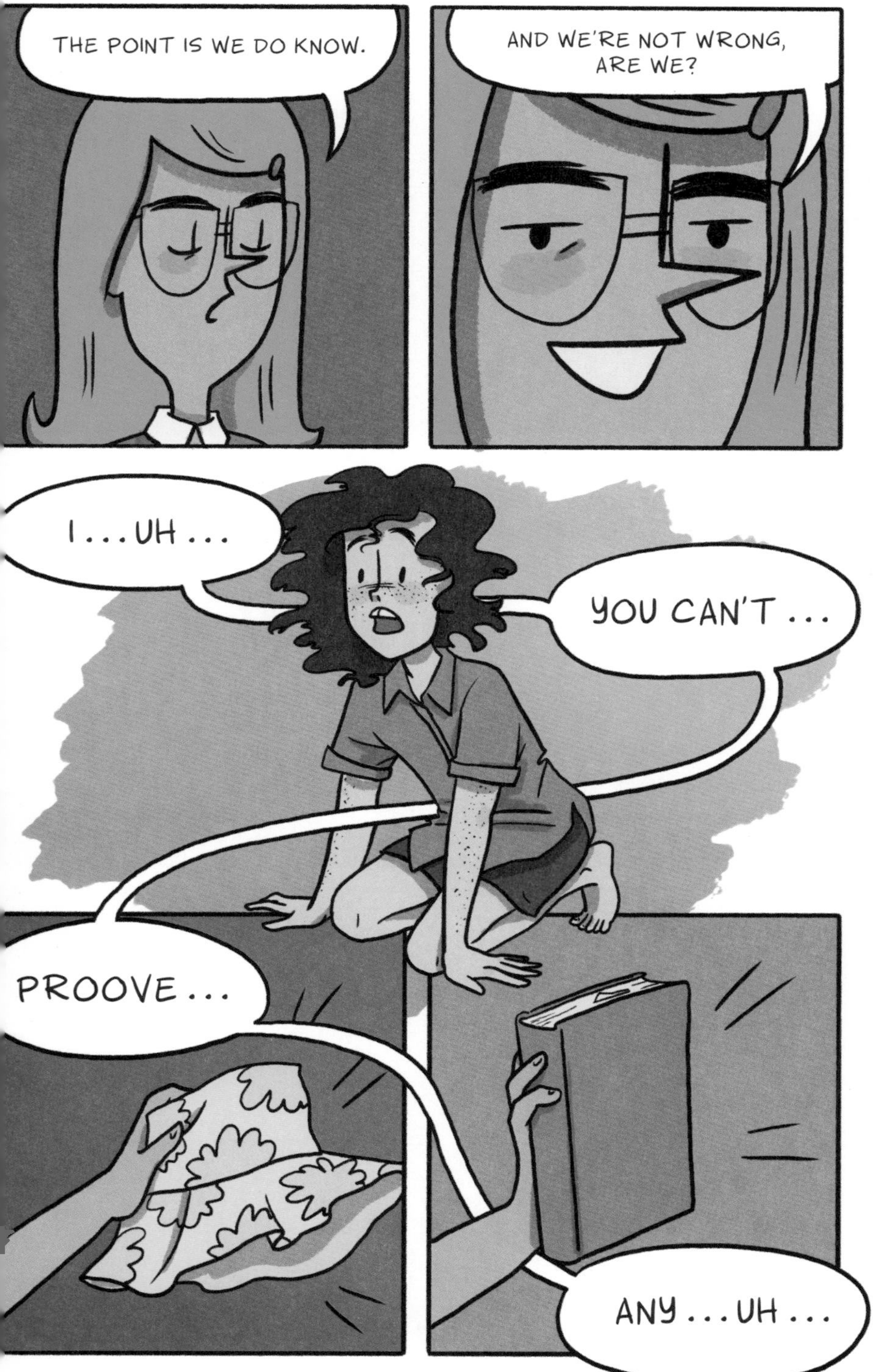
THE POINT IS WE DO KNOW.
AND WE'RE NOT WRONG, ARE WE?
I . . . UH . . .
YOU CAN'T . . .
PROOVE . . .
ANY . . . UH . . .

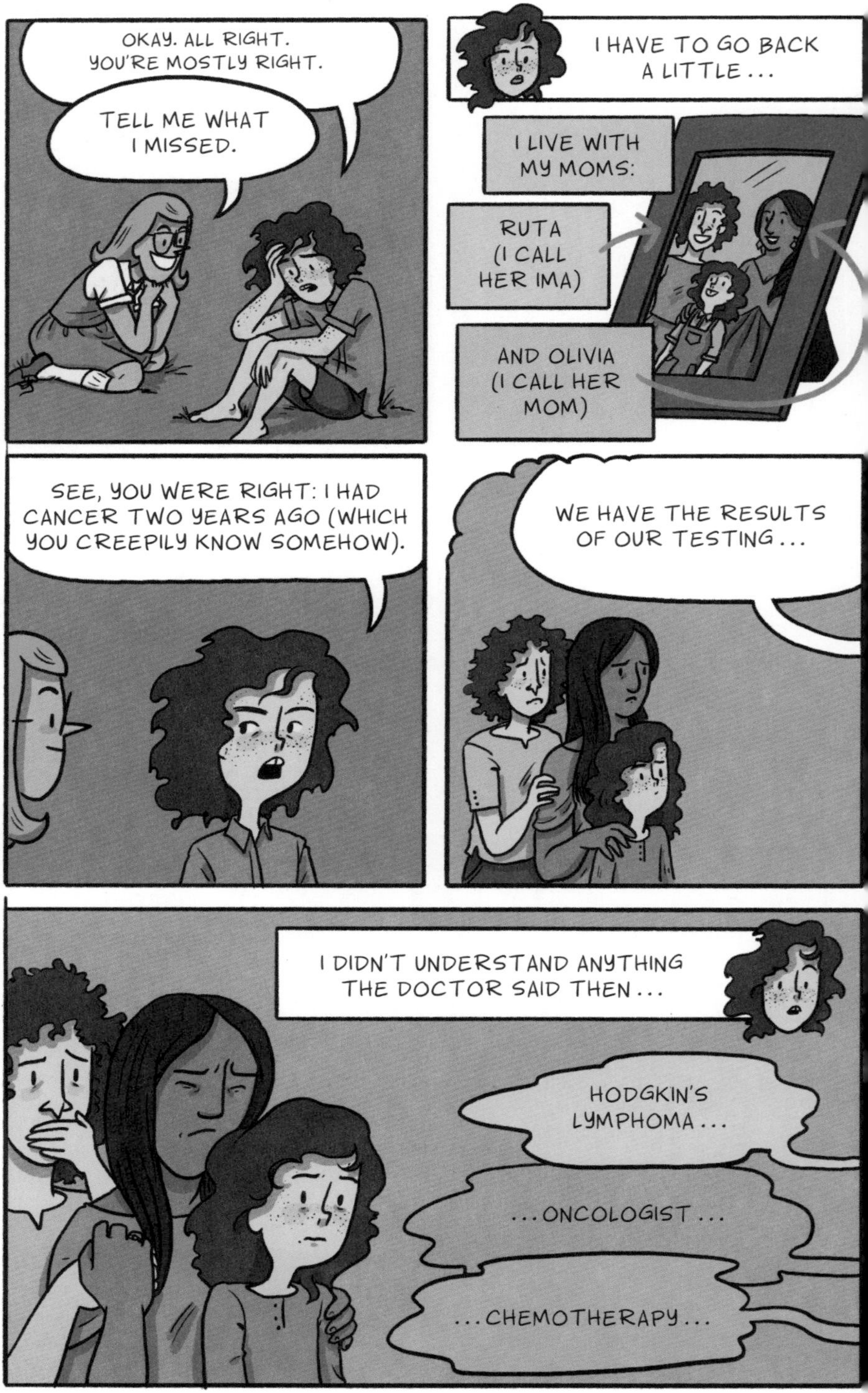
OKAY. ALL RIGHT. YOU'RE MOSTLY RIGHT.
TELL ME WHAT I MISSED.
I HAVE TO GO BACK A LITTLE . . .
I LIVE WITH MY MOMS:
RUTA (I CALL HER IMA)
AND OLIVIA (I CALL HER MOM)
SEE, YOU WERE RIGHT: I HAD CANCER TWO YEARS AGO (WHICH YOU CREEPILY KNOW SOMEHOW).
WE HAVE THE RESULTS OF OUR TESTING . . .
I DIDN'T UNDERSTAND ANYTHING THE DOCTOR SAID THEN . . .
HODGKIN'S LYMPHOMA . . .
. . . ONCOLOGIST . . .
. . . CHEMOTHERAPY . . .

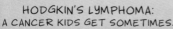
BUT I FOUND OUT **PLENTY** SOON ENOUGH.

HODGKIN'S LYMPHOMA: A CANCER KIDS GET SOMETIMES.

ONCOLOGIST: CANCER DOCTOR.

CHEMOTHERAPY ("CHEMO"): CANCER MEDICINE WITH SIDE EFFECTS LIKE LOSING YOUR HAIR AND BEING SO TIRED AND FEELING LIKE YOU HAVE TO BARF ALL THE TIME.

IT **IS** SERIOUS. SOME PEOPLE DIE FROM IT.

BUT **LOTS** GET BETTER.

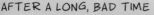
AFTER A LONG, BAD TIME

I STARTED TO GET BETTER TOO.

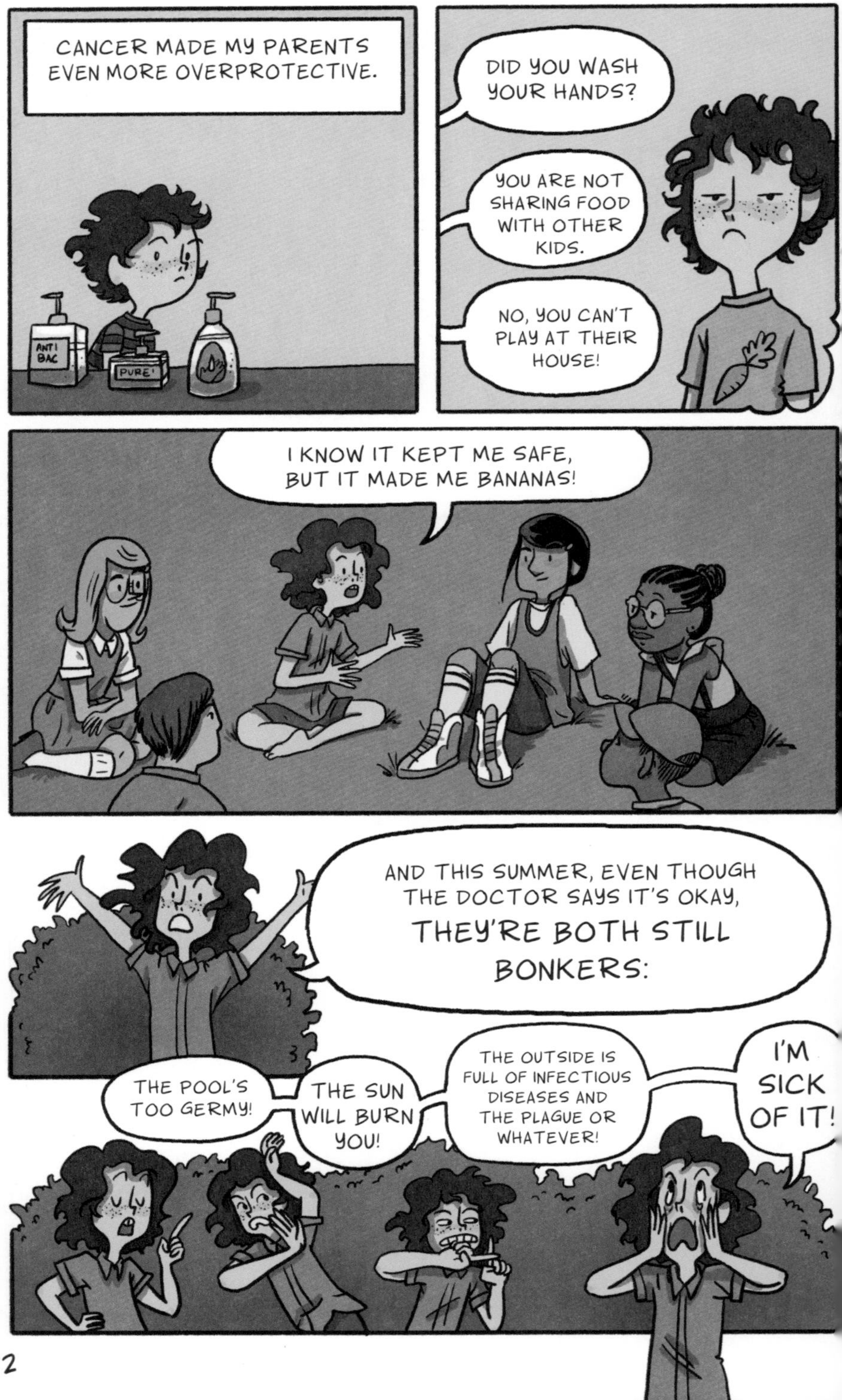
CANCER MADE MY PARENTS EVEN MORE OVERPROTECTIVE.
ANTI BAC
PURE
DID YOU WASH YOUR HANDS?
YOU ARE NOT SHARING FOOD WITH OTHER KIDS.
NO, YOU CAN'T PLAY AT THEIR HOUSE!
I KNOW IT KEPT ME SAFE, BUT IT MADE ME BANANAS!
AND THIS SUMMER, EVEN THOUGH THE DOCTOR SAYS IT'S OKAY, THEY'RE BOTH STILL BONKERS:
THE POOL'S TOO GERMY!
THE SUN WILL BURN YOU!
THE OUTSIDE IS FULL OF INFECTIOUS DISEASES AND THE PLAGUE OR WHATEVER!
I'M SICK OF IT!

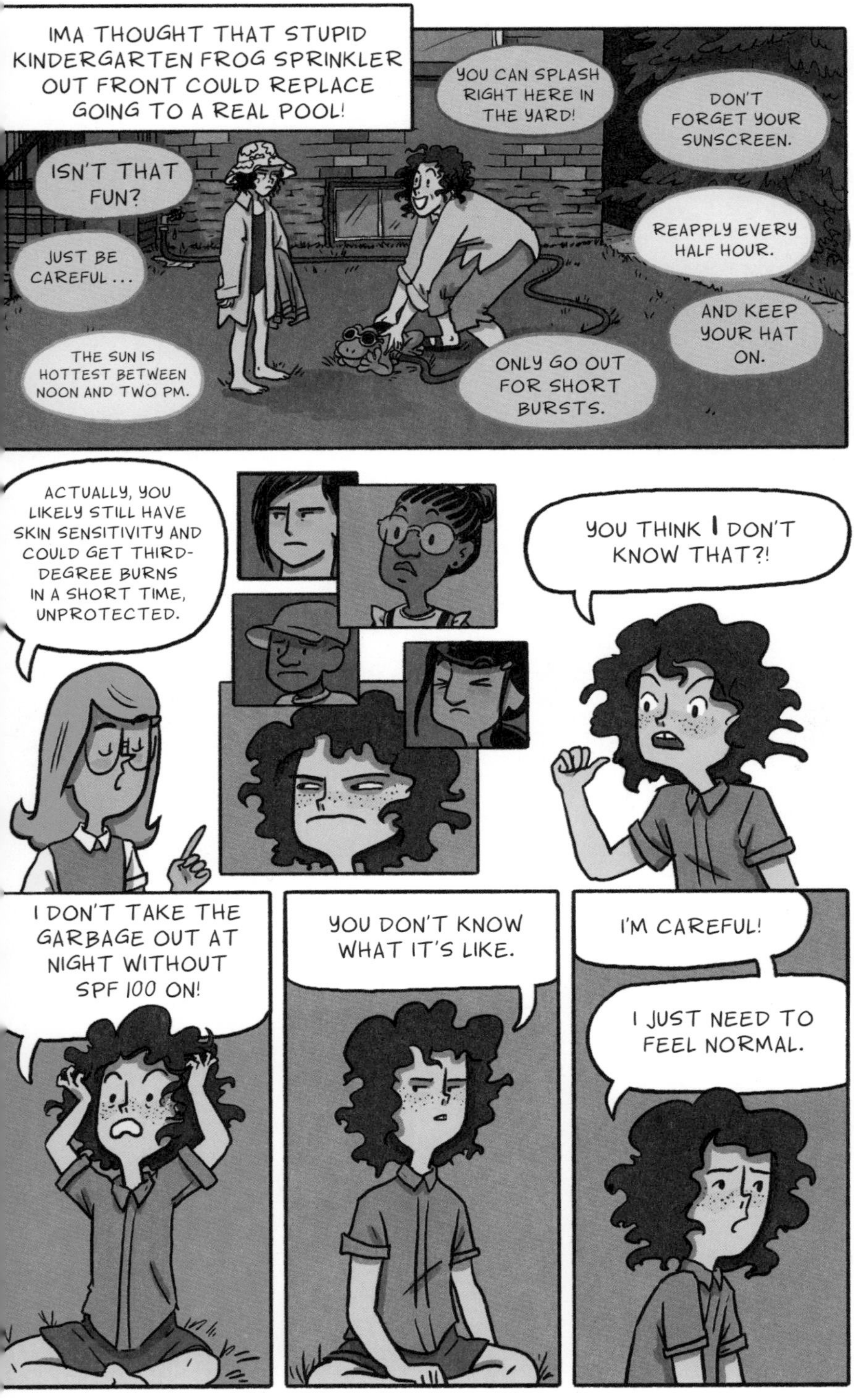
IMA THOUGHT THAT STUPID KINDERGARTEN FROG SPRINKLER OUT FRONT COULD REPLACE GOING TO A REAL POOL!
YOU CAN SPLASH RIGHT HERE IN THE YARD!
DON'T FORGET YOUR SUNSCREEN.
ISN'T THAT FUN?
REAPPLY EVERY HALF HOUR.
JUST BE CAREFUL ...
AND KEEP YOUR HAT ON.
THE SUN IS HOTTEST BETWEEN NOON AND TWO PM.
ONLY GO OUT FOR SHORT BURSTS.
ACTUALLY, YOU LIKELY STILL HAVE SKIN SENSITIVITY AND COULD GET THIRD-DEGREE BURNS IN A SHORT TIME, UNPROTECTED.
YOU THINK I DON'T KNOW THAT?!
I DON'T TAKE THE GARBAGE OUT AT NIGHT WITHOUT SPF 100 ON!
YOU DON'T KNOW WHAT IT'S LIKE.
I'M CAREFUL!
I JUST NEED TO FEEL NORMAL.

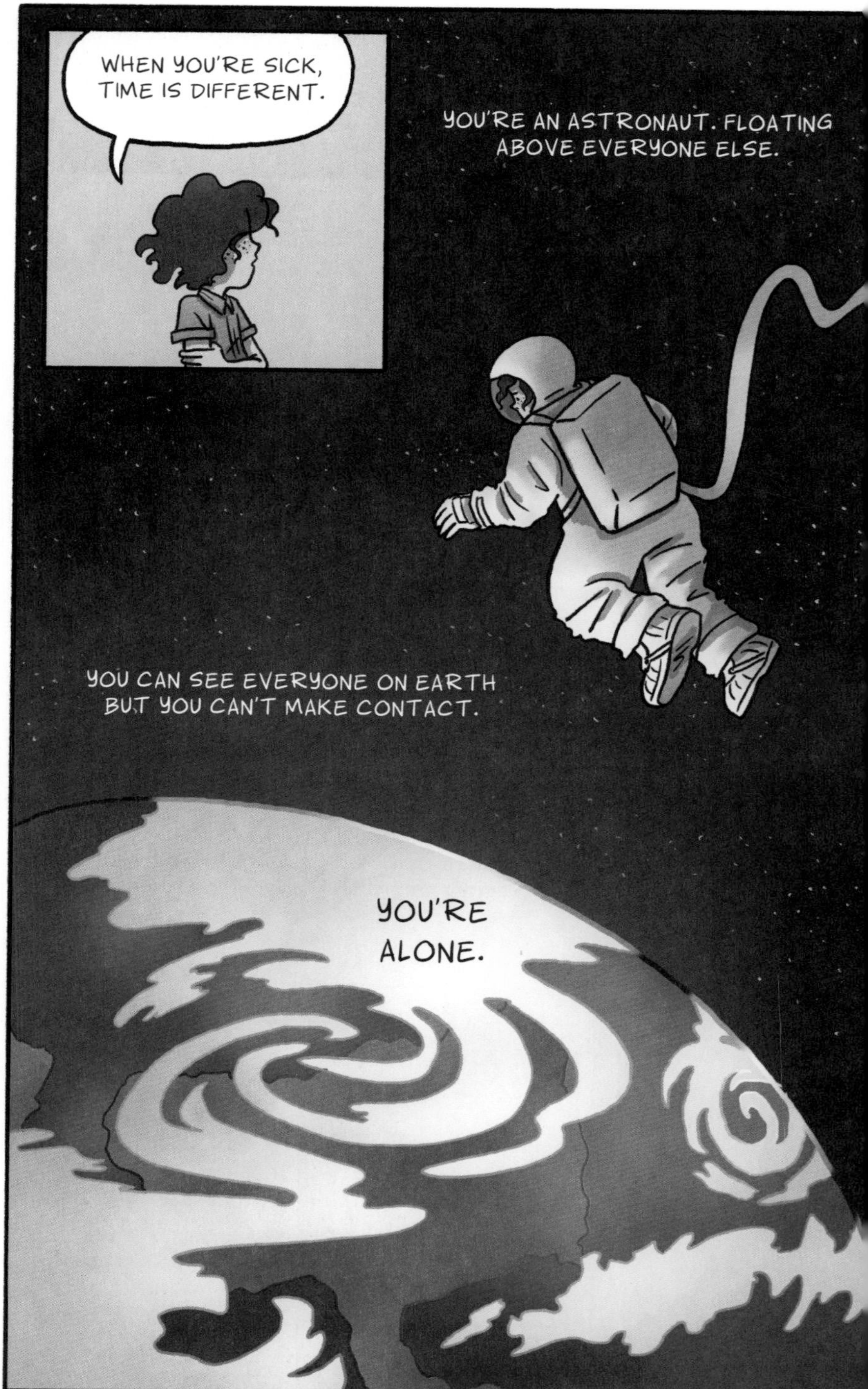
WHEN YOU'RE SICK, TIME IS DIFFERENT.
YOU'RE AN ASTRONAUT. FLOATING ABOVE EVERYONE ELSE.
YOU CAN SEE EVERYONE ON EARTH BUT YOU CAN'T MAKE CONTACT.
YOU'RE ALONE.

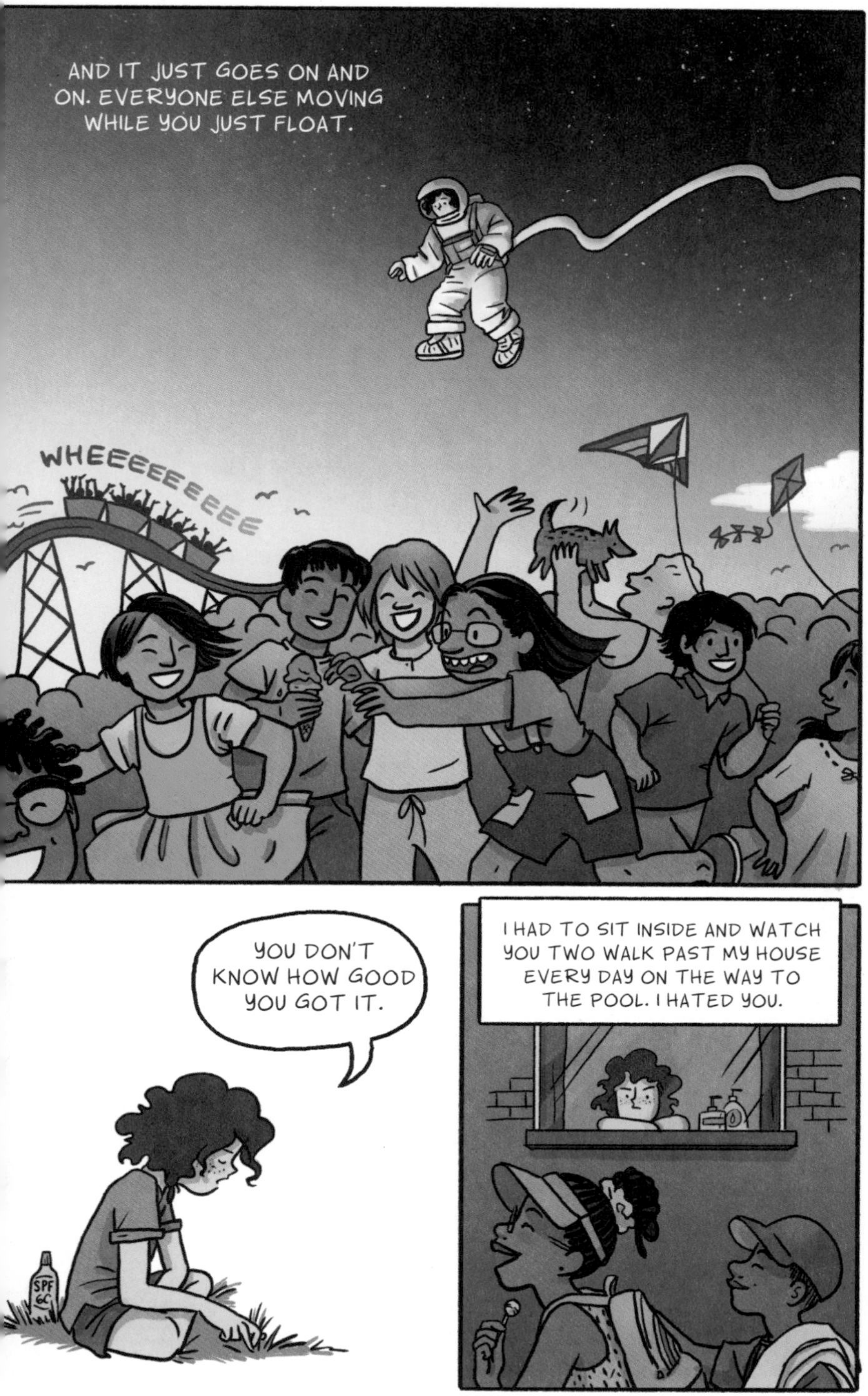

AND IT JUST GOES ON AND ON. EVERYONE ELSE MOVING WHILE YOU JUST FLOAT.
WHEEEEEEEEEE
YOU DON'T KNOW HOW GOOD YOU GOT IT.
SPF 60
I HAD TO SIT INSIDE AND WATCH YOU TWO WALK PAST MY HOUSE EVERY DAY ON THE WAY TO THE POOL. I HATED YOU.

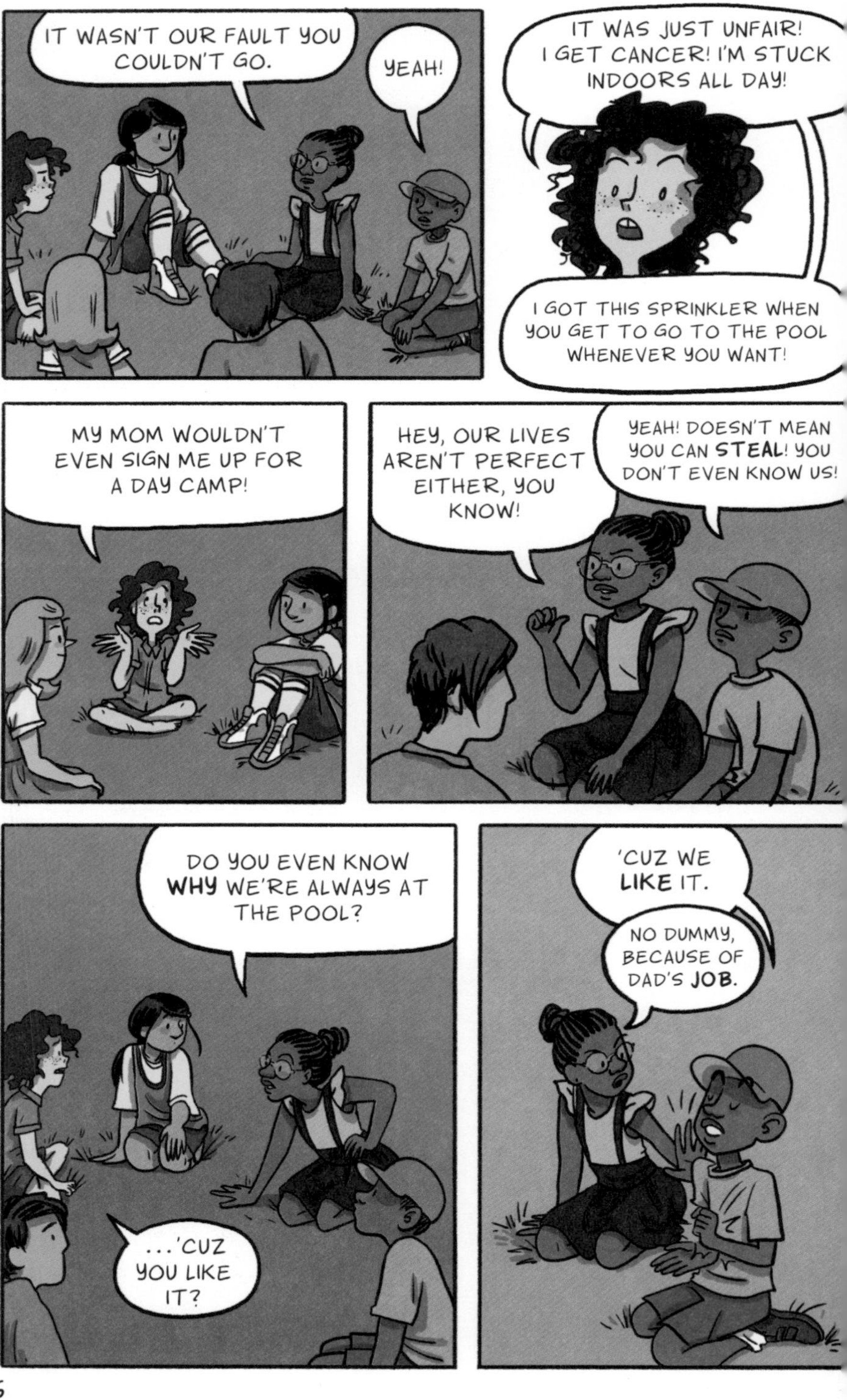
IT WASN'T OUR FAULT YOU COULDN'T GO.
YEAH!
IT WAS JUST UNFAIR! I GET CANCER! I'M STUCK INDOORS ALL DAY!
I GOT THIS SPRINKLER WHEN YOU GET TO GO TO THE POOL WHENEVER YOU WANT!
MY MOM WOULDN'T EVEN SIGN ME UP FOR A DAY CAMP!
HEY, OUR LIVES AREN'T PERFECT EITHER, YOU KNOW!
YEAH! DOESN'T MEAN YOU CAN **STEAL**! YOU DON'T EVEN KNOW US!
DO YOU EVEN KNOW **WHY** WE'RE ALWAYS AT THE POOL?
...'CUZ YOU LIKE IT?
'CUZ WE **LIKE** IT.
NO DUMMY, BECAUSE OF DAD'S **JOB**.

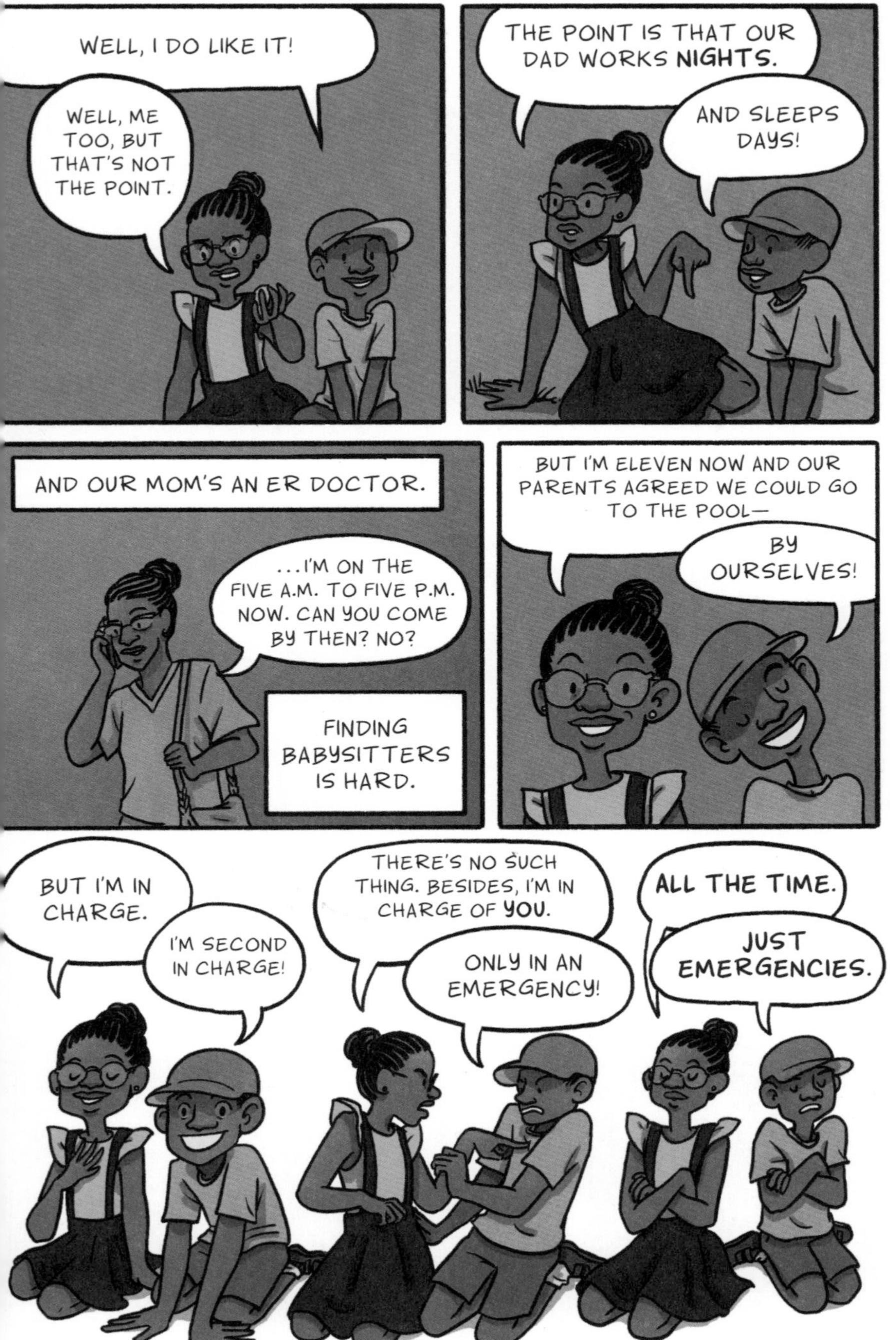

WELL, I DO LIKE IT!
WELL, ME TOO, BUT THAT'S NOT THE POINT.
THE POINT IS THAT OUR DAD WORKS **NIGHTS.**
AND SLEEPS DAYS!
AND OUR MOM'S AN ER DOCTOR.
...I'M ON THE FIVE A.M. TO FIVE P.M. NOW. CAN YOU COME BY THEN? NO?
FINDING BABYSITTERS IS HARD.
BUT I'M ELEVEN NOW AND OUR PARENTS AGREED WE COULD GO TO THE POOL—
BY OURSELVES!
BUT I'M IN CHARGE.
I'M SECOND IN CHARGE!
THERE'S NO SUCH THING. BESIDES, I'M IN CHARGE OF **YOU.**
ONLY IN AN EMERGENCY!
ALL THE TIME.
JUST EMERGENCIES.

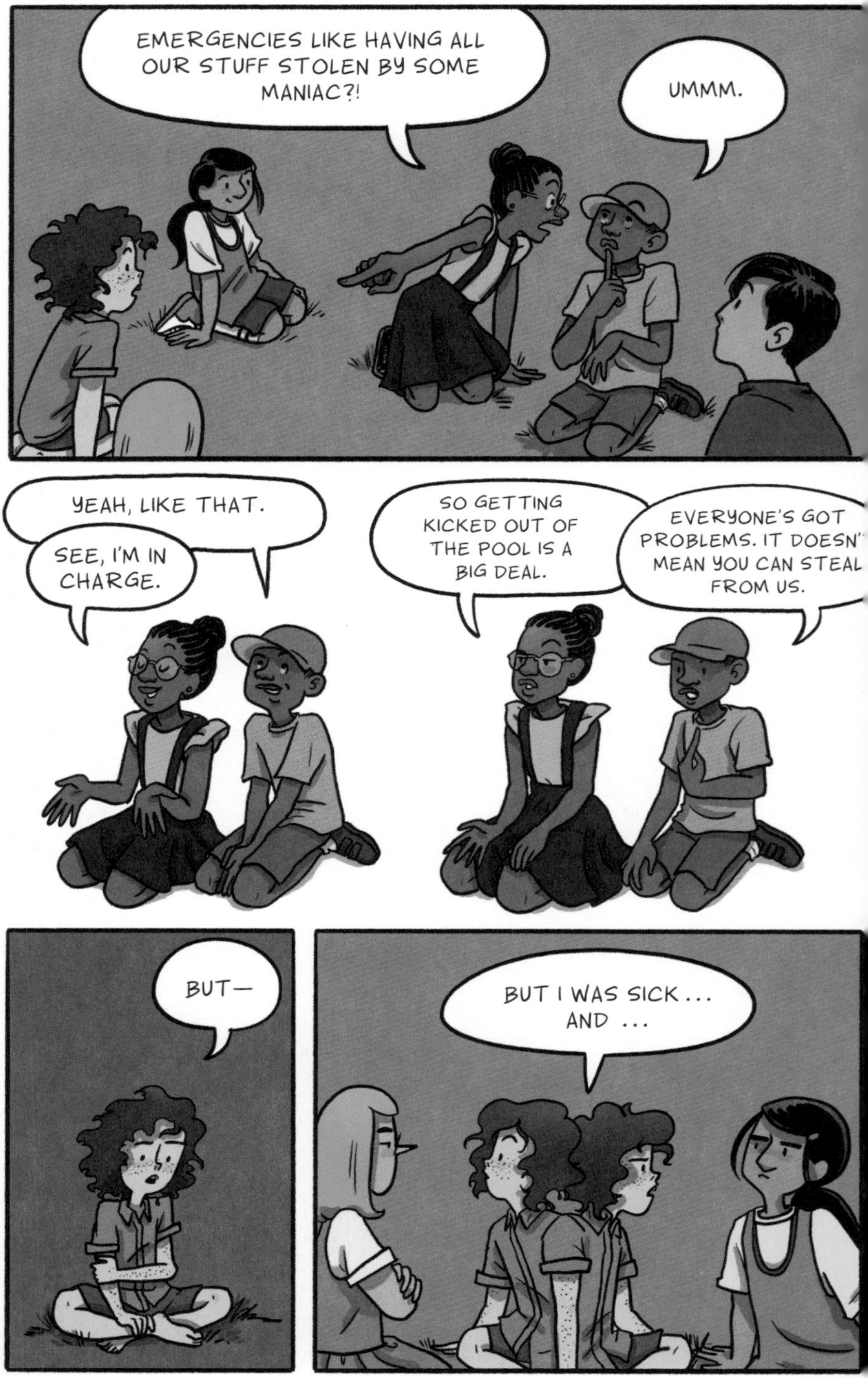

EMERGENCIES LIKE HAVING ALL OUR STUFF STOLEN BY SOME MANIAC?!
UMMM.
YEAH, LIKE THAT.
SEE, I'M IN CHARGE.
SO GETTING KICKED OUT OF THE POOL IS A BIG DEAL.
EVERYONE'S GOT PROBLEMS. IT DOESN'T MEAN YOU CAN STEAL FROM US.
BUT—
BUT I WAS SICK . . . AND . . .

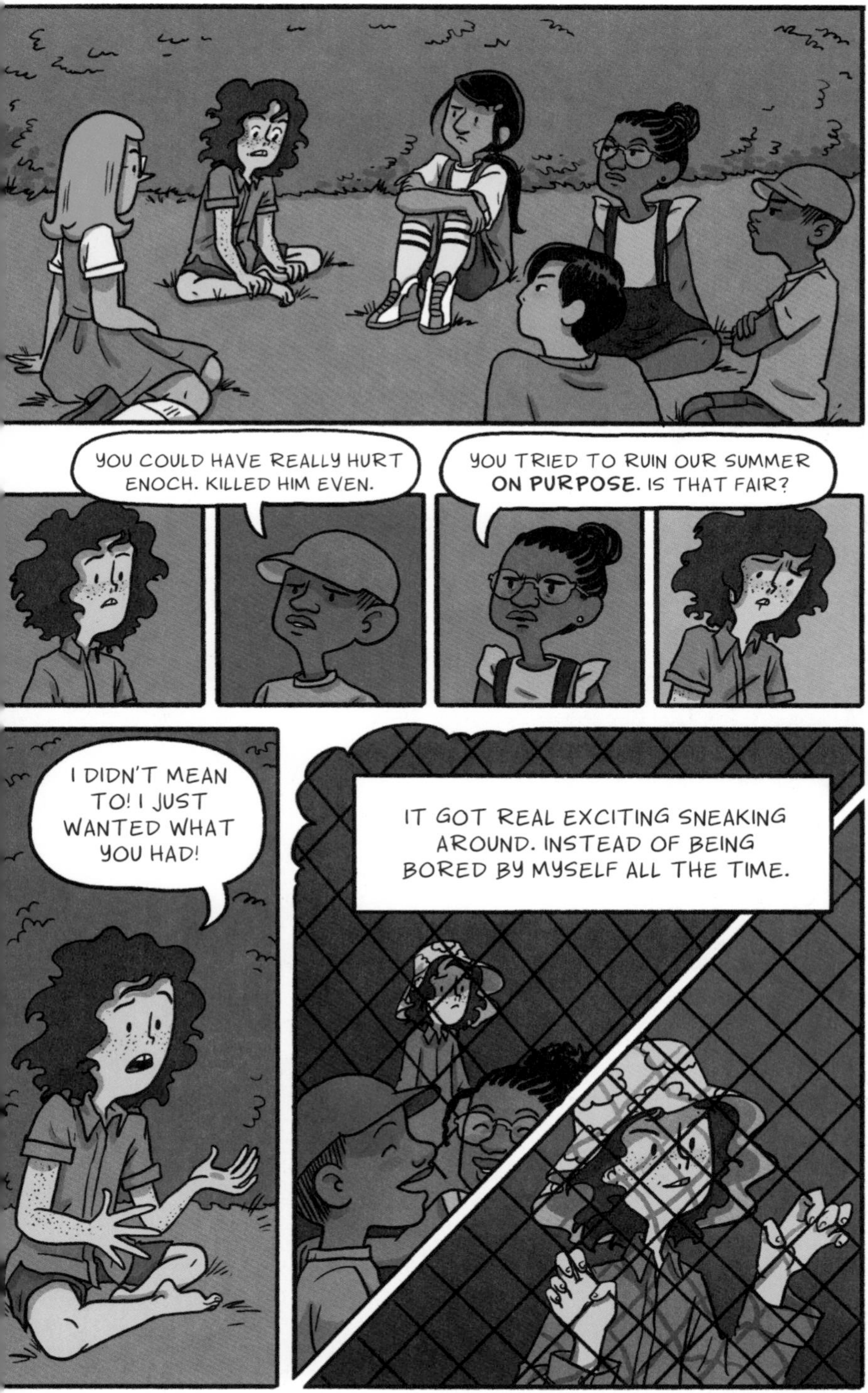
YOU COULD HAVE REALLY HURT ENOCH. KILLED HIM EVEN.
YOU TRIED TO RUIN OUR SUMMER **ON PURPOSE**. IS THAT FAIR?
I DIDN'T MEAN TO! I JUST WANTED WHAT YOU HAD!
IT GOT REAL EXCITING SNEAKING AROUND. INSTEAD OF BEING BORED BY MYSELF ALL THE TIME.

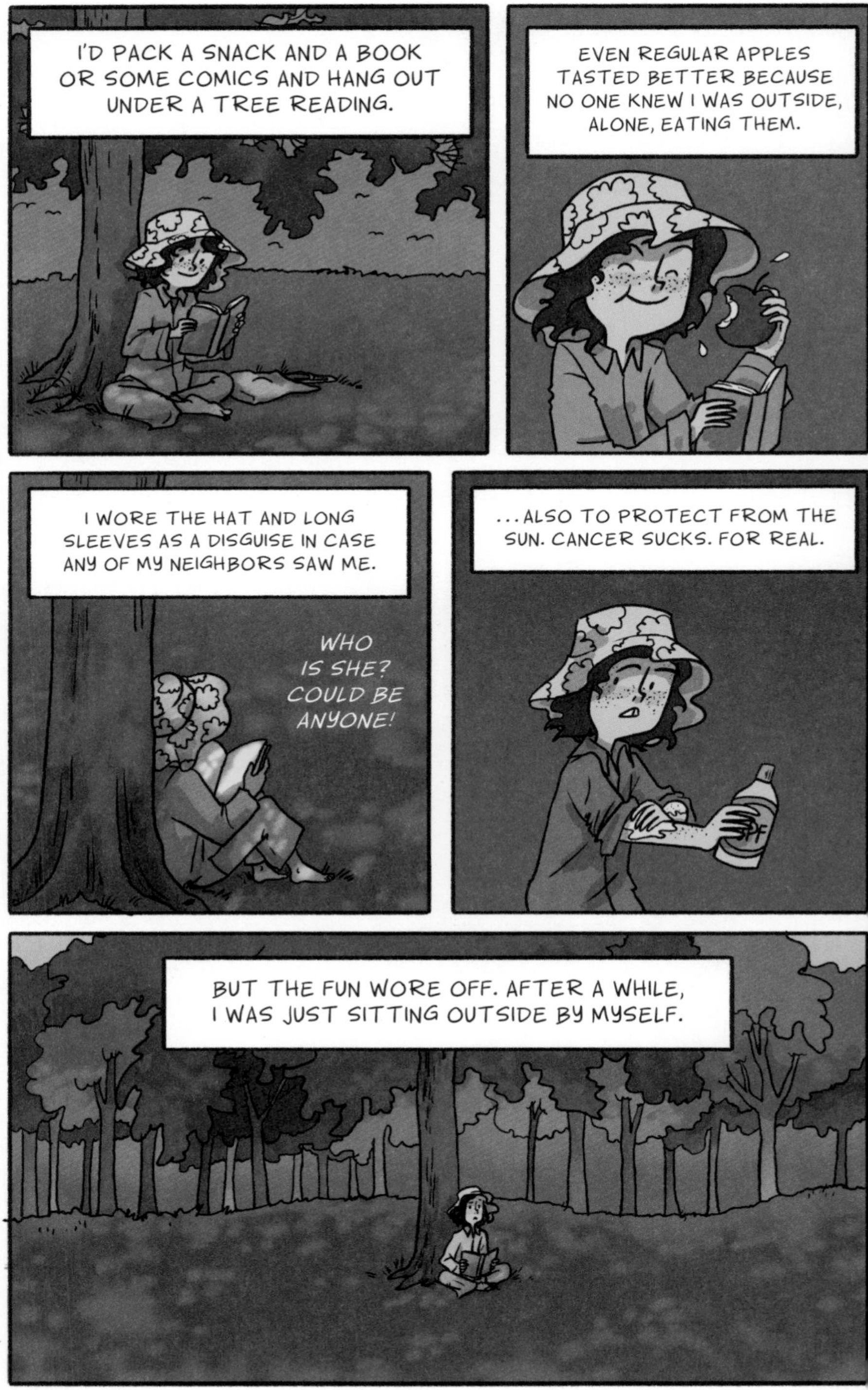
I'D PACK A SNACK AND A BOOK OR SOME COMICS AND HANG OUT UNDER A TREE READING.
EVEN REGULAR APPLES TASTED BETTER BECAUSE NO ONE KNEW I WAS OUTSIDE, ALONE, EATING THEM.
I WORE THE HAT AND LONG SLEEVES AS A DISGUISE IN CASE ANY OF MY NEIGHBORS SAW ME.
WHO IS SHE? COULD BE ANYONE!
...ALSO TO PROTECT FROM THE SUN. CANCER SUCKS. FOR REAL.
SPF
BUT THE FUN WORE OFF. AFTER A WHILE, I WAS JUST SITTING OUTSIDE BY MYSELF.

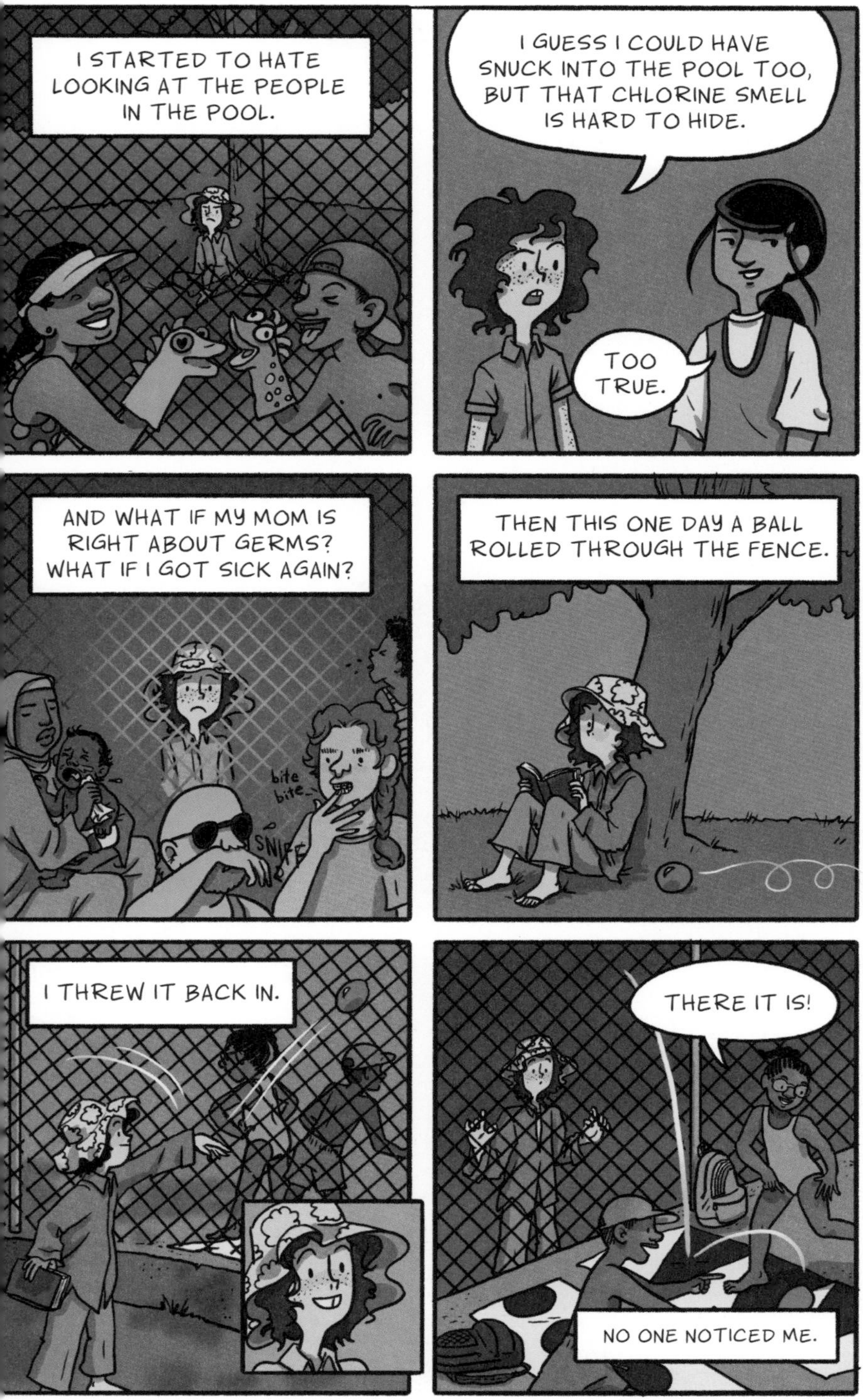
I STARTED TO HATE LOOKING AT THE PEOPLE IN THE POOL.
I GUESS I COULD HAVE SNUCK INTO THE POOL TOO, BUT THAT CHLORINE SMELL IS HARD TO HIDE.
TOO TRUE.
AND WHAT IF MY MOM IS RIGHT ABOUT GERMS? WHAT IF I GOT SICK AGAIN?
bite bite
THEN THIS ONE DAY A BALL ROLLED THROUGH THE FENCE.
I THREW IT BACK IN.
THERE IT IS!
NO ONE NOTICED ME.

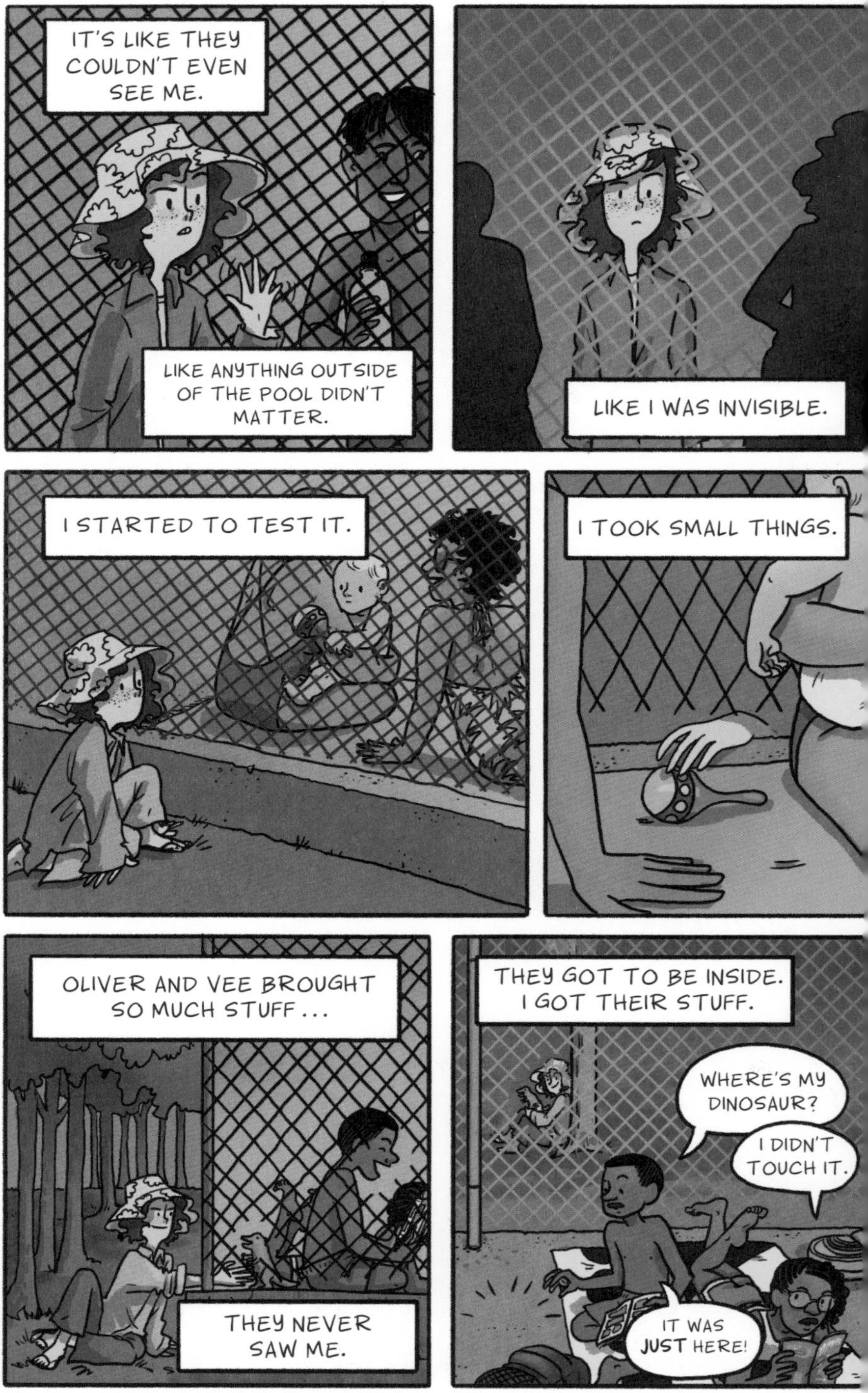
IT'S LIKE THEY COULDN'T EVEN SEE ME.
LIKE ANYTHING OUTSIDE OF THE POOL DIDN'T MATTER.
LIKE I WAS INVISIBLE.
I STARTED TO TEST IT.
I TOOK SMALL THINGS.
OLIVER AND VEE BROUGHT SO MUCH STUFF . . .
THEY NEVER SAW ME.
THEY GOT TO BE INSIDE. I GOT THEIR STUFF.
WHERE'S MY DINOSAUR?
I DIDN'T TOUCH IT.
IT WAS **JUST** HERE!

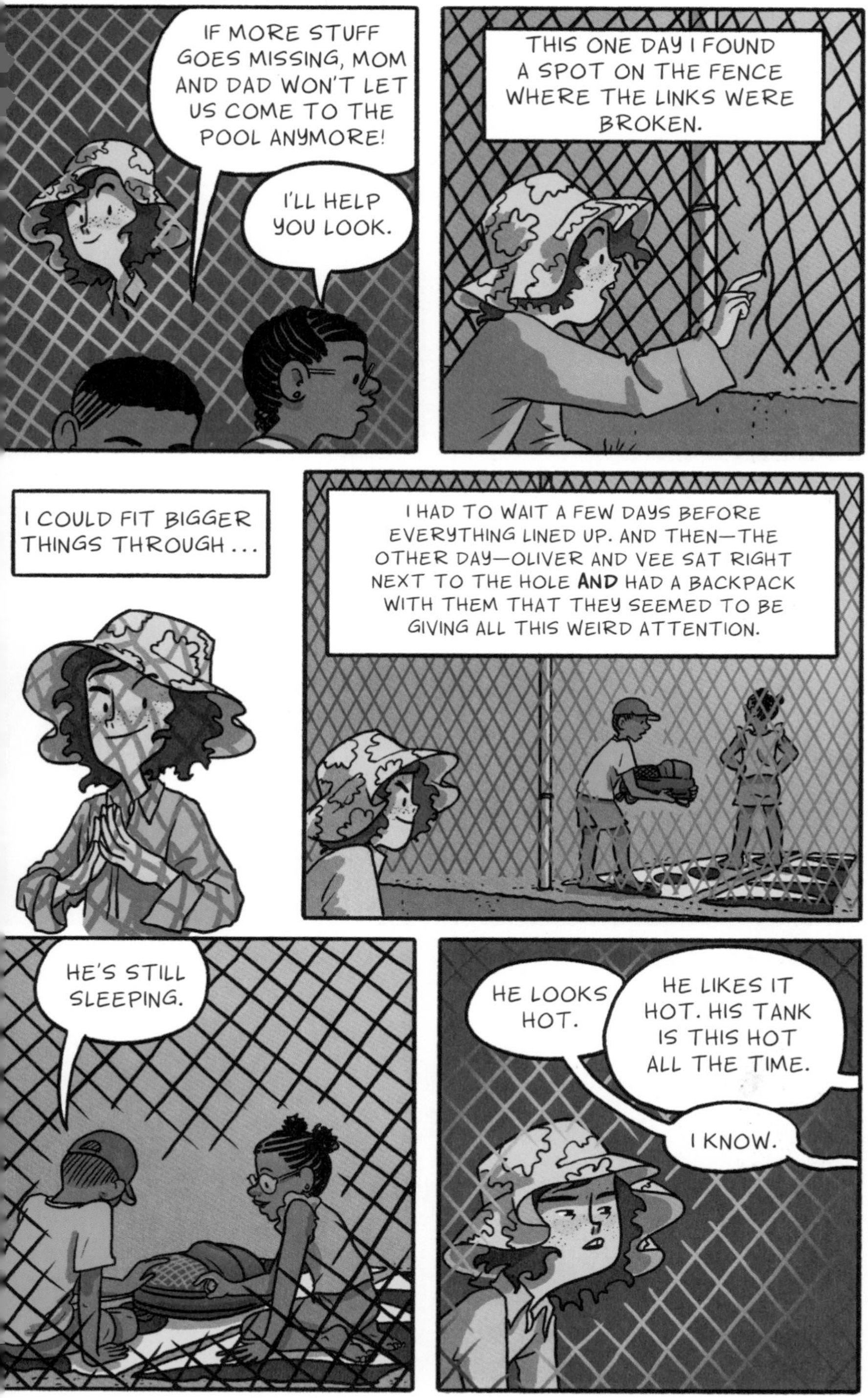
IF MORE STUFF GOES MISSING, MOM AND DAD WON'T LET US COME TO THE POOL ANYMORE!
I'LL HELP YOU LOOK.
THIS ONE DAY I FOUND A SPOT ON THE FENCE WHERE THE LINKS WERE BROKEN.
I COULD FIT BIGGER THINGS THROUGH . . .
I HAD TO WAIT A FEW DAYS BEFORE EVERYTHING LINED UP. AND THEN—THE OTHER DAY—OLIVER AND VEE SAT RIGHT NEXT TO THE HOLE **AND** HAD A BACKPACK WITH THEM THAT THEY SEEMED TO BE GIVING ALL THIS WEIRD ATTENTION.
HE'S STILL SLEEPING.
HE LOOKS HOT.
HE LIKES IT HOT. HIS TANK IS THIS HOT ALL THE TIME.
I KNOW.

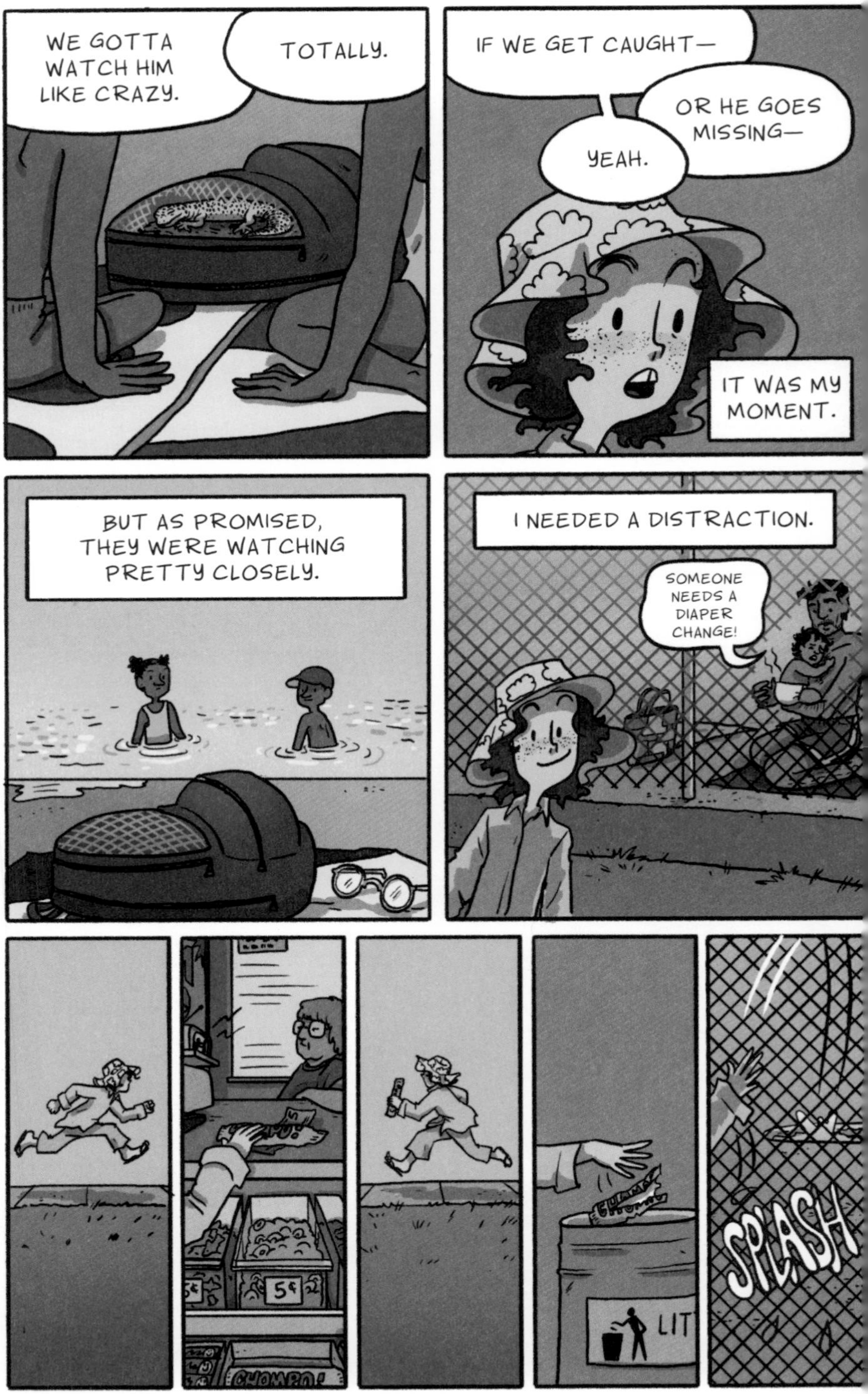
WE GOTTA WATCH HIM LIKE CRAZY.
TOTALLY.
IF WE GET CAUGHT—
OR HE GOES MISSING—
YEAH.
IT WAS MY MOMENT.
BUT AS PROMISED, THEY WERE WATCHING PRETTY CLOSELY.
I NEEDED A DISTRACTION.
SOMEONE NEEDS A DIAPER CHANGE!
5¢
5¢
CHOMBO!
LIT
SPLASH

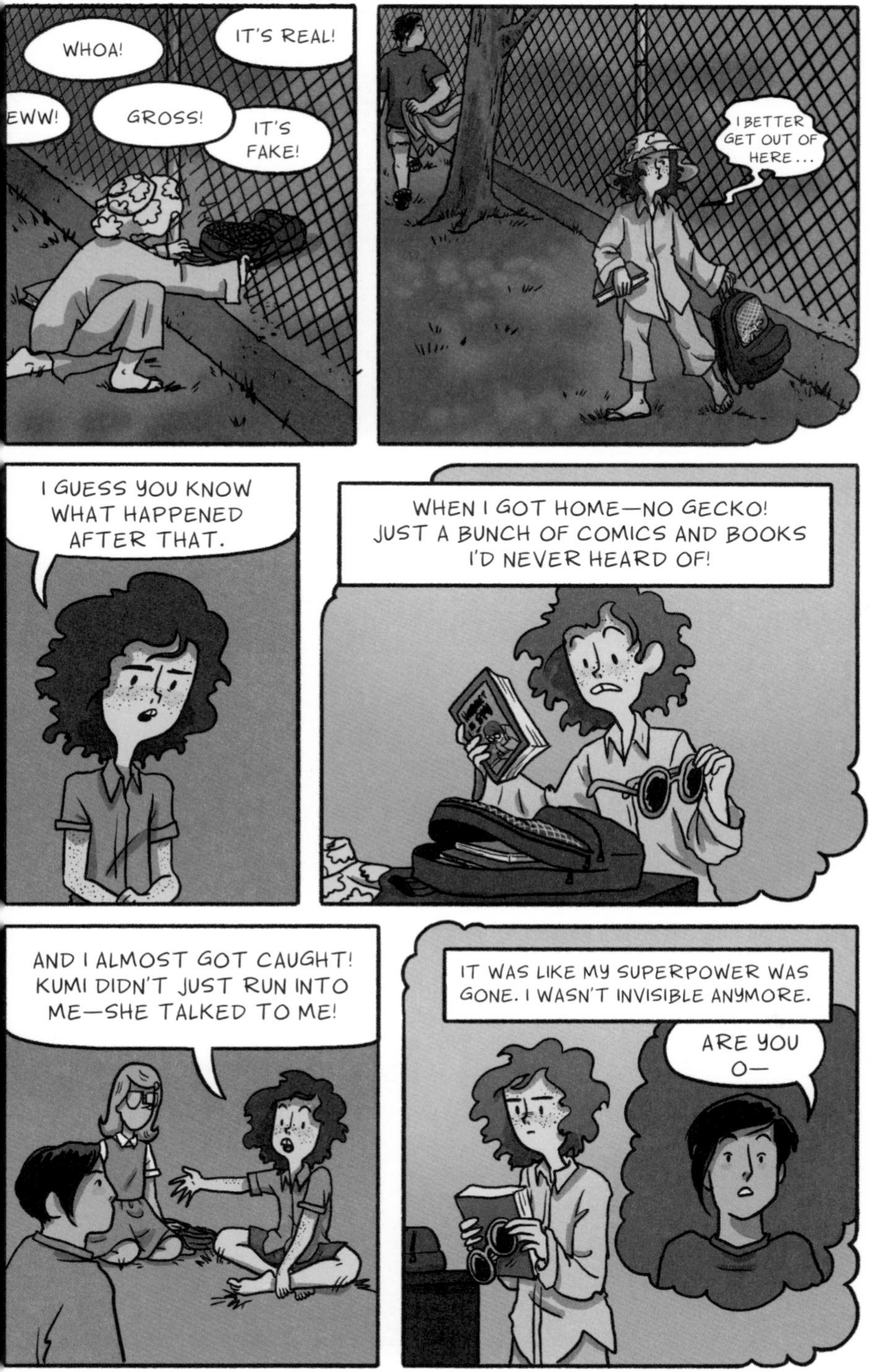

WHOA!
IT'S REAL!
EWW!
GROSS!
IT'S FAKE!
I BETTER GET OUT OF HERE...
I GUESS YOU KNOW WHAT HAPPENED AFTER THAT.
WHEN I GOT HOME—NO GECKO! JUST A BUNCH OF COMICS AND BOOKS I'D NEVER HEARD OF!
AND I ALMOST GOT CAUGHT! KUMI DIDN'T JUST RUN INTO ME—SHE TALKED TO ME!
IT WAS LIKE MY SUPERPOWER WAS GONE. I WASN'T INVISIBLE ANYMORE.
ARE YOU O—

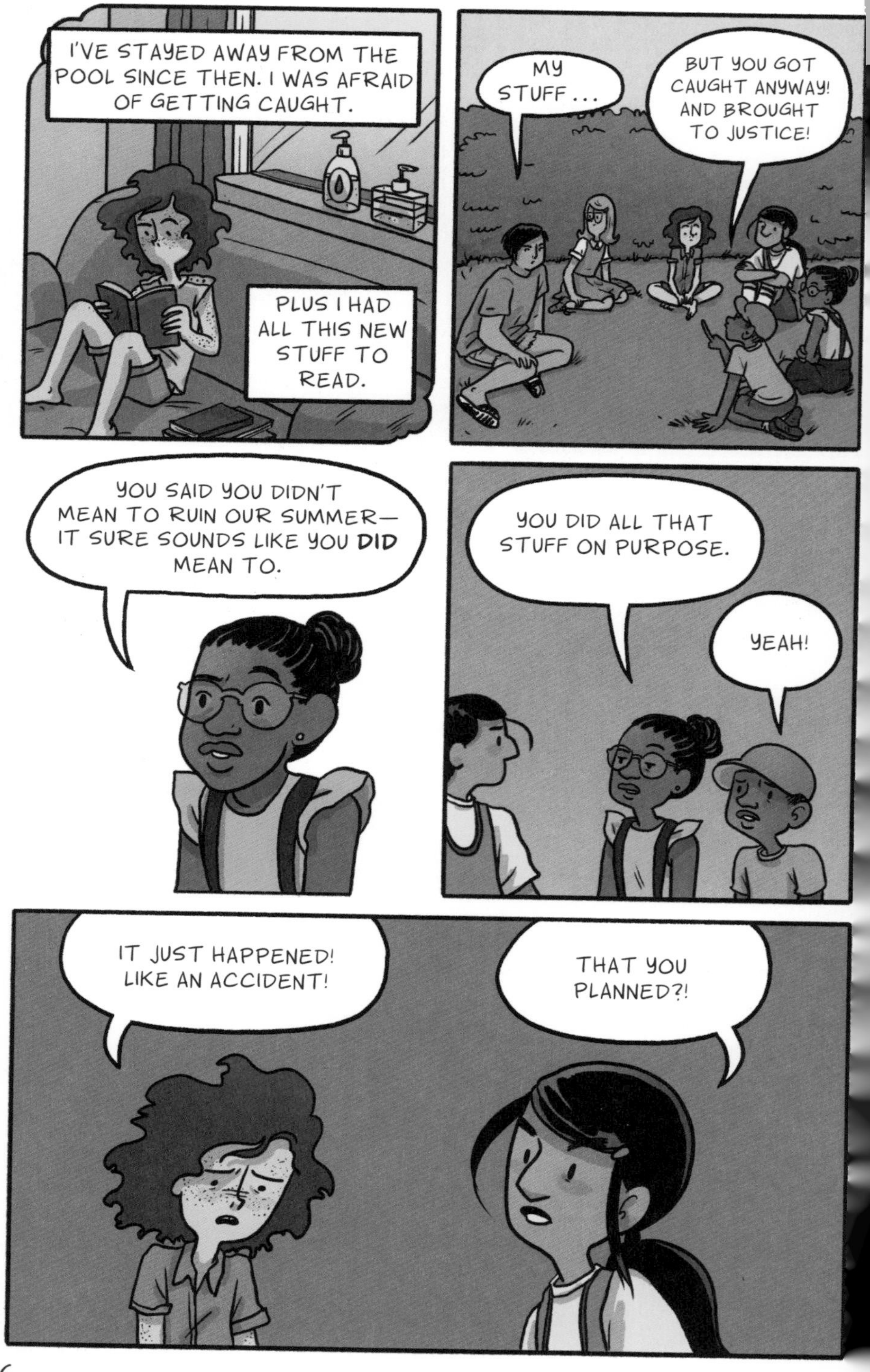
I'VE STAYED AWAY FROM THE POOL SINCE THEN. I WAS AFRAID OF GETTING CAUGHT.
PLUS I HAD ALL THIS NEW STUFF TO READ.
MY STUFF . . .
BUT YOU GOT CAUGHT ANYWAY! AND BROUGHT TO JUSTICE!
YOU SAID YOU DIDN'T MEAN TO RUIN OUR SUMMER— IT SURE SOUNDS LIKE YOU **DID** MEAN TO.
YOU DID ALL THAT STUFF ON PURPOSE.
YEAH!
IT JUST HAPPENED! LIKE AN ACCIDENT!
THAT YOU PLANNED?!

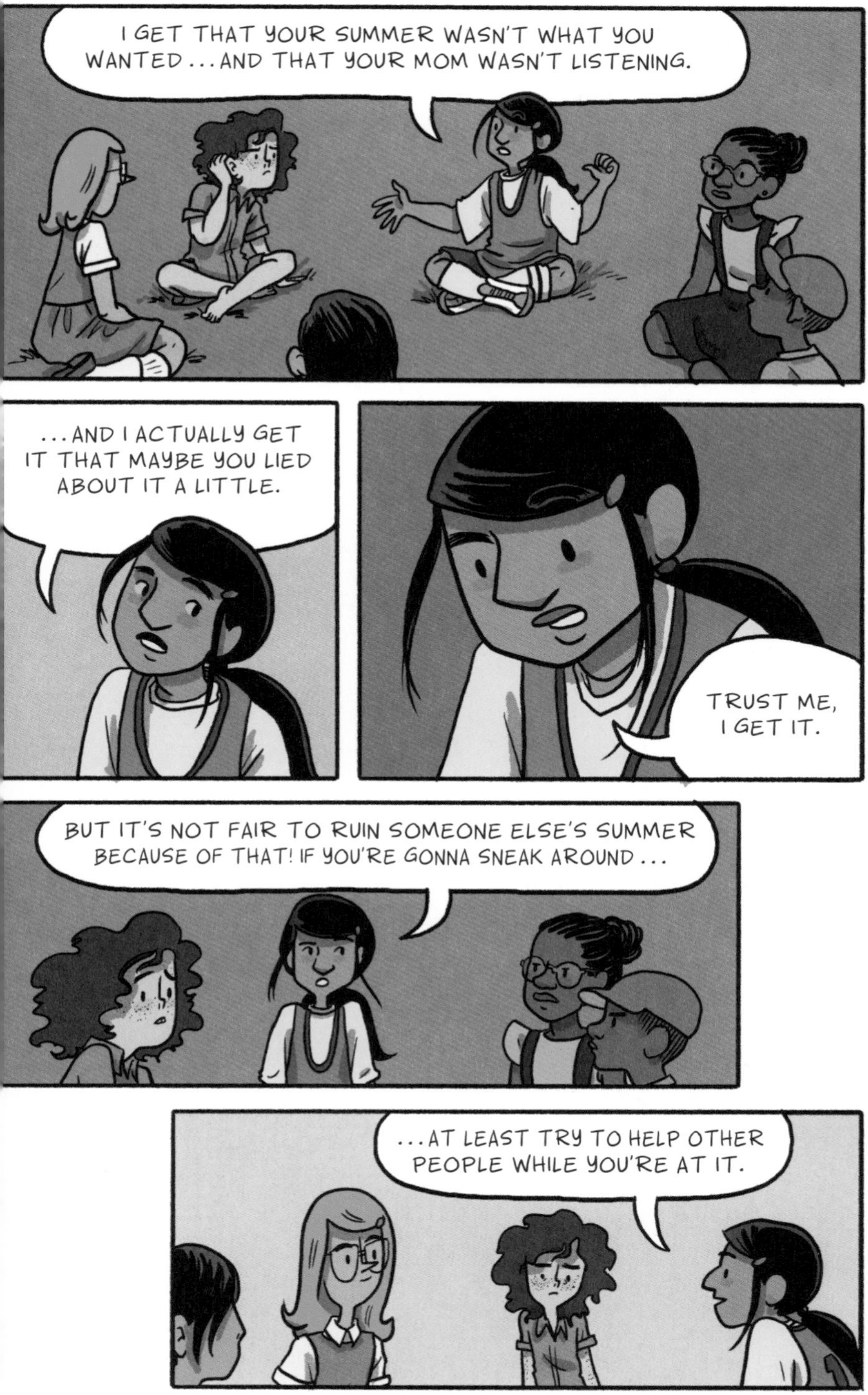
I GET THAT YOUR SUMMER WASN'T WHAT YOU WANTED . . . AND THAT YOUR MOM WASN'T LISTENING.
. . . AND I ACTUALLY GET IT THAT MAYBE YOU LIED ABOUT IT A LITTLE.
TRUST ME, I GET IT.
BUT IT'S NOT FAIR TO RUIN SOMEONE ELSE'S SUMMER BECAUSE OF THAT! IF YOU'RE GONNA SNEAK AROUND . . .
. . . AT LEAST TRY TO HELP OTHER PEOPLE WHILE YOU'RE AT IT.

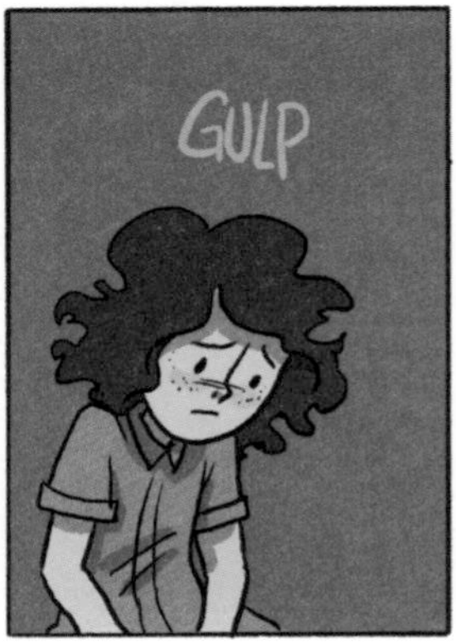
GULP

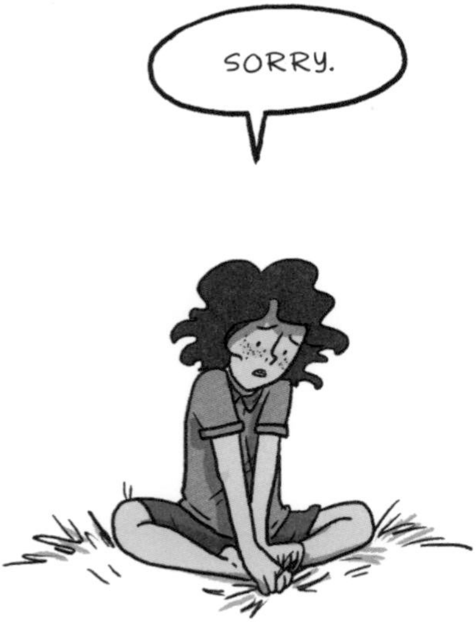
SORRY.

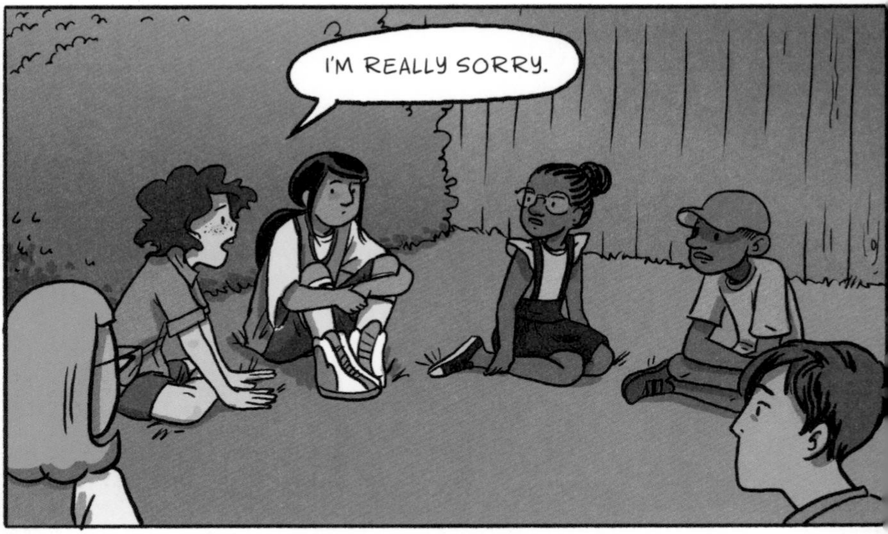
I'M REALLY SORRY.

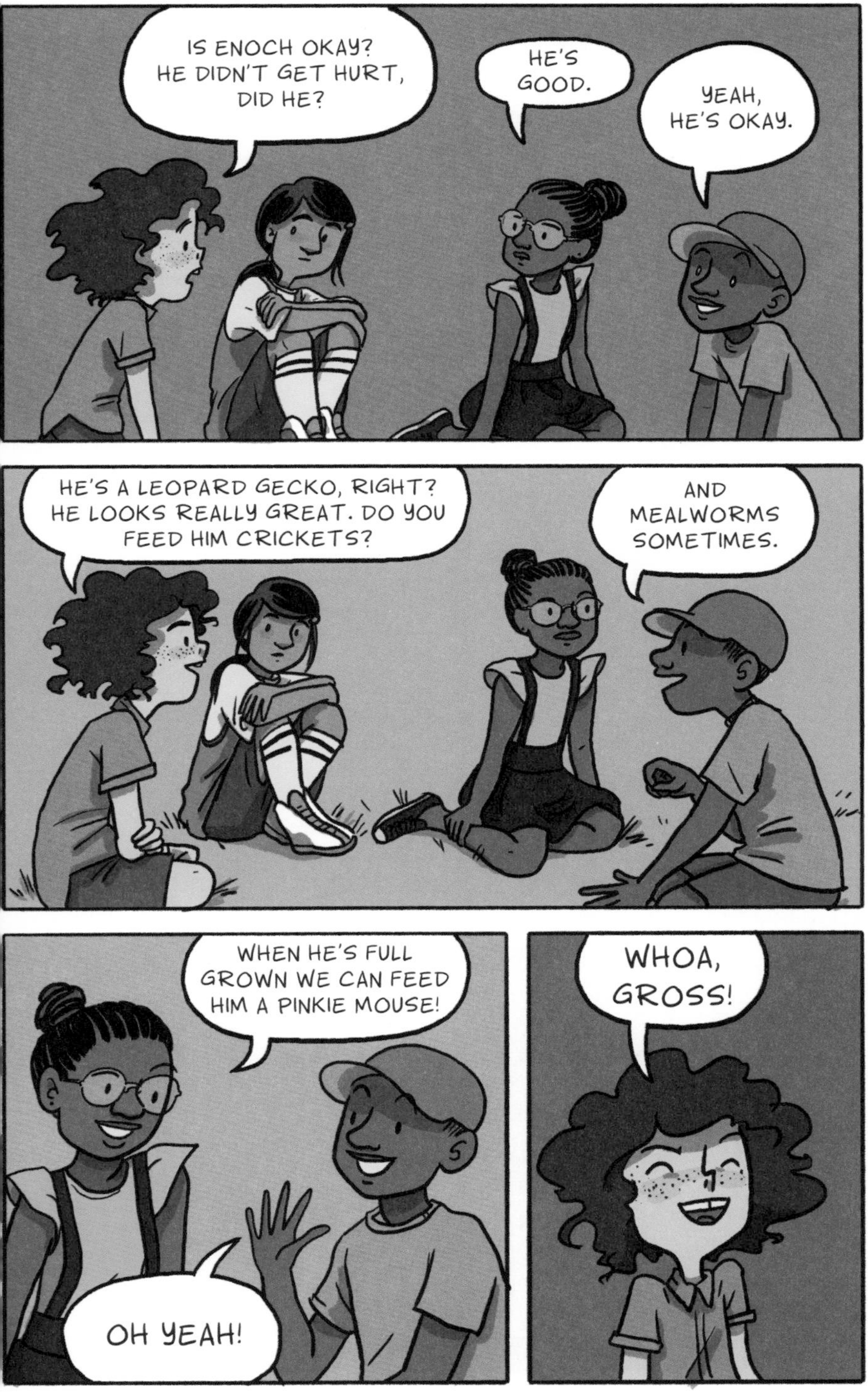
IS ENOCH OKAY? HE DIDN'T GET HURT, DID HE?
HE'S GOOD.
YEAH, HE'S OKAY.
HE'S A LEOPARD GECKO, RIGHT? HE LOOKS REALLY GREAT. DO YOU FEED HIM CRICKETS?
AND MEALWORMS SOMETIMES.
WHEN HE'S FULL GROWN WE CAN FEED HIM A PINKIE MOUSE!
OH YEAH!
WHOA, GROSS!

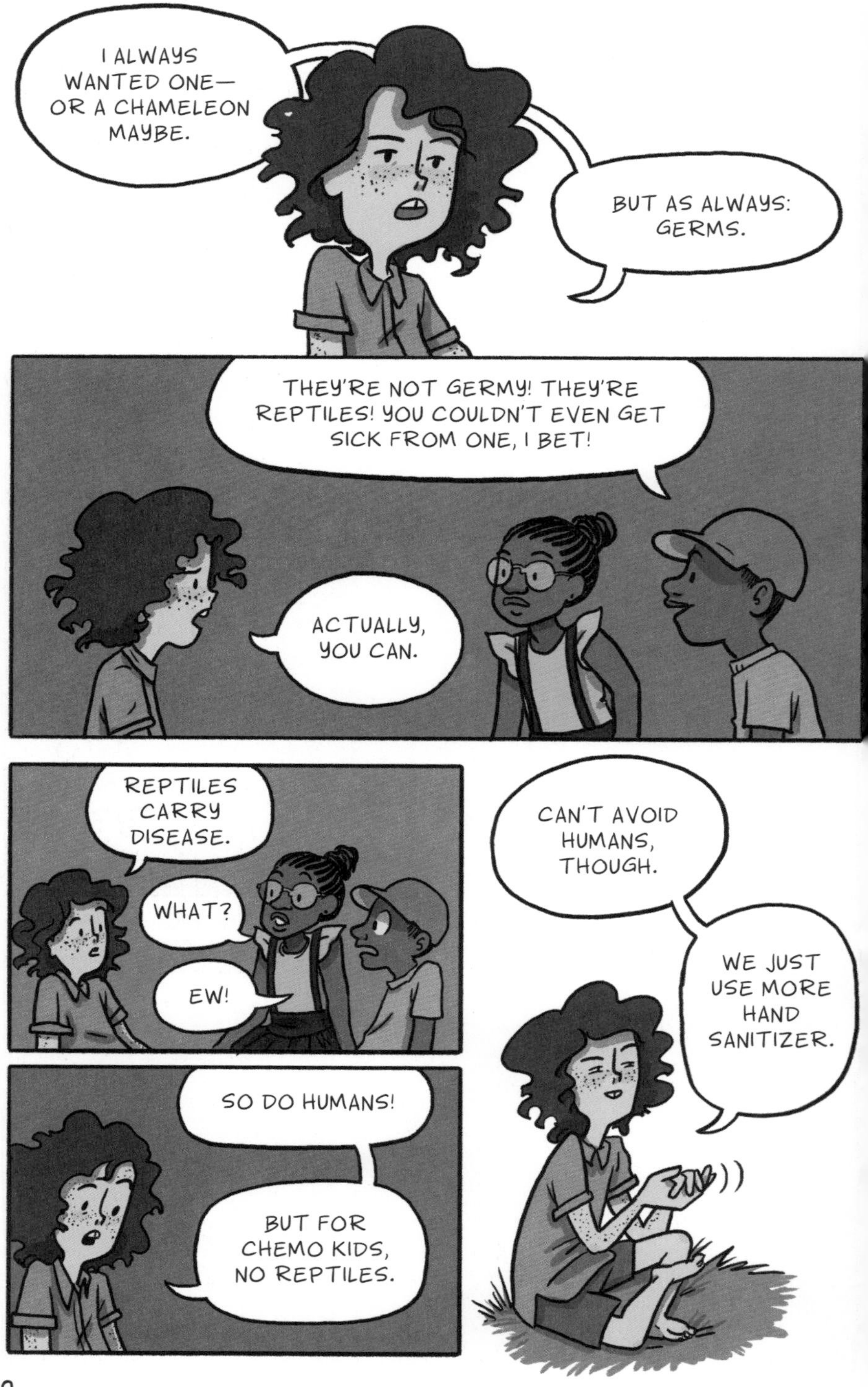
I ALWAYS WANTED ONE— OR A CHAMELEON MAYBE.
BUT AS ALWAYS: GERMS.
THEY'RE NOT GERMY! THEY'RE REPTILES! YOU COULDN'T EVEN GET SICK FROM ONE, I BET!
ACTUALLY, YOU CAN.
REPTILES CARRY DISEASE.
WHAT?
EW!
SO DO HUMANS!
BUT FOR CHEMO KIDS, NO REPTILES.
CAN'T AVOID HUMANS, THOUGH.
WE JUST USE MORE HAND SANITIZER.

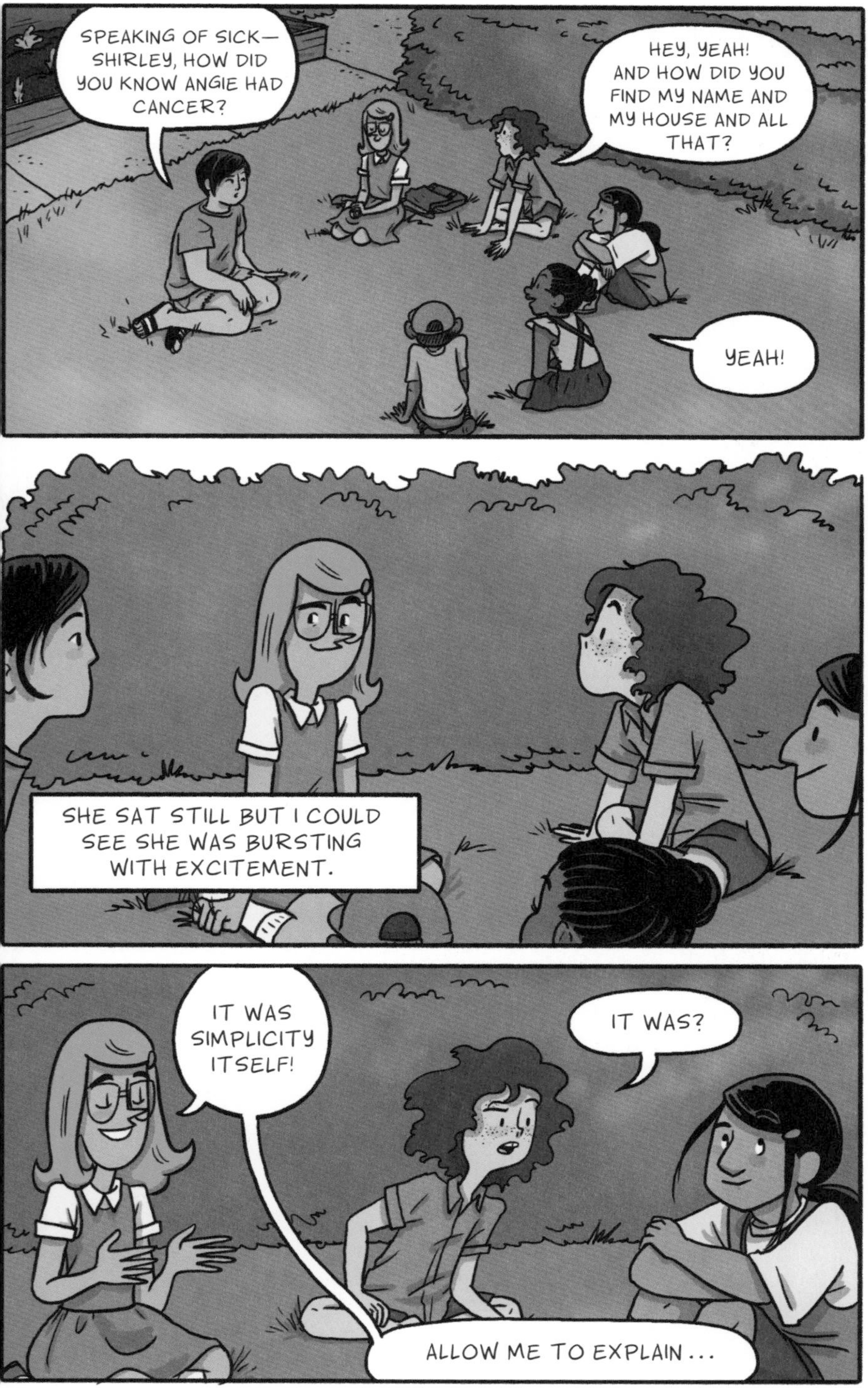
SPEAKING OF SICK— SHIRLEY, HOW DID YOU KNOW ANGIE HAD CANCER?
HEY, YEAH! AND HOW DID YOU FIND MY NAME AND MY HOUSE AND ALL THAT?
YEAH!
SHE SAT STILL BUT I COULD SEE SHE WAS BURSTING WITH EXCITEMENT.
IT WAS SIMPLICITY ITSELF!
IT WAS?
ALLOW ME TO EXPLAIN . . .

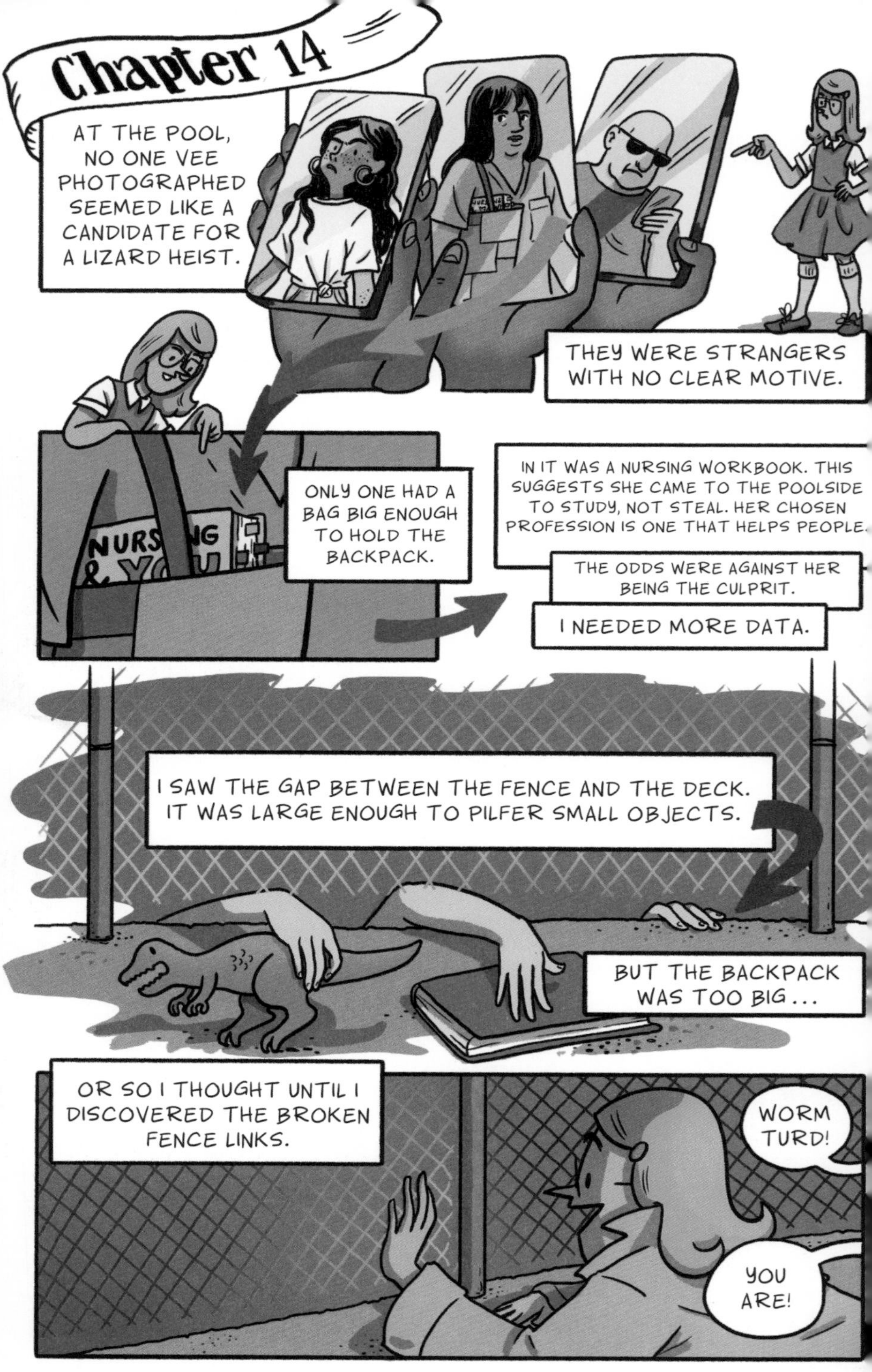
Chapter 14
AT THE POOL, NO ONE VEE PHOTOGRAPHED SEEMED LIKE A CANDIDATE FOR A LIZARD HEIST.
THEY WERE STRANGERS WITH NO CLEAR MOTIVE.
NURSING & YOU
ONLY ONE HAD A BAG BIG ENOUGH TO HOLD THE BACKPACK.
IN IT WAS A NURSING WORKBOOK. THIS SUGGESTS SHE CAME TO THE POOLSIDE TO STUDY, NOT STEAL. HER CHOSEN PROFESSION IS ONE THAT HELPS PEOPLE.
THE ODDS WERE AGAINST HER BEING THE CULPRIT.
I NEEDED MORE DATA.
I SAW THE GAP BETWEEN THE FENCE AND THE DECK. IT WAS LARGE ENOUGH TO PILFER SMALL OBJECTS.
BUT THE BACKPACK WAS TOO BIG . . .
OR SO I THOUGHT UNTIL I DISCOVERED THE BROKEN FENCE LINKS.
WORM TURD!
YOU ARE!

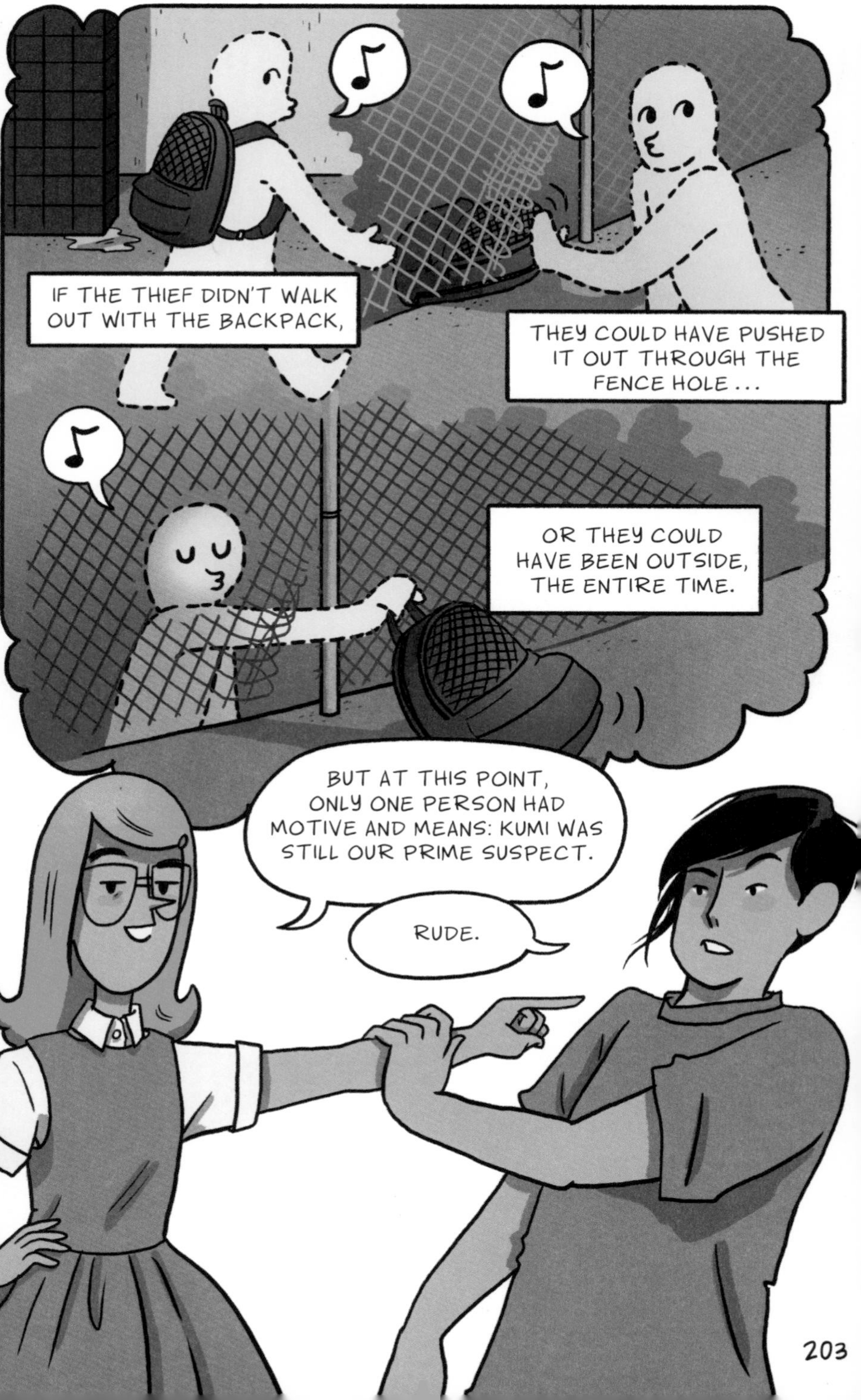
IF THE THIEF DIDN'T WALK OUT WITH THE BACKPACK,
THEY COULD HAVE PUSHED IT OUT THROUGH THE FENCE HOLE . . .
OR THEY COULD HAVE BEEN OUTSIDE, THE ENTIRE TIME.
BUT AT THIS POINT, ONLY ONE PERSON HAD MOTIVE AND MEANS: KUMI WAS STILL OUR PRIME SUSPECT.
RUDE.

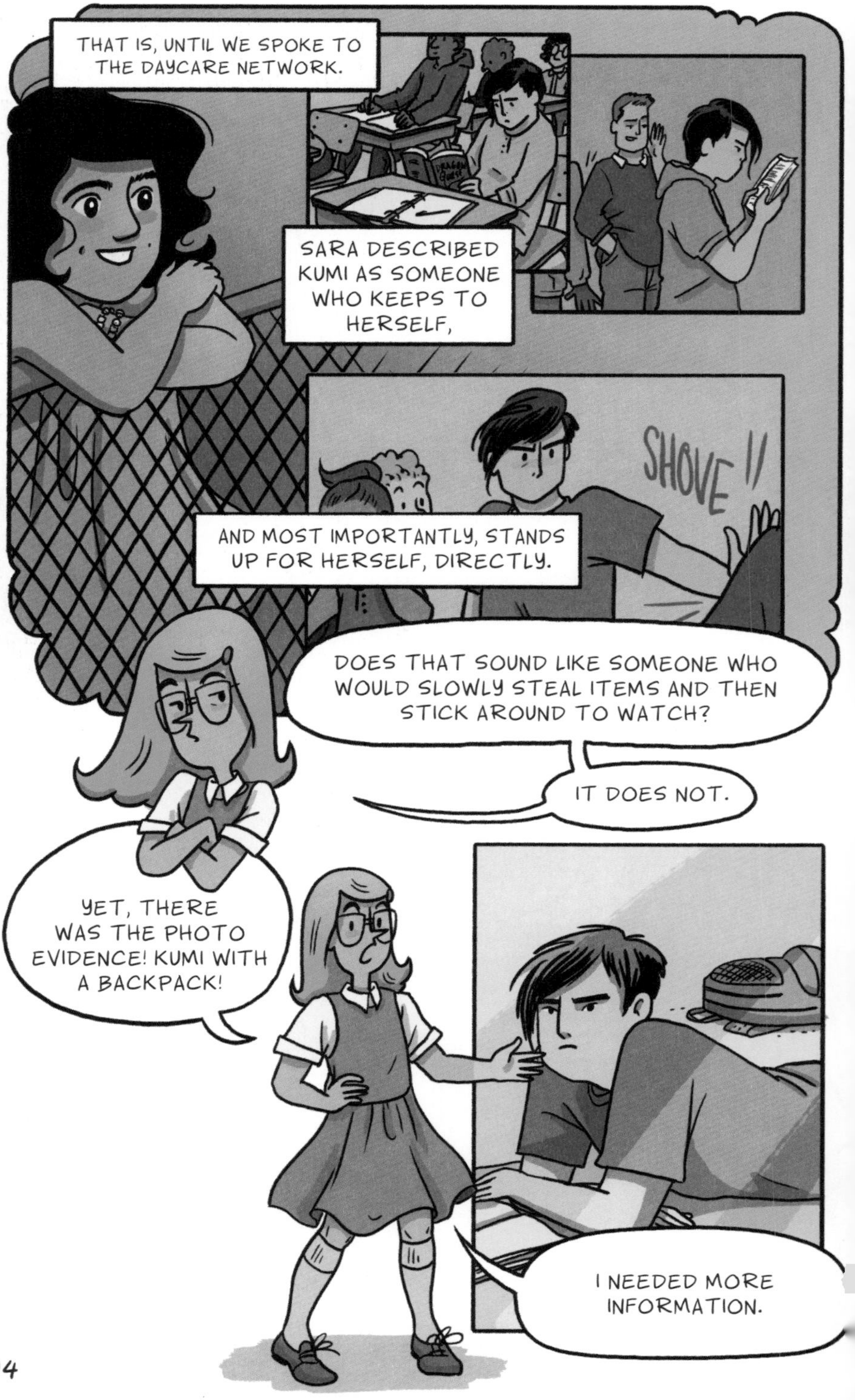
THAT IS, UNTIL WE SPOKE TO THE DAYCARE NETWORK.
SARA DESCRIBED KUMI AS SOMEONE WHO KEEPS TO HERSELF,
SHOVE!!
AND MOST IMPORTANTLY, STANDS UP FOR HERSELF, DIRECTLY.
DOES THAT SOUND LIKE SOMEONE WHO WOULD SLOWLY STEAL ITEMS AND THEN STICK AROUND TO WATCH?
IT DOES NOT.
YET, THERE WAS THE PHOTO EVIDENCE! KUMI WITH A BACKPACK!
I NEEDED MORE INFORMATION.

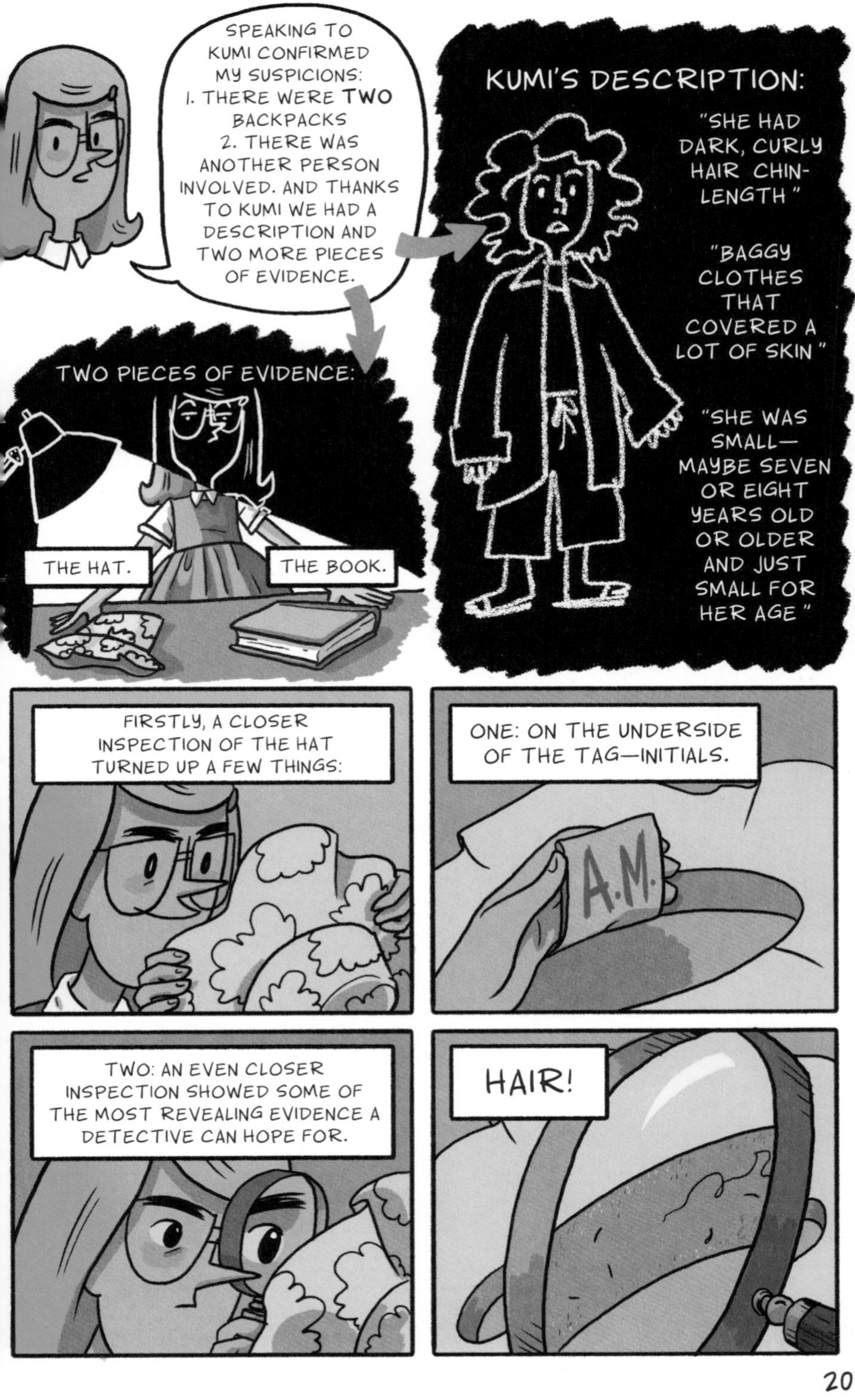
SPEAKING TO KUMI CONFIRMED MY SUSPICIONS: 1. THERE WERE **TWO** BACKPACKS 2. THERE WAS ANOTHER PERSON INVOLVED. AND THANKS TO KUMI WE HAD A DESCRIPTION AND TWO MORE PIECES OF EVIDENCE.
KUMI'S DESCRIPTION:
"SHE HAD DARK, CURLY HAIR CHIN-LENGTH"
"BAGGY CLOTHES THAT COVERED A LOT OF SKIN"
"SHE WAS SMALL—MAYBE SEVEN OR EIGHT YEARS OLD OR OLDER AND JUST SMALL FOR HER AGE"
TWO PIECES OF EVIDENCE:
THE HAT.
THE BOOK.
FIRSTLY, A CLOSER INSPECTION OF THE HAT TURNED UP A FEW THINGS:
ONE: ON THE UNDERSIDE OF THE TAG—INITIALS.
A.M.
TWO: AN EVEN CLOSER INSPECTION SHOWED SOME OF THE MOST REVEALING EVIDENCE A DETECTIVE CAN HOPE FOR.
HAIR!

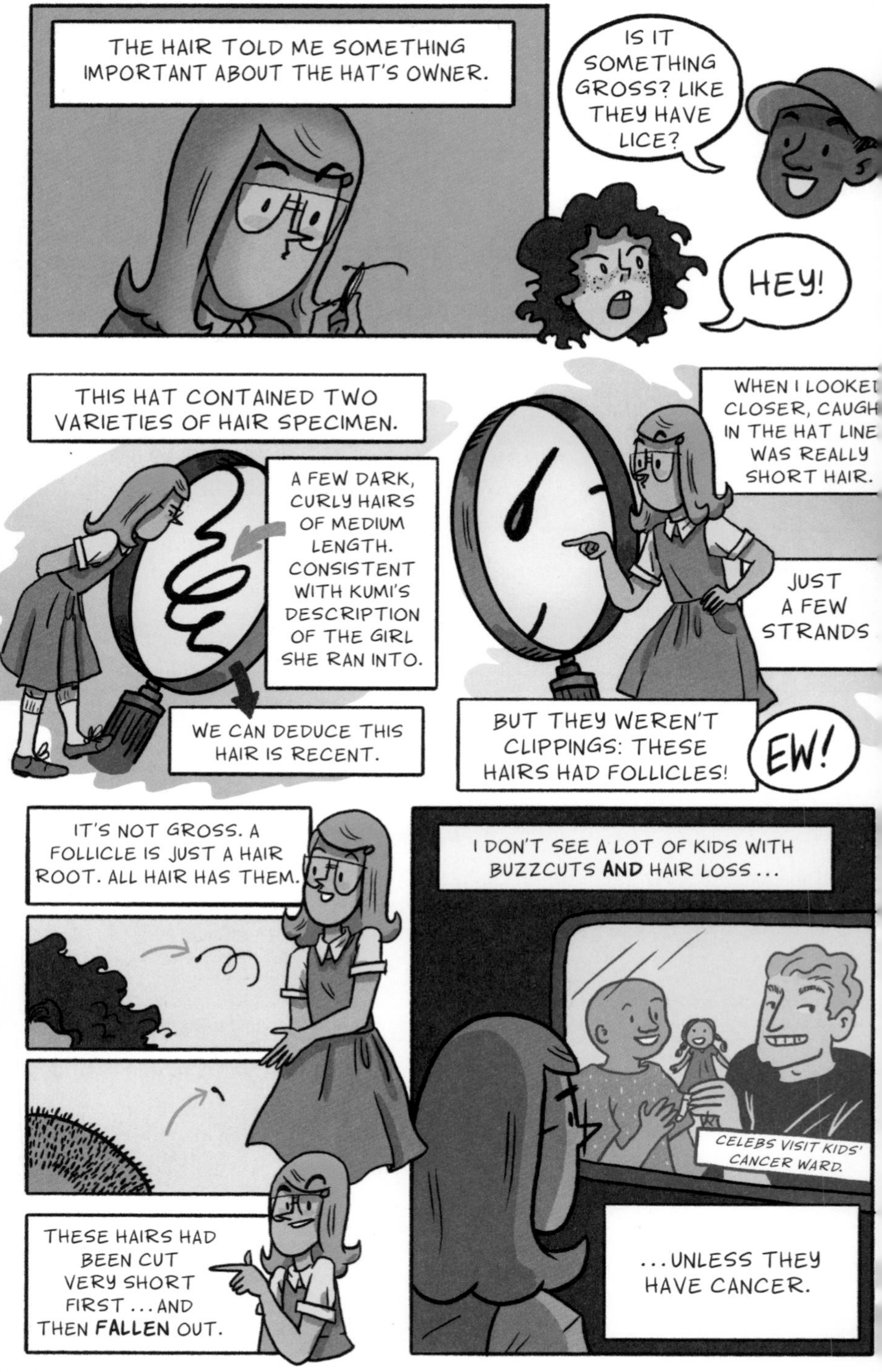
THE HAIR TOLD ME SOMETHING IMPORTANT ABOUT THE HAT'S OWNER.
IS IT SOMETHING GROSS? LIKE THEY HAVE LICE?
HEY!
THIS HAT CONTAINED TWO VARIETIES OF HAIR SPECIMEN.
A FEW DARK, CURLY HAIRS OF MEDIUM LENGTH. CONSISTENT WITH KUMI'S DESCRIPTION OF THE GIRL SHE RAN INTO.
WE CAN DEDUCE THIS HAIR IS RECENT.
WHEN I LOOKED CLOSER, CAUGHT IN THE HAT LINER WAS REALLY SHORT HAIR.
JUST A FEW STRANDS
BUT THEY WEREN'T CLIPPINGS: THESE HAIRS HAD FOLLICLES!
EW!
IT'S NOT GROSS. A FOLLICLE IS JUST A HAIR ROOT. ALL HAIR HAS THEM.
THESE HAIRS HAD BEEN CUT VERY SHORT FIRST . . . AND THEN FALLEN OUT.
I DON'T SEE A LOT OF KIDS WITH BUZZCUTS AND HAIR LOSS . . .
CELEBS VISIT KIDS' CANCER WARD.
. . . UNLESS THEY HAVE CANCER.

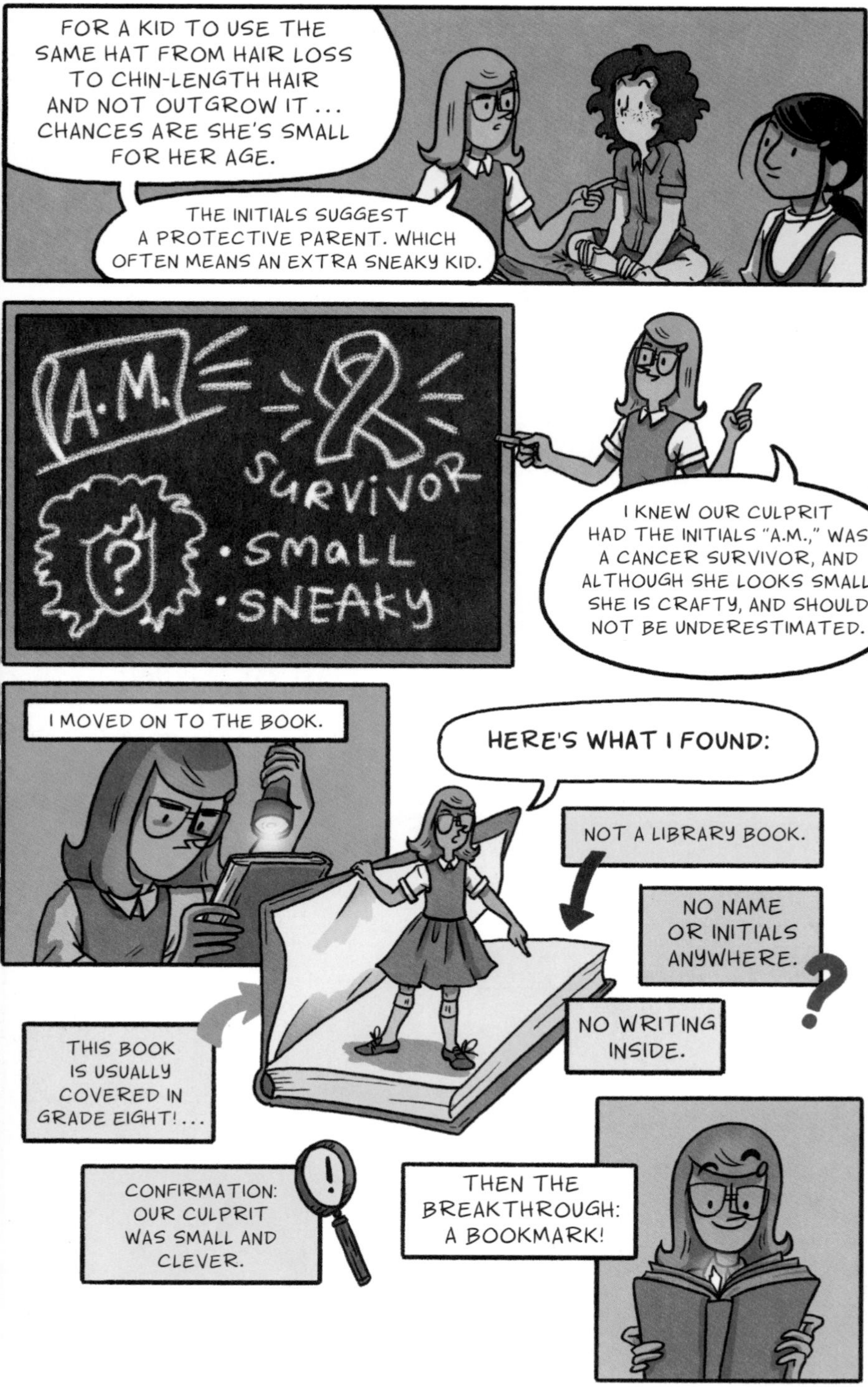
FOR A KID TO USE THE SAME HAT FROM HAIR LOSS TO CHIN-LENGTH HAIR AND NOT OUTGROW IT . . . CHANCES ARE SHE'S SMALL FOR HER AGE.
THE INITIALS SUGGEST A PROTECTIVE PARENT. WHICH OFTEN MEANS AN EXTRA SNEAKY KID.
A.M.
SURVIVOR
•SMALL
•SNEAKY
?
I KNEW OUR CULPRIT HAD THE INITIALS "A.M.," WAS A CANCER SURVIVOR, AND ALTHOUGH SHE LOOKS SMALL, SHE IS CRAFTY, AND SHOULD NOT BE UNDERESTIMATED.
I MOVED ON TO THE BOOK.
HERE'S WHAT I FOUND:
NOT A LIBRARY BOOK.
NO NAME OR INITIALS ANYWHERE.
NO WRITING INSIDE.
THIS BOOK IS USUALLY COVERED IN GRADE EIGHT! . . .
CONFIRMATION: OUR CULPRIT WAS SMALL AND CLEVER.
THEN THE BREAKTHROUGH: A BOOKMARK!

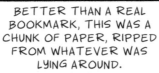

BETTER THAN A REAL BOOKMARK, THIS WAS A CHUNK OF PAPER, RIPPED FROM WHATEVER WAS LYING AROUND.

VOILA

RED DOG SECURITY
151 DUNDAS WEST   TORONTO, ON.
NOTICE OF UPDATE TO SERVICE
MALINOWSKI
BORDEN

I HAD A LAST NAME AND A STREET NAM

NOW IT WAS TIME FOR FIELDWORK.

THE NEXT DAY...

I'M LEAVING!

WITH JAMILA?

YES, MOTHER.

I HIT THE STREETS.

SO YOU WERE JUST GOING TO WALK UP AND DOWN BORDEN STREET AND HOPE YOU SEE A GIRL ON THE LAWN? BORDEN'S A LONG STREET!

IT SURE IS.

WELL...I MADE SOME ERRORS IN JUDGMENT THERE AND WAS ALMOST FORCED TO GIVE UP.

BUT I HAD A STROKE OF LUCK.

I'M LEAVING.

WHY CAN'T YOU JUST TELL ME WHAT'S GOING ON?!

WHY ARE YOU SMILING?

I WAS SMILING BECAUSE THE CASE WAS SOLVED.

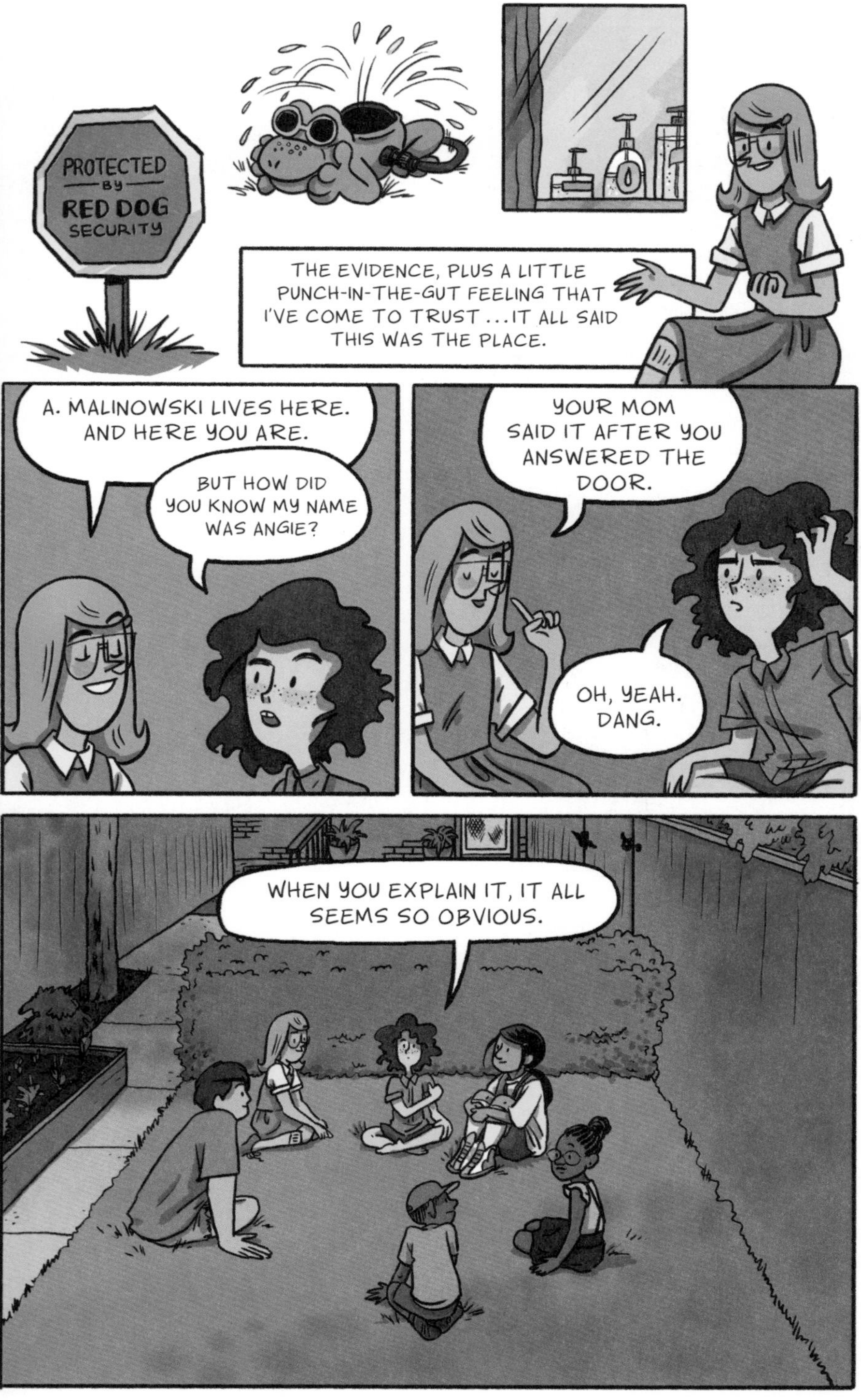
PROTECTED BY RED DOG SECURITY
THE EVIDENCE, PLUS A LITTLE PUNCH-IN-THE-GUT FEELING THAT I'VE COME TO TRUST . . . IT ALL SAID THIS WAS THE PLACE.
A. MALINOWSKI LIVES HERE. AND HERE YOU ARE.
BUT HOW DID YOU KNOW MY NAME WAS ANGIE?
YOUR MOM SAID IT AFTER YOU ANSWERED THE DOOR.
OH, YEAH. DANG.
WHEN YOU EXPLAIN IT, IT ALL SEEMS SO OBVIOUS.

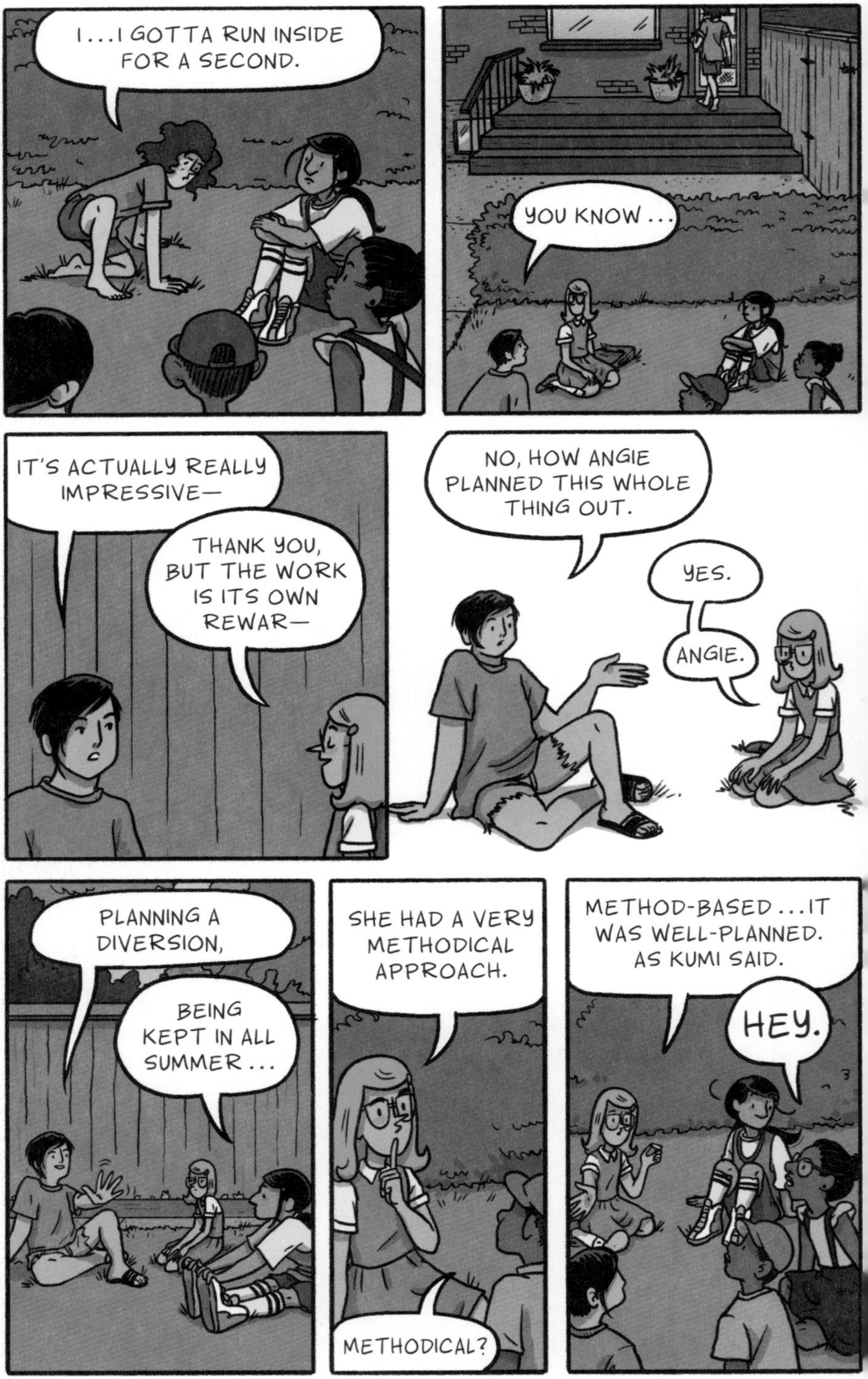
I...I GOTTA RUN INSIDE FOR A SECOND.
YOU KNOW...
IT'S ACTUALLY REALLY IMPRESSIVE—
THANK YOU, BUT THE WORK IS ITS OWN REWAR—
NO, HOW ANGIE PLANNED THIS WHOLE THING OUT.
YES.
ANGIE.
PLANNING A DIVERSION,
BEING KEPT IN ALL SUMMER...
SHE HAD A VERY METHODICAL APPROACH.
METHODICAL?
METHOD-BASED...IT WAS WELL-PLANNED. AS KUMI SAID.
HEY.

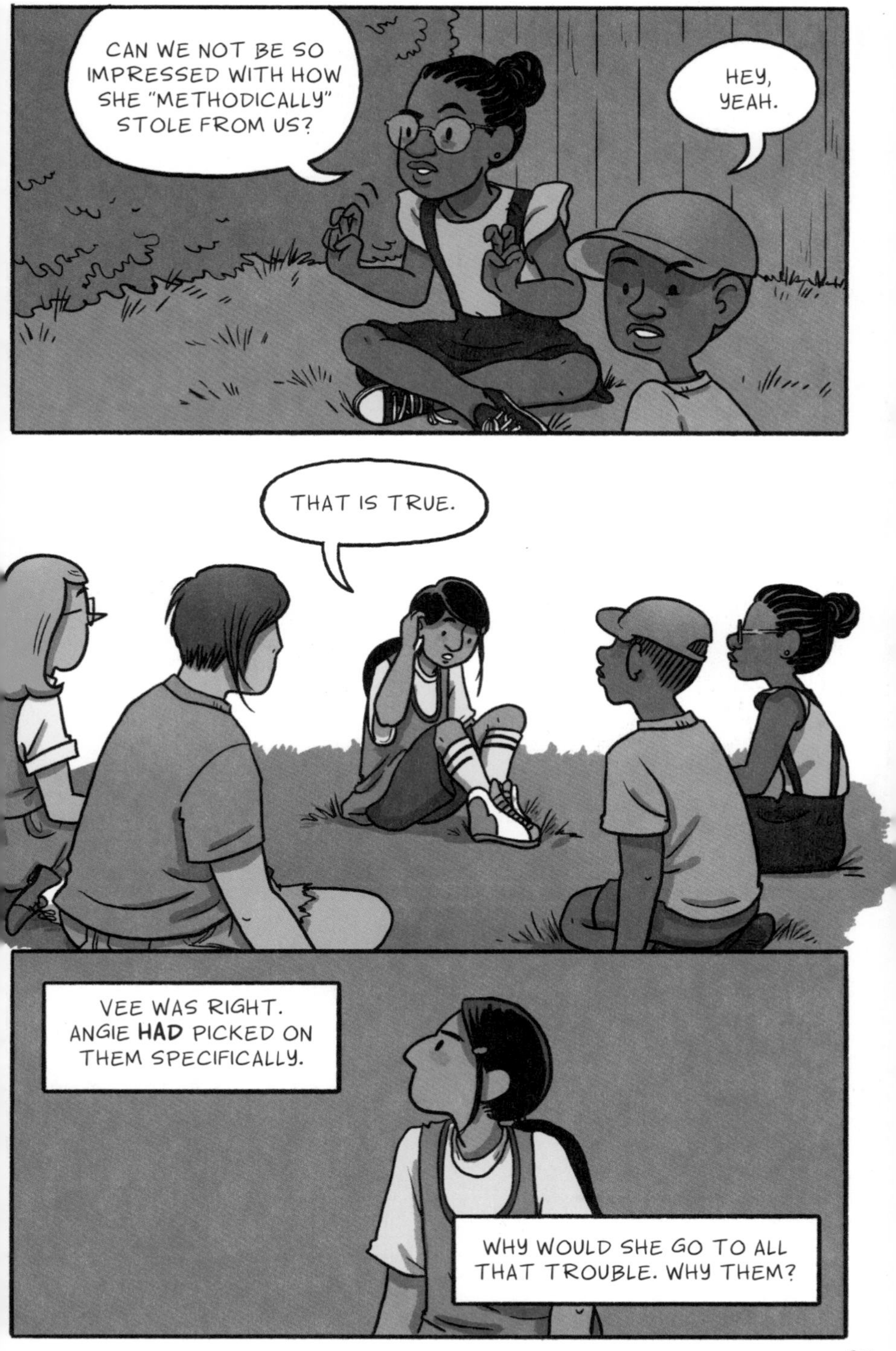
CAN WE NOT BE SO IMPRESSED WITH HOW SHE "METHODICALLY" STOLE FROM US?
HEY, YEAH.
THAT IS TRUE.
VEE WAS RIGHT. ANGIE **HAD** PICKED ON THEM SPECIFICALLY.
WHY WOULD SHE GO TO ALL THAT TROUBLE. WHY THEM?

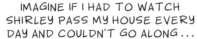
IMAGINE IF I HAD TO WATCH SHIRLEY PASS MY HOUSE EVERY DAY AND COULDN'T GO ALONG...

YOU'RE RIGHT.

THANK YOU.

IT'S NOT OKAY... BUT I THINK SHE PICKED ON YOU BOTH FOR A REASON.

OH YEAH?

SHE SAID SHE SAW YOU EVERY DAY AND WANTED MORE THAN ANYTHING TO GO **WITH** YOU.

IT GOT ALL ROTTEN WHEN HER PARENTS WOULDN'T LET HER OUT.

BUT I THINK SHE REALLY WANTS TO BE FRIENDS.

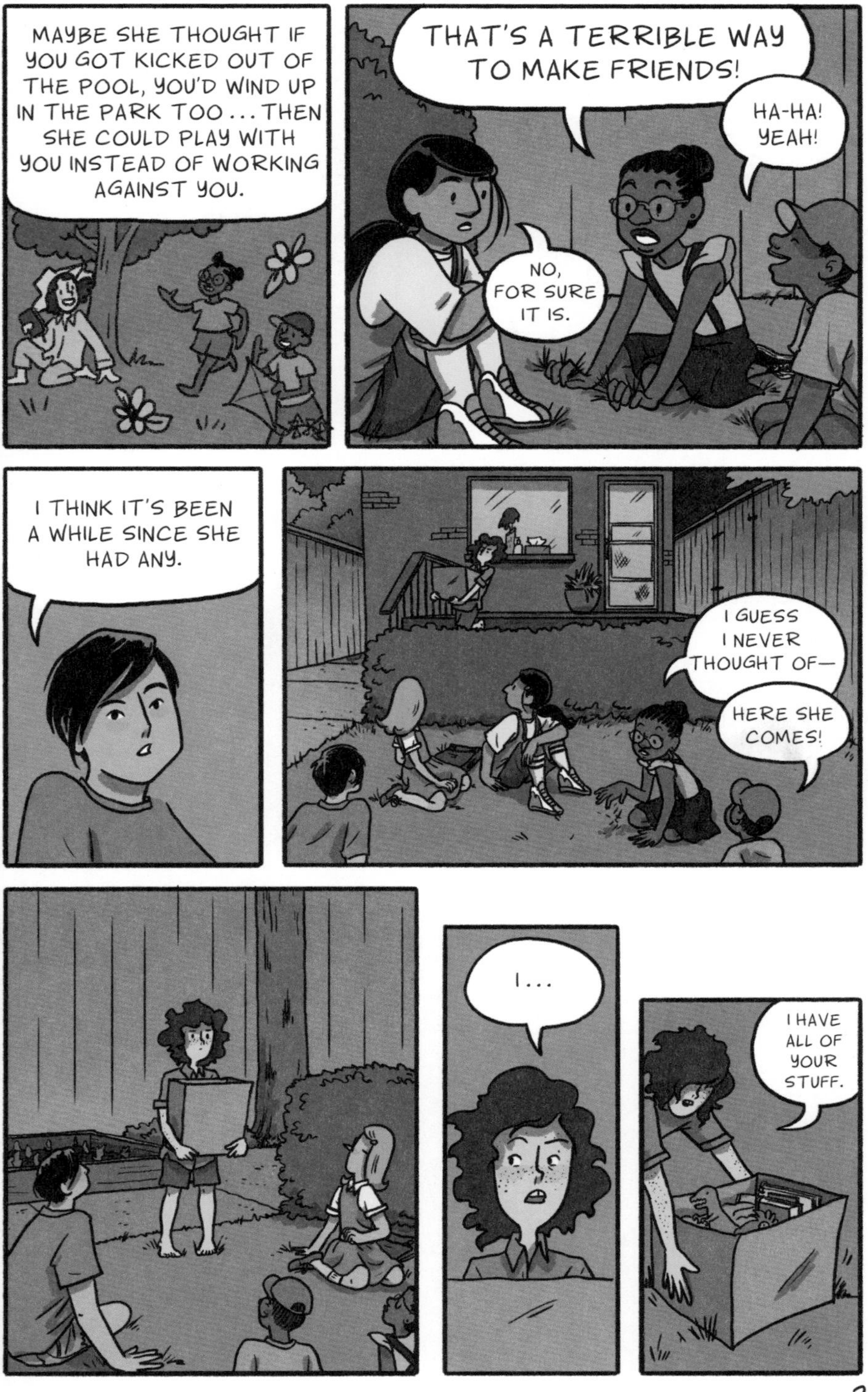
MAYBE SHE THOUGHT IF YOU GOT KICKED OUT OF THE POOL, YOU'D WIND UP IN THE PARK TOO . . . THEN SHE COULD PLAY WITH YOU INSTEAD OF WORKING AGAINST YOU.
THAT'S A TERRIBLE WAY TO MAKE FRIENDS!
HA-HA! YEAH!
NO, FOR SURE IT IS.
I THINK IT'S BEEN A WHILE SINCE SHE HAD ANY.
I GUESS I NEVER THOUGHT OF—
HERE SHE COMES!
I . . .
I HAVE ALL OF YOUR STUFF.

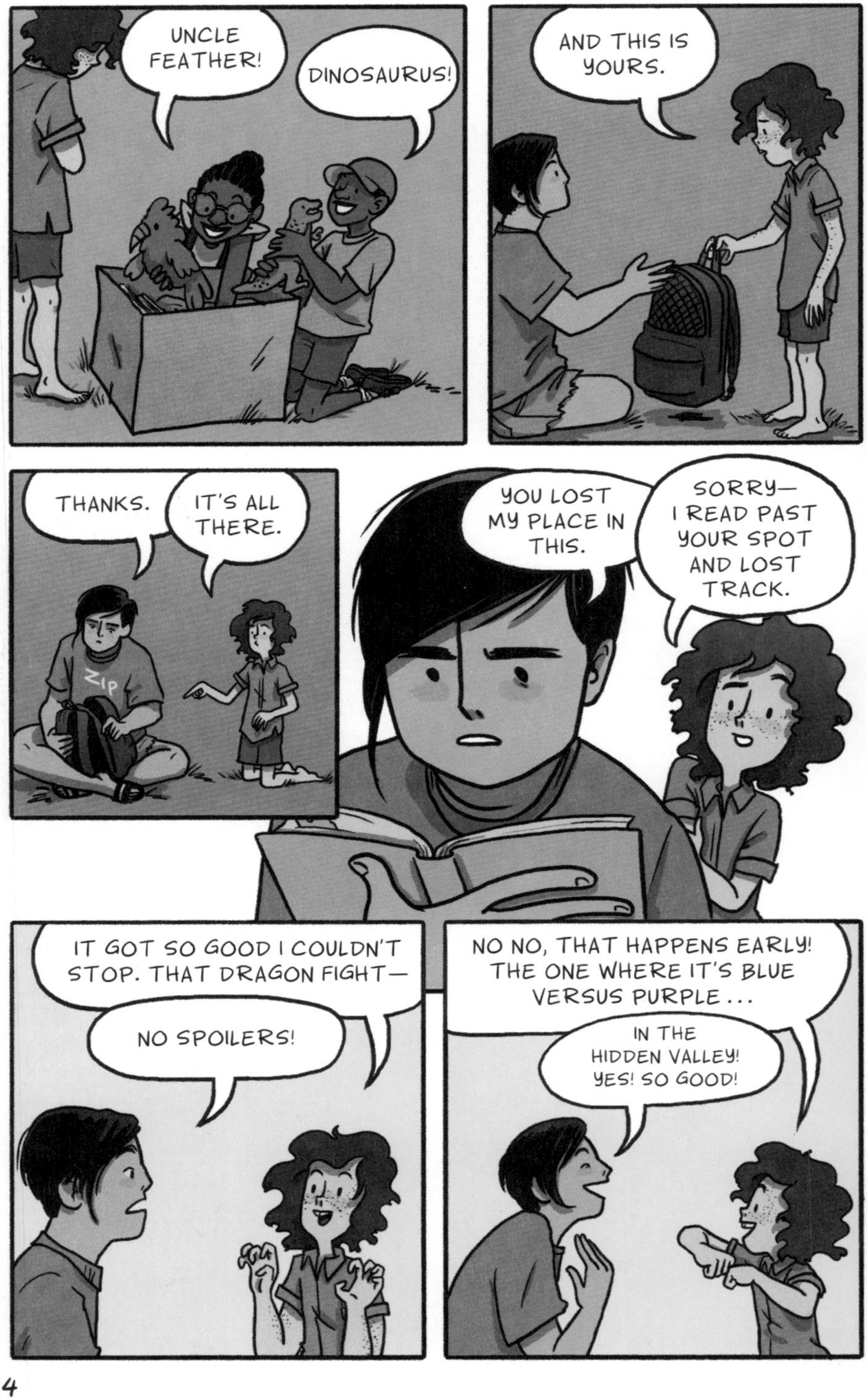
UNCLE FEATHER!
DINOSAURUS!
AND THIS IS YOURS.
THANKS.
IT'S ALL THERE.
YOU LOST MY PLACE IN THIS.
SORRY— I READ PAST YOUR SPOT AND LOST TRACK.
IT GOT SO GOOD I COULDN'T STOP. THAT DRAGON FIGHT—
NO SPOILERS!
NO NO, THAT HAPPENS EARLY! THE ONE WHERE IT'S BLUE VERSUS PURPLE . . .
IN THE HIDDEN VALLEY! YES! SO GOOD!

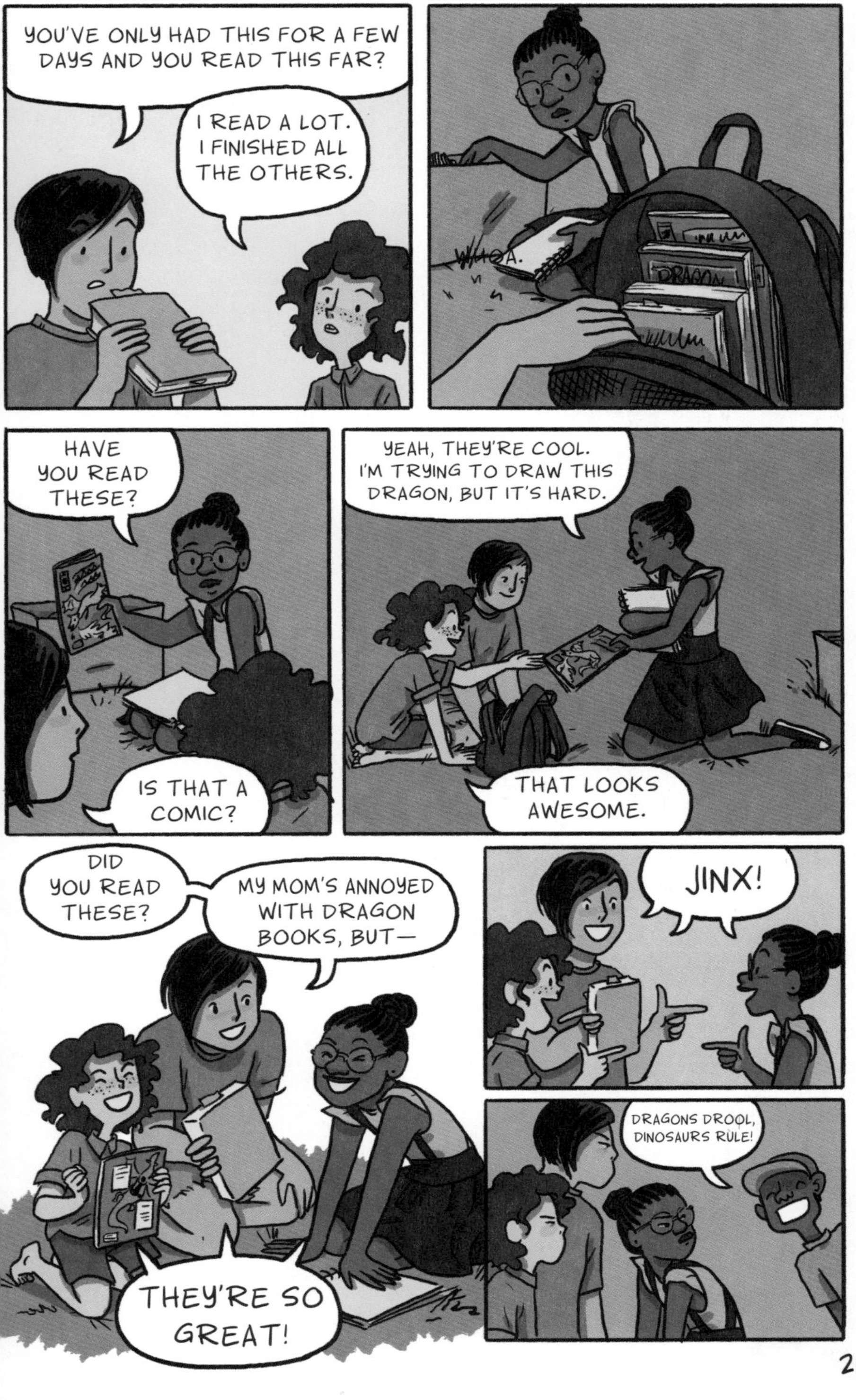
YOU'VE ONLY HAD THIS FOR A FEW DAYS AND YOU READ THIS FAR?
I READ A LOT. I FINISHED ALL THE OTHERS.
WHOA.
HAVE YOU READ THESE?
IS THAT A COMIC?
YEAH, THEY'RE COOL. I'M TRYING TO DRAW THIS DRAGON, BUT IT'S HARD.
THAT LOOKS AWESOME.
DID YOU READ THESE?
MY MOM'S ANNOYED WITH DRAGON BOOKS, BUT—
THEY'RE SO GREAT!
JINX!
DRAGONS DROOL, DINOSAURS RULE!

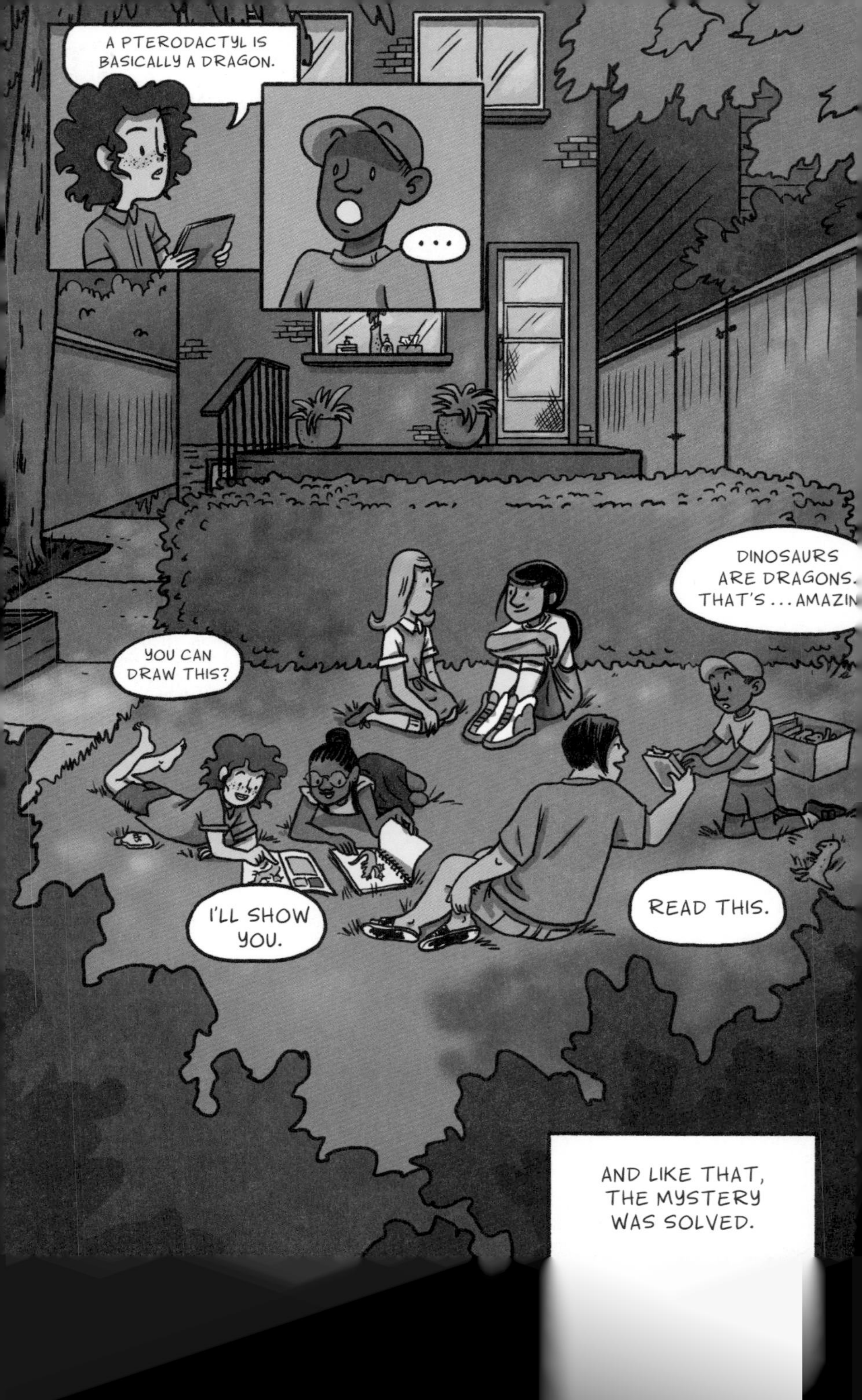
A PTERODACTYL IS BASICALLY A DRAGON.
...
DINOSAURS ARE DRAGONS. THAT'S . . . AMAZIN
YOU CAN DRAW THIS?
I'LL SHOW YOU.
READ THIS.
AND LIKE THAT, THE MYSTERY WAS SOLVED.

Chapter 15

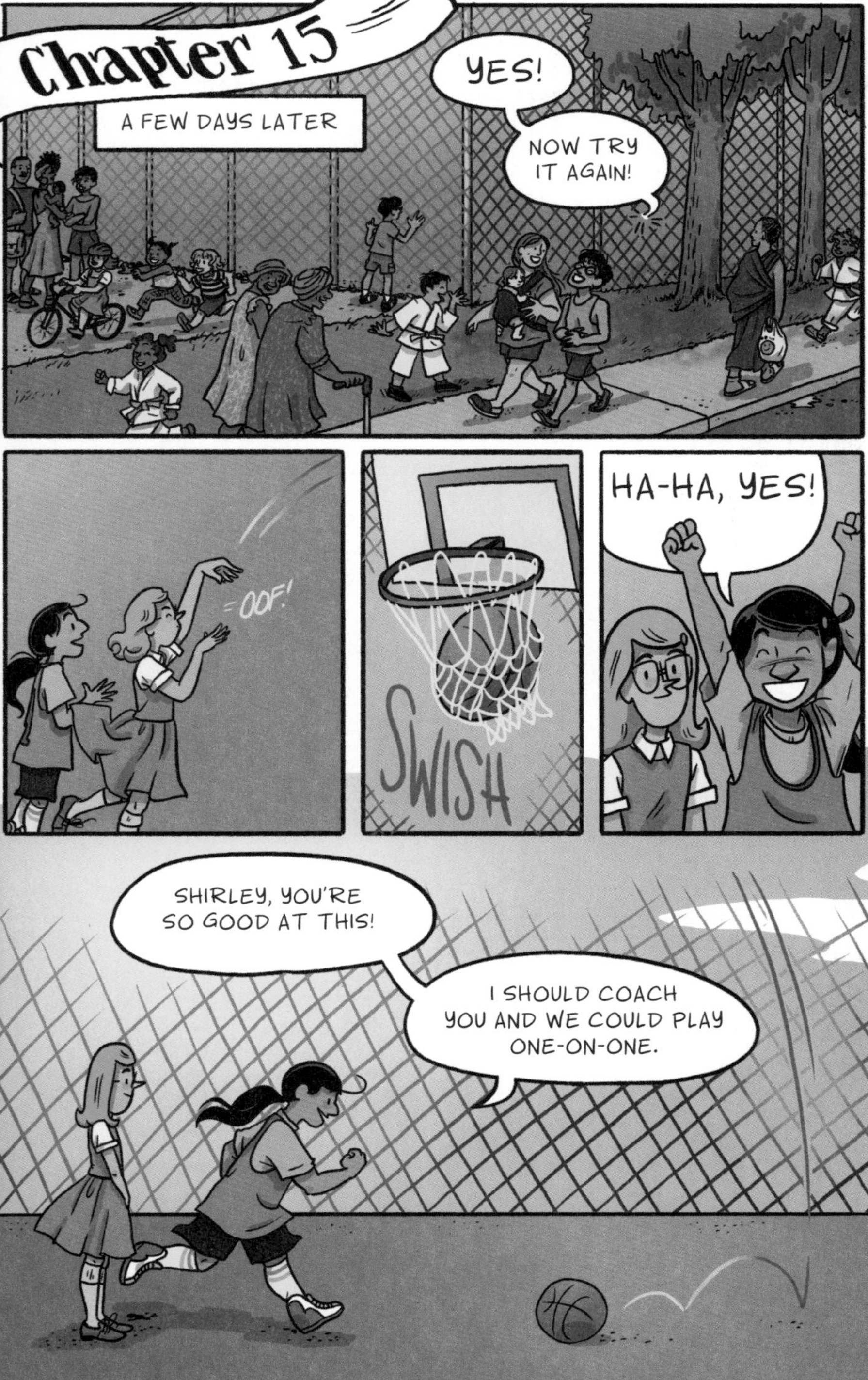
A FEW DAYS LATER
YES!
NOW TRY IT AGAIN!
OOF!
SWISH
HA-HA, YES!
SHIRLEY, YOU'RE SO GOOD AT THIS!
I SHOULD COACH YOU AND WE COULD PLAY ONE-ON-ONE.

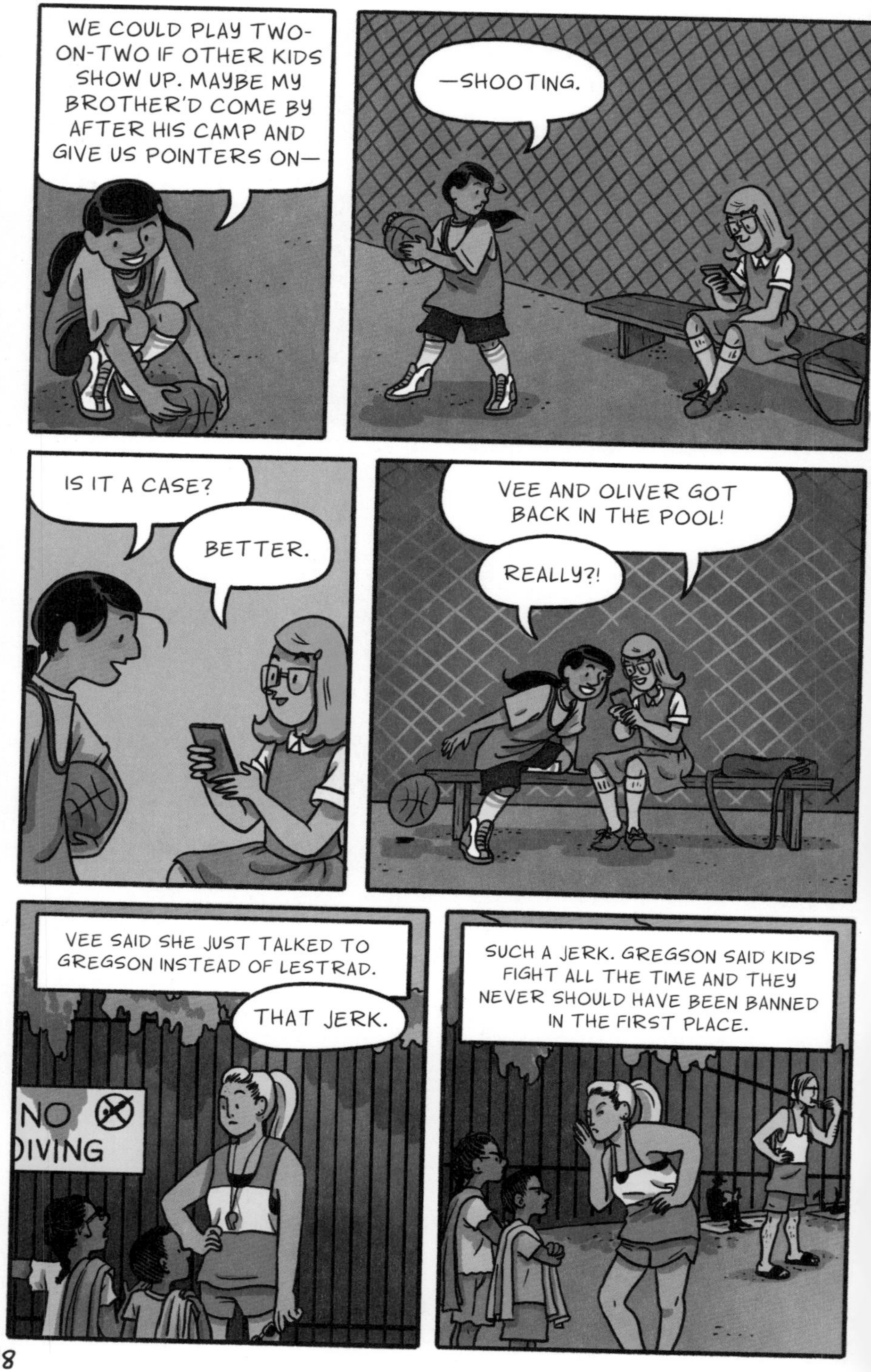
WE COULD PLAY TWO-ON-TWO IF OTHER KIDS SHOW UP. MAYBE MY BROTHER'D COME BY AFTER HIS CAMP AND GIVE US POINTERS ON—
—SHOOTING.
IS IT A CASE?
BETTER.
VEE AND OLIVER GOT BACK IN THE POOL!
REALLY?!
VEE SAID SHE JUST TALKED TO GREGSON INSTEAD OF LESTRAD.
THAT JERK.
NO DIVING
SUCH A JERK. GREGSON SAID KIDS FIGHT ALL THE TIME AND THEY NEVER SHOULD HAVE BEEN BANNED IN THE FIRST PLACE.

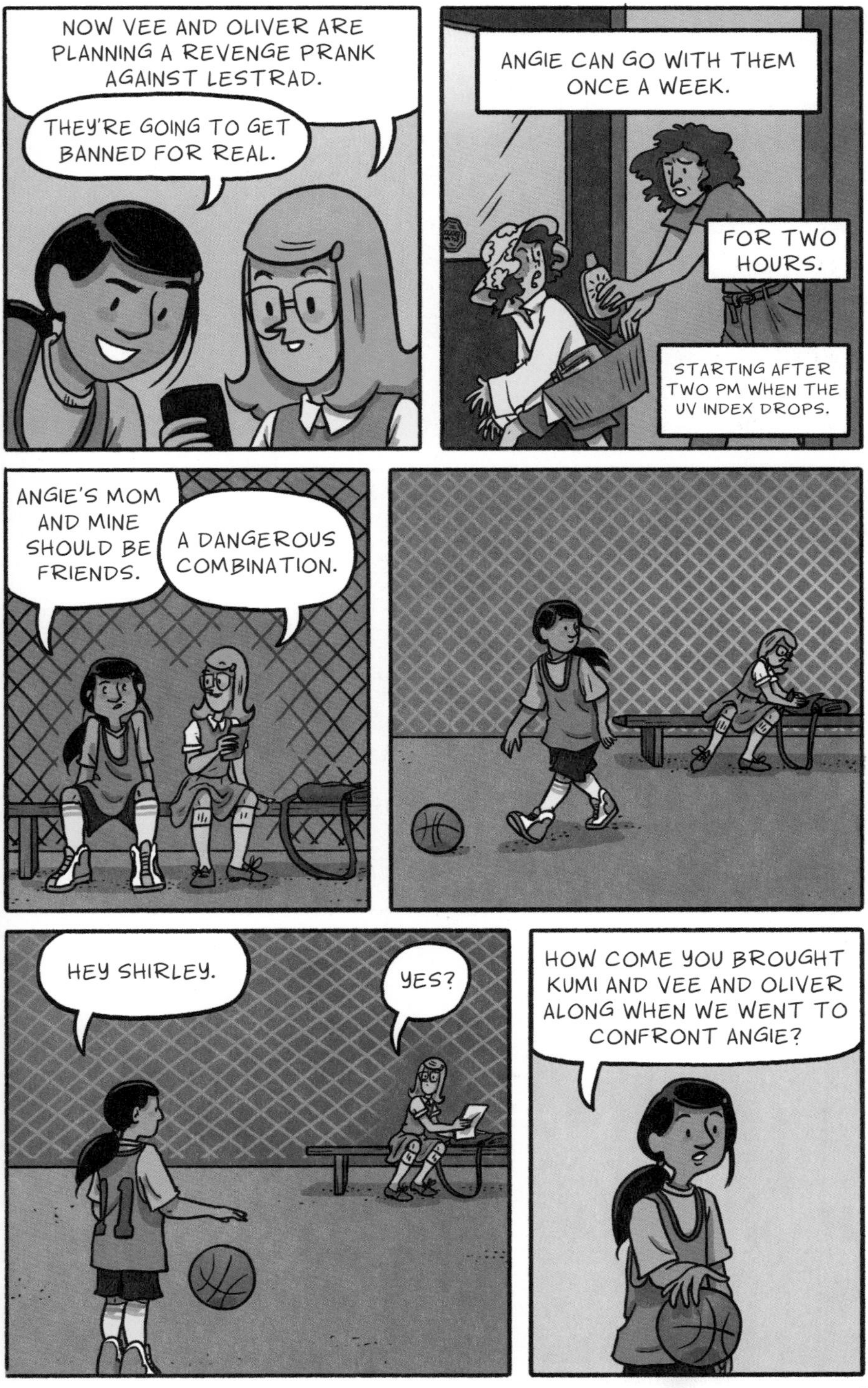
NOW VEE AND OLIVER ARE PLANNING A REVENGE PRANK AGAINST LESTRAD.
THEY'RE GOING TO GET BANNED FOR REAL.
ANGIE CAN GO WITH THEM ONCE A WEEK.
FOR TWO HOURS.
STARTING AFTER TWO PM WHEN THE UV INDEX DROPS.
ANGIE'S MOM AND MINE SHOULD BE FRIENDS.
A DANGEROUS COMBINATION.
HEY SHIRLEY.
YES?
HOW COME YOU BROUGHT KUMI AND VEE AND OLIVER ALONG WHEN WE WENT TO CONFRONT ANGIE?

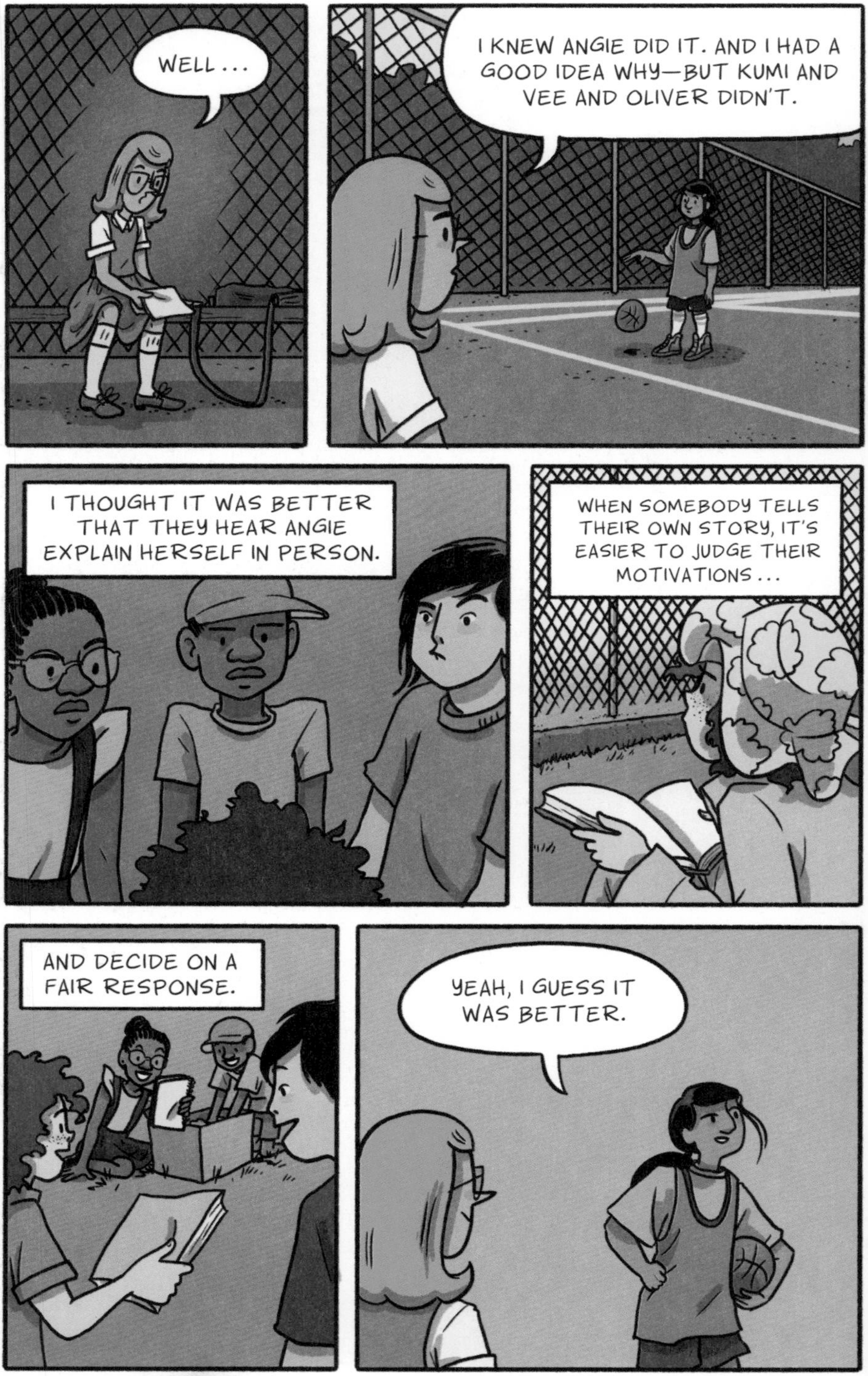
WELL . . .
I KNEW ANGIE DID IT. AND I HAD A GOOD IDEA WHY—BUT KUMI AND VEE AND OLIVER DIDN'T.
I THOUGHT IT WAS BETTER THAT THEY HEAR ANGIE EXPLAIN HERSELF IN PERSON.
WHEN SOMEBODY TELLS THEIR OWN STORY, IT'S EASIER TO JUDGE THEIR MOTIVATIONS . . .
AND DECIDE ON A FAIR RESPONSE.
YEAH, I GUESS IT WAS BETTER.

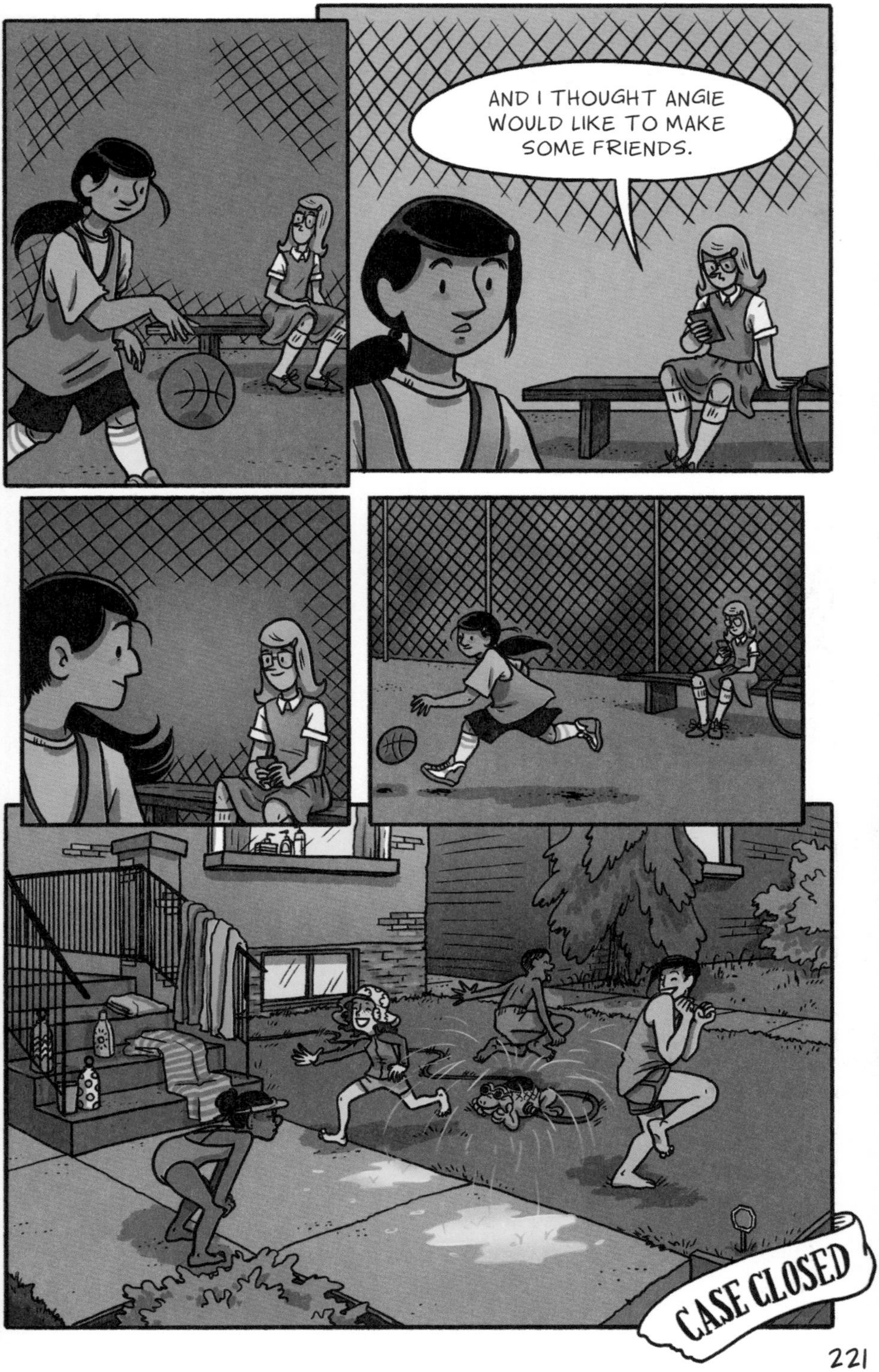
AND I THOUGHT ANGIE
WOULD LIKE TO MAKE
SOME FRIENDS.
CASE CLOSED

ACKNOWLEDGMENT AND ONGOING THANKS TO THE PEOPLE WHO SUPPORTED THIS BOOK IN SO MANY WAYS:

Mariko Tamaki, whose support and collaboration cleared this path; my agent, Anjali Singh, who helped shape this book in its earliest days & championed it onward, as well as Ayesha Pande and everyone at Ayesha Pande Literary; my patient and generous editor Dana Chidiac, designer Jenny Kelly, early editor & keen eye Namrata Tripathi, and everyone at Dial Books for Young Readers and Penguin Random House; Samra Habib, Ryan North, Aisha Jamal, Sameer Farooq, Sadiya Ansari, Sydney Smith, Jane Edmundson, Sel Ghebrihewot, Sana A. Malik, Teela Wyman, and Brooke Day, who read drafts, provided inspiration and context, and answered questions over the long course of several years; Kat Verhoeven, whose flatting skills saved my life, and for her contributions to page 169 in particular; Sam Maggs, Hope Nicholson, every one of my studiomates, Dustin McMurphy, Jaime Graves, David Ross, and Mikey Bennington; Alana and the whole Trumpy family for giving an only child a chance to see how a big family lives. Special thanks to Leigh Stein, Lux Alptraum, and the Binders. And to my mom, Lottie, who is included in the dedication.